SO MASTERFUL A LOVER . . .

Charles. He was her most shameful passion. Handsome, virile, fierce, yet living so treacherous a life. And now this man Pam desperately wanted to hate but couldn't stop loving was back . . . to remind her of betrayed dreams . . . to intoxicate her flesh . . . and, most dangerous of all, to stir the fire that raged between them into a spontaneous blaze of destruction. . . .

LOVE, SEX & MONEY

"JUICY, COMPELLING, ENJOYABLE!"
—*El Paso Times*

"EXCITING, DELICIOUS, ABSOLUTELY DELECTABLE!"
—June Flaum Singer, author of *The Debutantes*

Sharleen Cooper Cohen is a born and bred Californian presently living in Encino and Malibu. Her other novels include *Marital Affairs*, *The Ladies of Beverly Hills*, *Regina's Song*, and *The Day After Tomorrow*.

LOVE SEX & MONEY

SHARLEEN COOPER COHEN

A SIGNET BOOK

NEW AMERICAN LIBRARY

A DIVISION OF PENGUIN BOOKS USA INC.

For Marty
With all my heart and soul

PUBLISHER'S NOTE

NAL BOOKS ARE AVAILABLE AT QUANTITY DISCOUNTS WHEN USED TO PROMOTE PRODUCTS OR SERVICES. FOR INFORMATION PLEASE WRITE TO PREMIUM MARKETING DIVISION, NEW AMERICAN LIBRARY, 1633 BROADWAY, NEW YORK, NEW YORK 10019.

This is an authorized reprint of a hardcover edition published by E. P. Dutton, a division of NAL PENGUIN INC., and simultaneously in Canada by Fitzhenry and Whiteside, Limited, Toronto.

 SIGNET TRADEMARK REG. U.S. PAT. OFF. AND FOREIGN COUNTRIES
REGISTERED TRADEMARK—MARCA REGISTRADA
HECHO EN DRESDEN, TN, USA

SIGNET, SIGNET CLASSIC, MENTOR, ONYX, PLUME, MERIDIAN and NAL BOOKS are published by NAL PENGUIN INC., 1633 Broadway, New York, New York 10019

First Signet Printing, June, 1989

1 2 3 4 5 6 7 8 9

PRINTED IN THE UNITED STATES OF AMERICA

A novelist's imagination and the most dedicated research are rarely sufficient to bring fictional characters to life. To the friends, acquaintances and strangers on whom I imposed, questioning them at length about their experiences, I am extremely grateful. Their generosity revealed rich details of their worlds, and I could not have written this book without their help.

Nancy Cooper
Sheldon Brucker
Michelle Klier
Norman Ackerberg
Burton Fohrman, Esq.
Judy Leaf
Frances Enslein
Bill Waggoner
Lareen Fender
Caryl Goldstone
Marguerite Thomas
Linda Solway
Gene Bergen
Carla Munsat
Dorothy Eagleton
Alice Fisher

Sandi Gelles-Cole
Joe Singer
Edward G. Brown
Suzanne Barash
Hilary Berens
Olga Dytniak
Sgt. Robert Woodruff
Robert E. Blythe, Esq.
Ronald H. Cooer, Esq.
Alice Ovsey
Norman Leaf, M.D.
Timothy D. Gee, M.D.
Merrel Olessen, M.D.
Mary Harden
Myrna Lanier

And a special thanks to Steve Eisner for his vast knowledge of a fascinating subject.

They are one person,
They are two alone,
They are three together,
They are for each other.

BY STEPHEN STILLS,
"Helplessly Hoping"

BOOK
I

Yesterday

1

Joanne was in jail again. The call came into the dorm just as Pam was leaving for her last final. Now what? Pam tried to call the court, but couldn't get through. Damn. Bureaucracy in action. It would have to wait until she took her Advanced Corporate Management final!

But all during the exam, concern for Joanne intruded. Could she get to L.A. in time to get Joanne out tonight? Probably not. It would have to be first thing in the morning. Joanne's troubles always came at the worst time.

Pam wrote furiously, fingers cramped, shoulders knotted and hunched, more from juggling her responsibilities than from the difficulty of the exam. The question was a snap: "Compare the management techniques and philosophies of German and Japanese businesses with American corporations." She knew it cold, which meant she'd aced the final. She'd already made Phi Bete, now maybe she'd graduate magna cum laude. Those were the honors she needed for her future.

At 3:45, completing her last thought by quoting a recent article about the German industrial complex in *The Harvard Business Review,* she ended the paragraph with a definitive summation and closed her blue book. For a moment she just sat there, and then it shot through her. *You're through, Pam. College is over!* She wanted to shout with joy as she bolted up the stairs of the lecture hall two at a time; what a fabulous feeling of freedom. *Look out world, here I come!* But the mood was spoiled by obligation. Joanne again, tarnishing another wonderful moment.

It would take seven hours to get to the Van Nuys court, which would make it 10:30 P.M., too late to ar-

range a release for tonight. Poor Joanne. But in three
more weeks she would graduate and be free of Joanne:
disorderly conduct, bail $350—two months' worth of Pam's
savings. Every dime she'd ever made in her life had gone
to help Joanne. Well, not anymore. From now on, the
money she earned would be hers. And that's why she was
going to New York, where her father lived, to get the
kind of job she'd dreamed of ever since she was a child:
creating great, tall buildings in the city where they were
the most magnificent of all.

Two of the dozens of boys she'd dated in the last three
years stared at her as she passed. Boys had stared at her
all her life, but much more lately. "I'm all through," she
called out gleefully, still filled with that sense of release.
They gave her a thumbs-up approval. But beating the
system and taking her finals early weren't what had brought
that look to their eyes. College boys were satisfied with
only the basics. But somewhere in the real world was a
man who'd appreciate her for her brains and independence
as well as her looks. Being raised around unreliable men
had taught her that if she wanted the good things in
life—and she sure as hell did—she'd have to get them for
herself, the way she always had. That was why she'd
persuaded her professors to let her take her finals early,
even if it meant a grueling study schedule. Now she'd
have time to earn some extra money while everyone else
crammed for three more weeks. Nobody got away with
the things she did. Trish and Hillary were slightly scan-
dalized by her behavior. "If you don't ask, you don't
get," she always said.

The warm spring sunshine caressed her face, but she
couldn't stop to enjoy that either, now. *Damn you, Joanne.*
Trish had left the keys to her car as promised, and Pam
dumped her books on her bed in the dorm, scribbled a
note for Trish and Hillary, and then, out the door. She
gassed up the car on Euclid Avenue and drove onto the
freeway heading south, the late-afternoon sun to her
right, shining on the green waters of the bay.

With every mile, she felt lightheartedness slip away,
depression set in.

The bail bondsman knew her from the other times.
"You finished college, kid?" He looked up, studying her,
trying to be tough, but smitten with her like most men.

What did he see standing there, she wondered: a too-tall young woman with a light blond ponytail, a long neck, narrow hips, slender legs, and a good set—if she said so herself. But why did they all stare? She thought her cheekbones too prominent, jutting at a slant the way they did, her chin a touch too square. And her height drove her crazy. Pants that fit through the hips were always too short at the ankle, skirts that other girls wore below the calf hit her just below the knee. Taller than Joanne, nevertheless she was built like her: aristocratic bones. What a laugh. But she had her father's eyes, crystal clear, a light china blue that deepened to aquamarine depending on what she wore, and fringed with heavy lashes. She thought her eyes were too big, but she liked her smooth, unblemished skin that tanned without burning, and her teeth were great—thank God, no braces. Her mouth could be called overly generous, and her nose was straight, almost classical, though a bit narrow before it turned up at the end. In fact, she thought, all her features were over-large; everyone else thought she was exceptionally beautiful. The high cheekbones gave her expression a haughtiness that her dimpled smile softened, but what truly made men stare and then sigh with desire was her sense of herself, a combination of brains, beauty, and courage that no amount of hardship could diminish. She had developed that sense of self to compensate for her background, and now self-confidence blazed out of her like a banner that engendered hostility in jealous eyes and a recognition in others who tried like hell to fabricate it, that she was the real thing.

Joanne looked terrible—stringy hair, smeared makeup, Orlon sweater dirty and stained. Was anything tackier, Pam thought, than an Orlon sweater past its prime, fuzzy little balls under the arms and around the breasts, and the once-white color now the gray of a dirty cat. Joanne's black slacks were shiny and tight; her sandals revealed a deteriorating pedicure. Joanne didn't know Pam was watching her as she signed out at the release desk behind frosted panes of glass in a room with green institutional walls; then she turned.

"You came. Oh, baby, I knew you would."

"Hello, Mother."

Joanne started to cry. The tears made clean traces down her grimy cheeks and she clung to Pam. "I didn't want to stay there, but you shouldn't have spent your money."

"It'll be all right. I'll take you home." Seeing her mother's gratitude made the long drive almost worth it. Joanne was sad and vulnerable, her need as exposed as the sorry state of her clothes and her too-ripe smell.

Blinking in the bright sunlight of the San Fernando Valley morning, Joanne let herself be led to Trish's Corvair and got in.

"Barney's gone. Took off when the police arrived. The bastard. It was his fault I got arrested. He was the one who yanked me off the bar stool, and the stool broke. Is that any way to treat me?" Pam handed her a Kleenex. "And Barney takes off. Leaves me sitting on my keester screaming at him in the middle of Ray's on Sherman Way. The cops must have been around the corner, they got there so fast, or I'd have gotten up and gone after him."

Pam sighed. The same tired dialogue, a lifetime of lame excuses.

Joanne appraised her. "You don't look so hot yourself, honey. Those circles under your eyes? If you don't take care of yourself, it can catch up with you too, you know. Mothers know these things."

First came the warning, next would come, *See, you still need me. Better stick around here.* "I've been working hard, Mother." Sarcasm just popped out.

Joanne grabbed it and threw it back. "Heard from your father lately? Is he coming to graduation?"

Pam stiffened. She ached to have her father with her at graduation even more than at any other time in her life. This was the final moment of her childhood, the last father-daughter moment he would ever share with her, except her wedding, but there wasn't much chance he'd come. "He hasn't said definitely. You know he doesn't like to leave Jennifer and his sons. Maybe this time he'll be there."

"You're dreaming again, Pam. When has he ever done what he's said he'd do? Except help pay for your education. And even that wasn't much."

Joanne's words ignited her disappointment and anger,

but she held it back. At least her father had paid for her
tuition and books, though she'd paid for everything else
by working her tail off. But what good did that do? Her
mother would just go and blow whatever savings they
had, or just give it away to some guy with a sad story.
Why not? She hadn't earned it. But at least Joanne had
been there, not far away in Connecticut like her father.

Pam headed for Joanne's West Hollywood apartment,
where she'd slept last night. She didn't think of it as her
home; there wasn't even a real bed for her. When Pam
had first gone to Berkeley, Joanne had moved into this
one bedroom with a double bed, and Pam used the sofa
in the living room on her rare visits to L.A. Since childhood, her presence had cramped Joanne's style. Now was
no different. The men in Joanne's life were usually jerks.
Barney was typical. Pam couldn't wait to get away from
home; that was why she'd stayed in Berkeley during the
summers and taken classes, which had also enabled her
to graduate in three years instead of four.

As they pulled up to the two-story apartment building,
Pam said, "Have you got any food in the house?"

Joanne looked at her with that familiar expression of
guilt and defiance. "I wasn't expecting company, you
know."

"I'll go buy us some lunch," Pam offered.

Joanne nodded and got out of the car. "There's a
hamburger place on La Brea. And don't forget the beer."

Pam decided not to hear the request for the beer.

Pam had always worked. There was never enough money
to live on, let alone to buy luxuries. At eleven she was
the only girl in her neighborhood to have a paper route,
then she did some babysitting, sold subscriptions, and
later worked in the school cafeteria. The stigma attached
to a girl who wore a uniform and a hair net and smelled
of cooked cabbage was hard to overcome, but she did it
with determination and a sense of style. The older she
got and the taller she grew, the more she had to develop
her own look. Other girls could be cute, in ruffled collars
and flowered prints, but not Pam. She wore primary or
pastel colors mostly because people remembered prints
and she couldn't afford new clothes, but also the solid
colors enhanced her unusual beauty. At fourteen she

discovered the pageboy, and for her honey-blond hair it was the perfect hairdo, smooth and uncomplicated, it framed her flamboyant features. Always a leader, she was class president, student council member, and prom queen, and she got top grades by studying at night after dates. She'd be damned if she'd be cheated out of a social life just because she had to work. Her social life and her dreams kept her going, dreams that someday she would live with her father and work with him in his construction business. As a child, she imagined herself standing beside him, feeling the warmth of his pride as they controlled the movements of huge machinery together, digging enormous holes in the earth and then slowly filling them up with stately, tall buildings. When she grew older and understood how business actually worked, she was determined to be his partner someday and share his duties with him.

Her dreams nearly made the harsh realities tolerable, but not always: like at fourteen, when Pam developed breasts, and her mother asked to be called Joanne instead of Mom, so no one would know how old she was. And when she was fifteen, her mother's boyfriend Randall started giving her seductive smiles, watched her undress, and walked in on her in the bathroom. Once he even touched her on the breast. Frightened and disgusted, Pam knew Joanne would blame her, so she didn't tell. But then the nightmares started, followed by stomach pains so severe she kept missing school. Joanne's suspicion of doctors, based on her inability to pay them, kept Pam from being treated. By the time she saw a doctor he diagnosed a pre-ulcerous condition and ordered rest. Lying there in bed, doubled over with pain, she knew this was Randall's fault.

The next time she caught him watching her, she yelled so Joanne could hear, "What are you staring at? You're disgusting." Joanne got the hint, and soon Randall was out of their lives. But the pain didn't go away. Day after day, Pam came home from school in agony, praying she would feel better. But it only got worse.

Her life was out of control, and she had to do something about it. One thing was certain: if her father were here, none of this would be happening. Or if she were living with him in his beautiful home back East, everything would be different. He would love her as much as he loved his two sons and never forget her birthday. It wasn't his fault that he'd let her down, or hardly ever visited her and seldom wrote; it was Joanne's. Joanne had driven him away. She was weak and lazy, expecting everyone to take care of her without doing anything in return. She had made him so angry he couldn't be good to his daughter. Joanne's fault! Joanne had deprived her of having two parents as her friends had. Parents who stayed married, and ate real home-cooked turkey on Thanksgiving, not frozen dinners, who bought each other Christmas presents and took their kids for pony rides, made them tea when they were sick, bought them new clothes for school in September.

Suddenly she realized what was eating at her insides, rage at Joanne. But her realization only brought her more pain. She lay on her bed, bent almost double in agony, while an enormous scream welled up inside, terrifying her even more than the pain. If she ever let out that scream, she'd lose control and go mad. But she couldn't hide from the truth. Life would never be better until she was old enough to leave Joanne and go to her father. Her mother would never marry a decent man who'd buy them a house and support them so Pam wouldn't have to work while she was still in school. And her father would never show her how much he loved her while she lived with Joanne. Her knowledge finally overwhelmed her, and the cry that burst forth tore at her heart as she sobbed with pain and anger.

After a long time, when she couldn't cry anymore, she dragged herself to the bathroom and washed her face. Her puffy red eyes looked back at her, but maybe she saw a newly acquired wisdom in them. She wasn't so afraid of her feelings now. In letting go, she hadn't gone mad; in fact, she felt relieved. Perhaps in time she would understand that Joanne couldn't help the way she was.

But now, without hating Joanne, she felt only emptiness. She still loved her father, missed him, wrote him letters telling him how proud she was of him, of his work, told him about the building projects going on in Los Angeles, asked his advice about her life. His answers were brief and far between, but then he was a busy, successful man, just as busy and successful as she would be. And someday she would be completely independent and not need anyone at all, except her father. That's what she decided at fifteen. Her father was the only one worthy of her love, and she wanted to be just like him.

They finished eating their burgers, and Pam gathered up the wrappers and threw them away.

"What am I going to do when you go off and leave me alone?" Joanne asked. "You're heartless. Have been since you grew up. What happened to my sweet baby girl who used to love it when I bought her an ice-cream cone, and took her to the drive-in movies on school nights?"

"You know I'm not deserting you. I'll send you money. You have your friends and your life, even a job now and then. You'll be all right." The bleakness of her mother's life saddened her.

Joanne's expression said, *Don't lie to me, you know my life is nothing.* But that fear was too real to articulate. Without Pam's stability, she might slide down the hole she'd begun to dig as a much younger woman. Watching the fear on her mother's heavily made-up face, Pam had an awful premonition of Joanne becoming one of those bums who lived in the alleys and on the streetcorners of downtown Los Angeles. But Joanne's vanity would keep her going for a while, believing as she did that she was destined for wonderful things if someone would just give them to her. Pam worried that when Joanne's fading looks faded even more, there wouldn't even be a Barney to make life bearable.

"Why can't I go with you?" A lament born of desperation and spoiled dreams.

"We've been over this. I'm going to be spending a lot of time with Dad, and you know how awkward that would be for you."

"I'll believe that when I see it."

"You don't think he'll love having me there, after all this time?"

"I have no idea what he wants, Pam. Just don't set yourself up again, like you did every time you ever expected anything from him, that's all."

"Well, I'm going to be working with him, you know."

"Has he offered you a job?"

"Not officially. But I've written him about my plans."

"You're gonna need me to pick up the pieces."

When have you ever picked up the pieces? Pam thought. "It's more expensive to live in New York than in California. You hate the cold. Besides, you don't have the money to move."

"So damned practical. Always were. And unfeeling."

Pam felt tears stinging her eyes and willed them away. Hillary and Trish didn't think she was unfeeling. With her two close friends she even had a sense of humor. Only with her mother was she cold. She brushed the accusation away like eraser dust. She didn't hate Joanne anymore, or love her.

And yet she found herself getting up from the sofa bed where she'd been sitting, coming over to Joanne, and putting her arms around her mother. There was still compassion.

Joanne clung to her, their bodies so similar in height and shape. "I know you don't think this is fair," Pam said, "but life was never fair to me, either."

"So you're getting back at me, deserting me, for life's unfairness?" Her mother's petulance might have annoyed her, but for the fierceness of the return hug.

"I'm not getting back, Joanne. Just out. Out of this town, where I've never been happy. There's no dream for me here. I've always wanted to be like Dad, to work with him, and now is my chance. I've heard about New York, how tough it is there. I'm ready for the challenge. Besides, I want to meet new people who'll know me as I am, not as I was."

Joanne broke the embrace and stared at her daughter. "That's what I told them back home when I came to California, and look what happened to me. I was gonna make it big, too. But New York eats people alive. When you're born there, you belong, like your father. But otherwise you're never accepted, always kept out."

"Maybe in Dad's family, but not with other people."

Joanne defended her position, though she knew Pam was right. "Well, I've had friends who went there, tried to make a life there, and came back miserable."

"Don't start." Pam's voice was sharp. "Just don't."

Joanne sighed, defeat drooping her shoulders, a common posture for her. "I don't know what I'm going to do without you."

"You'll be okay. You coming to graduation?"

"Oh, Pammy, I don't know. I can't afford to fly. How else would I get there?"

This was a hint for Pam to borrow Trish's car once more and drive all the way back down to get her. "You could take the bus."

"It takes forever, and those bus depots are so depressing."

"I really want you to be there, but if you can't come, you can't. What about Hillary's parents? If they're driving up, maybe they can take you."

"Oh, I'd feel so out of place. You know how those Jews are, they think they're better than everyone else."

Pam's eyes glazed over as she withdrew from her mother's words. She welcomed indifference at moments like this. Mr. and Mrs. Markus were wonderful people, protective of Hillary, called her every Sunday, shared their lives with her, made her interests their own. Hillary's friends were like their own children; they included Pam every time they came to Berkeley. Without the Markuses, she'd never have seen the opera or the ballet. They had sent her birthday presents, bought her Samsonite luggage for graduation, listened to her plans, encouraged her, called her sweetheart. "Why shouldn't they act like they're better than other people? I think they are." It had just popped out, impelled by fury, the way roaches scamper out from a kitchen counter when the lights are switched on. Roaches and her words horrified them both.

"That's why I don't care to come." Her mother seized the swatter. "I can't stand to see you sucking up to those people. How low can you get, Pamela?"

"You're right." Pam's sarcasm outlined her words. "I wouldn't want you to see that. I'll send you a picture of me in my cap and gown so your visual experience can remain pure."

The comment went over Joanne's head. "I was planning to buy you something," Joanne said, at the mention of a cap and gown. "But I've been a bit tapped lately."

What else was new? Pam moved away from her mother. "I'm going back to school now, Mother. Have to study for my finals."

"I thought you said you were through."

Her mother seldom listened, but this time she had.

"No, I said I'd be *glad* when I was through."

A brief nod. Now they were both off the hook.

Pam picked up her gym bag with her overnight things, kissed her mother's cheek, and waved good-bye to her mother, to her old life and all its sadness, and then she walked out the door. It occurred to her that she might not see her mother for a long time, but that felt like a burden being lifted.

2

"Mel, we'd better stop," Hillary insisted again, pushing his hand away from the inside of her thigh. His fingers were dangerously close to the edge of her underpants. She struggled with herself even more than with him, wondering if anyone could see what they were doing, parked here on Grizzly Peak. But the windows of the car were fogged from the moisture of their heavy breathing and the chilly damp weather. *What are you saving it for?* she asked herself. *To be the last living virgin at Berkeley?*

"Oh God, Hillary," he moaned. "You're driving me crazy. Come on, baby, don't be a tease. We're not kids."

His mouth was on hers again, deeply probing, assaulting her resistance, pulling even more passion from already swollen, tender lips. His tongue was in her mouth, his other hand caressing her breast, silken touches; it felt so good. She smelled Aqua Velva after-shave.

"Mel, not here, not now," she whispered, trying to catch her breath, to keep her resolve. He'd gotten so good at knowing how to excite her.

"There's no better place on earth than right here and right now, Hillary." His mouth closed over hers again, his hand crept closer, teasing, touching. And then he whispered, "I love you."

She was stunned. *He'd actually said it!* It was like the right key in the right lock. Moisture flooded through her, melting her resistance even more. He'd never said it before. Never. Inflamed by his words as his hand reached closer to its mark, she felt herself letting go. Her body trembled with passion, swept away by her love for him. The aphrodisiac of his words blotted out everything else. So what if her friends sometimes criticized him, pointed out his faults? They'd never been in the dark with this love, when he took her in his arms and drove her slowly out of her mind.

She heard the sound of his zipper. "Do you really?" she whispered. The hardness of his flesh pressed against her. She'd never let him go this far before.

"Yes," he breathed, "yes."

He sat up and pulled off his cords, his head pressing against the top of the car as he struggled in the confines of the front seat. Then he turned and gently helped her pull down her underpants. This was an irrevocable step; in a moment there would be no turning back. Brazenly, she lifted her hips to assist him. She loved him so, how she loved him. Ignoring the armrest that pressed into the back of her head and the dashboard so close on the right, she was unable to think rationally anymore. He leaned over, kissing her, touching her there, right there, trying to enter her, and suddenly she was terrified. What if she got pregnant?

Sensing her hesitation, he covered her face with kisses, touching her in a way that sent shock waves through her. Even though he was so much taller than she, their bodies found enough room on this cramped seat. She closed her eyes, intensifying the sensation.

They were almost doing it, having sex, intercourse, the *F* word.

She wanted to do it with all her might, but all the warnings kept repeating, *Wait until you're married. Guard your reputation.*

No! Get it over with, a voice in her head said. *It's a natural function, for God's sake. Pam's done it, probably Trish too.* The endless discussions beginning in junior high. *What's it like? He puts his thing in* where? *Don't be a goose. Disgusting! I'll never let any man do that. And his tongue in, too? At the same time? No, stupid. Before and after. Yuk. Double yuk.* In this position, it didn't take much to keep him out. Then she thought, *No more fear of getting raped while I'm a virgin, or of dying as a virgin.* And she wanted him so much. Her fingers entwined in his soft, curly hair. "Do you really love me?"

"Yes, yes," he gasped.

She relaxed and opened up to him, finally letting it happen. It hurt and fit and felt amazing, so amazing. She stopped, wanting to hold this moment forever, but she was unable to think about it and do it at the same time. Then everything responded at once, reaching for him, new parts of her were born with instant knowledge.

"Oh God," he said, pushing in and out. He started slowly, and then continued in a steady rhythm, while she moved with him. She wondered if she was doing it right, then she didn't care. She could have gone on like this forever.

"I love you," she said, "I love you," grabbing on to him, sensing some kind of building within him and within herself. All she had to do was hold on and be carried with him.

"Love you too, you too, you too, oh, oh, oh . . ." His body shuddered and so did hers. It happened beyond her control. A spasm, an uncontrollable, funny kind of shockingly wonderful sensation. What was that? Could it be?

The more he moved for his own pleasure, the better it felt. She was trembling all over; a rush of heat suffused her body as she crested with him. It was a miracle, an orgasm the first time they made love. God meant for them to be one. Mel was slowing down, but she wasn't. The heat within her flared up, overtaking her.

And then it was happening again, or it had never stopped. Her body soared, carried on a cloud of heat; her brain was on fire, more pulsing; the uncontrollable vibrating continued and continued. She never wanted it to end. She felt glued to him. He was every man she'd ever loved, even Paul Newman. "Mel!" she cried out. "I love you, oh God, I love you." And she thrust her hips against him. But he was soft and was slipping out of her. Already? "No," she cried out, "wait." And the spasms happened again, simply by his pressing against her. Moments passed. Her body calmed down, though she didn't want it to, her breathing slowed until it was quiet and she could only hear the sound of her heart beating and the car creaking. The vinyl seat was stuck to her bare skin, and there was a terrible crick in her neck.

"Mel, Mel, I love you so much."

"Are you all right?"

"Yes, yes, I'm all right."

He stroked her hair, kissed her cheek. She could feel him smiling. She was in heaven. He pushed up on his elbows and she looked deeply into his dark eyes. "You're really something." He was grinning, both with surprise and self-satisfaction, looking boyish and unbelievably appealing, instead of serious as he usually was, this driven law student with whom she was so enamored.

"You're really something, too."

"I had no idea you were so passionate. I could barely keep up with you."

"Of course you could! You were wonderful. You made me feel that passion."

But his smile faded and she felt a chill. Something was wrong. She hated it when he got that way, quiet and distant, making her feel she ought to know what was bothering him but didn't.

He reached up and wiped a small circle in the foggy windshield, revealing a black hole. "Were you a virgin?"

A hot flush of embarrassment rushed through her. "How can you ask such a question? Of course I am, was. You know I was." Everything about her proclaimed how virginal she was. Couldn't he see? How could he question that?

He pulled away from her and moved himself around to sit behind the wheel. The sharp features of his profile were outlined by a glow from the foggy window. He seemed not only intense, but darkly foreboding; how fast his moods changed! The sudden loss of his body on hers made her want to cry. She pulled her leg out from behind him and sat up too. He wiggled his pants up over his long legs and handed her some paper napkins from inside the glove compartment. The feeling of desolation was overwhelming. After what they'd just shared she should feel closer to him than ever, but all she felt was terribly alone.

"There wasn't any bleeding, and it didn't seem to hurt very much." Now some of the harshness in his expression had softened.

"There isn't always bleeding, is there? I used to go horseback riding when I was a kid, and I've used tampons for years, but it hurt, believe me."

He seemed embarrassed, looked away. "I'm sorry if I hurt you."

She desperately wanted him to look at her. "What you said hurt the most. Don't you know you're the first? The first and only." He didn't reply. "Then what is it?"

"You're such a pistol," he blurted out, turning to her. "Shooting off twice like that. So fast. You didn't need me at all. I might have been anybody, for that matter."

There was a furrow between his eyebrows that she wanted to kiss and smooth away. But she was amazed by what he'd said. "That's not true! No one in the world could have made me feel the way you did. I would never have made love to anyone but you. Never!" She was going to cry, and then her mascara would run. "Here I waited all this time, and you accuse me of pretending. How can you be so cruel? Maybe I'm inexperienced, but I can learn. I only want to please you. If you don't like the way I make love, I won't do it like that anymore."

"It's not that, Hil." He took her hand. "I was taken off guard, that's all." His hand felt sticky, and it embarrassed her. But she didn't pull away.

"You've said no so many times, I couldn't believe you were finally letting me do it. And then you knew exactly what to do. You seemed like a pro at it."

"A pro? You mean like a prostitute? How can you say such a thing?" She felt the thrust of his words in her gut, harsher and more painful than the other part of him had been when he was inside of her. The warm semen he'd deposited was seeping back out, and she thrust the napkins between her legs. This was mortifying. She'd get icky wet all over his seat.

"I didn't mean an actual professional woman. I meant an experienced one."

"I only did what came naturally because I love you." In spite of her resolve, she was crying. "You're such a wonderful lover."

"Me?" She heard the surprise in his voice, saw delight change the expression in his eyes. "How could you tell?"

"A woman knows these things. Everything about you is wonderful." She looked at him, tears running down her face.

He wiped them away with his fingers, the sticky ones, and his smile turned into that boyish grin again. "I'm sorry for being so stupid. I know you're a virgin." Her heart soared, actually leaped out of its despair. He believed her, everything was all right—no, it was miraculously wonderful. "Want to do it again?" he asked.

"Again? We can't do it again, not until we're married."

"Who said anything about married? That's years away. What do you think, we're going back to necking after this?"

The terrible fear clutched her again that she had felt when they first started dating; every time he'd brought her back to the dorm, she'd never been sure she'd hear from him again.

"What we say in the heat of passion isn't always what we mean."

"You didn't mean it?"

"What?" He was teasing. "Sure, I meant it."

"And now?"

He smiled at her, and even more than his words, his expression told her the truth. "Yes, I love you. I've tried not be in love with you, but you're so lovable, I can't help it. Look at you." He pressed her cheeks with both his hands and kissed her puckered lips. They both laughed. She wanted to shout with joy. "I just don't want you to get the wrong idea."

"What idea?"

"That we're going steady, or that this is some kind of proposal."

"I know that." She stared at him. "But after what we've just done, I assumed . . . Do you think I'd ever be with anyone else after this? Do you still want other girls?" The thought filled her with an icy fear.

He considered her question. "No, I don't want anyone else. You're perfect for me. But I'm not ready to settle down."

The last thing she wanted to hear. "You'd better take me home, Mel."

"What do you mean, I'd *better* take you home? Or what?"

"Nothing." Except that she wanted to die. She'd given every ounce of herself, nothing held back, and it wasn't enough.

"Okay, I'll take you home."

Damn, he always responded like that to ultimatums—stubbornly. It wasn't what she meant, not after he'd said he loved her.

He rolled down the window, punched on the radio, and started the car, all in three fast moves. The fog on the windshield was clearing, and they could see the lights of Berkeley twinkling below them and three bridges beyond, lighting up the black waters of the bay. Chubby Checker was singing "Do the Twist." Mel accelerated and backed out of the dirt area among the eucalyptus and pine trees where they had been parked.

Panic struggled with fear. Had she ruined everything between them after they'd made love, an irrevocable act? And in her senior year. Twenty-two, graduation in three weeks. Would anyone ever marry her? Would Mel?

"Please don't be angry."

"Please don't be angry," he mimicked, and she burst into tears.

He stopped the car and turned to face her. "I'm sorry. Don't cry. I'm not angry, just disappointed. First you say I'm a great lover, then you say you don't want to make love to me again. What am I supposed to think?"

"You don't understand. Doing it once I can say was passion, but doing it again would mean I'm really . . ."

"What? Say it."

"A slut," she whispered.

"What!" he shouted. "You're crazy. Why would you think such a thing?"

She'd heard so many guys refer to girls as sluts once they'd slept with them. "I just do, that's all. It's wrong."

"So you equate sex, a normal, human function, with marriage. You'll only sleep with me if I propose to you? Well, no way will I be bullied into that. I've got graduation from law school this month, then I've got the bar ahead of me. Marriage is the last thing on my mind. I do love you, Hillary, and it was really good with us tonight, but either we're lovers or we're not. I don't want to play games."

She couldn't lose him, not now. The thought gripped her heart so hard she wanted to scream. "Oh, Mel. I just can't. I know you're right. But I'm afraid."

He took her hand and kissed it. She touched his smooth-shaven cheek, feeling reassured. She loved the way he looked, the dark curly hair, the expressive dark eyes, eyes that could be sad one minute, joyful the next, and then filled with intensity. He had dark skin, a strong, slightly hooked nose that added strength to his face, and a full, sensual mouth that grinned easily and sometimes pouted, but was usually set with determination. "You didn't say you loved me just so I'd give in, did you?" Hillary asked, breaking the easiness between them.

"Absolutely not. But my definition of love and yours are different. To you, 'I love you' means marriage and a family, and to me it means I care for you deeply, but no strings attached. I need my freedom. I don't want to be tied down yet. I've got years of living before that happens."

"I don't want to tie you down, Mel. I just want to love you." She smiled bravely, but her heart was throbbing painfully. There was nothing she wanted more out of life than to be Mel Robin's wife and bear his children and keep his house and make love to him anytime he wanted.

He leaned over and kissed her lightly on the cheek. "You're sweet, Hillary-Dillary. That's what I love about you the most. Don't ever lose that quality."

She sighed with happiness.

"Want to go to Carmel with me for the weekend? We'll study for finals together. Some of the seniors from Boalt are going. We could go down Friday night, have a ball."

This was it, the real decision. Even more difficult than the earlier one had been. She did love him. Couldn't let him go. Wanted to be with him with all her heart. She took a deep breath and let it out slowly. "Okay."

He was grinning again. "Hey, that's great. If you think tonight was good, baby, you ain't seen nothing yet. In between cramming, we'll cram some more." He winked.

His words embarrassed her, but a thrill of anticipation shot through her, delicious excitement mixed with a hard rock of guilt and a chill of joy. How wonderful it would be to wake up in the morning with him next to her. And even though she knew he meant what he'd said about not wanting to get tied down, maybe she could get him to change his mind. But underneath, she knew the only mind being changed was hers.

3

A feeling of disorientation made Trish dizzy, that and the hot sun beating down. The chancellor's voice floated out of time. "And, as you approach your adult lives, you will recall your days in this institution . . ." His voice drifted on the airless day. On her left, Hillary seemed to listen to every word, absorbed in the emotion of her college graduation. Her hands were folded in her lap, her full breasts jutted forward in the graduation gown; even in this shapeless getup she looked like an Italian actress. The bridge of her turned-up nose was moist with perspiration, her green eyes filled with tears of sentiment, her thick auburn hair curled around her face. The longer Trish knew her, the more beautiful she became, or had Trish ceased to see her as she really was, and now only saw her friend's inner beauty?

On her right, Pam sat tall, nearly a head taller than either Hillary or Trish, looking cool and serene even in this heat. Her legs were crossed, and her right foot tapped in time with the inner energy that filled her with a constant hum. She bet Pam would remember every word of this ceremony, quote it in years to come.

How Trish loved these two friends; loved them from that first week in the dorm in her sophomore year when they'd discovered one another, forming the bond that had kept them close all through college. Hillary was always ready to listen to Trish's problems, but then she listened to everyone's; Pam's beauty had set the dorm abuzz from the moment she'd walked in the door with two guys carrying her luggage, but she'd also turned out to be a brain. *And then there's me,* Trish thought, *my sketchpad in hand, pretending indifference while I study everyone for their secrets, the pseudointellectual, quoting passages from Proust.* She almost blushed to remember how badly she'd wanted to be their friend, and yet it had happened easily. The three of them had soon recognized that they were different, special, that they complemented one another; each added her special strength to what the others lacked. Trish emulated Pam's sense of purpose, applying it to her own burning desire for expression in art. And Trish's unswerving ability to work hard was what Hillary needed to inspire her plans to be a teacher. But Hillary had what they both needed, a loving warmth. The three of them had made other friends at Berkeley, but no one else as close. And yet Hillary and Pam were leaving Berkeley: Pam for New York, and Hillary for a student teaching job in Los Angeles. She would be lonely left behind. The thought of it gave her a feeling of emptiness inside.

There was a consolation. Professor Arthur Matalon. Just saying his name was enough. Thinking of him had saved her at dinner last night with her parents. And she'd needed saving; she didn't fit in with her parents anymore. It had been painful to feel them trying to reshape her into their mold again. Her parents looked the same, yet different too. She'd forgotten how their everyday comments jarred. Her brother, Tommy, had reached out and taken her hand when their father got started.

"Kennedy is dragging this country to ruin, and his crazy brother is even worse, with that damnable civil rights crap. Infuriating! Trying to jam the Negro's rights down our throats. The front of the bus, the back of the bus, integrated schools, votes for Negroes—well, the South isn't going to stand for it and I don't blame them. You can't change behavior ingrained for hundreds of years overnight."

She used to think her father's opinion was gospel, but now she knew how repressive governments could be— Poli Sci 129. Some students on campus were beginning to protest against certain organizations. She was drawn to them, but afraid to join—not Matthew and Patricia Baldwin's daughter!

Tommy's discomfort was obvious; her father didn't notice. Tommy stretched his neck up as though his starched collar irritated him, but that wasn't it. Blond, blue-eyed Fred Carmichael, Tommy's roommate at U.C. Hastings

College of the Law in San Francisco, looked down at his hands. They were polite, in league. Comrades, as she was with Trish and Hillary.

Her brother countered, "Bobby Kennedy's all right. He just gets carried away by his ideals." If only one of them had the courage to say what he felt to their father. They both thought Bobby Kennedy was wonderful. And when President Kennedy had spoken at Berkeley on Charter Day, she'd worked on the committee, shaken his hand. Thrilling!

Professor Matalon—Arthur, she sometimes dared—thought John and Bob Kennedy were Moses and Christ. Arthur Matalon consumed her thoughts. His eyes burned through her clothing, seeing her soul, her dedication to art; their intensity made her tremble. Rasputin eyes, even a touch mad at times, in a bearded face, above a lean body in an open, caftan-like shirt and drawstring pants: when she gazed at him she forgot to breathe and then found herself gasping for air, mortified. His home in Big Sur was permeated with the scent of fresh pine and linseed oil. It was a bohemian jumble, with piles of fabrics to drape over the model's stand, jars filled with colored paint, chunks of crystal, amethyst, geodes, and lace curtains on the windows that looked out to panoramic splendor. In his own backyard, redwood trees reached to the heavens, and in the front, a vast green ocean broke on strange, erotic rock formations, defying what one knew to be true, that this was Earth and not some alien planet in the galaxy.

While her parents talked about how engineering, her father's work, had once been a noble profession and was now a dirty word, her thoughts curled around Professor Matalon like smoke from his fireplace. An invitation to his paradise had come as a graduation present extended to several of his better students. And she'd worked her heart out to be one of his better students. Brad and James, two of her fellow artists, had come that day too, sipped wine, and then necked by the fire, openly. Arthur inspired that kind of freedom. Even now, sitting here surrounded by her entire graduating class, the memory of seeing two boys kissing sent strange feelings down her body. She'd been fascinated by them, stared until she'd seen Professor Matalon watching her. She'd had a crush on Brad as a freshman.

That day was like no other. Matalon had a parrot named Pegasus, a fish named Ahab. She'd stood on the redwood deck at the back of the house, feeling the fresh, moist earth of the garden and the encroaching wilderness envelop her; impossible to care about mundane realities there, with nature in abundance. Perils lurked too, adult perils, never encountered before, aberrant sexuality, secrets of countercultures beyond her ordered, family-dominated, father-dominated existence.

"Little Trish," Arthur Matalon had whispered, joining her on his deck, breathing warm air into her ear, sending shivers down her neck and chest, electrifying the nipples of her small breasts. "I know you think *fuck* is a dirty word, but I think *virginity* is. It isn't your body that's virgin, it's your mind."

"I'm not a virgin," she'd told him, embarrassed and bold.

"There are all kinds of virgins," he'd said, taking her by the shoulders then and turning her around to face him, noticing the erect pea shapes under her cotton blouse. With a brazenness that amazed her, she'd wanted him to run his palms lightly over her nipples; she'd feared he knew what she was thinking. "Such a young thing." His smile took the sting out of *young,* made it seem special. "There are wonders awaiting you. Someone will delight in teaching them to you. I'm sorry it won't be me." He saw her eyes widen. "Have I shocked you?"

She couldn't reply, dazzled by his power, the masculine force of him. He was everything she'd dreamed about, knowledgeable, brilliant, sophisticated. She imagined him touching her, making love to her. It showed in her gaze.

"We shall see a lot of each other during your graduate work. I'm aware of your talent, but it's untried. You need to experience the reality before you can express it in symbols. You have to feel everything." And he ran his hand along her cheek down to her neck, lightly caressing her. Her body flooded with desire. And panic. He sensed her fear and moved away. "I won't rush you. I promise."

She almost reached out to cling to him. Her parents were moving to Iran, leaving her adrift to enter this new

frightening, wondrous world of his. She'd be cut off from
their values, free to seek her own. What would hers be?

The undergraduates stood up to sing the school an-
them for the last time, hot and perspiring in their caps
and gowns, the sunshine blazing them a blessing. Trish
cried all the way through the school song; they all did.
She hugged Hillary and Pam and several friends nearby,
then they filed out of their row and went back across the
field to meet their families. In front of her, Hillary hooked
her arm through Pam's. "Don't go back to the dorm to
pack yet," she insisted, pulling her along. "Come to
dinner with my parents and Trish's. It doesn't matter that
Joanne isn't here."

"You have to come," Trish insisted, catching up, ready
to cry again until Pam agreed to meet her and Hillary
later. Trish's parents came up to her smiling, offered
congratulations. Other families were hugging; girls were
crying, engaged couples were kissing. The tumultuous
chorus of the ending of her childhood surrounded her.
She wanted to hold this moment forever. And then she
spotted Professor Matalon holding court with a group of
women from the Fine Arts Department. Trish hadn't sat
with the Art Department graduates because she'd wanted
to sit with Pam and Hillary.

"Won't you reconsider coming to Iran with us, Trish?"
Her mother's blond cap of Doris Day curls shone in the
sunlight.

Trish tried to get Professor Matalon's attention. He
was looking the other way. "I'll come for a visit," Trish
promised.

"We're embarking on quite an adventure, old girl,"
her father said. "Like Peter O'Toole."

"You mean T. E. Lawrence?" Tommy could be super-
cilious, she thought, the way he would never go out with
her girlfriends when she tried to fix him up. They weren't
good enough for him.

"Dow Chemical's loss is Shell Oil's gain," she said, to
soften her brother's remark. Professor Matalon saw her
and waved. She beckoned. He excused himself from his
group and came toward her. Her heart pounded.

"These are my parents, Matthew and Patricia Baldwin,
and my brother, Tom. This is Professor Matalon, a brilliant artist and my painting instructor." Her father and

her brother shook his hand. He looked regal in his faculty robe, the colored ribbon draped around his neck, even better than he'd looked at the awards breakfast that morning, when she'd been presented with a special award. He smiled warmly at Patricia. "Your daughter tells me you're moving to the Middle East. How I envy you that experience. Oriental subjects have always been a source of inspiration to Western artists."

Patricia was spellbound in an instant, but not Matthew. Sensing a rival for his daughter's devotion brought out the worst in him.

"Like I've been telling Trish, now that she's graduated it's time to settle down, get married." He turned to Trish. "Someone like that Brad you used to date. Whatever happened to him?"

"He's around," Trish said, feeling herself start to blush.

"Don't you agree, Professor?" Matt asked him.

A look passed between Trish and the professor, and his eyes twinkled in response. If her father only knew about Brad.

"But your daughter's very talented, Mr. Baldwin. We're happy to have her in our postgraduate program."

Matthew shook his head, patted his paunch. "This artist thing, well . . ." He was unwilling to give it any credibility. "No offense, you understand. But it's no life for a woman, except as a hobby."

Professor Matalon knew quite well that art wasn't a hobby to her, it was her life. But she'd hidden her passion, her compulsive need to do it, from her parents, as an alcoholic hides a flask. "Dad, I can be an artist and be married. It's not against the law!" She tried to change the subject. "Will you be taking some time off this summer?" she asked Professor Matalon.

"Yes, I'll be spending time down the coast. You must come and visit. You and Brad." He winked.

She could feel the color rise to her cheeks. He kissed her mother's hand in farewell.

"What a handsome man," Patricia said.

"If you like the type," Matthew replied.

Tommy was watching her. She glanced away.

Her father took hold of her arm firmly and started marching her toward the street, as if getting her away from something dangerous. Even he sensed the undercurrent. "I'll give you one year to get this out of your system, Trish, and then find a good business job or a husband, and that's that. The allowance and tuition will stop. Mother and I have paid for you children long enough; we have to start saving for ourselves. Certainly, Tommy, you know we'll finance your law school until you pass the bar," he called back to Tom, who was walking behind them, "but after that, you're both on your own."

Trish looked at her mother to see if this was true, begging for it not to be. Her mother looked away. Her father's words pulled the oxygen out of the air. If she couldn't be an artist, there was no life to look forward to. The thought of working in some office made her body recoil—being locked up, breathing cigarette smoke all day, typing, filing, smiling at the boss—to earn money so she could paint. She'd do anything for that. But the thought of being poor was frightening. They were paying for Tommy's graduate education, why not hers? How could she manage without their help? She'd never been without good clothes and food, and a beautiful home. She hardly had any job experience, not like Pam, who'd always worked. Artists often starved—part of the package; but could she do it?

They were walking through Sather Gate toward Larry Blake's, where they were meeting Hillary and her parents for dinner. People she knew waved at her and she waved back; most of them she would never see again.

"We got an offer on the house," her mother said.

Trish and Tommy exchanged a look; the family home sold out from under them, ranch-style in Pacific Palisades, where mornings were made misty gray by the onshore fog, but afternoons were clear and sunny yellow, as cool as the cherry creamsicle from Mr. Mahoney's market. Couldn't go home now, no choice. But her parents going to oilfields halfway around the world didn't make her as lonely as being left behind by Hillary and Pam. She was a baby newly birthed and terrified.

"Daddy, what should I do with my check stubs and bank receipts?"

Her brother snorted, "For God's sake, Trish, grow up."

But she hardly heard him. *What will I do if my car breaks down?* Her father had always taken care of those things. Panic goaded her, teased her throat near to closing. *What if they raise my rent? What if my landlord won't fix the heat? What if I get sick? Or have an accident?*

She looked at Tommy. *On your own, baby*, his eyes said. Why was he more capable of handling a crisis than she? But he didn't have a crisis, they were giving him money.

She looked at her deserting parents. *Arthur will help*, she thought, clutching at his essence with a drowning child's frantic hands. *Professor Arthur Matalon.*

4

Hillary cried during the graduation ceremony because of the poignancy of the occasion, but mostly because of what she had to tell her parents. This would be the hardest thing she had ever done. She explained to her brother Bobby that she wanted to be alone with Mom and Dad, and then the three of them walked through campus to the bridge in the leafy glen over Strawberry Creek.

"I can tell something is bothering you," her father said, putting his arm around her; she pulled away.

"Ben, leave her alone," her mother admonished.

Hillary stopped and turned. Her heart was so high in her throat she could feel it choking her.

"What is it, Hillary?" The color had drained from her mother's face.

"I'm pregnant, Mom," Hillary said, forcing herself not to look away.

The look in her father's eyes wounded her more deeply than she thought possible. Her mother gasped and clutched her heart, then tightened her trembling lips.

For a moment no one spoke. Only the sound of birds, the occasional break of other voices, and the water rushing over the rocks interrupted the silence.

Finally her mother said, "Are you sure, Hillary? There's no mistake?"

Hillary nodded.

"My God, Hillary." Her father turned away.

"Ben," her mother said, "what's done is done. Mel is a good boy. They'll be happy."

A sob caught in Hillary's throat and the tears spilled over. "Daddy, do you hate me?"

He turned back, even more shocked. "Hate you, Hillary? Never could I hate you, no matter what."

But the ever-constant glow of love in his eyes for her was now mixed with deep disappointment, and that cut like a knife. "I don't understand, Hillary. A young woman of your caliber, an honor student, a teacher, a girl with your upbringing, how could you let this happen? Your mother and I have always expected better of you." He turned away to hide his tears, or was it rage?

"It's not the most terrible thing in the world, Daddy." Her heart was breaking, absolutely breaking. "I love him. I made a mistake, but I'll make up for it." Sobs shook her body. She'd had no idea how much she would be hurting him. Nor was she ready to be a mother. God, it was awful. Didn't he know how scared she was, how sick, both in her body and her soul? Only last night she and Mel had settled it. For a while she'd thought it was all over between them, that she'd have to solve this problem on her own.

She was at a farewell dinner with Pam and Trish at Larry Blake's when Mel found her and dragged her away from the table. He knew she'd gotten the results of her test that afternoon. "Why didn't you call me?" he'd demanded when they were out in front of the restaurant.

"I did." Her voice rose with alarm. "I spoke to Craig Goldman, he said he'd tell you."

"Well, he didn't."

She couldn't meet his eyes.

"Well?" There was panic in his voice.

She nodded.

"Oh God," he exclaimed. And then, "I'll be damned if I'll be forced into this."

Her first impulse was to wring her hands the way her mother always did when something went wrong, and then she thought about falling on her knees, clutching at him, humbling herself, begging for his forgiveness, convincing him it had been an accident. But her pride won out. She held herself very straight and said, "I don't like being forced into it either, Mel. But you were as eager as I was, that first time. Neither of us worried about protection until we went to Carmel."

"So now what?" he asked, more of himself than of her. "I've got the bar exam in August. I'll never pass it with this hanging over my head. Do you know what percentage of graduates pass the bar the first time?"

"Mel, you're fourth in your class, and Law Review."

"It's no guarantee. Damn, Hillary. This is the worst thing that's ever happened to me. One time. One fucking time we fucked without a rubber. I don't believe it."

She winced at his words, looked around to see if anyone passing by had heard him. "Do you want me to go to some back-alley abortionist with a coat hanger?" She was willing to tear her heart out and serve it to him on a platter if that would do any good.

He looked at her then, realizing that this was probably the worst thing that had ever happened to her, too, and some of his anger dissipated. "Maybe you could go horseback riding."

"If you want me to," she said. "You don't have any obligation to me, Mel. I want you to know that."

"You know I do," he said. "And you know I'll do the right thing if it comes to that. I've just got to get used to the idea."

"I'm sure we could find a safe abortionist."

"They're never safe when they're illegal, Hillary. I couldn't let you take a risk like that." He sighed, and she saw tears in his eyes. "Why don't you go back inside with Pam and Trish, and I'll see you tomorrow at graduation. I've got a lot of thinking to do."

She felt numb, separated from reality as she turned to go.

"Hillary."

She stopped and looked at him, trying to swallow that huge lump in her throat. "I do love you. It's just such a shock." And then he was gone.

"I'm going to need your help," Hillary said to her friends when she got back to their table. "I've decided that if Mel won't marry me, I'm going to keep the baby. I'll raise it with my parents until I can make a life for the two of us." Trish and Pam gazed at her with pain in their eyes.

"How are you going to tell your parents?" Trish asked.

And Pam said, "Mel Robin had better run when he sees me coming."

Just then, there was a commotion at the door to the restaurant and they all turned to look. Mel had come back.

He made his way through the crowded room, embarrassed but determined.

His eyes met Hillary's as she gazed up at him. Then he reached out and took her hand, pulling her out of her chair. "I love you," he said, thinking she was the only one listening, unaware of people watching at nearby tables. "I'm sorry for the way I acted before," he said. "Will you do me the honor of marrying me?" And everyone in the restaurant had cheered.

As Hillary kissed him, she heard Pam say, "If he hadn't come through for her, I would have killed him."

"Ben," her mother said. Hillary knew a look had passed between her parents that said, *Leave her alone, already.* And then she felt her father's hand on her shoulder.

"Don't cry, darling," he soothed, unable to take her pain, especially if he was adding to it. "It'll be all right. You don't have to marry him if you don't want to. You can have the baby and give it up for adoption, or we can adopt it ourselves. You know we would do anything in the world for you, anything."

Tears blurred her vision, but she heard his concern, felt surrounded again by his love. "I could never do that, Daddy, give up my baby. Especially because I love Mel. Both of us made the mistake. Don't blame him for everything."

"She's right, Ben. It could be worse. Mel could refuse to marry her, leave her alone to handle this by herself."

Ben sighed, took hold of her chin, and raised her face to look at him. "At least he's being a mensch about it." He was trying to show her he would make the best of this. "You love him, this bum?"

"Yes," she whispered. "I really do."

He gazed at her, a long look that said, *Okay, if that's your choice, but it'll take him a lifetime to prove himself to me.* He sighed. "Look at it this way, we won't have to pay for a photographer at the wedding."

Her mother *humphed,* but Hillary's sadness began to lift, hearing the standard family joke. Ben was a professional photographer, and he never charged anyone in the family to take pictures at their weddings or bar mitzvahs; his photographs were the Markuses' contribution to the event. One time a little cousin had said, "It's too bad your father doesn't sell television sets. Then we could have had one of those instead of pictures."

Hillary could see what an effort her father was making to be fair. She'd never loved him more than at this moment.

Barbara spoke. "That assistant of yours—is he good enough to handle your own daughter's wedding, Ben? You can't do it. You'll be too busy walking down the aisle with Hillary, greeting our guests, and dancing with me to shoot the pictures."

"My assistant'll do fine."

Her mother gave him one of those looks, meaning, *We don't want to be sorry*.

"So how much time do we have?" Her father's ears reddened as he asked the question, and he looked away; his daughter's body would betray this secret in a short time, and in front of their friends.

"I'm sure it's very early, Ben." Barbara had the authority of a woman who expects this to happen from the moment she gives birth to a daughter. "We have weeks before she'll show; there's still time to make arrangements."

"Mel won't even be here to help plan the wedding," Hillary explained. "He has to go east to study for the New York bar exam."

"Maybe it's better," her mother said. "Saves aggravation, let me tell you, when fewer people interfere." And then she gasped and looked at her husband, whose face had suddenly turned as pale as her own. "New York?" they both said together. "He's going to practice law in New York?"

"You're not moving there?" her father asked.

"Oh my God," her mother exclaimed. "Ben, what are we going to do?"

And now it was a real disaster.

Hillary hadn't realized what the main tragedy would be. She'd been too concerned about her moral dilemma to think about what moving to New York would mean to her parents—or to her, for that matter. She'd totally avoided thinking about this; she was not just getting married, she was leaving home and going far away. "Please, we'll have to talk about this later. I can't take any more right now. I've hurt you both so much. Believe me, I don't want to go and live in New York. I hate the idea. But what can I do?" She was crying again, wondering if all this emotional upheaval could affect the pregnancy. Maybe she'd lose the baby and none of this would happen, marriage and parenthood and moving away, leaving her dear parents: her wonderful mother—who she'd always imagined would live next door to teach her how to cook, and how to care for the first grandchild in the family—would be in California and she'd be in New York.

Her mother came and put her arms around her. "You've got to go where your husband goes, Hillary. Whither thou goest, and all that." She smiled wanly. "New York isn't so far away." Now her mother was hugging her and crying, too. "Maybe when your father retires we could move there."

Hillary laughed in spite of her sorrow. "Mother, when New Yorkers retire, they come to California."

"I can't stand it, Ben. I'm losing my baby, and her baby too."

Her father put his arms around both of them. "When all the tears are over, Barbara, we'll be able to see this as a blessing. We've got our health, our daughter's marrying a smart boy who's going to be a success, and there's such a thing as phones and mail and photographs and vacations."

"I know," her mother said, still crying. "You're right, you're always right." She pulled away from his embrace and turned to Hillary. "I love you so much, honey. My precious Hillary. A wife and a mother." She shook her head then, and managed a smile through her tears. Then she pulled Hillary to her and hugged her fiercely; the two of them clung and cried. Finally it was Barbara who pulled away. "So tell me, do you think your cousin Judy would loan you her wedding dress?"

Hillary shrugged and smiled. "I guess so."

"Why shouldn't she?" Ben said. "I took the pictures of their wedding for free."

Hillary hugged her father tight. "Daddy, I'm so sorry. Tell me it's going to be all right. It is, isn't it?"

"You bet it is, sweetheart. 'Cause I'm gonna see to it. And if that Mel isn't good to you, he'll have me to answer to."

BOOK
II

Persistent
Memories

1

The July humidity hit Pam the moment she stepped off
the airplane—wet, oppressive heat that was at first a
curiosity and then a real discomfort, but she loved it,
opened up her arms to embrace it. Differences in the
people came next: more harried, tense, expressive, and
definitely more verbal, they called to one another, hugged
with emotion. By comparison, Californians seemed more
inhibited, more reluctant to show their feelings. She heard
the distinctive accents and smiled. They filled her with
excitement. She wanted to be a New *Yoarker* too, and
say it the way they did. She wanted to think of the Statue
of Liberty as a personal friend and the incredible sights
of Manhattan as part of her everyday world. She wanted
to talk like these people, who used their hands to express
themselves, who threw their arms around one another to
show they cared; she wanted to live like them, let the
pace of this world race through her blood, inspire her to
hurry up and get there. And tomorrow she would see all
the sights, the Lady herself, the Empire State Building,
the subway, the museums, Central Park, the Palm Court,
even if she had to walk her feet off. God, the anticipation
beat in her more intensely than the heat.

The bus ride into the Port Authority terminal in Manhattan was long and bumpy, but when she got her first
glimpse of the skyline she wanted to let out a yell. And
then she was on an actual New York sidewalk, gazing,
gawking, craning her neck like every other hick who'd
ever come here, clutching tightly to her suitcase. It was a
hell of a lot to conquer, but that was why she'd come.
But as the crowds jostled her and as the setting sun
sneaked its way between the buildings and the noise
enveloped, her, her bravado slipped. The massive struc-

45

tures were such a challenge. *Here we are,* the huge mono-liths called. *Come take us if you can.* And she realized how impossible was her dream. But then her eyes came down from the heights to the streets again and she saw they were filled with ordinary people who lived one day at a time the way she did. Some of them would make it—many of them, in fact. And if they did it she could too. She smiled at people and they smiled back, making her spirits soar. She was filled with such a joy that she wanted to embrace the whole island at once, see everything in one day, become one with her new city, the most exciting city in the world. She couldn't wait to call her father.

The Barbizon Hotel for Women was the least expensive place she could find, but on her budget Pam could only afford to stay there for two weeks. She was assigned a tiny cubicle for twenty dollars a day. It had a single bed and a sink; there was a pseudo-Impressionist print on the wall, and the bathroom was down the hall. The first person she met was the girl in the next room—Sandy from Minneapolis, who was giving herself a pedicure.

"Your feet are a major asset," Sandy told her, "so wear your most comfortable shoes when you're hunting for a job and an apartment. You can't believe how much you'll walk. And go down to Klein's to buy yourself some white gloves like these." She gestured to a pair lying on the dresser. "Everyone wears white gloves, but at Klein's they're a real bargain, hand-stitched, with pearl buttons at the wrist, made of cotton and polyester. After climbing onto buses and subways all day, you'll see how black they get, but these are easy to wash. You just leave them on when you wash your hands. Lather, scrub, rinse, and squeeze your fingers together." She had a friendly smile that bunched up her cheeks so that her eyes were hardly visible.

Pam thought the trick of how to wash your gloves was clever. "What else?"

"The Automat's just a cafeteria with food in machines. No big deal. The rents are worse than you imagined and the apartments are terrible. My lease starts in three days and I've already got two roommates, or I'd offer to share with you. I've been trying for two weeks, but no job offers yet, except with the employment agency I went to. They said they'd train me to be an employment counselor."

Pam tried not to be discouraged, but it was a bit overwhelming. "How do you meet men?"

"Get fixed up. I called this guy who's a friend of my mother's in Minneapolis. Back home, if a girl calls a guy first, her reputation is ruined. But here it's okay. He asked me for a drink. That's what they do in New York, ask you for a drink, 'cause the drinking age is younger here. But he didn't take me for dinner. Then a friend of his called me, so I'm dating him now. I could ask Lew if he could fix you up."

"That might be nice," Pam said, realizing that this wasn't college. She couldn't walk up to some attractive man and say, "I'm Pam, want to take me to dinner?" She didn't know a soul. But then, dating was not at the top of her list.

"So what do you want to be, an actress or a model? I'm trying for the theater."

"Neither," Pam said. "Ever since I was a kid I've wanted a career in real-estate development and construction. I was the only girl in my apartment building who played with trucks and dolls. My father is a general contractor. I'm going to work for him."

Sandy flung herself back against the pillows and stared at Pam, looking up and down the tall, narrow body, sizing up the square, sculpted jaw, the generous mouth, the pale blue eyes, the tanned, unblemished skin, the prominent cheekbones, the honey-blond hair pulled into a braid down her back; she took in the overall impact of her looks and the self-confident expression and said, "You sure could have fooled me."

First thing the next morning, Pam dialed her father and got his secretary on the phone. "May I speak to William Grayson, please. This is his daughter calling."

There was a long pause, and then the secretary said, "I'm afraid you must have the wrong number."

"No," Pam said. "I'm calling Grayson Construction Company, Mr. Grayson. Is he in?"

"Yes, but excuse me, miss, I've been with Mr. Grayson for twelve years, and he doesn't have a daughter."

Pam felt her cheeks burning. "Believe me, that's who I am. Please, may I speak to him?"

"I'm sorry, but he's in conference. Would you care to leave a number?"

That old aching disappointment began to overtake her. Leave a number? Oh God, not again. "I'll call back," she said. And she hung up.

Feeling humiliated, she could hear her mother's voice: *What did you expect?* Then she realized, *I'm not being fair. He doesn't even know I'm here.* She called back again.

"Please let me explain," she said quickly, after the operator had put her through to her father's secretary again. "What I meant to say was that Mr. Grayson has been *like* a father to me. Would you please tell him Pam is on the line?"

In a moment he came on the line. "Pam? Where are you calling from?"

Just hearing his voice made her heart pound.

"I'm here, in New York. I got in yesterday."

"I can't believe it. You wrote that you might be coming, but I never expected it so soon. How was graduation? I am sorry I couldn't be there. How do you like New York so far?"

"Oh, Dad, it's fabulous. There's so much to see, so much to do. I especially love . . . everything."

They laughed. Then silence.

"How long are you staying?"

Why was he asking that? It was all in her letter. Hadn't he read it? "I've moved here, Dad. I've wanted to ever since I was a kid, but, well, you know, the money and all." *Don't make him feel guilty, don't get off to a bad start.* "But now I'm here, and I'm hoping that you and I can spend time together, get to know one another. That's something I've really missed." Just saying it, knowing he was hearing it, made the emotion well up and she was afraid she would start to cry. The sadness of a whole lifetime without him threatened to come pouring out.

His voice wavered, and she sensed his discomfort. "So what are you going to do now?"

With great effort she controlled her emotions. "Well, I'd like to get a job. Which is another reason I'm calling. I was wondering if I could get a job in your company. I'd take anything available, just to get started."

"Just a minute," he said, and put her on hold.

Her heart was still pounding. This wasn't going the way she'd hoped. And though every ounce of her being prayed that he would say the right words, make the offer she'd wanted to hear her whole life—*Come work with me, come be my real daughter*—all the years of rejection had taught her that her expectations were naïve, that she'd never get what she wanted, and that this time wouldn't be any different. *It has to be!* she told herself. But a coldness crept through her, even though the temperature was in the high eighties. Here she was, a college graduate, dangerously believing in fairy tales. No, not just believing, but needing them to come true with every ounce of her strength.

"Pam, are you there? Now, where were we?"

The coldness had entered her voice. "I mentioned a job, with Gray-Con."

Again, silence. Then he said, "Why don't I speak to personnel and see if there's anything available?"

"Dad, it's your company. If you want someone, you can make a job available for them, can't you?"

"That wouldn't be right. I have partners to answer to. I can't just say to them that I want my—this young woman to come and work for me. And in what capacity?"

"I want to learn the business from you. I'm willing to start at the bottom, ground floor." She tried to make a joke.

No response. Then, "It's out of the question."

"But why? Ever since I was a child, I've dreamed of coming to New York and working in the business with you. You know that. I love what you do, I want to learn everything. Believe me, I'll work hard. I graduated with honors, majored in business because I thought it would give me a broader base than civil engineering, but I'm planning to go to graduate school and take some structural engineering classes if you think I need it."

"Why don't we have lunch and talk about it? Maybe sometime next week." She sensed his reluctance as an enormous weight she didn't have the strength to budge, like the feeling of trying to awaken from a deep sleep and not being able to.

"Dad, I don't want to wait a week to see you. I'm talking about coming to work for you now. I know construction is not the kind of business most girls like, but I do, especially if you'd teach me. I know I could learn."

"Teach you? Construction? You *are* kidding, aren't you?"

"No, not at all."

"I don't know what to say."

Maybe if I'd done this more slowly, she thought, *become reacquainted first, let him get to know me, see that I'm not a threat to his status quo. I won't interfere with his darling Jennifer and their sons. I'll never ask him for any more money. God, I can't believe this is happening again. It can't be, it just can't be!*

"Why don't I come over there and we can talk about it in person?"

"When?"

"Now. I'm at the Barbizon, and you're on Sixty-first."

"Now? Pam, that's impossible. I have to be on a job site in twenty minutes. Call me next week. I'll speak to personnel. Maybe there's something in the secretarial pool, or even bookkeeping, we have girls working there, but don't get your hopes up. I'm sorry, Pam, but I don't have time to discuss this right now."

Oh God, he was doing it again. The warmth she'd heard in his voice when she'd first called had shifted into something she couldn't penetrate; that same old shell encased him, she heard it, hated it, remembered it from every time she'd ever asked him for anything, especially his time. But those childhood needs were a thing of the past; the terrible, hurtful disappointments wouldn't tear her insides apart anymore. It wasn't like that now, she wouldn't let it be. How could she make him understand? "Dad, I miss you. I'd just like to see you. How about it?"

Another pause, a slight chink in the shell. "Maybe you'll come out to Connecticut for lunch on Saturday. Oh, wait a minute, not this weekend, we're going to Southampton. But the weekend after may be good, I'll have Jennifer call you. Okay?" *Jennifer? He's passing me off to her? The Wicked Witch of the East.* "And, Pam, it's nice of you to think of me, but there's nothing for you in my company. Construction is no place for a girl. Neither is New York, for that matter. Why don't you just stay for the summer, have some fun, and then go back to Califor-

nia? You're at the Barbizon for Women? A week from
Saturday, all right?" And he hung up.

That knife of pain was piercing her guts again. With all
her strength she kept it away. She heard her mother's
voice, saw her smirky smile, saw her finger pointing, *I
told you so*. He'd done it again. She should have known.
He didn't want her around, not then and not now. This
time she couldn't blame it on her mother. The thought
was too painful to allow; she set it aside for another time.
Somehow she had to separate their personal relationship
from the business one, make him understand that she'd
be damned good in his company. She could master it, if
he'd teach her. And if not, she'd learn it on her own, get
a job with another company, show him she was worthy of
working by his side. Maybe, once she proved how serious
she was, he'd believe her. Damn it, that was what she
had to do, and before a week from Saturday. She was
about to walk out of the room to spend her first day in
the city, determined not to let this temporary setback
stop her. But before she left, she sat down on the bed for
just a minute to think over what her father had said. And
suddenly, more than his words, that feeling of rejection
came flooding back. She tried not to let it, but despair
overwhelmed her and she threw herself on the narrow
bed and sobbed with a broken heart.

The secretary to the personnel director at Rosewood
Construction disapproved of her height, and especially
that she was from California. "They do grow them tall
out there," she said. "We'll have to get you an adjustable
typing chair and table." She handed Pam a standard
typing test along with her employment form.

"I'm not here for a secretarial job," Pam said, thinking
the woman had misunderstood. "I'm applying for the
training program either in management or as a consulting
contractor."

The woman's lips formed an even thinner line of disapproval. "Mr. Boylston will only repeat to you what I'm
going to tell you, even if you insist on seeing him. There
are no openings in our training program. We recruit on
campuses each spring and choose the finest young men
out of each graduating class in engineering. If you want a

job in the secretarial pool, I suggest you take this typing test now."

Pam rose with dignity and left the office.

It was the same story at Tishman Realty and Construction, Coldwell Banker, Helmsley-Spear, and William Zeckendorf. A woman's place was in the typing pool, and that was not what she had come to New York to do. She couldn't convince anyone that a beautiful young woman was truly interested in the construction of buildings. Well, if she was forced to take a job as a secretary, it would only be until she got a graduate degree in business and took some classes in engineering and real-estate management. Then she would have a better chance for a job in this man's world. But that would take money, something she had in short supply.

Sandy from Minneapolis was right: apartments were small, dreary, and terribly expensive. And how could she sign a lease without a job?

After two weeks of trying to get work other than as a secretary or gal Friday, she was running out of construction companies. Her father's profession was as impenetrable as he was. Yet wherever she went around the city she saw a familiar logo—Gray-Con—on buildings in various stages of construction. It was impressive; her father's company was one of the biggest. She tried not to feel resentful, told herself she'd put her childish wishes to rest long ago, that she only needed him as an adult needs an adult, as a business companion, but that child inside still wanted Daddy. She gazed at the Gray-Con sign with longing. Surely he could find something for her. He was her father.

The taxi that picked her up at the station in Stamford, Connecticut, wound through the quaint little town, but Pam could hardly enjoy the view for the knots in her stomach. It had been so long since she'd seen him.

Summer was in full bloom with an abundance of greenery. California was green, but not like this, green on top of green. Forests and vines encroached to the edges of park-sized lawns with buildings on them that looked like something from a Dickens novel—more like universities than homes.

The roads were narrow, tree-lined lanes, winding through

magnificent property. And the farther she rode away
from the town, the larger the expanses of land. Pam
began to realize what it meant that her father's house had
a name instead of an address.

The taxi driver slowed down in front of iron gates set
between cypress bushes. A driveway led from the gates
across a hill of lawn. There was no end to the surrounding stone wall, and no house in sight.

"Want to get out here?" the driver asked. "Or shall I
take you all the way?"

"How far is it?"

"A ways," he said, turning into the green velvet blanket. It took five minutes of driving, past the stables and
the caretaker's house, which was two stories high, built
of stone, and surrounded by flower gardens all in bloom,
before the main house came into view. Six round brick
chimneys arose from six different slate roof points; huge,
carved double doors gleamed in the sunlight; and leafy
trees shaded the approach to the house. She could hardly
contain her amazement, it was so beautiful, so enormous
and imposing. She fought back memories of how she and
her mother had lived all their lives in cramped apartments, making do on a waitress's salary, and for a brief
moment she understood her mother's bitterness. But she
wasn't bitter; she would hold a different place in her
father's life. Nevertheless, all this opulence made her feel
small-town and out-of-place in her white piqué dress, and
her heart beat with painful memories of miserable times
juxtaposed against all this splendor.

Just then the front door opened and a butler came out,
walked down the steps, and opened the taxicab door for
her. She paid the driver.

"Welcome to Briarwood, miss," he said. He wasn't
English, but Oriental. "Mr. and Mrs. Grayson are on the
terrace. Right this way."

It was Disneyland and a 20th-Century Fox movie.
Chandeliers, waxed parquet floors, a circular staircase,
delicate Impressionist oils, lemon yellow silk sofas, Sher-
aton tables, and a wall of leaded glass that opened onto a
huge stone terrace. Below, a turquoise pool sparkled in
the sun, and off to the side were two tennis courts. Two
young boys swam in the pool, cavorting, splashing, shouting. *My brothers*, she thought. She hadn't realized what it

would mean to walk into this house, this mansion, and come face to face with the living proof of her speculations. She followed the butler out to the terrace.

Jennifer had hardly aged at all, in her mid-thirties, beautiful even without makeup, her thick, dark hair in a ponytail. She was wearing tennis clothes, and her long legs were tanned. Pam had been six years old the first time she'd seen a picture of Jennifer in *Vogue*, modeling a taffeta gown. She was so beautiful. Joanne had pointed to the picture and said, "That's the woman your father is marrying." Pam had been in awe of her on the two occasions when Jennifer had come with William to California, but Pam had always sensed Jennifer's dislike. Now things would be different; she was an adult. It didn't seem possible that all this was real.

"Why, Pamela. How lovely you are." Jennifer extended her hand to shake. Pam approached and took it, feeling instantly relieved. She noticed the patio table was set as though an artist had done it, all gleaming silverware, china, and crystal, with pink flowers in the center. "Hasn't she grown up beautifully, William?"

Pam had been so dazzled with everything else, she hadn't really seen her father, but then she turned and looked at him and her heart caught in her throat. *Daddy,* she thought. Her father smiled awkwardly, and she felt a rush of love for him. Then she saw the shock on his face as he looked at her; he'd expected the coltish teenager she'd been the last time he was in California, and here she was, a woman. It made her proud, but also wary. She felt his arms go around her, smelled the scent of his cologne. He too wore tennis shorts and a shirt. The sun blinded her for a moment as she clung to him. Such a long time since she'd been held like this. She never wanted to let him go. She was in a fog, seeing him, the boys, this house. Being in his embrace felt so good she could almost taste it on her tongue. She tried to banish thoughts of Joanne and her apartment with the torn carpeting, that greasy old sofa bed—all she'd grown up with, compared to this.

"Sit down," her father said. His hand shook.

"Hey Dad, watch me!" one of the boys called out, as he jumped off the board into a cannonball splash.

"Is that Daniel?" she asked.

"Yes," Jennifer replied.

"They're so grown up," Pam said.

"Eight and ten," Jennifer told her. "Daniel will go to Choate soon; Billy too."

Pam could tell that was important from the way Jennifer said it.

"Pam." Her father spoke to her and she turned to stare into his daylight blue eyes, surprised at how much she resembled him. His sandy hair was getting gray, and she recognized the same cheekbones as hers, but his were lined, the cleft in his chin identical to hers. He reminded her of a blue-eyed Gary Cooper. "I can't get over how you've changed. I can't get over it." He looked away, as if the sight of her were indeed too much for him, then forced his eyes to meet hers. "There's something I have to discuss with you. I hope it won't embarrass you, but the boys don't know about you. They don't know I was married before. I told them you were a cousin from California. I decided they're a bit young to digest the truth. So, if you wouldn't mind, I'd like to keep it between ourselves, okay?"

His words were so hurtful that her brain refused to accept them. She almost started to laugh, and glanced at Jennifer as if to ask, *He doesn't really mean this, does he?* But Jennifer was smiling sweetly, as though this were perfectly natural. Only the white knuckles of her tanned hands, that clutched the arms of her wrought-iron chair, gave away her tension. No help there. The laugh died on Pam's face.

Pam was afraid she might lose control, but she held on. *Cousin from California? No!* she wanted to scream. "I understand, Dad." But she didn't. All these years he'd kept her a secret. Was he so ashamed of her? And Jennifer let him, probably encouraged him. She glanced at Jennifer and saw that same steely resentment was still there. "What should I call you, then? Uncle Bill?" The words stuck in her throat; the warm humid air closed in around her.

"William will be fine," he said, this time with no smile, merely an embarrassed flush.

She felt her lower lip quiver, and a sharp pain shot through her chest, but she fought for composure, took a deep breath. *No ulcer,* she thought, trying to relax. *Don't give Jennifer the satisfaction.* She reached for a glass of water, but it didn't help. Her apprehension was growing every moment; it had begun when she'd first called him, two weeks ago, and now it was setting in: her fantasies and expectations were leftover dreams, dusty on her tongue. The reality was that she could not become part of his family or work by his side if he kept her a stranger. Yet still she excused him, thinking, *He's not rejecting me, he's protecting his sons.*

"So. How do you like New York? And what are your plans?" Jennifer asked.

For a moment Pam couldn't speak, as she fought for composure. *Keep it light,* she told herself, *and sincere.* "Didn't Dad tell you? More than anything else, I want to work in the construction business with him. But since he didn't think that was possible, I decided to get a job with another company." She saw a look pass between Jennifer and her father; she smiled with forced charm. "Breaking into the construction business has been more difficult than I thought, even with a degree from Berkeley, magna cum laude. Nobody in the East is very impressed by a University of California degree. But maybe an M.A. would help, and some engineering classes, don't you agree?" She glanced at her father, who had pulled down that invisible mask again. The smile on her face was becoming a grimace. "Of course, classes are expensive, and I need to get an apartment, find a roommate, save up some money. Unless you could see your way clear to make me a loan?" She hurried to assure them, "I'd pay back any tuition you might advance me." Jennifer's tension was apparent, but Pam's appeal was to her father. "I really am serious about working for you, you know," she said finally, when he didn't comment. "I know I could be an asset."

"Five more minutes, boys," Jennifer called, interrupting her.

Groans and protests came from the pool.

Her father's expression had grown even more remote, until she saw a furrow between his eyes that she thought was disapproval, and it caused an icy tightening in her chest.

Her father glanced at Jennifer as if for corroboration,

then leaned forward and set his drink down on the glass table. She heard the cubes rattling, or was it her bones?

"I remember telling you, Pamela," he said calmly, but with intensity, "that after I paid for your college tuition, there would be no more money from me once you graduated. And yet here you are, asking for more. And not only that, you're still clinging to that harebrained idea of working with me in the business. I was sure you'd given that up long ago, in spite of what you wrote in your letters. I've never encouraged you, have I? I've told you over and over that it's not a good idea." He shook his head. "But you and your mother have always had crazy ideas. The construction business is a tough, dirty business. It isn't like selling typewriters for IBM, or soap for Procter & Gamble, or dresses at Bergdorf's. That's where you belong. Why don't you try those places? Ever since you got the idea about coming here, I've tried to discourage you. It wasn't a good idea for you to move to New York, but you never listened—stubborn just like . . ." He didn't have to finish the sentence. But she was picking up something else beneath his painful words, a kind of desperation to keep her away from him. Why? she kept wondering. Was she so bad? "You belong in California," he went on with that same need to convince, "away from my business. Frankly, I don't even like the idea of you being in the secretarial pool. No. Gray-Con is not the place for you. You say you're a grown woman; then prove it. Stand on your own two feet, and not in my world."

"All right," she agreed, feeling a kind of breathless pain fill her throat. He was so upset. The distance between them made her physically ill. All she wanted was to be held in his arms, yet she could plainly see that those arms were forbidden to her. Why? His words were strong, even tough, yet too intense. Would he be like this with Billy or Danny if they wanted to get master's degrees in business, or carry on the family name? Certainly not. Was this stranger the father whom she'd loved and thought about constantly? She felt utterly alone. It was a long way from here back to New York, and even longer back to California. Maybe she really didn't belong here. Then she remembered what life was like in California, with Joanne taking everything she earned. Perhaps he felt she was a drain on him, the way Joanne was on her. He had it within his power to give her the entire world. Her world consisted of two things, his love and the profession she'd always dreamed of, but he was denying her both.

The boys approached, wrapped in towels, large white monogrammed ones. A maid came out of the house and helped them into white terrycloth robes, also with monograms. They sat down as the first course was served. "Hi, guys," she said, forcing cheerfulness, not waiting for an introduction. "I'm Pam, from California."

They smiled at her shyly. They had freckles and reddish brown hair. She loved them instantly, had fantasies of spending Sundays with them at the zoo. Her very own stepbrothers. It had never occurred to her that she'd love them. They were a touching consolation. "This is some neat house you've got. And a pool. Which one of you is the better swimmer?"

They competed with one another for her attention, each claiming superiority. They told her about their horses, their school, their tennis lessons, and Boy Scouts.

"I was a Girl Scout," she said, but it was like ancient history to them. "I'd love to see your room after lunch," she offered.

"Oh, we don't sleep together," Billy said. "We each have a bedroom and a playroom and a study of our own."

"Of course," she replied, unable even to glance at her father. She felt cut off from him, as though she were an appendage he had no more use for.

Lunch continued. Another maid took away the cold potato soup—vichyssoise, Jennifer called it—and brought them chicken salad in a scooped-out pineapple, one half-pineapple for each person. Moist, thick chunks of chicken salad melted in her mouth, decorated with radishes and carrots cut like flowers with leaves of pimiento. Dessert was homemade blackberry pie. "We grow the berries ourselves," Jennifer told her.

Her father spoke very little during lunch; her sidelong glances were making him uncomfortable, but she couldn't help it. How could she get through to him? After lunch, the boys were anxious to show her their rooms, but after another meaningful look from Jennifer, her father detained her, his hand on her arm. It was the only time he'd touched her, beyond their first embrace, and her heart leaped with hope. "You two go ahead. I'd like to have a word with Pam, alone."

She turned toward his gaze, and their eyes met, hers filled with admiration, his with something she didn't understand. Pain? Embarrassment? Was he that ashamed of her? She shivered even in the warm, humid afternoon. How could she make this reunion coincide with her expectations?

"I appreciate your making the best of an awkward situation, Pamela," he began. She heard the pleading in his voice, but didn't know to whom it was directed. "Please understand that this is difficult for me to say, but I have to. We're getting the impression that you have some kind of expectation other than wanting to work in my company."

It was getting harder to breathe. "Like what?" she asked.

"Like becoming a part of this family." His embarrassment stopped him.

But Jennifer continued, "We don't mean to hurt you, Pam, but with things the way they are, it isn't possible. Your father cares for you, but it's been a long time since you and he were close."

So it was Jennifer who didn't want her around, making demands on her husband. The jealous stepmother was such a cliché, she'd always denied it until now. But just from the look on Jennifer's face it was clear. She would tolerate no interference in the way things were.

Her father went on, "I can't imagine, after what your mother must have told you about me, that you'd think much of me at all."

"She never said anything bad about you," Pam assured him, ignoring the looks she was getting from his wife. "She knows how much I missed you."

He was even more embarrassed now, and torn, yet he could tell she was lying; of course Joanne had talked about him. "Nevertheless, we think it's better that you not try to get too close to Danny and Billy. It only makes you harder to explain."

Out of the corner of her eye she saw Jennifer nodding. The bitch! And he was letting her do it, helping her!

Pain and anger forced Pam to say, "I'm not trying to

insinuate myself into your life. I thought I belonged here. I thought you cared about me. Dad—I mean William—I love you. Jennifer, I really like the boys; I want to get to know them better—they're my half brothers. I've never had any brothers or sisters. I've hardly even had a father. I thought things could be wonderful between us if we lived close by one another, if I were here without Mom. I know you don't like her, William, and I don't blame you. But I'm different from her. I take after you. I've got brains and ambition. I'm going to use them, too. I only wanted to make you proud of me." There was so much more to say, but Pam couldn't hold back her tears any longer and broke down, sobbing. As she cried, she cursed herself for giving in to her pain. It was the most humiliating thing she'd ever experienced, letting them know how much they'd hurt her.

"Pam, don't cry." Jennifer reached for her hand. Now she was remorseful, but Pam yanked her hand away. Her father handed her his handkerchief, but she declined that too, and searched for her own in her purse. "I don't understand," she cried. "Why are you being like this?" But the blankness of his stare made her want to escape immediately. If only he wouldn't keep colluding with his wife, looking to her for corroboration. Against the two of them she didn't have a chance. She stood up abruptly, using sarcasm to get her through. "If you'll excuse me, I'll go and see the boys' rooms. While I'm gone, would you please call a cab for me? I wouldn't want to overstay my welcome."

"Pam, it's not that you're not welcome," her father said weakly.

"Thank you for lunch," she said, and went into the house to ask directions to the boys' wing. The two of them watched her go; she felt their eyes boring holes in her back. She was exposed and raw, with a pain that cut through her harshly. She could hear her mother's voice: *You insisted he wasn't a bastard, only a misunderstood man, right? She dictates what his life should be, and he lets her. Now do you see?* Pam couldn't deny it any longer. The reality pressed against her heart. He really *had* ignored her all these years, had let his wife keep them apart. The excuses wouldn't work anymore. He'd broken all his promises, left her disappointed and empty, let her cry herself to sleep with only her mother for consolation, told her that circumstances were beyond his control. But there had been no circumstances except his choice to ignore her.

No more forgiving him, or believing in a dream. There was no dream. Yes, he'd sent money, but it was a pittance of alimony and child support, the smallest amount the courts would allow, and it never came regularly. Seeing the extent of his wealth made that unforgivable to her. There was an excruciating, tearing pain in her guts again; they felt ready to explode, like that time in high school. Joanne had borne the brunt of it then, but now it was directed toward her father, caused by her father. Remembering how long it had taken her to purge that rage, she knew she'd be in for a long night. *But, damn it, he wasn't worth it!* She didn't want to spend one more minute in agony over him. She was through with crying, in fact she wanted to scream with rage, scratch and claw and kill. *Enough, enough!* she shouted silently, fighting to keep the pain under control.

He was a weak bastard, a son of a bitch, just as Joanne had said. And cheap, guarding his life as though her presence dirtied it, holding on to his business as though it were his life force and she had threatened to steal it away. *Okay, you bastard, keep it! I wouldn't take it if you gave it to me.* But a lifetime of loving him, of waiting for this moment and then having rejection thrown in her face, was not easy to overcome, simply because she wanted to. The pain threatened to overwhelm her. But she would not let it. *I have value,* she told herself over and over. *I'll make it on my own. Someday I'll laugh about this. I'll be as big as you are, William Grayson, even bigger. 'We have the same name.' I'll say to people, 'but he's no relation of mine.'* Nothing in her life had ever made her feel this hurt and angry. Get-even angry. She wanted to do something, make a symbolic gesture. She would change her name, never again be known as his daughter. Then and there she decided to take her mother's maiden name, Weymouth.

When she came downstairs after seeing the boys' rooms, her father was more remote than before. It was clear that he'd retreat rather than fight. It made her more disgusted. He glanced at Jennifer, and she saw a look of helplessness in his expression; it made her gloat that he could suffer even the slightest. In that instant she hated him with the same intensity with which she'd always loved him. She exulted in it as it washed over her. And she let him see it, too. To his credit, he flinched.

As she was leaving the house, Jennifer walked out with her and handed her a piece of paper. "I've written down the name of the daughter of a friend of mine. I don't know much about the girl, but her mother and I used to model together and she's looking for a roommate."

Pam took it from her with a look that said, *Go to hell.* But if Jennifer was insulted, she didn't show it. "Good luck," she said, as Pam opened the door of the taxi.

Just then, a yellow Cadillac convertible drove up the drive, circled around, and stopped next to Pam's taxi. The man driving the car glanced at her as she got into the taxi, and she got a glimpse of a dark complexion, piercing black eyes, and self-assured defiance, but she ducked her head so he wouldn't see her.

"Hi, gorgeous," he said to Jennifer as he climbed out of the car. He was carrying a briefcase with the Gray-Con logo on the front, and he shifted it into his right hand so that he could put his arm around Jennifer as they walked together into the house.

Jennifer was laughing at something he was saying, her attention instantly diverted from Pam and her problems. She never looked back at Pam as her taxi drove away.

2

"Separate checks," Anita said to the waiter who came to take their deli order.

"Sure, sure," he replied.

"So, you need a place to stay, huh?"

"I'm at the Barbizon, temporarily."

"That is a lotta bucks. You fixed, or what?"

"I'm using my savings. What do you mean, fixed?"

"You know, got an old man? Mine's outta work. Never gives me nothin'. I mean bread."

"Your father's unemployed?"

"Not my father. My boyfriend, Silvio. Your timing's right. I'm stayin' in this sort of one-bedroom apartment on East Thirty-sixth, and my roommate moved out. I can't swing the rent alone, but with your half, we could make it. You got nice clothes."

Pam was wearing a black-and-white sheath dress with a white insert bib, and a jacket to match. She liked being complimented but she wanted to say, *I can't live with you, I hardly know you.* Then she'd feel foolish, like a hick. If this were California, she'd know exactly how to read this woman, but here all the signs were different. At home, she would have thought Anita was a tramp, but maybe girls were like this in New York. After all, Anita was the daughter of one of Jennifer's friends, a woman who had modeled with her. Just because she looked cheap didn't mean she was. New Yorkers were more adventurous, and she was a New Yorker now; why not just do it?

"Is the apartment nice?"

"It's a dump, but it's got four walls. Here's the key. Go have a look."

"You're giving me the key to your apartment? You don't even know me."

"Whatta you gonna do, take my stuff? I ain't got nothin' anyway." Anita had examined what Pam was wearing in detail when they sat down, but then had hardly looked at her again; she was too busy looking around the room, checking out everyone who came in or went out. Now Anita brought back her full attention as she asked, "You workin'?"

"Not at the moment, but I'll find something soon."

"So, MamZelle is looking for a showroom model who can also be fit in their patterns. You interested? Size seven."

"I'm a size six."

"That's close enough. Tell them Anita sent you. They're crazy about me there. I love to fool with them guys, have laughs, you know? Silvio gets jealous, makes him all hot and bothered. Those Hebe guys know how to spend, not like my wop. So tell Louie I said you're perfect for the job. You are, you know. Lend it some class."

"I've never modeled before."

"Nothing to it. Just put the clothes on over your girdle and walk around. MamZelle is a hot line, which is a good place to be, because when a line is hot, the place jumps, buyers every five minutes, production really hopping, everybody wants ya, you know what I mean? You don't wanna be in no place that's slow, got no business. You could go crazy like that."

"You came into modeling through a legacy?"

"A what?"

"A legacy, your mom."

"Naw, my mom did the photo bit, that's where the money is. I ain't photogenic, Silvio got me my job, he's connected."

"I really appreciate your offer, but I'm trying to get a job as a trainee in a corporation or maybe as a junior executive," Pam explained. "So far, the only offers I get are secretarial."

"With your looks? What a waste. You could be *goageous* with some makeup." She took out her compact and reapplied her lipstick in a fascinating ritual: foundation followed by powder, a pencil outline, then a brush to fill in the edges, an iridescent color in the middle, gloss on top of that, and finally a perfect blot in the center of a white paper napkin.

"Excellent," she decided, tilting her head and unwrapping a piece of spearmint gum, which she folded into her mouth. "If you like the apartment, you can move in right away." She swung her molded hips out from under the Formica-topped table, picked up her separate check, and made her way to the cashier. "Better pay your check," she called back over her shoulder. "They don't like you to hang around, lots of people waiting."

Pam jumped up, grabbed her check, and hurried after Anita.

After a few more fruitless days of job-hunting, her money was dwindling rapidly; in one more week at the Barbizon, she'd be using her capital, which had to go for a deposit on an apartment. Maybe she ought to consider modeling; it would be more interesting than being a secretary, and give her more freedom, as long as she went to graduate school at night and continued to look for a job in construction. If she kept at it, something would change eventually—it had to.

MamZelle was in a building on 39th Street off Seventh Avenue—a world unto itself. Racks of clothes were everywhere, on elevators, in corridors, being loaded into vans, and even coming up on lifts out of the sidewalks. Young boys, not more than seventeen years old, wheeled and pushed their racks around the streets, calling to one another in a language that sounded familiar, yet foreign.

Louis Goff, one of the owners of MamZelle, balding, pudgy, abrupt, and smoking a cigar stub, looked her up and down. Then he nodded thoughtfully and pursed his lips. "Leave it to that Anita," he said, "she's a pistol." His partner, Harold Miller, was tall, young, and attractive, with large brown eyes circled by dark rings of fatigue. Both men wore suits and ties to work, their jackets hung on a coat rack; now they were in their shirtsleeves. Obviously they preferred to be unencumbered so they could yell, and yell they did. During her interview they yelled at the cutters, the seamstresses, the models, the salesmen, and most of all at each other, but never at a buyer.

When a buyer was announced, they were honey and cream. Pam heard them offering tickets to the theater, dinners at "21," and a peek at something no one else had seen—though they had just shown it to a previous buyer. In the dressing room she heard the models talking about their dates and, in between, a Danish or a bagel, coffee regular, Coke, lotsa ice, pastrami on rye—where's the pickles? There was food everywhere, in the showroom, in the models' cubbyhole, in the designers' corner, in the office. A tumult of noise, smells, people, tension, and frenzy that somehow earned Harold and Louis over a half-million dollars a year—so Anita said.

"We'll start you now, see how you do. But get your hair streaked blonder," Louis insisted, a condition of hiring her. One of the models, Doreen, told her about an all-night beauty parlor on 57th Street that she could go to after work that day. After a tiring day on her feet, she hobbled over there. It was the most amazing place she'd ever been, crowded with people into early morning hours, with actresses still in stage makeup, and prostitutes in between johns getting their hair dyed, straightened, or bleached. And homosexuals. She'd never seen men wearing makeup and brassieres and false eyelashes before. Everyone seemed friendly, so she was surprised when her hairdresser said, "Hold on to your purse, honey, they'll steal it right out from under you."

Streaking her hair cost her twenty-five dollars, her food budget for the next two weeks, but it did make her look more glamorous, like a model. The hairdresser showed her how to wind her hair into a bun at the nape of her neck, instead of a ponytail.

The next day she moved in with Anita, though not to the original apartment. Anita had been evicted from the one on 36th, but had found another one on 14th between Second and Third, in a newly renovated building. Everything was freshly painted and clean, a miracle compared with what Pam had been looking at.

Pam gave Anita her share of the first and last month's rent—Anita was the one signing the lease—a total of $170 plus twenty more as deposit on the phone and utilities. Their only furniture was Anita's double-bed mattress and frame, which took up practically the whole tiny bedroom. She made it plain that she and Silvio would want to use it regularly, so Pam would have to sleep in the living room. Pam bought a sofa bed at Castro on time payments that would cost her three times the original purchase price; there was nothing else she could do but pay the $22.50 a month for something to sleep on. And now she was broke until she got her first paycheck in two weeks. Walking to work wasn't so bad, but she'd have to exist on the coffee and Danishes at the office and whatever she could manage to eat on a date, if she was lucky enough to get one.

The first man who asked her out was Art Percelli, one of the salesmen at MamZelle. He took her to dinner at the Grotta Azzurra in Little Italy; hearing him call her *babe* and feeling his hand on her thigh all evening was only slightly preferable to eating ketchup soup. The next meal she managed to get was at the stockboy Marvin's expense at Chock Full o' Nuts. She ordered both an egg salad sandwich and a cheeseburger, and wrapped the sandwich for later. And then it was Friday and she had an entire weekend ahead of her, no money and no food.

Anita took pity and bought her a carton of cottage cheese and a can of fruit cocktail. By Sunday night, after stealing an apple from a streetside vendor, she was tempted to try the New York shelters for indigents just to get a bowl of soup, but she was afraid. The fear of being penniless and alone in a strange city was overwhelming, and she cried until her eyes were puffy red slits. Everywhere she turned, she saw the logo of her father's construction company, remembered the extravagant meal he had served her, thought of the restaurant-sized kitchen that had prepared it. Damn him, she hated him. She cursed herself, too, for every quarter she'd ever squandered in her life in an amusement park or on a bus ride. If only she had them now.

On Monday night, Silvio fixed her up with his cousin Mario, a huge Italian man in his early thirties from New Jersey. Mario, a third as wide as he was tall, looked to be made of solid muscle, and spent most of the evening huddled in conference with Silvio at the other side of the table, while Anita complained, "You rats better start paying us some attention, or else!" Finally, Silvio reached

across the table at Vesuvio on West 44th, and slapped
Anita in the face, telling her to shut her yap. After that,
both girls sat there not saying a word for the rest of the
meal, except that Pam was shaking.

It had never occurred to Pam that Mario would expect
the same favors that Silvio enjoyed three times a week
from Anita, but when they went back to the apartment,
he followed them all inside and sat down on the sofa bed,
perspiring in his summer suit and tie. His slicked-back
hair smelled of pomade, and he wore a diamond ring on
his pinky finger. He was so large there was hardly room
to sit next to him, not that she was going to.

Pam felt captured, unable to hide in the bathroom,
which was inside the bedroom anyway, unable to escape
from this huge, dangerous man who never smiled.

Somehow during her attempt at conversation, after
Anita and Silvio had retired to the bedroom, Mario mentioned that his wife had taken their two children and
gone to Asbury Park for two weeks. Pam was shocked.
What must he think of her? That she was a tramp like
Anita, good for a roll in the hay while the wife's away?
She had to think fast and not insult this man, who was
too old for her, and dangerous. The only thing she could
think of to do was to cross herself and begin to pray out
loud to the Virgin Mother to forgive her for her sin,
unknowing though it was, of going out with a married
man and coming between him and God's sacred covenant
of marriage. Mario, a Catholic, as she supposed, was
chastised, and began apologizing. "Oh, honey, I'm sorry,"
he told her. "I didn't know you was Catholic." After
knocking on Anita and Silvio's door to say good-bye, he
left immediately.

On Wednesday morning, when the countdown was
only three more days to payday, Anita mentioned that
Silvio was taking her for a long weekend in the Catskills,
but Pam didn't give it much attention because she had to
catch the 8:15 train to New Haven, where MamZelle had
an additional factory. Harold wanted her to be fitted in
muslin by the pattern maker, whom she had met once
before in the New York showroom. He was a little old
Jewish man who offered her Sen-Sen while he pinched
her breasts for the bust darts.

Art Percelli was meeting her under the clock at Grand Central and escorting her there so she wouldn't get lost. But escorting her to New Haven was not uppermost on Art Percelli's agenda.

First he put his hand on her behind as they walked through the station, and then graduated to brushing against her breasts and touching her every chance he got. While she was being fitted in the muslin patterns, wearing a long-line bra and a taffeta half-slip, he stood by staring, until even Mr. Weisenthal, the pattern maker, who was as dense as they came, sensed her discomfort and shooed Art out of the room. He insisted on taking her to lunch, where he drank bourbon and water and began kissing her on the neck. She was frightened and intimidated, fearful of offending him and losing her job. "You're some gorgeous babe, you know," he whispered, as she sidestepped his latest embrace. "Lotsa class. You're wasting yourself at MamZelle. You could be a real model, in magazines."

Pam had never thought about photographic modeling, but those models really made money, and night school tuition was $378 a semester. "What makes you think so?" she asked, removing his hand from her thigh again.

"I'm around broads all day long. I've seen the best of them, and you're it. Not only beautiful, you've got a face that's interesting and sexy; the camera would really do it for you." He held up his hands in a square shape and looked at her as though through a lens. "Yep," he declared. "Perfect." His hand was sliding up her leg again.

She marveled at how fast he could move.

"I could help you, you know."

She let him inch just a bit higher. "How?"

He was perspiring in anticipation, but she removed his hand again, and then was saved by the waitress with their check.

"I'll tell you later, on the train back."

Pam hated to leave New Haven without seeing Yale, but Art couldn't have been less interested in this historical center of learning. He'd had a few more drinks, and by the time they made the 4:30 he was all over her again. "You were going to tell me about becoming a photographic model," she reminded him.

He pulled himself up importantly. She could see the

way his attitude changed; he wanted her to need him before he pounced. "Listen, babe, I know everybody in this town. I know the fashion people at all the magazines; they come to me for clothes for their layouts, don't forget. And I could recommend you. But first you'd need some photos."

"Of course," she said; it was impossible, given her current financial situation. To make money, you had to have money. "How much would photographs cost?"

"Two, three hundred, maybe, for a top-name guy."

Her heart sank. "I haven't got two or three cents right now," she confessed.

"I could fund you," he said, running his hand over her cheek and down her neck.

She moved away. "I could never let you do that."

"Call it a business proposition. I'll take a percentage of your first year's earnings, say forty percent."

"That's pretty steep, isn't it?"

"Naw, it's done all the time. A gorgeous babe like you would have it made, with my connections and your face and body." He whistled from a low to a high note. "Straight to the top."

Forty percent of her first year seemed like a fortune to her, but then forty percent of something was better than forty percent of nothing. "It would depend on how much I'd earn the first year. Would there be enough left over after your split?"

He laughed knowingly. "Are you kidding? You know what some of those horse-faces make? Forty, sixty, even seventy-five a day."

So much! How dumb she must seem to these sophisticated people. "And you'd loan me the money for the photographs?"

"Sure."

"You're really a nice guy."

"I'm a pussycat, babe. All you have to do is be real friendly with me." As if he weren't clear enough, he reached into her blouse and cupped her breast.

She felt her face turning red, felt the heat rising not only to her cheeks but to her brain as well. "Damn!" she swore, tearing his hand out of her blouse. "You're disgusting. Don't ever touch me like that again."

People on the train looked at them, amused, snickering.

Gone was his fake affability, and in its place was a sudden nastiness that frightened her. "You little cunt," he said, low enough so that only she could hear him. "You prick-tease. You've been letting me pet you all day, leading me on, and now you get all high and mighty. I'm disgusting, huh? Well, you'd better wise up to the real world, bitch. I make a bad enemy."

Every inch of her burned with embarrassment. She hadn't led him on, had she? She'd only been trying to be polite, not to offend him. Oh God, now what would happen?

The train was pulling into the station, and he was even more furious as he grabbed his briefcase and pushed past her. "You'll be sorry you ever messed with me," he said, and hurried away from her up the aisle.

Would anybody believe her? It was only 5:45; Lou or Harold might still be in the office. Maybe if she got to them first and explained that she hadn't meant to offend him . . . She literally ran from Grand Central across the avenues to Seventh, and down to 38th Street, praying that someone would still be there.

Everyone else had gone home except Lou. He was putting on his coat to leave when she arrived, breathless, her feet bleeding from new blisters.

From the look on his face, Art had reached him first. A phone call, one lousy dime, that she didn't even have. "Please, Lou—Mr. Goff—let me explain."

He just looked at her. Then he shook his head and came over to her, his arm around her waist, and led her out of the office, down the narrow, darkened workroom toward the door. "It's like this, honey. A girl like you is a dime a dozen: Art Percelli is my bread and butter. He knows the business, he's a top salesman, he travels, he fucks the buyers, he does his job. You know what I mean? You coulda been a little nicer, you know?" He patted her on the behind, as if to make a point. "And besides, I don't want no broads here who ain't happy, who're lookin' to leave as soon as something better comes along. I admire loyalty. In my business it's a rare commodity, that's why I grab it whenever I can, and toss out disloyalty whenever I catch it."

Her heart was pounding so hard she could hardly breathe. What was he saying? That she was disloyal, that she was expendable? My God, without this job, she could starve to death.

He seemed to sense her panic and stopped just inside the showroom door, led her to a sofa, and sat down next to her. "Life is full of give and take, Pam. A girl like you should learn that early, saves a lot of wear and tear later on."

"Are you saying I should have gone to bed with him and let him loan me the money he offered? That's wrong, Mr. Goff. It's like being a prostitute."

"Well, honey, it's a matter of how you look at it." He was patting her knee. Wasn't his hand a little too high on her thigh just to be friendly? She stiffened.

"Am I going to lose my job, Mr. Goff? I hope not. I've worked as hard as I could for you. I really like it here. Oh God." She started to cry, thinking of what the last two weeks had been like, and now it was getting worse.

His hand was too high on her thigh, and his arm around her shoulder was reaching for her left breast. "Let's say I'm considering whether or not to keep you, after Art's complaints." He pulled her closer. "Why don't we see if you can change my mind." He pulled her to him and kissed her. She could taste pastrami and cigars. She tried, she honestly tried to let him—not starving was very important to her—but she couldn't. Forcefully, but as gently as she could, she pulled away from him, unwilling to repeat the ugly scene of the afternoon. Tears were rolling down her face as she stood up and looked down at him. He looked up with a quizzical expression that said, *You're making a mistake.*

"I know," she said, as if he'd spoken to her. "May I pick up my check in the morning?"

"Suit yourself," he said, watching her go.

All Pam could think of on the long walk home, besides the blisters on her feet, was that at least she had Anita and Silvio to talk to. They'd never understand her reasons, but they'd be sorry she'd lost her job.

The first thing she noticed, when she turned on the light in the apartment, was that the sofa bed was gone.

For a full minute she stared at the wall where it had stood, not believing the reality of what she was seeing. The only proof that it had been there were the indentations in the carpet. Her heart pounding, she tore into the bedroom. The mattress was gone too, every stitch of Anita's clothes, and everything Pam owned in the world, except the clothes on her back.

3

A choking sensation constricted her throat. Like an insect captured in a jar, she bounced wildly from point to point, first the closet, then the bathroom, then back to the living room again. Gone. All gone, even her Samsonite luggage that the Markuses had given her for graduation. *Anita.* How could she have done this? *Call the police.* She dialed the operator, feeling lightheaded, as though she might faint.

The police would come by in the morning to make a report. No help until morning, not that they could do anything. *Oh God.* After only three weeks in New York she had no job, no clothes, no food. Joanne had been right. This city was eating her alive.

A key in the lock made her heart stop. It must be Anita returning to give everything back, to say it was all a mistake.

A balding man and a pregnant woman stared at her. "Who are you?" she asked, her voice trembling.

"I'm the super, lady. Your roommate said I could show the place as of tonight."

"My roommate isn't here anymore. She's a thief. She stole everything I've got!"

He looked around at the barren space and then back at her. "That's too bad." He turned to the pregnant woman. "These kids today." Then he moved back so she could step into the room.

"Wait!" Pam screamed. "You can't do that. We have a lease, we signed a lease."

"A lease? You crazy? This arrangement was strictly month-to-month, 'cause you two didn't have no security deposit."

"But we did!" Pam insisted. "I paid half myself, a hundred and seventy dollars. Everything I had," she whispered. "I gave it all to Anita."

74

"Boy, this place only costs a hundred and forty. She took you real bad; she never gave me no deposit. Just one month's rent."

"But we've only been living here two weeks, that means I've got two more weeks paid for." At least she wouldn't be thrown out on the street.

"Sure, but I gotta show the place."

She started to shake, and then her teeth began to chatter so hard her body was vibrating. When they had left, she wrapped her arms around herself and fell to the floor, rocking back and forth, until the dam burst and she sobbed.

When she had calmed down enough, she called Jennifer and told her what had happened. "Did you do this on purpose, to get rid of me once and for all? I know you don't want me around, but this is too much even for you."

"Pam, believe me, I had no idea what kind of a person she was. I knew her when she was a young child. I'm honestly very sorry."

"That's fine, but I've got to find her, make her give me back my clothes. I want you to call her mother and find out where she is."

"Oh, Pam, I wish I could. But Anita's mother, Pauline, died two years ago, committed suicide. I just ran into Anita a few weeks ago on Lexington Avenue and she mentioned she was looking for a roommate."

Pam couldn't believe she was hearing this. "A mark, you mean. A patsy, someone to steal from."

"I don't know where she is now, or who else might know her."

She put William on the phone. He seemed not only agitated but angry. "This is exactly what I was afraid might happen to you. My God, you're lucky she only stole your clothes. Let it go, Pam. If Anita is the kind of person you say, and her boyfriend is connected, that means the underworld protects them. You have no idea how fortunate you are that she's gone. Stay away from her now, even if you can find her. Write it off to experience."

"But she took everything," Pam said, fighting not to break down again.

His tone softened a bit. "Go home to California, Pam.

You'll end up on the streets. I know I said I wouldn't give you any more money, but I'll buy you a ticket home if you want it."

All they wanted was to get rid of her, both of them. "I wouldn't end up on the streets if you'd give me a job with your company." That would have been a great deal more helpful than a plane ticket home.

He sounded angry, defensive. "I explained it all before; it's not the place for you. I'm sorry."

The bastard couldn't even offer her a loan. "Don't worry, I'm not asking for money. But you're not sorry." She wanted to slam the phone down, but Jennifer came back on.

"I could give you some clothes, Pam. We're about the same size."

Strange, the idea of sharing her stepmother's clothes, especially her underwear. But she had no choice, if she was going to survive. "I'll take whatever you have Jennifer, and thank you. Especially if you have a suitcase to put the clothes in." The terrible reality was beginning to sink in. One by one, she thought of the belongings she'd never see again and the time spent in earning the money to buy them. Her two cashmere sweaters, her rain slicker, her Pendleton blazer, her bathing suit, even her pajamas and robe, were gone. All gone. They meant a lot to her because she'd had so little in her life, but they were only things. *Dammit, this will not defeat me! I will find a way out of this, no matter what it takes.*

"Put William back on," she said. And when she heard his voice, she said, "I've decided to take your offer and go back to California. And I promise that the price of a ticket is the last thing I'll ever ask of you."

"I know you're disappointed, but I'm glad you're being sensible," he agreed. "Be at my office around noon tomorrow. I'll have the ticket there for you."

"Don't worry," she interrupted him. "When I come to pick up the ticket, I'll tell everyone in your office I'm a distant cousin from Australia." And she hung up. For a moment her bravado slipped as she realized that her old standby, sarcasm, may have burned her last bridge with her father. Then fury and determination consumed her, and she didn't care anymore. *The stinking rat,* she thought. *It's his wife's fault I've been wiped out, robbed of every-*

thing I own, and he still won't do anything for me. Well, to hell with him! No more being naïve and dependent. It's not going to be so easy to get rid of me. I'll show them! I came here to conquer this town, and I'm going to do it. My name is going to be on those buildings, I swear it! And I'm going to get even with him someday, somehow! God, I'm going to get even. He's going to notice me! She almost screamed it out loud. Her fury toward her father and Jennifer was canceling out her fear of being penniless and desolate in this city. She would not be defeated, *she would not.* She took off her one dress, her one pair of shoes and stockings, washed out her one pair of panties and bra, and then covered herself with a towel she found in the kitchen, and lay down on the floor to sleep. It was only nine o'clock, and she was starving, but there was nothing to eat and no reason to stay awake. Yet sleep would not come, not until she had planned every detail of her immediate future. She lay there for hours, figuring out what she was going to do, planning it step by step, until she had it all worked out. And then she slept, knowing that tomorrow was going to be the most important day of her life.

At 9:30 A.M. she was at the MamZelle office to pick up her paycheck. She would have gotten there at seven, but the bookkeeper didn't come in until nine. The check was for $100. She cashed the check at the Chemical Bank in the lobby and then ate a meal of toast, eggs, and orange juice. It was the best meal she'd ever eaten. The next step was an appointment with Leonard Barash, a young fashion photographer she'd heard about from the models at work, new to the business and therefore not as expensive as the more famous ones. She needed to make a lot of money if she was going to support herself and somehow save to buy and develop properties. Barash could see her at one-thirty and would do a model's portfolio for her for fifty dollars.

At Macy's she bought a blue broadcloth blouse and a khaki skirt, clothes to live in for a while. In the photos they would also give her a different look from the black dress she was wearing. She was supposed to bring four changes of clothes to the session, but two would have to do.

At twelve sharp she was at William's office on the top floor, clenching her fists against the hope that rose in spite of herself: *Maybe after what I've been through he'll be softer, finally get the message that I'm the only daughter he's got.*

The receptionist greeted her, and then William's secretary came out and handed her a ticket on United to California, and a small leather suitcase. The woman stared at her curiously when she stood there waiting.

"Is there anything else?" she asked.

"I was hoping to see Mr. Grayson," Pam explained.

"Mr. Grayson asked me to tell you he's sorry he couldn't be here to greet you, but he had to be on a job. He said to give you his love and please to write to him." The woman's eyes were filled with sympathy, but Pam didn't see it. Something inside her broke. She actually felt every last ounce of her love for her father shrivel and die. She left without looking back.

The tan leather suitcase, only slightly scuffed, had Jennifer's initials in gold under the Mark Cross label. Even her castoffs were first-class.

Pam opened the suitcase in the ladies' room of the building and found a cotton print dress with a full skirt, a nylon nightgown and robe with lace trim, old slippers, a pair of clean white silk underpants, a full slip, a half-bottle of Chanel No. 5 perfume (the first she'd ever owned), a monogrammed handkerchief, a pair of white shorts with a striped cotton top to match, and a black sequined cocktail dress by Jacques Fath. The dress had seen better days, but it was the most expensive thing she'd ever had. It would add some elegance to her photographs; she'd wear it with her black leather pumps. *We're in business*, she thought, refusing to give her father or her stolen possessions another thought as she went to cash in the plane ticket.

Leonard Barash barely glanced at her when she came through the studio door, but his assistant told her to wait. When he did take notice, it was a long, intense look. Then he nodded briefly, told her to turn her head this way and that, and spoke to his assistant as though Pam weren't there: "Reminds me of someone. Sondra Pederson? Not Dorian Leigh, not Suzy either. Ali? Dinah? I know! A cross between Grace Kelly and Betty Bacall. Might be

interesting." Then he turned back to her. "We'll start
with head shots. Take off your underwear and wrap a
sheet around yourself. Carla will help you with makeup.
But don't take more than twenty minutes, I don't like to
waste time."

Carla whispered to her as she applied stage makeup to
Pam, "If he discovers a new face, it's good for both of you."

They worked for two hours on head shots while Pam
wore a sheet. Barash wanted to emphasize her features,
so he pulled her hair up high on her head and lit just her
eyes, keeping the rest of her face in shadow. "You've got
a long neck. That's wonderful, so does Audrey Hepburn.
Your features are large and unusual like hers—that's in
your favor too. I don't see you as a pretty face, you're
different. God, I could play with your face for hours.
Too bad you can't pay for it."

The more he worked, the more intrigued he became
with her, using her body almost as a sculptor works with
unshaped clay, laying her down, bending her over, still
wrapped in her sheet. When they finally graduated to
full-body fashion, he seemed bored. She needed fashion
shots for a portfolio, although he tried to talk her out of
it. "Your strength is in the exotic, not the junior miss,"
he said. But she put on Jennifer's black dress anyway,
the skirt and blouse for the junior look, and the shorts
and T-shirt for casual. Every time Leonard gave her
direction, she responded with natural ease. "Think of
murder," he'd say, and she'd picture Anita being stran-
gled. "You're young and innocent and he loves you,"
he'd say, and she'd think of Hillary on her wedding day,
smiling at Mel, kissing him, crying, with her father's arms
around her. "You've just lost the game," he'd say, and
she thought of last night, coming into her apartment and
finding it stripped and bare. "He just broke your heart,"
he said. That one was the easiest of all. "That's good,"
he said, "that's great. Great, she's great," until it had no
meaning whatsoever. "Not only does she look like roy-
alty, she can even move."

She hadn't expected to enjoy this so much; at first the
compliments made her feel better, then wonderful. And
every time he praised her, it meant a potential for money;
every dollar she could earn would bring her that much
closer to her dream.

The proof sheets would be ready in two days, and then they would know whether she could make a living at this or not. The camera could tell in an instant. Leonard Barash said he'd stake his life on it, but he was new to the game too.

The success of her future was riding on her face and body, not her brains as she'd always expected. But if it paid off, that was what counted. Three days later, Barash started sending her out on call. There were a lot of jobs she wasn't right for, but when she clicked, the designers were ecstatic.

Modeling seemed a game created by people who wanted to have a good time while they worked; it was easy to forget that models sold products. And to everyone she met, from the models in the waiting rooms to the photographers, the designers, the magazine people, and the assistants, the details of the shoot were life and death. For her, it all seemed trivial. And the work used so little of her potential that she felt as if she were cheating. Take rejection, for instance. For Pam it was part of the package; not every photographer would want her, not every article of clothing would be right for her, but when their bodies or faces weren't right, the other girls took it personally. Her appearance became a new toy, and she allowed others, such as hairdressers, lighting experts, designers, and makeup artists, to play with it endlessly, amazing her with infinite variations. Modeling was a vacation from serious life. And right now it was welcome as well as lucrative. Her hair—its texture, color, and style— was discussed with the intensity of negotiations at an international peace conference. Her weight was now of prime importance; the forced starvation she'd endured proved to be a boon because she'd already lost her extra pounds.

Soon after Leonard started getting her bookings, she received a call from the top agency, Brigitte James. Her name was being mentioned by Everyone, she was told. (Brigitte spoke certain words as if they were capitalized.) If Pam had what they wanted, they expected an Exclusive Contract. And if that meant more money for Pam, Pam would take it.

Brigitte, Jerold James, her husband, their assistants,

and a genius photographer named Sven Yanosh studied her portfolio, studied her, and shot more pictures. But first they spent hours with her makeup and hair, finally deciding it was best pulled severely back, emphasizing her unusual features. Leonard Barash's instinct had been right, but his work was unseasoned. And their experience proved invaluable. Pam didn't understand the difference until she saw the final results. In Leonard's shots she'd been glamorous, sophisticated, even pretty; in Sven's she was fabulous, possessing the mystery of a wood nymph, the regal bearing of a fantasy queen, or the freshness of a doe in flight. No one was as surprised as she. Brigitte and Jerold smirked slyly at one another—they'd done it again— and then they gushed, "Darling, you're going to be a sensation."

Her first assignment for the James Agency was for *McCall's*, a mother-and-child layout for Christmas—shot in July. She and the little girl wore nightgowns and robes of organdy, velvet, and satin, opened presents, hugged, and waved to Dad off-camera. For four and a half hours' work she earned two hundred dollars, less commission. And that was only the first day. Half of it went into her bank account. The work didn't seem that different from the jobs Leonard had booked for her. But then *Bazaar* did a spread where she was featured in nude body stockings and colored ones, her arms and legs encased in bracelets, and twenty necklaces wrapped around her long neck; her poses were almost contortions, with her head under her leg, and her leg over her shoulder. She'd never heard such raving.

Long before December, when these two issues hit the stands, she would be known as the hottest property, but all she cared about was how much she'd be making.

4

The desire to skip burst forth out of Trish's good spirits. Big Sur was heaven on earth. Not merely the majesty of the scenery with its massive jagged mountains, enormous, towering pine and redwood trees, huge blue sky, and vast ocean stretching out forever, but the life-style. Coming here on days off, she'd sing to herself while she burned the candle at both ends. Arthur had a house full of candles. He dripped them one onto the other. Some smelled sweet, others pungent. Their colors blended like her sleeping dreams and waking wishes.

After that first sensual brush of his hands against her face, he'd not approached her again. She waited, oh, how she waited.

She'd sat for him, white cotton blouse unbuttoned to bare her shoulder, a cat curled in her lap. He'd painted her in abstract, even her plaid skirt; he said she truly inspired him. He was her Picasso. And she painted him later from memory against a black sky, trying to capture his likeness peering out from between the enormous rocks on the beach; she remembered his intense, coal-burning center, the essence of his maleness lurking, ever there. It made her pulse race to think of him. How she longed to break free from the child she was. She looked to him for help.

On weekdays she was responsible; she attended classes, and sold furniture in Oakland for Manny and Sylvia Gold. On weeknights she baby-sat for families in Piedmont or Orinda, and then she'd come home to the room she'd rented in a house on Shattuck and sculpt or paint or weave or draw until four in the morning, feeling the passion of life surging within, needing to be expressed. Late night was the only time she had to complete her art assignments. She found herself spewing forth her interpretation of everything that had happened to her during the day; all her perceptions and feelings exploded into creativity. But the next day she'd resume life as an anomaly, her female passion locked behind a college girl's façade.

When she painted in Arthur's class, he admired her "creative fecundity," as he called it, if only she could lose her inhibitions. She was grateful he didn't coddle her, but he pressed, "Where's your heart, Trish? Still in the dormitory? Forget what you know, paint what you see. You've graduated, Rapunzel, let down your hair." All the students admired him. She'd look at his narrow, tanned chest peeking through the kaftan shirt and hardly hear him, feeling herself melting somewhere inside. An adult point of view and mature ideas were all well and good, but when he was standing there she was unable to be coherent. Each time class was over and she'd left his presence, she vowed to ignore him, to concentrate on her own sources; she'd insist that her heart slow its hammered beating, but it wouldn't.

Arthur had a friend named Thelma, a "lady friend," Trish's mother would have called her. Red lipstick and dark thick hair falling over one eye, round calves above high-heeled shoes. Divorced, self-assured, Thelma brought clients to buy his art, educating them in Abstract Expressionism. "The ladies of the Bay Area are boringly traditional, you know. They need you, Arthur." They drove Buicks and Chryslers and had Victorian houses to remodel. Trish wondered about her, about them. A comfortable manner existed between Thelma and Arthur that made Trish anxious. She cried often, and told herself she missed her family, but it really wasn't that. She was relieved to be without them; besides, they were with her whether she wanted them or not: *A lady doesn't kiss on a first date, and never in the car or on the front porch where the neighbors can see,* she recalled. (Hadn't been much chance of kissing in the house either, with a curfew of ten-thirty and her parents waiting up.) She wrote to them in Iran, dutiful, daughterly letters, but between the lines Arthur's name appeared. She told herself she was an adult. She cooked and cleaned for herself, paid for herself, too, though money was a constant worry. Her par-

ents sent her enough for tuition and art supplies, but the
rest was up to her. Her car needed repairing; the bush-
ings, whatever they were, cost her $82.50, a fortune. She
earned only sixty-five dollars a week. She drank coffee.
It was inexpensive and killed her appetite, and it kept her
awake during the day after working all night. Sometimes
she couldn't resist stretching out on one of the sofas in
Gold's showroom for a short nap. Mrs. Gold scolded her
and threatened to fire her upon finding strands of long,
dark hair on the sofa arm. Mr. Gold said, "Leave the girl
alone."

"Lazy young people, sleeping on the job. In my day
she'd have been out on her ear."

She agreed with Mrs. Gold. No sleeping on the job.

She kept her journal, saved her memorabilia from
childhood: report cards, watercolors from grammar school
done with tempera paint, stuffed animals, book reports,
certificates of merit, invitations to parties, and of course
her diary. She didn't know exactly why she saved these
things, whether for inspiration or a need for identity, but
if there was ever a fire, those boxes under the bed were
what she would grab first. Her early art had imagination
and childlike delight, but no purpose or direction; she
was working on that now—that, and Arthur Matalon. He
seemed to command two names, as though Art or Arthur
was too mundane for him. Fellow artists like Elmer
Bischoff and Richard Diebenkorn called him Matalon or
Matty.

Berkeley without Pam and Hillary wasn't the same.
But then, Berkeley was changing. Something called the
Free Speech Movement was just beginning and her classmates were caught up in discussions about off-campus
issues, like the Committee on Un-American Activities'
hearings in San Francisco the previous spring. Everyone
in the Art Department, except she, believed that the
government had no right to recruit for the armed services
on campus, nor should ROTC be part of the curriculum.
She thought the military was an essential part of the
country's defense, and ROTC trained future officers. It
was her father's opinion too, but then she thought about
the boys she knew being drafted and going off to war to
be killed, and it wasn't so clear anymore. The North
Vietnamese were supposedly supplying rebel forces in

South Vietnam, and our government was sending money and arms and soldiers to advise the army of South Vietnam. What if they took her brother, Tommy? Of course, he was safe with his student deferment until law school was over. But then what? This conflict wasn't the same as Hitler invading Poland. The ideology was as confusing as her own life right now. Arthur Matalon and Vietnam occupied dangerous ground, but she couldn't stay away.

Arthur invited Mario Savio, Berkeley's own radical voice, to his Big Sur retreat. As an undergraduate she'd stayed clear of political people and organizations like SLATE. *Don't join anything* was her middle-of-the-roader's credo. If her parents knew she spent time with a radical like Savio they'd be apoplectic. Mario and his friends talked rebellion: "We're fighting the same enemy in Berkeley as the civil rights marchers in Mississippi—depersonalized, unresponsive bureaucracy. The status quo has to be changed, even by force." She watched Arthur watching them, his presence creating as much controversy for her as their rhetoric.

She longed for the easy answers her parents supplied. What was it like in Iran? She looked for pictures of the Middle East and incorporated an Arabic feeling in some of her work, imagining the nobility of the male Arab as protector and lord of his household. A friend, Elizabeth McCracken, was in love with an Iranian from their art history class. That relationship was as odd to Trish as her infatuation with Arthur was to Elizabeth.

Most days a fever of excitement gripped her and she'd work until she dropped, painting her interpretation of her surroundings, but other times she'd weep with uncertainty and frustration, hating her work, unable to admire anything save the billowy white clouds against a sapphire-blue sky. She wondered as she typed purchase orders in triplicate and sent them to High Point, North Carolina—the mecca for furniture dealers in this country—if she could ever expect to earn a living as an artist. Selling furniture was how real people earned a living.

The Golds expressed much the same attitude about her painting as her parents did: she'd get over it and settle down, make someone a wonderful wife. Half of the time she agreed with them. She never got enough sleep, her eyes were grainy, her temples ached, and her stomach was queasy, but working in a furniture store stifled her and art set her free like it or not, satisfied with it or not, insecure about it or not. It was inescapable. And then there was Arthur; he was struggling the same as she was, on a much higher plain, of course, but they had that in common.

In the repair shop behind Gold's Furniture Emporium, Trish picked up odd bits and pieces of wood and fabric and foam rubber and carted them away in boxes for collages. Arthur called them her mishmashes, but she had done two on plywood boards and was trying to find a way to make them stand on their own, like sculpture, the way Manny and Sylvia Gold stood on their own, especially in the volatile atmosphere of Berkeley. They represented her past, Arthur Matalon her future. These two kindly, conventional people were bewildered by what was going on around them, and the furniture they sold appealed to people like them. Danish modern or Mediterranean offered no challenge; it was merely available, easy to place in an apartment, comfortable and currently in style. She named the two collages *Manny* and *Sylvia*. She wanted to do one of Arthur Matalon, a kind of sculptural tone poem, but the materials at hand didn't satisfy her. She searched through salvage heaps and railroad depots, looking for scrap metal that would represent Arthur Matalon better than would bits of contemporary furniture.

During the week—she worked at Gold's Tuesday through Saturday—she walked to work and saved the gasoline in her car for the drive down to Big Sur on Sunday. While she walked she daydreamed of sitting on the patio of Nepenthe, sipping spiked cider or rum and Coke, smelling the scent of burning wood in the fireplace, hearing the strains of classical music played by the guitarist. Sometimes Arthur would drive her down on Saturday night and she'd be in heaven, having him all to herself, listening to him discuss the early years of his education at the California School of Fine Arts, where Still and Rothko, the fathers of Abstract Expressionism, were his teachers. In 1948, when she had been eight years old, he had been twenty-one. He had voted for Truman and Stevenson. As a boy he had followed the battles in World War II as they happened; his parents had a friend whose son was killed in the Pacific.

While he talked, she studied his hands on the wheel, the thin long fingers, the raised tendons she wanted to touch. "I've been working on a combination of Abstract Expressionism and representational form, but it's discouraging, the work is neither here nor there," he confided, amazing her with his humility, "as though I can't commit to one or the other."

"There's always a time of insecurity when one attempts anything unique," she assured him, wanting to move her hand closer to his leg, just the slightest touch would be enough. And then he turned and glanced at her, making her feel as though he wanted to touch her, too. "You do understand, don't you? You have amazing empathy." He looked back at the road. "And of course you're talented. But you must keep working, never stop working. Did it sound too intellectual when I said in my lecture that I'm striving for the purity of form free from geometric shape, yet tied to the complexity of visual reality?"

"Well, the concept is intellectual, but sometimes that's the only way to express something as elusive as what you're doing. I think one of your greatest strengths is that you have the ability to translate the most complex ideas and give them the clearest meaning."

He squeezed her hand gratefully and grinned at her, and she laughed with happiness. If he only knew how she adored him.

She thought constantly about him making love to her. In a calculated move, she had gotten herself fitted for a diaphragm—but she and the diaphragm were still unused. "My work is so satisfying lately, it's draining my libido," she overheard him explain to Bart Pembrook, a potter who lived in Pfeiffer State Park.

"The next best thing to coming," Bart agreed.

She started reading articles like "I Was a Confessed Nymphomaniac." She also read the Kinsey Report and discovered that a great majority of women masturbated. She'd thought that only men did that, that you couldn't even do it without a penis. She wanted to try, but was too embarrassed to touch herself. Her own fingers caressing her body? Impossible.

One weekend at Arthur's, after drinking screwdrivers

all evening, she experimented with her eyebrow pencil, using the blunt end of the plastic cover to touch herself, trailing it over herself, finding sensitive areas, becoming excited. The impersonality of it allowed her response. She ventured down, touching herself there, gasping from the exquisite sensations, the control, light or firm, fast or slow, hers to know. Eyes open, gazing into the night, she had an orgasm. Nothing like the awkward and odd sensations she'd experienced with boys in college, when sex had been done hurriedly, in cramped surroundings, and with embarrassment or guilt. Now the luxurious feeling afterwards, thinking of Arthur before falling asleep, made her understand what all the fuss was about. Awakening in the middle of the night, she did it again, touching herself ever so lightly, imagining that it was Arthur, longing for him. The next morning when she woke up and saw the eyebrow pencil on the nightstand next to her bed, she threw it away, and then, when she got back to Berkeley, she hurried to Woolworth's on her lunch break and bought a dozen more, a week's supply.

She got a letter from Pam, with modeling photographs enclosed. Pam looked so different that Trish couldn't wait to see her, but Pam couldn't afford to fly to California and wouldn't be at Hillary's wedding. Trish drove to Los Angeles for the wedding and stayed with Hillary. The night before the ceremony, they each confessed something: Hillary to not liking Mel's mother, Trish to the eyebrow pencils. And Hillary said, "I think you should seriously consider getting married."

"And just whom would I marry? There isn't anybody."

"What about Mark Mason, the boy you went with in high school?"

"I haven't seen him since twelfth grade."

"Brad?"

Trish blushed, remembering about Brad. "Brad isn't interested in girls."

"What do you mean?" Hillary asked. "You don't mean he's a fag, do you?"

Trish nodded. "Have you ever wondered about two men doing it? Or two women?" she asked. "What do you think it's like?"

Hillary shrugged; these things did not really interest

her. "You're avoiding the subject. Do you want to be an old maid?"

"I can't just marry someone because I'm oversexed. I'll find a way."

But she was disturbed by what was happening to her body. She wondered if Jackie Kennedy ever had these feelings. Or her mother. No way.

She caught Hillary's bouquet.

5

Dearest Mama,

Your suggestion to eat soda crackers first thing in the morning is working. I keep them by the side of my bed and eat two before I even raise my head off the pillow. Mel hates it if I get cracker crumbs in our bed, but I'm very careful. In fact, I eat every crumb myself. Then I get up slowly, so as not to jar whatever it is that gets jarred and makes me feel so awful; and then I'm okay. No coffee or juice in the morning, just tea and toast. I'm losing weight, not gaining, which is amazing. I know what you're thinking, but don't worry. I'm perfectly healthy, thank God, but glad I never took tranquilizers last summer when I needed them. I could be having a thalidomide baby.

I finally said hello to the brunette in the elevator, remember the Janet Leigh lookalike? She only nodded back, certainly not interested in knowing me. She was wearing beige leather gloves, and the way she glanced at my white cotton ones I realized that not only are they tacky, but it's already too late in the season for white. Seasons are so definite here. It's beautiful now, but once it turns cold, there's no chance for warm weather until late spring. My first cold winter. What will this beach-lover do? Here I go again, crying at the drop of a hat (your favorite expression), but I'm so emotional lately. Mel is thriving here. He whistles as he walks to work. The results of the bar won't be out for a few more months. I hope he's passed. It means a raise of fifty dollars more a month, certainly not a lot, but every bit helps.

We're putting a partition in our bedroom so the baby can have its own space. I can't believe I'm living in an apartment you haven't even seen.

I never realized how much I took for granted growing up in California and having the same friends all my life. I never had to make an effort before to meet people and make new friends because my friends were always there. Here it's so different. I know what you're thinking, that I've got Pam. But she's single, and works every day. (You wouldn't believe what happened to her when she first arrived in New York.) I'd like to meet some young married women. Thursday night we're having a couple over for dinner. He's a lawyer in Mel's office, she went to Sarah Lawrence. I'm making your recipe for sweet and sour stuffed cabbage. Should I have mashed potatoes with it, or rice? Also, what about dessert?

Last Sunday, when Mel called his parents, his mother told him they were having Shabbat dinner with you next Friday. That's so nice of you to invite them, I know you aren't crazy about them. My mother-in-law hardly ever says hello to me when Mel calls her on Sundays, I know she thinks I'm a tramp because I had to get married, and to her son! She doesn't think I'm good enough for him. Do you think she's right? I wish we were coming to dinner Friday night too.

Your loving Hillary

P.S. *With all my heart I wish we were coming.*

"So what do you think of the new sofa?" It was the third time Hillary had asked Pam that question. It was the only furniture they had so far, covered with a blue-and-white quilted fabric with a straight ruffle across the bottom, and they were making payments on it.

Pam looked at her with an odd expression. Mel saw the look on Pam's face and sighed. "You girls don't mind if I watch some TV, do you?" And he got up from the table, turned on the set, and plunked himself down on the sofa.

Hillary blushed, and reached over to clear the dessert dishes.

"Let me help," Pam offered.

"You're the guest," Hillary insisted. Pam followed her into the tiny, narrow kitchen that was more of a closet than a proper room. The pots and utensils Hillary had used to make the dinner were already washed and put away, everything expertly organized.

"The veal was delicious," Pam said again, watching Hillary scrape the remains of the homemade apple pie into a bag and rinse the dishes carefully. Everything was done with ease and familiarity, no wasted motion. "I can't get over what an expert homemaker you are. You'll make a wonderful mother."

Hillary's green eyes filled with tears when she looked at Pam. Then she turned on the water loudly to drown out their voices, though the sound of the television would have done it anyway. "Do you think Mel is happy?"

"Of course," Pam said, almost wincing at the doubt she could see in Hillary's expression. Hillary could never hide her feelings, which were always written clearly across her face; intense joy, delight, devastating worry, whatever occupied her mind was there. It hurt Pam to see her concern. Mel had seemed awfully quiet during dinner; only once had he explained a case he was working on at the office, while she had chattered on about her work— the models she'd met, the idiosyncrasies of the fashion world—and Hillary had talked about her recipes and getting used to New York.

"I thought he was happy right after the wedding, when we first moved here. Lately he just seems depressed."

"Have you asked him about it?"

"He's got a short temper. Says nothing's wrong."

"Then maybe nothing is."

"I think he feels trapped. It's not easy, having to get married. At first you get swept along in the excitement and the plans, just being together. But then there's the morning sickness, and I can't help it, I'm very lonely for my family. And I'm gaining weight. It's only going to get worse, too. This is all the time we'll ever have to be alone, and we're not enjoying it. It seems too short, as though we've been cheated out of the best times of our lives."

Pam put her arm around Hillary's shoulder and hugged her. "There'll be wonderful times in your life ahead, honey. I know it. They say the first year is the hardest. I guess now we know why."

Something about what Pam had said struck Hillary as funny and she started to laugh, then just continued to feed on the mirth, trying to say what was so funny, but laughing all the harder every time. Finally she managed to sputter, "You may be one of the hottest models in New York, but you'll never make a philosopher. 'The first year is the hardest,' " she quoted. "Profound wisdom from Pam Grayson—I mean Weymouth."

Pam felt her defenses rising; she didn't respond well to being teased, but Hillary's mirth was infectious and she started to laugh too. "Okay, so I'm not Eric Fromm. But you have to admit, there's a reason for clichés."

"That's what I'm afraid of"—Hillary sighed, emptying the coffee grounds into the paper bag—"being a cliché."

Pam grinned at her friend, seeing her face flushed with the glow of health, standing in her kitchen, where her competence would put experts to shame, and she said, "If you're a cliché, everybody should be one."

Hillary turned and hugged her, pressing her soft breasts and round belly into Pam's ribcage.

Just then, Mel called, "Hey, aren't you two finished in there yet? It's getting lonely out here."

And Hillary pulled away, a blissful smile on her face now that Mel's mood had changed, and she hurried to finish in the kitchen so she could go and join her husband.

6

Dinner at Arthur's; Trish's turn to prepare. She brought the new soda, Diet-Rite, for everyone to drink, and made chicken curry from Mrs. Markus's recipe.

"How ever did you do this? It's so creamy," Thelma commented when she tasted the curry. "I always marinate mine in yogurt, or vinegar. That's how David Richards Brown of India House does his."

Trish had chopped an entire bag of peanuts by hand and toasted them with two boxes of Dromedary shaved coconut for condiments, along with Major Grey's mango chutney and raisins parboiled with cinnamon. Her white rice was lump-free too, bought at a Chinese restaurant in Berkeley and reheated, just in case. Now she wondered if perhaps Mrs. Markus's version was too unorthodox.

Color flooded her cheeks. "Is there something wrong?"

Dr. Fritz came to her rescue. "It's delicious, my dear, just as you are."

His smile warmed her, his grizzled hair, a Santa's cap and beard. He was in Big Sur to decide whether or not to affiliate with the newly built encounter therapy center, Esalen. Michael Murphy and Richard Price, Esalen's founders, who had brought him along, were deep in conversation with several members of Berkeley's Art Department. Trish was the child tonight, still wearing plaid skirts and penny loafers, longing to change, but into what? And how? She had no money for clothes, the ingredients for the dinner had cost her half her food allowance for the week, and she'd had to wade through a student rebellion at the Lucky Market to do it. Students protesting discriminatory hiring practices had thrown food all over the floor. Their destructiveness hurt their cause,

94

made the food inedible too. No matter, she rarely ate anyway—forgot to, more often than not.

Perls's steady gaze still held hers, giving her strength.

"You used canned mushroom soup?" Thelma laughed. "Is that how Protestants make curry?"

Trish's color deepened. Actually, it was Jewish curry, but she wouldn't betray Hillary's mom.

"Tell her to screw off," Dr. Fritz said.

But her mother had taught her that ladies never swore. Even if she'd wanted to, she couldn't say that in front of Fritz Perls, the creator of Gestalt. Perls was still watching her.

"It feels good if you do it." He smiled. She blushed even more, wanting to with all her might, but knowing that if she let loose, she might not stop. He patted her arm with understanding.

Arthur joined them from the buffet, and plopped down cross-legged on the floor, leaning against the sofa where she sat next to this riveting man. Arthur's plate was full, her Jell-O mold gleaming red, the recipe mailed to her by Hillary, typed on a three-by-five index card, and the curry, sprinkled with a glorious array of all her chopped condiments. Arthur's smile said, *I like it.* And then the ultimate compliment, a clean plate. She had been grateful for the turn to cook, to keep her mind off her obsession with her body. Each day she promised herself she'd never do it again, and each night, even in the early hours of the morning when she finally got into bed, her resolve disappeared in an instant as she thought of Arthur and her body made demands of its own. Afterwards, she often had languid dreams of him, but sometimes she had nightmares about her parents.

Sitting rigidly between these two men, whose laughter came direct and unencumbered, she longed to be like them. They had no cotton starched blouse to armor them; she was tired of not letting loose. Fritz took her hand, not quite fatherly; Arthur wrapped an elbow around her ankle as he stretched out, satisfied. She was a talisman between them; what she wanted to be was a maypole, all her ribbons unfurled. After a while their animated gestures and conversation moved away from her, and she escaped to take their plates to the kitchen.

Thelma apologized. "I was nasty before. The dinner

was good, actually." Thelma studied her as she would a piece of fabric for a client, hand on hip, hip extended, would this damask do? Trish was gingham to Thelma's Fortuny. "I fear he will choose you, foolish man. I know too much; you're a blank slate. And very beautiful. So tiny, delicate, not only are you young, you're childlike. You keep playing that role, don't you? You're smarter than you let on. He plumbs good depths. And of course adoration is an aphrodisiac. But let me warn you, he's extremely complicated."

Tabula rasa—her pulse raced. *Choose me? No way. If only he would!* Tuesday through Thursday, Arthur had little interest in her beyond the academic, pupil and teacher, but come Sunday he often had eyes for her, and smiles. But nothing more. If only he'd notice her as he once had.

Fritz joined her to do dishes. "Getting into any process is satisfying as long as it's all the way." He plunged elbow-deep into the suds, reminding her of her spaniel bubbling up his bathwater.

"I wanted to do it, you know, tell her to screw off."

"Conditioning dies hard," he agreed. "That's what Gestalt is all about, saying what you feel. Anything you feel."

"May I ask you something?" Her voice cracked. "It's about autoeroticism."

"Come on, just say it. You mean masturbation?"

She nodded, trying to sound clinical, impersonal. God, if he knew, she'd die. "It interests me, as a subject to explore—existentially, I mean." *Don't blush, Trish, don't!* "But I wondered, people who do it, can they stop?"

Startling her, he swore in German, shaking his head, maddened. "Why would you want to stop?" Then he spun around and embraced her, soapy arms and all, rocking her and crooning. "My child, *Gott*, what have they taught you?" He held her away, wet arm's length, fingers dripping, soaking into her blouse. "There is too much in front of your question, and too much in front of my answer." He looked at her. "What do you think?"

Tears sprang to her eyes suddenly, unbidden. "I don't think so."

"Self-love is part of sensuality, part of the integrated personality."

She felt filled with possibilities, attached to him. Permission was wonderful.

He lifted her chin and kissed her tenderly on the lips. She was surprised by the directness of it; his age almost disappeared.

Arthur materialized in the doorway. "Our little cook and bottle washer." An edge alerted her. She pulled away.

But Perls's gaze didn't waver, held her. "Come, my *liebling*, the world awaits you."

She understood, but it terrified her. She didn't want him to be the one to open her up—this stranger, physically old, yet so magnetic. Was she so needy that he could almost make her melt? Arthur's presence in the doorway drew her too. Aware and thrilled that he was jealous, she stayed, gazing up at Dr. Fritz. Then, coquettishly, she disengaged, cast her eyes down.

Perls sucked in his breath, watching her, and dropped his hands from her shoulders and back into the water. "Another time. I'll be there. Don't push the river, it pushes itself." He looked back at Arthur in the doorway, muttered under his breath, "You lucky son of a bitch." Then, "Send in the troops, I'm not doing this alone."

Arthur pulled her into an alcove behind the kitchen. "That's the last time I invite that lecher to my home. I'm sorry if he offended you."

She shook her head, no.

He wrapped his arms around her and smiled, a pleased, glowing smile, studied the curve of her cheek, her straight hair—getting longer from lack of time and funds for a trim—her small, turned-up nose, the expression of longing in her eyes, while she waited, her blouse damp. Slowly he came toward her until their lips met, tasting of raisins mingling, so sweet. She floated and pounded, pulse racing. Never again an eyebrow pencil when the real thing held her close, pressed against her. Wedded to his mouth, she received him so deeply. "You are a love," he whispered, pulling away. He opened the top button of her blouse and ran a finger, feather-light, into the cleavage. She moaned.

And then he let her go.

She asked Arthur for his opinion of her work; he

agreed to stop by her room. As his visit approached, the
meager space in her apartment shrank before her eyes.
An Indian batik spread, a brass student lamp with green
glass shade from home, her old gold and white provincial
dresser, a fur pillow and others of burlap that she'd
needleworked in a collage. Not much more than a dorm
room. Except for eyebrow pencils. She lit a candle in his
honor. The Jews and Catholics would have said a prayer.
She said one too: *Make him love me.*

They talked about him, he on the bed, she on the
floor listening. But something different was happening
tonight, a more intimate, deeply personal conversation.

"I've considered changing galleries; been with Phil too
many years. Not enough is happening."

She gazed up at him, remembering what Thelma said
about adoration being an aphrodisiac. "Since that group
show at the DeYoung in 1956 and the one that toured
Europe in 1960, there've been no other approaches." He
was gazing back, running his fingers over her hand. He
stretched out on his side. "Sure, there's been a piece
here and there in important collections, but I should be
having a museum show. If not a major one, such as
MOMA, then at least La Jolla or New Mexico." He
traced her cheek with his fingers, she touched his leg,
feeling the flesh inside his slacks, so daring. His eyes
pulled her into him. "Phil may be losing enthusiasm, a
change would stir him up. Of course, there's loyalty to
consider. He stayed with me through rough times." His
voice changed, deepened. "Speaking of stirring up"—he
was playing with her hair—"you do that to me." She
moved her head against his hand, kittenlike. "Your hair
is like silk, a dark river of it. Look how it shines, the
absolute absence of curl, like an Oriental's but with a
Western fineness. It symbolizes you, straight and pure."

She was shaking with desire, trying not to let him see.
"I longed for turned-up hair as a child, the kind that's
shoulder-length and just turns up at the ends. Mine would
never smile. We braided it, it slipped out." He leaned
over and breathed into it; shivers ran down her body. His
hand slid down her neck, caressed her shoulder under
her blouse. Her voice caught as she spoke softly: "My
mother used to pull it tightly to stay in and tell me not to
cry." There were tears in her eyes now, too.

He pulled back, trailing his lips along her cheek, talking softly in her ear. "I'd like you to meet Phil, see what you think of him. A gallery in Los Angeles is wooing me, but New York hasn't yet. So I'll stay here until my current work truly satisfies me. Then I'll go East. Not before."

She desired him so, his integrity, his sense of purpose. His lips grazed her eyes. Her lips trembled, waiting for his, remembering their first kiss; it was feather-light this time, instead of intense, as she longed for. He pulled away from her, leaving her shaking.

"What do you think of Hans Hofmann's work?"

"Somehow I associate him with Diego Rivera."

"Well, they both worked in the Bay Area in the early thirties, when Hofmann was teaching at Berkeley. But proximity is the only thing they had in common."

She racked her brain, not just for information about the artist, but for what she'd done to turn Arthur away from the discussion of her to something so impersonal. Her answer took on immense proportions, as if their relationship depended on it. Hofmann was from Germany, where he had taught, and founded the School of Fine Arts in New York, she was nearly certain. Worth Ryder, the founder of the Berkeley Art Department, studied with him. She ventured a guess. "His nonobjective painting was ahead of its time. I recall certain aspects of his theoretical synthesis of modern painting developed since Cézanne."

"I didn't ask you for an essay." But she could tell he was softening.

"I like him," she said. "But I don't think he had quite the originality of Still or Rothko."

He gave her a genuine smile this time. She hadn't failed. Would she have another chance?

Her creations surrounded them; he turned his attention there, sat up on the bed to study the assemblages, and communed thoughtfully. Did he want to rip them, praise them, improve them? Probably all three. Her natural ability to draw was sometimes a disadvantage to overcome, not to make things too realistic, stick to expressionism.

Suddenly he asked, "How do you feel about our age difference?"

A loaded question. She dared to gaze at him again. He was concerned about her reply, she could tell. "I've never thought about it much. Your soul is ageless and young, Arthur. The body is merely a shell."

He grinned. "You don't like my body?"

"No—I mean yes. I think it's wonderful. Very sensual and appealing."

"Not too thin?"

"No." Color flooded her cheeks. "Am I too thin?"

He leaned over, reached down to where she sat, placed his hands on her waist, and lifted her up, pulling her into his lap, cradling her. With a sigh, he buried his face in her neck, again breathing her in, then kissed her neck with light kisses. "To me, your body is your essence, strong, feminine, exciting," he whispered. "The childlike quality is what draws me to you, because I know you're a woman with strong needs and desires, I can feel them. But you make me want to take care of you." His hand on her back came around to her waist and up to her breast, bringing it alive. His lips were next to hers, whispering, "I see the sensuality in your work, shouting of passion and deep currents. Yet your face, your size and shape are like a nymphet." He was breathing rapidly; he pulled away to look at her. "Do you remember *Lolita?*"

She'd been upset by that book. "Yes."

"You're my wholesome woman-child."

His woman-child. *His?*

She looked deep into his eyes, light brown with flecks of gold, age-wise at thirty-five, and then forty, a dangerous age for a man. Was she his youth recaptured? Did she care? Was he a father figure? Did it matter? Spiritually, he was poles apart from Matthew Baldwin, though not so far removed from his age. Her father was forty-seven.

"Have you ever made love, Trish?"

"I've had sex, I wouldn't call it making love."

His smile was filled with longing. "Do you want me, Trish? I would never force myself on you. If we became lovers, I could not be your teacher any longer."

His closeness drove her mad. If only she had the courage to fling herself at him. "You're a wonderful teacher, so inspiring, fair and honest. Hard on me." She smiled. "I would rather be your lover."

He took her by the shoulders, his fingers reaching up

her neck into her hair. He held her head, bringing her
lips to his, kissing her between his words. "You have to
understand that I have friends, a life-style." His tongue
traced her lips. "That means female friends, like Thelma.
We're close, you know."

"I know. I understand." She waited breathlessly for
the next touch.

"And what about you? Would you need to experiment? You're young." His hand touched the smooth,
unlined skin around her eye.

She leaned into him, but he kept her a breath away.
She could barely breathe, yet her chest heaved. This was
actually happening, this petting, this fondling with long,
tapered fingers, playing the music of her muscles and
bones, her heart joining the chorus. "I believe in loving
one man. No pressure implied."

"None taken. I was thinking on a more permanent
basis myself. I think I could fall in love with you."

Love with you, love with you.

"Having you near me brings me joy and a peace of
mind I've never known. Your gentleness, your beauty,
even your mind excites me. There's so much I could
teach you. I want to." His lips were so close; she felt
moisture flood through her.

"Oh, Arthur," she sighed, pressing forward to kiss
him, finding their bodies against one another in her narrow bed, wanting him with every ounce of her being. As
their bodies pressed and clung, she realized she'd been
saved from her obsession; no more eyebrow pencils. She
had been trying to grow out of being gentle, but if he
wanted her that way, she would be gentle.

7

October 30, 1962

Dear Trish,

*Married life is wonderful, everything is new and excit-
ing, even saving coupons. Have you ever made Rice-a-
Roni? It's foolproof. But I miss California terribly. New
Yorkers push and shove, even when a woman is pregnant,
maybe it's because there are so many people but they're all
in their own world. I guess what I'm saying is I miss you
very much. Any progress with you-know-who? You wrote
me he wants to know everything about you, that you share
so much of yourself with him. I envy that. Mel is too
wrapped up in his work.*

*I've seen Pam a few times since last summer, she's so
busy. And our lives are so different already. It's funny
how fast it happened, she's got a career and I'm married.
Our conversations lag sometimes, unless we talk about
you (no gossip, of course, just that we miss you), or our
college days. And of course I love to hear about her work.
I'll let her bring you up to date herself on what she's
doing. It's very exciting. Speaking of exciting, I'm really
starting to show. Everything I eat falls onto my protruding
middle; all my clothes are soiled down the front like those
of an old woman who isn't in full control of her faculties.
Mel is always brushing me off.*

*The baby isn't due until February, but with the missiles in
Cuba and that terrible threat of war we had last week, I
keep wondering what kind of world I'm bringing him or
her into. (I really want a girl, someone I can identify with
and dress up, a little doll with curls to comb.) Thank God
we've got a President like Kennedy in the White House.
Isn't he amazing, getting Castro to dismantle those missile
sites? (Don't tell your father I said so.)*

*My mother is coming to stay with us when the baby is
born. Mel doesn't want her to, but I can hardly wait. He*

thinks that all mothers are like his, judgmental and picky, but if I criticize my mother-in-law, he's fierce in his defense of her. You know what she said to me? That I'd better not gain too much weight during my pregnancy or I would lose my appeal to my husband. Do you think Mel will find me unappealing when I'm big(ger) with child? Even now, when we go for a walk, I see him looking at other women, admiring their figures. I don't say anything for fear of being a nagging wife. I don't mean to complain, but there's no one here I'm close enough to who would understand. I remember your telling me about that pregnant woman who posed nude in Arthur's art class and how he said she was so sensual, and he touched her and laid his cheek next to her belly and talked to the baby inside. It made me cry. Mel is afraid to touch me when the baby kicks, as though he might hurt it. Oh, who am I kidding? There is a distance between us lately. It puts a definite strain on a new marriage to have a pregnancy so soon. Of course, if it weren't for the pregnancy, there wouldn't be a marriage. I'm so afraid that one day he'll walk in the door and say, "It was all a mistake, I want out." I would just die. I'm very careful what I do or say, so as not to annoy him. He gets angry very easily. Some nights I sleep for a while in the bathroom because I'm afraid to disturb him getting in and out of bed.

The part I find the hardest is ironing. Mel wears a clean shirt every day and then another one when he comes home in the evening. (His father does the same thing.) But his mother always had someone to do the laundry. Mel is very particular about his collars, and I try, but it's difficult to get them just right. We can't afford to send them out to a laundry, of course, so I keep trying. I'm getting better, but I really hate standing over the ironing board for hours. I can never get close enough, and my back always hurts. It's gotten so I dread opening the hamper to do the washing on Mondays and Thursdays. When I learn to iron a shirt properly in less than an hour, I'm going to teach it to my daughters so they won't feel as inadequate when they get married as I do.

Please write soon.

Love, Hillary

Hillary put a stamp on the letter and threw a coat over her shoulders to go down and mail Trish's letter. It wasn't until she was back upstairs again with nothing to do at eleven o'clock in the morning that she burst into tears. Now she regretted mailing that letter, it had been so disloyal. Some of the things she'd said were kvetchy complaints. What right did she have to say that Mel was difficult, or imply that he had a roving eye? Maybe she'd better call Trish and tell her to tear up the letter without reading it. But then it hit her that she couldn't afford to call Trish and that the things she'd said in her letter were true. Then she started to cry even harder.

Get hold of yourself, dummy, she thought. *Crying doesn't help.* She had to do something. Her mother would certainly not sit home crying and feeling sorry for herself. She'd be out doing something for others: volunteer work, or PTA. Well, it was a little premature for PTA, but maybe there was something else she could do.

She called Mel at the office to find out what time he was coming home tonight. But when he said sharply, "I'll be home when I get there, Hillary, don't nag," she almost lost her resolve.

"I'm planning a surprise for you," she said, before he could say anything else to spoil it, "so be prepared for a special evening." And she hung up.

Now how am I going to surprise him? she wondered, glancing around the apartment, wishing it were more glamorous or opulent, or somehow different. Then she remembered. There was something she'd wanted to do for a long time, ever since she and Mel had opened his Aunt Ruth's wedding present, but the idea was so naughty she'd never had the courage to tell Mel about it. Tonight she'd just do it and see what happened. Her brazenness amazed her, but she felt fiercely about her marriage and was determined to get some excitement back into their lives.

Her first stop was Gristede's, where she bought the ingredients for a dinner of poached salmon with wine sauce, scalloped potatoes, and fresh tomato bisque. Then she went across town to Sherry-Lehmann and splurged on a bottle of champagne. Then over to the yardage department of Alexander's for a feathered boa and two yards of chiffon. Finally she took the bus down to 42nd

Street, where she bought some other specialty items, in a
shop that catered to strippers and hookers. Looking at
herself in the dressing room mirror, she felt ridiculous.
With that profile, how could she ever hope to turn Mel
on? But then her naturally ebullient spirit took over and
she started to giggle. If this didn't turn him on, they
would certainly have a good laugh about it, and that
made it worth the effort.

Perhaps it was guilt over the way he'd snapped at her
on the phone, or the fact that he was really intrigued by
her surprise, but Mel was happy when he walked in the
door at six-thirty.

Hillary was wearing her wedding-night negligee, lace
across the bustline, but full enough from there down for
her to wear it in her fifth month. Only candlelight illumi-
nated the room.

She greeted Mel at the door with a lingering kiss, and
then helped him off with his jacket, loosened his tie, and
told him to remove his shoes and put on his slippers.

"I'd do it for you," she said, smiling, "but I can't bend
down so easily."

When he laughed, she knew they were off to a great
start.

First they sat on the sofa, eating canapés and drinking
champagne, while she gave him a few more kisses. And
then she told him to relax while she got dinner ready.

"This is really something, honey," he said, flattered
and pleased by all the attention. "I love to be pampered
like this, but I feel badly, you're the one who's pregnant.
Are you sure this isn't too much for you?"

"It's all part of the surprise," she told him. "So just lie
back and enjoy it."

The dinner was superb, as most of her dinners were.
But the champagne made everything seem like a party.
Hillary drank her share, knowing she would need plenty
of courage to do what came next.

After dinner, she stacked the dishes in the sink, which
was something she never did, but in honor of the surprise, she had decided not to break the mood with kitchen
duty. Then she took the rest of the champagne and their
glasses and led Mel over to the sofa and handed him a
note.

It said, "Wait right here until I call you, and think

erotic thoughts." He looked at her with such longing and surprise that she felt a thrill of anticipation. Daringly she reached out and caressed him, running her hand down from his chest to between his legs. He was getting hard already. She smiled and said, "I won't be long." Then she held her finger to her lips to keep him from asking any questions.

In the bedroom, everything was laid out on the bed; she'd tried on the paraphernalia earlier and had practiced what to do, so it wasn't very long before she was ready.

When she called to Mel and he came into the room, he gasped, for there she was, wearing a black bra with cut-out areas around the nipples, crotchless panties, a feather boa around her shoulders, and a piece of chiffon fabric draped over her body so that even if she did look a bit plump, she was certainly inviting, and damned sexy.

He started toward the bed, his erection pressing an obvious bulge in his trousers, but she held up her hand. "You can touch later, baby. Right now you're just supposed to look. And she moved the chiffon around, shifting her body, revealing parts of herself at a time, made so much more erotic by the blatantly sexy lingerie.

Mel stared, transfixed. Then he breathed, "You're gorgeous. When did you do this?"

"Shhh," she told him, turning on the bed in different poses, revealing a part here, a part there, while his eyes grew round with excitement.

"I don't believe this," he said, his voice husky and slightly embarrassed, but so filled with desire he wanted to jump on top of her and end the suspense.

"Do you want me?" she whispered, amazed at her courage, and yet so turned on herself that she didn't think she could wait much longer either.

"God, yes," he breathed, starting to unbuckle his belt and remove his pants.

"That's right," she urged, "take off your clothes so you can touch me. How I want you to touch me."

He hurried, unbuttoning his shirt, pulling off his T-shirt and socks. But as he was about to climb on the bed, she said, "Now comes the surprise."

"There's more?" he said in amazement.

Hillary nodded toward the dresser. "I want you to take Polaroid pictures of me. And you can tell me to do anything you want, anything at all, and I will." She put her finger in her mouth and sucked on it, then wet one of her nipples, which came instantly erect.

Mel gasped. "I'm shaking so much I don't think I can do it," he said, nearly overwhelmed by her offer.

"Yes, you can," she smiled. "Because that would make me very happy. And I'm sure you want to make me happy, don't you?"

He nodded and reached for the camera.

"The fixative is right there next to it," she instructed, feeling her heart pounding so hard she could hardly breathe. She'd never been so excited in her life.

He held the camera and looked through the viewfinder, then instructed her, "Move your leg, then open it a little more, no, now bend it. My God, Hil, I can see everything."

"Take the picture, Mel," she said. And he did, the flash popping in their eyes. He pulled the picture out of the camera and set it down, then turned back to her. "Take your hand and put it near your breast."

"Like this?" she asked.

"Sort of," he replied.

She could tell he wanted her to hold herself, caress herself, but he couldn't ask her to do it. So she did it, and he said, "That's fantastic." Another flash. This time he applied fixative to the first picture, which had developed while they waited. His erection was protruding straight forward, and when he turned around he said to her, panting with desire, "Honey, can't we make love now, and then go back to taking the pictures?"

"Are you sure you're ready?" she asked, feeling wicked and very much in control.

"God, yes," he breathed, but he didn't approach her until she said so. These were her rules, and he'd be damned if he'd break one of them even by accident and ruin anything.

"Do you find me desirable, even though I'm pregnant?" she asked, unable to resist.

He nodded, his eyes filled with so much love and desire that she felt she could live on it forever.

"Then come on," she said, opening her arms to him and moving over to the edge of the bed.

But when he got there, she reached around behind him

and pulled down his shorts, and then, because she couldn't resist, she took his erect penis in her mouth as far as she could. He came with a sudden explosion, and a moan of disappointment. "Oh, baby, I couldn't help it," he breathed. "You're so sexy, you're the sexiest woman in the world."

But she just clutched his butt and held him there, and swallowed, because a woman who'd just had her picture taken wearing crotchless underwear could certainly do no less.

8

Models met fancy people. They oozed out of the milieu like perspiration through Pam's pores after an all-day shoot under the lights. Beautiful people invited her places, and everywhere she went people fawned on her. Many times she'd invite Hillary and Mel along with her, not only for their company but as a reminder of reality, as she did tonight, to the opening of La Grenouille, on 52nd. Tables had been reserved for weeks; everyone in the fashion world was there; and Pam was one of the most photographed celebrities to arrive.

"This way, Pam," the photographers called, "over here, no, here, just one more, Pam, Pam!" Hillary's face was flushed with color as she watched her famous friend, but then her attention was caught by all the other famous faces jammed into the small space.

Inside, they were pressed back to back with the glamorous crowd. "It feels like work," Pam commented, noticing all the editors of *Vogue* and *Harper's* who were here, and the photographers she worked with every day. Strangers, too, recognized her, surrounded her, trying to be nonchalant while they stared. At gallery receptions she was sought out, at theater openings, charity fundraisers, or happenings.

"I put everything into what I do," she admitted to Hillary, "but I'm only biding my time. I know it's limited." As she glanced around the room, she recalled performing sinuous dances before the lenses of so many of the photographers who were here—Rik, Francesco, Oscar, Sven. Amazing how well she was compensated. She saw Richard Avedon come in with Jean Plimpton and waved. Richard eschewed dancing in front of the camera, the way so many others worked. He was all precision. How she respected him, the master of control.

He took hours to set the scene before the shutter clicked, placing a hand, a finger, a wrist, a chin, just so, or a knee, just so, or a hip thrust up, just so. "A halo," he'd demand of his lighting assistant. "More gloss on the lips, I said more lip gloss," to the makeup person. "Relax, darling," to the model, "don't stiffen up on me."

On demand, Pam could be wide-eyed, shocked, amused, anything at all; the other girls were adolescents. "She's so old," she overheard them say; she was going on twenty-three. "Luckily I do sophistication best and leave the junior scenes to my child competitors of seventeen," she confided to Mel, when he expressed concern over her longevity.

"Where do these young girls come from?" Hillary asked.

"Brigitte James finds them everywhere: Iowa, Kansas, or in villages and towns all over Europe. Göteborg, Sweden, is famous for its blondes; Brigitte brings them to New York, puts them up in her own home in a private dormitory, and watches their every move."

"Like a mother disguised in greenbacks?" Mel said.

"She's more concerned about her charges' behavior than my mother ever was about me," Pam commented.

"Speaking of mothers"—Hillary raised her voice to be heard above the din—"how's Joanne?"

"Complaining as usual. She hates her job, she's getting saggy under her chin, under her arms, and eyes. Everything's so expensive. She has a new boyfriend—Sam. Says he's the nicest guy in a long time. Works as a fisherman on his brother's boat out of San Luis Obispo. She met him at a restaurant in Santa Barbara during the Posada Festival. His wife doesn't understand him, but Joanne does. She's thinking of moving to Ventura to be closer to him. San Luis Obispo is a long drive from L.A. She tells everyone how famous I am, shows them my photographs in all the magazines. I send her money, but few letters."

"Have you heard from your father?"

"Not a word," Pam replied.

"Not even since you've gotten famous?" Hillary asked.

Pam shook her head.

How famous was she? The maître d's at top restaurants led her to tables whose location indicated her status, something important in New York, but it was rare that she came to parties like this because of her work schedule. Never a rule-breaker, she still wasn't. Except when she was working, she wore no makeup to let her skin breathe, slept eight hours every night, drank no liquor, ate nothing fattening, had regular manicures, conditioned her hair, exercised like mad, took vitamins; there was no time for anything else. After Anita, she vowed never to have another roommate, and the girls she met from her world didn't interest her—uneducated, unaware of anything beyond their world, and flattered by the attentions of wealthy men and their fans.

Pam wasn't. Men who wanted women to be ornaments and who treated them as acquisitions didn't believe her when she said that modeling was only a way station for her. It spoiled their pride in having her on their arm if she didn't think being a model was as wonderful as they did. There was a loose moral attitude both expected by an escort and adhered to by his latest status symbol. The girls behaved like colts out of the barn, unrestrained and glad of it. If one of them got in trouble—too much liquor, pot, or pills, too many late nights with Prince What's-his-name—she was sent packing. Brigitte wouldn't stand for a lack of morals, but other agencies weren't so particular.

Pam looked around the crowded restaurant at the people she worked with and thought about how every day brought her closer to her dream. By comparison, most of her co-workers felt insecure; for them, a party like tonight's was the highlight of their lives. They lived in terror of losing it, believing the criticism that their eyes were too close together, their necks not long enough, their smiles as dead as a lox, their sparkle permanently tarnished, ears too small or too large, noses too short or too long, hair too lank or too thick, bones too protruding or not enough. She didn't. It was a game she was playing for the moment, and which paid her a lot of money toward an advanced education; and her money grew because of her investments. Every day she learned more about how the world operated, and yet she made every effort to get to the top as a model and stay there. Her innate competitiveness wouldn't allow for anything less. Only performance counted; she focused on being more inventive than the other girls in the shot, more provocative or sensual or childlike or magnetic than anyone else, and making her disadvantages work for her. The over-large features, the long neck were now her trademarks. When she did a lipstick ad for Revlon and they photographed only her mouth, everyone knew whose mouth it was. So far, her career had proved she was the best at whatever she did.

The photographers used her, the clients loved her, and she set the tone, which was clearly self-determined; her effect was *in command,* whether freezing in Greenland in Maximilian furs, perspiring in woolens in Central Park in ninety-five-degree weather, or hiding her goosebumps in bathing suits in Atlanta in November. She was working hard, but having fun. Modeling made up for all the years of drudgery and colorless surroundings.

Vogue had sent her to Bermuda, and *Harper's* to St. Tropez, a lively resort/fishing village on the French Riviera, where the tiny shops were filled with chic sportswear and gorgeous jewelry and the girls wore the skimpiest bikinis. She went to dance clubs hidden in cobblestoned alleys, which didn't open until eleven-thirty at night. The clubs were jammed; DJs played the current American pop records at full blast while tanned young people did the newest dances like the twist and the jerk and the frug and shared a joint in dark corners.

Getting a taste of the world whetted her appetite. Her goal for 1963 was to do both the fall and spring collections in Paris. If she didn't get a direct assignment from Brigitte, she'd work out some kind of reciprocal arrangement with Wilhelmina or Dorian Leigh in Europe. In the meantime, she invested in the market so she could build financial security and have cash for her real-estate ventures. Some of her earnings went into blue chip, some into speculative stocks. She found a broker named Scott McDermott, who was willing to begin with her as a small investor, but soon she was one of his major clients. She read *The Wall Street Journal* every day, subscribed to the special market newsletters, listened to the stock reports, watched price indexes with particular attention to the cost of construction and real-estate prices, learned to read a financial report by studying the assets and liabilities of a company to determine whether the growth of revenues and growth of earnings coincided, and what the corporate net worth was for the current years, as compared to the previous two years. She became so adept at picking winners that her broker urged her to consider a career in investments.

At the Grenouille opening she told Mel about a conversation with her broker. "He said I have an uncanny knack. He's put some of his other people into my picks, like Royal Crown Cola and Brunswick Bowling and Occidental Petroleum. He said I've made him a hero."

"What made you pick Brunswick?" Mel asked.

"Their last quarterly report described how they were producing an improved mechanical pinsetting machine. When that machine corners the market, the stock will reflect it. Same thing with Royal Crown. I think Diet-Rite Cola is a winner."

"Every time I see your face in a magazine, I tell Hillary it's hard to believe a woman who looks like that is so shrewd. But you are, Pam."

Pam smiled. "I sold steel this morning. I wanted to get out before the price drops again. And I bought ten thousand dollars' worth of S.S. Kresge. They're opening some discount stores called K mart. My friend Eugene Ferkauf told me about it."

"Whenever I make some money, I hope you'll help me invest it," Mel said.

"You know I will," Pam assured him. "But my broker said I shouldn't listen to anything Ferkauf says. Scott says Ferkauf's Korvette stores aren't going to make it."

"I think he's wrong," Mel said.

"So do I. He just took over the W.&J. Sloane space on Fifth and 47th. Besides, it's my risk and my potential profit, right?"

"Right." Mel smiled, recognizing that tone of don't-mess-with-me in her voice.

It was exciting to make money in the market, but nothing interested her like the construction of buildings. Idolizing her father had gotten her started, but the dream was hers now. To own a piece of property, see its potential, find a way to build something huge and gorgeous yet utilitarian on it, and then watch it grow, that was what she wanted to do. She would be responsible for her own destiny, and not allow her life to be controlled by an impersonal institution like the stock market.

She had become separated from Hillary and Mel in the crowd, and then she spotted them; they waved that they wanted to go. She was making her way to the door when she heard her name and turned. Sven Yanosh was talking about her. "Pam is the one model who has changed the way we see women's beauty today. I think she's the most exciting face in a decade." Sven saw her standing there and said, "Speak of the devil." He reached out and took her arm, pulling her into his group. She had not seen who he was talking to until it was too late, and she was face to face with her father and Jennifer.

The three of them looked at one another in surprise, but Pam recovered first, giving them a slow smile and a cool nod. "Hello, William, Jennifer. How are you?"

It was the first time she'd seen them since that awful lunch at their home last summer. She'd come so far from that needy, insecure girl. She'd imagined what this moment would be like, wondered if they knew about her success; obviously they did. From the looks on their faces this was infinitely better than she'd imagined. She relished the moment, feeling the delicious warmth of vindication steal through her. It was also obvious from Sven's praise that she was on top. Jennifer was trying to ignore it all, but the effort was so great that the tendons in her neck stood out and her mouth was pulled into a tight round circle. In a sudden burst of insight, Pam realized that everything Jennifer had ever feared had come true. Pam had usurped her world; maybe she didn't have William, but she had the limelight, the youth, and the place of honor.

Her father looked terribly uncomfortable. *Good,* she thought, wishing Hillary and Mel were here to witness this.

"Jennifer," she said, "have you seen any of your *old* friends tonight?"

"A few," she replied, trying not to look Pam up and down, but unable to keep from doing it. "It seems you've done quite well for yourself."

"Yes," her father added ingenuously, "we buy all the magazines looking for your picture, and there you are!"

Pam almost laughed, seeing the look Jennifer gave him. And then the color rose in his face as he realized he wasn't supposed to have said that.

Then he said gruffly, "Your success is very impressive. I, for one, am glad you gave up that crazy idea about working in the building business. Jan and I knew that was no place for you."

"Oh, I haven't given it up at all," she said. "Modeling, as Jennifer knows so well, doesn't last forever. Building will be my next career." She'd kept up on what her father's company was doing almost as if he were a rival; she sought his name in print, and pounced on it with her heart pounding. But she wasn't about to tell him that. She knew all about his nearly completed building near Penn Station, with forty stories and 1.9 million square feet of office space. Occasionally she'd thought about calling him, but the pain was still too fresh, and now here he was, proving to her again, as if she needed reminding, how petty and small he was, how little they had in common. Maybe it was Jennifer's fault that he was so uncomfortable seeing her, unable to show her any affection, not even a kiss. But then she realized, with a feeling of exhilaration, that she didn't want his affection anymore; all she wanted was to get even. And tonight was just a small taste of what he and Jennifer could expect from her.

Mel and Hillary were standing at the door, waiting for her. "I must go," she said, kissing Sven good night. "We're booked for Wednesday, aren't we?"

"Yes, darling girl," he said. "I can't wait."

"And good night to you both," she said, studying them coolly. "I'm sure we'll meet again." She put as much challenge into her tone as she could. And then, without giving them a chance to say anything more, she left, smiling to herself with satisfaction.

The encounter left her with much to think about. It spurred her ambitions even more. She was almost impatient with her current career, wishing she could plan more concretely for her future. *I want to do something now,* she thought, knowing she wasn't nearly ready. But the world was going on without her. In California, Trish was in love with her art professor, and wrote letters about what it felt like to be a woman. The letters were so hot the paper seemed scorched. The protests in Berkeley over civil rights and the conflict in Southeast Asia were pinpricks in Pam's otherwise oiled, slightly tanned, and expertly massaged body. She read *The Feminine Mystique* by Betty Friedan, and thought of Hillary. Pam certainly didn't identify with it, nor did it remind her of Joanne. But Hillary didn't consider herself victimized by a system that encouraged her to find fulfillment through her husband and child, certainly not while she was fulfilled. Pam sent her the book, but Hillary didn't have time to read it.

Pam visited Hillary and Mel every chance she got. While she was there she envied Hillary, but when it was time to go she was glad to leave her there with her lamb stew on the stove, and her husband late for dinner.

In spite of Hillary's urging and attempts to fix her up, Pam hadn't had a real date in six months, though she was surrounded by good-looking men who assumed she was like all the other models, who smoked grass, drank vodka, and slept with one another's boyfriends or anyone with a title or a race horse. The models she knew were frantically trying to show themselves and each other that they still had libidos after parading around seminude all day in public. Pam wasn't certain she'd ever had one at all. "Sex loses something if it's too easy," she wrote Trish. "Give me a little old-fashioned forbiddenness or a touch of shame. Like the Beatles say, 'I Want to Hold Your Hand.' " It sounded as though she was a woman of the world, but she'd only slept with two men since college, and both times the passion had been short-lived. One's name was Barry, and he was Hillary and Mel's accountant. Sex with him had been too fast and unsatisfying. He'd wanted to do it with the lights on and her latest photos lying on the bed and propped up on her nightstand next to them. Afterwards, she realized that if you present yourself as a cardboard person, you'll only acquire a cardboard lover.

Finally she realized she couldn't wait any longer for her future to begin, and took her first step by enrolling at NYU's night school for a master's degree in business, with a focus on building development and engineering.

9

The tension of waiting for Arthur to make love to her almost brought her to tears, until he said, "I want you so much, my darling Trish, but our first time must not be here, like this, in this cramped garret. I want us to have time and space to savor and adore each other. Next weekend will be for us alone. I won't invite people, just us." He was still touching her, making her shudder with every caress. "Believe me, I have thought of nothing else but how to please you, darling girl. At first I thought your inexperience was a problem, but now I am thrilled by it. I shall truly be your teacher. I will be so tender and so passionate. But first, I want days of imagining how it will be, and when we think we can't wait a moment longer, that's when we'll make love." He smiled lazily, running his hand over her thigh; she felt the heat in his touch, and trembled all over. "I will send you special music to play, fabrics to move against your skin, then I will send you erotica to read. After that, I want you to touch yourself while you're thinking of me." His words were almost bringing her to climax. He was trembling too. "You are a kind of virgin, aren't you? A bride without a honeymoon. That is terribly exciting." He spoke softly in her ear, his voice low, his warm breath reaching right down into her. "In some cultures, virginal blood is considered the most potent aphrodisiac; it's given to old people to rejuvenate them, and to warriors before battle. It's said to have medicinal, even hallucinogenic qualities." He smoothed her cheek with his lips. "Dream of the magical time, Trish, when I shall be your lover." He kissed her once more, probing, exploring her mouth with his tongue, his hands on her body, in command, as a conqueror should be, though she felt him trembling too,

117

felt his hardness through the thin cotton of his slacks. "No matter what you imagine, it will be more, I promise."

He left her on the Indian bedspread, covers and countenance awry, to make plans.

But if she anticipated being with him any more, her trembling limbs and appendages would shake themselves right off her body, detach and refuse to reconnect.

All week she didn't eat, couldn't work, couldn't concentrate in class, painted sensuous abstractions that all looked phallic to her. He smiled at her when they met, a secret between them, kept his distance, and sent her something every day as he'd promised, along with passionate notes describing what he wanted to do to her. She was in a frenzy, and no one would understand. Surrounded by aliens amid an atmosphere of loosening attitudes, any reluctance she displayed would be ridiculed— but what if she disappointed him? She banished reluctance, yet wanted to turn and run. Her passions were so aroused she was terrified of losing control. What should she do, escape him or adore him? She adored him, it was that simple. Their religion was the same; they worshiped at the same shrine; and Arthur's statue was above the altar, phallus erect; she was going on twenty-three, *going, going, gone*.

The day finally arrived, unseasonably warm for late February. The mists burned off early, forcing dormant flowers to awaken and stretch when they'd expected to sleep all winter. She drove down the freeway, seeing every exit as a last escape, counting all the exits not taken as she passed them; they seemed to reach out for her with red and green signals, growing fewer and fewer.

Would he do it now, at eleven o'clock in the morning? God, she hoped so. Or perhaps he'd wait for the comfort of darkness. What if he hadn't kept his promise, and his entourage was there? There was still time to turn back, but the car wouldn't listen, took her in spite of misgivings.

She parked in an empty gravel driveway, heard every sound as if it were magnified by the stillness of the sunlit day. Her feet crunched as she walked, all of her focused and afraid, yet so excited. He had to have heard her, but he left her alone to enter the house.

It was filled with flowers, bouquets overflowing in bowls, vases, glass jars, a wedding of the senses. Vivaldi's music

danced in the air, more joyous for today than the usual
Bach. Scented candles flickered on every table and in
bunches by the fireplace, on the mantel. Jasper, the red
Labrador, had garlands of flowers around his neck. Arthur and Jasper both greeted her, Jasper's tongue lolling
from the heat. Arthur was cool and composed, but she
could see desire in his eyes.

"You're so beautiful," he sighed. She smiled shyly at
him, wanting to look away but caught by the love in his
eyes. "Are you as excited as I am?" he asked. He took
her hands, sat her down in that familiar lumpy comfort,
smiled, gazed, his joy contagious. In that instant, all fear
and parental objections fled; she caressed his cheek in
slow motion. He caught her hand and kissed it, his warm
breath mothlike on her palm. She whispered, "I love
you, Arthur. I love you with all my heart."

His lips brushed her ear. He whispered, "Did you read
everything I sent you?"

She nodded, dizzy with passion.

"Did you dream of me, touch yourself here?" he ran
his hand down her groin, lightly caressing.

Again she nodded, reaching out to touch him. He was
hard, and when her hand closed around him he groaned.
Suddenly he grabbed her, crushing her against him. He
kissed her, probing deeply with his tongue, and she felt
herself ready to explode. "God, I'm crazy about you," he
sighed, covering her with kisses. Her head fell back off
the sofa, baring her throat and her chest, heightening the
sensation as his hands sought her body and his fingers
searched between her legs. And then, as suddenly as he'd
started, he pulled back and stopped, panting, his expression a cloud of confusion. "You must think I'm ridiculous," he said, "acting like a college kid instead of the
seasoned lover I promised you. But that's how you make
me feel. Like a kid."

"No," she said, nearly crying with disappointment,
"you're wonderful. Your passion engulfs me."

He pulled her to him and put his arm around her
shoulder, holding her like that while he calmed down.
"You're so dear, aren't you? Well, from the moment you
walked in the door, my plans flew out the window. But
I'll be good, I promise."

She sighed with contentment. "You are good, you are only goodness."

He was smiling now as he leaned forward, turning his attention to the table in front of them; he spread something on a cracker, her first taste of caviar. He'd gone to San Francisco for it, the finest, all for her. And chilled champagne in a tin tub, flower petals floating in the water. His care and concern for the details of making her happy brought tears to her eyes. The wine was dry ambrosia; he dipped his finger into it, touched her behind the ear, and then licked it off. Smiling, they anointed each other with drops of the champagne, drinking and licking it off one another until she was doubly high, and then he offered her her first puff of marijuana—*pot*, he called it. This was truly tempting fate, but there was no resisting today. She'd bought a cotton voile print dress covered with flowers, rejecting plaid as too restricting. She coughed on the smoke, and then coughed again, thinking she couldn't do it. Then she held it in; after two more inhalations, her head floated off her shoulders.

"Do I need this?" she asked about the joint, but he hushed her with his lips and tongue and fingertips, lightly, expertly brushing her everywhere. As if it were part of a dream, he was unbuttoning her dress, down the front to the waist, until the flowers of her dress joined the flowers he'd prepared in bunches. The dress was peeled over her shoulders and tossed aside, the slip too, until all that remained was a passion so aroused she was amazed at having any coherence at all, yet she knew what to do as he touched her. His hands traveled over her small body, the thin neck, narrow chest, tiny waist, and slender legs, flooding her with desire. She wanted to grab him, to have him quickly, exactly the way he'd felt before; it was a defense against so much desire. But this time he made her wait. He kissed every inch of her, every part, his breath warm, his lips closed or parted, knowing when each would be perfect, and in the intimate places, when she flinched, he never let her cringe, or when her hand fluttered to stay him, as it often did, he moved it gently away, kissing her fingertips, implying that this was right, and this and this too, when he went in and out of those places, using both their hands in orchestration, making her touch herself wherever he touched her and watching her reaction, making her revel in her response to her moaning and shaking, until her head flung itself back out of control and she forgot to tell him anything, to feel anything but him inside of her, filling her to the brim, moving in exquisite rhythm and "Yes," she cried in a voice not her own. "Yes," and "more, more, more," until she was way up and over.

His own pleasure had no end, until she thought she would break, but found she only became more pliant in his hands. The ways he found to do it, the energy, the devotion to her enjoyment, were immense. As soon as it was over they'd begin again, while he took her hand, placing it here or there, wherever he would, gazing at her with eyes open, kissing her with eyes closed, the sun streaming in, the insects buzzing by. Nothing mattered, neither moles nor freckles, nor gray hairs on his chest, nor bulges around the middle, although his body for the most part was long and lean, especially with him inside of her, sliding in, amazing how it fit. Amazing, his stamina.

She lost touch of time, of counting, of wonder. There was more food, they were nude together in the kitchen, eating freshly baked wheat bread, honey, cheese, and apples. All the while they ate, she couldn't let go of him; if she stopped touching him she'd cease to exist, deflate like an old balloon. After napping, limbs entwined, more talking, more love, more pot. She loved it all, didn't realize that ever after she'd equate sex with marijuana, caviar, champagne, and a beggar's lunch. Just seeing them on a menu would evoke this day, or smelling or smoking pot would act as her aphrodisiac. Before today she'd had a choice; now she could never give him up. By the end of Monday, when it was time to go, she realized she'd lost all choice; he had the power to choose. And what if he didn't choose her?

10

A comedy of errors, having a baby. Not the conception or the gestation, but the birthing itself. Cars, your own or taxis, become unreliable beasts, breaking down on the way to the hospital. Rain or snow (in this case snow) is unrelenting, and husbands, nervous and excited, feel responsible and left out. Barbara Markus, Hillary's mother, watched it all happen, remembered her own experiences, two live, one miscarriage, and summoned a mother-in-law's patience from the gods who dole out in-laws' attributes in a miserly fashion. Ask any daughter or son-in-law to keep score and tote up the results: one's own mother 10, one's mother-in-law 2.

Mel was no exception. Since the day she'd arrived, a week ago, with too much luggage, according to him (one suitcase and a cosmetic bag), Mel had growled at her, low in the throat at first, like a dog who thinks he's heard a prowler and then recognizes the scent of the next-door neighbor's cat, giving a loud bark or two—"I need the bathroom in the morning at seven-thirty sharp, Barbara" —graduating to the frantic yapping that occurs when the UPS man is at the door: "I told you I can't stand the smell of broiled lamb chops in this tiny apartment," he complained, "and those frying onions are driving me crazy. We're not starving to death; your mother doesn't have to cook all the time."

"Okay, okay."

"And if it's a boy, we're naming him after my grandfather, not yours, because mine died last year and yours died ten years ago. And tell her not to pick up after me. I want *you* to do my laundry. It's embarrassing, Hillary, having your mother handling my underwear."

"Keep your voice down, she'll hear you." There was no privacy in this tiny apartment.

"Good!" Mel replied.

For some reason, Mel thought Barbara enjoyed sleeping on their sofa, ignoring the fact that at her age sleeping comfortably was such a necessity that without a good night's rest she was only half-alive the next day. There was nothing she wouldn't endure to be present at the birth of this child. But as much as she wanted to hold Hillary in her arms on the way to the hospital, when Hillary climbed into the cab next to her and put her head on her mother's shoulder, Barbara got out the other door and trudged through the snow to come around and sit in front with the driver so that Hillary could rest on the shoulder of her husband, where she belonged.

Throughout time generations of women had been witnessing this miracle—the birth of a grandchild—and Barbara Markus felt herself part of a great evolutionary force. At the moment she was glad to be the mother of a daughter; if it had been her son Bobby's wife giving birth, she might not have been invited at all.

"Oh, Mom," Hillary moaned. "I just got another one." The distance between the front and back seats of the cab prevented Barbara from reaching back and holding her daughter's hand, something she vowed to do all through labor, if they'd let her.

"Can't you go any faster?" Mel asked the driver, who dodged the uptown traffic on Park Avenue while overworked windshield wipers fought to keep the snow from obscuring his vision. Barbara was certain they were all going to die.

By the time Lori was born, twelve hours and eighteen inches of snow later, seven pounds, eleven ounces, Mel and Barbara had become enemies, cohorts, partners, and antagonists four times over. Barbara wished that kid gloves had been willed to her by some other woman who had survived a night like this. She discovered all over again that men would be men. Mel treated her like something between a decorative plant that he wouldn't mind lifting his leg on, and a flagpole at the top of which was a treasure chest of gold he had to reach, or starve to death. Her opinion was either supreme or worthless, her knowledge amazing or infinitesimal, her experience worth its weight in gold or ashes. And when they both saw Lori for the first time, they hugged and wept together and he thanked her with all his heart for being with him, and for allowing him to be so impossible, and for giving him such a beloved as Hillary.

Lori Jane was a dream, what else? She wiggled and mewed perfectly. Named after both grandfathers, Lewis and Johan, she had golden fuzz on her head and no birthmarks. Hillary nursed her; Barbara gave her water. Hillary slept; Barbara walked the baby. Mel sat on the sidelines and watched while mother and daughter established their ownership of baby with bottle warmers, electric feeding trays, vitamin drops, breast pumps, pads, and special bras; the baby's reactions punctuated all their sentences. Lori pooped and they discussed it; the mustard-yellow color looked just right. Barbara tested the temperature of the warmed supplemental bottle by shaking a few drops on her wrist, and the temperature of the baby's bath by dipping her elbow into it. Mel thought there was some mysterious and magical knowledge only she was privy to, and wished he had the nerve to ask her why she did it that way, but her air of authority kept him silent.

Lori stared straight at them, followed their faces without that squiggly, squirming lack of focus other newborn babies manifested. Uncanny behavior for an infant; did she know something fascinating was going on? It seemed that way. "Brilliant," Barbara pronounced. Mel agreed, totally.

Hillary had hemorrhoids; no one had told them about that beforehand. Barbara had remedies. Mel became the pharmacy's delivery lawyer.

And for Barbara, who had always been extra careful with money, it suddenly became no object. She bought little cotton T-shirts with ducks on them, baby equipment that strolled, swung, and hooked into the car, nightgowns that had flaps to cover the hands so that Lori wouldn't scratch herself, and strings at the bottom that you tied and untied like a surprise package to reveal bright pink chicken legs squirming inside.

Sometimes Mel was in awe of these women and what they knew. He was ashamed at wanting to curl up in Hillary's lap and nurse like his daughter and be cuddled. Then he wanted Barbara to go home so he could be in control again, get his hands on that baby for as long as he liked without someone snatching her away. How did they know so much? Why didn't he know it? He used to touch Hillary's belly and feel the baby moving and feel both repelled and amazed at that live thing within her—even envious, God help him, at what she was feeling. He once stood in front of the bathroom mirror, trying to see himself fully (which was impossible with the porcelain sink in the way), and imagined a womb growing there with a child in it, giving birth, the miracle of it. He loved Hillary more than ever, and yet resented her and her mother and his own daughter who would grow up to be just like them, a member of some unjoinable club, one to which he would never be accepted. Well, they couldn't join his, either, a consolation vehemently expressed and filled with pride.

We hold the power anyway, he assured himself whenever he felt these stirrings of insecurity.

Still, he watched with fascination and resentment their ministering, his reaction coming out in gruff pronouncements: "Can't you keep her quiet? I'm working," or "I won't be home for dinner tonight; you won't miss me, I'm sure."

"I will." Hillary was teary at everything these days, unable to do much but rest and nurse the baby. She was also soft and lumpy and puffy, with stringy hair; it took a major effort to wash it. Was this the voluptuous, sensuous girl he had married? Would that girl ever be back again?

Finally, when Lori was four weeks old and Mel thought he couldn't stand living like this for another minute, a miracle occurred. Barbara left. And then another miracle happened. He fell in love with his daughter and in love again with his wife. The first time he put the baby in her carriage and took her for a walk, there could have been no happier man on earth. When he was at work, he thought about the baby all day, her tiny hands, the buttery softness of her skin, the way she would grow and develop and he would be a part of it. On Sundays, when he and Hillary took her to the park or ran into people he knew on Madison Avenue, clients or fellow lawyers from the firm, he loved letting them admire her. If any of them said, "She's got your chin," or "She looks just like her daddy," Mel knew the meaning of bliss.

11

As a lover, Arthur wasn't what she'd expected. After the first few weeks of passion, he cooled considerably and his work took precedence again. Of course, no one could sustain the level of attention he'd showered on her at first, but that was what she wanted. The fear of losing him, of driving him away, filled her all the time. Yet she couldn't stop wanting more from him, and that made her become what she'd judged harshly in others: grasping, whiny, hurt, causing guilt. It was no way to keep him; she knew the rules of how to play hard-to-get, but was hardly an expert. Now she found silence for her own good eluding her. Her tongue wagged even if she bit it. "I hardly ever see you. Why can't we be alone this weekend? There are always people around. You never have time for me. You have two houses, in Berkeley and Big Sur, yet I'm living in this awful one-room apartment." He rarely invited her to his home in Berkeley, where he'd lived with his former wife, who'd gone back to Boston. Was he hiding something? A bevy of nymphets from the Art Department? She suspected everyone: Gloria the heavyset sculpture student from San Anselmo; Abby, into pottery, from San Diego; Julia from Chicago, who painted headless people, their necks ending at the top of the canvas. She, who found such consolation in her female friends, suddenly wanted to take a palette knife and scrape them out of his life.

She stayed away. That worked. Within a day he'd come looking for her in the graduate students' studio, or he'd grab her from behind and nuzzle her outside the ladies' room when no one was looking. "I missed you last weekend. Don't sulk, you know I care." She lived for those moments, hung on every glance, existing only for a repeat performance of ecstasy.

But his attention span dwindled. For a while they were an established twosome from Saturday to Sunday, but soon she was ignored until Sunday afternoon, when he'd light them both a joint and kiss her all over, ignoring her embarrassment and need for privacy. He'd lead her to the bedroom and close the door, while everyone in the next room knew what they were doing and she felt soiled. But she hungered for him so, she'd take what she could get. Only the pot lowered her resistance enough to allow her to truly enjoy making love under these conditions. *When is it going to be the two of us again?* she wondered, and sobbed herself to sleep because she was losing him. *I should never have told him I loved him,* she thought. *I should not have been so easy.* But everyone was easy these days. She just wasn't enough for him, young and unsophisticated.

Everything suffered; she had one cold after another, and her letters to her parents grew evasive, general. Next June she'd graduate with her master's and leave the cocoon of the university. The idea of real life preyed on her. She'd persuaded her father to fund the tuition for her second and final year of graduate work, but to keep peace she seldom mentioned her studies, focusing her letters more on her secretarial duties for Gold's.

Her father wrote back, "You are learning skills at Gold's applicable to any field of endeavor, something you can teach your children. Bravo, girl. But why another tuition bill? Aren't you through with that nonsense yet?"

Three pieces of her work were selected for the current student exhibition, judged by a committee of students and faculty members. When she thanked Arthur, he said, "I had nothing to do with it. I wouldn't support nepotism, Trish. I told you that when we got involved. In fact, to be fair, I pointed out to the committee the equivocation in your work. I couldn't allow myself to be accused of sexual favoritism; it's anti-art."

Dragging herself out of bed, body aching, head throbbing from the tension of not knowing how to rekindle Arthur's interest in her, she felt her life closing in. She didn't want Arthur's favors. The next time she went to his house in Big Sur, she "borrowed" three joints from his stash and stayed high for nearly a week. In letters to Hillary, she used hypothetical examples: "I have this friend who . . ." Since she didn't respect herself, she was afraid of losing Hillary's respect. If Hillary figured it out, she understood Trish's need for privacy and wrote back sound advice: "Tell your friend this man is no good for her." Trish's world was being liberated, yet still she outwardly clung to convention, at least with Hillary, the epitome of middle America.

Trish swore off pot and stayed home from work, leaving her more time to work. A fellow student, Luke Summers, invited her to dinner with a group of his friends. She liked him and his friends. The cook, Alice Waters, grew her own herbs and vegetables. Everyone sat around discussing the best way to prepare fresh trout, sautéed or fried or stuffed. Luke was about twenty-six. He'd been in the army before going to college, and was afraid of being recalled. It would be a shame; he was one of the more talented art students she knew. He didn't appeal to her. Tall and lanky next to her tininess, they looked odd together, but at least he was good company. She missed Arthur terribly. They watched a new English group called the Beatles on Ed Sullivan and ordered in pizza. Luke thought maybe he'd let his hair grow too, and wear it like one of the Beatles.

Since Arthur didn't mention the holiday, she made plans with her brother, Tommy, for their second Thanksgiving without their parents. She offered to roast a turkey and bring it into San Francisco. Tommy and Fred, his roommate, would make the trimmings. "Should we invite anyone else? Dates for you guys?" she suggested.

"No," Tommy said, "everyone's taken. Want us to find you a date?" he offered. She was already bringing one turkey, who needed two? Thanksgiving next Thursday would be a semi-family affair, without Arthur. That was Wednesday.

On Friday morning, a customer came running into Gold's and told them she had heard on the radio that President Kennedy had been shot. Trish and Manny Gold rushed to turn on a set just as Walter Cronkite announced with tears in his eyes that the President had died.

The incomprehensible horror shattered Trish's world; barely holding herself together, she ran to find Arthur. His comfort was essential now, far more crucial than her newfound resolve to be independent and not clingy. He already knew, and opened his arms to her and they wept together, watching, while the rest of the world wept too. By the time Thanksgiving came around it took second place to the events of the past few days. Trish roasted her turkey, and she and Arthur took it to a potluck supper that a group of local people were having in Big Sur. Tommy and Fred ended up eating in a restaurant with some of their out-of-town classmates. Nobody celebrated, least of all the new President and First Lady, or Jackie and her children, or Marina Oswald and her family. Everyone in the Art Department felt the loss profoundly. The campus was in shock. Kennedy's appearance the previous spring at Charter Day had given them a personal identification with him, charged them all with hope. After the assassination, student artists began expressing their rage and grief in hues of black and red, painting scenes of violence. And professors allowed the expression where it had never been acceptable before. Her only consolation was that Arthur clung to her as much as she clung to him.

For a week. While the incredible events unfolded, saturating their lives with despair, she discovered that the only way to survive was to allow the shock waves to make their own ripples. Her strength helped him cope.

Too soon, Trish felt him extricate himself from her grasp, one finger at a time, until she was slipping along the glass between them, unable to get a grip. The loss of his closeness and of her idolized President was more than she could bear. Only pot took the pain away. And what had turned his head? Thelma convinced one of her Bay Area clients to buy some modern art. The client gazed into Arthur's eyes while he described his philosophy, but she bought Diebenkorn instead. "A man with a *fu-chah*," she predicted.

The woman knew nothing about art, so the preference shouldn't have been personal; it might have been based on her favorite color. Arthur said it was a triumph for them all. Trish saw the pain in his eyes. It embarrassed him that she saw. He told her not to be an infant or to treat him like one. "I told her the truth, I'm glad for my colleague." The harshness of his tone struck her, implying that she'd be better off aborted than to be an infant. Then he said, "Don't come down to Big Sur on weekends for a while. Give us a chance to be apart, see what happens."

She turned away to keep her moony eyes from confronting him.

He put his hand on her shoulder. "I'm sorry if I've hurt you, Trish. I truly never meant to."

That officially ended it.

As the knife was thrust into her heart, she thought of dying. And for days afterward, that's what it felt like. But the pain didn't kill her; it just ached until she couldn't stand it. She decided not to do anything drastic, to wait and see if crying would help, but it hardly relieved anything. The only thing that helped was scoring pot on the street, but she had to stay high all the time. Mrs. Gold flared her nostrils in distaste that Trish was smoking. If she'd known what it was, Trish would have been fired.

A call to her parents gave no comfort at all. They sounded as far away as they were. "Are you being good? Are you working? How's the weather? What's new with Tommy?" She shouted her answers over the echo of her own voice. "I'll write," she promised.

He had loved her, he must still love her. She hadn't stopped, how could he? She hated herself; she was too young, to naïve, too thin, not talented, not enough for him. It was all her fault.

She lived in a foggy haze. One night she and Luke got high together and he kissed her. One thing led to another, and she was faced with a dilemma: should she sleep with him, or would that really make her loose? Sex before marriage was one thing if it was with the man you were going to marry, but having sex with someone you had no intention of marrying was something else altogether. But she had only Arthur's rejection to keep her company; finally she went to bed with Luke, who smelled of linseed oil, needed a deodorant, and had acne. It was like gritting her teeth and jumping into an unheated pool. Not only did she feel no passion, she almost burst into tears. Luke enjoyed it enough for repeat performances. All she did was long for Arthur.

Her friend, Elizabeth McCracken, said, "You can do better," and offered to fix her up with Achmed, a friend of her Iranian boyfriend. Trish wondered if her parents would approve. She didn't know whether their intolerance for minority races included Persians, now that they were living in the Middle East. She supposed it was difficult to remain aloof from your neighbors when you were beholden to them as your hosts for everything in your life. But then, the British had managed to do it in India.

Arthur saw her with Luke's arm around her, and her heart turned over. He didn't seem to notice.

Her work was hazy, like her brain, expressing befuddlement, especially when she was high, and denying the realization that the pain was constant and all-encompassing. Arthur's words became nails in her cross. "You are love; my dearest nymphet, you make me forget myself with delirious joy. Your body is a wonder, your soul akin to eternity. I don't deserve you." That much had been true!

She couldn't retrieve her innocence, but she could act as if she had. She got rid of Luke, starched and ironed her blouses, washed her hair three times a week, polished her loafers for hours, cleaned out her room and then cleaned it out again, stacked her junk in boxes with labels, and then made an index of the labels, never acknowledging her compulsion. She wrote her parents the first "up" letter in months: "I'm turning my life around, sweeping cobwebs out of the corners." Spring cleaning in January. Her desk at work was fiercely in order, papers stacked in perfect rows. Finally she stopped getting high, and allowed herself only one or two glasses of wine a day after work or after class at The Steppenwolf Café. Control was everything. If she could have seen herself, all starched and ironed, back erect as she sat on the Terrace—the outdoor student cafeteria—on sunny days, saying "Hi" like an automaton to whoever passed by, she'd have recognized immediately a woman close to breaking. But we never really see ourselves.

Students' clothing had changed dramatically; they wore loose-fitting, colorful clothes, and homespun shirts over their jeans. Her neat plaids and Shetland sweaters wrapped her in familiar security, small comfort against the constant ache inside. As she sat there, a fake shining smile on her face, sipping coffee, trying to plan her next project, she felt herself growing invisible, as though people could see through her and she was fading further and further into a mist. Only one person could bring her back, make her real, and he chose to ignore her.

The *Daily Cal* reviewed the student art show and gave her work the most space in the article. She saved six copies, and mailed two to her parents. Fellow students congratulated her, even as she felt their enmity. They thought she'd slept her way to being noticed. She began to see how destructive even a small amount of notoriety could be.

She ran into Arthur and Thelma. It was a shock, as if they'd thrown a bucket of ice water at her. This time, though she ached with pain, she had enough presence to toss her head and turn her back.

Enough, Patricia Baldwin, get on with it. If she didn't do something, she truly would break. Summoning up a frenzy of energy, she did her best work in months. In abstract form she depicted her loss, even separated from it and utilized its intensity. A bright yellow-white spot focused each piece, representing her essence.

High again on work, the pain was definitely less. A false euphoria set in. She even believed she could go to Arthur's again and be one of the group, that she was over him. She made plans, she'd flaunt her independence, maybe take her own fella. She looked for someone to invite.

She chose Rick Morrison. With cocoa-brown eyes, light brown hair, and a warm, friendly manner that inspired trust, he was a philosophy major working on his master's in history, one of the few people on the Terrace who responded to her hello. One day they sat and talked for hours until the sun set and the waiters cleared the tables away. He was her age and still wore plaid shirts and denim pants. They recognized each other from a geology

section in her sophomore year. He was sunny and uncomplicated after dealing with Arthur as Hamlet. Also,
he was surprisingly eager to see her. She began to sense
what she'd been missing for the past year: fun. Their first
date was to the movies in Oakland, to see *Goldfinger*.
Then he borrowed a car and they drove into the city and
ate at Tommy's Joint. But when he tried to kiss her, she
didn't let him.

"I just broke up with someone," she told him, "and
I'm not ready yet."

He was very understanding, but after a third date he
could tell he took it personally. She argued with herself,
This is stupid, he's a great guy, what's with you? She
honestly didn't know, since she was over Arthur. She
decided to confront her fear head on, and invited Rick
on a day trip to Carmel.

They drove down for lunch on a glorious spring Saturday, walked up and down the hilly streets in the sunshine
and had an hour at the beach, talking about their favorite
books and movies and artists. Their common interests
were making her giddy, like a dinner with too many
desserts. By late afternoon her hand tingled when he
held it, and so did her cheek, when he kissed it. She'd
been right to come here. Now to face the lion in his den.

It was Rick's suggestion that they end this idyllic day at
Nepenthe for drinks at sunset. Her subconscious was
applauding, while her conscious mind said, *No big deal*.

Just as they were seated in front of the windows over-
looking the ocean, Arthur, Thelma, and their group arrived. What if they hadn't arrived this particular day?
But she knew they would, it had to be. Her heart fell
through her knees when she saw him; his force was so
strong she nearly felt knocked over by him. He could so
easily have stayed home today, or gone to the Big Sur
Inn instead of here, but here he was, just to make her
doubt her own sanity. Rick was watching her, aware of
the currents.

"Isn't that Professor Matalon, from the Art Department?" he asked.

She nodded, unconcerned.

Arthur waved a gather-unto-us gesture, and she and
Rick were swept up with the Saturday *arterati*. She avoided

his eyes, feigning nonchalance. As soon as they were seated in the group, Rick decided to cuddle, or was just responding to the increase in her signals—more hand-holding, knee-touching. The affection she'd withheld all this time was being lavished on him. Arthur didn't like it at all. Good. After drinks she declined an invitation to go back to Arthur's for Thelma's beef bourguignon, saying that she and Rick wanted to be alone.

"Perhaps we'll see you in the morning." It was the first Rick heard he had a chance to score.

Arthur liked that even less.

She was delighted by his response, but why did he object to her being with someone else when he didn't want her? She'd thought this a habit peculiar to high school boys. Having Rick in her life suddenly made her able to recall the rules of playing hard-to-get: a man always wants what he can't have. She wasn't really using Rick. She was attracted to him, but if Arthur didn't know what was good for him, she'd show him. It felt good to know what she was doing for a change.

She and Rick rented a cabin in Pfeiffer State Park with a fireplace and a double bed. She told him nothing was going to happen, and believed it. But then they were in bed in their underwear, the fire playing romantic movies on the cabin walls and in the valleys of the quilt, and he kissed her. Damn, it felt good. For the first time she began to feel hope that Arthur hadn't ruined it for her forever. And why should she deny herself, when his touch felt so good? Was that what morals were, rules to protect us from what came naturally? Maybe his sweet-ness could help her forget Arthur after all, but when she closed her eyes, it was Arthur she longed for with every caress.

Breakfast at the Big Sur Lodge was a triumph. A foggy mist crept into the crevices of the mountains while they ate thick, crisp waffles with fresh maple syrup and drank steaming cinnamon coffee. Again, Arthur showed up, looking gray and hung over—Thelma must have gone back to the city.

"Professor Matalon, come join us," Rick called.

"He looks as if he'd prefer to be alone," Trish stage-whispered as Arthur approached, a bristle on his chin.

Her skin was fresh and shiny, still tingling from the shower she'd taken with Rick that morning.

She poured honey on her muffin, cheerful as a bee.

"One of the funniest things that ever happened to me was in the seventh grade on the playground." She continued the conversation as if both her lovers were not sitting here at the same table. "I was not feeling well, coming down with something awful, and at recess Colin Glazer pulled his pants down in front of me behind the handball board. I'd seen boys before, I had a brother, so I didn't even notice him. But at that moment the flu caught up with me and my stomach let go. Everyone in the entire school thought I'd gotten sick at the sight of Colin. It took years for me to live that one down."

"You never told me that story." Twelve years old was about Arthur's age at the moment.

"Didn't I?"

His chair scraped loudly on the plank floor as he pushed it back and stood to go.

"So long, Professor," Rick said, never taking his eyes from hers. She'd never noticed that Rick had long, thick lashes and golden flecks in his eyes, as she did. He would teach history, she art. Their children would have smart, artistic parents who philosophized about religion and psychology. On the drive back, they held hands and harmonized to "Shine On, Harvest Moon," "You Are My Sunshine," and "Me and My Gal."

Spring was imprisoned while it rained for a month. Arthur moped, grew a beard. Rick was even-tempered, giving her a wide range in which to use him. He knew that she was in love with someone else, but that she'd get over it. She started believing it too. He took her to see Joan Baez and Bob Dylan at the Berkeley Community Theater, music that was new to her and to which she responded instantly. They agreed with Dylan's hypothesis, that the times they are a-chayngin; his strange music fascinated her. Baez's tremolo held her in thrall, spoke to a place in Trish's soul that responded, the longing for passion. When she recognized that void, she became aware that sweet Rick couldn't fill it. He was too uncomplicated.

Two years of graduate school would be over soon, and then life loomed. More of the same, without classes and

students to commiserate with, teachers to rebel against:
"He doesn't know his ass. . . . He's university-bred, spouts
establishment rhetoric. . . . She's a dyke, can't you tell,
puts down anything feminine or traditional as nothing but
Betty Crocker. . . . Pop Art won't last another year,
either will Warhol, Rauschenberg, or Lichtenstein."

Trish bought a used Levi's skirt, a peasant blouse, and
a hand-tooled leather vest from a girl selling her clothes
on a corner. She intended to use them for her models,
but instead wore them herself every day.

12

Trish's days were filled with Rick and a compulsion to work. When thoughts of Arthur intruded, her eyes would glaze over and her face would reflect the pain, but Rick didn't mention it. His tolerance was nurturing. Spring progressed, and she took time off from work to go on picnics, drive to Sonoma, start a garden behind Rick's rented house. It reminded her of Arthur's home in Big Sur, how the flowers looked this time of year. The tomatoes, string beans, and sweet peas that she and Rick grew hid the marijuana plant. Theirs wasn't the only one. It got so they could spot that palmate leaf potted on every other sill in Berkeley. The whole town was going up in some kind of smoke, protest bonfires, incinerated draft cards, or hand-rolled joints. They hung out at People's Park. Antiwar protests linked to civil rights protests linked to protests against University repression were all anyone discussed. Trish and Rick attended rallies, but sat on the sidelines at sit-ins. And then one day she heard him running up the steps of her apartment and pounding on the door.

"It's open," she called, her hands filled with brushes.

He burst in, carrying a bottle of Chianti, his face red and perspiring. "I ran all the way from my house to the liquor store, and then all the way here."

"What is it?" she started to ask, but he burst out, "I've been awarded a Rhodes scholarship!"

She screamed, threw down her brushes and threw her arms around him, and they jumped up and down together, laughing and yelling. "I've never met such a superachiever as you," she teased. "You were Phi Beta Kappa, you ran track in college, you were vice-president of the student body, and now this. Just the kind of boy every mother wants for her daughter."

His eyes wouldn't meet hers. "Got an opener? I want to get drunk."

"What did you feel when you found out?" she asked.

"I was stunned," he admitted. "I've never known anyone who's been a Rhodes scholar."

"Neither have I," she said.

As the time grew closer, they talked of nothing but how it would be to be apart. Sometimes it would be good, other times the thought made them both cry. Finally, on the eve of his leaving, he said, "Why don't you come with me, babe? I may not be ready to make a permanent commitment, but I'd love it if you were there too. You could study and paint there just as well as here." The Rhodes was distinguished, but granted only to single people, and it provided only enough money for one person to live on.

A decision had to be made; Trish alternated between fantasies of going and the reality of staying, not admitting to herself that if she went she might never see Arthur again. "Studying in Europe would be a dream come true. I can't even imagine what it would be like to see masterpieces in person instead of on slides, especially my favorites. The thought of actually being there makes me quiver inside. But you know it's impossible to get a work permit in England, and my allowance from my parents ends this month after graduation. From now on, all my expenses are my own responsibility. I have no savings; I can't even afford the fare."

There were tears in his eyes that he couldn't hide from her. All this time he'd denied her subtext, which now came through clearly. "It's not money or your job, or your parents' disapproval of going to Europe with a man you're not married to, it's Arthur Matalon, damn his blackened soul." He'd known it in the way her body stiffened when the man's name was mentioned, in the look in her eyes at moments when a certain song came on the radio, or if he suggested Indian food. But the most telling thing of all, the thing that really hurt him was in the morning when he'd make the coffee, wake her with a kiss, and find that her first expression on seeing him was surprise followed by a flicker of disappointment.

"He's too old for you." It came out bitterly. "He's

tarnished brass, looking for you to polish him. But no matter how hard you try, you'll never restore his luster."

"You're wrong!" she insisted, unable to fully meet his gaze, knowing regret in a way she'd never known it before.

She sobbed at the airport, seeing him off to New York, where he would visit with his family before leaving for England. He'd been her buffer, and now the pain of not having Arthur hit her again with gale force. Would she ever see him again, this sweet man whose kindness had revived her, set her straight, but not ignited her, even though he was good for her? If only she could pluck her limbs free from the stalk that held them planted in this soil. But she could only stand and watch Jack as he made that famous climb, knowing he would make it back from the giant's castle in the sky with the golden egg.

After Rick left she was terribly low, but loneliness brought out good work, though she worked to exhaustion again, and smoked too much pot. What a strange phenomenon unhappiness was, a necessary catalyst, yet abhorrent.

"When are you going to get married and settle down?" her mother wrote. "Dorothy Platt's daughter is having her second child, and I got a second baby announcement from your cousin Carol. What's wrong with you, that no man has proposed yet? You might have to lower your expectations a bit, Trisha. Don't rule out any possibilities in the other denominations. I hear Mormons make wonderful husbands. Of course, your father draws the line at Catholics, and I wouldn't want you to marry anyone Jewish."

Her father wrote, "You're not getting mixed up in any of that craziness we read about in the papers going on in Berkeley, are you? We'll see for ourselves when we come for Tom's graduation from law school."

She both dreaded and anticipated their visit. To be with them again, to have their familiar touch and smell surrounding her; yet she ached with the need. But how to get ready for it? Her old clothes were out of date, and she had no money to buy new ones. Her mother would hate what she wore every day, and her apartment was especially open to ridicule. They might even insist that she go live with them in that far-off place. Tommy received his share of directives too: "We expect to meet a new, serious girlfriend when we arrive."

Rick was gone a week when she was awarded the Eisner Prize in art, a five-hundred-dollar fellowship. Her picture, along with that of the other recipient, ran in the *Daily Cal*. Everyone she knew, especially the classmates with whom she'd gone all through the Art Department, teased her by asking her for a loan or asking her to make an investment, or if she was now a capitalist pig? She hugged herself at night, thinking, *They liked my work. But was it really good?*

Hillary sent her wonderful pictures of Lori, a baby version of her mother. Trish stuck one of the photos into her makeup mirror. What would it be like to be a mother, to have that sweet little bundle dependent on you for her every need? Frightening and wonderful. Maybe it was Hillary's daughter that reminded her that time was passing, or maybe it was just now or never, but she requested a consultation with Arthur for his advice on her career. She made the decision to see him without mulling it over; she just plunged ahead. Of course, a part of her brain never stopped thinking about him, so going to see him was merely an extension of that. His student assistant gave her a time on a Tuesday afternoon. She washed her hair, which was getting long—it was easier than paying for haircuts all the time. Arthur had never seen it like this, almost to the middle of her back. Neither had he seen her in her new uniform—the casual look, complete with leather sandals.

It was his day to paint. All the members of the staff who were working artists were given studio space by the university in Kroeber Hall, and were only required to teach on alternate days. She envied the arrangement and wondered what it would be like to have students emulate you, admire you, criticize the hell out of you. Talk about confusion—one moment she wanted to be a mother, the next a teacher, always feeling that the two were mutually exclusive. Besides, one needed thick skin to be a teacher, and hers was far too delicate. And to be a mother? What kind of skin would she need for that?

The northern light streamed through the skylight of Arthur's studio, illuminating the paintings stacked around the room. He'd been busy painting these somber pieces;

not that his work was ever light or frivolous, but this new group was particularly dark. Foreboding swirls of paint, alleviated only by Prussian blue or black and gashes of gray heavily applied, plunged her into depression. She identified too easily, joined him instantly in that deep blue pool of sadness, an entire room full of sadness. In these past six months he had been productive (she thought about her own output, also prolific) but tormented. It was unrelenting, this thick emotionality, pressing on her heart with a steady heaviness.

He turned and saw her, paused to watch her approach. He seemed confused, not knowing whether he should stay where he was or swim to the surface of the grotto where he lurked. Then he put down his brushes and smiled, and his smile couldn't have expressed more delight. She could see that his eyes were unguarded, a direct one-to-one between them, and that familiar look took her breath away. Somehow the world had shifted; she saw possibilities there. He was walking toward her, but he seemed to float, and then he reached her, gazing down before he enfolded her in an embrace, as gently as waves at twilight hug the shore. She felt his ribs through his smock, the unfamiliar beard against her cheek.

His breath caught in a half-sigh as he inhaled her. "Have you come to say good-bye? To treat me badly by showing me your shining beauty and then snatching it away?"

"Good-bye? No. Why?"

"England. Your young man."

He was holding her away and then close again. Her knees were weak, actually weak. She'd heard that expression, but never believed it before. "Rick is already gone, I'm not going with him." She had thought there were many reasons, but there was only one.

"Why not? Didn't he want you?"

"Yes." She was instantly angry and he saw it.

"Forgive me. Of course he wants you. Anyone would. I'm being perverse because you've taken me by surprise."

"But you were expecting me."

"Not that kind of surprise. The kind that jolts me when I see the color of your eyes, smell your scent, like lilies of the valley."

She disengaged herself, felt the shock of air on her

body, away from his warmth. Half of her continued to talk, the other half stepped away and observed it all, amused by her attempt to be cool. "I came because I wanted your advice, a consultation." He'd once strewn flower petals in her path; she could remember the feel of them beneath her feet, their fragrance enticing her. Strong forces pulled her as she tried to stick to the point, that she was here for a reason, but her point seemed more and more obscure by the minute. She kept trying to maintain control. "I won the Eisner, you know."

"Of course I know. I championed you. Congratulations. Trish, you're ignoring me. You've never done that before."

They stared at one another while the air grew heavy with expectation. He drew closer. She thought, *Oh no, not again.* And then, *Of course, again.*

"Trish." There was a sob in his throat as he reached for her, hungry flesh needing to meld, and arms and mouths clinging, breathing in one another, her mouth surrounded by his grizzly beard. He leaned back against a counter and wrapped his leg around her. "God, I've missed you." His mouth was on hers; she swallowed the taste of him as though it were his essence.

She felt both their tears on her cheek.

"Thelma's gone. Boring company. She gave so little. Nothing like you. Do you know how much I love you? Even I didn't know. More than everything. Enough to marry you. Will you? You're not still enamored of that boy, are you? I waited until he was out of your system. Knew you needed someone else besides me before I could claim you. I couldn't be responsible for being your first and only. Too much power, and you know what they say about power."

She was unable to speak; he'd sucked the words out of her. Was all this true, that he'd loved her all this time, been giving her time to decide? Was he that wise, while she suffered? *Don't kid yourself,* a voice boomed in her head. *You saw him around campus. He couldn't have cared less.* Then what did he mean? He was kissing her hand, licking between her fingers, kissing her mouth, her neck, lifting up her blouse, pulling aside her bra to lap at her breasts. His hand up her skirt found the expression of her wonder at what was going on. "Marry me, darling,

please say you will. Let's have children, lots of them. I
want you to have my children. Will you? Are you afraid
because I'm older than you? Don't be. I'll be young for
you, I promise. I have magic potions to make us both the
same." She could feel him hard against her, fought sur-
render with all her might, and failed. He had her pants
off and his pulled down. He locked the door and was
back in moments gathering up her senses, splashing them
on the canvases around the room as he had done with
paint, with her life, for God's sake.

"Arthur," she cried out as he entered her, fevered by
his need, not knowing whether he was ravishing her or
she him. So often had she wanted this that the memory
was imprinted in her flesh, it knew what to do better than
she, gathering him up, joining as if by an osmosis in-
vented for their cells to merge all on their own. She
didn't even know if he'd really been expecting her, or if
this was a coincidence.

Afterwards, when she lay in his arms and he kept
kissing her face and cheeks, stroking her body, her eyelids, her nose, as though to memorize these new cells of
his, she asked him, "Marriage, really?"

His sigh was a deep, cleansing one. "With all my
heart."

Her response was joyous. Things like this didn't happen in real life, that a girl got to marry the man of her
dreams (and nightmares), the brilliant, successful, gorgeous, sophisticated artist, the articulate master of his
own life, and now hers. "Yes, I'll marry you, Arthur,"
she said, barely able to say it, knowing for the first time
the feeling of swooning. *I'll own him forever, and he'll
own me. We'll belong together, I'll belong to him.* It was
the greatest gift she'd ever been given in her life, could
ever hope to get. And then another thought struck her:
But I can't introduce him to my parents.

13

The Baldwins would be in San Francisco for two weeks, and Trish could not contain her excitement. At the airport she was so glad to see them that she felt whole again, and clung to them, kissing and smiling, wanting to absorb them into herself. She'd forgotten the way they made her feel, desperate to please. As she drove them to their hotel, if she managed to get a smile or a hug from them, it filled her with contentment. But by the time they had reached the Fairmont, reality had reasserted itself. "Why hasn't Tommy invited a date to join us for dinner after graduation? Honestly, that boy is impossible," her mother said. "And you?" her father asked. "Don't you know anybody besides that boy who went to England?" Her instinct had been right, they'd never accept Arthur. She wouldn't tell them she was getting married until they'd gone back to the Middle East, then she'd write them a letter. *Chicken.* She had to tell them. They had to be a part of her wedding.

"We'll take it in stages," she suggested to her fiancé, the word so new, so intimate it thrilled her.

Arthur was insulted by her reticence. "I'm a catch," he insisted. "I won't force you to tell your parents, but you must do it before they leave. Maybe they've changed after living among a foreign culture. In Iran, sixty-year-old men marry girls of seventeen when they already have wives."

Arthur didn't know her parents. Two years in Iran had not changed their attitudes; in fact, their lives were even more insular. Like the British in India, they lived within the compound of American life that flourished in a vacuum, making do with inconveniences and strange luxuries in spite of the exotica surrounding them. The customs

144

of the country only amused them. The Baldwins related incidents with a tone that said, You won't believe this! But underlying the tone was an unmistakable attitude of hypercritical disgust, mingled with superiority. And then they turned that attitude on Trish.

When Trish brought Arthur to Tommy's law school graduation dinner at Trader Vic's, Patricia remembered meeting him. "It's so kind of you to take an interest in our daughter," she said, and then tried to impress him by telling him about her servants in Iran. Matthew was less grateful; he thought Trish had brought this professor along as a ploy to justify her wasting her time as an artist. He couldn't possibly be her date. But as the evening went along, Matthew began to pick up an undercurrent between his daughter and this older man that made him extremely uncomfortable.

Arthur found Matthew insufferable, but he was on his best behavior.

Their second meeting was at brunch on Sunday, in the Baldwins' suite at the Fairmont.

The Baldwins were quite surprised to see Arthur with Trish again, but were polite enough not to mention it until Arthur and her father got into a political discussion about the bombing of North Vietnam.

"As much as I dislike Johnson," Matthew said, "who inherited Kennedy's mess, he's certainly doing the right thing by sending more troops to Southeast Asia. We have to prevent that domino effect. If we don't stop the Commies here, the rest of Southeast Asia will fall."

"That's a crock," Arthur exploded, unable to keep quiet a moment longer. "This war is something the French started in order to reestablish their empire in Indochina after the war. They drove out Ho Chi Minh and brought back the emperor from Hong Kong, where he should have stayed. They're the ones who created the puppet nations of Laos, Cambodia, and Vietnam. America paid nearly eighty percent of the French war effort to support Emperor Dai."

"That was in the fifties, this is now!" Matthew insisted.

"If Eisenhower had signed the Geneva Accords and compelled Diem to abide by them, none of this would be happening."

"And allowed free elections? That would have made it a Communist country."

"So what? It's not essential for American security. Those people want Ho Chi Minh."

"You're a goddamned Red, aren't you?" he said, standing up suddenly and pointing his finger. "Joe McCarthy was right, the universities are hotbeds of subversives. I suppose you think we should rebuild the stores and homes in Watts that the Negroes burned and looted?"

Arthur stood up to face him. "If you'd been economically oppressed and segregated from society, prevented from voting, and hated because of the color of your skin, you might want to riot too."

"Trish." Matthew's face was red as he turned to her. "I don't want you spending any more time with this . . . *man.* I'd like you to leave," he said to Arthur.

"Coming, Trish?" Arthur asked. There was a deadly silence in the room.

"She's not going with you!" Matthew shouted. But then he looked at Trish and saw that indeed she might.

Her body flushed with the heat of embarrassment; Arthur's eyes bored into her. If she didn't go with him now, he'd never marry her. It took all of Trish's strength to remove her napkin from her lap, push her chair away from the table, and stand up to go.

"I don't believe what I'm seeing," her father said, sinking back down to his chair. "You're not going with him? Are you a fool?"

But she followed Arthur, almost on tiptoe, shoulders hunched, as her father's verbal blows struck from behind. "That man is a Communist, a dangerous subversive. Stay away from him, Trish! Do you hear me? Patricia, do something! She's your daughter, stop her!"

"Oh, Matthew," her mother was crying. "She never listens to me, no one listens to me."

Trish could hear them all the way out the door. She grabbed Arthur's arm. "Arthur, I can't leave them like this. They can't help being the way they are. My father's politics are impossible, but he's got another side to him," she pleaded, wiping at the tears that were streaming down her face.

"The man's a bigot, Trish. After meeting him, I'm amazed that you're as open-minded as you are." She

clutched his arm, trying to stop his hurried, determined
march down the hall to the elevator. Finally, just as they
reached the front door of the lobby, he stopped and
pulled her fingers loose from his arm. "I'm not going to
force you to come with me, Trish. You're a grown woman,
old enough to make your own choices. Either you choose
me, or you choose your father." She went with him and
sobbed all the way home, while Arthur clenched his jaw
and glared at her.

Arthur refused to come to dinner on Monday with her
parents and her brother, so she went alone. It was a
disaster. Only by smoking a joint beforehand could she
get through it at all. They harangued her, denounced
Arthur, and insisted that she never have anything to do
with him again, until she felt she was being pulled apart
by two teams of horses. Finally, just as dessert was being
served, she burst into tears and told them, "I'm sorry you
two hate him so much, but he's truly the most wonderful
man in the world, and I'm going to marry him."

"Oh God," her mother said, "you can't be serious.
You see, Matt, I told you he'd had his way with her."
She never looked at Trish directly again that night.

For once her father was silent, waiting to regain his
composure along with the color in his face. Then he
found his voice. "To say I'm disappointed in you is an
understatement. That man is not only too old for you,
he's never going to amount to anything. He has the
opinions of a lunatic; he's a parasite on society, someone
who makes caca on canvas and expects decent people to
give him their hard-earned money for it. You can't even
tell what he's painting, for God's sake. I beg you not to
do this, Trisha. You'll regret it for the rest of your life. I
won't be a party to it. I won't. From now on you can sink
or swim all on your own; it's just too much for me to
swallow."

A needlelike constriction grabbed her throat too. She
would sink if left on her own, she'd always known that.
Was Arthur enough of a life preserver? In no way did he
resemble the much-longed-for son-in-law with a bright
future that her parents had always expected, someone
young and impressionable whom Matthew could influence. The dream of that young man had been gobbled up
by this dragon of a male—gray at the temples, no less—

who was rooting around Matthew's daughter like an old goat. Mortifying. Apparently, Arthur didn't give a damn what Matthew thought of him, hadn't even had the decency to show up and hear Matthew's opinion in person, but had sent a woman instead to face the music. The thought of him with Trish enraged Matthew so that when he could not change her mind, he too refused to speak to her or look at her. Again, she sobbed all the way home.

Of course, she had doubts about marrying Arthur. Most people, she assured herself, had doubts and insecurities when considering such a step. But now she had to bury them to defend Arthur to her parents or her parents to Arthur. Their mutual dislike was devastating to her. It took every bit of strength she had not to do as they asked and break off with him. She smoked another joint in the cab on the way home.

When she told Arthur what had happened, he attacked her parents with a fury she'd rarely seen in him before. "Those pompous assholes, those hypocrites. Your mother is a dandelion blown apart by his poison breath. There's no more strength in that woman than in a marshmallow, and your father's green with envy that I've got a luscious young thing with a tight ass and bouncy boobs to give me head, while he's stuck with your prune of a mother. No, I take that back, a melted marshmallow is what she is. His possessiveness of you borders on the incestuous. Are you sure you're not marrying me because of an Electra complex?"

Somewhere inside her there were tears wanting to get out, sobs that felt enclosed in cotton, already absorbed. She spoke hazily: "Don't be insulting, please, Arthur, I can't take it." Her cheeks were crimson from the battle of divided loyalties raging within her. Part of her cared deeply, the rest of her was numb. "We have to be understanding, Arthur. They're my parents."

"Fuck that," he shouted.

Tommy came to soothe her, talked about reasonable things. "Follow your heart, sis. Mom and Dad have done with their lives what they've wanted to do, so should you. They moved halfway around the world and didn't care what we thought. And now they're demanding that you serve up your life to them the way they want it. Screw that. Do what you want, and so will I. We'll both rebel, and damn the torpedoes."

"That's a laugh. You've never defied them, the perfect son. You want me to do the rebelling for you. Well, I hate it. I want their love and approval too." She felt the tears bubbling to the surface, but marijuana kept the sobbing encased.

"I'll talk to Dad. I'll make him see it's your life and your choice. He doesn't want to lose you, Trish, that's what all this is about. At least he loves you. Me he only tolerates."

"That's not true," she insisted, knowing he was right. Tommy had never lived up to their father's expectations, no matter how he'd excelled. He'd never been athletic or raunchy enough. His girlfriends weren't popular, his choices uncontroversial, his life too narrow for Matthew. She took his hand, he cried her tears. Did her father love her? If he loved her, would he refuse to talk to her, refuse to come to her wedding? She didn't think she could walk down the aisle without him. Certainly not without dope or booze. "What about Mom?"

"Whatever he says, she'll do."

Tommy was right.

Turning to look in the mirror, she was surprised to see herself as a bride. The day had finally come, though she'd kept herself inured. Now all the elegance seemed superimposed over her long hair and her artist's attire. Occasionally, in spite of a chemical crutch, the excitement of her engagement was pulled off-kilter by the disapproval of her parents. Her father didn't stay in California for the wedding, saying he had to get back to work, but her mother remained—a mixed blessing—to oversee the event she said was turning her gray overnight.

And Arthur was eventually understanding. When he saw Trish suffering because her father wouldn't reconcile with her, he held her and told her he would be her family now. It gave her great comfort. In fact, their only disagreement came when he wanted her to do what he wanted. If she went along, things were fine; if she didn't, he'd pout, accuse, and get angry. So she went along.

There were other subtle changes as well. He was an excellent cook, but now weekend potluck dinners fell to her to organize; if people hesitated when she asked them to bring something, she found it easier to do it alone, or if not easier, less troublesome. Many of his friends treated her as an amusement of Arthur's whom they tolerated, but Arthur said, "They're envious of your youth." Arthur had an entourage of friends who had achieved more recognition than he, yet his opinion held weight with them, his innovations inspired their work. Their success made Arthur pretend a largesse that he didn't feel and that only Trish knew to be false. His jealousy would be understandable if it weren't so hurtful. "Look at that crap," he'd say of a close friend's work. "I hope his brain rots." Her work, of course, was not considered in the same category as Arthur's, or even his friend's "crap."

He was also a difficult taskmaster, husbanding his praise. "Darling, the couscous was brave of you, but lacked flavor. Oh, and the rice wasn't dry enough. Don't you agree?" he'd ask the group. And then her couscous would be discussed, compared to everyone else's recipe or experience with the dish. (She had begun to attempt more and more exotic dishes to impress them, or to keep them from comparing: like rabbit pie with raisins, nuts, and cardamom, in a flaky pastry shell, sprinkled with powdered sugar. Her mother was now a source of Middle Eastern recipes.)

Of course, all her food tasted better and was easier to prepare while stoned.

She did not protest about the way their roles were defined, believing it temporary, waiting to become that treasured darling he'd described her as when he'd wooed and won her, but she did battle about where she was going to work. Arthur couldn't seem to find her any studio space in his houses in Berkeley or Big Sur; he was spread out all over them. Not to mention his studio on campus. And now she'd given up her apartment. She'd thought of keeping it as a studio, but her landlord rented it immediately, glad to get rid of her and her weird creations. The university facilities were no longer available to her since she'd graduated. Maybe small canvases and diminutive sculptures she could do at the kitchen table were the answer, but mentally it would cramp her style. She started looking for a garage space to rent.

And so here she was on her wedding day, a fatherless

child. At least he sent a telegram. She found a way to keep it from hurting too much. Her latest stash was Acapulco Gold, the mellowest. She thought there was no better way to get married than stoned in a meadow, with garlands of flowers in her braided hair that wound around her head.

Arthur came to get her and escort her to where the ceremony was taking place, on a tree-shaded bluff in Pfeiffer State Park. Tommy walked with them. Her mother cried through the whole ceremony, which made her sad; Tommy looked solemn; Arthur terrified. But Arthur squeezed her hand in his with a mixture of authority and nervousness. She floated. Today they were both so happy.

The minister stood facing them so that they overlooked the ocean, and spoke with a smile in his voice about these two dear people of talent who were joining their lives in these special times. "What passes for devotion and begins as an attraction between two people is the most private of emotions. No one else can tell what your special connection is. What we call love is ephemeral, an unknown, but it is that which has brought you together today." Listening to him, Trish felt giddy and giggly, thought about all her friends who were protesting the draft; at least that was something she'd never have to worry about with Arthur. She almost laughed, and wanted to tell him, but his tension held her in place, afraid of embarrassing him. She had a fantasy about flying over the crowds of friends and listening to their thoughts, hearing whether or not they really thought this wedding was such a good idea. But then she was grounded again, with "I now pronounce you . . . ."

A flutist and a violinist played music by Alexander Borodin, "Greensleeves," and one of the Brandenburg Concertos. Joints were passed, people sat on blankets in their velvet or dimity skirts, ice cream melted on the cake, while guests dipped their paper cups in the champagne punch. Faculty, students, and a few relatives attended the wedding, the Golds hugged her warmly. Her Aunt Joan and Uncle Ben from La Jolla came up to console her mother. Pam and Hillary sent flowers and gifts but couldn't come. How she missed them; she wondered what they would think about the wedding, it was so different from Hillary's. But then, her friends' worlds were different from hers. Photographs of Pam appeared regularly in high-fashion magazines. She wore skirts with clear plastic inserts banded across the thighs, false eyelashes, and bright bubble earrings. Hillary, in domestic seclusion, assisted at Lori's play school and volunteered at the Met. The only people at the wedding whom Pam and Hillary could have related to were Tommy and Fred, who served as a buffer between both worlds, and her father, if he had been there. She longed to have had her father walk her down the aisle—or actually the cow path.

Thelma came up to her after the ceremony, wearing flowered silk, looking bemused. "Well, dear, you have my sympathy. If you ever need advice, don't come to me. I might give it." Arthur threw back his head and laughed.

As the guests passed, Trish's mind wandered to Rick, studying in England; he symbolized her youth, the carefree things one did at twenty-five before marrying a man of forty-two, like getting stoned at rock concerts or going to the zoo on Sundays and acting like monkeys, or surfing in the freezing Northern California surf. She and Arthur were going wine-tasting in the Napa Valley for their honeymoon—he was replenishing his cellar—then on to Los Angeles, so he could visit artist friends and galleries and scoff at the L.A. scene.

She found Los Angeles artists friendly and willing to share, and even found a corroboration of sorts in what she'd been working on lately, a return to childhood for a more innocent view of experience. Everyone there was discussing Andy Warhol's Campbell's Soup cans, the Pop Art movement, and the death of Morris Lewis in '62.

In Los Angeles, on her honeymoon, she took something called LSD. It made pot seem like child's play. The colors were amazing, surrounding her with a reality she'd never imagined before, as though they were as alive as she, breathing, beating; then the awareness of the intensity of tactile experiences grabbed her. She believed she was journeying into her subconscious, communing with the source of her creativity. It manifested itself as a dark-haired child, the way she looked at seven; the child took her by the hand and walked her through each of her creations, letting the works converse with her, telling her what each of them meant in clear, precise terms. For the first time she was totally proud of what she'd done, but then everything grew distorted and nightmarish; she became frightened and overwhelmed by the images and feared she'd never get out of the distorted world around her. She huddled in a corner of their hotel room at the Hollywood Roosevelt, whimpering while darkness crept closer and closer, threatening to blot out all the light forever. When it wore off, she was exhausted from the ordeal, but somehow triumphant. Part of it had been good, even ecstatic, and the bad part had not been bad enough to deter her from trying it again. That heightened clarity and the vision of herself were too special to give up. If she could find it again and capture it, maybe it would be with her always.

14

September 25, 1964

Dear Trish,

The pictures of the wedding were beautiful, just as you described, informal yet charming. You glowed. I'm so happy you liked the toaster-oven, I use mine for everything. Enclosed is one of my favorite recipes for easy cheese-salmon croquettes. You make them on an English muffin in the toaster-oven. It's a perfect dish for a ladies' luncheon. I serve it with an antipasto salad and a pitcher of lemonade-tea, and get so many compliments.

The last time you wrote to me, you were trying to get over Arthur with Rick. I guess the cure didn't work.

You have no idea how much I wanted to be there, but we just couldn't afford it right now. We have to move to a bigger apartment; Mel wants to buy a house in the suburbs. Why, you ask? Are you sitting down? I'm pregnant. I just found out two days ago, so if this letter sounds disjointed, it's because I'm in a state of numbness. Lori is only seventeen months old, still in diapers. Of course, she'll probably be trained by the time the baby comes. I can't believe it happened again. But this time we didn't have the same traumatic reaction as last time. Baby Two is a little early, but it's one we eventually wanted.

I hate the idea of moving, but I'll be glad to get out of the city. There was a riot in Harlem last July, and every week there's some protest march. The beatniks are all over the Village, and there are radical groups on every corner soliciting funds or shoving a petition in your face. It's amazing how mobilized people are becoming over political issues—the Kennedy legacy, I guess. He filled us with hope that we could make a difference, and without him it's much harder to make it happen. And yet there's still so much apathy. I'm sure you heard about Kitty Genovese, that woman who was attacked on the street and

154

killed. Thirty-four people heard her screaming, but no one came to her aid.

Do you remember Les Wexler, from Dr. Popper's philosophy class? He rode on a bus to Alabama and was arrested and beaten. I saw him when he came back. The stories he told me were horrible. At least Johnson is strong on civil rights. I've been doing some volunteer work at the Johnson headquarters. We've got to stop Goldwater. The man is frightening, thinks we should escalate the Vietnam conflict. Mel has a draft deferment because of Lori, but so many guys we know are getting drafted.

Didn't you say you and Arthur knew Mario Savio? I remember what a buffoon we thought he was, now he's a big deal. Berkeley must be an amazing place to be. It's all we read about. Is the Art Department affected by what's happening on campus?

One thing I'll miss by having another baby is being able to go the theater. We can't afford tickets if we're paying more rent or a mortgage. We've seen Fiddler on the Roof *twice, and* Hello, Dolly! *and* Funny Girl. *They were wonderful, especially Barbra Streisand. She looks like my cousin Marlene. She sings a song in the show, "Sadie, Married Lady." That's you, babe (and me). Lori sends love to Aunt "Pish." Your name is the funniest thing to her.*

Mel and I wish you both as much joy and happiness as we have.

All my love,
Hillary

P.S. I'm seeing Pam today.

Hillary mailed her letter to Trish at Grand Central Terminal when she changed trains to the uptown IRT. Lori was squirming in her lap this morning, grabbing at people who were either jammed in next to her on the subway or standing in front of her. On rainy days the subways were extra crowded, and raincoats were soaked from the downpour up above. The air smelled of wet wool and perspiration. This was supposed to have been her Saturday for lunch with Pam, but the teenaged baby-sitter canceled and she couldn't afford to hire an agency sitter. Mel was going shopping on his one day off—she couldn't ask him to take Lori, no way. Pam suggested she bring Lori and they eat at Pam's.

The subway stopped four blocks from Pam's apartment; Hillary walked in the rain juggling the umbrella, the child on her hip, the diaper bag, her purse, and a bag of toys to keep Lori occupied while she and Pam ate. The two of them were soon dripping wet, and Lori cried, "Rain, Mommy, rain."

Pam's masseuse opened the door and gave Hillary an impatient stare. What good was having a massage, when your tranquility was disrupted by a friend bringing a noisy toddler to play?

Hillary took off her wet raincoat and Lori's, and then tiptoed around the apartment being quiet and holding Lori, whom she couldn't put down for fear of what she'd touch. She loved coming here, seeing all this elegance and sophistication. The apartment reflected Pam, eclectic and classy. The furniture was upholstered in a dark green velvet the color of moss in a forest. The area carpet, over dark plank floors, was woven to look like the skin of a leopard, and the draperies were a rust and green silk chintz trimmed with matching fringe, but Hillary liked the pillows on the sofa best; they were made of antique fabrics, pieces of old carpets, and paisley shawls. In the spring and summer, Pam slipcovered the velvet furniture with a flowered cotton chintz that somehow blended with all the other prints in the room, making the room into a spring garden. And the tables, the inlaid antique ones, felt so satiny to the touch. Hillary admired the parquet patterns, and the exotic woods.

Finally Pam appeared, wrapped in a terrycloth robe, her hair newly shampooed and hanging loose. All scrubbed and fresh, she looked even more beautiful than in the magazines.

"There's my little precious," Pam exclaimed, holding out her arms to Lori, who eagerly went to her. "How's my little pumpkin? You came in the rain to see Aunt Pam, aren't you delicious?" and she nuzzled Lori's tummy until Lori squealed with delight.

Hillary sank into a chair with a sigh of contentment. "I love coming here. It's so peaceful and roomy, and no baby's things all over the place."

Pam smiled, dancing in a circle with Lori. "Cha-cha-

cha," she sang, dipping and turning, "and boom, boom, boom." Lori was enthralled.

Hillary noticed that the dining table was set with Pam's beautiful crystal and china, and there was a high chair in the doorway of the kitchen, with a large towel under it.

"I borrowed the high chair from my neighbor so you could eat hands-free," she explained.

Hillary was touched by her thoughtfulness.

Just then the delivery boy brought their lunch, and Pam paid and tipped him. Then she turned to Hillary with a smile. "I ordered from D'Orsi's. Pasta, cold veal, ensalata—and zabaglione for dessert."

"This is heaven!" Hillary exclaimed, taking Lori and putting her in the high chair.

"I've got cottage cheese, Jell-O, and cold slices of liver for Lori."

"She'll love it," Hillary said, snapping on her bib.

"I have a surprise for you," Pam said. "After lunch, I thought we could put Lori down for a nap, or if not, I'll play with her and you can relax."

"Oh, that's not necessary," Hillary protested.

"Wait till you hear," Pam said. "My masseuse is coming back to give you a massage, and then André is coming over to do our hair, and bringing Estella to give you a manicure and a pedicure. The works, kid—on me, of course."

Hillary just stared at her friend. "I don't understand. What's the occasion?"

" 'Cause you deserve to be pampered. One baby, and another one on the way. I thought you might like a day of indulgence while I get to play mommy. It will do us both good. Say it's an early birthday present."

Hillary felt tears fill her eyes and she hugged Pam. "That's the most thoughtful thing anyone's ever done for me."

"Well, you deserve it," Pam said, always uncomfortable when Hillary got overly sentimental. She poured them each a cup of coffee and raised her cup. "To you, Hillary Markus Robin, my best friend."

"To you!" Lori mimicked, jamming red Jell-O into her mouth with her chubby little hands.

They both laughed at how cute she was.

"So how's young Clarence Darrow feel about the new baby?" Pam asked.

Hillary hesitated before replying. "He's happy, but he's so busy we don't have much time together."

Pam caught the note in her voice. "Mel's not God's gift to the world, Hil. He's just a man, and he's got the most wonderful wife in the world. Don't you ever forget it."

Hillary nodded, picking at her food. She was in the stages where nausea kept her appetite down. "I believe it when you say it, but sometimes my doubts get the best of me. Without me, Mel would be one of those swinging singles doing the frug at the Peppermint Lounge. And without marriage and a family, maybe I would be too."

"Single life's not so wonderful," Pam said.

"So why aren't you married?"

She shrugged. "I'm waiting to be swept off my feet."

"It doesn't work that way," Hillary said. "Love grows out of friendship and compromise when the heat of infatuation wears off."

"Spoken like an old married lady of twenty-four."

"Twenty-five," Hillary corrected her, then she sighed. "I guess I should take my own advice. I wouldn't give up my life with Mel and Lori, and now with the new baby coming, for all the single men in the world. I only hope Mel feels that way."

15

The European fall of 1964 enveloped Pam in a soft cloud of luxurious down, as well-groomed and heavily styled as the fur she was wearing, with its stand-up collar and cuffed bell sleeves. Being in Paris without a lover made her throat tighten with an unnamed longing, but it was better than not being here at all. Only her coat kept her warm, a fully let-out, natural lunarine mink, of all female pelts. She'd paid for it in cash.

She had spent 1963 earning her stripes, earning the right to her room with a view at the Ritz, and twelve messages waiting upon her arrival. There were famous models older than she, *grandes dames* such as Parker, Leigh, Wilhelmina, and MacGil, but, though new to the game, she picked up experience with Fire and Ice fingertips.

Photo sessions in the same couture clothes she modeled on runways in shows made them her own. Models could purchase their favorite designs at discount. She usually abstained, but on this trip she bought a custom-fitted Chanel suit, a Courrèges dress, Golo boots, a Balenciaga ball gown, and a cocktail dress by Dior. Paris made it seem fitting. Invitations came to her regularly, and to her young friend Astrid Bengstrom, Swedish model of seventeen who had accompanied her from New York. Astrid's family owned steel refineries in a small town outside of Stockholm, and Astrid lived life to excess. The delicacy of her spectacular beauty, her vulnerability hidden beneath a lacquer-hard veneer, brought out Pam's maternal instincts. The girl made all the wrong choices, opting to be a groupie for one of the musicians in the Rolling Stones instead of appreciating the young man who adored her, Nicki de Bonnedetti, of the Italian sports car family. Nicki was stalwart and loyal, but Astrid craved

159

rebellion. Pam saw her heading for disaster and tried at every chance to stop her. Raised by a close-knit, conservative family whom she now called hypocrites, Astrid defiantly threw away all restraints and Pam became her duenna, searching for Astrid in smoke-filled clubs and backstage at concert halls whenever they were in the same city as the Stones. In Europe, the wild, frenzied scene Astrid embraced was a step below decadent, close to frightening. Pam would pull her, loaded on drugs, out of someone's bed, and call Nicki, who would fly to their side in the de Bonnedetti plane; then they'd both sit with Astrid while she came off her high, or hallucinated through a bad trip. Pam tried to get her to stop taking drugs, but Astrid wouldn't listen.

But when Astrid was straight, her wit and charm enchanted everyone, especially the group of eligible men hovering around her who liked to date models. That autumn, through Astrid, Pam met Hoveland Thomas "Tommy" Maxwell, who would someday run his family's English bone-china manufacturing company; Khalil Sharma Amar, a Kuwaiti oil sheik; and Alfonse de Keirgen, heir to the famous watch and jewelry company, clockmakers to the King of Belgium, jewelry maker to the Court of France, established in 1740. These men were lobster mousse en croute, while Pam still thought of herself sometimes as macaroni surprise, the kind she used to get in the junior high school cafeteria. However, they were more interested in her as a person than were the American men she'd met. They listened to her dreams of becoming a real-estate developer, and encouraged her, shared information with her about their businesses and their own goals, and treated her as a woman with brains, and she grew fond of each of them. Tommy's effete manner belied a passionate nature. The one time he worked up his courage and kissed her in the backseat of a taxi, she responded to his enthusiasm, but declined his offer of going further in favor of continuing their friendship. Khalil Sharma, as shrewd as anyone she'd ever met, made his interest in her known from the first. Arab men rarely had women as friends, and she flirted with him more than with any of the others, but kept him at least as far away as across the table; Khalil tended to be all hands. Eventually she introduced him to Claudia, an Italian model

with a sculpted haircut by Sassoon à la Peggy Moffit;
Claudia's fiery nature suited Khalil perfectly, and from
then on he was content to be Pam's confidant, discussing
her investments with her, giving her his advice on diverse
money matters—advice that, when taken, nearly always
proved valuable.

And then there was dear Alfonse—Alfie, they called
him—one of the gentlest men she'd ever met. He had a
degree in gemology and business administration from the
Sorbonne, and was a combination of the artistic and the
pragmatic. He had wonderful ideas about the growth of
his family's company, which, though conservative by American standards, were radical where his board of directors
(led by his father and two uncles) was concerned.

They made a glamorous group, Claudia, Pam, Astrid,
Khalil, Alfonse, Tommy, and Nicki. After the fall fashion shows and magazine layouts were completed, they
took off en masse for Portofino to spend a week on
Khalil's oceangoing yacht.

Sipping cappuccino on the patio of the Hotel Splendido
under a canopy of morning glories entwined in the arbor
overhead, Pam looked at the Mediterranean spread out
before her, and thought about her mother. She could just
hear Joanne saying, "Do you believe this place? Right
out of Shangri-la. I'd swear I'd died and gone to heaven."
Joanne's crassness would always be embarrassing. And
what about her father? It still hurt to wonder. He'd
compare the place to Eden Roc, which had finer service
and superior cuisine. *Where do I fit in?* she wondered.
Her memories of her father still rankled, though being
with European men had given her insight into how men
behaved. Their families came third, after their personal
concerns and their business. Just like her father. She was
still bitter; she'd only seen him once since that night at
La Grenouille, and this time Jennifer had been more
blatantly vicious. She had hugged William's arm, smiled
at Pam through narrow eyes, and said, "Don't they ever
try to make you look beautiful, Pam, instead of weird?
They paint those awful colors on your face and give you
body stockings to wear. I'd protest, if I were you. You
don't want to be typed as odd."

"I like the way I look, Jennifer. Being unusual is far
more exciting than just being cute, the way they did

things in your day." It was hard to be civil; she had dropped names in their tea, hoping to splash them with scalding liquid. Seeing them merely added fuel to her ambition. *Someday I will surpass you, William,* she would tell herself after encounters with them, or whenever she caught herself lapsing into those childhood longings she'd nurtured for years. *Someday you'll see what I'm made of. I'll get you where you live.* In the meantime, she'd keep on with her graduate school classes and gather as much information as she could about his business, just in case.

People in the fashion world lived whipped-cream lives, rarely questioning themselves in spite of the intense questioning of today's youth who were fighting battles in the streets. Like Trish, for instance, who wrote, "I'm tortured by wondering who I am and where I'm going. Each day I pursue those questions with dogged determination. My work should reflect an opinion, but all it reflects is the quest for one. If my relationship with Arthur weren't so enigmatic, maybe it would help. He either adores me or ignores me. I'll never get used to it. When I wonder if I'll ever grow up, I console myself with the thought that Arthur hasn't done it yet, either." Pam marveled at how seriously Trish searched for the woman beneath her long flowered skirt and leather vest, while Pam was occupied with her next assignment or the growth of her stock portfolio. Hillary wore maternity clothes and thought about starting a nursery school. Hillary's interior woman was a mother and wife, no mystery there. *I'm the one who's enigmatic,* Pam thought, watching others necking, teasing, hot for each other, while she feared her brittle shell might break, Humpty Dumpty–like, if she gave in to those pursuits, never to be reassembled again. It was foolish of her, she was rodlike to the core, but her vulnerable spot—or maybe it was her strength—was in wanting to top William Grayson.

16

Thursday was moving day, when the rates were less expensive than on weekends. Mel was planning to take Thursday and Friday off and really help them move. But Wednesday night he got an emergency call to appear in court in the morning, and now Hillary would have to handle moving day without him, as well as finish packing, take care of Lori, and nurse three-month-old Stephen. And not only that, Mel had no clean shirt to wear to court; everything was packed. Hillary dug out the iron and pressed today's shirt, using the bed for an ironing board.

"You should have let my mother come," she said through clenched teeth, risking his reaction. Barbara had just spent three weeks with them when Stephen was born.

"You know I wanted us to settle in our new home without your mother deciding where the silverware should go."

"She wouldn't decide for us," Hillary said for the hundredth time. "I'd tell her what I wanted, and she'd do it."

"No, she wouldn't." His voice was rising to the exasperation level that made her want to yell back, but she didn't because the baby had finally fallen asleep. "You'd tell her where to put the silverware and she'd disagree with you and talk you into doing it her way."

Hillary suppressed a sarcastic comment. That was exactly what Mel did, not her mother. But she was too tired to argue. Anyway, her mother was back in California. Mel wanted Hillary to be like him, some kind of superperson who didn't need anyone. It was almost as if he'd planned this emergency just to prove to her that she could do it alone. The thought of what she had to do tomorrow, after being up with the baby at night, made her skin rash itch again. She'd broken out with it the day they went into escrow on the house.

Stephen was up twice that night, at one and at four. Lori got up at six o'clock for breakfast. The movers were due at eight but didn't come until noon, right at lunchtime. She nursed the baby again, gave Lori a sandwich, and packed the rest of the kitchen utensils. She and Mel had already made numerous trips to the house to take their smaller items in boxes so that the movers would only have the furniture and clothing wardrobes to take. It was a race against time to hang their clothes in the wardrobe boxes. She and Mel didn't have many clothes, but the boxes were jammed nonetheless. And the baby cried the whole time she was doing it. She had to stop and pick him up, or her rash would start to itch. And Lori kept getting in the way of the moving men, which caused Hillary to lose her temper and make Lori cry. Hillary had a terror of her child being crushed by a moving sofa.

Finally, at about 4:00 P.M., the truck was full of her belongings, and she and the movers set out for Crestmont, New Jersey, and their new home; Hillary drove ahead of the van to show them the way.

Trepidation and excitement had fought in her for weeks. Being house-poor was a new state of being. Years from now, if Mel struck it rich, they would be able to furnish. In the meantime they had a sofa, a chair, a bed, a dresser, baby furniture, and a dinette set. But it was worth it, for she finally felt as though she belonged. The suburbs were where she felt at home, not the city. Crestmont was a much more luxurious community than they'd ever expected to be able to afford, and best of all, their close friends Bobbie and Frank Lazar had moved there in December. Frank was in Mel's firm, and the two of them could commute together.

Bobbie was the first close friend Hillary had made since she'd gotten married; they'd hit it off right away when they met at their children's play school. Bobbie's daughter, Mitzie, was the same age as Lori. Bobbie was pregnant with her second child, but hardly looked pregnant even in her seventh month. She carried the baby like a small beach ball, right in front; the rest of her stayed slender, never puffy or swollen. Her skin kept its smooth tan color, her hair stayed lustrously dark and long, her face never broke out, her nails were pink and healthy. In short, she was someone to envy. But Hillary merely admired how lovely Bobbie managed to look, and wanted to be like her.

Bobbie didn't worry about the schools being over-crowded, pesticides poisoning the food, and natural resources being depleted. She wore simple but expensive clothes that she bought at discount, knew every bargain warehouse from Bethesda to Albany, and had an opinion about everything. She'd gone to the Fashion Institute but had no desire for a career; she loved to gossip, have a facial, and play bridge. Hillary thought Bobbie was an original until she met Faye, Bobbie's mother; they were exactly alike.

The baby was up most of the way to New Jersey, then fell asleep just as they were approaching the Crestmont turnoff.

"Are we there yet?" Lori asked.

Hillary scratched her rash.

Pride of ownership wrapped itself around her when she pulled up in front of her freshly painted new home and excitedly pointed it out to the moving men. But they were nonchalant, pulling into her driveway. Why weren't they blowing whistles and waving flags? Why wasn't the whole neighborhood, for that matter? This was one of the most exciting moments in her life. But she couldn't savor it because Lori was squirming to get out of her seat.

The house shone from loving care, and stood out like a spruced-up dowager looking wonderful, no matter that she was over sixty years old. They'd painted the wooden siding of the house a buttery yellow color, and the trim black. The shiny black front door was flanked by a pair of diamond-shaped leaded windows, the front porch railings were black like the trim on the house, and the shrubbery was all newly cut and trimmed. In winter, snow would cover the lawn like white crystal (clean after the dirt of the city), but now the lawn was emerald green. And inside, the newly polished floors and cream-colored walls, the kitchen with its original yellow tile and oak cabinets, the turned oak banister on the stairs, the bedrooms on the second floor, with their dormer windows and slanted ceilings, awaited them on this warm August day. The four of them would bring life to this doll house, like the one she'd played with as a child. And it was all hers, hers and Mel's and the bank's.

So lucky, she thought, opening the front door with her key and noticing her first delivery of mail; her heart did a flip. *McCall's* magazine had arrived, a wonderful omen. Hillary loved her *McCall's.* It told her how to style her hair, how to wear white fishnet stockings with a black and white houndstooth skirt, and what to make for dinner. There were arts-and-crafts projects so cleverly designed she simply had to make them, and the articles inspired her, helped her change, made her glad she was who she was. She savored the magazine during the few minutes a day she called her own.

Bending carefully, she picked it up so as not to jar the baby, then she called to the movers. "Bring the boxes from the trunk of my car first, and I'll make iced coffee."

Just then the phone rang, and Hillary went to get it.

"I wanted to be the first phone call you got in your new house," Bobbie said. "Am I the first?"

"Yes," Hillary laughed, "but I can't talk now."

"I just wanted to tell you we're bringing over dinner. There's a roast defrosting as we speak."

"Oh, that's wonderful," Hillary exclaimed. "But I won't be ready for company."

"I know that," Bobbie said, with that touch of wickedness in her tone. "I want to see the place before everything's in perfect order and put away. Besides, when you're exhausted at seven-thirty and yelling at Mel, somebody will have to fix you both a drink. See you later," she sang, as she hung up.

Hillary forgot what she was going to do next, and stood there with the phone in her hand. Lori clomped up the stairs, holding on to the railing the way she had been taught; and Hillary was caught by the sight of her daughter's short legs encased in her denim overalls, so round and pudgy, pulling her body up one step at a time. The sight filled Hillary with so much joy that her eyes filled with tears. She watched her daughter, knowing she was looking at the future; she and Mel and their children would be surrounded by the sounds and smells of everyday life, by birds chirping in the spring, and lawnmowers grinding, cornbread and baked apples and cinnamon buns, summer barbecues with friends, and maybe a large dog. And soon there would be paper drives at the grammar school, and Halloween carnivals. Tears rolled down her cheeks while she thought about her mother and father so far away, never near enough to come over for Friday-night dinners. But each day Mel would return home to the excited laughter of his children, to hear about their activities, to eat her lamb chops and banana bread and, best of all, to be held in her arms.

The baby stirred and woke up as the movers approached the front door with the first of the wardrobe boxes. They had to be unloaded right away, but just then her attention was caught by Lori, who had reached the top of the stairs, her baby face aglow with accomplishment.

"Look, Mommy," she cooed. "I did it all by myself. I got up to my new house."

Hillary beamed up at her daughter, wiping the tears from her face. "That's wonderful, darling," she said, pausing to give a prayer of thanks to God. And then she turned to direct the movers where to take the wardrobe boxes.

BOOK
III

Minor
Obsessions

1

Turbulent times had moments of brilliance. Flower children blossomed on corners and Trish admired the blooms, sat in People's Park smoking grass, talking, planning her next work, feeling mellow enough to postpone the fears of an unformed idea. The found objects she used in her assemblages assisted her creative process more easily than an empty stretcher. Empty stretcher bars without canvas were chasms to fill, just like her life. Routine bogged her down, though she clung to it for security. Arthur taught at Berkeley on regular days, painted on the others, came home late; she missed him when he was at work, waited anxiously to hear his car pulling into the garage, needing him to be with her, to tell her about his day, his work, to listen to her. He always had an opinion, and though it was seldom what she wanted to hear, he made her think. At least three weekends a month they spent at Big Sur; the fourth he'd take her for a walk around the Haight, score them a hit, drop acid with her, or plan a picnic with his friends in Golden Gate Park where they'd listen to Janis Joplin, the Jefferson Airplane, or Joni Mitchell, and he'd touch her perfect body with his mind. She went along with his preferences gladly, just as she'd always done in her parents' home. Lately her work consisted of knitting or crocheting her nightmares into webs. Sometimes she brought her work with her on weekends, looking like Madame DeFarge, while other women crocheted baby clothes and shawls. The results turned out to be loomed works on oddly shaped stretchers that she hammered together herself from old shipping crates. Entwined among the intricate tangles of yarn, rope, strips of fabric, and even horsehair were fantasy figures whose faces she painted on small canvas heads she fashioned herself, miniatures in an agony of self-discovery—sort of a cross between Edvard Munch and Marvel Comics. Occasionally a hand, fairylike and tiny, reached out from the labyrinth toward the viewer in a frightening re-creation of the last moments of *The Fly*, "Help me, help me." At some level, this was what she felt. But the desire to be rescued was buried deep in her subconscious and only tempted forth in periods of drugged hallucination. Most of the time, Arthur's presence was enough.

She wove flowers in her hair, which was longer all the time; she didn't comb it every day.

Arthur introduced her to a gallery in Oakland whose owners offered to include two of her knitted webs in a group show with the idea of signing her on if her pieces did well, whatever that meant. It wasn't a prestigious gallery, but their interest gave them an advantage. The effort it took to find a gallery, have slides taken of her work, and then convince the owners of her talent was terribly frightening, and after a few hits of pot it never seemed worth it.

Mondays were Sober Days. After a long weekend of doing drugs, she'd vow to lay off for good. But Monday afternoon would find her lonely again. She'd clean house, change the litter box, make an attempt at laundry, go to the market, plan her week, and put drugs out of her mind. If Arthur was in a good mood, which wasn't likely because he too was usually sober on Monday, she might last until Wednesday without a joint. But then she'd have a glass of wine with dinner on Tuesday, and that usually led to a toke or two; the rest of the week would take on a haze that never lifted.

Arthur handled the details of their lives. And he handled drugs better than she; he'd been doing them longer. He also managed to be productive, though she found it increasingly hard to work when she was wasted. But if she said no, it made him angry. "You're such a spoilsport," or "I don't want to get high alone. Come on, honey, just a few tokes."

It didn't take much to persuade her. Facing her own work, or the loneliness, or the fears that manifested themselves in her creations, especially those as yet undiscovered, was impossible without assistance. No matter how strong her resolve was on Sunday to go straight, she never threw out her stash on Monday morning.

When her first group show in Oakland, put on by Far Horizons Gallery, got reviewed by the Berkeley press as well as the Oakland paper, the critics singled her out. One said she had produced the most blatantly masturbatory work he'd ever seen; the other said it was either an abomination or appropriate for illustrating children's fairy tales. She'd never been reviewed by the legitimate press before. It was an experience she was willing to forgo.

Only three pieces sold out of the group show, and in spite of the review, one of them was hers. Too shy to meet the collector of her work, she photographed her first income check and signed a contract of exclusive representation with the gallery. Arthur advised against it: "You could hold out for better. Though better may never come." She felt loyal to Marlene Cuttman, who owned Far Horizons, and began working toward a show. The work she was doing now was totally different from what she had done as a student; she thought of herself as in the middle of her crocheting period. And after that, what next? The perennial problem for the artist loomed as a terrifying black hole, drawing her in.

The chilled, darkened interior of the foyer of the restaurant revived her after the furnace heat of the city. She didn't think such heat was possible; compared to San Francisco, New York was a shock. Their hotel room had an air conditioner in the window which blocked half the view of the brick wall across the airshaft; it rattled and whined, hardly cooling the hot, stale air. This city was excessive, possessing everything in overabundance, the crowds, the buildings, the merchandise in the stores, the dirt, noise, and heat, yet it met her expectations. For their second anniversary, Arthur decided they would come to New York for a cultural foray. It was less expensive in the summer. They visited artists in their lofts, exchanged ideas, though Arthur dominated most conversations. He was used to lecturing, and was articulate and subtly cutting. At his new gallery, Lois McGowan, on 57th Street— the real reason they had come—he was given prestige and promises. On the long flight east, Trish had made a vow to herself to speak up, not to let him mouse her into a corner, but whenever she tried, his glance withered her. When her tears bothered him, they'd make up, until the next time. Recently she had begun comparing him in her mind with a most unlikely parallel, her father. Who was she, anyway, was Arthur's attitude. A fledgling, was the reply. She'd just had her first one-woman show, which had consisted of a whole room filled with nightmarish crocheted webs (only this time they had been reviewed favorably).

The Village was the most exciting place she'd ever seen, an excess of the pleasures of the sixties. Head shops six to a block, leathercraft stores, bead vendors on every corner, flower children looking as if they'd come from or been to Berkeley. She and Arthur and new artist acquaintances sat at Café Figaro, discussing an article in the *Village Voice* that protested the U.S. bombing of North Vietnam. Everyone agreed the United States was committing criminal acts; the only thing to do was protest. Someone named Percy Sutton had introduced a bill in Albany to reform the state's abortion law. What a difference that would make in women's lives. Trish was an active supporter of changes in women's rights. She just hadn't gotten around to making them for herself.

Trish pushed open the inner, heavy glass door of the restaurant and stepped into the dimly lit interior, waiting until she could see more clearly.

"May I help you?" The maître d' fish-eyed her attire.

"I'm meeting someone."

Customers glanced at her, disapproving of her sandals, long Indian print skirt, and white cotton lace blouse. These patrons were from another era, in business suits and ties and tailored linen dresses, her parents' image reproduced in multiples.

"Trish?" She turned to see a younger version of her mother walking through the door wearing a seersucker blazer, an A-line navy skirt, and a pageboy hairdo.

It couldn't be. "Hillary?"

They stared, each taking in the other, keeping their mutual shock private. The differences were so blatant they stopped them cold, and then in a moment, those differences were flung away as they embraced. Trish's oil of musk, tinged with marijuana, mingled with Hillary's Jean Naté.

"I have so much to tell you," Hillary began, warming at once. "You look wonderful."

"So do you." They smiled shyly, unused to lying to each other.

"Did you get my last letter?" Hillary turned to the maître d'. "Mrs. Robin for two," she said. Hillary was so at ease here that Trish felt her throat constrict, a thin film of perspiration broke out on her upper lip, and she had the hysterical desire to fluff her hair, the way she used to do, once upon a time, when it was fluffable. Hillary led the way into a room of moving mannequins, assured that she was one of them. "Twilight Zone" time.

"My last letter," Hillary asked, "I sent you pictures of the house?" They were seated at a tiny narrow table pushed up to a long banquette where everyone was elbow to elbow. A single rose in a silver vase stood in front of them like a talisman. There were only inches between the diners sitting side by side, but there could have been brick walls separating them, for all they noticed one another. Trish faced Hillary across the table and didn't know what to say. And then she remembered what Hillary was really like beneath this conventional exterior.

"Of course I got your letter. That house looks like a mansion. You know what a terrible correspondent I've become, but I loved seeing it and hearing all about what you're doing. I devoured every page. Tell me, how's the baby?"

"Let's see, it's August, so he's fifteen months old. Can you believe it? Did I ever tell you the story of how I got pregnant with him?" She was trying to break the awkwardness, hoping her chattiness would do it. Trish was uncomfortable for Hillary as well as herself. "Mel and I had heard about this disco on 42nd where they have topless and bottomless dancers. We were so curious, but it took us a while to work up the nerve to go. Then Bobbie and Frank, you know, the Lazars, I wrote you about them?"

Trish nodded.

"Well, they wanted to go, too, so the four of us went. You wouldn't believe what goes on in those places. One gets used to it after a while, but at first I was stunned. You see everything."

"Yes, I've been to them in San Francisco."

"There's a two-drink minimum, so I had more than I usually do, and the show got me so turned on we forgot to use any protection that night. Nine months later, Stephen was born."

Trish gave what she hoped was an appropriate laugh, and then glanced away, thinking of all the times she had danced such dances for Arthur in the nude with tie-dyed silk scarves wrapped around her, an act guaranteed to give him an erection, which was lately more difficult to achieve. Pot excited her but did the opposite to him, and she was afraid to have sex while on acid after the last time, when she had hallucinated that she was being had by a disembodied fire hose that went on into infinity. She wondered sometimes if Arthur was getting it elsewhere, besides the occasional group thing, but she didn't want to know. She couldn't bear the thought. She could never tell that to Hillary, nor could she admit how plentiful sex was these days in her neck of the woods. She'd been tempted herself to join a group once or twice at a party, but somehow her mother's voice stopped her every time: *A lady doesn't participate in orgies*. She'd laughed to imagine the comment.

Hillary's anecdote about how she'd gotten pregnant had fallen flat, and there was an awkward silence.

"What do you hear from Pam?"

"She's in the south of France on vacation between assignments. The fall issues were shot through July, so she took August off."

It irked Trish that Hillary knew Pam's itinerary and she didn't. "I never expected her to become a model, not with her brains. I guess she cries all the way to the bank."

Hillary looked at her gravely. "I've never known you to be judgmental."

Trish was embarrassed. "Maybe it's a touch of envy." She sighed. "Her life seems so easy, not a care in the world, while mine is so filled with angst."

Hillary smiled. "Isn't that what inspires art?"

Trish smiled back, feeling her spirits lift a little. "I guess so."

"Speaking of art, have you seen the Warhol exhibit?"

"Yes, we met him. Arthur hates his work, pretentious and juvenile, he says."

"My friend Bobbie says Warhol is the quintessential representative of contemporary thought and mores, a genius, more so than all the other pop artists, like Lichtenstein or Oldenburg."

"Certainly not better than Rosenquist?"

"She didn't mention him."

"Arthur puts Warhol in the Peter Max category. But I think he's stimulating, makes one see the world in a new way, and that's always exciting."

"Whom do you like?"

"Willem de Kooning."

"Bobbie says de Kooning copies the master."

"All artists copy the masters, or are inspired by them. That's what art history is, each generation borrowing from, or being inspired by, or paying homage to what's gone before. And of course defying its predecessors."

"She was referring specifically to Picasso."

"Oh."

"Don't you consider him the master?"

The sudden tears in Trish's eyes stung. To her, Picasso was nearly a god, and to hear his name bandied about by Hillary's silly friend from New Jersey was more than irritating, it was close to sacrilegious. She forced a smile. "You're thinner, Hil. It looks like you've lost weight."

"I'm trying. But I go up and down. I have my fat clothes and my skinny ones. It took me a year to lose weight after Stephen was born. And Mel can eat anything and not gain. Like last night we went out with Bobbie and Frank to a new restaurant, Maxwell's Plum—you should see it, Trish, it's gorgeous. Ceilings covered with colorful stained-glass panels, and fabulous carvings, and statues. Bobbie calls it serious camp. Anyway, the food was great and the desserts even better. I nearly died watching everyone else eating chocolate mousse and tarte Tatin. But you obviously don't have that problem. In fact"—she looked at Trish's bony arms coming out of the short sleeves of her cotton blouse—"you're too thin, Trish. You're not eating properly."

Trish nodded, admitting to herself something she rarely thought about, that she usually forgot to eat. And pot no longer stimulated her appetite the way it had in the beginning; now she used it just to get through her day.

"What are you working on?" Hillary asked, eating her

hearts-of-palm salad in small measured bites. She explained that it was a way to stay thin, chew carefully, eat slowly, and put your fork down between bites. Her precise behavior annoyed Trish.

"I'm in a slump right now." Saying that made her feel like crying.

"That must be so difficult for you," Hillary said. There was something about the way Hillary was looking at her, with total concentration and empathy, that made Trish see beneath the trappings of the young New York matron to the loving heart within. Especially the way she now reached out and took Trish's hand, sensing her unhappiness. No one else in Trish's life showed that concern. "I've really missed you." Sadness welled up.

"What is it, honey, what's wrong?"

Tears rolled down Trish's cheeks. "I'm on a bad trip, I guess. My craft era, as Arthur calls it, has played itself out, and I'm searching for direction. The story of my life. But it was an intense time for me and I'm feeling the fall-off."

"It looks as though you're exhausted. What does Arthur say?"

She was surprised for a minute, thinking. "Arthur says I'm piddling around, playing, like a baby with finger-paints. He doesn't see what I'm trying to do. Thinks I should work in marble. I would die if I had to work in marble. That takes a clarity of thought I've never had. I'm too cluttered to carve smooth, glistening bodies or shapes that indicate bodies out of rock. It makes me choke to think about it. Arthur says I'll find myself soon." That last sentence was a lie, it was what she wished he would say. If only she didn't feel she was disappointing him all the time. Maybe if they had a baby, things would be different, he'd be proud of her. She knew he wanted a child, but she had mixed feelings about getting pregnant. Everyone they knew had babies, so many babies. She often felt like a baby herself.

Hillary's voice was low and soothing. "You know, we've taken a place in the country near Danbury, Connecticut, for four weeks through Labor Day. Come and spend some time with me. We'll laze around, and you can think about where you're going while I fatten you up.

We'll really catch up, not like this small talk we've been having today."

Trish avoided looking directly into Hillary's eyes, not wanting her to know how tempting it sounded to be out of her world for a while, lazing around. "I couldn't leave Arthur. Besides, he wouldn't let me."

"Then maybe you could both come."

Trish shook her head, thinking what Arthur would do to Hillary and Mel and their way of life. She could hear him now: "Those square, reactionary, no-taste, no-talent, uptight, white-bread friends of yours. So boring, the most exciting thing they do each day is move their bowels."

"You could visit us," Trish suggested slyly, turning the tables.

Hillary's expression revealed that she thought it was the same as an invitation to hell. But then she surprised Trish by saying, "You're not very happy, are you, sweetheart?"

It opened the floodgates and Trish started to cry, but quietly, so as not to disturb the people eating to the right and left of her. "It's hard sometimes," she said. "Arthur is temperamental and difficult to please. And he's so brilliant; the world just hasn't recognized his talent the way it should. Maybe with this new gallery it will. Our lives have no restrictions, and yet I feel as though I'm in a prison of my own making. I love him, but I want to be carefree, have fun. Everything is deadly serious."

"Do you ever hear from Rick?"

"Only at Christmas, he sends me a card. He's working in Pittsburgh."

"What about drugs, Trish? Are you still smoking pot and taking LSD?"

"Oh no, hardly at all anymore." Why couldn't she admit it? There wasn't anything wrong with it, not really. It was just that Hillary was so proper.

"That's good. I worry a lot about that. We hear so many horror stories about people overdosing or getting hooked on heroin, or catching hepatitis from dirty needles."

"What I don't need is a lecture!"

"I'm sorry. You're right. I just hate to see you like this. I wanted to see the girl I used to know, who was full of hope and expectations, who wanted to be an artist more than anything else in the world."

"She's still here." Wistfully, she was trying to convince herself as well as Hillary. "A bit wiser, is all."

"What are you really searching for?" Hillary asked.

Arthur's approval, she almost said. "My own truths, I guess. The same as any artist. I just hope to God I'll know them when I see them, the way Arthur does."

"But his truths can't be yours; they're different for everyone, aren't they?"

Trish stared down at the table, unable to answer that question. Logically she knew it to be true, but emotionally she believed there was only one truth, and Arthur knew what it was, just as her father had always known, but she didn't. It was a constant ache inside, her needing him to tell her, and he avoiding or refusing. Like two magnets at the same poles, she tried with all her might to pull him to her, to gain his truths, but the harder she pulled, the more he was repelled, and the more she resisted, the more she needed drugs.

They finished lunch, skirting the subject that had been exposed, with Hillary aware of a new awkwardness between them, and Trish denying it. Afterwards, on the street, blinded by the bright sunlight, they hugged, promising to write. Trish watched Hillary walk away, wanting to be carried away in her competent arms and nursed back to innocence, and at the same time wondering what in the world they had in common anymore.

Hillary thought about Trish, and her heart ached to help her friend, but she didn't know what to do about it. They each thought the other had no understanding of where they were coming from. They were both right.

2

It was more than two years since Pam had spent any time with her mother, so in December she invited Joanne to go with her to Puerto Vallarta for Christmas. The whoop of excitement exploded across the transcontinental phone lines. "What'll I wear? Bathing suits in December, I don't believe it! Is it safe to drink the water? Only a week, that's so short, can't we stay longer?" Already it wasn't enough. Dreading the ordeal, Pam wasn't deterred; Joanne was the only mother she had. She could hardly consider Jennifer her stepmother, since her father didn't admit to being her father. She wondered if that made her a bastard, and then decided that it made him one. One's real mother should have a treat once in her life, no matter if she'd earned it or not.

A few days before she was to leave, she got two calls. The first one was from William.

"I thought if you were going to be in town, you'd like to spend Christmas with us. We're having some people in."

She was stunned. Then she realized, *So, I'm finally socially acceptable. Even Jennifer's willing to have my name on her guest list.* "Isn't this rather sudden?" She couldn't resist. "Let's see, this is 1966; that means it's been a mere twenty-two years since we last spent a holiday together, when I was four. I'm overwhelmed by the attention. But how will you explain me to the boys?"

There was a silence while she thought, *You're an ass and so is your wife.* He sidestepped the issue. "How have you been, Pam?"

"Quite well, as you probably know."

"Yes, we still see your picture in magazines, and on the covers too. You must be doing great."

"Raking it in, actually. Would you be interested in an

181

investor? I'd still like to go into a real-estate deal with you."

Another one of those pauses. "I'm sorry, Pam. I really am." ·

She almost laughed, but then felt that old hurt àgain. "Sure, William, I know exactly how sorry. As for Christmas, I'm afraid I can't make it. But maybe we can get together a few years from now, something less than twenty-two but more than five. I'm taking Joanne to Mexico." And she hung up. .

Damn, he still had the power to hurt her. Every now and then he'd call and make some halfhearted attempt to be a father, but if she mentioned his business he would back away as if she'd given him an electric shock. It would be better if he'd leave her alone, instead of dangling a carrot in front of her that, dammit, she kept reaching for.

The second call was from Hillary to tell her that Trish was in the hospital in Berkeley. Since Pam was headed that way, Hillary asked her if she could stop off.

"What's wrong with her?" Pam asked.

"Arthur says it's a bad case of the flu, but from the sound of his voice it's more than that. I'm worried about her, Pam. She hasn't been herself for a long time. A dose of your pragmatism would be the best medicine for her right now." ·

"I'll leave a few days early so I can see her before I go to Mexico. I can't change those tickets, Hil, all the holiday flights are booked."

"That's fine, sweetie. You're wonderful to do it. I just wish I could go, but it's Hanukkah, and Mel has taken time off from work to be with us over the holidays. He'd never understand."

"When I see Trish, I'll try to pretend that I'm you," Pam said, knowing that was impossible.

"Call me from there."

"Will do."

"You're a model, aren't you?" the man across the aisle spoke to her as she settled into her seat. She nodded and ignored him, but his eyes bored through her, seeing everything she was. His gaze made her squirm like the princess-on-the-pea. Whenever she turned, he was staring. Something was familiar about him, some memory swam its way from her subconscious, but if she tried to remember by looking at him, it only encouraged him to stare more.

"Will you please stop?" she said, when they were flying over West Virginia.

"You're about twenty-five, but you can look eighteen or thirty-five, am I right? I don't read fashion magazines, but I bet you're in all of them. My wife reads them, though, wishes she looked like you. She doesn't, of course. Irma's short and busty, attractive enough. Not like you, you're stunning."

Pam shifted again, one leg over the other, trying not to pay attention. Finally she turned. "Shall I complain to the stewardess, or move my seat?" He smiled. Dammit, she found him attractive. Ruddy complexion, in his early forties, black hair graying at the temples, with silvery strands shooting through the rest, hard dark eyes and an even harder jawline. There was a rawness to his face, to the lines in his tanned cheeks, to the well-kept look, that covered something ominous. His intensity leaped the small distance between them as if they were actually pressed hip-to-hip without an intervening aisle.

She felt her cheeks getting hot, and cursed herself. She glanced at the papers spread out on his lap tray to distract him from noticing. For a moment she didn't see it, and then suddenly the logo on his letterhead gave her a jolt. It was the Gray-Con logo, her father's company. Something besides attraction was gripping her now. He did business with her father. Then, in a sudden rush, she remembered who he was: the man in the yellow Cadillac convertible who had pulled into her father's driveway the last time she'd been there—the only time—the day she'd found out what kind of a man her father really was. She had been terribly upset and furious from rejection, but she remembered this man, his easy familiarity with Jennifer, his assurance that he had the right to be where Pam didn't. And she remembered hiding her face so he wouldn't see her tears. She prayed he wouldn't recognize her.

"I'm Charles Meroni." He extended his hand.

Against all her instincts she took it. "Pam Weymouth," she said, realizing instantly that he was someone whose brain she could pick.

Just then the plane hit an air pocket and her heart skipped as if he'd known immediately who she was, but the name didn't mean anything to him. Certainly her father would never have spoken to him about her (or to anyone, for that matter). She did not want to get into a game with him of who-do-you-know-that-I-know, yet the questions she wanted to ask him were burning in her brain. She spoke to distract him.

"On your way to San Francisco?"

"Yes, but I could be persuaded to go on to Hawaii. The Islands have enormous potential."

"Potential for what?"

"Real-estate investment."

"Oh?"

"No place is as beautiful and romantic as Hawaii, besides being ripe for speculation. Why don't you join me? I'll show you what I mean."

His assurance drew her almost as much as her intense curiosity about him. This was fascinating. He could probably tell her everything about her father. "I'm on my way to Puerto Vallarta for the holidays, but I'm stopping off in Berkeley to see a friend."

"Puerto Vallarta is another resort that has called my name." He feigned a Latin accent: "Carlos, Carlos, exploit me."

She laughed.

"Real-estate investment in Mexico is complicated. You must have a Mexican citizen as a partner. The ownership of the land and the structure must be in his name. Comes a dishonest partner, or a revolution, and gringo is out." He shrugged, and she understood that a man as shrewd as he wouldn't put himself in that kind of position. "Are you married, Pam?"

"No."

"Engaged, or spoken for?"

"No." The politeness of that phrase, *spoken for,* was another generation's concept, inapplicable to the hopping in and out of bed she saw all around her. Even young men who were physically deferred from the draft and in no danger of being sent to Southeast Asia to be killed in some verdant jungle did it with any woman who was willing, at any time, egged on by a national insanity and the safety of birth-control pills. In truth, very few men she knew worried about the draft. Why was that, she wondered. Were they paying someone off?

"You wouldn't possibly be interested in a passionate one-night stand with a man who finds you exciting, sensual, and a challenge, would you?"

She burst out laughing and watched him flush, though he kept his composure. The more she tried to tell him what was so funny, the more she laughed, because that was exactly what she wanted from him, a one-night stand, plus a bit more—everything he knew about Gray-Con. Her heart wasn't racing because of what he knew, but because of his effect on her. She truly needed some passion and excitement, anything to wake her from the somnolence of her life. And not only was he vibrantly appealing, but learning about Gray-Con would really gall her father. William would hate for her to be involved with a close associate of his; the possibilities were exciting to consider. She jumped ahead to a time when she and this man might walk into a social event and there would be William and Jennifer. How delicious that would be. The idea truly amused her. But this Charles Meroni would never have anything to do with her if he knew who she was. She couldn't tell him, nor could she let this opportunity pass.

"How about just dinner?" she said, when the laughter ended, wondering how she could turn this encounter to her advantage.

"Would you consider a one-night stand if you weren't otherwise engaged?"

"No." She smiled. "Not with a married man." Their eyes met, and she felt exactly how tempting it was.

"Then dinner it is. Ernie's? You should have the most elegant setting in San Francisco. Their breast of capon papillotte à la Paillard is wonderful, and to start, excellent quenelles, made of sea bass and sauce Nantua."

"Have you memorized their menu? Or are you a gourmand?"

"I'm a sensualist. Food, fine wines, beautiful objects are the rewards for which I work long and hard. They make it worth the hours of travel and loneliness."

"You miss your family?

He shrugged.

"Then why the proposition?"

He sent her a look that made her shiver. "Appetite. Everyone who can afford it should develop one."

He's right, she realized. *And I've developed no appetite at all, missed savoring the pleasures other people seek with such enthusiasm.* What did she fear? Insatiability? Perhaps. Or was it her need to show the world who she was and what she was made of that gave her such singleness of purpose? Looking at him, she felt a zing of electricity race through her. At a crossroads in her life, she was ready for something to break through. Could he be the one? Obviously dangerous, the enemy's henchman. But what she might learn! And while she was learning, she would enjoy the hell out of playing with this big bad wolf.

During dinner she watched him, fighting his attraction. He ordered their food, certain that she would love his choices, and she did. He made her feel special, cared for, even though part of her resented his presumption. His decisions were delicious, slowly seducing her with the age-old temptations of fine wine, excellent food, a romantic setting, and forbidden love. The red velvet fabrics on the walls and draperies, the Wilton carpets, antique furniture, and Victorian opulence of Ernie's evoked the magic of another era and gave the evening a quality reminiscent of a time when women wore décolleté and long skirts and fanned themselves to express desire, distaste, or prudery, or fainted when necessary. Those feminine pretenses heightened desire, created a mystique, exactly the opposite from parading half-nude in a studio filled with people who were disinterested in her exposed erogenous zones but vastly preoccupied by her hipbones, her shoulders, or the angle of her head. That preoccupation during the day truly killed romance, so that after work she rarely sought it. Half the time she was embarrassed by what she did for a living, and now she was reminded by the close proximity of her alma mater—that citadel of learning, inspiration to knowledge, now a hotbed of scruffy, stubborn, and opinionated protesters, no matter how well intended—that her profession was either despised or ignored in the world of academia.

"It must be hard work, what you do."

"Any work that doesn't challenge one fully is hard. Do

you find your work challenging? I've seen your company's logo on buildings all over Manhattan. You do work for that company, don't you?"

"Yes, and we've done all right."

"What exactly do you do at Gray-Con?"

He studied her before answering, and she thought maybe he wouldn't tell her. "You're a fancy one, aren't you? I troubleshoot, or shoot trouble, whatever the case may be." He laughed at some private joke. "Actually, I'm what's called a consultant. I work directly with Bill Grayson; we split the workload. He makes sure the job is getting done, I make sure we're paid. It suits us both. He began life as a gentleman; I make sure he stays that way."

She saw his polish slip and recognized how different he was from her father. In fact, there was an unsavory edge about him; it made him all the more exciting. The color and cut of his silk-blend suit, the diamond on his pinky, even the pointed toe of his Italian loafer peeking out from under the tablecloth gave him away. More danger signs flashed at every moment, and she blinked to avoid their harsh light, more fascinated by him than she'd been by anyone in her life.

"So you think I'm fancy? Well, I'm not high society, just a poor girl making it on her own and getting my master's in business. I've always been more interested in your business than in mine."

"You mean power, don't you?"

She held his gaze, telling him he was right.

"Would you like to own your own modeling agency?"

"No, but I'd like to own your company. Is it for sale?"

He laughed with appreciation. "I'm going to have to watch you, aren't I?" He brought his wineglass to his lips, never taking his eyes from hers. "Why are you modeling, if you don't want your own agency?"

"To stake myself to an investment portfolio."

"I was right about you from the first moment I saw you sitting on the plane with your gorgeous legs crossed, driving me crazy; you've got a killer instinct." His voice deepened, roughened. "I want more from you than a one-night stand, baby." He saw her stiffen. "Relax, I'd never force you, there's plenty of time. But you'll come around; you have to."

She was hardly tasting her dinner, the excellent quenelles, the salad with walnuts and endive, so inflamed was she by his words and by who he was. "Tell me about your work and your boss. Are you the brains behind the throne?"

"You really want to know?"

She nodded, held her breath.

"Okay. I'll tell you. The construction business in New York, which is the only city in the world, has its own way of doing things. To get anything done you have to know your way around, know the ins and outs, know the right people and take care of their needs. It isn't Podunk, where a guy says, 'I'm building a building,' and then goes and does it. It's complicated. There are unions to deal with, for one thing; you have to have friends in high places, which I happen to have. We take care of each other. Pushing anything through the city takes patience and connections, and a lot of money. But profit is the bottom line. You have to know when to hang tough and when to sacrifice immediate money for long-range goals, when to pass costs along to the developer, which is an ultimate necessity, and when you have to eat them."

"Fascinating," she said, meaning it completely.

He was about to continue, pleased by her attention, when they were interrupted by a waiter who handed Charles a note. He read it with obvious concern and then glanced around the room until he spotted the people who had sent it. Four dark-haired, heavyset men in business suits were sitting in a booth across the room. When he turned and saw them, they nodded to him and he nodded back. He turned back to Pam. "Some friends of mine want to say hello. Will you excuse me?"

Pam could have sworn he paled under his suntan.

Charles walked across the restaurant to the booth where the men were sitting, and slid in. Pam thought it odd that not one of them shook his hand or greeted him warmly. In fact, they never smiled, though they seemed to know him well, so well that social amenities were unnecessary. She tried not to watch, but couldn't help it. The men spoke to him without expression or animation. It reminded her of being called to the principal's office, which had happened to her once in her school career when the boy next to her had copied from her paper. All four men were of different ages, but all were dressed exactly alike. Only a slight difference in their ties varied their appearance. The way the waiters hovered around their table bespoke more plainly than anything else who they were—men of great power, and probably not legitimate.

When they had finished talking, Charles embraced the man next to him, shook hands with the other men at the table, and returned to her. His smile was stiff and forced, his hands shook. The four men were paying their check.

"What was that all about?"

His eyes narrowed and his expression told her she shouldn't have asked. "Just some friends of mine," he said.

"Do you know a lot of people in this city?"

"My people are in every city," he replied, leaving no doubt as to who he was and who they were. Immediately she wondered if her father was one of "his people." It sent a chill of dread through her, and yet it was fascinating.

"Are those men involved in the building business in New York?"

"Not directly." His tone implied, *Enough questions,* but he answered, "They're in the waste-disposal business in New Jersey." The waiter brought them their dessert. The mood between them had altered, yet she was still enjoying herself immensely, growing more curious by the minute. He sipped his espresso, then caught her gaze again, trying to recapture the mood. "What do you think is the most commonly experienced sensual pleasure?" he asked.

From the look in his eyes, she surmised, "Sex?"

"No." He smiled that smile again. "But I'm flattered that it's on your mind."

She laughed with him, caught. "I know," she said, enjoying the repartee, "the most sensual pleasure must be laughter."

"No. There's something even more sensual than laughter or sex, something nearly everybody does three times a day on the average for their entire lives." He waited, but she shrugged that she didn't know. "It's eating," he told her. "Imagine how much time we spend eating, and yet we tend to ignore our most sensitive organ, the tongue and palate, or taste buds. Words have never been able to describe adequately the wonders of food. We say it's sensational, or delicious, or scrumptious. But those words hardly begin to do justice to this." He took another spoonful of one of the assortment of fresh fruit ices on the plate in front of them, each cradled in its own delicate, crunchy sugar wafer, surrounded by pieces of real tropical fruit to provide a contrast with the chef's enhancement of nature. He waited and watched her while she tasted the exquisite flavor on her tongue and she found that his description had enticed her completely; the feeling that suffused her was totally sensual, from her tongue downward throughout her entire body. He slid around the booth until he was right next to her, gazing at her profile in a most unsettling way. "Baby, I could give you the world," he whispered, tracing her jaw line with his finger, taking one of the chocolate-covered strawberries and offering it to her. His left hand on the table was tanned. She saw a whiteness under his wedding ring, felt his warm breath on her cheek, tasted the bittersweet chocolate and the tartness of the strawberry on her tongue. His lips grazing her cheek made her shudder. She willed herself not to respond, but it didn't do any good.

As though he had all the time and confidence in the world, he slid back to his place, still watching her. Her heart pounded with a fiery need that raged through her. Such magnetism had never pulled at her, ever. Her eyes told him what she was feeling. He stared back, willing her to come to him, almost begging. She felt fused with him in that moment, and desperately tried not to be. He was married. He worked for her father, doing what, God only knew. The temptation to be with him was overwhelming, but he was wrong for her. She had to withdraw.

The waiter offering them more coffee broke the spell. But when she looked at him again, she felt as though she'd lost something terribly important.

He'd picked up on her mood change, and his voice was flat; he was unused to not getting his way. "So you're actually going to Berkeley? Not a good place to invest in right now."

She was empty after throwing away what he was offering, but there was no alternative. Already he was slipping from her with his business talk.

"The San Fernando Valley has potential for development, and Tucson, Phoenix, and Palm Springs. I'm trying to get my partner to expand into owning what we build. He's a bit conservative. While I'm here, I'll be visiting a lab in Palo Alto that does windstress tests on the curtain wall—that's the face of a building."

His language was unfamiliar. Gels, sable brushes, wigs, proof sheets, key lights, those were her catchwords, signs for the verification of her existence. She and the other models bandied them about like familiar toys, pinning the words on each other's lives the way the clothes were pinned on them to fit, securely fastened. What he must know about the way things worked in his world, the world she'd always aspired to. He could be her shortcut, if she didn't get devoured along the way.

"Do you know what you're giving up by leaving me now? Do you have any idea what could be between us?"

She could barely breathe. Damn him for saying it.

They stood in front of the restaurant while his limo driver transferred her luggage to the taxi. With the look of regret on his face was a mixture of pain and anger. He was shorter than she, or perhaps the same height, she couldn't tell, but he was infinitely wiser. She felt as if she knew him well. He leaned forward and kissed her, absorbing her, teasing her, claiming her, proving—if she doubted it—what he was and what they could be together.

"This is only the beginning, baby," he said, a huskiness in his voice. His regret spread about them like the city's fog. "But you have to make the decision. Come to me, Pam," he said. "We'll never be apart again." He pressed a card into her hand. "This is where you can find me."

She got into the taxi and didn't look back, but his cologne filled her senses even after the cab drove away. She clutched his card in her hand and saw his face, felt his arms around her, all through that long ride back to the past.

3

The waiting room in the hospital lobby was deserted except for a man smoking a cigarette. Pam walked right past him, but Arthur recognized her. He seemed to belong here with his well-groomed shoulder-length hair, more silvery than she remembered. His dark eyes burned in a gaunt face shaded by heavy eyebrows; his sensual mouth was tense from pulling on the cigarette. He exuded sensuality, and Pam understood what Trish saw in him. He had a thin chest, thin body, thin beautiful hands. He reached for Pam's suitcase.

"What's wrong with her?" Pam asked as the elevator ascended. He wore love beads, faded jeans, a blue J.C. Penney work shirt, newly ironed; was Trish his laundress?

"She's dehydrated, undernourished, hallucinating. The doctors say she's coming out of it; they're worried about kidney damage. It kills me to see her like this. I've been living here at the hospital, haven't painted in days."

"What happened, Arthur?" In spite of her resolve not to, blame colored her question.

He ran trembling fingers through his silky hair, his expression showing genuine concern. "My fault," he breathed. "There's too much shit available around here, we're drowning in it. I should have policed her better. She expects me to be daddy and lover. I just want to be her husband. She's lost sometimes. It frightens me. We'll be flying, I think she's with me, and then she's gone, over the edge, off into some never-land I can't pull her out of. Don't look at me, Pam. She won't stop. I've tried."

"Not hard enough."

Instead of bristling as she expected, he smiled wisely. "None of us ever tries hard enough. There's always more

192

we can do, always higher we can reach or deeper we can sink." They got off the elevator. "Her parents really fucked her up."

They reached Trish's room, and Pam felt a physical shock when she saw her friend, gaunt and sunken, and recalled the times she'd seen her young model friend Astrid wasted on drugs. But this was Trish; how could this have happened? Her eyelids were blue-lined over sockets that protruded from her skull, her lips bruised, purple against the unhealthy paleness of her cheeks, intravenous lines in both arms, nails bitten down to nubs, her ribs showing pitifully through the thin cotton hospital gown, and then the added insult of hands held in restraining straps.

"She can't scratch anyone with those nails, but she hits and lashes out. I talk to her, try to soothe her. Sometimes I think she hates me."

Pam saw the pain in his eyes. He did love her, this child. *My age,* Pam thought. Trish looked like an ancient twelve-year-old, her hair left over from a long-forgotten fairy tale. Pam thought of Snow White, the green, rotten, poisonous apple made shiny red and appetizing by the magic of the wicked stepmother. That was what Trish had been feeding on, but who gave it to her?

Trish heard their whispering voices and her eyes flickered open. In that instant, Pam saw the terror of an abyss she could not fathom and would avoid at any cost.

"Hi, baby? How're you doin'?"

Trish's head thrashed on the pillow as though she didn't see them standing there. She was caught in her dark nightmare, and Pam's face was too alien and too normal to exist in it, so she denied it.

"Shh, shh." Arthur half sat, half lay down on the bed next to her, enfolding her in his embrace, gently stroking her face, her hair, her arms, as though calming a wild bird.

"Pam's here, darling, she's come to see you. Tomorrow she'll tell you all about what she's been doing and all the places she's been. Look at her, Trish. Doesn't she look wonderful?" He reached out to draw Pam nearer, but Pam felt squeamish, afraid of being contaminated.

The bony head looked through her and then recognized her and some of the wildness subsided. Pam felt tears welling up, but forced them away. *If only Hillary was here, she'd know what to do.* "Anything for attention, right, kiddo?"

Trish smiled. "I'm so glad to see you. There's so much to tell you. I've been away. I wasn't happy there. I don't want to go back. I don't have to, do I?" And then she was gone again, as though someone had kidnapped her, with eyes rolled back in her head, arms fighting the restraints, fighting the demons only she could see.

Arthur kept soothing and shushing for what seemed like forever, until she calmed down and fell asleep, gone again into yet another world.

Afterwards, Arthur stepped into the hall. "You must be tired," he said, handing her the keys to their house. "The night clerk downstairs in the lobby will call you a cab. Go on back to the house and get some rest. I'll stay here a while longer."

"Are you sure you don't want me to stay?" It had been an exhausting day, and she felt it catching up with her. The time change, the long flight, and then Charles. And now Trish. Her heart hurt, looking at her friend, seeing what she was going through.

"Go," Arthur insisted, carrying her bag into the elevator and pushing the button. "Don't let the cat out," he called as the door closed.

The house in Piedmont was suburban compared to the hippies who occupied it. Danish modern pieces mixed with Charles Eames, and an antique wicker loveseat. Plants grew on every table and bookcase and hung from the rafters. Arthur's paintings adorned the walls and stood in piles against the furniture. The master bed hadn't been made in days, the kitchen showed evidence of a bachelor's excess, newspapers were heaped in piles by the door, and the litter box smelled as bad as a litter box can smell, tainting the house with its odor.

Pam found the extra room and put away her things, then got to work. First the litter box, then she opened the windows to air out the house and attacked the kitchen, throwing out moldy food in the refrigerator, washing the stack of dishes in the sink. She squeezed two glasses of orange juice and left Arthur's for him in the newly cleaned refrigerator, topped with a sprig of mint she found growing on the windowsill. She plumped the cushions on the flowered sofa and redraped the Spanish shawl over the top where it belonged, retrieving it from between the sofa and the back cushions.

She stripped Arthur and Trish's bed and found a clean set of sheets. When that was done, she was too wired to sleep. The clothes hamper was in Trish's closet, and when she pulled it out to stuff the sheets into it, she saw a large plastic bag of dried green compost on the closet floor. She'd never seen so much pot before, four kilos at least, and next to it was a large bag of pills, all colors, shapes, and sizes.

The sight of those two bags hit her like a rock in the gut, and she felt chills all over her body and then anger. She grabbed the bags and carried them outside to the trashcan where she'd dumped the contents of the litter box and the moldy food from the refrigerator; she emptied both bags into the trash. Then she searched around the outside of the house until she found a hose, stuck the nozzle into the trashcan, and thoroughly wet the top of the noxious mixture. *There*, she thought. The cat litter stench and the garbage in the can, mixed with the drugs, made her physically ill. She shut off the hose and rewound it on its stand, feeling less helpless now that she'd actually done something to help Trish. Back in the house, she was too tired for a bath, so she crawled beneath the sheets and fell instantly to sleep.

"I'd love to stay here with you, but I don't have the heart to cancel Joanne's big moment in Mexico. The beach boys will go on strike if she doesn't show up at *la playa.*"

Trish giggled. In three days she had recovered most of her faculties, and much of her strength. She was sitting up in bed, wearing a lacy pink nightgown Pam had bought her, her hair in one long braid, and even a little lipstick.

Pam had awakened the morning after her arrival to find a bouquet of freshly cut flowers by her bed and a note of thanks from Arthur. He was off to the hospital early, to see Trish before class. He left her the keys to Trish's car. For the next three days, Pam either spent time with Trish or drove around Berkeley, seeing the old haunts, noting how much everything had changed. It had grown in a haphazard way, like the moldy food in Trish's refrigerator.

"You really have to get out of Berkeley," Pam insisted to Trish during one of their conversations. "Going straight is a lost cause if you live here. There's too much temptation."

Trish took her hand, gazing at her glamorous friend, who managed to look wonderful with no makeup, in a blue shirt of Arthur's over jeans and loafers. "You don't have to worry, Pam. After this, I'll never take another pill or toke again as long as I live."

Pam was silent.

"Don't you believe me?"

"I'm not the one you have to convince, Trish. What you tell me doesn't matter; what happens is what matters."

"That's great! You sit there and tell me I'm not cured. I've been through hell, you've seen it. What kind of an idiot do you think I am?"

"An addicted idiot, Trish," she answered softly. "You need the support of a therapy group or a private shrink to help you through this. Just saying you're through is not enough."

"You'll see. The minute I get out of here, I'm going home and throw away my pot, all of it, every damned seed."

"Is that it?"

"You're damned right."

"All the pot?"

"All of it. And the plants in the yard, we'll pull them out together."

Pam stared at her.

"Why are you looking at me like that?"

"What about the pills?"

"What pills?"

"The bagful in your closet, next to the pot."

"You saw that?"

"What do you think has been going on, Trish? You could have died. We thought we'd never have you back again, and you want to keep those goddamned pills?"

"No, of course not!" All the color had drained from her cheeks, and the two spots of rouge she'd applied stood out there like paint on a white doll's face.

"Don't worry, they're all gone. I threw them out the first night, into the garbage where they belong."

Trish's eyes grew huge and round. "You did what?"

The fear made her body quiver. "How could you do that?"

Pam grabbed her hand and squeezed it hard. "Do you hear what you're saying? Do you hear, Trish? I'm going to make them keep you here, or somewhere, until you are really through, forever!"

"But I am!" Trish cried.

"The hell you are!" she retorted, vowing to talk to Arthur and Trish's doctor and insist that they get her into a program before allowing her to leave the hospital.

Trish was sobbing; something Pam had seen her do many times in the past few days. But these tears were different, closer to reality than any she'd shed before when she was screaming that she was being eaten alive.

"The pills are gone, Trish. You've got a battle ahead of you, baby. But you'll do it, I know you can do it. Will you try, for me?"

Trish looked at her with a mixture of hatred and resentment. "For you? What the fuck do you know? Why should I do anything for you?"

"Because if you don't," Pam said, "I'll come back here and fucking kill you."

Trish was so shocked to hear Pam give back what she'd dished out that she gasped. "Where do you get off, talking to me like that?"

Pam, too, had shocked herself. "I don't know," she said. "I guess from watching my mother all those years ruin her life time and again with booze. And I have another friend, a model, much younger than we are, who's hooked. But I haven't been able to get her to stop. That helplessness and rage is all here inside of me. I won't let you do that to yourself. I won't. If I have to come and strap that damned straitjacket on you myself, you're going to get better, you've got to. You've just got to. There's too much to live for. You're young and talented, and you've got a man who loves you, and . . . and . . . ." She could barely say it. "And you've got my love too. I really love you, and I want this for you. Please say you'll try. You'll really try. And you'll call me anytime you need me, anyplace, any hour. I don't care where I am or what I'm doing, I'll be there for you."

Trish stared at her, the cool, self-determined young

woman who'd always intimidated her. "You'll be there for me?"

"You bet your ass I will!"

Trish gazed at her friend. The mountain she had yet to climb loomed between them. If she had Pam's strength, it would be so much easier. But if she had Pam's strength, she wouldn't be here in the first place.

"I don't know."

"Please, Trish, it's your life, for God's sake!"

"I'll try," Trish promised. "I will."

Pam felt the dread in Trish's words as they gazed at one another. They held hands and smiled bravely, trying to convince one another that the impossible could come true.

"I love you too," Trish said.

"I know," Pam replied.

4

Pam and Joanne stayed on the top floor of the El Dorado apartments, with a view of the aquamarine ocean surrounding the sleepy little town. Joanne would have preferred the luxury of room service, but the El Dorado apartments suited Pam fine—a stucco Mediterranean apartment with terraces, ceramic tile floors, and an orange round tile roof, twenty yards from the public beach. Joanne wanted to buy everything the local vendors were selling, and Pam indulged her. They sat in sling chairs on the sand, eating enchiladas with green tomatillo sauce, cheese crepas, and ceviche, a raw fresh fish cocktail. The cold beer made it all perfect.

But at night, when the fragrance of night-blooming jasmine wafted on the gentle air, Pam was consumed by thoughts of Charles, wanting desperately to see him again. But when she was forty, he'd be over sixty. An old man with a wife. Did Irma appreciate him, dote on him, take him for granted? Trish didn't mind the age difference between her and Arthur. Arthur acted young, though he looked to be well into his middle years. There was nothing wrong with being youthful, but Arthur's trappings were comical.

Charles challenged her, made her want to plunge into her dreams. But she was asking for heartache; a liaison with a married man was not in her plan. She had to forget the way his arms felt around her, the way her heart fell into her stomach when he looked at her.

Joanne could tell something was on her mind, but accepted Pam's explanation that she was worried about Trish.

And Pam sensed a lessening of her own hostility toward Joanne on this trip. Her independence gave her objectivity. Joanne was truly happy when someone took care of her. If no one wanted anything from her, or needed her, she could be appreciative and even gracious. In fact, she never stopped thanking Pam during the whole trip. When they said good-bye, the tears in Joanne's eyes were genuine. "You know I've always wanted the best for you, baby. And it looks as though you've got it."

But for how long? was the unspoken question. Being a top fashion model or building Manhattan skyscrapers was having the best, but being involved with a married man was not.

All the way from Puerto Vallarta to Los Angeles and then on to New York, Pam thought about Charles. The more she thought about him, the more unattainable he became. If *too old* wasn't enough, what about *too married*? And then there was *too involved with her father*. That sounded like three strikes to her, all you needed to be out.

New Year's Eve was lonely when there was someone you longed for, but she resisted calling him. *He's with his family!* she told herself. By the middle of January she had convinced herself he'd forgotten her, and had busied herself with work. But his face never left her thoughts or her dreams. She could almost feel him out there, willing her to call. And then February 14 arrived, a day for lovers. She denied the strength of her desire, fought it with all her will, and told herself that she'd just see how he was.

It felt as if someone were giving her orchids in winter when she finally picked up the phone, against everything she knew to be right. And even as she dialed, that inner voice warned her, but her will felt disembodied. Her body was whispering of passion in a language that bypassed logic; her fingers dialed on their own. Silencing that inner struggle with a wave of her hand, she just didn't listen.

He came on the line immediately, his voice vibrant with excitement and familiarity. When she heard him, she knew there'd been no contest.

"Every damned hour of every damned day since San Francisco I've waited for your call. I've driven my secretary crazy, asking for messages from you. I almost rented the electric billboard on Times Square to advertise my number. Pam Weymouth, you're really famous, aren't you? Your pictures are everywhere, and I'd never noticed. You're the only woman I've ever waited for in my life. What took you so damned long?"

"I'm here, aren't I?" she laughed.

"Where the hell is that?"

"Seventieth and Park, twelfth floor, number ten."

"Wait for me!" he shouted, hanging up.

She wished she smoked; it seemed appropriate at the moment to mark her descent into decadence. She surveyed the apartment she knew would be violated by his presence, surveyed her angular body in an emerald wool jersey, so expertly posed, about to be taken too, looked into the mirror, into her own blue eyes turned turquoise by the color of her clothes, noted the prominent cheekbones, the straight classic nose, the creamy skin, the square cleft chin, the shoulder-length blond hair that seldom ruffled, and the practiced haughty expression, wondering *What am I letting in?* Only a man, but so much more. There wasn't time to call it off, to make preparations, to leave. It didn't matter, he knew where to find her now. Always would. She'd have to change her name legally to Weymouth. Before now, she could pretend he wasn't real, imagine him when she wished, ignore him if she could. But she'd felt him pulling at her out there, unavoidable, over miles between them or only blocks away, knew he was searching, knew he'd find her scent, even in the February snow. And like a willing victim, she bared her throat.

He arrived wearing a fur-trimmed overcoat, a black, soft-brimmed hat, George Raft's clothes on Tyrone Power. The snowflakes made wet spots on the fur. He stepped into the room and dominated it, bringing too much of his world with him—even a huge, hulking man stationed outside the door, which meant he traveled with two, a limo driver as well as a bodyguard. The ghost of Irma stood beside him. Pam didn't let her in.

The coat was flung on a velvet club chair, the one she slip-covered in chintz in the summer, the hat tossed on the sofa among the paisley and brocade pillows she rotated for ruffled ones, à la *House and Garden*. "You're so much better than I remembered," he said, stepping toward her. "And I didn't think that was possible." He held her tightly to him and she remembered his shape, his danger, everything about him in that instant. And her fear.

Hands on her back, up her sides, inside her thigh, ruffling the silk of her flesh. She felt instantly invaded and set on fire. He grabbed her thighs, lifted her legs, and wrapped them around him, rocking her from side to side, gazing at her, and then finding her mouth to join and pull from her the admission that no defense be allowed. He let go of one leg and swung her around, picking her up in his arms as lightly as a child. His strength was as enormous as his power; she felt his muscles knotted, forming oval shapes around her. She clung to him with every fiber, and he moaned low in her ear. Then abruptly he let her down and held her against him, rubbing, thrusting fiercely again and again, holding her so that he could, and came, his head thrown back, hips jutting between her legs, the flannel of his trousers maddeningly impenetrable.

He was out of breath and dazed, but just beginning. He pulled up her skirt, pulled down her pants over her garter belt and stockings, then dropped to the floor and, holding her from behind, tongued her there, slowly, relentlessly, until her knees were weak and she too shuddered with the ecstasy he brought her. There was no stopping him, though all of her protested. She was nearly a virgin at this sort of thing, and her gasps and attempts to pull away made him want to hit her. She could feel it, as though she were a misbehaving child and he a furious parent. No man had ever put his mouth there before like that, and she was stunned by the sensation, weak from the aftermath, wanting to cover herself, but he stripped her of the rest of her clothes, quickly, harshly, all except her garter belt and stockings, then undressed himself, holding her wrist with one hand as if she would escape, pulling off his shirt with the French cuffs, his undershirt, alligator belt, slacks, silk shorts, shoes, and socks. He carried her into the bedroom, again with her legs wrapped around him, her heart pounding so hard she felt it beat against his furry chest, her moist center opened wide, tender and terribly vulnerable. He dumped her on the bed, pulled apart her knees, and gazed at her from top to bottom. She felt skinned of all reserve; a surgeon's knife couldn't have uncovered more.

"You make me crazy, absolutely crazy. What I want to do to you scares me." He was hard again, and his reddened penis stuck out at her, demanding. He approached her, unable to decide where to put himself, and then he was in her, kissing her, touching her in places she'd never been touched before, never been claimed before, sweeping her up with him so that her mind was not her own and her body shuddered out of control again, almost shocking her. He pulled out slowly, watching her, bending over to kiss her, running his tongue over her lips, into her mouth, under her tongue, down to her nipples, which he sucked on alternately, and from her mouth and from his exquisite movements in and out of her he pulled another convulsion she did not expect and had no will to stop. Her climax went on and on while he pushed up inside and held her tightly, grabbing her behind so hard she felt the bruises forming and she cried out, "Don't stop, oh, don't stop." And just as she subsided, he pulled out and climbed up the length of her to thrust himself into her mouth, where he came in a surging gush that nearly choked her, but she managed to swallow, and what she didn't swallow he rubbed over her upper body. Then he put his head on her chest, rubbing his cheek against the wetness, and said, "You fucking, goddamned bitch, don't you ever try to get away from me again. You're in my blood, you're in my soul, do you hear me? Do you?" He grabbed her by the hair, pulling her head back, licking her face, lapping the tears that squeezed from her eyes, licking his come from her chest, mingling his tears with his saliva. He stroked her face, stroked away the fear he saw there, gentling her, whispering, "It's all right, baby, it's all right, it's just love. Only love. Daddy loves you. Daddy loves you so much." Then he took her hand and put it on himself. "Feel my cock, baby, feel it." It was hard again. "That's what you do to me. I haven't had a hard-on for a broad like this in my whole life. I love you, God, Pam, I love you. I've been crazy without you, you're all I think about. I've been a monster to everyone because you didn't call. I wanted to buy you every dress in every store, every fucking diamond in every window, furs, perfume, cars, anything to claim you. I wanted to put you on top of the fucking Empire State Building like that gorilla and turn on the klieg lights so all this damned city could see the woman I love. And then I wanted to kill you, imagining where you were and who you were with. I've been crazy, crazy."

She felt his erection subside, felt her heart begin to slow down, felt the moisture of their lovemaking oozing out of her.

"I didn't know," she whispered.

"How could you not know?" he said, with a moan of desperation. If she didn't know, then she couldn't possibly return his passion, and if she didn't return his passion he would die.

"You're so worldly, so mature." She was overwhelmed by the fierceness of his emotions. "I never imagined you felt so much, I thought I was the only one, a silly girl with a crush."

"It doesn't work that way, baby. When the pull is this strong, it's got to be mutual. That's the only thing that kept me going. I couldn't understand how you could be so cool, or deny this need for so long. Then I thought, 'She's a cold Wasp bitch, ice in her veins.' But I knew it wasn't true, I knew you were made of honey, that you'd taste the way you do, like thick cream. You're a honey of a piece, baby, you taste like candy. You drive me crazy."

He was touching her again, and she was responding. She couldn't believe how completely he possessed her, how much she was in his spell, swept into his bear cave to be enveloped by his emotions. She *was* a cold Wasp bitch, compared with his fire. Did other people make love like this, this violently, this passionately? She felt like she hadn't known anything until now. Was this why Trish took drugs? Charles was a drug; she could feel him surging through her veins, making her high.

He took her arm and, with a deft pull, turned her over on her stomach. She felt like a doll, or his plaything, but her body burned as his hands touched her from her feet to her thighs. She felt his mouth licking her feet, sucking her toes, the thrust of his tongue between them in tender places that made her squirm, made her pulse race, shot bursts of wetness between her legs. He licked her all the way up, reaching her hips. She was writhing with pleasure, grinding her hips into the bed until he lifted up her backside to reveal her in a way no one had ever seen her before, felt his tongue in the crack and then inside and wanted to die from shame and pleasure, knew not to resist, torn between her censors flashing and the answering moisture of her body, felt his fingers in front, gently probing, again exciting, raising the sensations to a pleasure too strong to control. He sensed her reaching her peak, and lifted her up, sliding himself inside, keeping one hand between her legs and the other on her breasts, rubbing her nipples with dry, sure fingertips, until her whole body was up, up, and over and she screamed from the ecstasy of it, feeling him coming again inside her, joining them in this strange behavior forever.

He lay on top of her, finally spent, whispering over and over, "You're it, baby, you're it. There's no more to go, baby, I'm home, Daddy's home."

Later she felt him pull down the spread and move her around so that they were both under the covers and his body was wrapped around her, a soft fur rug, warming, holding her securely so she'd never feel anything but safe again. But she could never let him know who she was. In the morning she would call a lawyer and change her professional name legally to Weymouth.

5

There was a fever pitch to her life now, an edge that had thrust itself between normalcy and danger. On one side was her work, the routine, the familiar sameness, on the other dwelt an irrationality, an itch that no amount of scratching could ease.

He wanted her when he wanted her, and only the intensity of their work prevented his total intrusion. His work was even more demanding than hers. Yet, whenever he could, he'd show up on a shoot and grab her off the set, while the photographer fumed, the makeup and hair people raged, and the client threatened to fire her, and he'd push her into the nearest bathroom and lock the door or leave it guarded by Guido, his bodyguard, while they wrapped themselves around each other and made love within a matter of minutes. No place was sacrosanct: the vestibule of a church; the backseat of his limo, riding down Fifth Avenue; the elevator in her father's building, with the buzzer sounding in their ears from pressing the emergency stop between floors; the administrative offices at "21"; the ladies' room at Kenneth's hair salon, with conditioner on her hair and a plastic cap.

He bought her a silver fox throw for the bed to match the silver fox coat, hat, and muff he bought her, and they covered themselves with it after making love on it.

He said he wouldn't wash after leaving her because he adored the smell of her on his fingers, and if it wore off, he'd reach into his pants and rub his crotch, hoping to find traces of her to keep him hungry until the next time.

"Does Irma do this for you?" she'd ask, with her finger inside of him, thrilled with the power of watching him melt before her eyes, of seeing his need for her in the creases of his face, in the sweat he sweated when he held back to give her pleasure. "Irma's a sow compared to you, baby, my baby. No man will ever be to you what I am." And she knew he was right.

Winter gave way to spring, and flowers filled her apartment. Every third day, daffodils, jonquils, sweet peas, orange blossoms, anthurium, and tuberoses from Hawaii arrived. Finally she gave the florist his own key; he knew not to use it when Guido stood guard. Charles was the most romantic of men, and the most difficult. Better able to allow his passions to show than she, he'd forced his way into her vulnerability, and she was forever afraid he'd smash her to pieces. To hang on to what little autonomy she had left, she maintained an aloofness that drove him wild. And when he was driven wild, so was she. But she could not control him. If she made plans for them to be together and it wasn't in his schedule, she lost. He could be abrupt and hostile if she opposed him or interrupted him, but when he wanted her, she'd cancel any engagement, no matter with whom. In private he called her filthy names and used gutter language, which to him was the language of love and sex. In public he was overly attentive, polite to a fault, charming, elegant, almost affected in his assumption of her purity, firing her with sexual hunger equal to the hunger she had for the business he worked at every day. Sometimes she asked him so many questions about his work that he accused her of spying for the competition, and she had to be careful. But she learned almost more than she wanted to know about her father and his business.

"Every other man is out of your life now," he told her. "You're mine; I'll fulfill any need you have, any fantasy or desire. There's no room in your life for boys now. Do you hear?"

She heard, and thrilled to his command. And yet the part of her that wanted to learn all that she could refused to be conquered. She'd go along only so far. "What about the nights you're not with me?"

"See your girlfriends or your fag friends, but no boys." That was easy; no one else appealed to her anyway. Just as it was easy to promise on Tuesday that she belonged only to him when she'd seen him Monday, Wednesday, and Thursday. But when he was with his family in New Jersey from Friday through Sunday, it tore her

apart. The passion she felt for him threatened to consume her, and yet she reveled in it, knowing that his
essence was defined by what he did. Suddenly all the
sentimental love songs applied to her, and the blues as
well. Her co-workers remarked at the difference. She
was kinder, less abrupt, not as single-minded about her
modeling, but then, as their time together grew from
weeks to months, the real-estate business became more
of a reality.

Hillary didn't like Charles, wasn't swept away by his
sensuality. "This relationship will end up no good for
you, Pam. Being with a married man diminishes you.
You're better than that, you deserve more." When Hillary labeled Pam his mistress, it sounded like *whore*, and
meant the same thing, especially when she showed Pam a
picture from a New Jersey paper that showed Charles
attending a charity event with Irma by his side, or when
Pam read about his daughter's first communion party for
three hundred people at the Waldorf.

"You're jealous," Pam yelled at Hillary, "that I have
an exciting lover who desires me and treats me like a
queen and you're married to Mel, whom you cater to and
jump for whenever he says."

"My relationship with Mel has nothing to do with it,"
Hillary insisted, stunned by this vehemence in her friend.
Pam could be abrasive if she wanted to, but she'd never
been that way with Hillary. "You're too good to settle
for second place, and you know it. Why else would you
be so defensive?"

"Don't quote me that predigested psychology you read
in *McCall's* magazine," Pam said snidely. And then she
was immediately sorry when she heard the hurt in Hillary's voice.

"Maybe we'd better not talk about this subject," Hillary suggested.

"If you don't want to talk about what's the most important thing in my life, Hil, then maybe we'd better not
talk at all." And she slammed down the phone.

And then there was the subterfuge of her identity.

At first she hadn't told him William was her father,
because he'd never have had anything to do with her if
he'd known, and because it was a perfect way to find out
what she needed to know. Now she couldn't tell him

because too much time had gone by; if he found out she would lose him, and that would be unbearable. There was hardly any way he could find out, unless she told him, or unless her father bragged, pointing out her picture in a magazine, saying, "That's my kid." After all, her pictures were everywhere. But that was unlikely; her father didn't want anyone to know who she was. She was always on edge, afraid of some mishap, but when Charles told her the details of his latest venture, or when his hot breath warmed her and his hands and body possessed her completely, she pushed aside her concerns.

She was enthralled, fascinated, consumed by him every waking moment. And when they made love, his body on hers, her legs wrapped around him, her nails digging into his back, she'd cry out, "I love you, oh yes, I love you." But she wouldn't allow herself to say it at other times, no matter how she longed to, or how many times he said it. She was afraid to let go, to love another woman's husband, especially when that husband was as involved with his family as Charles was. But not saying it only made it more true. She did love him, with her entire being.

She apologized to Hillary, who, of course, forgave her, but there was a strain between them and they seldom spoke about Charles. Since Irma rarely ventured into the city, Pam soon met Charles's friends and associates. And they made their own friends, too, men from the same mold as he, with ties to the underworld, families in the suburbs, and babes-in-the-woods. But none of those men adored their extra women the way Charles adored her. She saw how their women were ignored and demeaned by a lack of power in their men's lives.

With her and Charles it was different. He shared his business with her, rarely censoring his phone conversations when he called his associates from her bed after they'd made love. She learned how his business operated from the inside, heard him discuss payoffs and contract sweeteners, knew the names of city officials and even met some of the ones who gave him inside information, who apprised him of the amounts of closed bids so he could choose any job he wanted and come in just under the lowest bid, saw how men in construction dealt with one another, when they used patience or veiled threats. She saw how they cooperated or called in their markers, how they kept the cardinal rule of always passing any increased costs on to the developer, convincing the developer it was all in his best interests. Little by little she learned everything he knew, how a project was financed, and how crucial a thorough feasibility study was to insure profitability. Most important of all, she learned that Charles not only had friends who were involved, but was definitely a part of the underworld himself. He had ties to the teamsters, the building unions, and to behind-the-scenes bosses. He even used henchmen to take care of trouble now and then. And he had an independent source of income derived from his relatives who owned waste-disposal plants.

At first she told herself his ties to organized crime had nothing to do with her father. But as she heard details of the deals he negotiated for Gray-Con with union officials, she began to suspect that her father was involved too. How much, she didn't know. Her father's reticence to have her in his business began to make sense. Maybe he'd been trying to protect her by keeping her away. But even if that was true, it still didn't excuse the way he'd treated her since she was a child. It was tempting to think about gathering enough information on him to get him indicted; maybe he'd lose his business. But that wasn't her style. She had to find a way to get him where it hurt, without sending him to jail and ruining the family name. After all, she had to consider her half brothers. Even though she'd suffered for being William's daughter, there was no reason for his sons to suffer too.

So she overlooked Charles's guilt by association, too intrigued by him to judge, for she too had underhanded motives. No matter what he was, he had her loyalty; she was thrilled by his conquests, even proud of his deals. And he never ceased to be impressed by her intelligence and comprehension.

Charles encouraged her to continue with the graduate business school courses she'd begun in the fall of 1963, even though it took her away from him many nights during that first year they were together. But at the end of 1967, when she finally graduated from night school with a master's degree in business, he and Mel and Hillary came to the graduation to see Pam Weymouth get her degree.

Bit by bit she became more helpful to him, so helpful that he relied on her advice, included her in dinner meetings with certain associates so that she might assess his opinion of them, and then began to include her in the discussions, asking for her opinion in front of them.

One night, when they came home from a meeting with a plumbing contractor who wanted Gray-Con to absorb the cost of pipes that had frozen after installation and had to be replaced, he said to her, "Come to work for me. Be my assistant. Let me put you on the payroll."

Her heart leaped at the idea. But of course she couldn't accept. "I'd love to work for you, Charles, and maybe someday soon I will. But right now my own career is too important to me. It won't last forever, we both know that. But I have to see it through, see how long I can stay on top." It killed her to say no. "I'm as flattered as hell that you want me in a man's world, that you think I could hold my own."

"There's no doubt of that," he told her. "I've seen you in action. Like tonight, when you reminded the plumbing contractor that he was awarded this contract on a favored basis and had not had to compete for bids, so he should have figured in enough extra to absorb unforeseen costs like the frozen pipes. Couldn't have done it better myself."

She thought about her father and how he'd feel if he knew that she'd found a way to be involved in his business, even without his invitation. For so long she had wanted to rub his face in it, show him how wrong he'd been. Her life was a dream come true; she was getting everything she wanted, entrée into a world she'd always coveted, the adoration of a man she admired and desired. And yet at any moment it could collapse into a nightmare. The strain was taking its toll; she had sleepless nights, and there were lines around her eyes and mouth. Since the camera picked up everything, she knew she had to eliminate all stress, but still she kept loving him.

Through the strain and tension, she somehow managed to enroll in real-estate school, got her license, and then went on to more specialized courses.

Charles knew the construction business, but when it came to investments she was the expert; her stock portfolio had grown tremendously over the past years, greatly increasing her profits. Finally, Charles asked her to take over all his investments too. He had huge amounts of cash to invest, which came from various sources, few of them legal. His occupation as William Grayson's right hand was only a cover, a respectable position to divert suspicion from his real work as an underboss in one of the New York syndicate families that controlled dumping and disposal. Gray-Con gave him a legitimate base from which to deal in the construction industry.

In time she pieced together the history of her father's involvement with Charles, and saw how deep it ran. Originally, her grandfather, whom she had never known, had owned a hardware supply company in New Jersey, which had grown into one of the largest plumbing supply companies in the East. But William wanted to become a building contractor, and left the family business to strike out on his own as a plumbing contractor, since he knew that part of the business well. Early in his career he hadn't been able to make his payroll, and had needed cash. Rather than go to his father and admit defeat, he'd borrowed money from someone in Charles's family and they'd gotten their foot in the door. When he'd branched out from plumbing to start Gray-Con, he'd thought he was free of the past, but the next time he'd found himself financially overextended, Charles's family had insisted William take a loan from them, and as reciprocation, they'd put Charles into the business as his partner and associate. Pam almost felt sorry for her father; he'd thought he could make a deal with the devil and not have hell to pay. It never occurred to her she might be following in his footsteps.

"You've got to tell Charles who you are," Hillary insisted, every time they talked. She knew Hillary was right, but she was unable to face Charles's reaction, and she still hadn't found a way to get even with her father.

Early in her relationship with Charles, he'd talked about their being honest with each other. As the months and then a year went by, he'd become paranoid about it, living in constant fear that she would find someone else or grow tired of their arrangement or, worse, lie to him about her feelings. His code of ethics allowed for illegalities, bribery, payoffs, intimidation, coercion, overcharging, even violence, but it did not allow for dishonesty in

anyone close to him. He did business with so many
dishonest people, it was rare to find any truth at all. She
knew this, and still lied to him. The longer she waited to
tell him, the worse it got. His finely tuned antennae,
which allowed him to survive in his dangerous world,
sensed an undercurrent and he questioned her in minute
detail about the time she spent away from him. He pressed
her for every nuance of her conversations with others,
looking for clues. He wanted to know about every bite of
food she'd eaten, the decor of the restaurant, the seat
she'd occupied at the theater, the cost of her cab fare,
trying to catch her in a lie. But she never lied about
anything trivial. She saw no other men, always went
where she said she'd been, showed him ticket stubs,
restaurant charges, and clothing bills, and gave him all
the descriptions he wanted. Still there was an undercurrent, and he wouldn't let it go.

But in time he was lulled into a sense of security, and
she began to believe everything was all right, that someday the opportunity would present itself to tell him the
truth about herself, and that he would understand, and it
wouldn't harm their relationship, or end it. And she
sensed that he harbored his own resentments toward her
father.

William Grayson was everything Charles wasn't, born
to the upper class, accepted without needing to try. The
right schools and bloodlines gave William effortless access to the best clubs and best friends, things Charles
longed for. William's only minor fall from grace had been
when he went to USC in his junior year of college, fell in
love with what his family called a California tramp, and,
according to them, got tricked into marrying her. Charles
speculated that William's friends overlooked his Mafia
connections as a minor infraction, much like marrying
the wrong girl; any one of them might fall prey to unscru-
pulous associates if they, like William, wanted to make
names for themselves other than the ones they were born
with. People of their kind knew they weren't business
sharks like the Jews and Italians. And certainly they
understood how William had fallen in with the wrong
kind of woman, given that he'd attended only boys' schools
until college. Charles also supposed that William's first
wife, though he didn't know he was talking about Pam's

mother, had been an okay broad. But just not his kind.
And in William's world it was what one did about one's
mistakes that counted. He had done the right thing; he'd
dumped Joanne and hurried back to the fold, where he
was soundly welcomed and slyly admired for having had
an adventure. As long as William never brought it up, no
one else did either.

As she heard Charles talk about her parents with such
intimate knowledge, Pam wondered if her bloodlines were
enough to overcome Charles's sense of betrayal when he
discovered who she was.

And her fear of discovery grew with her passion for
him. No more able to remain aloof, she was as obsessive
about their relationship as he was about honesty, ached
with missing him on the days they were apart, resented
his family and her second-place role, and began to suggest that the arrangement wasn't ideal. Gradually she
found herself turning into one of those women who complained all the time they were together about the time
they spent apart.

Time passed. By the middle of the second year of their
relationship, modeling had become just a job; she was
marking time until she could finally do what she really
wanted. The pace was still grueling, yet it had lost its
excitement, and she could not find her way out if it
meant confessing to Charles. She got her real-estate ap-
praiser's license and studied property management, but
their relationship didn't advance beyond what it had been.
Though Charles sometimes talked about leaving Irma, he
only did this when Pam cried and threatened to go out
with other men. She wanted a husband and children of
her own. He understood, soothed her, and promised that
things would be different, but when they remained the
same, and new presents were not what she wanted, he'd
grow cold and distant, and even punish her on occasion
with a sharp slap if she kept complaining, or by ignoring
her for days. Eventually she knew not to arouse his anger
too much because of his violent temper, but he was
always sorry for those outbursts, admitting that it was
only because he hated to see her suffer, knowing that he
was the cause. He knew how hard it was for her, it was
for him too; and since it was that old familiar pattern of
disappointment followed by complaint followed by apol-

ogy that she'd been playing out with Joanne since child-hood, she usually forgave him.

But being in second place was finally so intolerable that avoiding the subject or hitting it head-on did no good and she knew that somehow she had to rescue her pride. She loved him too much never to see him again, and the way things stood, he wasn't going to leave his wife. But perhaps there was something she could do to entice him into doing just that.

Gray-Con functioned strictly as a general contractor that built for other developers; Charles had talked for years about expanding into development, but William had always said no. For some reason, Charles wasn't willing to go into a deal on his own, though he knew that the real money was in owning the buildings one built. Pam agreed, but she could see that Charles wasn't going to take the risk. Perhaps he believed that development took a kind of skill he didn't have, or maybe the right opportunity hadn't presented itself, but Pam wasn't bound by the same restrictions, and since developing property was her ultimate goal, she knew now was the time.

She watched for an opportunity, canvassed the city, talked to brokers, gathered her data, and began looking in earnest for a piece of property. In 1968 the cost of construction, including the land cost, was nearly three hundred dollars a square foot. A 450,000-square-foot building would cost $135 million to build. But if she owned the property outright, she could line up a tenant, and that would allow her to get a construction loan to cover eighty percent or more of the costs. Her knowledge of the market convinced her that getting a triple-A major tenant would not be a problem if she had the right property. The secret was to find it. She had nearly $300,000 of equity in her stock portfolio. That was more than enough to cover a down payment on the land; she'd worry about the other twenty percent later. She had to find the right property, then apply everything she'd learned about real estate in Manhattan. If she could syndicate the difference between the construction loan and her own investment, using private money, she might be able to do it. And then she found the perfect piece of property.

On Madison Avenue, between 55th and 56th, were three lots, each fifty feet wide; each lot held a building three stories high, made of brick, and the one in the middle was for sale. The building in the middle wouldn't be of any value to a developer who wanted to build a high-rise, unless he could get an option on the two other pieces and buy them all at a good price, somewhere under market value. And so she proceeded to negotiate. The brownstone in the middle was owned by a widow in her sixties named Nancy Fuller; it had been in the Fuller family for thirty years, and now she was moving to Florida and wanted to sell. But her sister and her son owned the buildings on either side, and they weren't interested in selling, though countless brokers and developers had tried. Pam decided to give it a try.

She invited Mrs. Fuller to tea at Schrafft's, the widow's favorite restaurant.

"I always have the rice pudding," Nancy Fuller confided, "and I do like their pastries. You know, you seem more like a friend than a real-estate person. Only men have approached me before, and they had no time to listen."

"Tell me about your husband, Frank," Pam asked, thinking Mrs. Fuller was like no one she'd ever known before, so well groomed for a woman in her sixties, and slender, with carefully waved gray hair and a black worsted coat with a Persian lamb collar.

"We were married thirty years, Frank and I. I nursed him through several heart attacks before he died." She had tears in her eyes. "You can't imagine the terror one goes through with a heart attack. Especially more than one. But now I'd like to leave those sad memories behind, and enjoy the Florida sunshine. If only my sister would come with me. Jan never married, sort of lived through me and my family, always a bit envious, I guess. And now that I'd like to move to Florida, she's refusing to come with me, stubborn, says she's declaring her independence. Won't sell because I want her to." But Nancy understood how her sister felt. "She's afraid of change. And she is envious of me, but it's because she admires me. She only wants what I had, she wouldn't take it away from me.

"If you could convince Jan to sell her building and come with me to Florida, Miss Weymouth, you would be doing her a great favor," Nancy insisted. "She really can't get along without me, we're very close, and I'd miss her too much.

"As for my son, Adam, he'll never sell, no matter what Jan or I do. He has nowhere else to go. But it would be better for him, if we didn't live so close to each other. You see, my son's life-style is a source of pain to me. In fact, we hardly speak to one another. When we pass on the street, it just hurts us both."

"That's very sad," Pam said. "Perhaps you could overcome your differences."

Nancy Fuller sighed and shook her head. "No, you see, my son has blasphemed against God by his chosen life-style. He lives with another man, and they are more than friends." Her voice was low and filled with pain. "This man he's with is not the first. I thank God my Frank died before he knew what his son had become."

Pam thought of all her friends who were homosexual, the artistic, flamboyant ones, the shy, gorgeous ones, and particularly those who were kind and loving to her. Most were brilliant, creative, and successful. And yet their sexual behavior was still considered aberrant by many people. She had a new compassion for how they must feel, and wondered how many of them survived being condemned by their families, rejected by relatives.

The homosexual community was tight-knit, and it wasn't difficult to locate Adam Fuller's favorite hangouts. She invited Cary, a gay model friend of hers, to go with her, explaining the situation to him; he was happy to help, and in his company she felt more comfortable. They found Adam, a young blond man in his late twenties, slender and attractive, with his friend Dennis, at Jumper's in the Village. Dennis was muscular, with dark hair and brown eyes, quite gorgeous, but not as gorgeous as Cary with his almond skin, black hair, and blue eyes. The four of them hit it off right away, teasing and joking with one another. Adam was a set designer, Dennis was in cosmetology school. And as it turned out, they were thinking of moving to San Francisco; they wanted a house with a yard, somewhere they could have a garden and raise Siamese cats.

"Then why," Pam asked, "are you refusing to sell your property?"

Adam looked embarrassed as he glanced at Dennis. "I

guess I'm just being stiff-necked like my mom's been with me. She wants me to sell, so I won't. Anyway, he's still in school; we can't leave town for a while."

"But what if I let you occupy the building rent-free until you finish your training? It will take at least that long to work out the plans. You know you're going to sell eventually, Adam. Why not sell to me?" He was wavering. "Think of it as helping a soul mate. You're trying to make it in this world against great odds, and as a woman in a man's business, so am I."

He nodded. "I sure know how that can be. You're different from all the other people who've approached me to sell. I could always feel their disapproval."

"We have something else in common," she said. "My mother was impossible to live with too. Believe me, I could top you story for story." And they both laughed.

"I have another idea," Pam said. "You can go to San Francisco and find a house you want, in an area you choose, and I'll buy it. Then, when you're ready to move, we can trade. There are definite tax advantages to a trade rather than an outright sale." Pam held her breath as she saw him glance at Dennis, who raised his eyebrows ever so slightly. Cary was squeezing her hand under the table.

Adam sighed. "You'd do that for me?"

"Sure, if the house in San Francisco compares in price to your building here. You might have enough money to buy two houses and rent one out. Property there isn't as expensive."

His features softened and he smiled with genuine happiness. "Okay, I'll give you an option on my property if we agree on the price. I bet I can even persuade my Aunt Jan to sell to you too. The Tishman people have really been after her, but she listens to me."

"I'm paying your mother one-twenty-five," Pam said. "Is that all right with you?"

"I'm asking one-fifty," he said, staring hard at her with a challenge. But if she was ever going to get anywhere in this business, she couldn't let herself be outbluffed on her first deal.

"Listen, this is an unusual deal, Adam. I'll pay for your trip to San Francisco and expenses. You'll be living rent-free for maybe a year. But I've got my costs to consider. We're talking about three pieces of property, and I've worked my tail off to earn enough money for this project. Nobody's helping me, nobody's left it to me. Your property isn't worth anything unless it's part of a threesome, and I own the main parcel. I'll give you one-thirty, just so you can say you outnegotiated your mother. But that's it." She smiled to soften the hardness in her tone.

Another glance at Dennis, another raised eyebrow. And then he grinned. "Okay, you've got it." And he extended his hand for a shake. But Pam wasn't happy until she saw him sign the letter of agreement she had in her purse.

She and Cary relived the night and laughed with delight all the way home until their cab dropped him off at his apartment. That night she couldn't sleep for the excitement of wanting to share this with Charles. *So that's how it's done,* she thought. *Have a plan in mind, work out every detail, and be creative on a moment's notice.* Always know your opponent, Charles had said, know his weaknesses and his strengths. Know what he wants and then give it to him.

She got up and called her friend Alfonse de Keirgen in Paris. "Have I got a deal for you," she said, explaining to him about her idea to build a high-rise in midtown Manhattan, using private syndicate money for the difference between what the construction loan would cover and the final costs of the building.

"I'm interested, Pam," he told her. "Send me something in writing as soon as you can, and I'll consider it. The real-estate market in America is the talk of Europe right now. Your timing couldn't be better."

Next she called Tommy Maxwell at his London office, and made him the same offer. "Alfie is about to give me his go-ahead," she told him excitedly.

"Khalil is staying with me in town," Tommy told her, responding to her enthusiasm. "I'll see if he's interested too."

"No, I'll call him directly. I want to make sure he understands the details. You know how vague you get now and then." He laughed, and gave her Khalil's number.

The phone call to Khalil brought the excitement to a peak, for he was the most enthusiastic of all. "In my

country, investments in America are extremely important. This sounds like a wonderful opportunity, Pam, my
dear. As usual, your intelligence matches your beauty. If
the profit margin is as you say, I'm able to give you my
commitment right now for up to five million. Let me
know if you have trouble raising the rest of the money. I
may go in for the whole amount."

After that, trying to sleep was useless. It was happening, finally! After all these years of planning, of dreaming, of wondering if she could do it, she had. She danced
around the room. Opened her own bottle of champagne.
But she didn't want to get drunk and spoil this feeling of
euphoria. She wanted to fully enjoy the credit. She stood
at her window and looked out at the city, feeling a part
of it as she never had before.

Her determination to succeed in real-estate development, and her desire to offer Charles something that
Irma couldn't, had brought her to this point. Would it
make a difference to him? Would he want to be in this
deal enough to make a real commitment to her? *Don't
count your chickens,* she thought, *it may not work. And
as for the deal, only my option with Nancy has been
signed. I still have to get Adam's and Jan's deals worked
out. And Alfonse or Tommy or Khalil could change his
mind.* No, it was a long way from congratulations; and
yet look how far she'd gotten. Nothing could stop her
now!

The next day she couldn't wait to tell Charles what she
had done. But his reaction was not what she'd expected.
"You witch, you sly little bitch." He slammed his fist into
his palm. "I knew you were doing something behind my
back."

"Behind your back?" she said. "I was doing it for us. I
wanted to make you proud, to get us involved in something together."

He grabbed her arm and pulled her to him, his face
contorted with rage, much the way it looked when he
desired her. "Is that why you slid home while I was
covering third base? Damn you. I've had my eye on
those buildings for months. I've had insiders working on
it. What did you do, go through my briefcase?"

She was stunned by his reaction, wanted to cry with
disappointment. Now she'd never get him away from

Irma; in fact, this might have the opposite effect. "I had
no idea you were interested in those brownstones,
Charles." If she had, would it have made any difference?
She wasn't sure. This deal was so good, she could taste it;
it would be hell to give it up, for anyone.

He changed his tactic. "You bought it for me, didn't
you? This is a trick, isn't it?"

"No way, Charles," she said. "I've been wanting to do
this for a long time. The only reason I didn't tell you is
that I wanted to prove to myself I could do this without
any help. This is a big city; I had no idea you were
interested in the same parcel."

"Well, now that you know, you'll step aside, won't
you? You'll let me have it. You'd never want to snatch
away what's mine, would you? Be a snatch with a snatch."
He grabbed her between the legs and squeezed hard. It
infuriated her more than it hurt; she stared him down.
He was like a child losing a toy. Well, she'd be damned if
his temper would intimidate her this time. She was beginning to realize that nothing would ever pry him away
from Irma, and her anger made that easier to bear.

"Take your hands off me, Meroni," she said. "I don't
like the way you're acting. In the two years I've known
you, I've watched you search out and pass on deals like
this time after time. Why is this one different? Because
it's mine? Forget it. I'm going ahead with this project
alone. If I need you, I know where to find you, in New
Jersey with Irma, right?" The look in her eyes said, *I
don't give a damn what you want. Getting what I want is
worth any price, especially if it means getting back at you
in the process.*

He pulled her to him and pressed against her, letting
her feel what getting the best of him had done, and
especially what her defiance made him feel. The balance
between them was never stable, always wildly intense.
And she had wanted this piece of property as much as
he, she had lusted for it exactly the way he lusted for
what he wanted. If he'd been happy for her, not threatened by what she was doing, she would gladly have
shared it with him, but all the months of feeling power-
less next to his real life and real family had taken their
toll. She'd proved herself to be strong, able to cause him

pain such as he had caused her, and the look of fury and defeat in his eyes made her glad.

They fell on one another, tearing at their clothes, never parting long enough to breathe, devouring each other and feeding on each other's hunger as if it were the first time all over again.

At times like this she knew he was hers, knew that no wife in the suburbs or lies about her identity would keep him from her. She knew also that she could use what she'd learned from him to conquer others; she felt a fierceness growing in her, a wildness that animals possessed when kept from what they wanted. The times when she complained because he wasn't with her, hated herself for needing him so, and competed with his impenetrable citadel of hearth and home, seemed far away. When she was in that dependent state, she wanted to poison Irma, scratch her face, drown her whelps in some neighborhood pool, and walk away with the prize. But now she felt that heat between them, so hot it threatened to ignite them spontaneously in a blaze of destruction. For weeks afterward there was no bickering or complaining, but only that heightened state of passion that had originally drawn them together. She ignored the warning that playing with fire was a kid's game, and that adults knew better unless they were pyromaniacs. In her more lucid moments she tried to plan for a future without him, afraid that if she stayed with him, that was what she would become.

And then she got pregnant.

6

God knows, she didn't want to trap him. Given his erratic temper, she didn't even want to tell him. Besides, the idea of being pregnant was shocking; first she had to get used to it. She must have put her diaphragm in wrong. So many times she'd worried that this could happen; every woman she knew worried about it, waited anxiously to see if her period was late, no matter what kind of birth control she used. And now it had happened. The unmistakable signs, then a doctor's confirmation. If only she could have the baby, but there was no way. This was different from the time Hillary got pregnant in college. At least Mel was free to marry her. Charles wasn't. The sensible thing to do was to have an abortion, easier now than in 1962, when Hillary had considered having one. She wouldn't even tell Charles, just find a doctor on her own, though it would kill her to lie to him again, as much as it would kill her to destroy their baby. Their baby. She wanted it so much. But, no! She couldn't let herself want it. There was no way.

Charles had a right to know. But how would he react? Everything would change between them; their lovemaking would hold a different kind of danger now, their lives the guilt of destroying their child. Instead of the heady intensity of their battle for control over one another, now their being together would hold responsibility and consequences and guilt. She didn't want this to cause their ending. How could she be without him? Impossible. He was her focus, the greatest part of her life; yet what was there ahead for them but more of the same, only worse? Still, she had to tell him, though she dreaded doing it with all her heart; she needed his strength to see her through the ordeal ahead.

223

Side by side at the banquette near the corner of the room, their favorite table at Café Chauveron, she chose the most familiar and sentimental place she could think of. And it was too public for Charles to make a scene. Pam's tension mounted all during dinner as she planned her words, replanned them while answering Charles's conversational questions with "Uh-huh, I guess so," and "What do you think?" He barely noticed, fuming over a foundation inspector who'd been paid royally and now was holding up the final approval. "You can't trust any of them," he said bitterly.

Coffee and their famous chocolate mousse cake with sabayon sauce signaled the end of her stalling period. She powdered her nose, preparing her ammunition for the battle, then took his hand and stopped him midsentence with a kiss. It was their first of the evening. She remembered when they used to kiss so often he wore as much lipstick as she.

He responded to the kiss. "I've been preoccupied, haven't I?"

"You've been fine. I've been preoccupied. Might as well tell you right out what's been on my mind." She took a breath, plunged ahead. "I'm pregnant, Charles, but don't worry, I'm going to have an abortion."

He got as pale under his tan as he had the first time they met, when they had had dinner at Ernie's in San Francisco, and Vito Genovese had summoned Charles to his table (Pam hadn't known who it was at the time, but when she found out later, she understood why Charles had reacted that way).

His color returned, along with his excitement. "A baby? But that's wonderful! And you'll have it. I'll take care of you. No abortion, absolutely not. God in heaven, what would my sainted mother say if she knew my sweetheart wanted to have an abortion. I couldn't have such a sin on my conscience. Darling, it's our love child, everything will be fine. Don't worry, we've got plenty of money. You'll hire a nurse, move to a bigger apartment, that place of yours is too small anyway. I'll take care of you, I'll love our child, but no abortion, I'd never allow it."

Her heart froze with fear. If he decided she should have this baby, it would be hell opposing him. "Charles, I can't have a baby whose father is married to someone else. I've told you what it was like for me, being raised by my mother and never knowing my father. I cannot do that to my child. I cannot, I tell you. You would not be able to live with us, you'd never have a holiday with us, never, we'd always be waiting for you to give us your time and attention."

"That's not how it would be. I'm with you most of the time now. Why would I be any different from a father who travels a lot? I'll take care of you, I swear."

"I couldn't stand it. Every time you went back to your other family, your *real* family, I'd hate you. I couldn't hide my feelings from our child. Maybe I'd come to hate the baby. I can hardly bear our situation now; this would only make it worse. I know abortion is a sin to you because you're Catholic, but I'll accept it on my head. It's not your decision, it's mine."

He grabbed her wrist hard; she couldn't pull away and create a scene in this very proper, dimly lit restaurant. "Let go of me, please, you're hurting me."

"I said no abortion. I won't have it, I tell you."

She lowered her voice. "Let's go home, Charles, we'll talk about it there. People are staring." She could feel their eyes on her.

"I don't give a fuck about what people think, let them watch," he snarled.

On the edge of tears, she was about to reply when a familiar voice interrupted them. "I've always known you didn't care what people thought, Charles," he said.

Pam's head snapped up as she recognized the voice, and she nearly gasped; her father and Jennifer were standing in front of her table, staring at her in shock.

"It *is* you," William said. "What the hell are you doing with him? I told myself it couldn't be. I still don't believe it, I just don't believe it!" William kept blinking as though he could somehow make this apparition disappear. But the more the reality sunk in, the more stricken he looked.

Pam felt the bottom fall out. Nothing had prepared her for this moment of discovery, for the physical shock that jolted her at the sight of her father standing there. He had a look of such agony on his face that her heart actually skipped a beat and then slammed against her ribs, racing, leaping with wild irregularity. She couldn't look at Charles, couldn't breathe, wished she could faint, crawl under the table, die, be anywhere but here.

It took an eternity for Charles to react, to be anything but surprised. "You know Pam?" he said to William, who stared at him as if it were the stupidest question anyone could ask.

"Know her? Come off it, Charles. You look ridiculous, pretending to be naïve. I know why you're doing this, but I thought you had better sense than to screw around with my daughter!"

"I'm amazed at the both of you," Jennifer said. "This is despicable."

Charles had not let go of Pam's wrist, and now his grip was so tight she thought he might break it. He looked at her with utter disbelief and confusion. And then, when he realized the truth, his bewilderment turned to rage.

William saw the reaction and flinched. Hoping to deflect Charles's anger, he said to Pam, "Just like your mother. I guess becoming famous has destroyed your morals and your sense of decency. Or didn't Charles tell you he was a married man?"

Standing next to him, Jennifer radiated embarrassment and disapproval, but didn't say anything more. William's fury was palpable, covering his fear for Pam; helplessness only added to his frustration. Conversations at nearby tables stopped while people listened.

"I'd hoped you didn't hate me anymore, that you'd come to forgive me for my mistakes," William said, almost pleading with her that this be true. "And all the time you've known my closest business associate, *intimately*." His sarcasm spread like spilled oil, but she saw tears in his eyes.

"Bill, I had no idea." Charles's excuse sounded lame.

"Don't make me laugh." His voice echoed total disbelief. "You planned this, you found her, didn't you? No matter how I tried to keep her from you, you got to her anyway. Not enough humiliation, Charles? Not enough in your debt? How you must have laughed at me. What a joke, huh? Both of you."

"Bill, I swear, I didn't know."

Pam could not breathe.

"Don't bother, Charles, I know you. You'd never let something like this slip by you. And if it did, what else got by?" And then, with a shake of his head, he grabbed Jennifer's arm and hurried her out of the restaurant.

Charles exhaled, a grunting sound, like a fighter who's just received a knockout blow. For a moment he sat there in stunned silence. Then his rage exploded. He grabbed Pam's face between his fingers, pulling her to him. His eyes were forest things, glaring from the body of a beast, his breath hot and foul as he said, "You're the one who's been laughing, aren't you? His daughter! You scheming little bitch. Why the hell didn't you tell me?"

"Oh, please, Charles, I'm sorry. I wanted to for so long."

"You're a fucking liar, aren't you? Weymouth is your professional name. When did you change it? When you met me?"

The pain of his grip was minor compared to the pain in her guts. She couldn't speak, couldn't move, only managed to whimper. He shoved her away, nearly into the man seated at the table next to her.

"Get out of here and go wait for me in the car." Charles's hand shot up to signal the waiter while she pushed their table away and squeezed by the couple next to them. She was so anxious to get away that she knocked over a glass of water on the man sitting there, who'd been innocently included in this fiasco, and who'd stopped talking to listen to her and Charles. He'd gotten an earful, and a lapful too.

"For God's sake!" the man exploded.

But she didn't turn around, just skirted around tables through the red-flocked wallpapered room, past the sommelier, and a surprised Roger Chauveron, to the door, and out into the night. Blessed, cool night. She tried to hail a cab, to run away from Charles to her apartment, to bolt the door against his rage, but Guido stood there, instantly alert to trouble, a bulwark against escape. He opened the car door for her and made certain she got in.

Pam didn't see her father and Jennifer standing outside the restaurant until Charles came out and her father grabbed his arm. There was hatred in her father's eyes. Charles was caught off guard; he looked at William holding his arm and then yanked it away.

"We'd better not get into this now," Charles said.

But William would not leave it alone. "You're nothing

but scum," he said. "You used my daughter like a piece
of trash. Why don't you go back to your scum friends and
leave me alone? You invaded my business and now you've
dirtied my life. I ought to kill you." His fists were clenched,
and Pam was afraid he was going to hit Charles. She
wanted to leap from the car and stop them.

But Charles was extremely controlled. Pam had never
seen him like this; his control was more frightening than
his temper. "I didn't know she was your daughter,"
Charles insisted. "I swear to God. I knew you had a child
by a previous marriage, but I never gave it a thought.
Jennifer's the only wife of yours I've ever met, Danny
and Billy the only sons I know. Her name is Weymouth."
Pam could see that for all her father's anger, he was no
match for Charles. But Charles was still holding on to his
control with great effort.

"She used a professional name for my sake, because
the boys don't even know about her."

"There, you see. I wasn't the only one kept in the
dark. And I was nuts about her. But it's no excuse. I
should have known."

"How long?" William asked. She heard his anguish.

"Over two years."

"Christ, I really underestimated her. I did everything
to keep her away from you, I rejected her, deprived
myself of having her with me at Gray-Con. But she found
a way! She said she'd get into this business one way or
another, and she sure as hell did. It's in her blood, the
way it's in mine."

"Tomorrow, Bill," Charles said, turning to go.

"Wait a minute!" William insisted. "How close were
you?"

Charles stopped and turned back. "Too close."

"You told her things? About me?" He looked stricken.
Charles nodded.

"I didn't want her to know." William glanced toward
the car, where he knew she must be listening, but he
couldn't see her because of the darkly tinted windows.
Pam was embarrassed to witness his shame, and surprised to see how much of it there was.

"She'll never use any of it. I guarantee that," Charles
said, looking toward her. The enormity of his anger
blasted through her hiding place, and the threat that if

she ever used what she knew against them, she'd regret it.

"Don't threaten her, or me." William grabbed Charles's shoulder, turning him back. "You do right by her, or I swear I will kill you."

Charles's teeth were so tightly clenched, the tendons in his jaw stood out. "Nobody lies to me and fucks me over and gets away with it, Bill. Nobody, you hear? She's going to pay, I swear, I'll make her pay."

William shuddered. "And I'd give my soul to get rid of you, Charles. You're a malignancy that's been eating me alive for years."

"I think you've already bargained with your soul, Bill," Charles sneered, and Pam was horrified by the glee in his tone. "We've got you by the balls, and always will."

And now they have me, Pam thought.

Charles reached for the door handle, but William kept trying. "You do right by her, you hear me? Leave her alone!" William shouted. "Or someday I'm going to get rid of you, Charles. I swear I will."

Pam was amazed that he was defending her. She wanted to jump out of the car and run to him for protection, but it was too late. Charles got into the car, and the moment the car pulled away from the curb he burst out of control, attacking her with venomous rage, slamming her with his fists again and again, punching her with all his might on the head and face and shoulders, shouting, "His daughter? His fucking daughter? You had the nerve to smile at me, to make love to me, to suck my cock while you were using me? I'll kill you, you fucking whore bitch, I'll kill you. There is no baby, is there? Another one of your lies, your fucking filthy lies. You thought I'd marry you, didn't you? Using me, you've been using me." With every word he became more enraged, hitting her harder and harder. He couldn't have stopped if he'd wanted to.

She screamed and screamed, sobbing, begging him to leave her alone, not to hit her. She tried to protect herself, but he was too strong. One hand held her while the other hit her again and again. Her nose was bleeding, her eyes swelling, her head ringing, her ears too, until she nearly gave up trying to get away from him, crying as much from fear as from the pain itself. Her vision blurred and she felt consciousness slipping and started to pass out, grateful for it, but he grabbed her and shook her. "Don't you dare do that, you cunt. The only reason I'm not beating the shit out of you is that I want you to admit there is no baby. Tell me, say it!" he screamed.

"There is," she sobbed. "There is. I swear to God. You're killing it!"

And only that seemed to slow him down.

Mercifully, the car stopped in front of her building. Charles gave her a few more blows until it seemed he was spent, then reached across her, opened the car door, and pushed her roughly out of the car. She fell to the sidewalk. "Get into your apartment and stay there. Don't talk to anybody, don't do a fucking thing until you hear from me," he shouted. "Do you understand? Go with her, Guido. Make sure she does exactly what I say."

The car door slammed and the limo drove away, while she sat there on the sidewalk, shaking from terror and pain. The huge man stood in front of her on the pavement, which was damp from an earlier rain. Her stockings were torn, her knees bruised, her dress ripped, her face bloody and swollen. She couldn't move, could barely see.

Guido grabbed her by the upper arm and yanked her to her feet.

"Miss Weymouth." Edward, the doorman, rushed to her side. She turned her face away. "What happened? Shall I call the police?"

"She was mugged," Guido replied. "We've got it under control." And he pushed past Edward, yanking Pam with him, pressed the elevator button, not letting go of her until they were in her apartment. Then he pushed her so hard it sent her sprawling into the coffee table.

Oh God, let me lose this baby now, she prayed. *Let it be over so Charles won't come near me anymore.* But once someone crossed him, he never gave up until he'd paid them back.

Guido was in the kitchen; she dragged herself into the bedroom to catch her breath. *Think, think!* But dizziness befuddled her mind, which was already frozen with terror. Getting help was all she could think of. She took the phone into the bathroom, locked the door, and dialed Hillary's number.

Hillary answered on the second ring, and Pam barely

held on until she heard the familiar sound of her voice; the eleven o'clock news was playing in the background. "Hil, it's Pam." She started to sob uncontrollably. "Something terrible's happened."

"What is it?" Instantly alert, Hillary's mothering instinct took over.

"It's Charles," Pam was about to tell her, but a horrible cracking sound reverberated in the room. She screamed as Guido shattered open the bathroom door with a thrust of his shoulder, grabbed the phone out of her hand, and slammed it down. Terrified that he would take over where Charles had left off, she cringed, waiting for his blows, sobbing and helpless. He grabbed her under the arms, yanked her up, and turned her around to face the mirror.

She gasped when she saw herself, the swollen, misshapen features, bruised and bloody, mucus streaming down her face. She might never be the same, never earn a living with that face again.

"You see that?" he snarled. "You want I should do it to you every day for a month?"

"No," she moaned, terrified and sick.

He was holding her off the ground as though she were a weightless thing of no consequence. When he let her go she fell a good twelve inches, her knees buckling, but she grabbed the sink and stopped her fall. "Then don't make no calls, and don't try nothin' else till Mr. Meroni gets here. Or I will."

"All right," she sobbed. "All right. Just leave me alone."

As he left, Pam felt her stomach give way, and she barely made it to the toilet, where she threw up. When she was through, she rinsed her swollen mouth and the blood off her face. Desperate for some ice from the kitchen for her swollen eyes, she was too afraid to ask Guido for anything, knowing she'd better keep out of his way. The water from the tap made a cool compress. She changed into an old nightgown and robe, needing the comfort of clothing from a more innocent time. Then she lay down on the bed and tried to sleep, but her body was aching and trembling from the assault, her brain jumping, frenzied with fear, anger, remorse, self-pity. Flashes of Charles's face repeated, the feeling of his hands hitting her, the look on her father's face as he'd stood there condemning her, his meanest opinion of her corroborated. But worst of all was her condemnation of herself for doing what she'd done. She'd never forgive herself, never.

Time passed while her brain leaped in and out of jagged images. She heard voices, a woman's and a man's. Guido was arguing with a woman. She couldn't hear them clearly. "I'll call the police," the woman said. "Have to see her." And then someone came into the room and sat next to her touching her face gently. "Pam what happened?" It was Hillary; she'd come. Pam started to cry.

Guido stood in the doorway, outlined by the light from the living room, his nightmare shape like every monster in every terrible dream she'd ever had.

"Get me some ice!" Hillary snapped at him, "or I'll call the police like I promised. Don't just stand there. My husband knows I'm here, and if any harm comes to me, he'll know where to look."

He shuffled off to do her bidding, Kong intimidated by Faye Wray.

"Charles found out who my father is," Pam sobbed, her head in Hillary's lap. "I never told him."

"Oh, Pam, I thought you'd told him months ago."

Pam knew she deserved hours of lecturing, but Hillary just said, "It will be all right. We'll take you to a doctor and then we'll have that animal arrested."

Terror scalded through her. "No police. Please. It was partly my fault. I'll be okay. Nothing's broken." Charles had known exactly how far to go, she wasn't surprised.

"He's disgusting. You're well rid of him."

"I'm not rid of him. I'm pregnant."

"Oh, Pam, you poor thing." Hillary stroked her forehead, listening to all of it before she spoke. "Mel can stop him from harassing you, Pam. We'll get an injunction. We'll find someplace you can have an abortion; maybe in Colorado. You have every right to have one." She stopped. "I never thought I'd hear myself say such a thing. But I'm beginning to see that in some cases abortion is necessary. You can't go on with him any longer, or bring his baby into the world."

"I know," Pam whispered, regretting that the good

times they'd shared were lost; their passion had self-destructed just as she feared it would. "I love him so much and I've hurt him deeply."

"And what do you call what he's done to you?" Hillary touched the swollen places. Pam winced.

"Do you have bookings for tomorrow?"

"I can't remember. They're in my book."

"I'll cancel them."

Pam started to cry again. "Hillary, I'm so glad you came."

Hillary stroked her hand. "It took me so long, I thought I'd never get here. I tore down the turnpike into the city. Thank heavens, the traffic was light. Mel would have come too, but we had no one to stay with the kids. Anything he can do, Pam, he said to tell you."

Pam nodded. "Go on home to him, Hil. I'll be all right. Hold him tight tonight, count your blessings, remember how lucky you are."

"I don't want to leave you yet."

Pam sighed and held on to her friend's hand. "Maybe you could stay for a while. It helps so much, having you here. But if Charles comes, you leave. I don't want you involved."

"I'd like to see him try anything with me."

Alarm shot through her again. "Hillary, don't even say such a thing. He can be dangerous. I mean it, don't get involved. Promise me!"

Hillary saw how upset she was again. "All right," she told Pam, to calm her down. "I promise."

Pam nodded, slightly appeased, and soon fell asleep. Hillary sat with her for a long time before she felt it was all right to leave her and go home.

7

She slept fitfully; the soft touch of a hand on her face woke her. Her eyes were nearly swollen shut. "Hillary?" She couldn't see who it was.

Then she heard his voice. "Pam, what did I do to you? Oh, baby, I'm so sorry."

Charles.

She froze, her body rigid with fear, waiting to be attacked again. "Get your hands off me, don't come near me. If you hit me again, I'll call the police and press charges."

"No, sweetheart, no. I won't hurt you. God will strike me dead if I ever hurt you again, never again. Oh, baby, I'm so sorry. So sorry."

She heard the catch in his voice, knew he was near tears, didn't know what to think, trembled on the edge of incredulity, far from believing.

"I'm so sorry, Pam. I wish I had some way to say it."

She heard him crying, felt his hand on hers, gentle. He kept apologizing, begging her forgiveness. Maybe they could forgive each other. Something inside of her began to soften. "I'm sorry too, Charles." Tears squeezed from her eyes. "For lying to you, for betraying you. I knew your rage was my fault, that's why I haven't gone to the police or done anything else about it. But it's over now. I won't be hurt anymore. Do you hear me? Do you see what you've done to me? I'm so scared, I'm so scared of you."

He was really crying now, heavy sobs, coming out in a high-pitched sound.

It stirred her compassion deeply, touched the part of her that loved him. She almost remembered that love in spite of what had happened. "What we've done to each

other, Charles . . . there's no going back. There's not
enough remorse in the world to heal this. Thinking about
it all night was as bad as going through it. I couldn't live
with myself. I hated you, feared you, blamed you, blamed
myself. I'm sorry too, so sorry." The weight of her guilt
was too heavy to bear; she thought her heart would be
squeezed to death by the pile of stones that lay upon it.
And even worse, her fear and hatred of him had consumed her as much as her attraction to him ever had.

"Don't say any more," he whispered, trying to control
himself. He wanted to soothe her with his touch, but she
flinched, so he withdrew his hand, took a Kleenex off the
bedside table, handed one to her, and blew his nose. "It
has to be healed, Pam. You're everything to me. It was
the betrayal driving me beyond control. Of all the times
to find out, of all the ways."

"I know," she breathed. "It was awful."

"In that one moment, all my worst fears came true,
everything I've ever been afraid of happened; I exploded.
But it will never happen again, I swear. I felt so cheap
while I was doing it, so sick with myself for hurting you,
and sick with myself for having trusted you, loved you. I
thought you had dirtied everything pure we had between
us. I wanted to hurt you the way I was hurting."

"And now?" She was still wary, very frightened, fearing that any minute he might explode again.

"I see why you did it. I know Bill; I know what a
sonofabitch he can be. Never to acknowledge that he has
such a beautiful daughter, to take no pride in her accom-
plishments or share his life with her, it's criminal, as if
he's ashamed of you. And then to say he was trying to
keep you away from me—I'm a father and it makes me
sick. Who could blame you for wanting to hurt him? Is
that why you were with me, used me?"

"No, Charles. I just wanted to learn everything I could
about your business. I just wanted to rub elbows with
you, to be in the thick of it. I admit I wanted to find a
way to get back at my father for all that he's done to me.
But getting him would have meant hurting you. I fell in
love with you, Charles. I knew you'd never see me again
if you knew who I was. I'll never use any of the information I know about Gray-Con. Never. It's enough to know

William is not the example of purity he set himself up to be. It's enough just to know it."

"If only you'd told me."

"I was afraid of what you'd do. I guess I was right to be afraid."

"No. It was the shock, only the shock."

She forced her eyes open, and sat up to look at him. His pain and remorse were genuine. He flinched at her appearance, turned his head away. "God, Pam, forgive me. Sacred Mother in heaven, grant me forgiveness, for I have sinned." He turned suddenly, a new thought torturing him. "Is the baby all right? Nothing happened to the baby, did it?"

"No, the pregnancy seems all right."

"Will you marry me?"

"What!" It was almost a shout.

"I mean it. I'll divorce Irma."

"But you're a Catholic."

"I'll get a dispensation. It's possible, you know."

"But your children?"

"They'll still be my children. But our baby will be my life, like his mother. Marry me, Pam."

Every ounce of her cried out in protest. "I can't marry you. I want you out of my life."

"No, you don't. You love me, I love you. You've always wanted us to be together, didn't you mean it?"

"I meant it then, but this is different."

"I know you can't forgive me so soon, but you will, in time. Nothing like this can ever happen again, because this was a one-time thing. You know that's true."

It made sense, but still . . .

"Have I ever hurt you before?"

"Yes."

"Oh, a few little love-taps in two years' time. But I'll never do it again, I swear. Never will I lay a hand on you again in anger. I'll devote myself to you, baby. We'll be together, we'll work together. You'll be fantastic in my world. Give up the modeling and come in with me; you can do it now that your father knows. Won't it drive him up a wall, you and me together?" He chuckled and she couldn't help smiling with him, though it hurt.

No more Irma and the kids dragging him away. The baby would have a name, legitimacy.

But he beat me. But I deserved it.

"I'm a great father, Pam. I change diapers, I play horsey, tell stories. I love kids. We'll be so good together."

"You really mean this?"

He got tearful again. "Damn straight."

"If you ever raise a hand to me again, I'll leave, Charles. I won't be one of those women who lets her man beat up on her, I swear. I swear." She'd never meant anything so much in her life.

"I wouldn't love you if you did, sugar. I'll never raise my hand again, ever. I take an oath on my mother's grave."

"But why marriage now, Charles? A baby can't make that much difference."

"But it does. You've never had children, you can't possibly know. You'll see, it will change me. It already has. Last night I was an animal. Someone should have shot me for doing what I did. But it opened my eyes. When the anger burned out and I thought about you and why you'd done it, I realized how much you mean to me. I can't live without you, baby. I was hitting you, but it was me I was hitting, furious with myself for loving you so damned much that you could hurt me so bad. I had a meeting with your father this morning and I told him to go fuck himself. I quit. I wouldn't work for any man who could treat his daughter the way he treated you." He was watching her to see her reaction.

"You quit? But I thought you said we'd work together."

"He wouldn't let me leave. Gave me my own ticket. Said he'd apologize to you."

"I don't want his damned apologies."

"Forget about that, honey. Marry me. You know how crazy I am about you."

"I don't know, Charles." She thought, *Hillary will hate this.* "Give me some time. I don't want to see you for a few weeks, while I heal. After that, we'll see."

He grabbed her hand, held it to his cheek. "I'll make it up to you baby. You'll be so happy you won't know what hit you."

She looked at him and thought, *That's exactly the problem with us. From now on, I'll always know what hit me.*

The first trimester went by (when it was still safe for her

to have an abortion), but she didn't notice because she'd accepted Charles's proposal and was too busy and too content. Being engaged made a difference. By the end of her fourth month she barely showed and was still able to do fashion layouts. Eventually she'd be doing only fur coat ads, or head shots for shampoo and makeup. Her bruises had healed without a trace of the beating she'd taken, and her life resumed, but with a new focus, Charles and the baby. Charles bought her a magnificent diamond ring, and she hunted for an apartment for the three of them, something more lavish than she'd have needed only for herself and the baby. She interviewed nurses, nannies, and cooks, and started reading about Catholicism. Maybe she'd convert. Charles started proceedings with the Church. He was waiting for news of the dispensation for his divorce before telling Irma about it; no use upsetting her until he had everything in hand. Pam found an obstetrician, started asking Hillary questions about being a mother, considered names, dreamed about her child, and thought of nothing else. Hillary lodged her protest, argued every argument, but Pam knew that Charles would never hurt her physically again. The circumstances had been unusual, and she felt mostly responsible. Besides, after the first three months, being pregnant was wonderful; she was too happy to hang on to the past.

Hillary pulled her trump. "Before you walk down that aisle, take a look at these." She handed Pam photographs of herself right after Charles had beaten her. Pam gasped when she saw them; they were horrible. "Where did you get them?" she asked.

"I borrowed your camera that night while you were sleeping and took them in case you decided to do something about it. When you didn't, I thought I'd wasted my time, but maybe they'll still do you some good, if they keep you from marrying that man."

Pam handed them back to her. "Get rid of these, they make me sick."

Hillary put them in Pam's lingerie drawer, under the stockings. "Just in case," she said.

But Pam forgot about them as life went on. Charles traveled a great deal, more this year than ever, and she saw him less. When they were together he was considerate, careful of her. The time without him was busy, spent getting ready for the baby, working on the negotiations with the Fuller family members, calling Europe on the syndication of her financial group. Her contentment was apparent as she discovered a world of happy people she'd never known existed, married people who lived their lives in twos; she had conversations with other pregnant women like herself about childbirth and baby furniture.

She questioned Charles. "Are you sure you want to do this? Are you happy? Do you forgive me?" And his reassurances calmed her until she'd have a nightmare about that night, see again the rage in his eyes, feel the pain of his attack, and wonder as she awoke in a sweat, *Am I crazy? Can this ever work?*

By her fifth month, the Church had still not taken up the matter of Charles's divorce, and Pam started to worry. She wanted to get married while she could still wear a wedding gown, but the baby was growing, and soon nothing would be able to hide that fact.

In her sixth month, Charles got word from the Archdiocese that the matter of his divorce was under consideration and that it looked quite favorable. He planned to tell Irma and fly down to Juarez and get a Mexican divorce, and he and Pam would get married in one month's time. She ordered a maternity wedding dress and the invitations, but then Irma caught a virus that went into bronchitis and then pneumonia. She was in the hospital, and Charles didn't have the heart to tell her until she recovered.

Pam canceled the invitations and fretted about how far she could let out the wedding dress.

At the end of her seventh month, Charles had to go to Hawaii for two weeks on business, and Irma was not fully recovered enough to hear the news that he was divorcing her. Christmas would be here soon, and Charles couldn't ruin the holidays for the children. Pam understood.

"We may have to wait until after the baby's born to get married," he told her. But they set a tentative date for January 15, giving Charles two weeks after New Year's to tell Irma.

Pam was somewhat mollified, but fighting panic. She couldn't put her finger on why, because Charles would eventually get his dispensation, even after they were married. He was as disappointed as she about the delays, anxious for their life together to begin. They finally found the right apartment and made a down payment pending the co-op board's review, four bedrooms and a maid's quarters, a dining room, lots of light, high ceilings, and a view, at 57th and Third. But they were still not together.

On December 10, in the middle of her eighth month, Pam got a call from Rick Harris at *Vogue* to do a spring layout in Nassau. "We know you have a large bun in the oven, but we can use you for head shots; we've got wonderful silk shawls and sun hats for you to do, and some hand-embroidered maternity smocks. Three days in paradise, and you can stay longer on your own, if you like. Jeannie, Lacey, Giselle, Lina, and the boys are going. Do say yes, love. You'll be the only suntanned mommy in the maternity ward on February first." Her due date.

She discussed it with Charles, but he was against it. "You're too far along. It's risky to get on a plane and go to the Caribbean. You could get sick there; you'll be too far away."

She felt warmed by his concern, but a bit stifled. "It's only for a week. You won't even be here."

"If you must," he agreed with jaw clenched, dripping disapproval.

She ignored his irritation, and got excited about leaving the cold, rainy weather.

Her cab pulled up to the curb at the airport, next to a pile of skis and boots and Gucci luggage labeled for Colorado. She thought how glad she was to be going to a warm climate as she watched the interchange among the members of the family to whom the luggage and equipment belonged. The mother, in a silver fox hat and coat, like those Charles had given her, looked the picture of apple-cheeked health as she supervised her excited children, who were laughing, giggling, teasing one another in anticipation of their Christmas holiday with Mom and Dad. The driver of their limousine got into the car ahead of her, and she was struck by how much he looked like Fazio. She was so accustomed to seeing Fazio driving Charles's car that she automatically assumed it was he, just as this family, a picture of domestic bliss, reminded

her of what she was destroying by marrying Charles. And
then the father turned to tip the skycap.

It was Charles.

It can't be Charles, he's in Hawaii.

But it was.

He put his arm around Irma and the girls, laughing at
something Irma was saying as he led them into the airport. For a split second Pam was almost glad to see how
completely Irma had recovered from her recent illness,
and then a sudden sick feeling gripped her, a kind of
shock she'd never experienced before, as her entire world
turned upside down. Irma looked as though she'd never
been ill.

"You getting out, or what, lady?" The cabdriver turned
to her. The skycap had already removed her bag from
the trunk and had his hand out for her ticket and a tip.

She went through the motions of paying the driver,
barely holding on to her control, and stepped from the
cab keeping her head down so no one would see her.

Colorado? They were going together? Why wasn't
Charles in Hawaii? When did he get back? Why hadn't
he called? How could Irma be well enough to ski? With a
terrible, sudden realization, she knew! Irma had never
been sick at all, never been in the hospital! The truth
slammed into her. He'd had no intention of asking Irma
for a divorce. He'd been lying to her all this time.

She didn't notice that it was raining until she felt it on
her face, wetting her hair, soaking her clothes, but she
couldn't move. She stood there at the curb while her
control slipped away through the gash in her reality.

"You all right, miss?" the skycap asked.

She just stared, couldn't go into the terminal, couldn't
put one foot in front of the other. What could she do?
What would he say? The enormity of it was overwhelming; nothing made sense. She thought back, remembering
his coolness, his hesitancy to make love because of her
pregnancy, and the delays in their wedding plans. And
the aloneness. But no loneliness she'd ever experienced
before had ever felt like this. A sob welled up inside,
threatening to burst forth, but she held on, knowing that
if she let it out something terrible would happen.

The baby moved, breaking through her dim awareness.
Remember me? it seemed to ask; she'd totally forgotten.

She went inside the terminal, swept along with a group of people hurrying in out of the rain, a zombie on her way to voodoo land. Two of the models going with her were in the check-in line. One of them called, "Pam, over here." The skycap took her bag to the two girls and set it next to theirs. Pam stared at them, nodded to their questions, got through the line, followed them to the gate, not really there, not really anywhere. She knew they were talking, but their words made no sense.

"I can't wait to lie on that beach. I've got a French bikini in my suitcase. It's hot, honey, really hot." Their voices came as if through soundproofing. She followed them into the coffee shop, where they ordered three Cokes. She sipped hers like a live person, though she wasn't one, felt the baby kicking like crazy, felt her mind slipping into a canyon so deep she'd never pull it out.

They walked down the corridor to the boarding gate, the longest walk in her life over in an instant, while a silent voice inside of her screamed, *CharlesCharlesCharles*. She was dazed by the noise, smoke, people; several groups of passengers waited for different flights. Across the large circular space she saw him with his family, as if he'd been waiting there to provide her with proof that the world had gone crazy. He was holding Irma's hand. This was time-out-of-time in a surreal movie. She wanted to sink into the floor and become invisible, but she was rooted to the spot, staring. Their faces and figures grew and changed as though in a funhouse mirror, coming at her, moving away, growing larger or smaller, yet so grotesque.

Something drew him, made him look up, and he saw her. Their gazes locked, and he realized in that moment the incredible accident of their meeting like this. She looked away, felt her strength finally give out, and sank into a nearby chair, unable to hold herself up. The person next to her was smoking, and blew the smoke her way. It was a welcome reality, penetrating her haze, something else to hate.

He was standing in front of her. He looked happy, jaunty; she felt tears on her cheeks, didn't know she was crying.

"Well, I guess it's finally over," he said. On the surface he spoke with pleasant relief, but she felt an underlying hardness. "What a long haul. I ought to win an

Oscar for my performance. I guess you've realized I
never intended to marry you." And then his voice changed
to granite. "Nobody makes a fool of me and gets away
with it, baby. Nobody."

Later she would understand that her inane questions
came out of physical shock, but at the time they seemed
reasonable. "Our apartment?"

"A fake purchase, a phony agent. She's an actress I
hired."

"My ring?"

"Keep it, services rendered."

"The Church annulment?"

"Never applied for."

"All the times you said you loved me?"

"Takes a liar to be fooled by one."

Every glib, practiced answer felt like a nail in her flesh.
"Why would you want to bring a baby into the world to
be punished for our mistakes?"

"Oh, I want the baby, Pam." The cheerfulness was
totally gone as he sat down next to her; the smoker on
the other side had left. "I told you I wouldn't allow an
abortion. It's a mortal sin. If you hadn't believed I was
going to marry you, you'd have killed the child. It was a
perfect way to pay you back." The enormity of his hatred
burned in his eyes. "Perfect, perfect. Now you'll have it
and I'll take it away from you. My cousin Angelo and his
wife, Carolina, will raise it. They have one kid and she
can't have any more. It will be with a family who'll love
it. You'll never love it, you have no love in you at all."
He leaned closer. "You never loved me, did you? Admit
it. Did you?"

She felt his breath on her cheek, his rage beneath the
surface, knew what that rage could do if it was un-
leashed, almost welcomed it. "Yes, I loved you." The
feeling of death in her heart was making her physically
sick; the love she'd felt for him was decaying inside,
rotting, festering. She gazed at him with pain-filled eyes,
unable to bear this torture, wishing she could vomit up
that dead love and give it back to him, get rid of it so it
wouldn't feel like some tumor run amok.

"I'll never give this baby to you, Charles. It's my baby.
I've carried it, worried about it, protected it, loved it. I
want this baby."

"Alone? How will you manage, with a bastard child? Besides, I'll sue you for custody, and I'll win. I have powerful connections, Pam. You know exactly how powerful. Either you give me the baby or I'll take it. And I'll hurt you, Pam, really bad this time. And just when you least expect it."

His plane was announced and his children called, "Daddy, come on."

She couldn't speak, knew he meant what he'd said. If she didn't do as he said, she'd never escape him. If she defied him and kept the baby, all of their lives it would tie them together. She'd either have to give him their child, or he would maim her, perhaps kill her. At this moment, if she let herself, she'd go mad, slide into some dark derangement that, no matter how horrible, would seem a better alternative than this.

"So long, Pam," he said as he walked away. "See you when the baby's born."

So long, she thought, *so long*. It stuck in her brain, repeated itself, summing up what her life had suddenly become: *so long*.

8

She sat by herself on the plane, stuporous. Her friends flirted, paraded, partied, owned the plane of mostly vacation-bound passengers, who happily became an audience, eager participants, thinking they'd been included in this exclusive club, but they'd be dropped when the wheels touched down, except for one or two very hip, very chic, gorgeous guys whom the girls and the boys both liked.

Never intended . . . never intended . . . Why didn't I know? For services rendered. A vendetta for which our child will suffer for the rest of its life.

Why?

The word *why* had become like a swear word, like the dirtiest word she knew. The baby kept moving, pushing its elbows and knees forward, demanding awareness, as if she could forget. In today's world, a husbandless mother-to-be wasn't as stigmatized as she'd once been. But her baby deserved to be raised in Hillary's suburbia, not in another version of Joanne's existence. Tears seeped through the wall behind her eyes. She harbored too much hatred to allow a true release, hatred for him and for herself.

She had no alternative, no way to protect her baby. Okay, let him hurt her; let him kill her; he'd never get his hands on this baby, never. She'd fight him, take her case to the highest court, his court, take it to Charles's own padrone. They'd dined together, laughed together, the old man had held her hand, told her she was lovely. Would he be a fair judge, or divide the child in two?

What was hurting the most? All of it. The death of her dreams, no father for the baby, the end of their future, of her love; even the loss of less important things hurt, like a new apartment, someone to share expenses, compan-

245

ionship. It couldn't be measured; the list was ridiculously long. *So long.*

Nassau was warm and moist, an external heaven to compare with the hell inside of her. The bleached pink stucco walls of their hotel, shaded by leafy banana trees, briefly flickered across her consciousness. There were huge wooden shutters to close out the light and close in the pain. Her friends surmised what was wrong; they'd seen Charles talking to her at the airport, watched him walk away and board a plane with his family. Since the baby wasn't in any danger, her depression had to be the result of what they'd seen. Several of them had been dumped too, and knew what it felt like. But she shut them all out like the sun, though they tried to pry between the slats, peek in at her shame, see her there, stripped of everything, including her pride.

She shared a room with Giselle, who wisely left her alone. The shoot was scheduled for tomorrow, Thursday, and would continue through Friday and Saturday. Giselle, a blond giraffe from France, with sultry pronounced lips and small blue eyes that she enhanced with mink lashes, drew on a joint she'd scored at the Nassau airport. The smell of marijuana made Pam ill, that and life. She wanted to beat herself the way Charles had done eight months ago, to show physical evidence of the devastation within. She wondered if it would show in the portraits they were going to shoot of her. Her face was drawn, skin stretched over bone; she was all belly, no extra weight on her arms and legs. The baby ate it all. She longed for Hillary or even Trish to be here. Finally, she thought of Joanne.

She called L.A.

"You're in Nassau? In your eighth month? When's the wedding?" The voice of experience never believed the wedding would take place. Pam realized why she'd called. She still couldn't cry.

"He's a prick, Mom. Just like you said, like all the 'uncles' you ever brought home to me."

"He dumped you?"

"Yes."

"And you so gorgeous and famous. If you can't keep

them, who can? Kind of brings you down a peg, doesn't it? Maybe now you can see why I'm the way I am."

"Actually, I do."

"What are you going to do?"

Who the hell knew? "How's the weather in L.A.? It's eighty-five degrees here."

"Don't change the subject, Pam. You've got a hell of a time ahead, I know."

"So?"

"So what?"

"Aren't you going to say it?" She baited her mother, wanting to hear the words.

"What am I supposed to say?"

"You'll think of it."

"Well, I'm not sorry, if that's what you want me to say. The married ones are the worst."

Pam knew what was coming next, almost smiled in anticipation, mouthed the words along with Joanne.

"I told you he'd never marry you. I said he'd never leave that dumpy wife and those kids for you."

Pam sighed. "That's it, Mom."

"That's what?"

"Never mind."

"You're not thinking of coming to live with me, are you? I don't think that would work, Pam, honey. I'm too old to have a baby around crying all the time. And Barney's back. Did I tell you? All sweetness and smiles. You'd think I'd learn to say no. He made some dough working oilfields in Mexico. He's a real doll."

"I'll let you know, Mom."

"What?"

"When the baby's born."

"Oh, okay. God, me a grandma. That's something, isn't it?"

"So long, Mom."

So long.

The director wanted an early shoot to capture the sunrise. The models bitched about the 6:00 A.M. call. Photographers were notorious for getting an artsy bug up their asses when they went on location. Luckily, in December the sunrise was at seven o'clock.

A fleet of pink-and-white-striped open jeeps, looking

like toys, were parked at the hotel entrance to take them
to the location, a primitive fishing village in another part
of the island. The roads were terrible, rutted and unpaved, but the drivers drove over them like a Grand
Prix, to the accompaniment of calypso music blaring on
the radio. Pam grabbed the side of the jeep as they
jounced along over potholes that nearly threw them from
their seats. They dodged carcasses of animals, horsedrawn
wagons filled with hay or chickens, and other cars careened at them from the other opposite direction, driving
as fast as they were; those near misses forced their hearts
into their throats until one vehicle pulled off onto the
shoulder and let the other one pass.

The models griped, "I thought New York taxis were
bad."

"This guy's crazy enough to lead a revolution."

"That last bump dislodged my *kishkas.*"

The morning shoot went well; they lunched on freshly
caught fish prepared by a local restaurant, along with
pumpkin soup, cornbread, and cucumber salad. Pam almost forgot her troubles, surrounded by carefree friends,
the warm sun, white sand, a sparkling turquoise ocean,
and work to occupy her mind. When the afternoon session was completed, they peeled down to their underwear and raced for the water, their hot skin almost sizzling
when it hit the heavenly coolness of the gentle Caribbean.

I'll stay in Nassau, Pam thought. *Find myself a hut and
a female companion to take care of the baby. I'll lose
myself in some small village with no phone.* She wondered what the custody laws were in the Bahamas. Charles
couldn't hurt her if he couldn't find her. But her savings
wouldn't last forever. Eventually she'd have to go to
work. And a life of mundane labor was not for her;
solitude and anonymity could make her crazy. She knew
what it was like to be raised by one parent, and at least
she'd had a legal name. Sometimes she missed Charles;
despite the hurt he'd inflicted, she was amazed to discover that love didn't die so easily. She'd truly loved him
and believed him, just as he'd believed her. Now her
future was unknown, full of terrible possibilities.

They drove back toward the sunset; flashes of it blinded
them now and then as they reached an incline in the road
or a clearing in the vegetation. Pam was in the front seat

of the jeep, next to Giselle, who sat in the middle; Cary, Keith and Raymond, the three male models, sat in the back singing rhythm-and-blues songs, "Little Darlin' " and "Get a Job." She wanted them to sing "Shine On, Harvest Moon," so she could harmonize.

As they barreled around a curve, Pam's heart leaped; an ancient, rusted, battered truck was heading directly toward them. On their right, a row of closely growing trees; on their left, a drop-off of twenty feet, no place to go.

Giselle screamed, "Look out!", ducked her head, and braced herself for an impact, but Pam didn't have time to protect herself before she heard a crash, felt the shock of it reverberate through her. And then there was nothing.

Cotton was torturing her. Enormous bales of black, furry cotton entombed her, hurting her beyond pain. She smelled earth, gasoline. Someone shouted, others cried. She cried, her voice disembodied, the pain everywhere, in a tunnel, in the sky, broken body, no going back, ever.

Hillary glanced at Mel, where he sat dozing by Pam's bed, and blinked her eyes, trying to moisten them; they were terribly dry. The last time she had looked in the mirror they were hollow from worry, the circles deeply pronounced.

For ten days, Pam had been unconscious. And then, at six-thirty this morning, the doctor had awakened them to say she was regaining consciousness. Hurrying over to the small, white stucco hospital, where they'd spent every waking minute since the accident, they learned that Pam still wasn't fully conscious.

It was now seven o'clock in the evening, and only once, all day, had she opened her eyes.

Hillary had prayed to every God she could think of for miracles; she had made bargains, promises, pleaded with Pam to hear her, to wake up, but she was unreachable.

"A blessing in disguise," Barbara had said, when Hillary called her mother to bring her up to date. "Better she not know what's ahead for her."

Hillary had cried so much she couldn't cry anymore. She'd never seen anything like the pitiful sight of her friend's broken body.

A rustling in the bed brought her attention back. Pam's eyes were open.

"He's gone, he's gone," she whispered. And then her eyes focused on the room around her and panic flashed as she came into sharper consciousness and felt the excruciating fact of her constraints, her brutal injuries; a butterfly impaled but still alive in a display case, fluttering, fluttering wildly.

A moan-scream escaped. Her voice was very low, hoarse, injured like the rest of her. "What happened?" Eyes flickered, jumped. "Hillary? Why are you here?" She flinched when she saw Mel standing behind Hillary. He'd leaped to his feet at the first sign that she was awake, but his presence disturbed her terribly. "Oh God, Mel. You're here too. It's really, really bad." She squeezed her eyelids shut, but her panic was mounting. "It's bad . . . it's bad . . ."

Hillary rang for the nurse and shouted, "Go get someone, Mel, quickly! You know how slow they are. Hurry! Dr. Thomas said to call the minute she woke up." She turned back to Pam. "Honey, try to stay calm. I'll explain everything."

Pam's terror was spreading around the room. She tried to move her head, which was held immobile, and found that a viselike grip prevented any movement. A pitiful moan escaped her wired jaw.

"Pam," Hillary soothed her. "Don't move. Just take a deep breath and listen to me. Just listen, okay?"

Pam's eyes pleaded from behind the bars of a nightmare.

"You're all right," Hillary stated firmly. "You've had a serious accident, but you're all right. You've been unconscious, but you're okay now. You've had surgery."

Pam whimpered, tears filling her eyes. "Hurts, hurts," she cried.

"I know honey. Do you want something for the pain? They didn't give you medication while you were unconscious, but now they can."

"Yes," she breathed. "Hurts so much, so much." She was crying, a shallow, mournful sound as though she realized that any movement would tear her apart. Her eyes grew wild again. "The baby, baby . . ." Again the pleading look. *Brandon if it's a boy, Melissa if it's a girl.*

"The baby's alive!" Hillary told her. "He survived the

accident, but you had a broken pelvis, so they had to take him by cesarean. He's in an incubator."

"Alive? How long, how long? He's okay? Oh God, it's a boy," she whispered. "Brandon, oh God," she sobbed carefully. "Charles. Charles?"

"Shh, let me tell you, Pam. Try and listen. Don't talk. Giselle told me what happened between you and Charles at the airport. But I figured out what was really going on. He forced you to go through with having the baby by promising to marry you, didn't he?"

She pushed her words out through wired teeth: "Don't tell him, oh God, don't tell him . . . here . . . here."

Hillary wondered if her cryptic speech was just her initial grogginess, the wires holding her mouth together, or if she'd suffered brain damage, as they had feared. "We didn't tell him, Pam, but he found out. We couldn't keep it a secret. He's very concerned about you and the baby. He's called several times a day. It's been in the papers, Pam."

Pam's eyes flickered wildly back and forth; she tried to turn her head but cried out in despair and frustration as the awareness flooded through her that she literally couldn't move. She began to hyperventilate as panic gripped her.

"No," Hillary cried, stroking her hand gently. "Be calm, try to be calm. There, that's it, shhh, I'll tell you everything, just be calm and listen. You're all right, you're all right." She repeated it many times before Pam heard her. "Your leg is broken and it's in traction."

Pam tried to focus on her leg, hanging from a contraption above the bed; though it was right in front of her, she couldn't see it.

"Your head is in traction too, you had a skull fracture. I told you about the pelvic injury, and there was damage to the bones in your cheek. A plastic surgeon from New York who was on vacation here performed the surgery on your face. It will be fine, honestly, Pam. He's an excellent doctor. He says you'll be as beautiful as ever." This wasn't exactly true, but he'd made Hillary promise to minimize the extent of Pam's facial injuries. Hillary was trying not to cry, but Pam's expression tore her apart. All these days of waiting, praying for her to wake up, and now she had awakened, only to face this horrible reality. The surgery to repair the right side of her face, crushed when her head hit the pavement, had been the most delicate of all; the doctor who had put a pin through her skull to hold the cheekbones in place was not actually vacationing in Nassau. He had been flown here by William, who had paid his expenses. William had wanted to come himself, but was afraid that it would upset Pam more than help her. He swore Hillary to secrecy, knowing how fiercely independent Pam was, and that she would not want his interference in her life. But he also wanted to do something to make up for the hurt Charles had caused her, though Hillary had not told him all the details, just that the engagement was off.

Hillary's nightmares replayed the details. She saw the jeep rolling over on top of Pam, crushing her leg and fracturing her pelvis, saw it continuing to roll, felt the horror Pam and her friends had felt. Most of the other passengers had been thrown clear, and had ended up with minor injuries like bruises and sprains. Only Pam, who was thrown out the open door on her side of the car, had sustained so many injuries. The obstetrician who had performed the cesarean section didn't expect the baby to survive, but he was still holding on, tiny, monkeylike; his little bones barely covered with flesh, his silky blond hair like his mother's, and he made sweet mewing sounds in his sleep.

Pam's life had been shattered along with her body. Hillary saw the pieces strewn all over. *Damn that Charles to hell,* she thought, for the twentieth time that day.

Now that Pam had regained consciousness, Mel would want to go home. They'd telephoned Joanne and told her about the accident; she'd called several times, but didn't have the money to get here. Hillary considered sending her a ticket, but she didn't know if Joanne would be of any comfort, and she was reluctant to spend any more of Pam's money. She was going to need every cent she had for her medical bills. The money Hillary and Mel had spent flying Barbara to New York to take care of their children, and then coming to Nassau, had used up their vacation allowance for the next two years. But there had been no question that they'd come.

Dr. Thomas, Pam's orthopedist, arrived, a man in his late forties, with steel-wool hair and an ebony face. Slightly out of breath from hurrying, he'd been keeping a vigil too. "She's awake?" Then he spoke to his patient for the first time. "Oh, I see you are. Do you understand what's happened, Miss Weymouth? Your baby is alive. You were badly injured, but you'll mend in time." He began to fuss around her, checking her physical functions.

Pam's eyes showed her exhaustion while she struggled to say what she felt. They could see she knew that her normal life had been hacked apart as though by a chainsaw. Its hellish work had misshaped her world, leaving its convoluted pieces raw, exposed, and excruciating.

Before she could speak, the nurse came in with a hypodermic. "If you'll all please go out," she asked, enjoying her official role as room-cleaner-outer.

"Come back, after," Pam said, wincing from the effort. And Hillary nodded. She tried to smile at Hillary, but discovered that her face wouldn't let her. The scabs and the pin in her cheek hurt with any movement. She cried out, barely managing to say, "Thank you."

The nurse was giving Pam a shot as Hillary's control broke. She hung on to Mel as they came out of the room, and cried in his arms, sobbing with relief and pity and fear for what lay ahead for Pam and her baby.

9

Drugs were a blessing and a curse, inflating her nightmares to the size of nimbus clouds in a black sky. Surgeons and nurses in greens became Egyptian torturers mummifying her alive, cutting out her organs while she lay pinned and helpless; their painted talon fingers shot electric sparks, pointed to raw nerve endings, wizardly magical torture with which they zapped her while they weighed her heart, liver, and lungs to be placed in canopic jars.

Awake, her breasts leaked milk for an infant cut from her body and encased in a metal and glass box as she was encased in plaster. There was nowhere to turn without torture. Every inch of her screamed in protest, whimpered in misery, groans escaping on their own.

Charles kept calling the hospital; though she refused to talk to him, he offered to take the baby so she could recover. If he did, she'd never see the baby again. It was a godsend that Brandon was still in an incubator and unable to leave; in fact, it took three weeks before he was strong enough even to lie in the crook of her arm. In defiance of all the odds, he'd survived. When the nurses brought him to her, she sobbed with joy, giving herself the luxury of a release she'd denied, stonelike, less it diminish whatever minute amount of self-control remained.

He looked up at this strange, blubbering person above him. Unable to turn her head or look down, she couldn't see him until a nurse held a mirror above his head. *Little son of mine, so wondrous and small. What kind of life can I give you? How can I protect you? And from your own father? Is there any way?*

In moments he was gone, both of them exhausted by

their introduction; but touching and holding him gave her new purpose. He had to be protected at any cost.

How?

Her nightmares reflected reality, though these drugged dreams terrified her even more, dreams in which Brandon was grabbed by men in black suits, torn from her arms and taken to hostile environments away from sterile safety, while she lay pinned and helpless, weighed down by something so heavy her brain turned it into bales of cotton, and then, as she lay there unable to move, the bales were set aflame and she woke up screaming in agony.

She clutched at the practicalities of life in momentary snatches between shots and pills and hallucinations, dreading the time when the baby would be allowed to go home. That was when she would lose him. Stock prices were up, and she sold what remained; soon her money would dwindle to nothing. She had very little left after buying the property in Manhattan, which she had to hang on to at all costs, and she was determined to find a way to protect Brandon.

The neck traction came off. Finally she could raise her head, turn it ever so slowly as it creaked. Smiles were still limited by the metal pin inserted from left to right through her skull, protruding from her left cheek with a small cork on the end; forget about laughter. No walking or holding the baby for weeks, until her pelvis and leg fractures mended, and then what? The doctors shook their heads over her slow progress, but worrying about the baby and their future together sapped her strength. What, what, what could she do? The logical answer was her mother, but every fiber in her being fought against it.

She made the call, knowing her son's life was riding on the whim of a deadbeat. She needed Oliver Wendell Holmes to plead her case. But perhaps knowing how tenuous the thread of life was that Pam clung to, how much she'd suffered and lost, Joanne would rise to the occasion.

"So. I'll be laid up for a long time," Pam said, after covering all the details. "Can't walk or care for the baby."

"It kills me to think of you lying there like that, all this time," Joanne said. "Yet you're lucky to be alive. I don't know how you stand it, Pam."

"I've got no choice."

"But still."

"You know the baby is almost well enough to go home now." Pam had waited for Joanne to ask about him, but she had not done so; it was a glaring omission.

Hesitation. "That's wonderful."

"I don't know what I'm going to do. I need a full-time nurse for me and one for him, that costs a fortune, and so do my medical bills. The insurance only pays part of it."

"You're telling me."

Pam clenched her fist so hard that her nails dug into her palm. *Keep it casual.* "I don't suppose you'd consider coming here to take care of Brandon for me until I'm on my feet?"

Silence. And then a sigh. "I know I should do it, Pam. You'll think I'm a shitty mother if I don't. As a matter of fact, I was afraid you might ask me to do this."

"Afraid?"

She rushed on. "It's just that I'm no good with babies. Your father took care of you more than I did when you were little."

It was the most absurd piece of information she'd ever heard. Bitterness seeped into her tone. "William never struck me as the paterfamilias type."

"The what?"

"Never mind."

"Well, it's true. He was the only one who could make you stop crying. Used to pick you up and walk you for hours, sang fraternity songs and college songs to you, even Christmas carols, anything he knew. It used to amaze me how you'd shut up to 'Ninety-nine Bottles of Beer on the Wall.' "

Pam couldn't picture it either. "Then he loved me?"

"Sure. He loved us both. We had some great times, me and your father, before we broke up. Bill just wasn't used to a tough life, the way I was. We should have been careful, but we weren't. Kids are so dumb. Next thing I knew, I was in the family way."

The quaint phrase for being knocked up betrayed Joanne's Iowa background.

"When Bill found out, he was okay about it. We were in love; what else was there to do? We drove to Vegas to get married, though his parents were fit to be tied when they found out. Cut him off without a cent. Once I even heard Billy crying on the phone with them. But we got through it. Bill got a job selling plumbing equipment for a company in Whittier.

"And then one day when you were about three, Bill came home to our apartment and caught a friend of his making a pass at me. He just blew up. We had a big fight and Bill accused me of leading the guy on. I never did. But he wouldn't believe me. Probably was looking for an excuse to run home to Mom and Dad. We would never have lasted, but at the time it was the worst thing that ever happened to me." She paused. "We weren't exactly suited. He used to get mad when I put his beer on the table in a bottle instead of pouring it into a glass. Did you ever hear of such a thing?"

Pam felt close to her mother at this moment. Hope was rising that she would take care of the baby. *If only she would help me long enough for my body to heal. Maybe if I could think clearly, I could figure out what to do.*

There was another long pause before that hope was dashed. "Honey, I'd really like to help you with Brandon, but I'm being honest with you. I'm not good with babies. You'd be better off with someone else."

Pam felt the fall of her expectations like a sharp knife in her guts, and cursed herself for forgetting even for a moment what Joanne was like. She wanted to scream, *You're my last hope!* But instead she said, "I can't afford anyone else, Joanne."

"Then let Charles pay. He's loaded, isn't he? He wants to help, doesn't he?"

Pam couldn't tell her why she must not turn to Charles. The fewer people who knew about it, the better. "Yeah, sure. Charles will pay for a nurse."

"That will work out better for all of us. You'll see."

"Sure," Pam said, hanging up. Despair washed over her again, along with the crablike fingers of pain. God, was there no way out except to ask Charles for help? She'd be better off dead. Not that she wasn't grateful to be alive. But still, it would be better if Charles thought she was dead.

A kernel of an idea began to form. *What if Charles thought the baby was dead?* It was such a horrible idea, she hated herself for thinking it. But she was in a horrible predicament. Tentatively she approached the idea, pleading with God not to make it come true just because she was thinking of it.

What if she told Charles the baby had died? Would he believe her? Only if she showed him proof, made it convincing. How could she pull that off? Perhaps get the hospital to issue a death certificate. They'd never do it. What about a forgery? Maybe. Then where would she go? To Australia. She'd raise the baby on her own. Charles would never find out. Like hell! Anywhere in the world that she took the baby, he'd find her; how well she knew his suspicious nature. Okay, then she'd put the baby somewhere else for a while. Maybe leave him here in Nassau while she went back to New York and pretended the baby had died. She could resume her career, and in six months she could tell the agency she was moving to Europe. She'd pick up the baby and go to New Zealand. Anyplace where he couldn't find her.

No such place. He'd always keep tabs on her, if only to make her life miserable on general principles, and to make sure she never made public what she knew about him and her father. As long as she had the baby, they'd never be safe from him. He'd never stop trying to take Brandon away from her. But could he? Of course. He had the money to keep her in court. She didn't. He knew judges, paid judges. It was too risky.

Then what?

When the solution finally occurred to her, she cried for so long her temperature rose to 103 degrees and she had to be sedated. For three days she thought about it, weighed every aspect, felt a kind of death occur within her, allowed herself to mourn, hated herself and Charles with every ounce of strength she had left, then somehow found the courage to set the plan in motion, and made the call to New Jersey.

Hillary was glad to hear from her. "Pam? It must be telepathy. I was just going to call you. How are you feeling?"

The sound of Hillary's voice almost ruined her resolve. If she started to cry, it would be all over. "Hillary, don't say anything. Not a word, just listen. I'm going to ask you to do something, and then I'm going to hang up so you can think about it. Don't call me back until you've thought it through completely. Talk to Mel. The two of you must give it every ounce of consideration. And while you do, know that I've really thought this through myself. Believe me, there's no other way to solve my problem." Hillary inhaled sharply as though she was about to interrupt, but Pam said, "No, don't say anything. You won't change my mind. Are you ready?"

"I guess so."

Pam's voice quivered, stumbling over the words, but she managed to say them. "Will you and Mel adopt my baby?" And she hung up.

Hillary sat there stunned, the receiver in her hand, her pulse pounding in her ears. How could one person's life be so tragic? What Pam had just asked her weighed on her so heavily she bowed her head from the feeling of despair that swept over her. *Imagine being in the hospital, so far away, facing your tragedies and pain all alone.* Raising her head, Hillary looked around her cheerful kitchen. The January sun streamed in through the blue checkered curtains. In the front yard she could hear the sound of Mel's snow blower grinding its way down the path to the street. In the family room, Stephen was watching Saturday-morning cartoons; Lori and her friend Mitzie were upstairs, playing a game. She was so fortunate compared to Pam; everything she loved was in this house, serene and secure, while Pam was forced to contemplate giving up her child. Another wave of sadness engulfed her, and her throat tightened. To her, the anguish of someone she loved meant that something had to be done, and she was the one who had to do it. But what could she do? She didn't even have to ask Mel to know his answer. No way! He'd remind her that adopting Charles Meroni's son would be a foolhardy, dangerous thing to do. She couldn't pass the baby off as her own; Charles knew she wasn't nine months pregnant (Pam would have told him), and if she were to adopt an infant he would figure out immediately whose baby she'd suddenly acquired. From the way Charles threatened Pam, their own family could be in danger for getting involved.

And even if she could get around Charles, supposing that he wasn't as astute as she believed—which, from what she'd seen, wasn't the case—adopting her best friend's child would certainly kill their friendship. Pam would be tortured every time she saw the baby, wanting him and yet unable to have him. And Hillary's own guilt would be impossible to live with, wondering if she was raising the baby the way Pam would have, feeling as if she were profiting from her friend's loss, maybe even resenting Pam for being his natural mother while dividing her loyalties between her own children and Brandon. Mel had no desire to adopt a child, and might not be able to love him as his own. Selflessness wasn't Mel's "thing," as they said nowadays. Mel's "thing" seemed to change with the times. He envied the radical dropouts who felt no need to succeed in a competitive world, and he longed to have the experiences they were having; she could see the longing in his eyes whenever he read an article about the new sexual freedom and mores.

But as much as she wanted to help, there was one major obstacle that made the adoption of Brandon out of the question; if Pam hadn't hung up so fast, Hillary would have told her the news she'd been keeping from her since the accident, knowing it would upset her. She was four months pregnant herself with her third child. How many babies could a person deal with at one time?

"They're a bright, loving, sincere couple, Pam," Mel told her after he'd contacted an attorney friend of his, who had gotten in touch with a childless couple named Matthews, and arranged for the adoption. Under the terms of the agreement, Pam wasn't to know the new parents' identity and they wouldn't know hers, though they knew a lot about her. They'd been waiting for a child for some time, so in a matter of days, Brandon would be theirs.

"What are they like?" Pam wanted to know. "Can they provide him with a good life?"

"They're blue-collar people, Pam, but honest and sincere. I thought it best not to place him with people who had any sort of visibility, because of Charles. You know Charles has unlimited resources. I looked for people who were not of Charles's ethnic background, or who would have any possible connection to him."

Pam knew he was right, but it was important to her that Brandon not be poor, as she'd been. Finally she agreed.

It was not as difficult as they'd thought to fake the death of an infant, especially one who'd had such a precarious start, but the details were crucial to the success of the venture. Pam knew that Charles would thwart her plans by finding Brandon, no matter who adopted him, if he knew Brandon was alive; thus there was the need for this elaborate subterfuge.

Hillary flew back to Nassau, took a room in a boardinghouse, and, with Pam's permission, took Brandon to stay with her. The next day she gave him a mild sedative and waited for him to appear limp and lifeless. Then she called all the people in the boardinghouse to come and see, crying and pretending frantic concern; her adrenaline level was so high from fear of discovery, or that something would go wrong, that it wasn't difficult to pretend. She made sure that enough witnesses thought Brandon was near death. Those kind black faces weren't as upset as she'd expected; they often dealt with this kind of tragedy. They stood and watched while she drove off with the baby in a basket, ostensibly to a hospital, to try to save his life. Actually she took him to Mel, who gave him to a nurse who was taking him to his adoptive parents.

Mel had found an elderly local doctor who was happy to make an extra thousand dollars to fake a death certificate after they told him about Pam's predicament and about Charles's associates and his violent, vindictive threats. Mel had gone to the trouble of searching out the oldest doctor he could find; once the old man passed away, no one could ever prove that Brandon was still alive.

Later, Mel came back to the boardinghouse to pick up Hillary's clothes, and told the residents there that the baby had died.

The nurse flew back to the States, taking Brandon with her. And Mel went to the hospital and officially informed Pam, as they'd planned, that her infant had died while in Hillary's care. Then he told the hospital staff the sad news. It was terrible for everyone. Even though Pam knew it wasn't true, her reaction was the same as if it had been; giving away the baby she adored was almost as much of a loss as his actual death would have been. Mel and Hillary hated lying to the people who had worked so hard to keep Brandon alive, but even that was necessary, because when Pam asked the hospital to inform Charles of his son's death, they did so—making it official. Hillary spoke to Charles, who was upset about the loss, and agreed to allow Pam to arrange for the burial.

The three conspirators could not have managed a fake funeral, so they told everyone the baby had been cremated. Hillary and Mel stayed on for a few days to comfort Pam, whose bereavement was genuine.

"Did Charles believe you?" was the first thing she wanted know.

"I'm sure he did," Hillary assured her. "He asked what had happened, and I told him. And he requested a copy of the death certificate. He wanted to know how you were taking it."

"You mean he wanted to know that I was suffering?"

"I told him you were devastated."

Tears streamed down Pam's face. "Goddamn him! I hope he rots in hell for this."

"I'm glad we went to all this trouble, Pam. It was really necessary."

Then Pam asked, "Mel, are you sure that Brandon's new parents will love him? Will they be tender with him? He's so delicate. Did he wake up from the medication? It didn't hurt him, did it? Oh God," she cried, trying to be strong. "Does the nurse know all the special instructions?" Mel did his best to reassure her, but her pain cut through him. He thought she was the bravest person he'd ever known.

The three of them sat in Pam's hospital room and watched the clock, imagining the plane arriving after its flight, wondering how the new parents must be—tense, excited, and insecure, taking Brandon as their own. They all felt this as if it were a real death, but knew they'd done the right thing. Before deciding on this course of action they'd discussed it endlessly, argued passionately to convince each other there had to be a better solution, only to come back again and again to the same conclusion. Brandon could not be used as a weapon, or torn away from Pam so that Charles could wreak more vengeance. Nor could she risk further bodily injury for trying to keep her child.

Mel, who was usually calm and practical, found the pain of this ordeal terrible to endure. "I didn't mind the risk to my career as much as the moral issue," he said. "The least of my sins was breaking the law by obtaining a fake death certificate. The worst of them was not being able to come up with a less painful solution."

Pam tried to make him feel better. "Brandon deserved better than Charles's cousin as a parent. That man is an enforcer for the mob, for Christ's sake—one of those people who'll never do anything but follow orders all of his life, terrible orders. One day he may be arrested for extortion or murder."

"I don't know, Pam. We're playing God. Those kinds of people love their children too," Mel said.

"Charles is the one who wanted to play God, only his work was more like the devil's."

Hillary listened to them talking, remembering all the dishonest things she'd done over the past few days, and now she smelled the fetid odor of their success. Like a psychic, she envisioned the future, while the agony of this reality plagued her. "You'll never be free of this, Pam. You'll always wonder about him, long for him, and so will I." She patted the growing child within her. There couldn't be any pain worse than giving away a child you loved, knowing he was alive and never seeing him again.

Pam's amazing courage gave out and she started to cry, deep, wracking sobs. "It was my choice. The only choice I had."

Hillary was so overcome by exhaustion she was unable to cry anymore. Of course she hadn't been allowed to meet the people who adopted Brandon, nor was she supposed to know who they were, but she had been unable to let go completely, and had done something even more dishonest by peeking into Mel's file and reading their names before those names were changed to protect Pam's and Brandon's identities. It was the first breach of trust she'd ever committed, not only in her marriage but in her life. Yet her need to help Pam overshadowed right and wrong. She had some idea of being able to keep tabs on the baby and to make sure he was all right. Brandon had been taken from *her*, too. Her almost-son.

A sidelong glance at Pam revealed the flesh on her abdomen, the residue of pregnancy, spilling over the edge of her jutting hipbone. The leg cast had been reduced in size, but still covered her from her waist to her toes. Her skin was dry and scaly, toenails in need of clipping, fingernails too. Glamour was a stranger to misery. Her cheeks were sunken, arms bony, hair lank and uneven, face still distorted from the scar on her cheek where the pin had been inserted. Plastic surgery would take care of that scar, but nothing could ever eliminate the emotional scars. And worse than the condition of her body, or the pain she still endured, was the wounded, hollow look in her eyes. The vibrant flash of fire that was Pam had been doused by suffering and tears.

BOOK
IV

Sometimes
It
Works. . . .

1

Berkeley,
1967–1971

When they finally released Trish from the hospital after her overdose, it was February. Seeing Arthur straight was as bad as being straight herself. Every enlarged pore and whisker on his face magnified itself two thousand times, while Trish's own skin flaked; each dry particle made her wince as it peeled from her face.

He put her into the car, tucked a lap robe around her, and told her he had to stop at the store on the way home. "I want to make sure there's food in the house." She was even more his possession, a beanbag shaped by someone else's opinion. She would collapse without his structure, her corners blending into blobbiness.

While Arthur marketed, Trish sat staring out the window of the car, feeling newly released from jail, or like a bird without feathers. He put the groceries into the trunk, got back into the driver's seat. "Are you warm enough?"

"Yes."

"Comfy?"

"Don't fuss so."

"You've been very sick, Trish. Scared the hell out of me. Didn't know if you'd pull through."

"I can't get over Pam coming here to see me. I never knew how much she cared."

"I care too, button. Was it my fault?"

"Of course not." *When had she become a liar, too?* The telephone poles sped by, each a sentinel marking her return, their monotonous regularity like a prophecy. Would the next be better than the last? Sometimes when stoned, and even in the hospital, she'd get hooked on a sound, say every word she could think of beginning with a certain letter; like echolalia, one word led to another: "Pudendum, penumbra, pubescent, pot. Pot—cannabis . . ." *See how it leads?* she thought.

"What are you muttering?"

"My *p's* and *q's*" she snapped, caught. "You always wanted them minded, didn't you?"

He ignored her black mood, drove the rest of the way in silence. At home, he brought her a glass of cider with ice and opened a new package of oatmeal cookies with raisins, the soft kind made with molasses, shoved the cat off the chair, and sat down beside her.

She glanced around, bewildered, then went mentally from room to room; everything was a mess, in need of repair. *Just like me.* The kitchen tiles were chipped; there was wax buildup on the perimeter of the discolored vinyl floor; dust mice under the bed scurried ahead of the breeze. *Laundrylaundrylaundry.* The bathroom mirror needed resilvering; specks of brown dotted its face, crackles pitted the edges. A rust drip stained the bathtub as though someone had spilled a bottle of iodine; plants grew spindly in need of cutting back; kitchen towels had unraveling holes in their middles; chipped china was stacked on the shelves; seams were split on quilts, chair cushions, and cereal boxes. After being away for so long, she saw it with sober eyes and it was *messymessymessy.*

The reality was dawning on her that she was really going to have to do it, to care for herself as well as for him. The responsibility made her heart race; adrenaline shot through her in a sudden spurt; her eye started to tic; her lungs to pant; and she hadn't even approached the spare bedroom where she worked, hadn't seen her most recent paintings stacked against the walls, her supplies caked with paint, brushes needing to be soaked, others drying—the ones she'd been sober enough to wrap in waxed paper and clip with a paper clip so they'd dry firm and straight. She remembered leaving flowers in a jar. They were long dead by now, the water breeding pollywogs. *That's a good* p *word, pollywog,* she thought.

"Take it easy." Arthur stroked her hand, put his arm around her neck, pulled her head to his shoulder, a hand on her forehead. "Shhh," he gentled her.

She needed his attention so, his forgiveness. He was only attentive like this when she was sick. Would it last? Better not to speculate. She'd always loved his being gently paternal, but he did it by combining the autocrat with the overseer. That was fine for a real father, but in a husband it was smothering. Maybe she'd asked for everything she'd gotten, couldn't really blame him at all.

"What's wrong with us?"

"Nothing. Just stress."

The itchy, crawly feeling of withdrawal crept up her arms, down her legs; tension grabbed her shoulders, knots impossible to untie. "I'm going to jump out of my skin. I'll never make it. I won't. I need something so badly."

"You'll make it, Trish. I'll help you. Lean on me."

His arm was still around her, and she pressed her cheek firmly against his chest, bones and flesh built to be leaned on. If only it would last. "I hate therapy. I hate those groups." She spoke in an imitative singsong: "What did your mother do to you? What did your father do? Trish, I think Natalie is hostile toward you." She resumed her normal voice. "It's all such bullshit, I can't take it."

"You haven't even started."

"I've had five weeks of sessions. You call five weeks not even starting? I hate all those druggies, those junkies. I don't belong there. And Dr. Rennie thinks he's so fair, with that kind, dispassionate voice. 'How does it make you feel, Trish, when Merv says you're hooked on drugs?' Like screaming, I said. I wanted to scratch all their eyes out!"

"It takes time," he assured her.

She sighed, needing him, or needing some chemical so much she ached for it. But she stayed clean.

In two days his ill temper surfaced, and he began barking orders. "Where are my shirts? Why isn't the bed made? Can't you get anything done?"

She retreated into work. It felt wonderfully easy, compared with staying clean.

He said, "You call this work? You painted better stoned, and that was really shit."

She crumbled, too quickly for him to catch her, and stumbled toward the closet where she used to keep *it*, B.P., Before Pam. Crawling frantically around on her hands and knees, she groped into corners, under shoes, for anything that might have fallen out of her old bag of tricks.

Arthur was instantly sorry for what he'd said. He chased her; his arms went around her, pulling her to her feet.

Skin and bones was all she was after eight weeks in the hospital. She clung to him, whimpering, "I'll never make it, I want to give up."

Responding once again to that childlike need, he encouraged her. "Your work is good, Trish, keep at it. All of us have doubts, even hate what we do, find the result inferior to the intent. All of us know the breakthrough is in us, if only . . ."

"If only . . ." she repeated, trembling.

"If only," he continued the litany, "the medium we've chosen is the right one to convert our ideas into reality. Should I give up painting for sculpting? Turn from abstract to realism? Combine the two? Difficult decisions are what pave the road to hell, not good intentions."

"I'm decided out," she sighed with fatigue, felt her energy drain from her like spilled milk. The compulsion to get high, get loose, get lost, get drunk, whatever was handy, beat through her with every thump of her heart. Arthur's arm around her was the only deterrent. *You call this work?* he'd said. Like her father, he could be so kind one minute, so critical or demanding the next.

She clung to him; he led her into the bedroom, folded her under the blankets, tucking her in, straitjacket-like. That felt safe and secure, necessary to keep her from climbing the walls.

She fell asleep to her vow. Tomorrow she'd paint an hour at a time, watching the clock, giving herself credit for going through sixty straight minutes. The group demanded that her house be clean of any drugs, including liquor, but Arthur refused. First there was his wine collection, then there was scotch, vodka, and beer, a part of living, as American as Hallmark Cards. "You can be strong," he said. And she was. Her body vibrated with the effort of trying. She tossed her head back and forth to rid her brain of those insidious spiders crawling in from every webbed corner; each hairy leg carried a drink, a pill, a joint, a fix.

"Let me out of here!" she cried silently, until she slept.

Fatigue never left her. The drug rehab group insisted that fatigue was a result of unexpressed emotions. During group she fell asleep when someone else was talking. It was the only place she relaxed; she certainly didn't sleep in bed.

Everything continued to deteriorate: the rust stain in the bathtub spread accusingly; tiles in the kitchen chipped all by themselves; the ice compartment in the refrigerator crusted over with white coils of frozen water, huge prehistoric worms re-created by inadequate technology. She'd boil a pot of water and set it inside, watch the steam melt the outer white fuzz, until the white worms were smooth and drippy. Then she'd close the door and forget about it until later, when she'd find the pot of water frozen in with the rest.

Only work soothed her. She didn't show it to Arthur. But it was the best work she'd ever done. All pretense was gone, externals stripped away, essence revealed in self-portraits. Eventually he wandered in to see. He held in check his propensity to criticize, knowing how fragile she was. Or because the work was good? She couldn't read him. His unstated opinions hovered like heavy black storm clouds, but she kept her back to the wind, dug in her heels, and let it blow. If he said one harsh word, just one, she'd lose it all. She could tell he wanted to, but he didn't. She kept working without input, just as she had in the old days, until finally a glimmer of self-satisfaction began to glow, a single ember in the frozen, undefrostable part of her psyche. Painting on regular-shaped canvas, conventionally acquired, as opposed to the odd-shaped crocheted pieces she used to do, represented her return to normalcy, even though the figure from the crocheted pieces appeared as herself—a tiny, fairylike female creature still reaching out, but unfettered now, floating in a pool, in the ocean, in space, in weightless environments, in lily ponds, an homage to Monet. These were Trish's first tentative steps as a whole person, so there was a wait-and-see quality to the work, and yet it expressed a beauty and joy in life that she'd only hinted at before. The better it got, the more work she did, the less she thought about drugs. One life, Pam had said, her life. *If only*.

2

"I can't stand the way she's always sketching us," Natalie whined. "Thinks she's so clever. The artist. She's invading our privacy."

"Trish, your work should be left in the studio. This place is for another kind of work, just as serious and important." Dr. Rennie was being fair again.

Trish felt the color rise to her cheeks, yearned to tell them to fuck off, but refused to descend to their level. She put her sketchbook aside; she was never without it, her trusty companion, the way her journal had been during schooldays.

"Did you want to say something?" Attention was focused on her.

"I think Natalie has the floor—the one with the complaint. I've complied." Steam was coming out of her ears. *Hold it, Trish, hold it.* She held her breath, held on. *Good girl.*

Dr. Rennie studied her, elbow on the arm of his chair, chin in hand, his plaid slacks crossed over bony knees, open-collared shirt, T-shirt showing above his buttons, like a nerd. She smiled, suppressed it.

"What is it?" he asked, the mild-mannered therapist.

She burst out with a guffaw. "Your T-shirt shows, and it's corny."

The rest of the group laughed too, even Dr. Rennie, all but Natalie.

"And you're so gorgeous," Natalie said to Trish. "Miss Skin-and-Bones."

Dr. Rennie hooked his finger over the neck of the T-shirt, pulled it away from his body, and let it snap back. "My wife says the same thing—square dresser, she calls me." He waited until the mirth had subsided. "But you wanted to get angry, didn't you, Trish? Instead, you found something to laugh at."

She felt a sudden sensation of drowning, as though she had plunged into an aquarium and was gazing at the others from inside the glass as the water level rose higher and higher; they just watched her drown. Ben to her right, layers of fat hanging over the edge of his seat, stared and perspired. Natalie, pinched face, wires of gray in her curly hair, glared. Then Dr. Rennie, then Ida, in her sixties, and Larry, nineteen, on her left. The water in her closed-in prison climbed higher, up to her chin, over her mouth, above her lip, over her nose. There were tears in her eyes. *Hold on, Trish, hold on.*

"Well? Aren't you angry at Natalie for making you stop sketching?"

"I chose to stop." She clamped her mouth shut, forgetting that if she talked underwater she'd drown. She put her head in her hand, closed her eyes.

"Baby doesn't get her way, so she's crying."

Trish's head snapped up. Natalie's beady eyes swam before her own. Then, slowly, deliberately, she reached over, picked up her sketchbook and pencil, stared at Natalie full on, and began to draw her with an evil leer, two fangs, and long hairs on her chin.

"Give me that." Natalie snatched the sketchpad away before Dr. Rennie could intervene, but he leaped to his feet and took it away from her.

"We don't touch one another in a hostile way, or grab each other's possessions, Natalie. Either abide by the rules or leave." An august command from the good doctor.

Natalie slumped back in her chair, chastised.

Trish glared.

"Yes, Trish?" Dr. Rennie again.

Hold it, hold it. Oh God, she couldn't hold it any longer. She had held it in for years. That goddamned Natalie, she was nothing. Why should Trish hold it in for her? She hated her, hated them all. She felt the aquarium start to crack, tried with all her might to hold it, but for someone like Natalie it wasn't worth holding on. The aquarium crack grew longer, snaking along the glass surface until the pressure inside suddenly cracked it wide open and the words came pouring out. "I hate you,

Natalie," she screamed. "You're the smallest, pickiest, nastiest person I've ever known." Her fists were clenched and she pounded on her knees. "Natalie, go fuck yourself, go to hell, jump in the lake, eat shit." There weren't enough angry words to say what she felt. Natalie's face swam before her eyes, and suddenly she saw the face of her mother there, and then her father. It shocked her so deeply that she shut up. And then she started to cry again, crying until she was all cried out, until at last she felt purged, let out. What a feeling. And then the group was hugging her, clapping her on the back. Ida and Larry both took turns. Dr. Rennie beamed, even Natalie grinned, and Ben jiggled on the chair next to her.

"Good girl," they were saying, "good girl," and she was amazed to be getting approval for losing her temper.

The months ran together in a blur, individualized only by the pain of discovery as she traced back her precepts, one by one—parentally based. Girls *shouldn't,* girls *never,* girls *didn't.* To look at Mom and Dad for the first time out of context was so hard.

And Arthur was no help. He hated talking about her sessions, resented her time there, the way she quoted Dr. Rennie. A constipated voyeur, Arthur called him, behaving as though she were sneaking off to see a lover. She learned that she'd re-created her family's structure in her own marriage. It turned out that Arthur was like her father in many uncomfortable ways. Her father dominated her mother, and guess what? Arthur dominated *her.* She was angry at her brother for abdicating when it came to admissions and discovery, and eventually told him so and they grew closer than ever before. Arthur would have none of it. Their conversations ended up in arguments, and then in bed. His own aggression excited him.

New ideas occurred to her, ones she wanted to share, but she feared being laughed at. She waited until after lovemaking, when Arthur seemed mellow, to venture into those areas of conversation. "Every woman ought to examine herself inside; we're a mystery to ourselves, too shy and afraid of what we look like and what we feel. When I think of how ashamed I used to be to masturbate. . . ."

He raised himself on his elbows, alerted. "You don't still do that, do you?"

His tone stopped her from telling him. "What if I did?"

"I'd take it personally. I'm not enough for you?"

"Don't you masturbate?"

"That's entirely different."

Why? she wondered. "Still, women should be familiar with their bodies."

"Don't tell me you believe that absurdity?"

She dropped the discussion, bought a speculum from a hospital supply company, and took a look at herself, at that mysterious inner rosebud, the entrance to life for every human being ever born. Even Christ was born of woman, though conceived by God, and came into life through such a place. The idea changed her. It dawned on her that women had power. Men needed them to procreate, to immortalize themselves. Women had so much power, maybe that was why men were terrified of them. She considered the historical images of women in art: glorified, madonnaized, idolized, attacked, even raped. It amazed her to think those images hadn't just happened, that they were socially significant, mostly painted by men. She'd been exposed to those ideas before, studied them, but they'd never felt so personal. Wasn't Georgia O'Keeffe sly, painting vaginas to look like flowers, or vice versa, glorifying femaleness, getting to the essence and saying, *Here's the mystery, the beauty, the wonder of women. Isn't it about time we flaunted it?*

"If you're so fascinated with your cervix," Arthur said, "why don't we have a baby? You know how much I want children. If you think you can handle it, that is."

By way of repairing the ideological rift between them, he'd found her weakness. She took it to mean that he loved her. Was the timing right? She discussed it in group, and eventually decided that she was ready, felt whole enough within herself to be able to give to another human being, to care for an infant of her own. She'd spent a year free of pills and dope, had accumulated a new body of work approaching completion. Maybe she'd have her second one-person show and a baby at the same time.

*   *   *

Arthur's gallery on Sutter in San Francisco, Bergeron-Sykes, liked her work; of course, they were anxious to please Arthur, who insisted they be impartial. But then they—and he—decided she shouldn't be handled by the same gallery that handled him, so they sent her to Leacock's on Powell. Jarmin Leacock, a slender, balding man from an old San Francisco family, studied her slides for weeks before calling, while she barely slept.

"Should I call him, or wait to hear? Should I send the slides to another gallery at the same time? What's the protocol? Don't you think Leacock is stuffy, too proper for my work? He'll never like what I do; it's too far out for him."

"You'll hear from him, Trish. And he won't take you if he can't do you justice. He knows his clientele. His gallery isn't stuffy anymore, not since he acquired Still and Smith. He's committed to the contemporary scene and taking chances. I've been interested in the gallery myself."

Arthur didn't take her fears seriously. Leacock would not want her. Bergeron-Sykes was the top contemporary gallery in the city, and Leacock was a close second in prestige. She was basically a beginner, maybe aspiring too high. She'd felt guilty leaving Marlene Cuttman, but Marlene's gallery, Far Horizons, hadn't grown beyond the local Oakland scene, and it was time to move on, even though Leacock's was so lofty. Marlene was pissed.

"That's gratitude for you," she said, when Trish told her she was looking for a new gallery. "It's tough out there, lady. Don't say I didn't warn you. And don't let your husband's fame go to your head. That's your work you're peddling, not his. I think you should do more time in the boonies with me than try for the big stuff before you're ready. You have a long way to go, kiddo, let me tell you."

Trish didn't need to be told. Marlene knew her exact weak spot and, in a burst of sour grapes, pressed it hard. Trish dearly wanted to stay clear of Arthur's coattails.

Amazing—Leacock liked her work, offered a limited arrangement. She was an old hat at those. He'd take a few pieces for a group show he was putting together entitled "Esoterica: From the Sixties Looking to the Seventies." Would Arthur consider putting some work in the show too?

Arthur declined—contractual obligations prohibited him—but she saw a spark of something in his eye. He and Jarmin Leacock were kindred souls; they even curled the sides of their mouths upward in the same cynical way. Whenever she and Arthur spent time with Jarmin, he and Arthur overlooked her. It made her feel like jumping up and down and waving her hand to be noticed.

The show was reviewed and Trish's work praised. "Her otherworldliness, juxtaposed with the exquisitely rendered figure dominating the paintings, leaves a haunting impression. Trish Baldwin combines the best of surrealism with reality in the abstract; she celebrates the joy of womanhood in a time when discontent is rampant among women." Best of all, the pieces sold.

After the review, Leacock offered her a one-woman show, schedule permitting, in eleven months, which would be December, a long time to wait, he said. She said coolly, "I don't mind." And then, when she'd left his blasé presence, she leaped and jumped with glee, shouting, yelling, laughing. There had never been such a high. She held the feeling to her heart with such tenderness, as though it were the baby she'd been trying to have. For the first time she actually felt worthy. Recognition. It was finally happening. She called Hillary.

"I'm so thrilled for you," Hillary gushed. "It's fabulous. Maybe Mel and I can come to the opening in December if we go to California for the holidays."

"That would make everything perfect," Trish told her, feeling as if time were short.

She had three paintings completed that had not been in the group show, and would have several more by December.

In 1968 her own world had a rosy glow, even though the rest of the world was in turmoil. But the assassination of Martin Luther King in April and Bobby Kennedy in June, even the terrible escalation of the war in Vietnam and the impending presidential race between Richard Nixon and Eugene McCarthy, didn't prevent her or Arthur from working to capacity. It was a productive time for both of them. Trish anticipated her first one-person show with joyous excitement, and spent evenings during the middle of her monthly cycles trying to get pregnant.

In September, Arthur had a nasty fight with Claude

Bergeron and severed his relationship with the Bergeron-Sykes Gallery.

Jarmin, who had become Arthur's close friend, commiserated and offered to represent him. Arthur agreed, and Trish grew apprehensive, wondering how this would affect her career.

Two weeks after Arthur signed his contract with Leacock's, Jarmin called. "Trish, I'd like to take you to lunch. How's Paoli's, twelve-thirty?" Jarmin's voice always jarred, made her pulse race as though being with his gallery were a dream, and she'd awaken to find it had all vanished.

She stammered, "I never go to lunch, Jarmin, it breaks up my workday. In fact, I never eat lunch."

"It's important, Trish."

She could hear that it was; all the more reason to stay home. She'd been afraid to relax lately, unable to ask Arthur why it was all right for Leacock to represent both husband and wife, but it hadn't been all right for Bergeron-Sykes. Had that policy, which she'd thought was written in stone, been shattered? Or was it just Arthur's sense of whimsy? Leacock was *her* gallery, tenuous though it was. Would Jarmin drop her? No way, she told herself over and over. Arthur was unapproachable, his sole response was, "We'll work it out."

"I'm coming to you," Jarmin insisted, when she kept refusing lunch. "I'll bring a basket of goodies like Little Red Riding Hood."

Trish hated the analogy. "Wine or beer?" she offered, when he arrived.

"Neither, we'll need vodka, for the caviar."

She began to shake.

Jarmin looked guilty; that tightness around his eyes must be guilt. Carefully he opened his lunch, a tray of finger sandwiches, watercress, sliced olives, anchovies, and then caviar, sour cream and crackers, and ratatouille. Chocolate wafers for dessert. She poured him a vodka, herself a 7-Up.

"So?"

They looked at each other across the book-laden coffee table; she watched a fruit fly hover over the bowl of apples and grapes. Clear September weather etched the Berkeley hills sharply against a white-blue sky. Zinnias cut from the garden filled a water bottle; the cat purred on the sofa next to her.

"I have some news." His eyes were focused just slightly to the left of her ear; she wanted to turn and see the person he was talking to, but it was she.

She plunged ahead, noticing that she couldn't get his attention even when Arthur wasn't here. "Are you ready to photograph the announcement card for my show? I haven't picked the painting yet, can't decide. I need your expertise. Have you heard any more about the catalogue? What did the San Jose Museum say?"

"There isn't going to be a show or a catalog, Trish," he blurted out. "At least not with me, not now. I've had some difficulty with my calendar. Marilyn Johnson is ready much earlier than I expected, and Jake Berman must have January, and now, with Arthur joining us, the rest of the year is taken. I'll have to move you back at least another twelve months. It's not fair to you. I know it's not. I can't expect you to wait another year for a show after all your hard work. You're free to go, if you wish. I'm letting you out of your contract."

The bottom dropped out. A knee-jerk reflex: she put out her hand to stop the fall but fell anyway, scraping her heart on the way. Her hand grabbed the nearest thing for support, the vodka bottle. The liquid in the bottle in its iced container somehow made it into her 7-Up, into her mouth, down her throat, before she even tasted it. The warm glow from the liquor sprang instantly to her thighs, turned them into mush. No matter, she'd already fallen. A voice somewhere inside was crying, *Noooo!* But all she said was, "No show? I don't understand."

He tended to become short-tempered easily, another similarity between him and Arthur. "I explained it quite clearly. You are the newest member of my group—well, actually, Arthur's the newest, but you have the least exposure."

"I'm the most expendable."

"I wouldn't put it that way."

"Does Arthur know about this?"

"Let's not bring him into this."

"I thought we were going to work it out."

"Work what out?"

"Us both being represented by your gallery."

"There's no conflict with that, it's a scheduling problem, dear." The more she pressed, the snappier he got. "I explained it clearly," he'd said, implying *If you can't understand, it's too bad*.

She understood. The pain of understanding pounded in her head. "If Arthur hadn't been available for you to represent, this wouldn't have happened."

"Yes, it would," he insisted, too rapidly. "I was overextended when I took you on. Besides, a man in my position can't afford to turn down an artist of Arthur's repute."

"You have many artists who are more famous and whose work is higher-priced than Arthur's."

"He's on the verge of a breakthrough, Trish. I'm going to see that he gets it. You wouldn't stand in his way, would you?"

God, she was thirsty. "It looks like he's the one who's standing in mine." Like a hypnotic suggestion made during a trance, something made her stand up abruptly, as though she were forcing him to keep her place in spite of Arthur. Her sudden movement knocked over the pedestal dish of chocolate wafers; the cat came to life and made a lunge for the one that fell on the floor. The room tilted; her head felt heavy, as though it might topple off like the wafer, pulling the rest of her with it. Something smelled fishy, then she recognized the scent of anchovies. Poor cat, the scent was probably driving him crazy.

She turned too fast toward Jarmin, spilling some of the drink she'd just refilled. The room spun. "Get out," she said, not as firmly as she'd have liked. "Take your food and shove it." She raised her glass in silent salute to her group training, picked up a caviar sandwich and tossed it to the cat, then ate one herself. "I've lived with Arthur long enough to know when he's instigated a situation." She was slurring her words; more vodka would take care of that. "He once instigated me into marrying him. And he once instigated himself into an orgy. Said it was 'one of those things.' I was too stoned to care. And now he's instigated himself into your gallery and me out of a show, and you've let him. You're as bad as he is." Rambling now, how embarrassing. The thought of her paintings without a show to show them made her so sad. Tears spilled over from the well of sadness inside, she licked them with her tongue as they rolled down her cheeks. The vodka was keeping that well of sadness from gushing forth.

"I thought you were leaving," she snapped. "Go on!"

He was at the door, looking back at her, unable to go or stay. "I'm sorry, Trish. You're a fine artist. Any number of galleries will snap you up."

She tried to snap her fingers, but no sound occurred. "Just like that," she said, "no snap. It's a snap. No, it's a cinch." She sat back down on the sofa, unable to get up. Such a long time without a drink or a pill or a hit, and for what? "For an asshole like you?" she said, out loud, waving him away as though he were inconsequential. "Arthur's gonna hear from you!" she said. "No, that's not right. Arthur's gonna hear from me, and you're gonna hear from Arthur."

Jarmin left.

"Jarmin the varmint," she said, reaching for the bottle. She finished two-thirds of it before passing out.

Angry silence pounded in her head, along with dizziness and pounding of another kind. "Oh, baby, I'm so sorry," Arthur apologized. "I never thought he'd do that to you. But you can't let it beat you, baby. He's right, someone else will grab you. That bastard—do you want to sue Jarmin?"

"What good would it do?" The defeat had worn her down. "If I forced him to give me a show, there wouldn't be any honor in it, and it would take longer than another year."

"Then I'll drop out of the gallery too. He can't do that to you and get away with it."

"Okay," she said, slurring her words. "Drop out."

"I will," he said. "We'll discuss it when you're sober."

"I can't let you do that," she said, wanting to cry again but feeling plugged up.

"Well, maybe it's not such a good idea for both of us to be looking for a gallery at the same time."

The vodka wore off but she scored some uppers and had the best sex she'd had in months, hating Arthur with her entire being for supplanting her, making her obsolete, but needing him to fill the awful void inside. It wasn't his fault; he felt terrible. But his ego wouldn't allow her go to Bergeron-Sykes, and she couldn't go crawling back to Marlene Cuttman, either. Anywhere else she went, it would take a year to get a show, not to mention doing the rounds again, poised for rejection—no, poised to be poisoned. Any way she looked at it, it stank. In a fit of despair, she sent her slides to McGarrity's in New York, the new contemporary gallery in Lower Manhattan that had caused a stir by discovering so many pop artists who were becoming famous. They were located in SoHo, the area south of Houston Street. She didn't tell Arthur she'd sent the slides, didn't talk to Arthur, except to make love to him. She blamed him, even though it wasn't his fault. Maybe it was the blame, but the baby they both wanted wouldn't get made. Just as well; she was empty of everything, good for nothing, wanted to destroy her work, Arthur's work, hated the feelings of resentment and jealousy she felt toward him. And he was so understanding, so kind. He championed her, made suggestions, praised her. "You'll get something soon," he assured her.

In November she got a letter from her mother, asking them to come to Iran for a visit. It seemed like a good idea.

"We can't leave now," Arthur said. "My show is next month."

"What show?" Her question echoed in a hollow cavern.

"The one I've been working on. The one with Jarmin."

A show? "You're having a show next month?" She stared at him. "You didn't tell me it was this soon." She was completely unprepared, felt her insides ripping apart. If only she'd known what he was going to say, she'd never have been sober. "You got my spot, didn't you?"

Two circles of bright color sprang to his cheeks. "It wasn't your spot. The show set for January wasn't ready to be moved up a month, and I was. I was supposed to be shown in February, but they needed someone to fill December. It just worked out that way."

"It just worked out that you took my slot? That was my show! Jarmin lied to me. You both lied to me. What did you tell him? That you wouldn't sign with him if he still handled me? Is that it? What were you afraid of, that the reviewers would mix us up because we're married? We don't even have the same last name."

"Of course not, baby. I'd never do anything like that to you."

But he had done it. She knew it by looking at him. Her own husband. The enormity of it slugged her again and again in the gut, ripping her apart even more. Unbelievable. She wanted to claw and tear at him. She was looking at him, and he looked the same, but she was seeing him for the first time. All that blame and resentment she'd been feeling guilty for had been justified. He deserved it and more. "I must be a damned good artist, Arthur, for you to be so afraid of me. Or did you tell yourself I'd gotten some kind of unfair advantage? What kind of a husband are you? You destroy, that's all you do, destroy! Well, I won't let you destroy me! Not anymore."

He stared at her, caught. "You don't know what you're talking about. You're acting crazy, Trish."

"You cheated me out of this show and this gallery, and you say I'm crazy? Didn't you, didn't you?" she screamed, wanting her fury to attack him the way his betrayal had devastated her. "Well, it doesn't matter, it doesn't matter what you try to do to me. Because I'm younger than you, baby, and I'm a good artist, maybe great; I have a lot to say and I'm not afraid to say it." It sounded good, but it wasn't altogether true, only in her good moments. She was usually terrified to say out loud what was inside of her, she only knew how terrified she was when she got wasted and saw the difference between facing her realities head on and dodging them with dope. She turned away from him and went into the bedroom, took a suitcase down from the top of the closet, and began to pack. She was shaking with fury. *And I wanted to have his baby*.

He followed her, stood in the door. "What are you doing?"

"What does it look like?"

"Where are you going?"

"Away from you."

"But where?" He sounded genuinely scared.

She was scared too. She'd never been anyplace without him since they'd gotten married. "To see my parents."

"Don't go, baby. I'm sorry. I'll make it up to you."

She turned to look at him; how different he looked,

suddenly older, lined, not so glamorous, definitely hateful, almost repulsive. How amazing that his ego couldn't take the competition with his own wife. His own greed was driving her away, and she'd loved him so much, gloried in his success, admired him, revered him, wanted to impress him. Well, she never could, not if he was threatened by her. The way he was made her sick. In a flash she thought of all the times in their six years of marriage that she'd overlooked this. He'd never praised her, always made her feel small, put her down, suggested that she quit, courted her failure, and now, the final blow, he'd sabotaged her. The fight with Bergeron was probably his subconscious making its first step in an elaborate plan to hurt her career. Of course he'd deny that; he didn't even know he was doing it. To him, self-protection was paramount; he always made sure he got his before anyone else. The way he'd wormed his way in with Jarmin, oozing pleasantries—Arthur was seldom pleasant. Male bonding, she knew all about that. Some men were threatened by capable, strong women, wanted them weak. And she'd married one, played right into his hands. God, had she been weak. The knowledge was too much to take all at once. He was standing there and she felt the sudden pain of losing him; he was still Arthur, sexy, brilliant, exciting Arthur Matalon. She remembered when she used to think of him like that, first and last name together, the Art Department's lion, king of the nubile students. He protested against university restrictions, unless his fellow protesters were militant females, and then he'd call them dogs, dykes, hoggers, or no-talent cunts. "You're really a sonofabitch, aren't you?" She wanted to cry, but she was so filled with hate that tears wouldn't come.

"You knew what I was when you married me."

"No, I didn't," she said, "but I do now." And she turned back to her packing.

3

Whenever her anger waned, urging forgiveness, Arthur fanned the flame. His natural belligerence rose to the top like the seeds in her orange juice, making it impossible to watch him steal what she'd worked so hard to achieve. Be the dutiful wife? Not this time. Arthur took her to the airport.

"Don't go, Trish, it's nearly Christmas." Anguish made him youthful again. She remembered the first time they'd made love amid the flowers; he had barely aged since then. She had, a lot. At least she *felt* old, at twenty-eight.

"Goddamn you. You're so stubborn. We can work it out."

She heard the Beatles singing it; their version was better. "You always say that."

"Don't expect me to be waiting for you."

"I won't." His threat was like a bee sting.

"And what are you going to do over there? Join some fucking harem?"

Sadness enveloped her, something inside closed itself to him. She'd never felt as strong as this before, almost autonomous. The "almost" part was because she was leaving but she wasn't really alone; she'd be with her parents in Iran. It took courage to go from one authority figure to another. Arthur had a new respect for her, she saw it in his eyes. *I'm lucky we couldn't make a baby.*

Her plane was announced, and Arthur grabbed her and hugged her tightly, bones embracing bones. He was trembling. She assumed it was a hangover rather than emotion for her. He held her at arm's length. "Little Trish, take care."

She was reminded of going off to camp.

As the plane taxied off, she sobbed, feeling torn from

her moorings; the pain was excruciating. If the plane had had engine trouble and turned back, she would have kissed the ground at Arthur's feet and begged him for another chance. But there was no engine trouble. The plane took off smoothly and kept on flying, taking her away from the man she loved, and hated.

Shortly after takeoff she started to feel sick to her stomach, and for the entire flight she couldn't keep any food down. Between trips to the closetlike lavatory, she slept. The plane stopped in Rome twelve exhausting hours later, and, after a layover of two hours, flew on to Tehran. The sight of Mount Demavend, Iran's highest peak, rising above the city, covered with snow, helped her forget about her physical distress; glimpses of the desert terrain were exactly as she'd imagined, familiar, like the land around Palm Springs.

But the moment she disembarked she sensed the difference of a totally alien environment. At once joyous and intrigued by this adventure, yet lightheaded and ill, she'd have run away if she'd had the chance.

Her parents looked both self-assured and nervous. Her mother smiled and waved shyly; her father's officious expression said, *I know just what to do here.* And he did. He got her through customs, though it took forever. Several times her belongings were searched, which kept her from her parents and allowed her to bridge the gap, to overcome the estrangement of the different cultures between them. Her artist's eye took in details of this city: women wrapped from head to toe in black or navy *chadors,* others dressed in Western clothes, looking fairly cosmopolitan; officials repeating the same function, each distrusting what the other had just done; vendors carrying trays on their heads filled with steaming cups of tea; fruit peddlers; toothless people, aimless people; children sleeping, crying; flies buzzing; and obvious drug deals being made from hand to hand in handy packets. It was both exotic and vile. She couldn't wait to paint what she was seeing.

Her parents stood out like actors on location, Dorothy Malone and Leon Ames, good old Mom and Pop. Her mother was exactly the same but heavier: her face powder too white, her blond hair combed into a perfect cap, wave on top, large curl over one ear, her eyes round and startled. Her father's face was lined, more severe, and he'd lost weight, which could account for the increase in lines—no more portly Matthew. He was a new person without his stomach protruding, almost dapper. She wondered what he patted now with satisfaction after a meal. Certainly not his wife's knee. He was more military than ever, and Trish felt wary of him, guilty, from seeing an obvious drug deal being made. Getting high could certainly soften her reaction to her father. Her parents were making progress with her entrance visa, and kept smiling, gesturing, and not looking at her directly, to avoid revealing how appalled they were at the way she looked. She wore her usual handmade sandals, batik blouse, love beads, braid down her back, and leather miniskirt; her purse was made out of the top of a pair of blue jeans. She was kindred to a million undergraduates and postgraduates in America, but here life was *different*. When she realized how they felt, all the progress she'd made—in therapy, in her life, in understanding herself—disintegrated. She was their little girl again, anxious, timid, inadequate, feeling her happiness deflate.

Finally she was through customs, briefly hugged as one hugs a servant, and off they went in their American car to their Americanized Iranian home.

On the way, the sights and smells flung themselves at her. "You're not taking Pahlavi Boulevard, are you?" her mother said. Matthew ignored the advice.

Suddenly sirens began wailing, heralding a line of jeeps full of soldiers in a procession. Matthew pulled over while they whizzed by, followed by cars full of official-looking men, then a long, shiny black Rolls-Royce with two men in it, and finally an identical car with two women in it. Along the four-lane highway, citizens waved Iranian flags of white, green, and red for their Shah, his wife, Queen Farah, and members of the government who were entertaining the premier of Italy and his wife.

"Whenever the Shah leaves his palace, the streets are blocked for twenty minutes to two hours," her mother explained, "which is why I didn't want to take this route."

"It didn't take long, though, did it?" her father snapped. Trish had forgotten how the sound of anger in her father's voice affected her, an exasperated tone that she now understood to mean, *Even here in this foreign coun-*

try, Patricia, you're still the same. Then, as though he wanted Trish on his side, he reached back and squeezed her hand. "It's wonderful having you here, honey." It made her want to cry.

Exhaustion overwhelmed her; her body didn't know what time of day it was, but she fought sleep for the need to see this amazing land.

Her parents lived in Shimran, a suburb on the outskirts of Tehran, but at a higher elevation, so it was cooler in the summer than in the heart of the city. The Shah's summer palace was here, in the village of Tajrisch, and the important Iranian families had summer homes here too; foreigners like her parents lived here all year. The house was typically Iranian, a huge, two-story monstrosity completely enclosed by a high wall that opened into a Persian garden, in the center of which stood a sparkling swimming pool. The brown-yellow bricks of the house were made in Tehran. Most of the residences Trish saw as they drove through the city were built of these bricks.

Her mother was eager for her company, touched her hand and brushed wisps of hair from her face, which both saddened and annoyed Trish. If only she'd been like this when Trish was growing up.

There were many servants, each employed for a different function. The gardener and his family of three children lived in the small gatehouse, another servant greeted them at the door, still another ran to get the tea service, and several young women stared and giggled at her from various vantage points.

Patricia showed her to one of the many bedrooms in the house, and she climbed gratefully into the bedding on the floor that a servant had prepared for her.

Once she was awakened by the unfamiliar sound of a call to prayer chanted from the rooftops in the neighborhood, but then she sank back into her Persian bed and slept until daylight.

The first morning in a strange land was like awakening to a new life. Off with the old world, on with the *new* old world. Her room overlooked the pool and garden, where a profusion of flowers bloomed and the aquamarine water sparkled in the sun. She could see herself taking a swan dive off the balcony into the pool below, though she'd probably crack her head open if she tried. But the sight of the clear water and colorful flowers made her want to soar.

In search of breakfast, she wandered around the upper floors, and then the ground floor, looking for the kitchen. When she found it, a shock awaited her. The kitchen was separate from the house and hardly big enough for two people to work in, though there were three people in it now, seated on the floor, preparing food. There was no counter space, but only an open charcoal-burning stove, with two huge copper kettles next to it. Just then her mother appeared, and led her, as though she were demented, back upstairs to the dining room, far away from the sights and smells of that terrible place. She explained that since servants prepared all the food for wealthier Iranian families, kitchens were not built for convenience or comfort.

"We have our own garden where we grow things ourselves, and we have our own well, so the water is pure. You don't have to worry about dysentery," her mother assured her. She studied her daughter. "You're so thin, dear. I know it's fashionable in the States, but here a woman is considered beautiful if she has meat on her bones. One of the highest compliments a young girl can receive is to be told that her face is shaped like the moon."

Trish smiled, thinking "moon face" had always been such a joke in college. Her mother, always so thin and conscious of her weight, was obviously glad to have an excuse for her extra pounds.

"Tell me about Arthur. How is his career going?"

What about my career? Trish wanted to ask, but she squelched the bitterness. At least her mother was being civil about Arthur.

"Didn't you write me that he was having a one-man show this month? I was surprised that you weren't staying home to be there with him. Such an interesting man he turned out to be. Even your father is interested in what he's doing. I'm sure he's going to be very famous one day, even more than he is now. Many of our friends here, some of the professors at the university, have heard of him."

So that was the reason for the change in heart about him. It would have been amusing if it weren't so sad.

Since her parents liked Arthur now it was more difficult to confide in them. "We've been having some problems," Trish said.

"You know how these artists are, Trish. Be flexible." The subtext: *You might lose him.* Trish nodded politely. *You never forget,* she thought, *like riding a bicycle, how to behave when you're with your parents.*

Her mother lived like an empress, with servants at her elbow. Trish watched, surprised, how she directed them with ease and control. The tea was poured steaming hot from a brass teapot into attractive china cups, the honey cakes were gooey and dripping, the bright orange melon slices tasted like ambrosia. There were dry, ricelike cakes as well as sugar buns, blood-red orange juice, a hot cereal, warmed goat cheese, and toasted brown bread with preserves. Trish ate hungrily, realizing that she'd lost every meal she'd eaten since she left Berkeley, but after a few bites she seemed to lose her appetite.

"Where's Dad?" she asked.

"He's gone to Riyadh to confer with the Saudis."

The moment I arrive, he leaves, Trish thought, feeling rejected and yet relieved that she could postpone her father's interrogation.

"The Fluor Corporation there is developing a technology that could be useful to our oil industry here, and he's checking it out. He just couldn't rearrange his schedule." Her mother sensed her disappointment, identified with it. Trish had never realized that as women they had much in common. Whatever their men wanted came first.

"Saudi Arabia is an interesting country, but much less developed than Iran. I'm ever so grateful we're living here. The Saudis don't allow nearly as much westernization of their women as the Iranians. And the social life here is quite active, actually more than I can handle. Tonight, for instance, there's a reception at the university for the Italian premier. The Shah will be there. And tomorrow night, I thought I'd have an informal reception in your honor, invite some of our dear friends here in Tehran, introduce you to the young set."

Reception?

"I'd rather you wouldn't," she said, but didn't stay to argue because her breakfast was coming up. She barely made it to the bathroom. Later, when she was lying on her bed mat again, Patricia brought her some herbal green tea, a local brew said to soothe the stomach.

"It's my bridge day, dear. Don't forget the university party tonight. It's black tie; do you have a formal gown with you?"

Trish suppressed a laugh, wanting to say, *Do you prefer my patchwork jeans, or the Indian cotton skirt?* But she decided to feign illness for tonight's formal gala, give herself time to acclimate.

She spent her first day in Iran exploring the city, driven by Mohammed, the gardener, who doubled as her driver while the chauffeur drove her mother. They careened through narrow, winding, unpaved streets, dodging people who meandered back and forth, peddling, shopping, bargaining, surviving while cars nearly crashed into them at every turn. And wafting through the air more often than she could stand was the unmistakable odor of hash or pot. She'd come to the source and hadn't even realized it. Or had she? Insisting that Mohammed let her out to walk, though he protested vehemently in his limited English, she managed to score a small amount of hash before Mohammed forced her to get back into the car. The hash helped her ignore the fact that she was still unable to keep food down.

By Friday night she was ready to meet people, and for the party in her honor she wore a white antique lace blouse, a long black velvet skirt that had once belonged to a San Francisco dowager, and her mother's pearls. She entwined flowers from the garden in her waist-length hair. The group was gray-suited, brocaded, and fond of alcohol. Anachronisms kept walking through the door, as though the sixties hadn't happened. Hillary would have been right at home. Nibbling on soda crackers, the only thing she could tolerate, she stared vacantly at the faces of the Americans in Iran—businessmen and their wives, professors from the university—and at the well-dressed Iranians who spoke English and had been educated in America, their wives arriving in *chadors* that they unwrapped to reveal French couture silks. Everyone asked her about her husband and his work, and thought she was very modern and courageous for traveling here by herself. If she approached a group long enough to join in the discussion, it invariably focused on trouble at home:

student rebellions, the outrageous behavior of young people these days, the proliferation of drug use, sex (the word spoken in a hushed tone), and how glad they were that they were raising their children in a normal environment. They blithely disregarded the terrible poverty of this country and the implicit caste system it perpetuated, the lack of democracy, not to mention the blatant oppression of women, the exploitation of the poor who served their every whim, and the brutal treatment of political dissenters. Trish laughed to herself as she realized that, to them, she was the expert deviant. She didn't withhold a thing.

"Yes, orgies are commonplace now. I've visited a few myself—never participated, actually, but I know people who have." That bit of news spread through the room like a noxious odor. "Everybody does drugs. It's part of the creative process." Not quite as shocking as the first bomb she'd dropped. "No, I don't think we should be in Vietnam. Why do you think there was a national turn in Draft Card Day, November fourteenth? The government lies to us, you know. Sure, I march and protest, I've been arrested many times, hasn't everybody?" One by one, her parents' friends withdrew, solidly turning their backs, until finally her mother took her aside and, with a face red with anger and embarrassment, ordered her to stop. She agreed.

Tonight's party was a stand-up, Iranian style; guests stood around the buffet table, which was laden with immense platters of meat, fowl, rice, vegetables, breads, fruits, and flowers, and ate from small plates, using fruit knives and forks. A hostess could serve more people that way than at a sit-down, and the number of guests one entertained increased one's status proportionately. Patricia had gone all out for this one. Strings of flashing electric lights outlined the entire house, the enclosure wall, and all the trees in the compound. Strings of lights were very big here all year long, one of the guests explained; since the country was Moslem, no one thought of them as Christmas decorations.

Names and faces ran together like their after-shave and eau de cologne. She found herself dancing with one military haircut after another in old-fashioned suits. Only one man wore his hair in the current style and sported

bell-bottom pants with his doublebreasted jacket; he stood
out among the others. His blond hair fell in bangs over
his forehead, and his sideburns came down in front of his
ears. His wife was dressed in a brocade miniskirt and vest
to match, square-toed shoes with buckles on the tops and
a daring silk chiffon see-through blouse, which would
have revealed her flat chest if it weren't for the vest.
They were Connor and Maureen O'Brien, and they were
in their mid-thirties. He was in computers, and she was a
fashion designer not too happy about being transferred to
this unfashionable desert.

Trish introduced herself and found them intriguing,
especially his gray-blue eyes, when he looked directly at
her.

"Can you believe it?" Maureen said. "I'm at the height
of my career, with a boutique on Carnaby Street, and he
takes this bloody assignment." Her hostility burned. Maureen was Irish, with dark red hair, pale skin, red lipstick,
and black eye makeup, and had been born in Ireland;
Connor was Irish-American. They'd met in England, where
his company had sent him to open their English branch.
Married six years, they had no children; Maureen's career came first. "Mary Quant inherited all my customers."

Trish watched Connor while his wife complained. He
knew Trish was observing them, and it embarrassed him.
Trish found that endearing, felt sorry for him that his
wife was so insensitive. "Couldn't you get someone to
run your store while you're here?" Trish asked Maureen.

"The shopgirls steal you blind if you're not around,"
she said. "Besides, London inspires me; that's where I
need to be, to observe the street scene, see what's happening, you know, be in the thick of things. It's such an
exciting time. *In England.*" She gave her husband a nasty
look then, and walked away, leaving him there. He watched
her go, and ran his fingers through his hair, as though
controlling exasperation. He had a bump in the center of
his nose, and Trish wondered if he'd ever broken it. It
gave character to his otherwise handsome features, his
deep-set eyes, wide forehead, and strong jaw. The Irish
coloring, the freckles, the large frame, made her think of
a Nordic warrior. But Trish had never seen anyone so
wound up before. When she bumped against him accidentally in conversation, every muscle in his body was

tensed as though he were performing isometrics. She wanted to reach out and gentle him, as one would a nervous animal.

Suddenly he turned and looked straight at her, and she felt his eyes boring into her. "What kind of art do you create?" he asked.

The question surprised her. "My own kind," she said. "I hope it expresses me, and yet involves the viewer emotionally."

"I'm glad you didn't say 'pretty pictures.' "

She laughed. "Now do I look like someone who would make pretty pictures?"

He smiled, and she was amazed to see how young he was. She hadn't noticed before that he was her age. "Would you like a glass of wine, or a whiskey?" she offered, wishing she could somehow calm him; the energy emanating from him unnerved her. His eyes bored through her again, and she saw dark flecks in the gray-blue color. "I don't drink. You shouldn't either, if you're not feeling well."

She didn't recall telling him. "You're in computers?" She knew nothing about them and cared less, but he was the only person in this entire room she identified with even slightly. She'd had no idea that being in a foreign country would make her feel so completely alien, or that it would be the Americans who would make her feel foreign herself.

"Yes," he replied. "Sorry about Maureen, she's not too happy here. How long are you here for?"

Meanwhile, his eyes cased the room, clicking over each face. She could tell he knew some of them, didn't know others. He seemed like a computer himself, but there was more to him than he let on. Then he turned his attention back to her. "You really haven't been well lately, have you?" As he said it, she realized she still wasn't.

Odd, but he seemed worried about her. He took her hand in his, as though to ward off danger. She was picking up the strangest vibes from him—more mixed messages, she thought, than a drunken fortune cookie stuffer. Her hand felt small and protected in his larger one.

"I've got some kind of bug, from traveling. I may have to make a dash."

He moved his hand up to her wrist and held it, looking at her, trying to figure something out. Her stomach began to quiver again; she didn't want to have an accident all over him. Then he placed a warm hand on her forehead, surprisingly gentle; energy vibrated from him like the tight muscles of his body. He stared into her eyes. "There's no fever, so sign of infection, your eyes are clear. It's something else." He moved close to her, studying her intently; for a crazy moment she thought he might kiss her.

"What is it?" she asked, when she realized he was assessing her. She thought, *It must be psychosomatic. I'm making myself sick because I didn't want to leave Arthur but couldn't stay, and I don't want to be here either, and yet I can't leave.*

"That's not it," he said, as though he'd read her mind.

It made her feel so strange; she yanked her hand away from him, feeling chills go through her. Suddenly she didn't want to know what he thought. She turned to go, knowing she'd be lucky to make it to the bathroom in time.

His voice followed her through the crowd. "I know what it is. When you're ready to find out, I'll tell you."

This is too much, she thought, reaching the bathroom just ahead of one of her mother's guests. Connor O'Brien's odd behavior made her shiver as she retched. She decided to avoid him. But when she came out and he was gone, she felt a sense of loss.

4

Lying by the pool, being waited on by servants, suited
her while she floated, trying to assess her life. Arthur was
cut off from her by distance and by her need to keep him
away. It proved easier than she'd expected; as more time
passed, he assumed an aura of unreality. Maybe it had
something to do with Connor O'Brien. She thought a lot
about him, but kept reminding herself that he was married. Her parents would be furious if they knew what she
was thinking, especially her father. But Connor was the
first man she'd ever been attracted to like this, except
Arthur. Eventually she'd have to come to some conclusion about Arthur, but not now; whenever she was awake,
he was asleep, and so they were distanced by time. Being
so far away had rearranged her references; she felt encased by this new life, the way its women were encased
by their *chadors*. She wanted to explore, to find inspiration for new work, but couldn't go places alone because
women didn't do that. So she accompanied her mother
on her daily outings: volunteer day at the hospital, a
meeting to plan the spring charity flower show, trips to
buy Christmas presents, and lunch in other women's homes
or at the American Embassy club.

There was tension between her parents that she'd never
recognized before—a dissatisfaction with one another—
though her father was kind to her. "I should have been at
your wedding," he told her. "I've regretted it." Then he
hugged her. Had it always been like this? She couldn't
recall. Her mother was frightened of her father, and
Trish could see why. He was demanding, judgmental,
fault-finding. Iran's ethic of male supremacy had gone to
his head. Aware of Trish's disapproval, he circled her as
an animal circles an interloper, in wide circles at first,
sensing danger, then narrowing the circles with every

turn until he was ready to pounce, to force her back into the mold from which she'd been trying to escape.

While she watched her parents spar, two weeks passed and still she felt listless, her stomach upset with a nonspecific malady. It could be from the altitude (Shimran's elevation was two thousand feet), the time difference, the dry climate. She thought it probably was from taking drugs after abstaining for so long. If that was the case, then more drugs would help. Hash was sold on the street in small quantities, and if she was going to buy, she might as well get enough to take some home. Maybe she'd even sell some of it, make a bundle.

She celebrated Christmas with her parents, exchanged gifts, and called Arthur in Big Sur, where he was spending the holidays.

"Hi, baby. How's everything? I missed you at the show. It was a huge success. The reviews were mixed, but I got one great one."

"That's nice." It was as hard as she'd thought it would be.

"When are you coming home?"

"I don't know."

"This is getting stupid, Trish. Embarrassing. Everyone wants to know what's going on with us. I don't know what to tell them."

"Tell them I'm fine."

"I want you to come home. Right away. Definitely by New Year's, you hear!"

"I'm not ready, Arthur."

"Goddamn you," he shouted, "then you can go to hell." And he hung up.

Later, at a party for Shell Oil executives and their wives, she looked for Connor, but he wasn't there. Her disappointment was acute, and she redirected her anger at Arthur toward Connor instead. If she didn't diffuse it, she felt that havoc would ensue. Finally, her mother's friend's chauffeur told her about a hash dealer in the city who could get her all she wanted; he would be her intermediary. She agreed.

The next day he came for his money, but she knew enough not to hand him two hundred dollars for a kilo of hash, or she'd never see him again. They arranged for him to take her to the dealer for a twenty-five-dollar fee, a month's salary for him, a lot of money for her, too.

Ali drove madly down one narrow, twisting street, nearly killing everything in his path. She bounced wildly in the back seat of Lillian Burton's Mercedes, carpeted with Persian rugs, thinking herself mad to be doing this. The *chador* she had borrowed from Kooba, one of her mother's servants, was hot and smelled of body odor, but gave her anonymity. Strangely, it encased her body, yet allowed her fantasies free rein, stimulating her imagination. Wearing native dress made a difference in the way Persian men regarded her, with a kind of possessiveness they didn't express when they knew she was an American. Bondage had interesting aspects, so long as she could go back to being free and independent anytime she chose.

The longer she remained in Iran—and she realized three weeks was not much—the more she was incensed by the way Moslems treated women. In her world, women marched for equality and spearheaded changes in society; here women were in a dark age, grateful that their status was now more liberated than it ever had been in the history of the country. The veil was not required (though it was worn anyway), and women could vote and were in college and business. Yet the majority considered it a sad day when a daughter was born. Women were thought of as weak; through them dishonor might come upon a family. It was infuriating to be so discriminated against, never to be able to show yourself in public, never to be allowed to touch or kiss your loved one if a third party was present, to be forbidden to swim in the ocean, to join in male social company, to hold public office, or to inherit money or property equally. And not only could your husband have another wife, but he could divorce you simply by saying "I divorce you" three times before a magistrate. And Iran was more liberal than other Moslem countries.

The car stopped suddenly, throwing her forward against the front seat. Ali shouted at the car that had swerved in front of them and stopped at an angle, blocking their way.

Now the two drivers would get out and argue furiously over whose fault this was; it could take hours before they agreed on anything.

A crowd gathered, cars were backed up in every direction, drivers begged to be let through the narrow *kutche*. But Ali stood his ground, protecting the car of his employer. After forty minutes of this, her patience used up, she reminded Ali that they were meeting someone.

He sprang to life, glancing up and down the narrow, twisting street in confusion. Obviously the twenty-five dollars she'd promised him was an incentive. Then, ignoring the furious protests of the other driver, he took her arm, walked her forcefully through the crowd surrounding them and down a nearby *kutche*, this one with a stream, or *jube*, running through it. "What about the car?" she asked, amazed that he would leave it.

That stopped him for a moment while he considered. "We come back," he decided finally, leading her away, while drivers honked and swore.

The muddy, deeply rutted street was difficult to walk on and she was sure they were lost, but Ali walked hastily, turning at corners and alleys. As they were walking along past stalls, shops, and cafés, Trish glanced into a café and noticed three men having coffee. Two were Persians, but their blond Caucasian companion caught her eye. Connor O'Brien. Her heart bumped when she saw him, and she wondered what he was doing here. He glanced up just as she passed by, but she ducked her head so he wouldn't recognize her.

It was getting late, and Ali kept looking at the sun, trying to judge how much longer it would be before it was time for evening prayers. Trish could tell he was concerned about leaving the car. Then, from far away, they heard the undulating wail of a siren approaching; Ali grew agitated as it came closer. Finally he stopped and pointed to a street of shops covered with fiberglass and canvas roofing. "You go there," he said, giving her a shove, "I go car. Meeses no happee, no car. Poleece take. No good, no good. I go now, I find you." And he took off at a run, leaving her there alone.

She turned to where he'd pointed and saw a typically crowded bazaar, dirty and hectic, similar to all the other bazaars, but this one was covered. Did that make it an obvious drug market, she wondered. And where was the dealer? The purse she carried suddenly felt transparent, as if every vendor in this tightly packed, frenetic place could see the money inside. She was grateful to be wearing a *chador,* and wished she knew more of the language than just a few words. The street was filled with rug merchants, brass dealers, bead vendors, jewelers, grocers, and every other form of shopkeeper, all hawking their wares. She kept her head down and her eyes averted as she moved through the crowd, excited by the adventure. Her stomach was getting queasy again, but the danger of being alone was enough to make her feel ill. The farther she wandered, the fewer women there were, but she didn't realize that until she looked around and saw she was the only woman here. A group of scruffy Persian men in a café stared at her, gesturing about her in a universal language every woman understands. Realizing what an idiot she was, she turned around and started to make her way back.

"Pssst!"

Someone called to her. A dark-skinned, nearly toothless man in a laborer's gray, pajamalike outfit beckoned; he was even more filthy than was generally acceptable. He stood in the doorway of a shop that looked like a blacksmith's supply, but the interior was dark.

A thrill of fear shot through her; she ignored him and kept walking while her heart pounded. Was he the dealer, or someone who wanted to harm her? She'd never felt so sorry for her actions in her life, and kept walking, back to where she'd come from. He was alongside her in an instant; she smelled his odor, even more pungent than the smells of food, dirt, smoke, and animals that filled the air.

"You buy, you buy," he said, tugging at her purse. "You buy. Many dreams, you buy."

Her heart lurched and she tried to keep away from him, walking as rapidly as possible, less aware of direction than of trying to get away.

The man had a large bag slung over his left shoulder made of pieces of carpet sewn together with wool; he shifted the bag to his right shoulder so it was between them; she felt it push against her hip. There was a hard, brick-shaped object in the bag.

"You look," he said. "Look, look."

But she kept walking until he nudged her hard with his elbow and held the bag open so she could see. More hash than there was in the whole world.

She glanced around, wondering if anyone else had seen, but in this crowd he'd been unobserved. If this was the man she was supposed to meet, he would know how much she'd agreed to pay for the hash, but these people always bargained for everything and she didn't speak his language. Ali was going to do that, damn his miserable driving skills. Suddenly she realized that she ought to get back to Ali by now, but nothing looked familiar. In her nervousness she had gotten lost.

The man stuck to her side, no matter how she tried to get away from him. She forced herself not to panic. Keeping her eyes down, she walked with purpose, as if she knew where she was going, while the dealer kept pace. "You look, Meesey, you buy. Have dreams."

He was eyeing her purse, and eyeing her as well, she could tell. He was taller than she, thin and wiry, and she wondered if she could outrun him. "No dreams," she said. "Go. Go." She gestured to him to leave her alone.

But instead of leaving, he got furious, grabbed her arm, yanked her to him, and stuck something into her side; she tried to twist free, but he held her hard, pressing a sharp, pointed object into her.

A knife.

For an instant her brain didn't grasp it, but when he pressed the weapon forcefully against her waist, she couldn't mistake his meaning. Terror shot through her.

This can't be happening.

Ahead of them and to the left was an archway over a darkened alley. He was pulling her toward it. If he got her in there, they'd never even find her body. *Think, my God, think.* She reached into her purse and took out some money. She waved it at him and threw it into the air, then started yelling, "Yaa, yaa!" over and over, at the top of her voice. The man at her side was startled for a moment as people in the street noticed the money and began yelling and diving for it. But her abductor didn't let go of her. In fact, she could feel the knife pressing into her so hard it was cutting her. She was crying and still screaming in a kind of Arabic wail, so as to cause a disturbance. Her right hand clutched more money from her purse and she waved it at him, wishing she could see his reaction, but he was behind her and she was afraid to turn, with that knife pricking her skin.

Just then a young Arab boy darted toward them from the right, snatched her purse out of her hand, and shoved something at her abductor with a violent thrust. She heard a popping sound. Her abductor fell forward, trying to catch himself by grabbing her, but instead the knife he was holding plunged into her side. An excruciating pain shot through her, and she cried out as she stumbled. Nearly unable to get free of him, she pushed him away and almost fell over him. He lay on the street in front of her, a scarlet pool of blood spreading from a bullet wound in his chest. His eyes stared at her, glassy and in shock.

In terrible pain, she sank to her knees, feeling the warmth of her own blood flowing down her side. She still didn't understand what had happened. Her hand closed over the bag of hash he'd been carrying, and she picked it up, forcing herself to stand again. She had to get away from here.

As she stood, the knife that had stabbed her fell to the ground; she heard it clatter and then felt another gushing sensation from her side. She pulled herself away from the man while people rushed over to see. She nearly fainted.

The people crowding around were bumping into her and she cried out in pain, terrified that she was going to be trampled to death right here in this fly-infested alley. She grabbed hold of a nearby wall and helped herself up, sidestepping away from the body. Then she slowly moved back through the crowd of wailing, shouting people, trying to avoid notice. Frantic with fear, she fought to stay conscious, feeling more alone than she'd ever felt in her life. The blood still oozed down her side.

Again she was jostled, and more pain shot through her and she nearly fell, but someone grabbed her arm, and this time she cried out, "Oh God, help me."

A man's voice said, in English, "I'll help you."

She turned and looked into the eyes of Connor O'Brien.

5

"What are you doing here?" she gasped, clutching him so she wouldn't fall down. "Did you follow me?"

"Yes. Just keep moving."

"But that man was shot." She was crying from terror and pain, which was so agonizing she could hardly keep from screaming.

"Let's go!" The tense muscles of his surprisingly strong arms half carried her along, but the pain became her entire world.

"I'm hurt," she managed to gasp, and he realized that she was. He touched her there and she cried out, her head reeling.

He stayed calm. "My car is just around here." He pointed to another alley. "Can you make it?"

"I don't know." She wanted to, but the world tilted crazily, and darkness formed a circle over her eyes, closing off the light in the center.

He caught her as she fell, lifted her up, and carried her the rest of the way. She was conscious when he put her into the backseat of his car, but then lost awareness again except for an occasional jerk or bump as the car raced along, until they reached the American Hospital.

He carried her into the hospital and she heard a commotion as the nurses said, "She's a Moslem woman, they prefer not to be treated here. Unless you're her husband?"

Connor O'Brien swore at them. "She's an American, dammit, the daughter of an executive with Shell Oil."

Then hands lifted her from him. Light, she was so light, she floated through the air, settling on a bed that rolled down the corridor. On her side, her good side, she saw him hurrying next to her. He was carrying the bag in his hand. *Where did he get it?* she wondered.

"Tell the radiologist I have to talk to him," he said.

"Yes, yes," the attendant was saying. They wheeled her into a brightly lit room; she felt as light as a feather on a sill, ready to blow away with the slightest breeze.

A man's voice spoke firmly to O'Brien, quieting him. "We'll take her to X-ray right away, just calm down. Is she your wife?"

"No, no, a friend."

Floating away, from grayness to darkness, and darker still.

But she heard, "You don't understand," and sensed a terrible urgency in Connor's voice. "You can't X-ray this woman."

Why not? she wanted to ask, but feathers didn't speak.

"We have to," the doctor said, "to determine the extent of her injuries."

Then she heard him say, "You have to be careful, because she's pregnant."

Before she lost consciousness again, she thought, *So that's what's been the matter with me.*

Her mother hardly left her side. The professional volunteer finally had a worthwhile cause.

Arthur called and offered to come and be with her; she said yes, wanting him desperately, but in the middle of their conversation they were suddenly cut off and he didn't call back. For the first time she broke down and sobbed, though crying made the pain in her wound much worse. She needed Arthur's arms around her, wanted him to hold her the way he had the last time she'd been in the hospital. She forgot about what he'd done to her, she only needed him. She hadn't even told him about the baby. *My God, a baby. I could have lost it before I even knew it was there. How did Connor know I was pregnant?* She couldn't wait to ask him.

Her mother's friends paid her visits, asked the same questions as her father: What were you doing in the streets all alone? Why were you wearing one of those Arab dresses? What's the matter with you, are you crazy? Aren't you lucky that Connor O'Brien happened to be there? *What was he doing there?* she wondered, and then recalled seeing him in a nearby café.

To call her lucky was an understatement. Every time the door to her room opened, she hoped it would be he, but he didn't come. She asked the nurses if they'd seen him, told her mother she needed to thank him. No one knew that she wasn't the one who'd told him about the pregnancy.

She'd lost a lot of blood from being stabbed, but fortunately the injury wasn't serious, though the knife had missed her kidney by centimeters.

"We're very grateful to O'Brien, of course," her father said. "But any one of us would have rescued you under the circumstances." There was resentment in his words. *But why?* Trish wondered.

"His wife, Maureen, is coming to see me tomorrow," she told her parents.

"How kind." Her mother fidgeted. Matthew did too, making Trish even more curious.

"His wife's a lovely girl," Matthew said.

"Do you know them well?" Trish thought of Connor O'Brien as her hero. He'd saved her from death, but could he save her from herself?

She wrote him a note, hardly adequate to express this bond between them, and gave it to his wife when she arrived, embarrassed that Maureen might see how she felt. But Maureen didn't notice.

"Connor's gone back to the States on business," she explained. "Told me to tell you he's glad you're well. As the French say, *pas de quoi.*"

She was terribly disappointed. Once she left Iran, she might never see him again.

"Your parents are delirious about the baby, your dad especially. Beaming, he is."

Her father beaming? Amazing.

Her mother opened the door to her room and, finding Maureen there, smiled a sick-sweet smile.

Maureen's thick false eyelashes, over her Irish green eyes, batted politely. Her auburn Ann-Margret hairdo crackled with electricity from the desert dryness.

"How are you, Pat?"

Trish felt tiny electric shocks shooting through the air, and wondered if her mother's hair might begin to stand on end. She was mystified as to whose movements on the carpet had caused the charged atmosphere.

Maureen waved good-bye and sauntered out, swinging her round, narrow hips.

Tears were rolling down her mother's cheeks. Trish wondered if the baby in her womb would someday be as confused by her as she was by her own mother. "What is it?"

"I think your father is *interested* in her."

The pain in her stitched-up back throbbed sharply as she caught her breath. The irony was too incredible. *Like father, like daughter?* "What the hell does that mean?"

"She's a home-wrecker is what it means," her mother said, wiping her face with a handkerchief. "Of all the couples in Iran, why did you have to get friendly with them?" The anger was turned on her now. "You really know how to attract trouble, don't you? Ever since you got here. My friends are talking about what a scandal you are, the way you dress, the things you say. You told Marian Wilson she was behaving like an ugly American when she fired her maid. But the woman was stealing from her. And you lectured Mariza Assiz on women's rights, got her all stirred up. She's a Moslem, for heaven's sake, what can she do? I'll tell you what she did; she talked back to her husband and he's threatening to send her home to her family. Do you know what a disgrace that would be? You can't come in here and expect to change the order of things. One can see you've become a liberal. I surely hope you haven't become a Zionist, too. And going to that bazaar dressed like a beggar woman. I'll never understand you risking the life of your child on a whim, for curiosity and adventure. This isn't Berkeley, it's Tehran. More goes on here than meets the eye. I don't know, sometimes I think I've failed with my children. You're a hippie, an embarrassment to your father, and your brother is . . ." A sob caught in her throat.

"Tommy is what?" she asked, afraid to hear what her mother would answer.

"He's a disappointment to us. Thirty-one years old and never married. Isn't anyone good enough for him? When was the last time he dated a girl on a steady basis, I ask you? It's really affected your father. He would never have looked at a creature like Maureen if he wasn't so disappointed in his children. Neither one of you has turned out the way we expected. Maybe it's the times, but it's hard to be a parent."

Trish heard her mother's words as arrows of pain.

She'd always known that was how they felt, but now, hearing it firsthand, it hurt terribly. She turned away to hide the tears that swam to her eyes. *It will be different for us,* she told the tiny fetus in her womb. *I'll listen to you. I won't force my ideas on you. I'll let you be who you are, and love you no matter what.* Her mother was crying now.

"What do you mean, Dad's interested in her?"

"He'll get over it," her mother said, reaching for her compact to pat away traces of unhappiness. "These things happen in the best of families." End of discussion.

For days after she was released from the hospital, she thought about her father's interest in Maureen O'Brien, another woman, right under her mother's nose, a social acquaintance, here in this tight-knit community where everyone knew everyone else's business, in a country where a wife could be executed for adultery. How could Maureen prefer her father to Connor? She felt so sorry for her mother, yet admired her courage, the way she carried on in the staunch British tradition of her heritage. But most of all, Trish wondered what had caused this chink in her father's armor. In a strange way, it made him more human—that he could feel passion. The idea embarrassed her. How little she knew him. He had disappointments too, dreams of his own. It was easier to believe she was the only one capable of dreams. Was that why her father opposed her being an artist, because it reminded him of what he hadn't done? Neither of her parents would talk about their problems with her, or with each other. Now she could see why it was impossible for her to confide in them.

Two days before she was scheduled to return home, she asked to have lunch with her father at the office.

"Sure you're well enough?" he asked, pleased by the request.

She was nervous, anticipating what his reaction would be if she pried into private matters. Yet she just couldn't leave, couldn't go back to the States, without broaching this subject. She wanted to understand.

The executive dining room could have been in any city in the United States, except for Iranian food served by Iranian waiters.

She borrowed an outfit from her mother, a fitted suit

from the fifties by the California designer Adrian. It had shoulder pads, a peplum over the tight, straight skirt that hit her just below the knees. Pregnancy had filled out her figure and she felt quite womanly in the costume, as she thought of it.

Her father's pleased expression when he saw her touched her, and she smiled at him. Then she realized how so much of what she'd done in the past had been designed to displease him. He pulled out her chair for her, beckoned to some of his associates, and introduced her. "My daughter, Mrs. Matalon, about to make me a proud grandfather."

Maybe she wasn't such a disappointment to him after all, or he to her.

"So," he began, and she was reminded of the tea parties she used to have when she was a child, pretending to be grown up. "Quite an adventure you had. I thought your mother would faint when they said you'd been stabbed." She thought she saw tears in his eyes, but he turned away. "I was pretty upset myself." He composed himself and turned back. "Why didn't you tell us about the baby? Well, no matter. I'm sure Arthur will be glad to have you home, though we'll miss you."

"I'm sorry we didn't have more time together," she said, suddenly aware that he was telling her he cared.

"I envy you young people these days, free to have the kinds of marriages you do, free to experiment. Not like us old sods, stuck in our ways, forced to remain there. You know what you want, and it's different from what we wanted. So many more opportunities for you than there were for us. You think I'm not aware that I'm reactionary. Well, I notice, believe me. The sixties have affected me too. All this free love. Nobody's a virgin anymore when they get married."

She couldn't believe her father was saying such things. "Does it matter?"

"Not really. Besides, you're a married woman now, about to have a child. You know, having my first grandchild is a milestone in my life, too. Makes me think how time flies. Better take your chances now, before it's too late. If it isn't already."

"What are you saying, Dad? What chances do you want to take?"

"My career, for one. I was passed over as senior vice-president. Should have stayed in the States and protected myself. The company need top people to come to these outposts, but then we lost our place in line. Out of sight, out of mind, when it comes to executive promotions. Don't mind telling you, I was bitter. I've given up a lot for this company."

"Like what?"

"America, for one," he said, leaning forward forcefully, bumping the table and rattling the glasses. "You think it's easy living here? Ask your mother, though she makes the best of things."

"Do you?"

"What?"

"Make the best of things?"

"Certainly," he insisted, blustering.

How strange to find herself sitting across from this reasonable father assessing his life, looking at the scheme of things at fifty-five years old. What had erased that judgmental, austere parent, allowing this confidence? Maturity in her? She hoped so. This new Matthew unsettled her, though she liked him better. Then she saw a flicker of the old Matt as his expression changed, stiffened; she followed his stare and saw Connor O'Brien coming toward them, his nervous eyes darting around the room, never connecting, until they connected with her.

"Hello, Matt," Connor said, "Trish." His voice softened when he spoke her name. The two men shook hands. Trish watched them for signs of awkwardness and found plenty, but then they were both awkward men.

"You're back, I see," her father said. Connor's body exuded wariness, and a sadness, too, that Trish felt in her bones.

She gazed up at him. "I'm so glad to see you." And she realized how much she meant that. "I'm going home in a few days and wanted to thank you in person. I didn't think I would see you."

He nodded almost jerkily, ran his fingers through his thick, sandy-colored hair, turned his haunted gray-blue eyes on her. "Maureen gave me your note before she left."

"She's gone?" Trish asked.

"England," her father answered.

And then she knew it was true; her father was seeing this man's wife. A woman her own age. She looked from one to the other. Would they come to blows? She wanted to cry with anger for them, for herself, for her mother. How guilty she felt for her feelings about Connor. How casually she'd accepted the reality of infidelity. *He's having an affair, she's screwing her brains out, happens every day.* But not to her parents. *It's okay for you, and not for them?* She felt her cheeks get hot; again, O'Brien seemed to know exactly what she was thinking and was embarrassed for her. And yet everything was left unspoken, and politeness governed.

"You never told me why you were in that bazaar that day," she said.

"You never told me, either."

"You knew though, you found my package."

"I was in the area on business."

"What package?" Matthew asked.

"What business?" Trish asked. "Certainly not computers."

"None of yours," O'Brien replied.

Hurt, she turned to her father. "I was buying dope." She wanted to shock him now, hurt him too.

"Lower your voice!" Matthew said.

"What did you do with it?" she asked Connor.

"Threw it away," he said. "I knew you wouldn't want it, once you knew about the baby."

"You didn't know about the baby?" her father said.

"But I do want it." She ignored her father's question, wanting to shock Connor too, blaming him for his wife's behavior. "You had no right to dispose of it without my permission. I paid in blood for that package."

"Then you're stupid. Isn't it time you grew up? You can't be both a child and a parent."

She resented him for seeing her so clearly. "How did you know about the baby?" It was as if they were the only two people in the room.

"I read the signs, they were all there. You just hadn't looked. It was a very stupid thing to do, to ignore what was happening to your body. That's what dope does to you, makes you a dope."

"I don't like the way you're talking to my daughter, O'Brien," her father said.

How can you tell I'm still a child? she wanted to ask him. *And if you know that, do you know how I can grow up?* But she didn't dare, when he was looking at her with such disapproval, as though her father's behavior were all her fault too. Then, without giving her any answers, without responding to her questions, though she knew he'd heard them, he turned and walked away.

"Insufferable bastard," her father muttered. "Heard a rumor that he's CIA."

So that's it, Trish thought.

"If he's CIA, I'm the Queen of Sheba."

"And listen to who's talking," she nearly shouted, overcome with disappointment that O'Brien was walking out of her life and she'd never see him again. "Is your behavior so exemplary that you can criticize him?"

Matthew's temper flared. "How dare you talk to me like that. You're nothing but a filthy drug addict. I won't allow that tone, do you hear me? I may be ashamed to admit it sometimes, but I'm your father, and you'll show me respect."

There he was again, the father she'd always known, so certain of his position, capable of meanness, treachery, and betrayal, yet still demanding respect. Something about this situation was terribly familiar. She had a sense of déjà vu. And then suddenly she saw Arthur's face superimposed on her father's. They were so much alike. For the first time she saw it with total clarity.

She wasn't certain to whom she was speaking, Arthur or her father, or her fantasy of them, but everything came pouring out. "You have the gall to tell me how to behave, when you're cheating on my mother with another man's wife? That man would be justified in hating you, but instead he saved my life and you don't even thank him. You're the one who should be ashamed!"

He stared at her, stunned that she would breach the etiquette of family silence. In their family, no one ever said what he meant or what was true; truth was couched in euphemisms and shadows. Then what she'd said really sank in, and his fury and rage exploded. "You loud-mouthed brat, you'd better apologize this instant for overstepping your bounds."

But there were no more bounds for her to overstep, not where he was concerned. Only truth. She waved it like a flag of emancipation, her private declaration of independence, the first step in growing up. "Look, Dad, I don't mean any disrespect, but you're acting like a fool. Maureen is too young for you and she's boring, she's shallow, lower-class. You think she'll recapture your youth for you. Well, no one can do that. It's gone, Dad. Face it! She's using you to hurt him, though what he's done to deserve it, I can't imagine. But she enjoys torturing him. You're nothing but a toy to her. I can't believe you'd be fool enough to be used like that. You must be desperate." Insights came pouring out; she attributed them to O'Brien, as though his apparent ability to read minds had rubbed off on her. Or maybe the insights came from being married to Arthur and being held in bondage by just such a man as Matthew.

Her father was staring at her in disgust as though she'd let out a foul odor. "I think you'd better leave."

Quite calmly she said, "No, Dad, I think I'll stay. I'm not through. And don't use that tone of general to lowly private with me. *I'm* disappointed in *you* this time. I'm hurt and upset and I want you to know how much I hate what you're doing."

Her father stared at her for a long moment while neither of them breathed. She had no idea what was coming, but his face got redder and more furious. And then he just crumbled. He put his face in his hand, and his shoulders shook. At first she thought he was laughing, but then she realized he was crying. Matthew Baldwin crying, no, sobbing. She reached over and covered his other hand with hers, waiting while he cried, holding in the sound, except for the rapid intake of air. Her heart ached for him.

Finally he quieted, wiped his eyes, blew his nose, sighed deeply, and took a drink of water. He couldn't meet her eyes. "If you don't mind, I'd like to be alone for a while. Why don't you stay and order lunch. I'll see you at home tonight."

"Don't leave, Dad," she pleaded. "Stay and talk to me." It was the first time she'd ever felt close to him in her life, felt she'd gotten through his austere façade to the real person inside, and now he was shutting her out again. "Please stay."

He looked up at her with such sadness it made her

want to cry along with him. "I'd like to, Trish, but it wouldn't be right. Your mother needs you even more than I do right now. And I really wouldn't know what to say." He pushed his chair away from the table and left, stopping only to arrange with the captain to pay her bill.

She felt so badly for him; obviously his well-ordered life had come unraveled and he was clutching at the pieces. She hoped for all their sakes he could make it right.

Watching him go, she thought of herself and Arthur; the two of them were just like her parents, and it was a disturbing thought. She'd be damned if she'd allow herself to have the look in her eyes she'd seen in Connor O'Brien's, or the expression on her face she'd seen on her mother's. She had to think of her baby now, she couldn't bring up a child in a home where its parents didn't nurture one another, help and support one another. Marriage was not every man for himself and every woman for him too. Then and there, she made a decision. When she got home, she would ask Arthur for a divorce.

6

When she came out on the street into the bright light of the afternoon, Connor O'Brien was waiting for her. The sadness of her encounter with her father still hung there, clouding her greeting, but seeing him lifted her spirits, even though she was annoyed with him too.

"I have to talk to you," he said.

"I thought you did that already. I'm a child and you know best how I should live my life. It's amazing how all the men in my life feel they can tell me what to do. It must be something about me. And yet every one of them is really screwed up." She was including him in that group, but realized, after her conversation with her father, that she could not let Connor O'Brien be one of the men in her life.

"Come inside." He took her arm and led her back into the building, into a small deserted conference room off the lobby. They sat on a sofa, facing a flower-filled garden with a fountain in it. Trees shaded the circular walk around the fountain. The sound of splashing water added a sense of peace to the room.

"I feel I must explain something to you, even though it might not make much sense." His eyes gazed steadily into hers, no nervous darting here and there, such as she had seen before. But his hands were tense; she could tell it was from wanting to reach for hers and thinking better of it. "As you must know, I have to get my life in order. So do you. I surmise you've been thinking about a divorce. I have too. But since I met you, it's become more urgent."

Now it was her turn to be surprised, and she was. "I make it more urgent?"

He leaned forward, his elbows on his knees, his head down. She saw him swallow, saw his Adam's apple move slowly up and down in his throat. Then he sat up and looked at her, and she felt jolted by what she saw, felt something warm and tender enter her with his gaze.

"I have no right to say these things to you. There should be at least be preliminaries between us, a coffee date, or dinner and dancing." He smiled. And again, she realized his smile was wonderful. "I would love to take you dancing, somewhere on a moonlit terrace. But you're leaving now, and neither one of us knows what will happen in the near future." He sighed. "I just feel that preliminaries aren't necessary with us. We shared something that day in the bazaar that makes them obsolete. What I'm trying to say is that I feel connected to you. I have this desire to protect you. I care, that's all. I'd better leave it at that."

She didn't know what to say. But she felt the truth of his words. The two of them were connected. She cared about him too, a lot, and she was definitely attracted. "All those days in the hospital, I prayed that you would visit me, and when you didn't I felt terribly sad."

"I left Iran because I didn't trust myself to be with you. I don't know what it was, but from the moment I met you, I wanted to be with you."

"It could be that you're just clutching at me because of Maureen. Afraid to face the hurt you must be feeling."

"I thought of that. I don't think so."

"I have the same reason to be drawn to you—a terrible marriage."

"But you have a child to consider." He shook his head as if this was all so impossible, then looked at her as though dismissing the impossibilities. "As I said, we don't know what the future will bring, but I think you and I are important in each other's lives."

"As friends?" She smiled.

He grinned, and then laughed. "You know better than that." The expression in his eyes made her feel glad inside.

She leaned forward and kissed him lightly on the lips. Then she pulled away and they just stared at one another, acknowledging this new bond between them. "When I get my life in order, where can I reach you?" she asked.

He handed her his card. "They'll always know where I am."

She nodded and took it. "I can't make any promises, Connor. As you said, neither of us knows. This is very awkward. I hate the idea of going home and wondering whether you and Maureen have worked things out. For my parents' sake, I want you to, but for my own, I don't. I can't plan my life based on what you do. I don't even know you."

"It's the same for me. And you're pregnant."

"But my marriage is over," she stated, surprised at how sure she felt.

"Then will you let me know?" She didn't know he was holding her hands until he let them go. "When you're ready for me, I'll be there." He placed his hand on her cheek, caressing her for a brief moment, then he stood up and left without looking back. She felt a terrible emptiness overtaking her. But then in a moment the emptiness was gone along with the guilt, replaced by a buoyant sense of happiness.

Something about a long flight of many hours prepares one for a shift from one world to another, the way a journey by covered wagon once did for the American pioneers, or the way a long sea voyage did for early travelers. Trish cried after leaving Iran. But by the time she got to Amsterdam for her flight home, she was ready to get back. She had a lot to do to get her life in order. And being pregnant and on her own frightened her terribly. She'd have to earn a living. She doubted that Arthur would be generous with her. And now that she was faced with the reality, divorce sounded ugly. She'd be one of *those* women, someone who'd failed.

She slept a bit on the flight over the Pole, and when the plane touched down in San Francisco and she saw the skyline of the city, the whole experience of the Middle East seemed like a dream, except for the reality of Connor.

She searched the crowd awaiting the arriving passengers for Arthur, but he wasn't there. There was only a tall, slender man with brown eyes who resembled him, but this man had fashionably coiffed gray hair and was wearing a business suit and tie. The man grinned at her as she approached him and she smiled back, and then it hit her. It was Arthur.

His arms were around her before she'd recovered from

the shock. "I didn't recognize you," she exclaimed. "What have you done to yourself? The beard is gone. You've cut your hair. I've never seen you in a suit. What are you doing?"

He was laughing gaily. "It's a new me, Trish. I had to find a way to show you how much I've changed."

She was stunned by what he'd done. He wasn't the same man, not at all. She looked at him as they walked through the airport to get her baggage, finding that she was disappointed by the change, and yet intrigued. He was so different physically, and so full of enthusiasm. She felt herself almost being drawn in by him, and held back only with effort.

"I had to show you how overjoyed I am about the baby, Trish. I'm so excited I can't sleep at night. How I've wanted a child. For years. The first time I was married, I wanted one, even three children, but it wasn't possible. And now you're pregnant." He stopped and turned toward her, taking her by the shoulders. His abrupt move caught her off balance and she nearly fell, but he caught her. "Are you all right?" He was terrified that he'd hurt her.

"Yes, I'm fine. I'm only pregnant, Arthur, honestly." Her reluctance to care about him was still very strong, and yet so was his appeal. But the hurt, the betrayal, had come flooding back the moment she saw him, and her scars were reopening.

"I know how angry you must be at me," he said. "I don't blame you. I got caught up by my greed, I admit it. All those years of being an almost-made-it had really gotten to me, especially when I saw the excitement you were generating at such a young age. It brought out the worst in me. And it was all for nothing. The show didn't do for me what I wanted. The critics still aren't raving. And I almost lost you because of it. God, I've beaten myself up about that. But I'm really going to change, Trish. You'll see. It's going to be different now."

She stepped around him and kept walking toward the baggage, her heart pounding with tension. This wasn't what she'd expected, not at all. She'd imagined him to be defensive, blaming her for staying away so long, for jeopardizing herself the way she had, for being infatuated with another man; even if he didn't know, she thought maybe he could see the truth on her face the first time he looked at her. But he wasn't aware at all, didn't blame her, was operating on another set of assumptions entirely. As he talked, proclaiming his love for her and his desire to change, she reached into her pocket and closed her fingers around Connor's business card, which she had kept there during the flight, like a talisman. She could see Connor's face before her, his smile, his intensity, but Arthur's voice and presence superimposed themselves.

"Oh God, Trish, don't ignore me like this. Say something, will you? I've been desperate, waiting for you to come home, praying that you'd forgive me, that we could have a second chance. Don't write us off too soon. We're going to be parents. Doesn't the baby deserve to have both a mother and a father?"

"That's not fair," she snapped, her frustration boiling over. She was surprised at how furious she still felt. "You can't lecture me on parenthood and marriage, and promises to change and expect me to just open my arms to you. Not after what you did to me. How do I know you won't do something like that again? You can't be sure yourself. And now we're bringing a child into our mess. It would be better to make a clean break of it now."

She'd never seen a look on his face of such anguish. "You can't mean that, baby. You can't be that cruel."

They were standing in front of the baggage carousel, and Trish spotted her luggage. Arthur grabbed her bags and escorted her out. She was glad for the break in their conversation. But he wouldn't be deterred. They drove out of the airport and she felt enormous fatigue descend on her. The pregnancy, the flight, her surgery, and now this. Not to mention the strain of meeting Connor and finding herself so drawn to a stranger. Everything had taken its toll.

"Arthur, let's wait awhile until I can get acclimated to being here before we start making plans for the future."

"Then you are coming home?" he asked. "I was afraid you might go directly to a hotel or something."

Her head snapped toward him. That's exactly what she had been thinking, but when he greeted her so eagerly, so full of plans and needs, she couldn't do it. She was still stunned by his appearance. He looked so *establishment*, like the men her father worked with, she couldn't get used to it. And then the importance of what he'd done began to sink in. He'd changed his appearance for her, altered what he looked like to express his change. She'd never have done that for him.

He saw her staring. "Takes getting used to, doesn't it? It was a shock to me too. But I like it. I feel different. Certainly more responsible. Not like the man who was so envious of his wife's talent and so desperately insecure about himself that he'd stoop to sabotaging her career."

She felt tears burning her eyes, and fought the desire to let go. She was so terribly tired. "I'm touched that you care enough about me to do something so drastic. I know how the way you looked suited you, how much it reflected who you were. I just can't get used to this. But I will in time. I'm sure it will only take time."

His hand closed over hers. "I love you, Trish. I'm so sorry for what I did. I hope you can forgive me. Can you, do you think?"

He glanced at her, but she stared straight ahead, watching the towers of the Bay Bridge pass overhead.

"Please say you'll forgive me. I need to hear you say it."

"I don't know, Arthur. I really don't. I guess we'll have to give it some time and then we'll both see."

"We have plenty of time, don't we?" he said, taking her words as a promise. "There's no need to rush things, there's no deadline on it. And in time you'll see how much I've changed, I'll prove it to you so that you'll really know, so that you'll trust me." She felt trapped, as though her former life had tightened around her, pulling her down, like a swimmer caught in an undertow.

She nodded without answering, and turned her head to try to see the blue-green water of the bay over the side rail of the bridge. But all she could see was Connor O'Brien's eyes, the image of his face already fading.

7

It was the middle of February 1969 before Pam was able to return to New York—to cold and snow and desolation. Her father offered to meet her plane, but he was the last person she'd let see her in such a deteriorated condition. Limping slowly through the terminal, relying on the aid of the airport personnel, she felt helpless and demeaned. She expected the cabdriver to be brusque or rude, but he took one look at her and helped her into the cab and then helped her out again when they arrived at her building.

Her apartment was silent, empty. When she entered, she wept from weakness and despair, remembering the dreams she'd had. Charles's presence was everywhere. Hillary had gotten rid of the baby paraphernalia Pam had bought before the accident, and her cleaning woman, Angela, had put food in the refrigerator. But nothing was the same. Photographs of herself around the apartment gazed at her haughtily, mockingly, reminding her of a time when she was unscarred and beautiful. Even after her face healed, she'd never again assume an attitude of elegant superiority, or expect that life was hers for the taking, that she was impervious to the problems that beset others. She'd never model again; that part of her life was over, along with the fantasy of happily-ever-after. Somewhere in this world, her child was being raised without her. Some other mother was rocking him to sleep, brushing his blond, wispy hair, making him smile. She was only twenty-eight years old, but from now on life would never be totally filled with joy again, not in the same way.

And physically she was still having problems. The first week at home she couldn't get out of bed, until Hillary and Dr. Baer, her plastic surgeon, forced her. Then she started going the rounds to her new team of doctors

320

assembled by Dr. Baer, an orthodontist, an internist, an orthopedist, and of course her gynecologist.

Her vision had been affected by the accident, and she was terrified that the condition was permanent. For weeks she didn't tell anyone. Besides, there were so many other things wrong. Her leg muscles were atrophied, and she had physical therapy four times a week, which was excruciatingly painful. Her back ached all the time from the pelvic injury. She still had headaches from the skull fracture, and new procedures were being done on her daily. Her prison-camp thinness proclaimed her suffering for anyone to see. But she didn't see anyone. Afraid and ashamed to go out, she sat at home, staring at the television, not even seeing it.

Her friends and family worried about her, conferred with one another behind her back. Trish called Hillary, Hillary called Joanne, and William called her. After listening to them prod her to snap out of her depression and begin life again, she realized she couldn't regain her momentum until she knew for certain that Charles had accepted the story of Brandon's death. The fear that he would find out what she had done was always with her. So she accepted an invitation from William for lunch. All she'd told him was that when the baby died she'd decided not to marry Charles.

William took her to Madrigal, but Pam didn't want to be seen and declined a front table, making her way slowly and painfully to the back of the restaurant. The effort of getting dressed and going out exhausted her. People stared at the red scar on her cheek, at her emaciated appearance. She ignored their concerned expressions.

"You've really had a terrible time," William said. He was nervous, unable to find the right words. She wanted to ask about Charles, find out what he knew. Even if it depicted her, she'd replay the tragedy of Brandon's death to convince her father.

"You know I was against your staying in New York. I was afraid something like this might happen to you."

She picked at her warm lobster salad, then sent it back in favor of a plain hot consommé. "I-told-you-so has never been a favorite expression of mine." She was surprised that the old resentment and desire to get him were still there. All this superficial fatherly concern would never erase them.

He revolved his glass in a small circle on the table, took a sip of water, trying to find words; but there were none. "It's terrible about the baby, Pam. I'm sorry I never got to see him. I can't imagine what it was like for you. And for Charles too. He was really upset."

"What did he tell you?" Her heart was racing.

"He blamed both you and Hillary. Said you risked the baby's life by going away so late in your pregnancy, and that Hillary was incompetent. She should have hired a trained nurse for the baby."

"Hillary feels terribly responsible, but it wasn't her fault."

"I'm so sorry for you, Pam," he repeated. And she could see that he meant it. If he believed that the baby was dead, then Charles believed it too. That meant Brandon was safe, finally safe. Relief flooded through her.

"What are you planning to do now?" he asked.

Exhaustion overcame her again, and she wished the lunch were over. "I'm going into real-estate development. I've got a project that I started before my accident."

Several expressions flitted across his face, none of which reassured. "I don't think you've quite thought this through."

The consommé warmed her; she was always cold. "Yes, I have. It's time for me to do what I've always planned. I need something real to help me go on." Her pulse was pounding, and she paused to catch her breath. "If I ever get my strength back."

What she always had thought was his anger, she could now see was anguish. "I blame myself for what you've gone through. It's because of me you got involved with Charles. But I'll say it again, Pam. Being a builder is not a business for a woman. Believe me!"

"You still don't get it, do you. I don't give a damn about your opinion anymore. You think you've been noble, protecting me from Charles. But what about the rest of my life? What were you protecting me from then, a father's love?"

He flinched. "You've always wanted more from me than I could give. Ever since you were a child, it's been that way. And I failed you. But in this, I know what I'm talking about. You're free of Charles now, Pam. I am grateful for that. Don't put yourself in a business where you're bound to run into him. I should think that would be intolerable for you too, after what's happened."

"You've never been generous with anything but discouraging advice. That you hand out gladly. But you're the one who screwed up, didn't you?"

"Yes," he admitted. "In many ways."

"Do you think you deserve to walk away from this without paying anything?"

"No. But I pay, believe me."

"Are you into Charles's associates that deeply?" She wanted to hurt him the way he had hurt her.

He flushed a deep red and nodded.

"What are you going to do if Billy and Danny ever want to come into the business?" It had never occurred to her before that her stepbrothers might find themselves rejected too.

"Jennifer and I have not encouraged them to consider it," he said, unable to meet her eyes. Then he signaled the waiter for the check. "I guess this lunch wasn't such a good idea after all."

She realized how furious she still was at him. He'd sold them all out, and all she had left was a need for revenge. "I never thought I'd say this to you, but I'm sorry for you, William." And without waiting for the check, she pulled herself out of the booth and limped slowly out of the restaurant.

It was weeks before she ventured out again, and then only to see Dr. Baer. He was her savior, the only sane person in her insane world. He'd been wonderful to her, patient, caring. He'd even flown back to the Bahamas to check on her postoperative condition after the initial surgery, because she couldn't travel to him. They'd seen one another so often that they'd gotten to be good friends, but his follow-up care went beyond the ordinary doctor-patient relationship. She had developed a dependency on him that he seemed to welcome, and that was turning into a strong attraction. It kept her going. Seeing him was the only thing she looked forward to in weeks that focused on pain and limitations. Knowing that he cared about her, sensing his attraction for her too, made her feel there might be a life out there beyond her own problems. He was the one she turned to when the lunch with her father made her feel like giving up again. He

encouraged her to talk about it until she'd put it to rest,
called her every day until her spirits improved, and promised to make her beautiful again, though she could tell
that in his eyes she still was.

"Look up, Pam," Dr. Baer said, examining her eyes,
when she finally admitted to him she had a problem.
"What do you see?"

"I still see double. It's been like this since the Bahamas."
Exasperation and fear lived with her moment by moment.

"Well, it's not your vision or the eyeball itself that's
damaged. It's the eye socket. The malar fracture caused
a disalignment. That's what's causing your binocular vision difficulty. The inferior rectus muscles may be pre-
venting the eye from rotating upward. We won't know
until we go in and see."

"Go in where?" her voice quavered.

"We'll incise right below the lower eyelid, and recon-
struct the floor of the orbit with silicone if necessary.
Perhaps there's an entrapped muscle. It's an easy operation, Pam. Don't worry."

Her eyes filled with tears. Another operation. More
pain, anesthetic, recovery time, depression on top of
depression, and loneliness.

Dr. Baer gripped her hand with sympathy. "Is there
anyone you'd like me to call, to be with you?"

She thought of Hillary, but shook her head. Hillary
would be there for the surgery. She always was.

Dr. Baer turned her face to the side to look at her
scar. "It's softening up nicely. Another month or two and
we'll take care of it. Shall I book you into Manhattan
Eye, Ear and Throat? Or NYU this time? I can do the
eye surgery the day after tomorrow."

"So soon?" She started to tremble. When new procedures were thrown at her, it took time to adjust.

"Better sooner than later. We don't want to give those
muscles any more time to atrophy."

She sighed. "Thursday's as good as any other day.
You'll be there every minute, won't you?"

He was still holding her hand. "Haven't I always been?"
he asked.

"Your wife is a lucky woman," she told him that day,
as she was about to leave his office. She'd admired the
picture of his family every time she saw it displayed

prominently on the cabinet behind his desk, of a happy, smiling woman with long, dark hair and a vibrant expression, her three children looking like a combination of their parents, smiling mischievously. He'd seen her looking at it, but had never commented. This time his curt nod made her reconsider; maybe they weren't as happily married as they looked.

The morning of the surgery, Hillary picked Pam up and brought her to the hospital at 6:00 A.M. Hillary had left her home in New Jersey at 5:00 A.M. to get there on time. Hillary wouldn't think of allowing Pam to take a cab.

On the way, Pam talked about Mark Baer. "Why do you suppose he doesn't talk about his family? I know he's still married because his wife calls him during the day. He always takes her calls. And one day when I paged him, I heard a child's birthday party in the background."

"He is handsome," Hillary agreed. "Those soft brown eyes, curly brown hair, the teddy-bear type, very cuddly."

"I like the way his smile lights up his face."

"We were impressed with him that night after your accident, when he came to the hospital."

"His confidence made me feel I would pull through," Pam said, remembering how he used to tell her he would do the smiling for her when she couldn't. She'd be crying and in pain, and he'd say, "You really want to smile, don't you?" And he'd give her a lopsided grin, then insist that she tell him exactly how wide to make it. "No, not quite that wide," she'd say. "Yes, a little bit more. Okay, that's just fine." And soon, though she couldn't smile too, her spirits would be lifted.

"You're not going to fall for another married man, are you?" Hillary asked just before surgery.

Pam shook her head slowly, getting groggy from the preoperative medication. "No way, Hil. I'll never fall for another man again, period!"

"Sure," Hillary said, as they wheeled her out of the room, but Pam didn't hear her.

The next thing she heard was Mark Baer's voice as she was coming out of the anesthetic. "Everything's fine, Pam, went very well. The problem should be solved."

"Thank you," she whispered, feeling tremendous gratitude.

Her eyes had to be bandaged for twenty-four hours, an uncomfortable feeling, but she slept a great deal. And then the next morning, as she was waking up with her eyes still bandaged, she heard a soft knock on her door.

"Pam?" a woman's voice said. She could hear the sound of metal clanging, the slow shuffling of feet. "I'm Diane Baer, Mark's wife. May I come in?"

Pam's body stiffened in surprise, picturing the beautiful dark-haired woman in the photograph, in contrast with the way Pam must look right now. Recovering from her embarrassment, she stuck out her hand, but Diane didn't take it. Pam let it fall to her side.

"You have me at a disadvantage, Mrs. Baer. I wasn't expecting company." The annoyance in her voice at having her handshake rejected was plain.

"Please call me Diane," she said. "I'm sorry I can't shake your hand," the woman explained. "I have to be careful of infection."

A real nut, Pam thought. And then said, "Oh, I get it. You must work here in the hospital, right?"

"No," Diane laughed. "Why would you think that?"

"What else are you doing here so early in the morning? I'm sure it's not just to do rounds with your husband, is it?"

"Mark said you were extremely perceptive, besides being brilliant. He's told me a lot about you. In fact, he's talked of nothing else since your accident. He said you had tremendous courage."

"He's a wonderful man and a wonderful doctor, your husband," Pam told her.

"I know," she said softly.

Something was coming, but Pam couldn't imagine what it was. She was starting to feel guilty in the presence of the wife of the man who made her heart beat a little bit faster. But she had no designs on Mark Baer; she could assure Diane of that if the subject came up.

"I wanted to meet you," Diane began, "because I was curious to see how you were dealing with what's happened to you. I wanted to know what you did when despair overwhelmed you. I thought maybe we could compare notes."

"Are you conducting some kind of psychological study?" Pam snapped. "Because I don't appreciate being a guinea pig."

"No," Diane's voice quavered. "I'm so sorry if I've misled you. I thought you knew, that Mark might have told you. I'm in the hospital as a patient. I had a mastectomy two years ago, and after the first series of chemotherapy treatments they thought I was cured. But it's back, and has spread quite a bit. I'm on chemotherapy again."

Pam was stunned. It was the last thing she'd ever expected. "I didn't know," she said. "I'm so sorry."

"Yes, so am I. You see, the loss of my hair for the second time, even the pain, is nothing compared with not being able to take care of my children." She stopped talking, and Pam knew she was trying not to cry. "Please forgive me," she said, finally. "I should never have bothered you. I get a little crazy sometimes. It's the dope I have to take for the pain. Things get mixed up in my mind."

Just then, someone came into the room. "Mrs. Baer!" Pam recognized the voice of the floor nurse. "What are you doing down here? And dressed like that. You'll catch pneumonia in that thin nightie. You wait here while I get a chair to take you back up to your room. I swear," she muttered, and was gone.

Pam heard the sound of metal rattling and clanging again and realized it must be Diane's IV, that she'd wheeled it down here with her. The image of her physical beauty and what she must look like now began to seep into Pam's brain, and she too wanted to cry.

"I don't have much time," Diane said. "Not with you, maybe not at all. So please just listen. I thought that it might help you to know that there are others, like myself, who are worse off than you are. Someone with whom you would not want to trade places. And even though you will recover and I probably won't, I would not have been able to stand the pain of losing my child the way you did, on top of suffering the kinds of injuries you sustained. So you see, I wouldn't want to trade places with you, either.

"But the other thing I wanted to tell you is that I'm aware my husband likes you. Not just as a patient, but as a woman."

Pam could hear in her voice how difficult this was for her to say.

But she went on, "I think that his liking you is a way of helping him to survive what he's going through on my account. He's going to have so much to bear, raising our children alone. I wouldn't want to trade places with him, either, and watch him suffer and know I was going to lose him."

Her voice caught in her throat and she was silent, trying to catch her breath, to go on. Pam was trembling from emotion, and from the tremendous empathy she felt for this woman.

"Please, Diane. Don't talk this way. You don't know what's going to happen. Don't give up."

"I'm not giving up," she whispered. "But I must prepare as best I can. I wanted to tell you that if Mark should turn to you afterwards, if you can help him, it's all right. Just know that it's all right. You deserve happiness too."

The nurse arrived, bumping through the door with a wheelchair. "I've brought you a blanket too," she said. She was trying to help Diane into the chair, but Diane cried out in pain as she lowered herself into the seat. And then the two of them turned to go, with the accompanying noises of metal wheels and poles clanging against a glass IV jar.

"Wait, please," Diane said to the nurse with some exasperation.

Pam identified with her, knowing how it felt to be weak and in pain and at the mercy of someone else's will and agenda. "Thank you for coming," Pam said.

"It was good to meet you," Diane replied. "I've admired your photographs in magazines. I'm sorry I can't shake hands with you."

"I understand," Pam told her. And as Diane left, Pam said, "I hope things go well for you."

"You too," Diane called back.

As she heard the door close, she reached up and touched her breasts, feeling Diane's anguish. It was overwhelming.

She'd been warned that crying would increase the swelling in her eyes and slow the process of healing, perhaps even damage the surgery, so she clenched her arms around her body against the intense need to burst into tears. She could barely catch her breath. She'd never felt such despair for someone else's pain, never seen such courage. It made her want to run and leap with the joy of being alive; instead, she got up out of bed and felt her way to the window, touching the cold glass, knowing that tomorrow she would see the street below, that soon her body would heal, but Diane's wouldn't. She felt that fury again, against a God who could take this woman from her family, the same God who'd taken Brandon from her arms. But it was selfish to think that way. Diane was unselfish.

She knew that somehow this encounter had to make a difference. Making her way back to the bed, she thought of how Mark Baer had given to her at a time when his own life was in agony. She settled herself in bed again, and gripped the sheets with her fists, picturing the faces of his children, imagining their lives without their mother. Diane's words rang in her brain. *You deserve to be happy.* How could Diane not be bitter? Yet she wasn't. Her body might be wasted, but it was still a temple of love, capable of nurturing. The beauty of her soul had lit up the room. Even though Pam couldn't see her, she knew Diane's concern for the well-being of her family was greater than her fear for herself. And she'd been able to surmount self-pity when Pam had not. Pam had wallowed in it by comparison. It was as if Diane Baer had been sent to teach her that. Well, she'd learned it. Never again would she feel sorry for herself. Never again. She'd had painful times, hard times, but they were over. It was time to move on, away from that self-doubt and depression. She had to let it go.

And then she couldn't hold back any longer and let herself cry, sobbing for the pain of the Baer family, for her own loss and suffering, for the unfairness of life. And as she sobbed, she knew it was the last time she would cry like this. She had passed into a new era of her life. She was now finally an adult, about to take her place in a grown-up world.

8

Once Pam learned about the troubles in Mark's life, she knew she could not lean on him, and renewed her own determination to forge ahead in spite of the continual setbacks. In five weeks' time she had nearly completed her physical rehabilitation. The surgery to repair her vision made an enormous difference, since now the headaches subsided; through her newly reconstructed eye sockets, life began to look beautiful again. She increased her physical therapy sessions from three to six days a week, and went on a health regimen that included balanced meals, meditation, and study. During her meditative periods she gave herself positive suggestions, read books on how to overcome adversity, and applied the principles. If she felt herself slipping into discouragement or depression when she thought about Brandon, she diverted her attention to something happy, something pleasant. But the loss of her child was nearly impossible to forget. Yet she knew that if she was ever to go forward, this was her testing time. The one fantasy that worked to divert her darker thoughts was to imagine herself actually building a high-rise office complex on her Madison Avenue property, floor by floor. She read books on architecture and urban planning, reread *The Fountainhead,* and would not allow herself to slip back. And strangely enough, it was Diane Baer who often kept her on track.

After an initial awkwardness, Pam and Diane became friends; Pam visited her often. They grew close in a short time. The suffering they had both endured made a bond between them that others did not share and enabled them to reveal themselves to each other easily and quickly, recognizing that they couldn't afford the luxury of a long period of introduction. Mark kept Pam apprised of Diane's medical progress; unfortunately, it was in a steady decline. But Pam wouldn't accept that.

"She's so full of hope, Mark. Other people have responded to chemotherapy, I know she will too." Now it was Pam who was giving the pep talks.

Diane loved hearing about Pam's real-estate developing, and wanted to know every detail. "My friends are so careful of what they talk about with me; they're afraid to tell me if they're having fun, because I'm not. So there's not a lot to say. I don't want to talk about my nausea, or weight loss, or pain medication. I want to hear about their lives, or yours, how you put together a financial syndicate among your wealthy European friends."

And since Pam didn't want to talk about her physical rehabilitation or the loss of her child, instead she described Tommy, Khalil, and her other partners.

"My father would be impressed by you," Diane commented. "He always wanted a son to follow in his footsteps as a general contractor, but he only had daughters. It never occurred to him, or to me, that I might be able to work with him in his business. Construction was only for men, a philosophy ingrained in us for as long as I can remember. But you don't accept that, do you?"

Pam laughed. "No, but I've heard it often enough."

"You're amazing," Diane told her.

"And so are you," Pam said.

But Diane shook her head. "No, I'm just trying to survive."

As Pam's body rebuilt itself, so did her future. Her friends in Europe were still committed to her project, and she was finally able to send them a financial breakdown. After much discussion they agreed on the details. Each member of the syndicate would have an owner's share of the building, commensurate with the amount of his investment as a limited partner. As the general partner, Pam became president of an autonomous company called Weymouth Development Corporation, which was responsible for the actual construction of the building. Pam's initial investment in the project would be her time, expertise, and initiative, and for that she would receive the equivalent of a million dollars of investment. And once the limited partners recouped their investment, Pam would receive twenty percent of the profits and they would get eighty percent. The syndicate was also reimbursing her for the down payment on the property. She would draw a salary from the construction loan during the development period, while the building was being completed, and then while it was being leased.

She explained to Diane, "Having private seed money to finance this building gives me a real advantage, because I don't have to establish initial credit with a bank. When you're first starting out as a builder, it's almost impossible to get seed capital because you have no track record. And not only that," she added, "but because I was willing to give up some equity in the building, I won't be carrying any debt until we go for our construction loan."

"But your responsibilities are enormous," Diane pointed out. "I know what it takes. The success of the entire project rests on you, and you're the one on the hook for the loan."

Pam shrugged. "Don't remind me, will you?" The responsibility weighed heavily on her, and was sometimes frightening. The syndicate might be putting up the actual cash, but she would be doing everything else, such as dealing with the lawyers over technical issues, hiring the architect to do the feasibility studies, working with the engineers on the final plans, pushing everything through the city's bureaucratic approval process, and then, most important of all, trying to find tenants. As soon as possible, she needed to find a major company that would lease a large portion of the building, someone whose name on the lease would bring in other tenants.

She talked to leasing agents, but they wanted enormous fees and jealously guarded any information they possessed as to who was looking for available space. For her first venture, she would have to lease the building herself. She pored over business magazines and journals, and then wrote letters to the companies she read about that were in growth phases, offering them prime midtown office space. She made calls to companies that were looking to move to larger quarters, and advertised in the *Times* and *The Wall Street Journal*. Soon, prospective tenants began calling her. Fielding their questions, showing her projected architectural studies, talking about rent per square foot and the proposed date of completion, one day she suddenly realized, *I'm actually in business!* And now the excitement that filled her days kept her in its grip. The only cloud on her immediate horizon was Diane's condition. She was still not responding to therapy.

Talking to Diane became a habit. Sometimes Diane called in the middle of the night when she couldn't sleep, knowing that Pam would be awake. For Pam, a full night's sleep was a thing of the past; adrenaline kept her going. Especially when she got a call from the New York National Bank, telling her they wanted to lease the entire ground floor for a midtown branch, plus four upper floors for offices.

"That's fantastic," Diane said when Pam told her the news. She was full of enthusiasm, even though she was in pain. "Having an A-one tenant almost guarantees your profit, doesn't it?" It was wonderful, having someone who truly understood.

She got a feeler from Rensselaer Publishers, who were willing to take ten additional floors. With two major tenants she'd be able to carry the cost of the building until the rest of it was leased.

She celebrated by bringing Diane a hot fudge sundae, but ended up eating most of it herself because Diane had so little appetite.

Diane was getting worse every day. Mark spent most of his time at the hospital; the children came often for brief visits, but Pam stayed away during those times, knowing that they all needed to be alone with one another. She tried to immerse herself in her work so as not to think about Diane, but it was always there, like a dull ache in some inner part of her. Sometimes she was surprised at how deeply she cared about Diane, and she wished she could spare herself this concern, aware that she had somehow transferred her thwarted need to be maternal to Diane, who was certainly needy. But then there were Diane's special qualities, which were undeniable. Pam just didn't want to lose her.

Pam interviewed more than a dozen construction consultants who were to oversee the actual construction of the building, but she found every one of them reluctant to work for a woman. Not only did she need someone who would be on her side, but someone whom she could trust. After all, she knew she would be a target for every kind of overcharge and price scam imaginable. Her construction consultant would be the key to her success, and she would be at his mercy, a place she did not want to be.

It had been a particularly discouraging day, with men not only treating her with disdain, but amused by her. She was looking forward to telling Diane about it, when she arrived at the hospital.

Mark was waiting for her outside of Diane's room. The look on his face told her immediately.

"She's gone, Pam," he said, his voice quiet and withdrawn. "It happened a short time ago. I was with her until the end."

Pam started to cry, and they held each other. "I don't believe it. It can't be true. I was coming to tell her about my day. She would have laughed so much. Oh, Mark, I'm so sorry. She was very brave, and she suffered too much."

"At least that part is over." His face was as white as his jacket. He seemed empty.

"How are the children?"

"They're okay," he said. "I spoke to them. I'm glad they weren't here. Is it selfish of me to want to be with her alone?" His head fell forward as he cried, repeating her name over and over. "I don't know how to go on without her."

"Let me take you home, Mark. The children need you, and you need them."

He let her lead him down the hall. "Would you come by sometime soon? It would help me to see you."

"I'm coming now, Mark. I'll stay as long as you need me. I'm sure there are arrangements to be made. You have family to help you, don't you?"

In a way, she dreaded the ordeal of seeing Diane's family, of being in her home, meeting her children, seeing firsthand the life that had been so cruelly denied her. But she knew that it would be good for her to have something to do. Anything to ease the pain inside.

The Baer apartment on Central Park West was furnished with English antiques; a plaid sofa and chairs stood on a needlepoint rug. A collection of porcelain dolls and miniature teddy bears spoke of Diane's hobbies, and her entire home reflected her warmth and love of detail. By the time they got there, the apartment was filled with family and friends. Watching Diane's three children hugging their father was painful for everyone in the room. And then Pam embraced Diane's mother, who was barely able to hold herself up. Pam met women the same age as Diane, friends whom Diane had described to her. Their children had grown up together, and some of them had gone to school together as she and Trish and Hillary had done. They were grieving for their friend, recalling special moments in Diane's life, comforting one another's tears. One of them, Carole, came over to Pam. "Of all of us, you were the one she turned to at the end. I must confess, it was too hard for me to be there for her, watching her suffer. So many times I was grateful to you for doing what I couldn't do. And a little envious. You made her laugh, you brought the feeling of being alive again back into her life when she needed it most." And she hugged Pam.

As Diane's friends and family kept thanking Pam, she suddenly realized why she had been Diane's friend in spite of the pain of losing her. It was because she alone had been able to do something for Diane that the others hadn't. And in that moment she realized that not only had she hated Charles for making her give up Brandon, but she had hated herself even more. And now she could begin to forgive herself; her friendship with Diane had shown her that she was still a worthwhile person, even though she'd given away her own child.

While she thought about this revelation, Pam made herself useful, ordering food from the caterer, making coffee, emptying ashtrays. Mark sat on the corner of the sofa, receiving friends, hugging each one in turn; he was in shock, as though the light in his life had gone out.

Two days later, after the funeral, they were again at Mark and Diane's apartment. New people to greet, more heartache to bear. Sometimes there was laughter; life, after all, went on. She wandered into Mark's study and found a group of men gathered around a heavyset man smoking a cigar, who seemed to be holding court. She turned to go, so as not to intrude, but a booming voice called out, "You're Pam, aren't you? I'm Diane's dad. I've been wanting to meet you."

He had reddish gray hair, a large frame, and fading

freckles on his leathery face. He wore an alpaca cardigan
over red plaid pants, and brushed the edge of his mus-
tache with his left hand while his right flicked ashes from
his cigar. He stood up, towering over her. "I'm Jake
Harrigan. And you're the lady builder Diane told me
about. Said you were pretty, and she was right." The way
the rest of the men stopped talking briefly to look at her
made her uncomfortable. These men were all in construction, she could tell by their tanned faces and rough
hands, by the way they deferred to Jake and wore their
suits as if they were armor. She nodded a greeting; these
were the men she'd soon be working with, but they
ignored her as if she was of no consequence, just another
woman.

Pam took his large hand in hers. The sadness in his
eyes was obvious to her. Tears came to her eyes and she
reached out and hugged him. "I'm sorry about Diane,"
she said in his ear. "She was one of a kind. You must
have been very proud of her."

She felt his body stiffen as he tried to control his
emotions. He let her go, and nodded, gazing at her with
steady green eyes. "That she was, my little girl. That she
was. Said the same about you. Said you and me had a lot
in common. That we're both fighters." His back was to
his friends so they couldn't see his tears. "Think she gave
up?" he asked, really wanting to know.

Pam shook her head. "No way, Jake. Sometimes there
just isn't any choice."

He nodded again, wiped the back of his hand across
his eyes, and then turned back to his friends with an
expansive gesture. "I'd like you to meet the boys. This is
Curly Miller, he's in masonry; and Bart McCallum, one
of the best electricians you'd ever want to meet; and over
there is Pete DiMaggio and his brother Dino, they're
foundation men; and this here's Federico Pollianno, a
genius when it comes to marble."

Pam smiled, and shook their calloused hands. "Maybe
I should ask you all for your business cards," she said.
"I'm going to be putting plans out to bid for my first
building in the near future."

They just stared, as if she hadn't spoken. "I'm serious,
I'm developing three lots near Fifty-fourth on Madison.
We're nearly ready for demolition."

"You somebody's secretary or something?" Dino DiMaggio asked.

"No, I have my own company."

"Sure, honey," Bart McCallum said with a laugh. "And your building's gonna be unfinanced and empty unless you team up with someone with a track record."

Some of the men nodded, and then elbowed one another. "I do need to work with the right person," she conceded, "but I'll manage the financing and the tenants, Mr. McCallum. And if you don't need the business, I'm sure there's an electrician in this city who does."

Curly Miller shook his head. "Ain't no place for a woman."

"You may be right," Pam said, truly considering his opinion. "And then you'll be able to say you knew it all along. But I'm going to do it anyway, and love the hell out of trying."

"Is this a joke?" Pete DiMaggio asked.

"No," she assured him. "I've got my financing and I'm fifty percent leased."

"No disrespect intended, ma'am, but you're gonna fall on your keester," Pete DiMaggio said.

"If that's all that happens, I'll consider myself lucky."

Pete and his brother Dino both chuckled with knowing smiles that Pam took to mean, *She hasn't got a chance.*

She refused to let herself believe they were right, yet that heavy anxiety lay beneath everything she did.

Jake intervened. "Wait a minute, you bums, my daughter was buried today, and this woman was her friend, and that makes her my friend. Are you pussies so afraid of someone without a beard that you have to make the old lion roar? We've all heard of women's lib. Well, it's starin' us in the face. We're not gonna give her trouble, are we?"

They looked at one another and shook their heads. She wasn't consequential enough to be any trouble. "Not me," someone said, as though speaking for the group.

"But she's gonna give us work, you dunces."

"Her?" someone said with disbelief.

"Sure."

Jake put his arm around her and led her toward the door. "Come on, honey, let's leave these bums to themselves. They're too dumb to know how much nicer it is working for someone who smells like you than for someone who smells like me."

Pam's delighted laughter sparked Jake's, and they fed on each other's mirth. Even the men in the room joined in and laughed too. Jake waved a dismissive gesture at them, and he and Pam walked down the hall to the living room.

"They're right, you know. You won't have an easy time of it."

"I will if you'll help me," she said.

He took his arm away from around her shoulder and looked at her.

"I have a proposition for you," she said. "Can we meet tomorrow?"

He shook his head. "I've got a helluva day, honey. I start early and go till seven, then I'm expecting a shipment in from Cleveland tomorrow night, and may have to be up most of the night."

"I'll meet you anytime, anyplace you say."

"Okay," he challenged, "6:15 A.M., Charlie's Coffee Shop on East End and 38th; it's near my job site."

"You got it," she said. "I'm buying, and you won't be sorry."

9

Charlie's on East End was crowded at 6:15, mostly with construction workers. The cold morning air made her scar stand out brightly against her pale skin, and people stared. She stared back until they dropped their gaze. Mark had said that next month he would be able to repair those two lines that bisected her cheek from her right eye, ending at a V above the edge of her lip, but she was beginning to get used to it, even to regard it as a symbol of her triumph over adversity.

Jake waved to her as she entered. He was sitting in a back booth that overlooked the street, but the steamy windows obscured the view of bundled-up people heading for work. The hot interior of the coffee shop smelled of breakfast. He wore a heavy, army-type jacket, down-filled and scarred with hardened plaster, grimy around the cuffs. His wool cap had left marks across his reddened forehead, and his gloves were piled on top of the cap on the seat next to him, next to a scruffy set of rolled-up blueprints.

Pam's impression was that almost everyone in this coffee shop knew one another. They must come here often. The customers looked at her, an interloper, with undisguised curiosity. The DiMaggio brothers nodded in recognition but not in friendship.

"So, little lady, how can I help you?" Jake asked, after she'd ordered breakfast. She saw three cigars sticking out of the inside pocket of his jacket and was grateful that he hadn't lit one yet.

She pulled off her mittens, slipped out of her coat, and settled back. "So, Jake. Are you interested in success?"

"Sure am."

"I am too. I've already been successful in one business—

actually two, investments and modeling. And I've learned that to be successful you have to have a dream."

"That's true." She had his full attention.

"Do you ever think of how some people get to be a success?"

"Hard work and some luck, I guess."

"If that were true, a man who works as hard as you would be way up there. No, I think it has to do with that dream again, first of all believing you can have it. Then taking a series of steps, one after the other, to make it come true. If there are obstacles, you find a way around them. But each step makes sense only if you know where you're going."

"Seems as if you do," he commented.

"Yes, I do. And last night, when I found you, I think it was a lucky step."

"Remains to be seen," he said, and she knew she had a lot of convincing to do.

"You've probably heard that I've been turned down by several construction engineers; seems they don't want to work for a woman. But I have a feeling you're different, Jake. I have a feeling that you and I could make gorgeous buildings together—the kind that would be the envy of every developer. But no matter what you say to me, whether it's yes or no, eventually I'm going to do it. I'd rather do it now, that's all."

"Do what?" he asked.

"Make Weymouth Development Corporation the biggest in this city. I may look like only one inexperienced person to you, but I've already got a sweet setup. I have my own financing syndicate providing me with money below prime. I've got an excellent piece of property and two A-one tenants promised, one to take the ground and first four floors, the other to take a third of the building. I've got a master's in business and a real-estate license, and I can do my own property appraisals. Plus, I've got terrific ideas on building management. But most of all, I'm fired up, Jake. This is something I've wanted to do since I was a kid, and now's the time. I need someone I can trust, who won't screw me, on the job and off."

"What makes you think I wouldn't screw you?"

She gazed into his green eyes, remembering the pain he'd felt over the loss of his daughter, the way he'd jumped to her defense in front of his associates, and the things his daughter had said about him. "You just won't," she said.

He nodded, as if to confirm her opinion.

"I don't have any connections yet. In fact, I'm trying to keep away from some I don't want."

"Anything I should know?" he asked.

"Maybe when I know you better," she said.

"Were you referring to Charlie Meroni and his cronies?" She felt her face begin to flush. "So you knew?"

"New York is a huge city, but a small town."

"Then you understand how I know you won't screw me. I didn't connect you with Diane until we met, but I've heard Charles talk about you. You're not one of his favorites. It irked the hell out of him when you got that Ravenswood project out from under him."

Jake was amazed that she knew about that, and laughed with satisfaction.

"But I don't know the subs at all," she continued, "and I don't know the teamsters the way you do, though I have a good idea of what goes on. I've sat in on meetings, I've been privy to negotiations firsthand. I know about zoning variances and how to acquire air rights, and how much to fork over when certain hands go out, and which wheels to grease."

"You really do know how it works. But you only know the men Meroni deals with. There are plenty of others."

"Then the smartest thing I can do is find myself an expert like you who can play defense for me, and who's clean. One thing I don't want to do is get involved with the syndicate. And you're squeaky, as they say. I'll pay you whatever you ask. A straight fee or a percentage, whatever makes you comfortable. But there's one thing, I'm going to be a hands-on employer. I don't want to be insulated or protected from this job. I have to be informed every step of the way what's going down on my job site. And while you're building my building, I'm going to be looking for our next property. I can keep you working double-time until you retire or holler uncle, whichever comes first. What do you say?"

He shook his head and grinned at her. "You are a chip off the old block, aren't you?"

"You mean my father? I wouldn't know about that."

"You are, I tell you. It's amazing," Jake said, drinking scalding coffee as though it was cold milk. "I've worked with Bill on a few large jobs in the city. He's singleminded, just like you, doesn't tolerate nonsense, and gets right to the point. Too bad that rotten group got hold of him."

"How did you know he was my father? I thought it was a well-kept secret."

"I read about it in the paper when you had your accident, just like everybody else. And then there was some talk among the subs. We've all heard of each other or worked for one another over the years, you know how it is. As I said, New York can be a small town."

She nodded, wondering if her half brothers had read about the accident in the papers too.

Jake sighed, turning back to her offer almost as an afterthought. "I don't know, Pam. I'm loaded with work as it is. I don't think I can take on any more responsibility. At my age I should be cutting down. And you are a beginner. I'd have to wet-nurse you all the way. And a girl to boot. I'd be fighting a few battles over that one. It might not be worth it."

"I've always thought it was what's between your ears that counted, not what's between your legs."

He threw back his head and laughed loudly. People at nearby tables stopped to watch. He slapped the table three times for emphasis, repeating her comment. "I'm gonna quote you on that one," he said.

She waited until she had his full attention again, so afraid that he was going to say no, in spite of her eagerness, her enthusiasm, and her salty language. "What if I offered you a profit participation, Jake? What about a partnership? Aren't you tired of working on a salary? Wouldn't you like to step up and be one of the big guys?"

He stared at her, and she could see she'd really gotten his interest this time. "Just how much participation are you offering?"

"You'll make your usual fee and override, and I'll give you ten percent of anything I own. That goes for this building and all the future ones, as long as you stick with me and I'm pleased with your work."

He rubbed his chin, and whistled. Then he grinned. "You could have had me for five percent."

"I know." She grinned back. "But I want you happy, Jake. Real happy."

He reached out and took her hand in his, in a gentle, fatherly way. She fought the tears that threatened to spoil the moment. "I'm proud to accept your offer, Pam. I think you're gonna make a helluva partner. You'll make us both rich." He paused, and his voice caught in his throat. "My little Diane, the Lord bless her, was right about you. You're something special."

10

(Brian's four weeks old today)

Dearest Trish,

I'm sending you a box of baby things, some that I've treasured from my own brood, and some of the things Pam bought and was sadly never able to use. A few of the items I'm sending I couldn't live without, like the plastic-lined terrycloth bibs. They snap on real easily behind the neck, and they're large enough to cover everything, especially when the baby starts feeding himself. You can't believe the sight of a twelve-month-old, sitting in the high chair eating Jell-O and cottage cheese with his hands. But I recommend that as the best way for them to learn to feed themselves. You'll also find some hand-knitted sweaters and hats that my mother made. Send them back when the baby outgrows them. Of course, hand-knitted sweaters should be saved, but lately I've become a packrat, saving newspapers, aluminum foil, and especially cans for recycling. I'm trying to get a recycling center erected in our town. We really must preserve our natural resources.

At first I couldn't imagine Arthur as a father, but from what you've told me, he's very happy about your being pregnant. I'm glad you reconsidered getting a divorce. To err is human, but it's divine to forgive. I can't believe I just wrote that. I sound like my mother, always quoting homilies. But it's true or it wouldn't be so quotable. A child deserves to have both parents. I'm of the school that believes that relationships must be worked at, not discarded along with yesterday's disappointments.

Your fears about the baby's health due to your drug use seem to have been unfounded. You look wonderful in the *photograph, but so thin. Are you sure there's a seven-month baby under there? As usual, after giving birth, I'm a house, it's starvation time again. Nursing usually helps me lose the weight, and this baby is a dream. Eight pounds, fourteen ounces at birth, we make them big. He's chubby and sweet and fits right in with the family routine. He has to. I was up and out by the sixth day to drive the car pool, and Brian was right with me. It's better giving birth in the warmer months. Babies seem to stay healthier longer.*

I saw your work in the group show at McGarrity's Gallery in SoHo. I'm so proud and awed by the response you're getting. The gallery people have great expectations for you, and judging by the way your work is selling, I can see why. Don't worry about finding time to paint after the baby's born, the little ones sleep most of the time. When you have a baby, a three-year-old, and a six-year-old, it's like juggling a set of flaming torches. Maybe you should plan to take a few months off, I'm sure the time off will help your work. You've said yourself that the major part of creativity is the thinking and the planning, and the rest is hard work, with a fraction of talent thrown in. So use the time to renew yourself.

Listen to who's talking. I've been around children so long I'm beginning to talk baby-talk myself, between leading Lori's Brownie troop and Stephen's nursery play group, and now goo-gooing to Brian, my brain capacity is shrinking every day.

But sometimes I'm reminded that I'm a person and not just a mommy. I have a story for you. You know how being pregnant doesn't show when you're sitting at a table or driving in the car? Well, it doesn't show when you're sitting in the theater, either. Bobbie and I went to see a matinee of Hair *when I was in my seventh month. I'm sure you've heard about it, it's a musical about the protest generation, antiwar, antiestablishment, pro-drugs, pro-sex, and pro-love. The format is like nothing I've ever seen before. I found it so exciting, the music's wonderful. The audience was standing in the aisles, singing and crying and yelling. You must see it if you can. Anyway, we were in the second row on the left aisle, almost on the stage. During the show, one of the lead performers, a gorgeous black guy, picks me out to sing to. He was grinding his hips to the songs right in front of me, staring, flirting every time he came to our side of the theater. (Bobbie was jealous, but he only had eyes for me.) There's a song in the show where the female lead sings about black boys being so sexy, and he sings back to her, that white girls are really sexy. He's supposed to sing the song to her, but he sang it to me. People were looking at me, and I was blushing. I kept thinking that if he knew I was pregnant, he wouldn't be interested at all. After the show, an usher came over to me and gave me a note. This actor was inviting me for a drink at Sardi's! I sent the usher back with a note telling him I couldn't meet him, I had to meet my husband for dinner. Five minutes later, just as Bobbie and I were leaving the theater, he caught up with me.*

He looked at my basketball middle and smiled. Said he knew I was the earth-mother type. Bobbie hung around, wanting to meet him, but he ignored her. He was so gorgeous, and kind and sure of himself. Stared into my eyes until I felt faint. I kept thinking, "This can't be happening," but it was. He told me he was from Chicago, his name was Ben, and this show was going to make him a star. I believe him. Such talent and magnetism. He told me I was exactly like a girl he was in love with in high school, but she would only be friends with him. No white girls dated black guys back then. But things are different now, he said, and when he saw me he knew we had to meet me. He said, "This is the Age of Aquarius and he have to let the sun shine in." (Those are titles of songs from the show.) He said I was one of the most beautiful women he'd ever seen, and he kissed me! Right there in the lobby of the Biltmore Theater. It was a wonderful kiss. Very loving and gentle. He said if I ever wanted to be with him to let him know, and then he left.

I was shaking so much I thought my legs wouldn't hold me up. So many emotions went through my mind, mostly about how much life is changing, and how much I've missed, living in New Jersey, raising children, staying in my insular world. It took this stranger to shake me up, make me see how exciting life is, how unexpected. I was flying after that. I didn't know how I could face Mel, knowing I had a secret, that I'd felt desire for a total stranger, let him kiss me, and in my seventh month!

Bobbie swore to me she wouldn't tell, but later on at dinner (we met Mel and Frank in the city and went home together) she looked as though she was going to burst a seam. I know she's my friend, but she takes advantage sometimes. Like that night, she wore a suit without a blouse, and her cleavage kept showing. Mel kept looking, too. I don't blame him. I'm beginning to see what he's been talking about all these years, about the new mores. I've wondered for weeks what it would be like to go to bed with Ben, not that I ever would. But what would it be like?

I'll bet you're amazed that I, of all people, could be writing such a letter, having such thoughts. I'm amazed myself.

Destroy this letter after reading it. Or leave it alone, it will probably self-destruct.

Good luck in July! Brian is looking forward to his new playmate.

All my love, Hillary

11

On July 20, 1969, the entire world watched a miracle: the first man walked on the moon. In Trish and Arthur's life, another miracle occurred: their daughter, Kelly, weighing 2,400 grams, was discharged from the neonatal care unit at Children's Hospital and placed in their arms so they could take her home.

Actually, Kelly was placed in Arthur's arms because Trish was too weak to carry her, weighing only ninety-seven pounds herself; the trauma of the pregnancy and Kelly's premature birth had taken their toll. Trish's brother, Tommy, drove the three of them home from the hospital, smiling with pride at his niece and his sister, slapping Arthur on the back, snapping pictures of the event. It was finally time to celebrate.

From the moment she'd discovered she was pregnant in Iran, Trish had stayed off drugs; the child growing within her made it easy. Once the nausea and bouts of vomiting stopped, she felt better than she had in a long time. And Arthur lived up to his promises. He was devoted to her welfare and the baby's. Gradually she began to believe they could be happy again, and she tried to put thoughts of Connor out of her mind. At first it was impossible, but as time went on, and she and Arthur rediscovered their feelings for one another, she felt she'd made the right choice.

Amazing energy and creativity filled her days. During her pregnancy she plunged into work, inspired by her trip, the people she'd met, the insights she'd had. Her work took on a new richness and maturity. Something was clicking, and it excited her. As she worked, she talked to the baby. "What do you think? Is this the way it feels to be in a bazaar? Is this the color that expresses my terror when that man stuck his knife into me?" And the baby would answer with a push of an elbow or a knee. If, on occasion, Arthur's old envy of her productivity surfaced, she overlooked it. If his advice was opposed to what she knew to be right, she found the strength to follow her way and not his, against his disapproval. But he didn't punish her with it; he was too happy about the baby.

In the early weeks of her return, when Connor's presence was still so strong, she painted several likenesses of Connor, capturing that strange, tight, tortured expression in a multi-image collage painting that taught her more about him in retrospect than she had learned in person. She pined for him, missed him, tried to keep alive what they almost had, but there was so little between them that it was not possible to hang on. She wondered how he and Maureen were doing, but she couldn't write and ask her parents.

And then she began to have problems with the pregnancy. At first she wasn't gaining enough weight, so the doctors put her on a weight-gain regimen, but the nutritional supplements didn't work; she wasn't able to ingest enough calories to feed herself and the fetus. She lost weight. Arthur tried bullying her into eating, which never helped. Then, in her seventh month, her hands and feet began to swell. At first they thought it was normal, but when her blood pressure rose, the doctors diagnosed her condition as toxemia and insisted on performing a cesarean section immediately; otherwise, either the baby would die, or she would. She fought against them, fearing her child's death more than her own, but as she was deciding, nature answered the question and she went into labor.

At the onset of yet another of Trish's physical problems, Arthur began to return to the old behavior. Either he was unable or unwilling to support her through another illness, and this one, though not her fault, he blamed on her earlier drug use. He discussed her prior narcotic addiction with every doctor on her case, wanting someone to say that Trish's condition was a result of her own actions. His fear for the baby's safety turned into blame, and a coldness grew between them that made her sick at heart, for she too blamed herself for all the problems she was having.

After a long and difficult labor, Kelly was born at

thirty-one weeks, not yet fully formed. She had a fine fuzz of hair on her reddish body, her skin was uncreased, like a rubber doll's, and her breast buds hadn't formed yet, nor had her earlobes. But her Apgar score, based on the group of tests given to all newborns to assess their heart rate, respiratory effort, muscle tone, reflex, and color, was 8 out of a possible 10, and the doctors were optimistic. Within hours, though, she began to breathe rapidly in an attempt to get air, and her chest X-ray showed evidence of Respiratory Distress Syndrome. A tube was put down her throat to her lungs, and she was put on a respirator. Every hour of Kelly's new life brought more fear and anguish until Trish could barely stand the guilt she felt. Seeing that tiny, helpless infant subjected to the cruel measures needed to prolong her life made Trish's day unendurable. By the next day Kelly was blue and just lay there. Then she began to have seizures.

After the long labor and hours of watching Kelly, Trish was totally exhausted, but when Arthur came into her room and started to cry, she somehow found the strength to comfort him.

"She's convulsing, Trish. I couldn't watch that tiny little baby caught in those uncontrollable seizures. It's the worst thing I've ever seen." She squeezed his hand so hard her own hand turned numb. If she didn't hold on, the pain and fear for her child's life would cause her to convulse too.

Amazingly, an intravenous dose of glucose stopped the seizures, but Kelly's bilirubin test, which measures the liver function, began to rise. Fluorescent therapy didn't help, so the doctors performed an exchange transfusion. Kelly stabilized, but now she had to be fed by a tube in the stomach because she was too weak to suck. Trish tried to nurse her, but her milk was drying up, despite efforts to use a breast pump. Arthur became frantic. "She needs nourishment, Trish, especially your milk for immunity. You've got to do something." But there was nothing she could do.

Whenever anyone told her not to worry, she got angry, especially when Kelly forgot to breathe. The hospital staff were used to that phenomenon, and put Kelly on a monitor attached to her chest by two sticky electrodes; a bell rang whenever her breathing stopped, and a member of the staff would prod her into breathing again and see if she needed CPR. It terrified Trish. Once, it happened when Trish was visiting the nursery and the nurses were galvanized into action. But Trish nearly collapsed from fear. *What if she didn't start breathing again?* Afterwards, she heard that bell in her nightmares.

Statistics were against Kelly's survival. Over half the babies who had such a low birth weight died, and of those who survived, half were severely retarded and had cerebral palsy. But somehow their prayers were answered and Kelly pulled through.

The joy of bringing the baby home that warm day in July was tempered by her delicate condition and their fears for her future. But the sun shone brightly through the nursery window, and Tommy and Trish and Arthur toasted Kelly with orange juice. Later, Tommy brought in a pizza. It was the calm before the storm.

Caring for an infant, especially a first child, is an exhausting full-time job for most new mothers. Taking care of a sickly infant who requires feeding every two hours and constant monitoring takes the endurance of a saint. Trish and Arthur were not saints. He felt helpless with the baby, afraid to hold her, afraid to do something wrong, so he was little help at all. Trish spent eighteen out of twenty-four hours feeding and holding Kelly. Whenever there was a problem—and they occurred with constant regularity—Arthur blamed it on Trish's inadequacies as a mother, or on her former drug use. She could not combat him and defend herself, so she cried. Later, she read articles on the results of drug abuse on infants and fetuses, and found that, indeed, some of Kelly's problems might have been caused by her drug use. There was no consensus of opinion, but INAs (infants of narcotic addicts) were often born prematurely, with symptoms of addiction; they were subject to more infections and had a lower rate of survival. The fact that Trish had not been addicted for some time didn't matter to her; she blamed herself because she had used drugs and alcohol during the time she conceived and during her first weeks of pregnancy, the most critical time for an embryo. And now she had no milk for her child, or physical strength to care for her. And Arthur was nearly useless. Whenever Kelly stopped breathing and the shrill bell sounded at all hours of the day and night, they had to get her breathing again by prodding her or using CPR, and then had to check for any signs of blueness around the mouth. Every time the monitor sounded, the incident had to be logged into a report, even if the baby dislodged the electrodes accidentally by her movement. Each nurse they hired would quit, fearing the responsibility if Kelly died. And Kelly cried a great deal, either from digestive problems or from the tense atmosphere around her, and Trish had nowhere to turn; between blaming herself, dealing with Arthur's anger and the baby's demands, she could barely function.

One night at two o'clock in the morning, when she hadn't slept for days and the baby had been crying for hours, she called Hillary in desperation. It was 5:00 A.M. in New York, but Hillary answered the phone, instantly alert.

"I don't know what I'm going to do," Trish whispered, so exhausted she could barely speak.

Hillary listened while Trish poured her heart out, questioned her, soothed her, calmed her down. Finally, when Trish had told her everything, she said, "I'm coming," and then she hung up.

The very next evening Hillary arrived with three-month-old Brian in her arms. Brian was still nursing so she couldn't leave him at home. When Trish saw the cab pull up in front of the door and Hillary's beautiful face smiling through the window, she felt as though she'd been saved from an avalanche. "I would have been here sooner," Hillary explained, "but I had to wait for my mother to fly to New Jersey to take care of Lori and Stephen."

If Hillary was shocked when she saw Kelly—still bruised from the many intravenous needles, the side of her head shaved where a needle had been inserted, and as tiny as a chicken—she didn't show it. In minutes she had Kelly comfortable and gazing up at her.

Hillary had a system for everything. Diapers were washed first thing in the morning, then bottles were sterilized and formula made. She found a market that delivered groceries, and restaurants that delivered too, and ordered lunch and dinner nearly every day. She cleaned the nursery and bathed the babies on alternate days, and set up a nap schedule for Trish and herself. The rest of the house was cleaned by a cleaning lady with her own car, whom she hired from an agency. "When everything is running smoothly and you're calmer, it affects the baby. It took me a while to learn that," Hillary explained. "But if ordering in meals, having groceries delivered, and finding a cleaning woman with a car is too expensive, then I stop spending money on anything else in order to pay for it. I'd even hock my jewelry if necessary. Besides, you only have to do it until you're stronger and the baby isn't in danger." Her methods did reduce stress, and everyone calmed down.

Hillary sang as she worked, rarely lost her temper, and when Kelly screamed, she cooed and sang to her, rubbing her tummy in firm, circular motions until the screaming stopped. "How do you know what to do?" Trish asked.

"Experience gives me confidence, I guess. Kelly is the fourth baby I've taken care of." She smiled at Trish's hopelessness. "You'll learn; you have to believe that what you're doing will work." Her cheerfulness was contagious.

"I'm thinking of partially weaning Brian," she assured Trish, "so I can nurse Kelly every other feeding, and we'll give Brian a supplement if he needs it." Trish watched Hillary nursing her daughter, who took to the cuddling and mother's milk instantly, and wondered whether women like Hillary had more than enough milk because they were born nurturers, or whether they were nurturers because they had so much milk. Being with Brian, who was chubby and healthy, gave Trish hope that Kelly would soon grow to be normal. The only problem was Arthur. He felt invaded by Hillary. Never having had a mother-in-law to contend with, he resented her. She expected him to do his share with Kelly, and when he refused, or took his time about it, she admonished him. Once he stormed out of the house in anger, and Hillary looked at Trish bewildered, as if to say, *Husbands aren't supposed to behave like that.* Trish was mortified. But all she could do was shrug and say, "That's Arthur."

Even with the two babies, Hillary still had time for Trish. She read the articles Trish gave her about infants of drug users, and found flaws in Trish's arguments. "First of all, many women have toxemia who've never even taken an aspirin. And remember, you suffered a physical trauma in the first month of your pregnancy. You had a knife wound and major surgery! That's enough to affect an embryo." Trish hadn't even thought of that. "Even if your old life-style did affect the baby, what good does it do to punish yourself? You're devoted to Kelly. She's responding well, considering your problems. Guilt is a waste of time, Trish. Let's move on."

If only Arthur would let her. His antagonism grew daily. The baby's condition was Trish's fault. And not only was she to blame for his child's suffering, but she had given him an imperfect offspring. What could he hope for from a child with Kelly's early handicaps? He did not hide his bitterness. Hillary defended Trish, which only made him dislike Hillary more. He made her feel unwelcome.

Hillary stayed two weeks, long enough for Trish to regain her strength and learn how to care for her child alone. But mostly what Trish learned from Hillary was to have confidence in her own intuition, and to take a no-nonsense approach to a life-threatening situation. After Hillary left, Arthur called her a busybody, scoffed at her methods, and tried to undermine Trish's new-found dignity, but she wouldn't let him. A sick feeling was growing inside that she'd made a mistake by staying with Arthur, but now she didn't have the strength or the inclination to do anything about it. Soon, she told herself, she and the baby would be healthy enough to extricate themselves from his anger and his domineering presence, but not yet. And so she held herself aloof from his bitter onslaught, using Hillary as an example. And occasionally thinking about Connor.

12

At five months old, Kelly was still tiny and delicate; and even though Trish had recovered her own strength, taking care of Kelly was a herculean task. Sometimes Kelly smiled and cooed, but she could barely lift her head off the mattress and hadn't yet turned over. Trish was tormented, wondering whether or not she'd suffered brain damage. Kelly could see the mobile above her crib, but rarely reached for it. The episodes of apnea were less frequent, but they still happened and were still terrifying. Kelly had been hospitalized twice with high fevers, and Trish spent her days with her, but Arthur stayed away. At first, when the doctors feared that Kelly had pneumonia or hepatitis or some worse kind of virus that could result in brain damage, Arthur said it was too painful to watch, but as Kelly started to improve, he said, "She doesn't know I'm there. It's not like I can carry on a conversation with her, or anything. You're her mother, she responds to you more than to me."

The second time she got a fever, Arthur said it was because Trish hadn't taken proper care of her, that she shouldn't have gone to the park, where Kelly could be exposed to other children's diseases.

"We didn't see any other children there, Arthur. The doctor told me for my own sanity and the health of the baby to take her for short outings when the weather is good." She'd sat on a bench for fifteen minutes next to an elderly woman who was feeding pigeons.

"Doctors don't know everything," he insisted. "You could have brought her to visit me at the university. That would have been safer."

Trish told him why she hadn't visited him with the baby. "When I see you at work, the new canvases you've produced while I do nothing but take care of the baby, it makes me envious." Arthur just shrugged. Even though she adored the baby, it had been months since she'd worked, and her work had always been crucial to her survival. Arthur did not acknowledge that, nor did he share Kelly's care with her. He played with the baby, but refused to change diapers, make formula, or bathe her, and not once had he offered to stay home for a day so Trish could work. She knew all the reasons by rote. *(1.) Those are women's jobs.(2.) One of us has to earn a living to pay these astronomical medical bills. (3.) Kelly's illness is a result of your abuses; who else should take care of her but her mother? (4.) You're so selfish, all you think about is your own career when your child's life is at stake.*

She waited for the day when she could be free of him, and only her fantasies of Connor kept her going. Often she was tempted to write to him, but didn't. She wanted to come to him a free, self-supporting woman with a healthy child and no encumbrances. She was grateful that Arthur wasn't interested in sex anymore; they rarely talked, except to argue over Kelly.

And then Kelly developed a hernia, a fairly common occurrence among premature babies, owing to early feeding in the incubator. But another surgical procedure so soon after a hospitalization was dangerous. On her way to the hospital the morning of the surgery, Trish came into the kitchen to find Arthur's breakfast dishes still on the table, the trash can overflowing, and spilled coffee grounds in the sink. He was reading the paper, making no attempt to clean up after himself. Her impulse was to tear the paper out of his hands and throw the dirty dishes out of the window along with him. But screaming at him would do no good.

"I think it's time we called it quits, don't you?" she asked, getting his attention grudgingly away from Herb Caen. Suddenly, everything overwhelmed her; again the baby's life hung in the balance, and she was the only one who cared. "You blame me for everything that's gone wrong, but Kelly's the one who pays. It doesn't do any good to blame, it doesn't change anything."

"Oh, you'd like that, wouldn't you? I'm supposed to turn the other cheek, overlook what you've done to our child. My only child." Suddenly he started to sob, letting out his bitterness. "She's so pathetic, Trish, and she suffers. I can't stand watching it. I can't stand listening to that monitor screaming at me in the middle of the night, saying, 'Your child is dying again, she's dying again!' Or have some doctor tell me she may not pull through another procedure. God forgive me, sometimes I wish it were over. I wanted her so much, my little girl. And then she was born with all these problems. I think of you swallowing that shit, and I can't stand it. I want to kill you. I hate you so much, so goddamned much, Trish! I hate you!" he screamed.

"It's not my fault!" she cried out, stunned by his vehemence, almost knocked over by it. "What if it's not my fault, Arthur?" she asked. "What then?"

He looked up at her, his face red and tear-streaked, venom filling his eyes. "But it is!" he insisted. "And no one will ever tell me different."

"What if this is just the way God intended it?"

"Don't invoke the name of God to me! This is God's punishment to you, only I have to pay for it too, and so does Kelly, goddamn you!" he shouted.

Something snapped, she couldn't stay with him a moment longer. It had been a mistake to reconcile, but that was past now. Time to go on. Just she and Kelly, God willing.

She turned around and walked away from him without another word, not caring if she ever spoke to him again.

Later she called her brother and got the name of a divorce lawyer.

Ron Slezak's office near the courthouse building was furnished with Victorian antiques; Boston ferns hung from the acoustic-tiled ceiling; his desk chair had wooden spindles across the back; and his desk had a green leather top with gold stenciled edges, and drawers in front as well as in back. There was a potbellied stove in the corner of the reception room. Trish felt comfortable here, but that quickly changed.

Slezak was in his fifties, nearly bald on top, but he had enough hair to grow long sideburns. He smiled at her as he said, "So, another love child bites the dust."

She was embarrassed.

"Don't get me wrong. Lately my women clients are

getting shafted. Frustration is the nature of my business. I know you want what's coming to you, but you probably don't have a good chance of getting it."

"But I haven't even told you anything yet."

"Trish, may I call you Trish?" She nodded. "I've been in this business a long time." He paused. "Let me guess. You were married in a field of poppies and your favorite music is Crosby, Stills, Nash and Young, and Simon and Garfunkel." She nodded. "The trusting type," he sighed. "I knew it. Your brother told me you're an artist; does that mean candles shaped like flowers, and quilts?"

"No, I'm a painter."

"Okay, at least you're serious. But most ladies who come here have crystal prisms hanging in their windows, a stained-glass lampshade in the breakfast room, a brass peace symbol around their necks, and no idea of how to protect themselves financially. Yet they expect me to make it come out all right. It rarely happens, rarely. If you want some advice, you're better off making the marriage work. At least he's supporting you. Let him join the commune, or leave the commune to become a stockbroker. Is it so bad?"

"It's nothing like that." Slezak was so discouraging she felt like crying. "My husband is an artist as well as a professor of art. He doesn't want to change his profession. But I want a divorce."

He sighed. "Okay, why don't you give me a picture of your financial arrangement with your husband?"

Her heart began to pound with a sudden awareness. "Arthur pays . . ."

"The bills," he finished for her, "and you get an allowance to pay for the groceries, the cleaning help if there is any, your toiletries, and some secondhand clothes. You save all this money for him, never thinking that it's half yours too, right? Am I right?"

He was right.

"That's what I call living in the dark ages, not our current society. I can't perform miracles and help you divorce a husband who's more like a father, plus find you enough money to pay my fees, support yourself, and pay for a sick child's medical expenses." He lifted up his eyes as if to say, *What am I going to do with her?* Then his sad eyes met hers. "When are you people going to wake up and start taking responsibility for living in the world of today?"

"By 'you people,' do you mean women?" she said, getting offended. She stood up so quickly it surprised him. "I'll bet some of us women pay you sizable fees, don't we? Just as I expect to. Well, I don't appreciate being patronized, Mr. Slezak. My brother Tom recommended you, but I can find another lawyer if my case is so impossible."

His tone changed considerably. "Mrs. Matalon, I didn't mean to offend you. I just don't believe in stringing you along, telling you things are hunky-dory, when I know they're not. Sometimes I feel like Goldwater when he told us that war in Indochina was inevitable and we ought to send troops right now, before the Communists got too strong a foothold in the area. Real popular opinion, wasn't it? The country thought he was a dangerous man, and gave him the worst defeat for a presidential candidate in decades. And now we're eating Vietnam for breakfast, lunch, and dinner." He sighed again. "Why don't you think of me as your own private Barry Goldwater? Sit down, please." She was softening a bit. "If you're interested in the truth, I'm the one who will give it to you. I apologize if I patronized you."

She sat down again.

"Here's the situation," he said, his voice more sympathetic, yet realistic. "Your husband owns both your homes, and they're in his name. You've never earned money toward their upkeep, which might have made them more subject to community property. You have no control over your husband's assets, and very little of your own. You have no access to his funds, you can't withdraw money and have no credit of your own. You'll be without his medical insurance, though the baby is still covered, and it will take a long time to resolve these matters. In the meantime, how will you live? It's a good question. Have you got the money for my retainer?"

At least she'd anticipated that. "My gallery in New York is sending me a check for a recent sale. It's for eighteen hundred dollars."

He smiled. "You get a good price for your work. Do you sell paintings very often?"

"Yes," she acknowledged. "But I don't earn nearly as

much as Arthur. And then there's his teaching salary and benefits, but I made twelve thousand dollars last year."

"What happened to the money?"

She felt her face turning red. "I spent it on baby furniture and a visit to my parents and on . . . other things. But I don't do that any more."

"You mean drugs?"

She nodded, and he said, "Your brother mentioned that you'd had a problem. I hope it's in the past. Your husband could sue you for custody of the child and win if it can be proved that you're unfit."

"That won't happen. Arthur doesn't want Kelly, he could never take care of her."

"He could hire someone to care for her and sue you for custody just to be vindictive. I've seen it happen."

She felt the color drain from her face at the thought, and her hands perspired. Arthur could be vindictive. He'd told Trish proudly how his first wife had gone back east and left him full ownership of both their homes, rather than fight it out with him.

Slezak was making notes on a yellow legal pad. "You could get a job, couldn't you, teaching, or waitressing?"

"The baby needs full-time care. I haven't painted since she was born. I haven't anything to send to my gallery."

"So it's up to the generosity of your husband until we get a temporary support order. What about your family?"

"My parents are out of the country, and they're opposed to divorce. I don't think they can help. But my brother might loan me some money for a while."

"Do you want to retain me as your attorney?"

"Yes," she replied. "I want you to go ahead."

"How is your daughter?" he asked.

"The hernia surgery went well, but the recovery has been slow. I'll be taking her home in a day or two. I'll speak to my brother about a loan, and find a place for us to live right away. I know Arthur won't move out."

He stood up and offered his hand. "Let me know where you are, and how things are going."

"Isn't it your job to let me know?"

"Trish, it never goes quickly. If you're prepared to wait, you'll be better off. The idea is not to let it get to you, but I've never seen anyone yet who can avoid that."

She nodded, shook his hand good-bye, and left the office. She stopped at a pay phone and called her brother.

But when she told him why she'd called, there was a long pause, and then he said, "I'm so sorry, Trish. But I'm completely tapped out. I just made a major investment in a nightclub in the city. It's called Bluebelles, and I didn't tell you about it because I didn't want Mom and Dad to know; you know how they are about any investment that isn't ITT. Everything I've got is tied up there."

"It's all right, Tommy," she sighed. "I'll work it out. Maybe I'll ask you for a job as a waitress," she said.

There was another long pause. "I don't think so, Sis. The club caters to men only."

"You're not investing in a place that discriminates against women, are you?"

"No, it's not that. Women are welcome, if they want to come."

"Tommy, what is it?" she asked, mystified.

"It's a gay bar, Trish. Where men can go to meet other men. Men like me, Trish. I'm a homosexual."

Her first reaction was sadness, and then she thought, *I'm not really surprised.* But she didn't know what to say. She thought about her parents' reaction, felt heartsick for their sakes. This would kill her mother and her father, for different reasons. Her thoughts rambled. The silence on the phone was painful. Finally she said, "Thank you for telling me, Tommy. It must have been a very hard thing to do."

His voice changed, as if he were trying not to cry. "I've wanted to tell you for a long time, but it never seemed right. Now especially is the wrong time, with Kelly in the hospital and you getting a divorce. But I needed you to know, Sis."

"It's okay," she said, not believing it. For him it would never really be "okay" again. She thought about the way they had ridden their bikes together as kids to the Bay Theater on Saturday afternoon; how they had played marbles and skated on the sidewalk. Her big brother, how proud she'd been of him. He'd played baseball in the street with the boys, had girlfriends in high school. None since. Never since. *Fred,* she thought. *His lover is Fred.* And how many others? What will people think? Will they shun me? Shun him? My brother! God, it was hard. She wanted to scream at him, to hurt him the way he had hurt her. In a way, he had just died, the Tommy she'd always believed was real. She'd never have any nieces or nephews now, never have a sister-in-law like her mother had, to share the cooking tasks on Thanksgivings: *I'll make the turkey and dressing, you make the vegetables and desserts, Aunt Marge can make whatever else we need.* No sister-in-law.

He was crying.

She started to cry too. All her self-concern went in an instant, and all she could think of was his pain. "I love you, Tommy," she said. "Don't cry. I love you."

She heard his sobs subside, and then he said, "Thanks, Trish. Because I love you, too. I'm sorry I can't help you this way, but I'll do what I can."

"I know you will."

"Trish?"

"Yes."

"Are you going to tell Mom and Dad?"

"Do you want me to?"

"No, not yet."

"You'll do it, won't you?"

He sighed. "Yes, only not yet."

"Okay," she said. "I'll talk to you soon." And she hung up.

13

Divorces are often nasty. Couples who fool themselves into a truce, believing they are fair-minded, become angry, envious, bitter, and betrayed, a lethal combination. Perhaps it's the death of expectations, of happily-ever-after, that makes them suddenly enemies. In Trish's case, it was bitterness over the sacrificing of her own happiness and fear for her future that made her want to get Arthur. She'd believed him when he'd said he'd changed. He hadn't. And she had probably lost her chance at happiness with Connor by waiting so long. Arthur, on the other hand, was experienced at this sort of thing, and knew exactly how to proceed. And being the basically self-centered, penurious person that he was, he was out for himself.

Her days were unrelieved by change; she was alone in the house. At night when the monitor rang, occasionally he'd get up. Now Trish was afraid to sleep for fear she wouldn't hear the shrill ringing of the bell. What if she slept through it? Once was all it would take. Sleepless nights took their toll. Loneliness and fear caused a constant ache inside. How could she manage alone? In spite of Arthur's warnings to her to find her own place, she waited for him to come home and discuss the details of their separation, but he stayed away. Her money was running low. The daily tasks of caring for the baby never ceased. She wanted to work, to pour out her creative expression the way she always had. She'd become accustomed to saving up pieces of her life as they happened, using them in her work and leaving the understanding for later, postponing her reactions until she'd worked them into a sculpture or an assemblage, or painted them onto a surface. In reality, her work was psychotherapy without the couch or the therapist. Even if she didn't come to any conclusions, she felt relief after working, as though she'd consigned her worries to the muse. Now, a volcano of unresolved feelings gathered. She clutched at the thought of Connor as the only one who could save her. But she didn't even know where he was. And maybe he was an illusion. *How little I understand men,* she thought. *What poor judgments I've made.* She realized she had turned to drugs in the past to keep from examining herself, her reactions, her core beliefs, fearing that there might be nothing there.

The baby needed her desperately, and she responded to that need, focused on keeping her daughter alive. Without her constant care, Kelly could die; Kelly's needs became her drug.

Kelly was so precious, so sweet; the taste of her soft round body, the smell of her flesh, the smile in her deep brown eyes were Trish's only joys. The baby knew Trish, though in a limited field of knowing, as no one else had ever known her. Trish was the goddess in her universe, and Kelly reached out for this giver of life who kept her from danger. Trish called Hillary and told her what was happening. Hillary offered to send money, but Trish said she had to do this on her own. "I remember everything you taught me," Trish told her. "Before I do anything for the baby, I ask myself, 'How would Hillary do this?' But now it's up to me to be the nurturer."

She had to be so careful, fanatically guarding against germs. She boiled all utensils, disinfected all clothing and furniture, washed walls and floors, wore masks if there were the lightest sneeze in her head, gave away the cat for fear of allergies and germs. Kelly could not be exposed to one unnecessary microbe. Other mothers could take their six-month-old children to shopping centers, to play in sandboxes; they could have lunch with their friends while their babies sat in strollers and gummed their zwieback. But Kelly was too delicate. Trish couldn't even tickle her and make her laugh, for fear the laughter would irritate the membranous tissue in her lungs. And now their germ-free environment was to be invaded, and Kelly would be exposed to God knew what. Trish wanted to scream in protest. In getting a divorce, she was risking Kelly's life.

On the fifth day after she'd asked him for a divorce, she came home from a doctor's appointment with Kelly to find that Arthur had packed most of her clothes and the baby's things into boxes and suitcases and their belongings were sitting in the kitchen; he was literally kicking her out. It filled her with a complete sense of helplessness. All she could think of was Kelly's apnea monitor. She had to take it with her; it was a matter of life and death.

"What are you doing?" She choked on her words, her face drained of color, her always thin body shaking with rage and fear.

"What does it look like? I've stayed away long enough. This is my house and I want you out. Now, today."

"You can't mean it."

"Oh no?" He picked up the largest of the suitcases and pushed past her, banging into her. She was holding the baby in the infant seat and swung Kelly out of his way, jerking her. Kelly was startled into a loud cry. He took the suitcase out to the car and was back in a moment. Trish was crying too as she soothed the baby.

"Jesus Christ!" he exploded. "You're as bad as she is."

Trish was afraid that Kelly would rupture her newly sutured abdomen and stifled her own tears as she desperately rocked and crooned to the baby. Finally Kelly stopped.

Arthur was coming in after another load. "Don't look at me as if I'm heartless or cruel, Trish. I'll pay for a motel until you find an apartment. You can have all the baby's furniture. For now, I bought you a port-a-crib. It's in the car. I have to do this," he said, his eyes filling with sudden tears. "I need my life back." He was hurting too. For a weird moment she felt sorry for him.

Then he said, "When you destroyed yourself you destroyed our daughter too. I hate you for that."

"And you had no part in it?"

"I'm not the drug addict." Self-righteousness was his shield.

"You took drugs for years. That could have affected the baby. You're the one who introduced me to drugs, to LSD, pot, hash, pills, and alcohol, your favorite. Even without a chemical dependency, your attitude would have driven me to it."

"What attitude?"

"To be on top by putting me down, making me feel inferior."

"No one can make you feel inferior, you are!"

"You bastard," she said, fighting not to believe it, as though he were throwing her backwards into a deep well and then holding her head under until she drowned. *Inferior, like hell!* Suddenly she knew why he was saying these things, why he'd always said them, his own insecurities.

"What are you staring at?"

She could feel her posture changing; she stood taller. "I'm not inferior, Arthur, as a person or as an artist. I'm good. Really good. Maybe I can even be great. I don't copy anyone, I'm not derivative like you." She advanced on him, her insight propelling her. He stepped back, and she almost smiled to see him retreat. "It's always killed you that Bischoff and Diebenkorn traded work with me and not with you. I saw the look on your face when Claire Falkenstein said she wished she had my level of insight at twenty-nine, instead of fifty-nine. But you always reinforced my doubts. And when I trusted my instincts and rejected your advice, it killed you, didn't it?" He looked startled, cornered. It felt wonderful to be on the offensive. "I knew you were trying to destroy me. I'd see your fury, and I'd die inside. Well, how does it feel to see mine?" She advanced even further until she was very close to him, glaring up, her fists clenched. "I knew you were wrong, and that made you hate me all the more. Didn't it? Didn't it?" She wanted to pound her fists into his chest. "Kelly is only an excuse for hating me; you're scared of me." She knew she was right and it made her strong. She was glad she'd come back to him for this past year; she'd learned so much, truly finished with him. Now, when she walked away, it would be without any remorse.

He was staring at her, horrified, as though she were a snail who had just shed her shell and crept toward him, trailing green slime all the way. "You're out of your mind."

"No, I'm not," she insisted, taking one more step until his back was pressed against the refrigerator, "not crazy at all." But the way she was staring at him made her feel a little crazy at the moment.

"You're a nothing," he spat. "You'll always be nothing. Get out of here, I want you out. And take that damaged child of yours, or I won't be responsible for what I do."

Trembling and afraid of her own rage, she picked up her purse and the baby, feeling relieved to be leaving, pushed open the door, and marched down the walk to the car.

She strapped Kelly into the infant seat in the car. The baby smiled and cooed at her. She wanted to grab her and hug her, bury her face in that soft, delicate body, breathe in the scent of new life, of downy softness, feel those little hands caress her cheek. How could he not adore her too?

The car was piled with their belongings. She realized with a start that this old Chevy wagon was Arthur's too. She had nothing that was hers, except for her clothes and her paintings. *My paintings*, she thought suddenly. *I can't leave them here, they're not safe with him.*

He stood in the doorway watching her. She wished she could flip him the finger, back the car out of the drive, and pull away in a dramatic exit. But he knew exactly what her work meant to her; if she made him too angry, he would never let her have it.

"I'm coming for the rest of my things tomorrow," she said, "while you're at work."

"You'd better, because tomorrow afternoon I'm having the locks changed."

She wanted to scream with frustration, and thought diabolically of driving the car forward and smashing him against the house. The baby started to fuss. It was close to her feeding time. At least there was a bottle in the diaper bag, left over from this afternoon's visit to the doctor. First they'd have to find a motel with a kitchen, and then shop for groceries. No one would be there to help her unload their belongings from the car, or find Kelly's things among all the boxes. Wherever they went, she'd have to clean it thoroughly before they could stay there. Now that her anger was dissipating somewhat, she could feel the hopelessness; this was a nightmare.

Arthur reached into his wallet and took out some

money and brought it to her. "I'll give you your usual allowance for the next month. By then we should have some temporary financial agreement." He turned and started to walk away.

"I need money for the first and last month's rent on an apartment," she said.

He shrugged and kept walking. "You'll just have to manage, I guess."

"Arthur," she said, wanting to scream again.

His eyes were as cold as she'd ever seen them when he turned back. "You've gotten everything from me you're ever going to get, kid. There isn't any more."

Trish closed her eyes and clutched the steering wheel. She detested needing his money, but the baby's health was at stake. Arthur glanced at her again and came walking back. It seemed as though he would relent. *I knew we couldn't be that heartless. He knows I can't care for the baby all by myself* Trish thought. But just then Kelly started to cry again, and Arthur stopped in his tracks, abruptly changed direction, and went into the house without a backward glance. There was nothing she could do but drive away.

She found a motel room with a kitchen in the neighborhood, put the baby down on the floor in the infant seat, and began dragging in their belongings from the car. She borrowed some cleaning materials and a vacuum from the hotel manager, and cleaned the room as best as she could. Then she ordered some Chinese food to be delivered and set up the port-a-crib, installing the electronic sounding device in the bed. Once the small beige pad that monitored Kelly's movements was in place, it gave her a feeling of relief. At least some things were under control.

After dinner, she bundled Kelly up and went to a nearby market for baby supplies. By the time they got back, Kelly was overheated from crying, and had a fever. Fighting a feeling of panic, she sponged the baby with alcohol until it brought her fever down.

The tiny motel room, piled high with their belongings and bags of groceries, looked like someone's storage garage; she could barely move around. She would have loved to take the baby into bed and sleep with her cuddled up in her arms for comfort, but Kelly had to

sleep on her movement monitor. She plugged the electronic pad into an outlet in the kitchen, where she had
set up the port-a-crib, attached the electrodes to her skin,
and finally Kelly fell asleep. Trish covered herself with
the spread and fell into an exhausted sleep. It had been
eight nights since the apnea monitor had rung, but this
night it rang twice, filling her heart with that same ago-
nized fear as she jumped out of bed and prodded her
daughter into breathing again. *When are you going to
grow out of this, Kelly?* she wondered. *When will you be
out of danger?* The fear haunted her so, especially now,
when she was Kelly's only source of assistance. She had
difficulty falling back asleep in anticipation of the next
time, and thinking that tomorrow she'd have to find a
place to live and somehow find the money to pay for it.

There was so much to do, she didn't know where to start.
First she arranged for a moving company to meet her at
the house at one o'clock; then she called a nurse's registry and hired a practical nurse for the day. By the time
the woman arrived, Trish had made several appointments
to see apartments.

Trish opened the door and let her in.

But when Mrs. Spindler, the nurse from the registry,
saw the motel room, she looked at Trish as if she were
crazy. "You expect me to work here? Why, this isn't
suitable. Not at all." She turned to go.

"Oh, please, Mrs. Spindler, don't leave," Trish begged.
"It's only for today. I have to find an apartment. The
baby needs a home. Please, I need your help so much."

The woman was trying to judge her sincerity. Trish
gave it her best smile. "I know it's crowded, but it's
clean, I cleaned it myself. And the baby is wonderful.
Won't you meet her?" She led the way to Kelly's crib.

As if on cue, Kelly grinned and waved her hands.

Mrs. Spindler sighed. "Why don't you show me what
I'll need to know."

Trish almost hugged her.

Rents in the Berkeley area were high, but she finally
found an apartment in a rundown neighborhood in Oakland for $325 a month, first and last month's rent re-
quired on deposit. The building was a converted house,
with a kitchen unit built into the dining room. The walls

were peeling and in need of paint; the cabinet doors were old and warped; the closet smelled musty and ancient; there were no light fixtures except a bare bulb in the living room—which was heated by an old radiator—and a lightbulb in the ceilings of the bedroom and the bath. But it had hardwood floors, easier to keep clean than carpeting, and it was on street level, which was convenient. All she needed was the money to pay for it.

At one o'clock she drove to Arthur's house to meet the movers, Phil and Larry. They were waiting for her, but when she put the key in the lock, it wouldn't open. He'd already changed the locks.

"Damn you, Arthur!" she shouted at the silent walls and empty windows.

"What do you want us to do?" Larry asked. "Call a locksmith?"

She looked up and down the street as though searching for someone to come and help her, but there was no one. She picked up one of the loose bricks lining the flower bed outside the kitchen door, and took a few steps back.

When the movers saw what she was going to do, they tried to stop her.

"It's my house and my belongings. I'll be damned if he's going to keep them from me," she said, heaving the brick through the window in the back door.

The shattering glass made a satisfying crash.

Trish reached in and unlocked the door and then showed the movers what to take: her books, some small appliances and kitchen utensils, the baby's furniture, the rest of her clothes, and her paintings. She was surprised to see how many works of art she had accumulated, and how many paintings she'd been given by artist friends over the years in exchange for her own. Even Arthur had given her pieces of his own work as gifts, for birthdays and anniversaries. Those paintings would pay her rent.

The moving van followed her back to the motel, where they loaded the rest of her belongings into the truck while Trish cuddled Kelly for a while, taking strength from her sweet body, and then reassured Mrs. Spindler she'd be back for Kelly by four o'clock, when Mrs. Spindler's day ended. The moving van was costing her thirty-five dollars an hour, and Mrs. Spindler was costing eighteen. She didn't have enough money to pay either of them.

She took two paintings—an abstract in ochers and browns that Arthur had given her, and a small Diebenkorn oil of his Ocean Park series—and drove into the city across the Bay Bridge. There was nothing else she could do but sell these paintings, though it felt like she was cutting off her arm. Claude Bergeron gave her three thousand dollars for the Diebenkorn, and Jarmin Leacock gave her two thousand for Arthur's abstract. Both pieces were worth six times as much, but she took the money gratefully and sped back through the late-afternoon traffic to pay Mrs. Spindler and pick up Kelly.

The moving van was waiting for her in front of her new apartment on Chestnut Street. Phil and Larry helped her assemble Kelly's crib; she moved the apnea monitor from the port-a-crib to the main crib herself.

By seven o'clock she was finally moved in. The nursery furniture was set up in the bedroom, along with the single bed she'd taken from Arthur. Her art supplies were in the living room. The toaster and blender were plugged into the kitchen, her electric blanket and clock in the bedroom, her hair dryer in the bathroom, and the small TV-radio combination she'd brought with her was in the living room. These meager belongings were all she had taken that Arthur wouldn't miss, besides the vacuum cleaner. Tomorrow she'd unpack her belongings and buy a chest of drawers, and a TV table and chair to eat on. She didn't need any other furniture; besides, she was afraid to spend any more money than she had to. She needed to guard every penny so she'd never have to sell anything again as precious to her as her fellow artists' work. Even Arthur's work was precious, though he wasn't.

She sat with Kelly on the bed, singing to her and rocking her until the baby was nearly asleep. Trish was so exhausted she could barely stay awake herself, but there was much more to be done. She decided that the first luxury she'd allow herself would be a light fixture to cover the bare bulb in the ceiling. And the second luxury would be to contact Connor. *I'm kidding myself* she thought. *He doesn't want to hear from me.* But she knew she had to do it.

"We're going to be all right," she said to Kelly, who

was nodding off as she transferred her to the crib and attached the monitor. "We're going to be all right." As if Kelly knew it was true, she wiggled her bottom up high in the air, and sighed as she fell asleep.

Then Trish began to clean the apartment, scrubbing the floors on her hands and knees with disinfectant. It took her five hours in the bathroom and kitchen alone. It was after one o'clock when she checked on Kelly once more and finally fell into an exhausted sleep herself. Her muscles ached and her body was just too tired and sore to go on, but when she finally slept, she dreamed that Connor stood watching her with a mysterious smile on his face while she scrubbed floors and walls that would never come clean.

Trish awoke from a deep sleep, instantly awake. With a sudden start, she bolted up in bed. *Where am I?* She didn't know. Frightened, she looked around the unfamiliar room. And then she remembered.

The sunlight pouring in from the uncurtained window blinded her; the sun was high in the sky. It was late! Kelly was still asleep in the crib next to her. She glanced at the clock. It said three o'clock. In the afternoon? It couldn't be! Not three o'clock. She picked up the clock. No humming, total silence. *But it's still plugged in.* The second hand had stopped, the clock had stopped. *It must be broken.* She felt so relieved. She reached over and picked up her watch from the floor. Ten-thirty. It was late, but not as late as she'd thought. She'd slept through the breakfast hour. So had Kelly. Poor baby must have been as tired as she was. But it didn't make sense, Kelly must be hungry.

Suddenly her heart fell with a sickening thud.

Oh God.

What if the clock wasn't broken; what if it had stopped because of a power failure? That meant there was no electricity at all.

"Kelly!" she screamed, leaping out of bed, grabbing her daughter up in her arms. The shock of that cold, limp, lifeless body almost made Trish drop her.

Oh God, oh God, no!

There had been a power failure. Kelly had stopped breathing and the monitor hadn't warned her. "Kelly!"

she cried, frantically shaking the child in her arms, laying her down on the bed, trying to breathe life back into that whitish-blue body. It was no use. Soon she realized it.

That was when the pain hit, like no pain she'd ever felt before, a searing, white-hot iron boring through her very center. She cradled Kelly in her arms, breathing shallowly against the force of it, rocking the baby, moaning, making primitive sounds she was unaware of making.

When some time had gone by and nothing had changed, when the coldness in her arms did not stir, gave no sign of life, she started to scream. And she screamed until someone came and found her and took the baby away.

BOOK
V

Where Have All
the Flowers
Gone

1

"What's on your program today, Hil?" Mel was sitting on the bed, tying his wing-tips. It was still dark outside at 7:10 in the morning.

Hillary hummed along with the radio. Carole King singing "You've Got a Friend" always reminded her of Trish and Pam. She pulled the green hand-knitted sweater on over her head and thrust her arms into the sleeves, trying not to shiver. So far, November had been freezing.

"There's a repairman coming for the dishwasher," she told Mel. "This morning I'm stuffing envelopes for Save the Seals. I have to pick up the cleaning, have a haircut at one, and take Brian to the pediatrician after school. Then I'm buying the invitations to Stephen's birthday party. Stephen wants us to take him and his friends to see *The Godfather* for his birthday. I'm more inclined to take eight-year-olds skating." Mel's face had an odd expression as he listened to her daily tasks. "Something you want me to do?"

"I thought maybe we could have lunch. You'd come into the city."

"Oh, honey, not today. How's tomorrow? I could cancel my lunch with Bobbie."

"Tomorrow?" He sighed, looking at her sadly. "Okay."

"What's wrong, babe?" she asked.

He shrugged. She could feel his tension. "I don't have time to go into it now; I'll be late for my train. You've got a million things to do."

The sounds of Lori and Stephen arguing over the bathroom again interrupted them, but Hillary tuned it out.

Mel stood up and she came and put her arms around him. "None of the things I have to do are as important as you."

He pushed her away. "Bullshit, Hillary."

377

"Mel, what is it?" She stepped back, away from him.

He plopped down again on their four-poster bed with its antique crocheted Colonial string canopy, and put his head in his hands. Then he groaned. "I didn't want to tell you like this, but I can't keep it in anymore. I want out, Hillary. I don't want to be here anymore."

A chill shot through her, and she held it off, but it was like trying to stop a wave at the shore with her hand. The chill washed over her, filling her senses with bitter salt water. He'd finally said it.

"I need some time to myself."

A wounded-animal sound bubbled forth as she stared at him. More and more, this was happening to people she knew, but not to her! *God, please, no!* "You can't mean it."

He looked up at her; how could a torturer have those brown eyes? "Hillary, please don't look at me like that. I put a deposit on an apartment in the city, but just for one month. I thought I'd move out this weekend."

"Just like that? Without any warning?" She felt the air being sucked out of her lungs.

"You can't be totally surprised." His voice tightened defensively. "We've talked about this hypothetically; what we would do if either of us ever wanted out."

Stupidly, she grabbed at the details of their lives, examples to change his mind. "What about dinner this weekend with Bobbie and Frank? And Friday night Lori is giving the opening prayer at Shabbat service."

"For God's sake, Hillary, we'll cancel Bobbie and Frank; they'll understand."

"Don't you love me anymore? Don't you love us?" This wasn't happening, it was a joke. In a moment he'd tell her he was just kidding. But the longer it took for him to tell her, the longer she was forced to play out this hideous charade. "You can't leave us; we're your family." Her eyes were dry, painfully dry. She blinked them. No moisture at all. It was surreal; she was standing outside herself, watching herself plead with her own husband not to destroy their lives. "Mel, we made love last night. What was that all about? How could you make love to me and not tell me what you were planning? That's why I can't take you seriously. I refuse to take you seriously. Nobody could be that cruel."

Her words seemed to knock the air out of him. He exhaled with a grunt. "I wanted to tell you, but I couldn't." His eyes pleaded with her.

"So instead you made love to me?" She was in shock, remembering last night. Their lovemaking hadn't been outstanding, but it had been enthusiastic. "Was it the sex?" she asked. "I thought it was wonderful. Didn't you like it?"

"Stop!" he nearly shouted, anguish in his voice. "It's not you, it's me. You're a great lover. You're a wonderful wife. No man could ask for anyone better than you. I love you. But I've got to get away. I'm feeling smothered. I feel that life is passing me by. I'm stuck in this velvet rut we've made for ourselves. I've got to have some time alone, some time to see who I am, where I'm going."

His words echoed off the walls, rattled the lace curtains on the wooden rods. Through her incredulity and shock, she felt anger boiling up. "Get to know yourself? Now that's bullshit!" Hillary shouted. "You just want to get laid, don't you? Don't you?" She advanced toward him, her fists clenched, but was stopped short by the look of surprise in his eyes. He tried to cover it, but she'd already seen it. She'd really put her finger on it this time. She felt fury boiling even hotter inside. God, for so long she'd been afraid of this. And damn him, he'd finally done it. Finally said it. He looked different to her, less appealing. And then from somewhere came the strength to know exactly what to do. She crossed over and closed the door so the children couldn't hear them, then came back to him.

"Okay, Mel. If that's what you want to do, it's fine. Go ahead. Rent your apartment, have your time alone. Even fuck your brains out, if you have to. But just understand this, you're risking everything we have together. And for what? It's all the same in the dark, baby. All the same."

"How would you know?" He shouted back. "Who else have you ever had? I've only been with two other women besides you in my life, and I was so young I didn't know what the hell I was doing."

"And now you're such a wonderful lover that you're going to do the things we do, that are ours alone, with

some other woman? God, the thought makes me ill."
She felt her stomach churning.

He shook his head and turned away. "I didn't want to
tell you like this."

"How did you want to tell me? During lunch at Côte
Basque, sipping our white wine? 'By the way, darling,
I'm leaving you.' 'Oh, really, darling, how nice. What a
jolly good idea.' Well, it sucks, Mel."

"I'm not actually leaving, Hil, I'm just taking some
time off. We've been married for ten years; it's 1972, and
the sixties passed me by. I'm thirty-five years old." He
raised his shoulders in a shrug. "I know it sounds inane."

She folded her arms across her chest, holding on, her
attention caught by the chrysanthemums on the dresser.
The water needed changing. *What strange things we think
about at times like these,* she thought. Again, she had this
unreal feeling that part of her was reacting and part
observing. The reacting part was doing an admirable job
under the circumstances, bringing her an awareness of
things she'd never known before. Why wasn't she falling
apart? She was surprised at herself. "You know something, Mel, I'm glad you made this decision. I know it
was tough. But at least you did it. For ten years now, I've
been scared to death of this moment, waiting for it to
happen. And somehow I knew it would. When I got
pregnant with Lori, you did the right thing. And then
with Stephen, you took it like a champ. You've been a
good father, an excellent provider, even a loving husband. But all these years I've felt second-class, like I was
not your first choice, like you got stuck with me and
made the best of it. Well, guess what I just realized?
That I got stuck with you, too." She started to laugh, it
just bubbled forth. "I got stuck too!" The look on his
face stopped her laughter.

"Maybe it's time we *both* figured out whether we'd do
it again if we had the chance," she continued. "I thought
I knew the answer to that question, but maybe I don't. I
do know that if abortions had been legal, we wouldn't
have had Lori or Stephen. My God, that's frightening. I
can't imagine my life without them." She paused to listen. She could hear Lori saying to Stephen, "You always
steam up the bathroom so it makes my hair curly. You

do it on purpose!" Even when they were obnoxious, they were so precious to her, how could he do this?

She looked back at Mel. "Okay, go ahead. You go off to New York and screw your secretary or the new legal intern or whoever, and I'll do the same. There are a few men in my life that I can call." She turned to look at herself in the mirror, to assess the goods. She was thirty-four; her hair was still a lustrous auburn, long and curly; she'd been a size eight for two years now, and worked out three afternoons a week. There were a few lines around her eyes and at the edges of her mouth, but the dimples were still perky, even if her breasts weren't. She turned back. "We'll have a trial separation, Mel, like separate vacations, meet back here in a month, compare notes. Is that all right? Sound fair?"

No answer. He was staring at her. This wasn't the same woman he'd married and gotten bored with. This was a new person. She almost felt herself transforming right before his eyes. "That's the best I can do for you, Mel. That's it." She raised her hands for emphasis, and then, with a continuous motion, swept her hair off her face. In spite of the pain in her guts, she really did understand what he was going through, but by God, what was good for the goose was good for the gander. She turned toward the door, fighting the urge to throw her arms around his knees and beg him not to do this. But that was the old Hillary. The new one felt triumphant that she had not acted like a fool.

He caught her at the door. "You don't mean it, do you?"

"What?" She turned back, not willing to give him any more than she had to. Something subtle was shifting between them at this moment, some balance of power.

"About seeing other men?"

"Why not? I'm on the pill."

"Hillary!" He sounded like her father. "You can't do that."

This time she didn't let the smile out that tickled the edges of her lips. "It works both ways, Mel. That's how I feel about you being with other women." She prayed not to betray her glee. "We've been approaching this for years. You do what you have to, and so will I." She was amazed at the clarity with which she was seeing things as something else occurred to her. She considered not saying it, but it would be easier now than later on. "You know what, Mel? I'm tired of having a husband who's doing me a favor by being married to me. If I'm such a fabulous wife, then I should be treated like one. And if you can't do that, then maybe you're not right for me, either."

He seemed stunned, as if he'd just opened his familiar underwear drawer and found something foul and disgusting in it. "I can't believe you're saying these things. I've always thought you were so content, that it would destroy you if you knew I wasn't happy."

Now the tears that had refused to come earlier filled her eyes. "I've always known, Mel. And it does hurt. More than I can say. But it's not destroying me."

"What should we do?"

She reached to take his hand, but then decided not to. He flinched as she withdrew. He was bewildered. At this moment she knew she could convince him to give up this idea. But it would only rise again.

"You go to the city for as long as you want. I'll tell the kids you went on a business trip, or that you're working on an emergency case. They'll be all right."

"And you? Will you really be going out with other men?"

"I will if you go out with other women," she said, studying him, surprised at how confused he seemed. She had never felt clearer in her life.

"That's crazy, that's unfair."

"I think it's very fair."

"But how will you know if I do?"

Now she let the smile out. "I'll know, Mel, because you'll tell me."

"I could lie," he said, almost defiantly.

She raised her chin, stared him straight in the eye, and said, "So could I."

2

"Do you see a road?" Hillary slowed down and peered through the dust that caught up and then surrounded them.

"I see it, Mom!" Stephen's excited voice rose higher. "Over there!" He pointed to a narrow lane between two bushes of sagebrush. Hillary saw a row of four mailboxes that had once been painted a bright blue and yellow; now they were weathered and cracked.

She swung the car to the left off the dirt road and onto a rutted lane. "I swear, I don't know how Trish lives out here," she commented, rolling up the windows so the dust wouldn't come in.

"So this is Santa Fe," Lori commented, nodding wisely, her father's daughter.

"Boy, I wish Dad could see this. Are you sure you're not getting a divorce?" Stephen asked from the backseat.

"I told you ten times that Dad couldn't come with us because he's got too much work at the moment, Stephen. Now enough with the questions, all right?"

"I have to go, Mommy," Brian said, next to Stephen in the backseat.

"We're almost there, sweetheart."

"That's what you said an hour ago." Lori was definitely preteen at ten years old.

"I see it, there's the house," Stephen shouted in her ear. She turned to look, and almost ran the car into a rock that jutted out. "Damn," she muttered, swerving to avoid it. "All I need is to have an accident in a rental car."

"No big deal," Lori said. "The company will have it fixed for you. At home when the car needs fixing we always have to do it ourselves."

Hillary laughed. "You're right." She peered at the

four dilapidated New Mexico–style stucco-and-tile houses all nestled in a group. "Which one do you think is hers?" Rusted cars were parked here and there among the scrubby brush, also a truck and a red VW bug. There were even some scrawny chickens walking around, and behind one of the houses was a corral with two horses in it.

"Oh, wow!" Stephen said. "Can we ride the horse, Mom?"

"We'll see," Hillary said, feeling sorry that she'd dragged the children out here to the wilderness without thinking it through. And from the looks of this place, she might really be intruding. But last Tuesday, when Mel had said he wanted some time to be alone, all she had thought of was needing to be with Trish. And Trish had said to come. So she'd packed up the kids and jumped on a plane. If it didn't work out, they'd stay in a motel and go home tomorrow, on Saturday, instead of Monday. In any case, it would be an adventure.

"Isn't that Trish?" Lori asked, pointing to a woman in jeans and a rust-colored sweater who'd come out on the veranda of one of the houses. She was shielding her eyes from the bright rays of the setting sun and watching them approach. In the past, Trish would have waved with excitement; now she just stood waiting. Seeing her, Hillary was glad they had come.

They pulled the car up to the front of the house and got out. And then Trish was hugging her and Hillary was trying not to cry because the children were watching.

"I can't believe how you've grown," Trish exclaimed, hugging each child in turn. Brian didn't want to let go, and Hillary had a bad moment, wondering how Trish would take to being hugged by a small child, but she just hugged him back until he broke away. Brian had a special love for Trish because he'd been told about his visit to Berkeley when Kelly was born, and he'd seen the snapshots in the album, so that of all the children, he felt the closest to her.

"Are you all right?" Lori asked Trish, expressing motherly concern. Even though Kelly had been dead three years, Lori still talked about it as if it had just happened. Hillary was sure Trish talked about it that way too.

Trish nodded to Lori and smiled, taking her hand. "Anyone for cider and cookies?" Trish asked, leading the way into the house. "Me, me," the children chorused. Inside, the house was a lot better than it looked from the outside, with its peeling stucco and cracked tiles on the roof. Hillary recognized some of Trish's things from her home in Berkeley. The Spanish shawl lay over the back of the sofa; her books were stacked in piles in a bookcase; there was the upholstered chair that rocked, a wrought-iron plant stand, and Trish's baker's rack with brass trim. The Indian rugs on the floor Hillary had never seen before, nor had she ever seen a ceiling like this, made of narrow cedar logs still covered with bark, and attached in parallel rows that were bisected by round wooden beams. A fire blazed in the oval plaster fireplace, and Kachina dolls adorned the rough-hewn wooden mantle.

"You're all so welcome here," Trish said. "You're the only visitors I've ever had." She smiled at Hillary over the heads of the children while they ate their snacks.

"If you don't want us descending on you," Hillary said, "we can go to a motel in town."

"No, that's too far away. I'd never get to see you."

"Well, I brought the kids' sleeping bags, just in case, and I can sleep on the couch."

"We'll work it out," Trish said, shaking her head as if she couldn't believe what she was seeing. "You look wonderful, Hil. I've never seen you in jeans, with your hair pulled back like that. You look seventeen."

Lori looked up, instantly alert to women's talk. "But she still looks like Mom, don't you think?" she asked Trish.

Trish agreed.

"Do you work in this room or the other one?" Lori wanted to know.

"The other one," Trish answered. "Would you like to see?"

Lori nodded, but Stephen said, "I want to go see the horses. Can I, Mom? Please?"

Hillary looked at Trish.

"It's fine," Trish said. "The people who own them are away now, and I'm taking care of them. I'll teach you to ride if you want," she said to Stephen.

Stephen was in heaven.

Hillary took Brian to the bathroom while Trish took

the older children out to look at the horses, and then Hillary and Brian came out to join them.

The air was cold, tingling her skin, making Hillary feel alive and invigorated. The desert was bathed in a golden light, and the sagebrush and the soil glowed pink and blue in the late-afternoon sunlight. Hillary could see why so many artists loved to paint this unique landscape, which looked to her as though it were filled with rare treasures. The light was truly different here from the light back east. She breathed in the sweet air, felt it fill her with renewed life. Then she overheard Trish warning the children about rattlesnakes, and she wanted to bring them into the house and not let them out of her sight until Trish assured her that they'd be fine if they explored carefully and stayed out only until dark.

"You'll watch Brian," Hillary cautioned the two older ones. "Don't go off and leave him, and don't boss him around."

The children were in such good spirits they would have promised her anything. As she and Trish turned to go back to the house, Stephen called, "Hey, Mom, this place is supercalifragilisticexpialidocious."

She nodded and waved, but it was clear that Trish didn't know what Stephen was talking about.

"It's from *Mary Poppins*. Didn't you see that movie?"

"Out here?" Trish laughed. "We're lucky to watch television."

"Have you been keeping up with details about the break-in at the Watergate Hotel?"

"We do get the papers out here, even *Time* magazine."

"Fancy that," Hillary teased back.

They settled in front of the fire with glasses of wine, and Hillary began to relax.

"Why don't you go first? I want to know everything, like whether you're really all right, and if you're glad to be back at work after such a long time, and if you miss Arthur. You know, all the superficial stuff."

Trish smiled. "I was just thinking about that lunch you and I had in Manhattan when I came there with Arthur in 1966. God, I was so young. I thought you were Mrs. Uptight from New Jersey."

"I was," Hillary admitted. "But I thought you were going straight to hell."

"I did," Trish said.

Hillary nodded. "What about Arthur?"

"He's still teaching, still considered someone of only local importance."

"And what's with your career? Are you showing your work? Selling? I haven't received any notices from galleries, unless you've taken me off your list."

"Don't be silly, I'd never do that." Trish paused to study her. "You know, I think I detect a touch of brittleness about you I've never seen before." She cocked her head. "What's going on?"

"I'll get to it," Hillary promised. "But don't evade the subject, tell me."

Trish's gaze was caught by the flames leaping in the fireplace. She spoke slowly, unemotionally. "I didn't paint at all for the first year. When I got back to it, it was like learning to walk again. Eveything creaked, the bones of my body and my creativity were atrophied." She glanced up, still keeping her emotions in check. "I wanted to die when Kelly died, but I didn't. I just shut everything out. Never answered the phone, or letters."

"I know," Hillary told her. "A few of mine came back. It was a helpless feeling, being so far away and not being able to reach you. I prayed for you. It was all I could do."

"Maybe I felt it," Trish said, looking up at her for a brief moment. "I don't know. Pam wrote too, and called. I appreciated it, but I couldn't respond." She glanced down at the fire again, and the light played softly with her features, her small body, her long dark hair, her workman's hands with their nails cut short, the freckles sprinkling her nose and cheeks, but she still looked young, even childlike, except that the suffering in her eyes made her old. "The second year, I went back to work and never came up for air, breathed nothing but the smell of turpentine and oil paint. I had no direction, but was obsessed with trying to make sense of what had happened, though I couldn't stop crying. I painted faces and bodies turning away, looking within, hands pulling away from one another, eyes cast down, expressions of anguish. I experimented with new methods. Sometimes I applied paint heavily, other times my canvases were smooth and I used a fresco technique. I spent some time in Los

Angeles, but I was a recluse, not seeing people for days at a time. I'd gotten used to being alone. Sometimes I fooled myself into thinking that where I lived would make a difference. It didn't."

She took a sip of wine, and their eyes met. Hillary could see the weight of the years she had suffered. *I can't even imagine,* she thought.

"One day," Trish continued, "I smiled at someone, I bought flowers. Two years had gone by without my noticing the seasons or the holidays. That was when I moved to Santa Fe and started painting figures who raised their heads, who looked forward to what life offered. About then, I stopped aching all the time, but that had its own kind of pain because of what it meant—the letting go. I had looked at children with complete indifference, but if I heard a baby cry, I had an overwhelming urge to run and comfort it. That began to ease, too."

She stood up and motioned to Hillary. "Come with me, I want to show you something."

They went into Trish's studio, a large oblong room off the living room. It had an opaque skylight and a window that looked out to the barren fields dotted with yucca trees and brush. Trish's work was piled against the walls and hung on display. Most compelling was a series of collages depicting gestation and birth among a carnage of infant bodies. The images were violent and shocking, for Trish had applied parts of dolls to the canvas in a jumble of infant body parts, so that the effect was stunning and graphic.

Hillary felt a shudder go through her. "Powerful! I never would have thought it possible to capture the emotion of your . . . ordeal, but you have."

Trish studied the work dispassionately, obviously inured to their impact. Then she nodded. "I guess these helped me put it to rest."

"Has anyone seen them?"

"I sent some slides to my old gallery in New York. They didn't like them." She smiled ruefully. "Pat McGarrity wrote me a scathing letter. 'These works are an abomination. They show a seriously disturbed mind at work; I suggest you seek professional help,'" Trish quoted. "I memorized the letter." She laughed. "After I got over the shock of the rejection, I thought maybe he had a point. I did see a therapist for a while in Santa Fe. But my work didn't get less violent. In fact, the therapist thought it was cathartic for me. And she was right. The work has calmed down now. I should send my slides out again, but I just can't face another rejection." She shrugged.

"But you're so talented, you can't just let your career flounder. If you haven't been selling your work, how do you live? Arthur?"

"God, no. I wouldn't take anything from him. After the settlement money was gone, I waited tables for some friends who have a health-food restaurant in Santa Fe, and saved up enough money to live on while I painted. I'll probably go back to waitressing soon. My money's running out."

"What about your parents?"

"They did what they could, but their marriage was in trouble. I couldn't lean on them."

"How are they now?"

"Better."

Hillary admired Trish's courage and lack of self-pity. It was quite a contrast to the girl she'd known, who had been dependent either on her father or her husband. "Could I take some of your slides home? I'd like to show them to Mel. I'll return them to you."

"Sure," Trish agreed, leading the way back into the living room. "It's getting dark, we'll go find the children."

Hillary followed her outside to the porch. Brian and Stephen had fallen asleep on the old-fashioned upholstered porch swing that hung on chains from the rafters. Lori was sitting next to them, stroking Brian's hair and rocking the swing while she gazed out at the desert. She looked up at Hillary and Trish and smiled, then yawned. "I'm starved," she whispered.

"I've got a chicken roasting in the oven," Trish whispered back.

"Do you have any Chinese checkers?"

Trish nodded and laughed. "Play it all the time."

"I challenge you to a game after dinner," Lori said, getting up from the swing carefully so as not to awaken her brothers. "Want me to make a salad, Mom?" she asked.

Hillary looked at Trish, who nodded. "I wouldn't miss

this for anything," Trish said, opening the screen door and pointing the way to the kitchen.

"They're wonderful children," she said to Hillary. "Just what I would have expected from you."

"They do have their moments," Hillary said.

After dinner and three games of Chinese checkers, the children finally went to sleep, and Trish said, "It's an odd thing about mourning. People say, 'Time heals all wounds,' or 'You'll learn to live with it.' They all give advice. But that's a fallacy. It isn't time passing that helps, it's what you do with that time that heals. If you let yourself mourn, feel the wall of pain that is unsurmountable, that scrapes your fingers raw if you even try to climb it, then sometimes there is relief. I was tempted to go crazy at times; that's the easy way out. I cried until my guts were wrung out of my body, night after night, knowing that there were still so many more tears, so much more pain—unending. If I talked about it as much as I wanted to, and I never wanted to stop, people got tired of listening; they didn't know what to say."

She reached back and took hold of the long braid that cascaded down her back, bringing it forward and untying the fastener at the end. Then she began undoing the long, silky hair until it was all undone. She shook her head, letting it flow free. The firelight caught silver highlights of the dark river of hair flowing over her shoulders, and accentuated the tiny lines around her eyes and mouth from exposure to the desert air and sun. As if to underscore the way she looked, she said, "I'm different now, Hillary. I'll always be regarded as the woman who lost her child. No matter how I smile or wear my hair or manage a routine existence, they'll always think, 'Look how well she's doing, considering.' So I talk to myself, write poems, and paint pictures, paint, paint, paint. Whatever helps. Nothing helps."

Hillary came and put her arms around Trish, and they held one another for a moment. "It's so good to have you here," Trish said, pulling away. Surprisingly, neither of them cried. "I haven't talked like this since Kelly died, except to my therapist. It feels good."

"What about men? Have you dated at all?"

She shook her head, and her hair undulated in waves from her scalp all the way down the long strands to the ends. "There was someone, a long time ago. I thought he would make a difference. But after Kelly, I knew I wouldn't be good to anyone ever again, so I let it go."

"Maybe you'll change your mind."

"No," Trish said, dismissing the idea. "Romance is over for me. I couldn't risk another involvement and a possible loss. Never again." Her expression said the subject was closed. "We've talked about me all night. What about you?"

Hillary wished there were something she could do to help Trish end her isolation, but all she could do was hope. And yet she sensed a feeling of peace here that Trish must have discovered too. Hillary's expression reflected that sense of well-being, easing the furrow between her eyebrows, adding a sparkle to her eyes. She gazed at Trish, trying to convey her gratitude. "Before I came here, I thought I had a crisis. But I see how small my problems are."

"You mean compared to mine?"

"Frankly, yes."

Trish nodded, smiling at the truth of her statement, not offended, like a nun who can feel compassion for a conjugal relationship in the abstract.

"Everything's going to be all right, I'm sure of it now."

"But problems only get solved if you work at them."

"That's true," Hillary agreed. "And that's what I intend to do."

Hillary and the children flew back to New Jersey on Monday, so Stephen and Lori missed only one day of school. But when Hillary came into the house that night, carrying a sleeping Brian in her arms, her new sense of determination and inner peace deserted her. She missed Mel terribly. The house felt lonely, its emptiness mocking her. The phone rang. She reached for the receiver by the stairs.

"What's going on, where have you been?" Bobbie demanded. "I've been calling since Friday night. You didn't tell me you canceled our date to go out of town. But Frank told me about Mel's apartment. You poor thing," Bobbie commiserated.

"I'll call you back," Hillary promised. "We just walked in the door."

"I can't talk now." Bobbie sounded breathless. "Frank is waiting for me. I just had to know how you were."

"I'm fine," Hillary assured her, wondering if it was true. She didn't feel as fine as she'd felt in New Mexico.

"I think it's a mistake to sit and wait for him," Bobbie stated. "You've got to hang tough. Want me to fix you up? I've got a couple of guys who'd call you in a minute."

For a moment Hillary didn't believe what she was hearing. It was one thing to bluff Mel, another really to go out with someone else, maybe even to bed with him. She hoped it wouldn't come to that. Then she realized what Bobbie had just told her; she really *knew* men. "Bobbie, are you saying what I think you're saying?"

"Sure, it's kicks. I never told you before, because you wouldn't have understood. But now I think you do."

"Does Frank know?"

"No way. And don't you tell him!" There was touch of panic in her voice.

"I wouldn't tell him, you know that. Bobbie, I've got to go, Brian weighs a ton. I'll talk to you tomorrow." And she hung up.

She turned to carry Brian upstairs, where Lori and Stephen were already getting ready for bed, when she heard a key in the lock. She held her breath and her heart began to pound. It was Mel.

He saw her on the stairs in her jeans and down jacket, saw the suitcases and sleeping bags on the floor. There was a stricken look on his face. "Are you coming or going?"

"We just got home. I took the children to visit Trish for the weekend."

"All the way to Santa Fe? And you didn't tell me?" He was halfway between whining and furious.

She couldn't resist. "I was giving you your space."

"Here, I'll take him." He reached for Brian, who stirred as Mel lifted him.

"Just put him to bed in his clothes," she said. "I'll change him later."

Mel gave her a look as if he'd never seen her before, and climbed the stairs to Brian's room. Hillary heard the excited greetings from Lori and Stephen, telling him all about their adventure. And then he was downstairs again, still in his overcoat.

"Are you staying?" Hillary asked, indicating his coat. "I mean, just for a visit?"

"That's what I wanted to talk to you about. But first, what is going on here?" he asked. "I can't believe you did this."

She ignored his question, took off her jacket, sat down on the sofa next to the fireplace, stretched her feet out on the coffee table, and looked around the room with contentment. "It's good to be home." It felt even better now that he was here.

"Yes, it is," he said, as though he too meant it. He took off his coat and sat opposite her on the other sofa.

"Do you want a fire?" she asked.

He shook his head. "It's too late to start one now. It would burn all night, and that makes me nervous."

"But you won't be here, and it doesn't make me nervous." She leaned over and turned on the gas, lit the flame under the logs, and closed the screen.

Mel was holding his temper. They were both awkward, partial strangers, semi-siblings.

"Did you come home for some clothes, or something else?"

He shook his head again, looking down at his hands. "I came home 'cause I'm an idiot, Hil. After two days away from you, I felt lost. I missed you. I missed the kids, I missed our life and our home. And then I didn't know where you were. I imagined the worst, that you'd gone home to your mother, that you were getting a divorce. God, the tortures I put myself through. But you knew I would, didn't you? Is that why you went away, to hurt me, to make me think you were with someone else?"

"No, actually I was thinking about myself, about how I was going to manage. But I was with someone else, Mel. My friend Trish. We talked and shared our feelings and laughed and cried. It was great."

"And what about me?"

"What about you? You wanted this."

"Quit reminding me."

It was heady, having the upper hand, and she was tempted to rub it in. Only four days of freedom and already he wanted to come home, she could tell. But what did she want, for him to grovel? Or to have their marriage back where it belonged? Of course she wanted it back, but never again on a trial basis.

"How was your weekend otherwise?" she asked. "Did you *play?*"

"Only racquetball. I rented a bike and rode through the park. I had lunch with a lady." That gave her a pang. "But I thought about you. It finally came home to me what I was risking. That's why I'm here. Not to apologize, but to see if we can work things out. It's true, I've always felt I was shortchanged on a carefree youth," he admitted. "But I've gotten so much more in return." His eyes were guileless, his expression pleading. "I want to call off the game-playing, Hil. I don't want anyone but you."

She was surprised and thrilled to hear him say the things she'd always wanted to hear. But she was afraid to believe him. "Of course you want other people, Mel. So do I. That's only natural. But it's not worth the risk, is it?"

"No," he said, smiling at her. "It's not worth losing us."

"Do you really mean it?"

He nodded, smiling that smile that always made her melt. But she couldn't melt, not yet. "What's going to prevent this from happening again? I don't think I could take another few days like the ones I just spent. I was terrified that I'd lost you too."

"I can't guarantee I won't be discontented sometimes. But I've done what I said I'd do, and it didn't work, baby. It just didn't work."

"You don't think some other body, some other woman, would be exciting, desirable? Make you feel different?"

"Yes," he admitted. "But it's you I love."

"I think we need more time, Mel. This is too sudden. You just left a few days ago, but it took you years to get to this point. You can't have come to a permanent solution in such a short time."

"You're wrong, Hillary. Actually, I realized it before I left, but I'd have felt like a wimp if I hadn't gone through with it. I do know myself, Hil. I talk a good story, but I don't want to play if it means losing you." He had tears in his eyes.

But still she needed more. "Are you saying you're not

going to complain anymore about what you've missed? About having to get married? There's not going to be that subtle discontent pervading our lives?"

He gave her that grin which made her forgive him almost anything. "I'm not promising miracles," he said.

She laughed.

"But there will be no more discontent," he promised. "I finally understand that you too had to make the best of the situation. And as you said, other people do look appealing from time to time."

"By 'people,' you mean women?"

He smiled again, nodding. "But it's you I love, baby, only you."

She was afraid, in spite of his assurances, that this problem might crop up again. How she wished there were guarantees. But all she could hope for was the strength to handle it as well the next time as she had this time. She got up and came over to him and sat on his lap, winding her arms around his neck. He just held her. Then she lowered her head and kissed him, lingering, tasting, pouring out her love. She could feel his response where she was sitting.

"Oh, Hil," he moaned. "Let's go upstairs."

She got up and took his hand and led him up the stairs. Halfway there, she said, "I've got an idea. Why don't we ask my mom if she'll come and take care of the kids for a week, and you and I can go play in your New York bachelor's pad."

His hand cupping her behind, and his kiss on her neck, told her exactly what he thought of the idea.

3

THE YEAR'S MOST FASCINATING WOMAN

Still stunning at 37, with the hint of a faded scar across her cheek from a near-fatal car accident that cost her a career as a model, Pam Weymouth is this year's new kid on the block threatening to unseat the all-male stronghold of Manhattan's building industry giants. Grudgingly or not, they're making room for her. At a time when real estate has been in a devastating slump, she is still building high-rises. Her first venture was a 60-story commercial building on Madison Avenue in midtown, fully leased prior to breaking ground.

Teaming up with construction old-timer Jake Harrigan, who keeps the sub-contractors and business agents in line, leaves Weymouth free to acquire properties and develop new projects. In the last five and a half years they have built and developed seven commercial high-rises in midtown Manhattan, and two luxury condominiums. This year, with two hotels planned and one under construction, Pam Weymouth has entered a new phase.

"Hotel rooms bring the highest rent per square foot of any kind of property," she says, but refuses to address the complexities of managing and running hotels as opposed to managing and leasing commercial real estate, in which she is a proven expert. "We're setting up a hotel management division of Weymouth Development, and I don't anticipate problems. If I allowed my limitations to stop me, I'd never have entered an industry where I was the only woman."

It's true. She is the only female builder to this date in New York City.

Because she was on the outs with her father, William Grayson, of Gray-Con, one of the older established construction companies in the city, her father's connections and experience were not hers to use. "My father thought I should teach kindergarten," she says with a touch of bitterness. Now an active member of the Builders Association task force, she has worked to reform the building business. "I've learned to play ball," she stated, "but if some of those loopholes between management and labor were closed, fewer rats could slip through. The owners and builders in this industry must band together and muscle back those who are muscling us. It's the only way to keep the cost of construction within manageable limits. The outrageous cost of building is only going to continue to escalate. That means skyrocketing rents to offset the bloated cost of labor."

She knows of what she speaks. The new labor contracts being negotiated right now to increase the minimum wage per hour of several crucial trades, such as electricians, drivers, and demolition teams, will add millions of dollars to the overall cost of a building. Weymouth, however, isn't hurting, with a ski chalet in Aspen, a home in the Hamptons, and a fourteen-room penthouse in her most recent condominium project on Third Avenue, she has helped create and is a charter member of the new consumer society. As far as marriage and a family are concerned, she's content being single and relishes her little time alone. Shown here on the deck of her East Hampton home with longtime acquaintance and investor Alfonse de Keirgen of the jewelry dynasty, Ms. Weymouth insists, "We're just good friends."

—*Forbes,* October 15, 1974

Jake came into Pam's office, carrying four copies of *Forbes* magazine with the article about her in it. "Have you seen this?"

She nodded.

"Can't top you at anything," he said. "Got these from

a friend of mine who works at the magazine, out of the first batch off the press." He plopped down in a chair opposite her. "How'd you get yours?"

"Malcolm Forbes," she told him.

"What a bunch of bull. This writer glossed over our major problems. We're in the worst cash crunch we've ever experienced, and it's all because of the economy and those damned hotels."

She leaned back in her swivel chair. The honey color of the suede upholstery blended with the color of her hair; she put her arms behind her head and lifted it off her neck. It was ninety-five degrees today, and the sun was beating in on her back. "We can't control the economy, but we can push for completion, Jake. Once the hotels are open for business and filled to capacity, the cash crunch will pass. You planning to bronze those?" She nodded at the magazines in his lap.

"No, I thought I'd cut them into long strips and wind them around the holder in the bathroom so Your Majesty could put them to good use."

Pam laughed. "If I wasn't afraid of the newsprint coming off on my bum, I'd think it was a good idea." She let her hair fall to her neck, then returned her chair to its upright position. "They just write articles like these to convince people that things aren't as bad as they are, that the city isn't facing bankruptcy, and the stock market hasn't just fallen a hundred and fifty points."

She leaned forward, elbows on the desk, the excitement of an idea lighting up her eyes. "You know, everybody's predicting more doom. But I'm not. I took a walk downtown yesterday, the area in the low thirties east of Fifth."

"That just borders on Murray Hill?"

She nodded. "I think it's ripe for redevelopment. I'd like to buy up several square blocks and plan a major project, like a mini-city."

"You're crazy, Pam," Jake almost shouted. "I'm tearing my hair out over our situation, and you're out in left field. If our tenant occupancy falls any lower, we won't be able to service our debt. We could have lenders foreclosing on us in one month's time." He reached into his pocket for a cigar, saw her look, and put it back. The rule was "not in Pam's office."

"As tight as that?" she said. "I thought we had more room."

"You didn't read those figures I sent you last night, did you?"

"No," she told him. "I can't let details get me down, Jake. I have to be the visionary."

"Oh, great. You ignore everything we're going through and dream about a mini-city."

"Why not?" She always got hot when opposed.

"Acquiring the property, for one thing. Mini-cities are usually built on large available parcels, like Century City was in L.A.—Alcoa acquired that land from 20th-Century Fox in one huge parcel—or they're built on property that's been condemned by the city, or else on reclaimed land or man-made tracts. But once you start to buy up occupied city blocks, you'll get nothing but headaches. To get possession, you have to have the tenants vacate; very expensive on a big site, especially with rent control protecting residential tenants. And besides, there are a lot of other areas in the city better than that one for redevelopment."

"Name two," she challenged.

"Times Square, the entire theater district, the south-west tip of the island, if you could get the city to approve a landfill. Even Wall Street needs upgrading, and those areas would not only draw top tenants, but you'd get zoning breaks and tax incentives, too."

"Don't be so negative, Jake. As long as you're in the city, location isn't that crucial. Any space can be made appealing."

His eyes grew wide. "This can't be the Pam Weymouth I know. Your epitaph was going to be 'Location Is All.' "

She smiled. "You remembered."

"And how the hell are we supposed to pay for this little venture of yours? We're out of money, lady. We are facing the end. It could happen next month!"

"And what about our class-A building in the airspace over de Keirgen's Jewelers on Fifth? We acquired those four adjacent buildings for this project."

"Those plans are coming along, Jake. But don't dismiss this other idea, okay? It would be a lot better for the city than another glamorous building, even if it is *our* glamorous building."

He threw up his hands. "You're unbelievable. How are we going to pay for everything, dammit?"

She sighed. "I don't know yet."

He shifted in his chair and crossed his legs. "You think this is a good idea?"

Her eyes got that look of excitement again. "It's fantastic."

"Then we'll have to sell something."

"I know. I've been getting calls on the Madison Avenue building," she said quietly.

He just stared at her. "That's our baby. Our firstborn. You dedicated it to Diane, you can't sell that. And besides, nobody is buying New York property right now, they're stealing it."

She sighed. The last thing she wanted to do was sell the Madison Avenue property. Not after what she had gone through to build it. Charles and Brandon and her whole other life were tied up in it, her flagship. But Jake was right, they were in a precarious position right now. She had read the figures and they terrified her. She couldn't let everything go, just to hold on to something she loved. "Listen to me, Jake. That building, of all our properties, has the highest potential for profit and it's the most desirable because of the long-term, blue-chip tenants and the rent escalation clauses. That building got us started, and it's the only one that can save us right now."

"But nobody's putting money into New York right now."

"There are still some people in this world who believe there's never been a better buying opportunity for Manhattan real estate than now, when everything's depressed. The Manheims in Canada believe it, and so do I. They've been secretly buying up Manhattan property, and they want the Madison Avenue building. I keep telling them no way, but their CEO has called me every week for the last two months asking me to reconsider. The sale of that building, with the profit margin we've got in it, could service our debt until the hotels are finished, and get me started on my mini-city. Now don't look like that, Jake. I need to keep my dreams alive. Madison Avenue was the past. Murray Hill, or some other location, is the future."

He looked away, pretending to be angry, but it was to hide his sadness.

"Jake. Diane's memory lives with us, whether we still own that building or not. You know that."

He turned back and nodded, but she felt like crying too. Every loss in her life reawakened all the other losses, starting with her father and ending with giving up Brandon.

"I'm going to fly to Canada and talk to the Manheims, see what they've got in mind. Maybe I can strike a deal where we won't have to sell the property. But I've got to have the leeway to do it, if I think it's best." Again he nodded, and they went on to discuss other projects. But all day Pam worried whether she was doing the right thing. Sentiment was nice, if one could afford it, but she couldn't allow her empire to collapse because of sentiment. And her original syndicate investors had a right to their profit, too. Maybe it was worth sacrificing her first building for the idea of amassing a huge block of land to use however she wanted—within the zoning restrictions of the city, of course—and for the need to make a profit. It would place her in a category that only a few people had achieved. And none of them were women.

The next day she walked the area that she'd seen the day before block by block, ignoring everything but what she would do here if the property was hers. And the next day she hired a helicopter to fly her over the city, which was illegal, but she was lucky and didn't get caught. There it was, teeming below her, the city in grid form, the blocks and streets of her future and her fortune. Gleaming gold, iron, and steel, there for the taking. Exhilaration blew through her like a Santa Ana wind off the desert. She felt as though she owned the world. *And someday I will own it all,* she thought. *And if not all, then as much as I can possibly imagine.*

The helicopter escapade turned out to be lucrative as well as intoxicating, because while flying over the spires of the buildings, she got a unique overview of Manhattan, and also found the perfect location for what she wanted to do.

Just before she was to leave for Toronto, she got a call at home from Jake.

"I got word that the banks will not give us an extension next month," he told her. "And we've run out of cash. If you don't make an amazing sale on the Madison Avenue building, you can kiss everything good-bye!"

His panic had gotten to her. She could see it all slipping through her fingers. Her compulsion was to call the Manheims and say, "Take it, it's yours, just bail me out." But she wouldn't do that. Too much was riding on it. She had to present herself as the one who was doing them a favor. Thank God, the property she had to sell was a plum because of its massive cash flow. That was why they'd kept calling and asking her to sell.

By the time she got to Canada, she had worked out her strategy, but it proved unnecessary. The Manheims were delightful to do business with. Soft-spoken and courteous, they offered her top dollar for her building, and she made the deal. They promised to leave in place the plaque dedicating the building to Diane Baer.

When she got back to New York, the news was all over the street that Pam Weymouth had received the highest percentage sale over cost of a building of any sold in the past year. But, better than that, with her newly acquired fortune, she could go ahead with her project.

Experience had taught Pam that it was tricky to buy or option large pieces of property in any major city in the country, especially Manhattan. If the owners of a targeted area found out they had something desirable, the price would rise accordingly. And if speculators found out, they would buy parcels to resell at a quick profit, costing her even more.

First she contacted Mel Robin, whose law firm handled her legal matters. Mel recommended Marshall Levine as a discreet real-estate broker and an expert in acquisitions. Levine, along with his brother and another young man, headed an aggressive, innovative brokerage house. At their first meeting, Levine included Jayson Mowbry, who headed his own title company. They would also need to do discreet title searches of the property they wanted to acquire.

"You understand," Pam cautioned them during their initial meeting, "that I don't want any of the owners in the area to know who's making the offer on their property. We'll set up different corporations for each separate parcel we buy, and try to acquire a cluster of buildings large enough to build something on, so we can always use it. Then, if the owners of these separate clusters gossip with one another, they won't know that the same company is buying it all."

Levine made notes of her suggestions and brought out a map of the area with dimensions of each parcel they'd need to acquire. His preparation was impressive, especially when he discussed his battle plan of going after key parcels so that the other ones would fall more easily into place. "And we'll try to get you the square footage price you've specified," he assured her.

"Just remember, the more you save on the cost of options and prices for these properties, Marshall," she told him, "the bigger your bonus will be."

"I think that sellers will respond to a bona fide purchase rather than an option. I've had a two-page offer drawn up that's been approved by the New York Real Estate Board."

Pam glanced it over. "I see you're offering a nonrefundable cash deposit that the owners can keep if the deal doesn't go through."

He waited for her explosion. After all, he was giving away her money.

But Pam nodded. "I think it's an excellent idea. Just keep the deposits to a minimum if you can."

"There's something else about this deal that we'd better discuss now," Levine told her. "Acquiring this property can take years of secret maneuvering. You'll have a fortune tied up in options, only to find that someone or something has blocked your way—a difficult or reluctant seller, or the city, or even the state."

Pam looked at each of her advisers in turn. "We'll deal with every obstacle as it occurs, gentlemen. But we're going to succeed," she insisted. "I won't consider anything else."

As the weeks and months went by, Pam followed the details of the property acquisitions with great interest, contributing her own ideas whenever necessary. And her innovative thinking often persuaded an otherwise reluctant seller to sell.

Most buildings were not owned by single individuals, but by groups of people who rarely agreed on how the property should be disposed of. And when a corporation owned a building, the details got even more complicated because of special tax considerations, tenants' leases, or the corporation's own plans for the property. But bit by bit, Pam could see the area of the city that she'd designated for her new project becoming hers.

4

"We are approaching Kennedy Airport and will be land-ing in about fifteen minutes," the captain's voice an-nounced. The passengers burst into applause. A violent rainstorm throughout the Eastern Seaboard had nearly diverted this flight to Atlanta, and it had been so bumpy that many people had gotten ill. The stewardess had told them they would be the last plane to land in New York for many hours to come, maybe days. "Please make sure your seat belts are securely fastened, return your seatbacks to their upright positions, secure all tray tables, and place your carry-on luggage under the seat in front of you. And thank you all for flying with us today. . . ."

Welcome to New York, Trish thought, feeling surpris-ingly happy in spite of the inconvenience of a rainstorm and a terrible flight. She reached again for the letter in her purse from McGarrity's, wanting to read it over once more, still unable to believe what he'd written. She was about to become one of the new celebrated artists of the seventies.

God bless Hillary, she thought. Without Trish's knowl-edge, Hillary, acting as her agent, had taken the slides of Trish's work to the galleries in New York. When she informed McGarrity that she was seeking other represen-tation for Trish, she discovered that he had been looking for Trish to clear up a mistake. Pat McGarrity had been in the hospital with a gallstone when Trish sent him her last group of slides. An assistant who no longer worked for him had written that terrible letter to Trish, and McGarrity wanted to apologize. He insisted that he was still a loyal fan and supporter of Trish Baldwin, but thought that she'd stopped painting. He asked to see her new work, and fell in love. They signed a contract and he sent her an advance. The money got her out of debt, and almost everything Trish sent to him sold, so she paid back the advance immediately. She'd had to work eighteen hours a day to get together enough work for a show. And now that show was scheduled for next month, September 1976. She and the nation's Bicentennial were making a splash together.

The wheels of the plane touched down with a jolt, jerking her forward. At last, New York. After all this time, she was ready. How she looked forward to a reunion with Pam and Hillary. For the first time since college, they'd be living in the same city again.

She managed to find a cab that was willing to take her into the city despite the storm, but whose backseat was so broken down she couldn't see out the front window. Every bump sent a shock through her spine. But she was too elated to care; her past was truly behind her now. She'd rent a loft as soon as possible; she could afford it, finally. Having her own place in New York was a dream come true, all part of the progress she'd made.

For some time now, she had been able to think of Kelly without that terrible knifing pain inside. Imagining Kelly at two years and at three, taking her first steps, speaking her first words, brought her comfort. She even created a grown-up Kelly as a whole, strong little girl, a bubbly child, bright and funny, seeing her each year, at four, and then at five, running on the grass, riding a pony, playing at the shore. If Kelly had lived, she might not have grown up straight and tall, spoken words or sentences, or put toddlers' puzzles together. But Trish wouldn't have cared what her limitations were, she'd have given anything to be able to care for her, to hold her child in her arms again, whole or not, perfect or not. But it wasn't to be. Not ever.

If only she could convince herself that her drug-taking and her hasty departure from Arthur hadn't caused Kelly's death. Somehow she would have to learn to live with that. She wondered if Pam blamed herself for her baby's death, but didn't have the nerve to ask her.

Trish walked home from her art gallery opening at McGarrity's, still excited from being the center of attention. What a night! The crowd had pressed around her, heaping praise on her as she stood there, surrounded by her paintings, which contained her whole life, reconstructed and all for sale: the pathos, the struggle, the indecision, the insecurity, the tragedy, and now the triumph. As promised, Pat McGarrity had caused a stir in the New York art scene by promoting his latest find, and causing a stir of this magnitude was not easy among the established giants of contemporary art. But Trish's career was on a wild high. Her work was featured in an article in *ArtForum,* and the *New York Times* review was a rave. She could hardly believe the famous artists who had come tonight and complimented her: James Rosenquist, Roy Lichtenstein, Helen Frankenthaler, Robert Rauschenberg, and Andy Warhol, who remembered meeting her with Arthur years ago. And best of all, her dear friends had been here tonight too—Pam, looking wonderful in tangerine silk, Hillary and Mel, and her brother, Tom, who had flown in from San Francisco for the event.

The champagne she'd drunk had not clouded the excitement of the evening or her feeling of fulfillment. But still, in one corner of her heart was a dark hole that no amount of success or celebration could heal.

The highlight of the evening came at 9:30, past the time when the opening was supposed to end. McGarrity had winked at her and nodded across the room to one of the curators from MOMA, who stood enthralled by one of her works. As she watched, the curator motioned to McGarrity. Pat raised one of his bushy eyebrows at her and went to do his job.

She still couldn't believe that the Museum of Modern Art was interested in acquiring one of her works. Her feet barely touched the wet pavement as she walked down West Broadway and turned left on Broome. And then her stomach rumbled and she realized she was starved, hadn't eaten all day. The door opened for her at Café Arts and some people came out. She waited for them, lost in thought, but one of them called her name and she looked up. Connor O'Brien was standing there.

Her heart thudded as she recognized him. Everything came flooding back in an instant as she gazed at him. He was tan, but there were white lines around his blue eyes that the sun couldn't reach. His sandy hair was still thick, though not styled the same as she remembered, and now shot through with some gray. He had a mole on his cheek that she'd never noticed before, and an even deeper furrow between his eyebrows. She didn't dare look down at his hands, those hands that had held her life in them, kept her from dying. She adored his hands, and his wide smile that gave her comfort and security all at once.

"How are you?" he asked. "I'm so glad to see you. What are you doing here?"

"I live a few blocks away," she said. She was grinning back, silly, childlike, wonderful, but then she felt the smile start to change as she thought, *You can't do this, Trish.*

"I've wondered so many times how you were." He was studying her, still reading her too clearly.

"What are *you* doing here?" It was an insane question, but seeing him made her feel fluttery inside. Here was the one person she'd not allowed herself to want in all this time.

"I'm living in New York," he said. "Actually, I'm in the neighborhood because I heard about your opening tonight and I wanted to go, but thought you might not want to see me there."

She glanced away, feeling so many emotions—happiness, fear, and awkwardness—all at once.

"Are you meeting someone?" he asked.

She shook her head.

"May I join you?"

She hesitated. "I don't know, Connor."

"You're not still angry at me about Maureen, are you?"

"Why would you think that?"

"You only answered one of my letters, the one after the baby died. I figured you were angry."

She sighed. "I wasn't."

"Come on." He took her arm. "I'll buy you dinner."

She let him lead her into the small, crowded restaurant, but a feeling of panic was beginning to rise within her. He gave their name to the hostess and turned to her.

"I was glad to hear that your parents patched things up. You know I got divorced?"

"Yes." She avoided his eyes because they threatened to absorb her.

Someone who'd been at the opening came up to her and offered congratulations. She welcomed the interruption. Connor's presence next to her made her heart beat wildly. Finally they were alone again among the crowd, and she turned to him. His eyes were so kind, so intense, she looked away. "I didn't mean to hurt you by not writing back. I didn't write to anyone. There was no place for you or anyone in my life. Not even my parents were invited."

"Somehow I thought I was different. Egotistical of me, wasn't it?"

She shook her head, at a loss for what to say. She'd thought of him constantly . . . until Kelly died. That had changed everything.

"How about now?" he asked, trying to keep it light, but there was anxiety in his tone.

She shook her head. "I'm sorry, Connor. Not ever."

The color drained from his face. "You don't mean that. I know it's been a long time, but I always thought —no, I knew—there would be a time for us."

She steeled herself and looked up into his eyes, letting him see the dead place within her. He flinched, and his eyes filled with tears.

"How stupid of me," he said. "I'm so sorry for you, baby." He spoke softly but she heard him perfectly, though the room was filled with the din of voices. Yet, this time, she didn't allow the power of his presence and emotion to reach her.

"My work is all I can manage, Connor. It takes all I have left; there isn't any more."

"That will change," he said.

"I don't think so," she answered. There was a coldness within that made her shiver when she thought of how long it had already been without any change. Her appetite was suddenly gone, and she knew this was the wrong place to be. "I think I'd better go," she said. "It was good to see you." And she left him there without turning to see the hurt she'd inflicted, especially since she felt it more than he did. His presence had stirred up so many feelings again, feelings she couldn't afford to have. She could not stand the pain of another encounter with him, and yet he lived in New York; she might see him at any time. As she hurried away from the restaurant toward her loft, she promised herself that if it took every ounce of her strength, she would forget about him, ignore his presence in this city, and if she ever saw him again, she'd walk the other way.

"Why don't we introduce ourselves by going around the room so each of you can tell me your names?" Hillary said. The group of seven-year-olds sat cross-legged on the floor in front of her, in a circle around Mel's reclining lounge chair, gazing up at her. The family room was silent on this October afternoon, except for their fidgeting.

"I'm Mrs. Robin," she prompted. "I'm going to be your Cub Scout leader. And this is Mrs. Murphy, my co-leader."

Estelle Murphy, the mother of Andy, one of the boys in the group, perched on the left arm of the recliner, smiled at the group. "Hello boys."

"We have a wonderful year of activities planned for you, and I've asked my two older children to come here this afternoon to tell you what to expect." Hillary indicated Lori and Stephen, standing behind her. "Lori is thirteen and Stephen is eleven, and both of them have been Scouts. Lori was a Brownie and then a Girl Scout for four years. Stephen was a Cub Scout and is now a Boy Scout in Mrs. Warren's troop." Hillary bent down and put her hand on Brian's towhead. "And this is my other son, Brian, whom many of you know. Bri, why don't you start the introductions and show the others how to do it?"

Brian flushed slightly, but spoke up. "I'm Brian Robin. I'm seven years old. I'm in Mr. Gleason's class at Crestmont Elementary." He turned to the boy on his right and gave him a nudge with his elbow; Craig Weinberg introduced himself, and next came Kenny Trowbridge, then Dougie Brown, and Marshall Daniels, Andy Murphy, Kevin Matthews, and so on. Hillary studied each one; some wiggled, others giggled, the quiet ones, the nervy ones, the naughty ones. She would have skipped right by him, but there was something familiar about the face of one of the boys.

She came back to him, interrupting John Wexner. "Excuse me, but what did you say your name was?" she asked the boy with the blond hair and large green eyes.

"Kevin Matthews," he repeated, quietly, wondering if he'd done something wrong.

Hillary stared at him. *Why was he so familiar?* "Have I ever had your brother or sister in one of my groups?"

He shook his head.

But she couldn't stop staring; it was right at the edge of her brain, she just couldn't place him. Brian was watching her, noting her odd expression. Her youngest child was her most observant, and the one most in tune with her feelings. She realized she was being rude and winked at Brian; he tried to wink back, but hadn't yet mastered the skill and ended up looking slightly cross-eyed as he blinked both eyelids. She giggled and Brian laughed. "Go ahead," she said, turning her attention back to the group and letting the boys finish their introductions. She tried not to look at Kevin, but found her eyes turning to him again and again.

Lori and then Stephen explained the goals of scouting and what the Cubs could look forward to in the future, and then she took over.

"I always give this little speech to my new den, guys, and you'll get to know what I mean as we know each other better. But one of the goals of scouting is to learn to be good citizens. And one of the things that teach us about that is to take care of the world around us."

Kenny Trowbridge raised his hand, and she called on him. "Is that when we save things, like soda cans and bottles and stuff?"

"Yes." Hillary smiled. "We'll learn all about the environment, and how important it is for each of us to preserve it." She saw the look of indifference on their faces. "But we'll do other things too, like visit the fire department and the Museum of Natural History. I promise, you'll like it." Then Hillary gave the boys a list of what to bring to the next meeting, talked to them about their uniforms, and taught them a song. She loved hearing their young voices singing about the kookaburra in the gum tree. Then it was time for refreshments and the meeting was adjourned.

She'd been a Scout leader for Lori with the Brownies, and for Stephen too; now it was Brian's turn. Although they expected it of her, each child was afraid she'd get tired of being a leader and he wouldn't get his turn, but she loved it as much as they did.

In the kitchen, the sound of children's conversation created a din; they were crowding around Lori and Stephen, asking them questions. She moved over to where Kevin Matthews was drinking his punch and eating his cookies, still drawn to him for some reason. "Is everything all right?" she asked.

"Oh yes. You have a lovely home, Mrs. Robin," he said to her.

Polite, she thought. *Well mannered, well taught.* She noticed that his flannel shirt cuffs were frayed, the sleeves too short for his arms. Glancing down, she saw that the laces on his shoes were knotted in two places, and there was a patch on his knee. *Not exactly a wealthy child.*

"You're Kevin, aren't you?"

"Yes, ma'am," he answered, looking up at her with doe eyes.

"Are you new in Crestmont?"

"No." He was relieved to talk about mundane matters. "I live in Rutherford, but the troops in my school were all filled up, so me and Bill and Angelo got to transfer to your troop. It's okay, isn't it?" He seemed afraid that this magical opportunity was going to be taken away from him.

"Yes, that's okay," she assured him.

"My dad's gonna drive us home, and Billy's mom's gonna drive us here, 'cause my mom doesn't get off work till six," he explained.

"What does your mother do?" Hillary asked, wondering if she knew his mother.

"She's a secretary at Crane Chemical," he pronounced, obviously by rote.

"I see." That didn't seem familiar to her.

"And your birthday's in December, Kevin?"

His eyes grew even rounder as he stared at her. "How did you know?"

She smiled. "It's on your enrollment card. I thought maybe I'd met your mom in the hospital when Brian was born, but he's a little younger than you."

"My birthday's December twenty-second, Mrs. Robin. I'm old enough for Cub Scouts, aren't I?"

"Yes," she assured him, "you are."

He sighed with relief and she moved on to talk to the other children.

But the child's sweet face stayed with her from Thursday through the weekend. And then on Sunday, as she was sorting through some old magazines for the Cub Scouts to use for collages, she found some of Pam's earlier modeling pictures. Suddenly she knew why Kevin's eyes were so familiar. They were Pam's eyes. That was when she knew who he was. *Pam's son, Brandon, is in my Cub Scout den.* A shock ran through her, a jolt of electricity. She remembered the name Matthews; that was the name of the people who'd adopted Brandon, she'd seen it in Mel's file when she'd sneaked a look at it so many years ago. They'd named him Kevin.

Her heart was racing. She could barely think of what to do. She tried to calm herself. *Wait until I tell Pam,* she thought, and then immediately realized she could not tell Pam. And she could not tell Mel, either. Mel would be furious that she had breached his trust. Pam could never know that her beautiful, precious, bright son was not only living here in New Jersey, but by some amazing quirk of fate (which had provided too many seven-year-olds in Rutherford this semester who wanted to be Scouts and not enough leaders) he would now become friends with Brian. She recalled his face, trying to remember if there were any signs of Charles. She hadn't seen any. He was the image of Pam: slender body, cleft chin, the same nose and eyes. Looking at him, Hillary realized Pam must have been a beautiful child. *How many people would love to meet you, child,* she thought, thinking of Pam's mother and father, not to mention Pam herself. Even Charles—no, especially Charles, with his grown daughters—would be in love with this little boy. And it was her secret to keep, hers alone. Eagerly she looked forward to their next meeting, when she could learn more about him, meet his parents, see for herself how he was doing. She was very grateful to fate for having given her the opportunity to become reacquainted with this child. She almost felt like his fairy godmother. Brandon —no, Kevin—had been brought back into her life. She'd make sure never to lose sight of him again.

5

Hillary was rarely late. An evening with Pam and Trish was something she adored, but on this sweltering July night, reluctance detained her. She knew why, but that didn't help. *How can I tell her?* she thought over and over, during the ride into the city. *I promised myself last fall that I'd never mention a word about Kevin. But now she's got to know.*

Hillary rang the bell and Trish opened the door, carrying a glass of wine. It was blessedly cool in the loft.

"We were getting worried," Trish said. "Not about you, just your fabulous salad." She took the Tupperware bowl from Hillary and gave her a kiss on the cheek.

Pam was curled around a pillow on the floor of the cavernous space, wearing pale pink linen pants and a shirt to match. "Hi, toots. How are you?" She threw her a kiss. "Do you realize this is only the third time the three of us have gotten together since Trish moved to New York last August? I've really missed you two."

"Let me get you a glass of wine," Trish offered. "We were just discussing old times. Remember philosophy 1A and 1B with Dr. Popper, being and becoming, 'I think, therefore I am'?"

"No," Pam corrected her. " 'If a tree falls in the forest, is there any sound without a mind to perceive it or an ear to hear it?' Which philosopher was that, Hil?"

"I don't know," Hillary sighed.

"Yes you do," Pam insisted. "You remember everything."

"George Berkeley," Hillary replied, slightly annoyed.

Pam picked up on her tone. "What's wrong? Are you okay?"

Hillary didn't want to get into this now, especially in front of Trish. Trish handed her a glass of wine and she

415

sat down on one of the pillows. "It's hot, and I've got a lot on my mind, that's all."

Trish glanced at Pam, who raised one eyebrow. "You're the one we look to for our pep talks, and you come in like a summer storm. Want to talk about it?"

"I said no," Hillary snapped, and then hastened to apologize. "Let's drop it, okay?"

"Okay," Pam agreed.

"Berkeley's theory was supposed to prove the existence of God," Hillary said. "There is sound, even if a human ear doesn't hear it, because the mind of God, which perceives all, hears it." *After what happened to Kevin*, Hillary thought, *there is no God, but some cruel demon sitting on high, causing suffering*.

"See?" Pam said. "I knew she'd remember." Her words were slightly slurred; obviously she'd been drinking wine for a while.

Of all the nights, Hillary wanted her to be sober on this night.

A timer bell rang and Trish announced dinner. The three of them came to the table as Trish put the cannelloni down next to the salad. Pam had brought brandied peaches for dessert. Hillary pulled a black director's chair up to the gray marble table and sat down, but she had no appetite. All she could think about was getting Pam alone so she could tell her what she knew, and yet she dreaded doing it more than anything she'd ever done in her life.

"In college I worshiped the Renaissance painters," Trish said, dishing out the cannelloni, "and the Impressionists and then the Abstract Expressionists. But now I understand what we all have in common, the struggle to find a unique way of expressing ourselves. Of course, some are more unique than others." Her eyes twinkled with mischief as she began to eat her dinner. "So. Do you think I want to be one of the unique ones? Bet your ass I do."

Hillary heard the self-confidence and determination in Trish's voice and realized how much she'd changed.

Pam clinked her glass on Trish's. "Here's to my gods, all with feet of clay, Harry Helmsley, Bill Lefrak, Bill Zeckendorf, Ernie Hahn, and the Tishmans."

"How's your pet project doing?" Hillary asked, referring to Pam's hush-hush acquisition of a large part of the city that had been going on for years. Hillary knew about it more from Mel than from Pam.

Pam, sitting next to her, had an odd look on her face. "There's been a new twist to the everlasting saga. I finally found out the identity of the owners of one of the last holdout buildings we've been trying to acquire. The owners' names were buried under a pile of dummy corporations, as well hidden as we are. But my detective is better than theirs, or else my connections are. If I can buy their building, three of their neighbors will agree to sell, and that's almost the whole ten blocks."

"So who is it?" Hillary asked.

Pam took a slow sip of her wine and said, "My father."

"My God," Hillary exclaimed, giving the reaction Pam had expected.

"That's too ironic," Trish said. "What are you going to do? He won't sell to you, will he?"

"No way," Pam exclaimed. "If he knew what we were planning he'd take pleasure in blocking me."

"I can't believe that," Hillary said, ever the optimist.

"That's because you judge everyone's father by yours. And even if Bill didn't try to stop me, Charles would."

That Hillary agreed with.

"I'll find a way," Pam declared. "I didn't spend three years of my life and twelve million dollars in options and deposits to have it all go to waste now."

Trish was feeling the wine too, and she lifted her glass. "To Pam and Picasso, the two people I admire most."

Pam laughed. "Have you decided what to do with this loft?"

Trish raised her glass to the empty room. "Do you think I should build partitions, or leave it more open?" Pam was the expert at space-planning. "I'd like it to be gorgeous—minimal, but luxurious. You know?" At the moment its dark corners were piled with works in progress.

"Any new romances, Trish?" Hillary asked.

Trish looked at her and shrugged. "No one interesting."

"Was that man you met in Iran really in the CIA?" Hillary asked.

"So I heard," Trish replied, indicating that she didn't want to discuss it.

"How's work?" Pam asked Trish. And while Trish

went into a lengthy discussion, Hillary realized she felt ignored. Her questions were answered in monosyllables, while Pam's rated dissertations. Ever since she'd arrived, she'd felt her opinions were of less consequence than theirs, her life-style less important. She'd forgotten how it felt to be the third member of a group of two, but she remembered now with a pang. Sometimes in college she'd felt ganged up on by the two of them, the superachievers. She was the one who was honored to be their friend, special, because she'd been chosen to be with these incredibly special people. She always wanted to be with the in-crowd, but they never gave it a thought because they *were* the in-crowd. Others wanted to be with them. Their talents were so obvious, hers nonexistent. And that created a tie between the two of them; their wavelengths were direct, while hers wavered in the air, never truly connecting. Sometimes in college they had made her feel not good enough; now they were making her feel provincial, and that pissed her off. And yet they'd needed her, turned to her, still did. *I'm the one with the husband and the children,* she thought, and then felt guilty. Thank God, she hadn't said it out loud. Only a twist of fate had given her so much while taking away everything from her friends. No one knew that better than she. That tiny coffin being lowered into the ground, Trish sobbing next to her, calling, "Good-bye, my baby, don't be cold. It's all right, it's all right," trying to reassure herself over and over when everyone knew it wasn't all right.

They were finishing their iced coffee when Pam set her glass down on the table and pushed her chair back. Hillary could tell she was about to leave. *I'll ask her to drive me to the train; when we're alone I'll tell her.* Her heartbeat started to race.

The lights went out. It was suddenly pitch black in the room. The air-conditioning unit, which had been hissing, sending down wonderful cooling air, stopped. The refrigerator gave a rattle and died. Everything was silent. Then, in the street, cars began to honk.

"What day is today?" Trish asked.

"July thirteenth," Pam answered. "Why?"

"I thought maybe I'd forgotten to pay my water and power bill."

Groping in the dark, Hillary made her way to the

window. There were no lights anywhere, except for the headlights of cars. Across the street, someone was shining a flashlight out the window. Eerie.

"The end of the world as we know it," Pam joked.

"Do you have any candles?" Hillary asked.

"Does the Pope pray?" Pam laughed. "Asking Trish if she has candles is like asking me if I work. And it's all I do."

"I know what you do," Hillary snapped, nearly losing her temper. In the dark she couldn't see Pam's expression, but knew she must be surprised.

"My trusty Sony," Trish said, coming toward them with a candle and a portable radio in her hand. She tuned into one of the emergency stations which were broadcasting.

"At 8:31 P.M., Eastern Daylight Time, a series of lightning strikes caused the third power plant at Buchanan, New York, to shut down, resulting in a blackout that extends throughout most of Manhattan and Westchester County. It is not known how long the situation will last, but emergency crews are working on the problem. You are requested to stay in your homes. Do not go out. Repeat, do not go out. Those of you who are stuck in elevators or on high floors of buildings, don't panic, help is on the way. Repeat, help is on the way."

The three of them stared at each other through the flickering candle, and then started to laugh. "Oh God, I don't believe this," Pam said. "The lumbering giant Manhattan is out of commission. Reminds me of Gulliver and the Lilliputians."

"I hope Mel and the kids aren't worried," Hillary said.

"Oh, I'm sure they're not." Trish put her arm around her. "This reminds me of People's Park in the sixties. 'World Under Siege.'"

"I have this mad desire for ice cream," Pam said. "Just think, all the ice cream in the city is melting. We'd be doing Baskin-Robbins a favor. Aren't you dying to go outside and see what it's like?"

"They want us to stay in, Pam. You heard the announcement. It could be dangerous out there. Who knows what could happen in the dark?"

"Don't you ever get tired of being good, Hillary?" Pam asked, making her way to the door.

"Don't be bitchy," Trish admonished, following Pam. "I think I'll have Jamoca Almond Fudge."

"Is it good when it's melted?"

"That's the best, ice cream soup." The two giggled the way Stephen and Lori did when they were doing something they shouldn't. After seeing Kevin today, Hillary couldn't be jolly or daring. She sat alone in the dark, feeling sadness envelop her. *Must be getting my period.* It was the usual reason for her mood swings. But it wasn't her period; it was being far from her children, concerned for their health, afraid for their future. What was Mel doing? Had he gotten home before the blackout? Or was he stuck in his office on the thirty-third floor? Would he spend the night there? And if he did, would he be alone? She called his office, but there was no answer.

Such dour thoughts. She had no reason to doubt Mel; he'd always been there. He complained a lot, still flirted sometimes, but he was there. And he was half of her. She couldn't imagine what it was like to be Pam and not look to someone else for completion. Not that it was negative to be a part of a duo, but Pam was sufficient unto herself. She never concerned herself with keeping a spark alive in a relationship the way Hillary did, and Hillary's needed reigniting; they'd have been married fifteen years next month. She and Mel could go to Atlantic City and stay in a heart-shaped room with mirrors on the ceiling. She'd buy a shortie nightgown (if she could lose eight pounds first), and they'd drink champagne and watch sexy tapes on the video, forget about everything else. Without warning, she was sobbing. *Damn, I must be getting my period.*

She groped her way to the bathroom and found the john in the dark, splashed some water on her face, and then made her way back to the living room. The place was scary in the dark. Her footsteps echoed. The heat was oppressive. She must have dozed, because finally Trish and Pam came back with two containers of melting ice cream. "We didn't know what flavor you wanted, so we thought you could share ours," Trish said, thrusting a soupy mixture at her. She took a taste; it was delicious.

"When in doubt, eat," Hillary said, laughing in spite of herself, taking another spoonful, trying to feel more carefree. "If only food didn't taste so good, but it always does the job, instant gratification. It's like I'm having a romance with it."

"If you're having a romance, I'm a rival for your lover," Trish said, taking another spoonful for herself. Cars were still honking outside.

"Well, what happened?"

"It's crazy out there. We heard that thousands of people are stuck in the subways and elevators, can you imagine? In this heat? The traffic is unbelievable because the signals aren't working. Mounted police are the only ones who can get around easily."

"So what do you want to do? Stay here? We can put my mattress on the floor and use these pillows, too. I'd like to open the windows, but I'm afraid someone might climb in. The fire escape is easy to use."

"Leave it closed," Hillary said.

"I think we can brave the streets," Pam said. "My chauffeur will get here eventually, and I'll take Hillary to the train."

"What if the trains aren't running?" Hillary asked.

"Then my chauffeur can drop me off and take you home."

"Pam," Trish said, "don't you live on the fortieth floor? And aren't the elevators broken?"

Pam shrugged. "So I guess I'll stay here. But my chauffeur will drive you to the train, Hil."

Then I won't be able to be alone with her so I can tell her, Hillary thought. "Pam, I know this may sound silly, but will you drive with me to the station?" Pam was about to protest when Hillary lowered her voice so Trish couldn't hear. "I have to talk to you."

"Sure," Pam said, studying her friend.

Hillary said good-bye to Trish, and Pam said she'd be back. As soon as they were down on the street, Pam asked, "Okay, what's going on? Something has been bothering you all night. And it's not the blackout."

Hillary felt her throat constrict with fear, her pulse begin to race. "First of all, you have to know, I didn't want to tell you this. I still don't know if I'm doing the right thing, but there's no one I can discuss it with. I've gone over the pros and cons many times, trying to find an answer, but neither way seemed right. Telling you is the lesser of two evils."

"For God's sake, Hillary, you're scaring me. What is it?" Hillary heard that cut-the-bull tone in her voice.

"I have news about Brandon."

All the color drained from Pam's face, and she swallowed hard. "What news? How the hell could you have news of him?"

"When he was adopted, I looked at the file. I've always known the name of his parents."

"And you didn't tell me? How could you not tell me?"

"Please, Pam. Mel's career was at stake. That's confidential information. And you didn't want to know, did you? Or you'd have asked me to look, wouldn't you? I know you would have."

Pam turned away, her eyes filling with tears. "I wanted to ask you, but after what you'd done for me, I couldn't. Oh God, this hurts. I can't believe how much this hurts." She looked back, wiping her face hurriedly, forcing her strength to prevail. "Okay, tell me."

"Last fall he joined my Cub Scout den."

"He lives in Crestmont?" She was incredulous. "I don't believe it."

"No, he lives in Rutherford. But the dens in his area were all filled up. He joined ours with two other boys on a temporary basis until another one formed in his area. Oh, Pam, I wanted to tell you. He's so beautiful."

"Tell me," she said, grabbing Hillary's hand, squeezing with eagerness. "Is he tall? Is he shy? Outgoing? Oh God, if only I could see him. Pictures? Do you have any pictures?"

Hillary nodded. "I didn't bring them, but I have them. I took as many as I could without making the boys suspicious." She laughed. "I was afraid someone was going to accuse me of having an unnatural relationship with him, the way I stared and asked questions. He's terrific, Pam. And he has so many friends. He's very bright. He's a leader; the other boys look up to him. And he always makes them laugh. His parents are good people; you did the right thing. Because Charles would never have let him go, not this boy. He's special, just like you."

Pam burst into tears. After a while she said, "The hard-bitten executive has turned to mush. If the union negotiators could see me now." Finally she stopped crying and blew her nose. Something in Hillary's expression stopped her. "Why did you tell me now? There's more, isn't there?"

Hillary nodded. "Kevin—that's his name now—didn't come to the last few Cub Scout meetings in June. Then the semester ended and I forgot to call and see how he was. And then Frances Matthews, his mother, called yesterday. She wanted to know if Brian would write him a letter, and if I could ask some of the other boys, too. Kevin is in the hospital. When I found out, I went to see him." She bit her lower lip, trying not to cry. "Apparently he's not the only one. Several children from his gramar school have been stricken. Some have died. They think it might have been due to exposure to some toxic substance."

Pam gasped. "What's wrong with him?"

Hillary clutched her hand. "Pam, Kevin has leukemia."

6

He cannot die! she told herself, over and over. No God could be that cruel to take him from her now that she'd found him again. Besides, it was far too early to know his prognosis. Worrying wouldn't help. Seeing him would. *No! I must not go near that hospital. It wouldn't be fair to him, or to me.* But how could she stay away? She'd give everything she had to actually see him, if only for a moment. *I'll walk by quickly, just take a look.*

But days went by and she didn't go. The fear of seeing him was overpowering. How could she see him and not talk to him, and how could she talk to him and not claim him? But she had no claim. No claim! Better not to go, not to put herself through the torture of seeing him, only to lose him again. What was the saying? What you don't know won't hurt you. Sure.

She called Mark Baer. "What can you tell me about leukemia in children? One of our employees' children is sick."

"What kind? Acute or chronic?"

"Acute, I think—lymphocytic."

He sighed. "That's the most common kind in children."

"You were thinking of Diane, weren't you?"

"Actually, no. I was thinking of Allison, Peter, and Jessica, I would never be able to handle it if they were sick."

"I'm sorry, I shouldn't have asked you."

"Yes, you should." He was exasperated with her, an emotion she often generated in him. "You know I want to be of any help to you that I can, Pam. God knows, you need me little enough as it is."

They had a warm, caring relationship. After Diane's death they had spent a lot of time together and eventually their attraction for one another had resurfaced, but Pam realized that what Mark needed was not what she was able to give—a mother for his children and a loving companion for himself. She got along very well with his children, and became a close friend to them, but her work schedule left little time for parenting and long weekends in the country. At first Mark had insisted that whatever she could give him was enough, but soon he came to realize that she was right; he was used to a different kind of relationship and wouldn't be happy with less. It was a disappointment for them both, but neither of them could really change. Maybe someday, Pam thought, but not now. Mark kept hoping.

"Will you get me the information I need or not, Mark?"

"Of course I will." Now his pride was hurt. "But before you hang up, let me give you some advice from experience. A great deal has been written about cancer and its treatment, especially in children. But usually people who are ill or who find their loved ones stricken don't read books about it. They're too shocked and stressed."

"So what should I do?"

"Tell your friend to take his child to a medical facility where they specialize in that kind of illness, no matter how far away it is. Being in a place that has the latest techniques and treatments available will give them a sense of confidence."

"That's not always easy to do."

"No, but it's worth it. They'll find an attitude among the staff and the patients that's reassuring. They will have seen it hundreds of times, so to them it's nothing new, and that diffuses the terror, brings it down to manageable proportions. There's something to be said for everybody being in the same boat. And that's not the same as 'Misery loves company.' "

"Thanks, Mark."

"Pam, the latest statistics for leukemia treatment are very good. Fifty to seventy percent of children live five years, and close to fifty percent are cured."

She thanked him again and hung up before she let herself cry. Then she called Hillary.

"His doctor's name is Pearl Friedman," Hillary told her. "She's on staff at a small hospital in New Jersey where he was being treated. He was an outpatient at the

beginning of his induction therapy—that's the first stage
of treatment—but he caught a cold. His white count was
too low to fight the infection and he had to be hospitalized. Now his parents have gotten him into Sloan-
Kettering. I've seen him twice since he's been there. He's
such a good kid. Brave. Wants to play soccer in September. And you know, I think he will."

"What about this hospital in New Jersey; is it considered good?"

"Not as good as Sloan-Kettering, where they have the
latest research and specialize in treatment of children."

"Why wasn't he taken there in the first place?" Pam
demanded to know, her anxiety increasing.

"I think it's a question of money," Hillary replied.

But I have so much money, she thought. *I have to find
a way to help him.*

The French decorating firm of Marchand et Fils, whom
Pam had hired to do the interiors of the Weymouth, her
first hotel on 57th Street, were due in the office in twenty
minutes; but she didn't give them a thought as she got off
the elevator in Pediatric Oncology and walked down the
hall. Her desire to help Kevin had finally propelled her
here, but now that she was actually going to see him, it
hit her squarely in the gut and she could barely put one
foot in front of the other. How many times had she
imagined him? There was no counting. The ache to hold
him, to touch him, to hear his voice never left, never. It
lay in her heart like a rock, taking up space, leaving a
pain that radiated from her heart to every nerve in her
body every time she took a breath. Once she'd gone to a
doctor for tests to see what that pain was, thinking it
might be a heart attack or her old ulcer, not believing the
truth. But there wasn't anything physical. Only the vision
of a tiny blond baby, skin like silk, growing up somewhere without her, featureless until today.

Hillary had told her where his room was. She would
just walk by, take a casual glance. That would be enough,
all she'd ever want. But her body was shaking so badly
she was afraid she might faint, her heart pounding, her
hands perspiring. There was a dull throbbing in her temple. She got as far as the door to his room and found it
was closed. *Of course, dummy, what did you expect?* And

she couldn't just walk in. Or, even crazier, hand him a packet of money or steal him away.

The nurses' station was busy; staff members, visitors, patients milled about. People looked at her, wondering what particular cross was hers to bear. The cheerful atmosphere surprised her. She felt totally conspicuous. A woman came walking down the hall and glanced at her, but Pam could tell she hadn't really seen her. The woman, in her early forties, knew where she was going, but her expression was anguished. She wore her graying hair short, with sideswept bangs over her forehead; she was plumpish, busty, not too tall—a pleasant, motherly woman. She took a deep breath and recomposed her features, then walked directly into Kevin's room. *That must be Frances Matthews.* The door swung wide and Pam looked in. One small boy in one bed, the other empty. Get-well cards were taped around the bed, wherever there wasn't equipment, and two huge eyes looked not at her, but at his mother. He smiled a weak but contented greeting, and the door closed.

Her knees gave way, literally would not hold her up. She clutched the edge of the nurses' station counter or she'd have fallen. As it was, two people rushed to help her—a man sitting nearby, and one of the nurses.

She smiled and waved them away. "I can't understand what came over me," she laughed. In a place like this, they understood perfectly. When she had regained her strength, she stood there reliving the vision of him over and over, tasting it on her tongue, placing the image of him on that sore place in her heart. For the first time since she'd last held him in her arms, that pain eased.

As an excuse to be here, she took a magazine off a table in a nearby waiting area and found a chair she could move until it was against the wall facing the door to Kevin's room. Then she sat down and pretended to read, her heart pounding with tension as if she were breaking into a bank. Every ounce of her begged for another look, as an addict begs for his drug.

And then a nurse went into his room; the door swung wide again and she cranked her neck to see, but this time Kevin was lying on his side, his back to her. The nurse came out, and Pam heard him call to the woman in a gravelly voice. "Good night, Mrs. Calabash, wherever you are."

A comedian? My son is a comedian? How could he know about Jimmy Durante? Someone must have told him. I've just heard him speak for the first time. What a sound. Jimmy Durante, one of my favorite people. Someone around him has a sense of humor. What things would I have told him if I'd had the chance? Stop it, Pam. Stop it!

Sitting there waiting for the door to open was both torturous and mundane. Like an episode in a television drama, scene by scene, she was putting together pieces of his life, and all she had were the meagerest scraps. For a moment she forgot why he was here, but only that he was; she had seen him, heard him. His gravelly voice had sounded like fairy bells. What a fool to think one glance would be enough! Her mind raced, searching for more crumbs of him. If she came at night, maybe she could sneak in and touch him, just his hand, or his forehead. *Sick, you're sick. You can't do that. You could get arrested for child molesting.* She suppressed a laugh, thinking of what a story it would make.

A female tycoon was caught sneaking into a seriously ill boy's room late at night, but denied knowing anything about the five thousand dollars' cash found at his bedside. "I only came to pick up his toys," she said.

Time ticked by; she barely thought about her obligations at work, about her designers, the Marchands, whom she was ignoring and who must be driving Jake crazy by now, while she played hooky. But she wouldn't give up one moment of the most exciting thing she'd ever done in her life. Maybe she'd never leave. Like some apparition in a science fiction story, she'd become part of the wall, part of the fixtures, sitting there hoping for a glimpse. She'd learn the hospital routine, how many times his door opened during the day, when he would actually get up and come out of his room. Oh, the joy, the amazing joy of actually seeing him standing there before her, not noticing her, of course, she was only the wall; but she'd get to see him for as long as she wanted, pour the sight of him all over her, his shoulders, his hips, his knees, his calves, his feet, his hands. He might even wave to her, smile at her. It was getting so late, she couldn't stay here any longer. She'd come back again, only early, before that woman got here. She'd never envied anyone as much in her life as she now envied Frances Matthews. And then she realized what she was thinking: *Envy a woman whose child may be dying? Nuts, Pam, you're nuts.* It was time to go.

She stood up, testing her strength, only a touch of dizziness from sitting so long. She was about to leave when his door opened again and Frances came out. She called back to Kevin, "I'll leave the door open for a few minutes, baby, so you can see what's going on out here. I'll be right back." And she headed for the ladies' room down the hall.

Pam froze where she stood, afraid to move. He was looking right at her. And then, as though his eyes didn't see her, he glanced away, lost in his reverie. What did a boy of eight and a half, sick in the hospital in the middle of summer, think about when he was alone? *Bet he wants to go swimming,* she thought. *Bet we wants to go to the beach, or to camp with the other kids.* Could they afford to send him to camp? How, when they couldn't even afford the proper treatment? He had to get the best medical treatment! Money must not be a consideration. But how could she arrange that? He looked back at her again, blankly. He looked a little like her half brothers. No, he looked like *her.* Her hand reached out to him of its own volition; she traced his cheek on the air. She knew in the first glance that he wasn't feeling well. The glassy look to his eyes. Was he in pain? This was impossible! She wanted to scream with frustration, hated herself for staring at him but couldn't stop. Then he noticed and turned away. *Oh, I don't want to bother you, sweet baby,* she pleaded. *It's only me, only me.*

She would have given anything she owned to be invisible. And to hold him, just for a moment, she'd have given her life. Helplessness squeezed her heart like a relentless fist, pinned her to the chair. She didn't know how much more of this she could take.

Just then, Frances returned from the bathroom and closed the door behind her. The sight of him was gone;

the fingers of the fist let her go. The light went out. Pam got up from the chair, picked up her purse, and made her way slowly to the elevator because there was no more energy left in any of the muscles in her body.

7

Through August and into September, Pam called the hospital daily to see about Kevin's condition. Every time she heard he was still there, she was both concerned and relieved. Concerned because he wasn't well enough yet to be discharged, and relieved because, since he was still so close by, she could see him. And she went often, in the early morning hours, late at night, and sometimes at lunchtime. Sneaking past his room, time after time, made her feel like a teenager when she and her friends would drive by some boy's house that they had a crush on, scared that he might see them, and hoping that he would.

Of course the nurses noticed her, recognized that she always sat in a chair across from wherever Kevin was, if he was having chemotherapy or was back in his room. She lived in fear of his family finding out who she was and of being kicked out. Unlawful visitation of a patient was her crime. She even thought about doing volunteer work at the hospital so she'd have a legitimate excuse to be there, but her schedule wouldn't allow it. When she wasn't at the hospital, she was on the job by 6:00 A.M. to confer with Jake, and rarely left the office before eight or nine at night. But with Kevin in the hospital she let everything but work go, such as her countless city committees, her board of directors' duties for two banks, and chairing a fund-raising gala for hereditary diseases. At the moment, she and Jake had three major projects under construction: two additional hotels, and the ultra-luxurious building on Fifth Avenue that would incorporate the landmark structure housing de Keirgen's jewelry store; above it would be a shopping complex, offices, and luxury condominiums of magnificent and unprecedented proportions. And of course she and Jake were still trying

431

to acquire the building that her father and Charles owned.
She needed to have it as a part of Weymouth City. So,
while she met with union negotiators, subcontractors,
designers, inspectors, filing clerks, city officials, state officials, tenants, loan officers, accountants, secretaries,
lawyers, and her stockbroker, trying to keep them from
ruling her life, she thought about Kevin and the officials
who ruled his life: lab technicians, oncologists, nurses,
therapists, administrators, hospital volunteers, fellow patients, radiologists, hematologists, and pediatricians.

From her first visit to Kevin in August, until well into
September, she had nodded to Frances Matthews whenever she passed. But with every nod, Pam felt her facial
muscles tighten with instinctive hostility. She could not
help resenting this woman who had raised and cared for
her son, even though she'd apparently done a good job.

One day in early October, they were standing next to
one another in the cafeteria line, and in spite of her urge
to leave, she was irresistibly drawn to the woman and
what she might say. She hungered for any personal news
about Kevin. On Frances's tray was a plate of lasagna,
French bread, a green salad, carrot cake, and a Coke.
Pam, who was having toast and coffee, pretended not to
notice.

For the first time, Frances spoke to her. "Do you have
a child in the hospital?" she asked. Her voice was low
and hoarse, like a whiskey drinker or a smoker, though
there were no cigarettes on her tray.

Pam's hand shook so that she sloshed the coffee onto
her saucer. "Yes," she replied, turning away.

"So do I," the woman confided. "I guess she doesn't
want you with her?"

They were paying for their food. "Why would you say
that?" As was her habit, Pam automatically handed the
cashier a twenty, indicating that the money was for both
of them, though she had no intention of becoming friendly
with the woman, only to pump her for information.

"Oh no, you can't buy my lunch," Frances protested.

But Pam gave her a look that said, *Forget it*.

"I'll get it next time," Frances said, moving over to a
table, assuming that they would now eat together. In
spite of the pounding of her heart, Pam followed her,
pulled out a chair, and sat down. "I meant, because I

always see you sitting alone in the hall. I never see you with your child."

Pam nodded. "Yes, you're right, doesn't want me around too much."

"Kids can be so difficult. How long has it been, for your girl, I mean?"

"I don't have a girl," Pam said, sorry she had sat down, yet unable to leave. This was the closest she'd come to Kevin in weeks—a rare opportunity.

"Oh, I'm sorry, I thought you said . . ." Pam's austerity was putting her off. She ate her lasagna. Apparently she was the kind of woman whose spirits couldn't be dampened for long. In a moment she started up again. "Kevin, that's my son, has had a terrible virus. We were afraid of pneumonia, but he's getting better. He has leukemia, he's on chemotherapy. The blood picture is looking good, but his resistance has been lowered, so anything he catches, even a cold, could be fatal." She glanced away, lost in thought, and Pam wanted to reach out, take her hand and say, I know, I know. But she sat there, stiffly, sipping her coffee.

"The pain has eased somewhat, that's a relief."

"What pain?" Pam had been told there wasn't much pain with the disease, only a terrible fatigue and lethargy.

"Bone. His bones ached and his glands were swollen. That's how we first noticed he was sick. God, you always think the worst with your kids, and when it is, you don't believe it. I didn't. It's really killing my husband. Kevin is everything to him. He's an amazing child, smarter than both of us put together. He's so mature I forget how old he is, and an athlete too, and what a sense of humor. Cracks me up. Our daughter misses him so much."

"You have a daughter?" Pam was shocked; she'd never considered that. *If you have another child, couldn't you just give him back to me?*

"Su Mei, four years old. She's Vietnamese, we adopted her."

"That takes a lot of courage."

"You mean to raise a minority child?"

"No, to have two adopted children." She didn't realize her mistake until Frances gave her an odd look.

"What makes you think Kevin is adopted?"

Pam felt her heart skip. "I just assumed. I'm so sorry."

"No, you're right. He is. But we don't tell people."

"Does he know?"

"No, we haven't told him. I know there's a lot of theories about that, but Gil and I think of him as ours. We couldn't love him more if he was. Of course, now, because of his illness, we're very curious about his family's medical history. We're trying to discover if cancer ran in his family, or if he has any brothers or sisters. Sometimes, in rare cases of leukemia, children are treated with a bone marrow transplant if a sibling's blood type matches. I've gone crazy thinking about all these things, watching him go through this. It changes you. I guess I don't have to tell you. What about your son? What does he have?"

"I'd rather not talk about it, if you don't mind."

"Of course."

Pam had finished her toast and coffee, and there was no reason to remain any longer. She pushed back her chair to go, but the woman thrust out her hand.

"I'm Frances."

Pam took it. "My name is Pam." She smiled for the first time.

"It really helps to talk sometimes, especially to a stranger. Everybody else gives you such sad looks." She smiled as if remembering something. "Kevin and I had a talk a few days ago. He told me he thinks of his illness as bad luck, but that it isn't going to get him down. And so far it hasn't. He jokes with the doctors and the nurses, has pet names for the technicians. He calls them the bloodsuckers. Knows just how to make things easier for himself, and he won't let them do it wrong—you know, stick him with a needle the wrong way, or give him a test before he's ready. He has this inner strength. He keeps my spirits up, I tell you."

"He sounds very special." She turned away and wiped at her cheek as though it was something other than a tear.

"Oh, he is. Maybe you'd like to meet him sometime?"

Pam turned back to stare into her guileless brown eyes, radiating friendliness; she felt suddenly lightheaded. "I'd love to meet him. Any time."

"Well, now's not a good time, he's having a bone marrow test and he always hates those so. But next time I see you around, I'll introduce you, okay?" When she smiled, Frances's lined face became softer and more attractive, the type of woman whose devotion to her family was easy for her.

Pam felt relieved; Kevin's mom was a wonderful person. Her jealous feelings had miraculously disappeared. After all, they were allies, weren't they, with Kevin's best interests at heart? Pam only wanted to help.

She sat back down, but now it was Frances who was anxious to go. She glanced at the round clock on the wall, and tilted her head apologetically. "It's getting late. Kevin will be back to his room and wondering where I am."

"Of course," Pam said. "I won't keep you." She thought of all the people she was keeping waiting. "I wanted to ask you something; it's rather personal."

"Shoot," was the reply; no artifice, no hesitation.

"I know that your medical bills must be enormous. Where your son's health is concerned, I'm sure you want only the best."

Frances started to laugh. "Don't tell me—you're an insurance saleswoman! Is that why you hang around hospitals?"

Pam laughed too; it was a logical assumption. "No, I'm in real estate," she said. "I was just asking because I belong to an organization that helps pay for catastrophic illnesses when a family has the need." She was making this up as she went along. "It's not exactly charity—far from it." She saw the tight muscles in Frances's face relax when she said that. "It's a fund. A fund collected from people who have lots of money, more money than they need, and they want to help. And it's there if you need it. If ever you need it. I can get your bills paid like that." She snapped her fingers. "No problem. Kevin could see any specialist you'd like; be treated right here in this hospital until he's well again. You could hire a full-time nurse for him, or a baby-sitter for your daughter so you could spend more time with him, or a driver to take you into the city in bad weather for your appointments. Anything you might need, I—we—could provide."

"My goodness." She sat back in her chair. "You're a regular Saint Nicholas, aren't you? What do we have to do to get some of this help? Oh, you can't imagine what it's like. The hospital in New Jersey doesn't have the same experimental program that they have here, and then there's the travel expenses, and staying in a hotel. In New Jersey we can stay at home." She raised her eyes to the heavens. "I can't sleep at night, thinking that if we can't afford this hospital it could mean Kevin's life."

"Oh, you can't let that happen," Pam said, alarmed.

"My husband will not take charity. He's very proud. But paying these medical bills is taking everything we have. We have a health plan with the company where we work, but it only pays so much. I had to take a leave of absence from my job as a secretary; I'm working evenings waiting tables at the Red Lion so I can be home with Kevin in the daytime to take him to the doctors and still pay our bills. Su Mei has to go to day-care; that costs money. Gil is working two shifts, one as foreman at his regular job, and driving nights for a waste disposal company. We're both so tired we can barely talk to each other. I can doze during the day when Kevin's resting, but Gil never gets a chance." She shook her head. "But Gil wouldn't take charity."

"It's not. It's rich people who want to help, who love children, who have more than enough money, who are looking for people like you to help. Maybe your husband wouldn't have to know where it came from."

"We don't keep secrets, Gil and me."

"Then maybe you could say you inherited it?"

"That's a laugh. My people are strictly blue-collar, honey. My dad drove a bus before he died; my mom worked in a factory, and my brother's a cop. He's got six kids. And Gil's family are mostly gone, not an heiress among 'em."

"I could be your rich cousin from California."

"My mama would tell him in a minute."

For the moment Pam was stumped, but now that she knew how much they needed her, she could not give up. "Let me talk to him, Mrs. Matthews, I'll see what I can do."

"Frances," the woman corrected her. "Did I tell you my last name?"

Pam bit the inside of her lower lip. *Careful, you'll blow it.* "Of course you did. Anyway, let me talk to your husband, approach him in such a way that he'll agree."

Frances stood up to go. "He's pretty stubborn. But I'm game if you are."

They shook hands again, and Pam wrote down her number. "I'll call him tonight."

"Should I mention our talk?"

"Yes, go ahead. Tell him you met some crazy lady who wants to pay your bills, but you told her he wouldn't take charity."

Frances nodded. "You really are crazy, aren't you?"

Pam nodded. "Takes one to know one." And they both burst out laughing.

Did she want to meet Kevin? Did Billy Martin want the Yankees to beat the Dodgers and win the Series this month? But she was worried. What if Frances noticed the resemblance between her and Kevin? If she knew who Pam was, she might get a restraining order to keep Pam away. Would she tell Kevin if she knew? Pam hoped not. She didn't want Kevin to learn the truth now, maybe not ever. But certainly not now; he had enough problems to deal with at the moment. No, her main concern had to be to persuade Gilbert Matthews to let her pay for Kevin's medical bills.

She considered the possibilities: she could say Kevin had won a jackpot or a scholarship, but that would mean lying. She didn't want to involve Kevin in a lie. She'd just have to convince the father it was in his son's interest to accept financial aid, and do it so he wouldn't sacrifice his pride.

Male pride, she came up against it all the time. Many men she worked with had chips on their shoulders; they thought of her as a nosy rich bitch. They resented her having money, whether she'd earned it or not, and the fact that she was their boss made her more of a target for their resentment. When she found incompetence or mistakes on the job, she couldn't afford the luxury of losing her temper the way Jake did; she had to be diplomatic. The one time she had yelled on a job, when some plumbing pipes had been stacked in such a way that they could roll off and injure someone, the plumber had walked off the job. First he'd tried to blame the supplier's driver, but when she'd pointed out that it was his responsibility, he'd said, "No bitch can talk to me that way."

Jake had smoothed things over, but she'd learned her lesson. Jake could say things like, "You sonofabitch, get your ass over here now, or it's fired," but she could not. Typically, she said things like, "Could you please tell Mr. O'Rourke to restack the plumbing pipes? They have somehow been unloaded incorrectly." Pause, smile. "And please ask him to do it right away because of the danger." If there was an accident, it was on her head, nobody else's, because it was her job, her insurance carrier, her liability. Sure, she could go after the subcontractor later on, but that would take time and money, while right now lives were at stake. The business agents of some unions could always find an excuse to slow a job down; they knew how it hung up the builder, how it ate into the narrow profit margin, how the threat of a slowdown always brought higher wages in negotiations, payoffs to certain officials, impossible concessions, just so the builder could get the job in on time. So she knew about tact, and male pride. And she would be extremely careful with Gilbert Matthews.

She made the call.

After a few pleasantries, he said, "My wife says you have a sick child too?" He was being cordial, but she heard the defensiveness in his voice.

"That's not why I'm calling. I think Frances spoke to you about my offer to help?"

"And I think she told you what I would say."

"Yes, she did. And first of all, I want to say that I understand how you feel. You've worked hard, and you've sacrificed a great deal for your son. Having him ill must be a nightmare for you."

"You don't know the half of it."

"If you had one dream in the world, one wish, and it could be granted, we both know what it would be, don't we? That Kevin would get well."

"He's *going* to get well. I believe that."

"But have you considered that you'd be helping Kevin to recover by accepting my help—I mean my organization's help?"

"How do you figure?"

"I'm sure you know how important it is for him to have the finest care, which means keeping him at Sloan-Kettering. And I know how expensive that is."

Silence.

She had to convince him. "But, as important as the proper treatment is, you must know how important a positive attitude can be in a patient's recovery. Well, if Kevin knows how hard you're working to pay for his treatment, and he sees how tired you and Frances are, and what a strain this is on the family, it will be more difficult for him to feel positive. And we have all this money sitting here, waiting to be spent, while Kevin's bills are getting bigger every day. I understand he's about to start the second stage of his treatment. They call it CNS preventive therapy. CNS stand for central nervous system, I think."

"Yes. He's pretty worried, too. They may have to give him radiation of the brain as well as spinal injections of chemotherapy. They say the leukemia cells can hide there otherwise, and come back later on."

"Shouldn't he have that treatment where they have the most experience? And he may need hospitalization, certainly many years of follow-up care. How can he remain positive, when you, the most important person in his life, can't be with him during that time? And what kind of quality time can you spend with him when you're half dead from working two jobs?"

"He's my son, I don't mind."

"But your daughter needs you too, Mr. Matthews. And so does your wife. Who's going to explain to them why you can't be with them at this crucial time, when I'm offering you a way?"

"You don't know what you're asking."

"I'm asking you to let me help. There are times when all of us need help. I've been down myself, badly injured, nearly dead. I couldn't have rebuilt my life without the help of my friends." She thought she was getting through to him, but she couldn't tell. "You know, Mr. Matthews, money is only important if it can make life easier, not as an end in itself. Your son is a hurt little boy right now, and he needs more help than you can afford at this time."

There was another silence while she heard him breathing heavily into the receiver. "You're pretty persuasive, aren't you?"

"Your wife told me how special Kevin is, how much you care about him."

"This is very hard, ma'am."

"Mr. Matthews, please believe me. If I had a son like Kevin, I'd want him to have the finest medical care money could buy, and if someone called me up and offered me a way to get it, I'd grab it so fast you wouldn't see my shadow. Please don't deprive your son of any chance he has to live." She was crying, he could hear it in her voice, and if he was surprised, he didn't show it.

Finally, after what seemed like a long time, he sighed. Then he said, "Hospital bills only. Nothing extra, like presents or anything. I can still provide for my family."

"I know you can. Your son is a wonderful example of how well you provide." Her relief was exquisite.

"What do we do now?" he asked.

"I'm going to send you some envelopes with stamps on them, and whenever there's a bill you want covered, you just mail it to . . . our headquarters. I never want you to worry about paying those bills again. And you tell Frances to quit her job at night so she can stay home with your daughter. I'll be in touch soon."

There was another silence, and then his voice caught as he said, "God bless you, woman."

8

Pam was supervising the installation of the magnificent slabs of lapis lazuli she'd gotten from South America for the inner face of the atrium of Weymouth Towers when she got a call on her beeper. She went to the construction phone and called her service. It was Marshall Levine.

He nearly shouted when he heard her voice. "Pam, we've finally found a way to get the building we want away from your father and his partner." His excitement was contagious. For nearly a year, they'd approached this problem without any success; they'd made offers that were turned down, upped the offers, and had them turned down again; they'd even offered to buy another property to swap for William and Charles's building, one with a better location, other tax advantages, and worth more money, but Charles and William wouldn't sell, saying they had plans of their own for its use. It was infuriating, almost as if they knew who it was they were opposing, though there was no way they could know. She'd had investigators trying to find ways to entice them or force them to sell, but no one had come up with anything.

"What is it, Marshall?" she said. "I can't believe there's really a way."

"Stay there," he said. "I'm coming over to tell you in person."

In fifteen minutes he had arrived at the construction site, but before he could tell her his news, he was awestruck by the beauty of her building. "I've never seen anything like it," he raved. "The plans and the models in your office were nothing compared to seeing it in person."

"Thank you, Marshall. It is gratifying."

"I know what you've gone through with zoning regulations, and the city approval not coming through until the

441

last hour. And when you demolished Atkinson's Furniture, you donated the art deco frescoes to the Met, and saved the wrought-iron railings and parquet floors. That cost you more than they were worth."

"I just couldn't destroy them."

"And then there were those protests over the unusual shape of the building; the press has had you for breakfast for months, haven't they?"

"Don't remind me."

"Well, when the public sees this, you're going to be a hero in this town. You alone may be responsible for New York surviving the recession."

Pam laughed at his superlatives, but she was proud of this beautiful building and the fight it had taken to build it. At the moment, however, she was anxious to hear his news.

They went into the construction office and she cleared everyone out and closed the door. Marshall took off his coat, removed a cigarette from his jacket pocket, and offered her one. She declined.

"Your connection to Graham Weston Development paid off," he began. "Remember last fall, when you suggested we might try looking into Gray-Con's business dealings? Well, the acquisitions person under Graham Weston, whom we've been paying under the table, called. They've been trying to buy a corner property on West Seventy-fourth, because without it they can't go ahead with an apartment complex they've got planned. Only we just bought the building they need."

She looked at him and shrugged. "What's the connection between Graham Weston's corner and Bill and Charles's building?"

He leaned forward excitedly, trailing ashes across the construction plans on the desk, and wiping them away with his hand. "Gray-Con is the builder for Graham Weston's complex. We contacted Graham and told him we'd sell him the building he needs, if Bill and Charles will sell us what we need. Weston is putting pressure on them as we speak. First of all, Gray-Con can't afford to lose this construction contract, and they can't afford to make an enemy of Weston and his group. This is a major deal for them, they don't want it going down the tubes."

His fervor was beginning to get to her. Maybe it was

possible. "Bill and Charles are in a tough position? You're sure? Weston is forcing them to sell to us?"

He nodded, a broad smile breaking over his craggy face. "So that Weston can get the property he needs. We told him we'd be glad to sell ours for theirs."

My God, she thought, *this may be it.* The excitement was beginning to lift her out of the chair. "What was our last offer to Bill and Charles?"

"Top dollar; we doubled it from the time before."

"Offer them half."

"But, Pam, we want this property badly, we can't dick around."

Her eyes narrowed to steely slits as she looked at him. "I said half, Marshall. That offer ran out months ago, we have no obligation to it. Everything's tough these days: interest rates are thirteen percent and climbing, inflation is double-digit, there are vacancies all over town, foreclosures everywhere. You know that as well as I do. The city is bankrupt and nobody's giving money away, least of all me. And since we've got the upper hand, baby, we're going to play it."

He sat back in Jake's huge chair and felt it lean under his weight. "I've never seen you like this before," he said.

She was about to retort, but he held up his hands. "But you're the boss. I'll make the offer."

"And be sure we make a profit on the building we bought out from under Graham Weston. They're *connected,* Marshall, they can afford it."

"How do you know?" he asked, sitting forward again, and snubbing out his cigarette among Jake's cigar butts.

"I make it my business to know who's connected," she said, "so I can avoid them."

"Okay." He stood to go, putting on his coat. "I'll call as soon as I get to the office."

She gazed up at him, watching his discomfort grow as she stared, but didn't let up. "Uh-uh, call now. Call from here. I want to listen."

"But, Pam," he protested, "I've got all my notes on my desk, everything's in the file, in case they want to refer to something from the past."

"I know the details, I remember exactly what's on

every page." She handed him the phone. "Make the call!"

He sat back down and dialed information, but she stopped him by telling him Gray-Con's number from memory. He gave her a look of respect tinged with apprehension, and dialed.

Countless times Marshall Levine had called Gray-Con, attempting to buy this building for his anonymous client, and had been kept waiting. They played with him, took up his time, gave him false hopes and then dashed them every time. He'd hated dealing with them and had forced himself not to feel humiliated by the way they laughed at every offer. But this time was different. The moment the secretary said, "Just a moment," and put him on hold instead of telling him Mr. Grayson and Mr. Meroni were not available, he knew it was different.

William came on the line first, and then Charles. Marshall put his hand over the receiver and said, "They're both on the line."

"Put it on the speaker," she said.

He shook his head. "They'll be able to tell."

She realized he was right and pressed the line button, carefully lifting the receiver to listen.

"I'm sorry we've been so hard to reach, Marshall," William said. "But you know how it is."

Pam heard a tinge of anxiety in Bill's voice and knew she was the one who had caused it. Her blood began to race.

"Sure," Marshall replied, "I know how it is. And I appreciate your attentiveness to this matter. I guess you know why I'm calling; I'm still interested in your building on Twenty-sixth. My client is one of those sentimental eccentrics, wants to own the place where his parents first lived when they came to this country. Sort of a family shrine."

Pam raised her eyes to the ceiling.

"Well, due to a change in our circumstances, we're prepared to sell," Charles chimed in, "for your last offer."

It had been so long since she'd heard Charles's voice, it made her shudder. She glanced up at Marshall to see if he'd noticed, but he hadn't. She clutched the arm of her chair for a feeling of solidity and safety. Just hearing Charles had made her feel vulnerable and frightened again.

"I'm sorry," Marshall said, "but we're only prepared to pay you twelve million."

Bill and Charles both protested. "That's crazy. What's going on?"

Her mind drifted. This was the victory she'd waited for! Not only was she getting back at her father, but at Charles as well. If they knew who was buying it, they'd probably forgo their construction fees with Graham Weston to stop her. And if they knew what she wanted it for, they'd never let her have it, no matter what it cost them. But she'd outsmarted them, both of them. She was bigger than they were, and better too. And it felt wonderful. How she'd love to let them know it was she, but she couldn't. Not until everything was signed.

"Goddamn you," Charles was saying. "You've got us with our pants down, and we can't do anything about it, but don't think I'll ever forget this, Levine. You'd just better watch out for me. And tell your client he'd better watch himself too."

"Shut up, Charles," William said. And then, "I'm sorry for my partner's outburst, Marshall. Just have the agreements in our offices as soon as possible and we'll conclude this right away. As you know, Graham Weston is anxious to begin their plans."

"Fine," Marshall said. "So long."

But William said, "Wait. Before you hang up, there's something I want to ask you. How did your client know to buy a building that Graham Weston needed so badly that they'd force us to sell ours in exchange, if he's just a sentimental son of an immigrant?"

Marshall saw the smile of satisfaction on Pam's face turn into a wide grin as he said, "Well, Bill, I guess in addition to being the son of an immigrant, he's also a son of a bitch." And he hung up.

Large square pieces of fabric were folded in a pile in one corner of the conference table, so that Pam could see the overall designs of the smaller swatches attached to the layout boards. Marchand et Fils had done a superb job of designing the interior of the Weymouth Hotel. She leafed through the photographs of the French antiques they'd acquired for the hallways and public areas of the hotel.

Of course, the Weymouth was not the first hotel to use such luxurious appointments, but the hotel suites themselves were also to be furnished in authentic pieces. Ordinarily, Pam would have been effusive with praise over such wonderful results. Today she merely nodded.

She leafed through the fabrics one by one, opening them up, enjoying their luscious colors, the Boussac chintzes, the Clarence House velvets, the Scalamandré silks, but her mind wasn't on it.

She forced herself to listen to Jacques Marchand. "The Weymouth on Fifty-seventh will have a French motif because of its smaller size, but Weymouth House on Seventy-second will be totally English. As you specified, malachite faucets, tortoise mirrors, and faux ivory tables. We've located a collection of fine English prints for all the rooms, while at the Weymouth we shall use some original Impressionist artists' proofs or lithographs—only numbered and signed series—as you insisted."

Jake sat there gnawing his unlit cigar as though smoke were already coming out of his ears, but she ignored him. He always reacted like this to high-priced items.

Finally, when they came to listing and pricing the art they had placed on hold in galleries in the United States and in Europe, he exploded. "You can't use original art on the walls, it's a waste of money," he scoffed. "It will be stolen or defaced."

"Like hell it will!" she shouted back, as eager to snap at him as he was to oppose her. "If it were up to you, we'd have girlie pictures on the walls."

He looked at her in disbelief; this was so unlike her. She ignored his reaction, and stuck out her chin to match his.

"This is the craziest, most lame-brained idea you've ever had, and you've had some beauts," he said.

"They usually pay off, too," she said, hoping he'd keep quiet. But once he'd let loose, there was no stopping him. She knew that about him, and yet she'd baited him all morning. She just couldn't help herself; some angry beast inside kept snarling to get out—the Marchands be damned.

"If it weren't for me, you'd spend every nickel you earned, and you know it."

They sometimes battled like this, but only in private.

Today something was prodding her beyond good sense. "Do I have to remind you who I am, Jake? And I don't mean majority owner of Weymouth Development, either. I'm the one who's socially acquainted with the prospective guests of this hotel, people who are used to living with the finest furniture and art. They will take care of it and appreciate it, not like the conventioneers who stay at the Hilton or the Waldorf and piss in the halls when they're drunk."

His face reddened from her rebuke. It was wrong of her to point out their class differences, but at the moment she didn't care. His anger only increased. "The prints will be enclosed in glass, Jake, and the frames attached directly to the walls. We can even alarm them, if you wish." Sarcasm lined her words. "I can just see the typical Weymouth guest asking a bellboy to please remove the art from his room and carry it down with the luggage. After all, he wouldn't carry his own belongings, even if they were stolen, now would he?"

No chance of a smile at that joke. He was frowning so hard his eyebrows came together in a single line across his forehead.

She turned back to the cost figures for the interior furnishings. Six million—about what she'd expected, though she had no intention of paying what they were asking. There was always room to negotiate. Her tone sweetened, and she smiled. "Monsieur Marchand, the designs are lovely, really exceptional. But they are far too expensive, *plus cher*. If it were up to me, I'd give you my approval in a minute." She shrugged, giving Jake a glance to back her up; in spite of his anger, he did. "But you see, we have an investment board that controls our expenditures." She played the game, shaking her head as if this were a difficult moment for her, then looked up at him as if she'd just gotten a wonderful idea. "Perhaps you could rethink these expenditures. Maybe cut out some frivolities. If you can see your way clear to bringing the job in for around four and a half million, we could go ahead immediately. That's all our budget will allow."

"Ah, Mademoiselle Weymouth, *c'est impossible*," he began, starting the standard speech about the quality and rarity of the antiques, the high price of fabrics and labor these days.

But she cut him off, unable to go through the motions today, and looked at him so directly he lowered his eyes. "Take it or leave it," she said, sensing Jake's surprise.

"Ah, you drive a hard bargain," Marchand said, reaching for the cost lists. "But let me go over the figures again and see what I can do."

She gave him a curt nod and got up to leave the conference room.

Jake followed her into her office and slammed her door. "Don't you ever pull rank on me again, Pam Weymouth, or I'm out of here. If you've got some bug up your ass, leave it home. I don't give a shit about your fancy friends, and you know it. You don't give a shit either, so what's going on? And why play games with Marchand? When you hired that man and his company, I thought it was the second coming. You've been creaming over their ideas for months, even flirting with him besides. Don't give me that look, I saw you. And now you shoot him full of cold poison. I don't get it."

She turned on him, her eyes glaring. "Stay out of it, Harrigan. Just stay out. You're so stubborn, opinionated, and narrow-minded. I can never get anything done without a battle with you."

He stared at her for a minute, knowing this was crazy. Then he said, "It's something else, isn't it? I've been married long enough to know that when the wife yells at me about the smell of my cigars, or that the furniture needs re-covering, or to turn off that damned baseball, I know she wants some attention, maybe a nice dinner out, or she wants to get laid. But you've got everything you want, including making a jackass of your father, which you've been wanting to do for years—that prince." He thought for a minute. "It's that kid, isn't it? The one who's got cancer."

He'd been picking up her signals. No wonder she depended on him, he was always right with her. She hadn't realized how much she'd been talking about Kevin until now. She took a deep breath and held it against the fear, and then let it out slowly. "I'm going to meet him today for the first time. He's been having radiation treatments and is losing his hair. His mother told him I belong to an organization that helps pay medical bills for sick kids. I don't know what to say to him, Jake. I'm scared to death."

"You, scared? Don't kid a kidder. Remember how you were with Diane? No pity. Just compassion. This is no different. He's just a kid, remember that."

He's not just a kid, she thought, wanting so badly to tell him. "But he's very sick."

"We all die, Pam."

"Don't say that, he's so young."

"Is he dying?"

"We don't know. So far, he's looking pretty good."

"So talk about that."

She nodded.

"You could pass on seeing him, you know."

Her look said, *Are you crazy?*

He held up his hands. "Okay, so see him. Pam, what's so special about this kid?"

She stared at him for a long moment, feeling her lower lip tremble and a kind of heat suffuse her body. She couldn't hold this in any longer, and Jake was like a father to her. If anyone would understand, he would. "This is not for publication, Jake."

"Honey, you know I'm no talker."

If she could trust him with the rest of her life, she could trust him with this. "He's not just any kid, Jake. He's my son. My own child."

"I had no idea, Pam," he said. "Where has he been?"

Her eyes filled with tears and she turned away; the relief of telling him and the sympathy on his face were making her break. "I gave him up for adoption, rather than let his father have him. Right after he was born, I told his father that he'd died. I know it was a terrible thing to do, but I had no choice."

He was quiet for a moment, and then he said, "His father is Charles Meroni, isn't he?"

She couldn't look at him, so she didn't know if he was shocked or not. After a moment she felt him come up close behind her, felt his hand on her shoulder. "You can't ever tell anyone, Jake. It could mean my life, even my son's."

"I'd never tell anyone, you know that." And then he said softly, "That's why you've been paying all his bills?"

"Yes." She felt her strength beginning to desert her,

her shoulders sagged, she couldn't hold back any longer and the tears came. "I'm sorry I've been so rotten to you lately."

"You poor kid," he said, turning her around to put his arms around her, "what you must have gone through."

And she just sobbed.

The expression on Frances's face was a mixture of apprehension and deference. Ever since Pam had begun paying Kevin's medical bills, Frances had treated her differently—like a celebrity. It made Pam uncomfortable, but she couldn't get Frances to feel at ease, or recapture that easy familiarity that had first sparked their friendship. Now, as she stood outside Kevin's door, Frances's body language said it all, the way she hesitated, shoulders forward, chin slightly down, apologizing for something that needed no apology.

"Kevin's very thin right now, hasn't been eating well lately. And his hair is kind of patchy. He's embarrassed about it."

Pam gave her arm a squeeze. "I'll wait out here," Frances said, as Pam went past her, opened the door, and went into the room.

He was gorgeous.

Up close, he took her breath away. Gray-green eyes, a heart-shaped face, blond hair carefully combed, still enough to cover his head. But the familiarity of him was what grabbed her the hardest, that and the way he was looking at her, with all of life's wonder in his eyes. He was wearing flannel pajamas with footballs and baseballs on them. She stuck out her hand. It was trembling.

"I'm Pam."

He'd been lying down, but now he pulled himself up to a sitting position to take her hand. "Hi," he said shyly.

She could see he was studying her, peering over her shoulder. She looked at him questioningly.

"My mother said you were an angel of mercy, but you don't have any wings."

At first she took him seriously, but then she saw he was kidding. She grinned. "I left them home, they get kind of heavy on my shoulders." She pulled up a chair to sit next to him. "I understand you've been going through some rough times."

"There's other kids here who are worse," he said matter-of-factly.

She nodded. "So tell me about school. Are you able to go to classes?"

"Yeah, sometimes, but it's a bummer 'cause I can't play sports. No energy. I'm afraid I'm gonna turn into a girl."

"What do you think, girls are the weaker sex?"

"Well, sure. They're not as strong as boys, you know."

"They can't play sports as well?"

"Nah."

"You know, I have a friend named Lori . . ." She almost told him Lori was Hillary's daughter, but then thought better of it. She couldn't let Kevin or his mother make the connection between her and Hillary. "Anyway, Lori is thirteen years old now. But when she was eleven she wanted to play Little League, and they said no girls."

His eyes widened to deep pools of blue as he listened. "What did she do?"

"She fought for the right to play and made them put her on the team. The boys on the team resented her, they were embarrassed to have her with them. They ignored her, called her names. The coaches were angry at having to accept her, but she stuck it out. Her determination needed another kind of strength than muscles."

He was enthralled with the story. "How'd she do?"

"She turned out to be the star hitter, voted most valuable player, and caught more fly balls than any boy on the team." Pam was touched by the way he listened to her, so fully, all his attention focused. She wanted to find other stories he would love.

"Yeah?" he said.

"Cross my heart." This was all going so fast she couldn't take it in. She was here, actually here, talking to him. She reached out and took his hand. "Give me a squeeze."

He wasn't very strong but he gave it all he could, scrunching up his face with effort.

Pam pulled away and shook her hand as if it hurt. "Not bad," she assured him. "You might beat a girl someday."

He blushed, ducking his head to hide it. "I was just kidding. Girls can do lots of things. Your friend Lori's okay, I guess."

"Speaking of baseball, who do you want in the Series?"

"Yankees, for sure. Don't you?"

"I'm from California, so I guess I want the Dodgers."

"Haven't got a chance," he predicted with grave assurance. He was staring at the faint scar lines on her cheek. "Can I ask you something?"

She touched her face. "You mean about this?"

He nodded. "What is it?"

"I was in an accident, a long time ago. And then I had plastic surgery to repair the damage. I think it looks pretty good, don't you?"

"Yeah!" he said with enthusiasm. "You're really beautiful." And then he blushed. "Did it hurt?"

She forced back the tears that sprang to her eyes. "At the time. But it's only a memory now. Physical pain is like that. When it's over, you don't remember it at all. Just like these bad times for you. Someday you'll forget all about them."

He nodded thoughtfully.

"Do you know what I do?"

"I'll bet you pay bills."

She laughed. "You said it, baby. No, I mean what I do for a living, to earn the money to pay my bills?"

He shook his head. For an instant she saw one of Charles's expressions in the set of his mouth, and then it was gone.

"I'm a building developer. I build tall buildings."

"Like with a single bound?" he joked.

"Not exactly. More like a series of tiny steps, but I'm the only woman in the city of New York who does what I do."

"I bet there's not many women in the world who do that, either. That's what my mom said."

"You could be right." The pride that filled her was the sweetest feeling of her life.

"That's really *tough*," he said.

She took it to be a supreme compliment.

"I've always wanted to do that," he confided. "Ever since I was a little kid, I wanted to build bridges, or houses."

She felt a chill run through her. "Did you really? You're not just being diplomatic?"

"Heck, no. I don't believe in kidding with the truth.

It's too hard to pretend. Like with some of the doctors and nurses, and even some of my friends, they pretend like everything is fine when it's not, and I'm supposed to pretend too. Not that everything's always bad, it's not. But sometimes this is hard to take!"

"I guess it is," she agreed.

"I really do want to build bridges someday. I'm good at building things with Lego. I started with Lincoln Logs when I was four. But sand castles are my favorite. I like to build tunnels and bridges and castles and forts. My sister steps on them, though. She's five."

Sister. Family. She was abruptly reminded, almost gasped from the shock of it. "Listen, Kevin, I promised your mom we'd only have a short visit. But if you like, I could come back."

"Sure. You could wait in line." He was teasing again.

She smiled. "You've got a great sense of humor, you know that? Where do you get it?"

He stopped for a minute. "My mom. She's pretty funny sometimes. She told me so much about Jimmy Durante, I dreamed I was him in another life." He looked at her, trying to be serious. "Don't tell anyone," he said, making a circular motion with his finger at his temple as if they'd think he was crazy.

She wanted to hug him very badly, but instead she stood up and turned away to steady herself. She was afraid of exposing him to infection or overstepping her bounds. Besides, if she hugged him, she'd never let him go. She turned back. "I have a secret for you, too."

"Yeah?" He was delighted that she was playing his game.

"Not only do I believe you, I know for a fact that you're right."

"How?" His eyes grew round with curiosity.

" 'Cause I was once Mrs. Calabash," she said, blowing him a kiss good-bye, turning slowly, and, tilting an imaginary hat, she did that Durante walk, feet apart, one foot after the other, head shaking, hand waving, singing "Ink-a-dink-a-doo," all the way out the door to the sound of his laughter.

"Hey, pretty cool," he called as she closed the door.

The hospital corridor startled her back to reality. Such a mixture of feelings assailed her. Wonder headed the list. What a miracle he was. God wouldn't let him die. And he was like her, genetically like her. The lack of reverence for adults, she'd had it at his age. That offbeat way of looking at life. That persistence and self-confidence. He was her son, whether or not she'd raised him. And he'd never known the heartache of a broken home, never had to watch two people express their bitterness by hurting him, never had to be torn between them. She'd given him that. He believed in happy endings, and that alone might pull him through. She was so elated, her feet hardly touched the ground, though it was a bittersweet happiness because part of her was deeply sad. Sad at his suffering, sad at her own, even sad for what she'd missed in her own childhood. But most of all there was a feeling of joy that she really had done the right thing for him. She knew that now with all her heart.

9

"Honey, come to bed," Mel called. "You know I can't sleep with the lights on."

Hillary was sitting on the john, reading the latest reports from the New Jersey Department of Environmental Protection. She'd been on their mailing list for years. But in spite of her concern and their effort, New Jersey's environment was becoming more polluted every day. Preparing for the dinner party she'd given tonight had prevented her from reading the reports until now.

The article that leaped out at her was about something that had happened in March of 1977, and this was November. *Where was I in March?* she wondered. That was when the state epidemiologist had informed a town meeting in Rutherford that the number of cancer cases in both children and adults was even higher than they'd thought. Out of thirty-two cases, thirteen of them leukemia, six involved youngsters between the ages of five and nineteen, and all six had attended the same elementary school. Kevin's leukemia was discovered in June, and he attended that school! Her hands started to shake. Rutherford was so close to Crestmont. She read on. Technicians from the state were testing air, soil, and water for possible contaminants. Two of the mothers of the children who had been stricken had brought these statistics to the attention of the state.

"Hil, please!"

She put down the reports, shut off the light, and went in to bed, but all she could see were those sweet faces, feel those parents' pain. Her hands and feet were freezing, and she put her feet on Mel's warm thighs.

"Jeez," he said, "that's really gonna put me to sleep."

455

"You don't mind, do you?"

"No," he said, snuggling closer. "Honey, why didn't you make your veal in Calvados tonight? I've been raving to Jordan about it, but tonight you bought the dinner from Alfredo's. You've never done that before, Hil. When Luanne asked you for the recipe, I thought I'd choke. I was sure you were going to tell her you didn't make it."

"I was, but your look stopped me, so I changed the subject and she forgot about it."

"Why were you going to tell her? It's bad enough to buy the food, but to confess makes it even more embarrassing." He sighed. "This evening didn't turn out at all as I expected. You kept talking about the pollution problems in New Jersey, even though nobody else was interested. It's difficult enough to get those people to come out here from the city without you boring them to death with our local problems."

Hillary moved slightly away from him. "What would you have preferred me to discuss, Mayor Koch's love life?"

"What's with the sarcasm?"

"Mel, people are dying. Children, the same ages as ours. People are getting poisoned, breaking out in rashes, babies are being born deformed, pregnancies aborted. Even fish and game are being massacred, and you talk about the dinner."

"Not this again," he said.

She felt him stiffen. This was not the time. It was just that she was so filled with horror, she didn't know how to express it. Wait until she showed him what she had read; then he'd understand her obsession. "I'm sorry, honey, I didn't mean to attack you. You're right, I did say I'd be cooking tonight. And I'd planned to, but I got so busy with the brochures about pesticide control that I didn't have time." Lately, since Kevin's illness, she'd been too preoccupied with environmental issues to bake her usual double fudge mousse cakes, or iron Mel's shirts herself. The environmental situation in what was ironically called the Garden State was appalling, dangerous, and all-pervasive. It embarrassed her that it had been going on around her for years and so little was being done. She'd been incensed by the articles about the death of wildlife and the illegal dumping in the wetlands, and she'd been involved in committees to help, but it had been a side issue with her. Those things had happened in other people's backyards, not hers, so she'd told herself that others would take care of them. Now she was ashamed of her negligence. She'd forgotten John Donne, who'd said that "no man is an Island"; she'd forgotten her parents, the altruists, and how they had raised her. Well, no more. She was about to declare her own war.

The facts were these. The state of New Jersey, the most concentrated center of chemical manufacture in America, was one of the worst polluted states, with a shockingly high incidence of cancer. There were so many offenses and probable causes that it was impossible to know where to begin. But she would begin; that was a promise.

She put her hand on Mel's thigh and pulled her feet away, now that they were warmed. "I'm sorry for boring everyone tonight, sweetheart. You're right, talk is cheap. Actions count."

"Does that mean that you'll make dinner next week for the Blakes and the Winslows?"

"Uhm-hmm," she said, not really hearing him, too busy thinking about what she was going to do next to help the environment.

"Crestmont Realty."

"Bobbie Lazar, please, Hillary Robin calling."

Bobbie came on the line. "I'm with a client, Hil."

"This will only take a minute. What's going on with that acreage adjacent to the industrial park near the county line? It borders on Crestmont, doesn't it?"

"Yes, at the west end."

"The 'for sale' sign is gone. Do you know who bought it, what they're going to do with it?"

"I only deal in residential, you know that."

"Could you find out?"

"Can't this wait?" Bobbie sounded tense, as usual.

"No," Hillary insisted.

"Just a minute." She put Hillary on hold.

Hillary finished slicing the carrots and potatoes for the soup, and reached for the zucchini.

Bobbie came back. "Lloyd, our commercial expert, says some large corporation bought it; he doesn't know what for."

"What's the zoning?"

Bobbie called out across the room, and repeated his reply. "Light and heavy industrial."

"But it's next to residential."

"Tell it to the state, babe. I've got to go."

"Wait! Can you get me the name of the corporation?"

"Christ, Hillary, I've got to go."

"Bobbie, I need the name."

Again she called out across the room and repeated the answer. "Chemicals for Safe Environment," she said, "headquartered in Elizabeth." And hung up.

The name sounded innocuous enough. *Let's hope it is.* She dumped the vegetables into her slow cooker with the lamb shank, bay leaf, and other soup ingredients, then she prepared an afterschool snack for Brian and set out for Elizabeth, New Jersey.

What she found out was terribly upsetting. Chemicals for Safe Environment was a wholly owned subsidiary of Jersey Chemical in Elizabeth, where much government action had been focused lately. It had been storing toxic substances improperly, and the contents were seeping toward an aquifer only a half-mile from thirty public drinking-water wells. As if that weren't bad enough, they didn't have the proper permits. In spite of a possible fine of three thousand dollars a day, nothing had been done. There were toxic chemicals stored in open-topped storage tanks and fiberboard containers that were leaking, even toppled over, and there was chemical ooze all over the ground. Hillary could see it from the street where she parked nearby, and smell it too, a noxious odor that permeated the air. And this was the same company that was moving into her backyard to build a chemical storage facility like this one.

In Crestmont, the facility would be partly below ground, and that meant the chemicals would be even closer to the water table. If there was any leakage, Crestmont's water supply would be polluted.

She had to stop them. She drove back to Crestmont and asked Casey Sullivan and Flo Goldman, who were as concerned about the proposed chemical plant as she was, to meet her for coffee in the village.

"Mayor Godfrey is in favor of this new facility, and so is the town council," Flo said, after listening to Hillary. "You know what an economic boon this can be for our community. We've been in a recession; inflation is killing us all; and this company will mean more jobs for the depressed local construction companies, as well as for middle-income families. Opposing this won't make us popular at all."

"I don't care," Hillary insisted.

"Neither do I," Casey agreed.

The three of them stared at one another.

"So what do we do?" Casey took a sip of her coffee.

"We have to organize a local opposition group to try to stop them from using that property for chemical storage."

"I wouldn't know where to begin," Flo said, folding her arms across the fullness of her chest.

"I do," Hillary said. "I come from a long line of organizers. My parents have always worked for political causes and charities."

Casey smiled. Her copper-brown eyes, flecked with gold, matched the color of her hair. She put on an Irish brogue: "Saints preserve us, we had a do-gooder hidin' here all the time."

Hillary smiled. "When you hear what we have to do, you'll think I'm more of a do-badder. We have to go door to door until we've spoken to every citizen of Crestmont."

"Door to door?" Florence groaned. "I hate the thought of that."

"It's only the beginning," Hillary promised. "This is going to take all our time and energy for months to come. But we can do it if we work hard."

"Oh, I don't know. Like my Joe says, you can't fight city hall," Florence said.

"But we've all seen what the efforts of ordinary people can do. Look at the civil rights movement. People just like us banding together in a common cause." Just then a bee buzzed by, landed on the edge of Hillary's coffee cup, and fell into it.

"I hate those things," Flo said, moving her chair backwards. "They drove me crazy all summer. Enough already."

Hillary reached into the cup with her spoon, scooped the bee out, and deposited it on the table, where it dried itself of the coffee and flew away. They watched it soar through an open door, over the patio, and away.

"You know what it's buzzing now that it's safe, don't you?" Casey said, winking her eye at Flo. "It's saying, 'Our Savior Hillary, Our Savior Hillary.'"

The three of them laughed.

"I'm going to remind you of this moment, Casey, when you're hating me for making you work your manicure off."

"Manicure?" Casey scoffed, looking down at her unpolished, housewifely nails. "Irish Catholics don't paint their nails. We're very sensitive about the mere mention of the word." She rolled her *r*'s, crossed herself, and then did an imitation of Jesus on the cross, arms outstretched, head to the side.

"Oh, you're bad," Hillary said, laughing at Casey's irreverence. "You're really going to be tested, my dear, just be sure you keep the faith."

"I will," Casey assured her. "Don't you worry. I will."

Hillary nearly ran a red light, screeching to a stop just in time. There was never enough time lately to do everything she was doing with Cub Scouts, running the house, and organizing the opposition committee. Her clock on the dash said 5:15; baseball practice had been over since 4:45. Brian would be worried, and she hated to worry him. She turned in at the parking lot of the field and sped down to where the diamonds were. Deserted. *Oh, God. Brian, where are you?* A car. Someone must have waited with him. Then she saw him and her heart lifted with relief. He wasn't alone; Kevin and his mother were there. She'd forgotten that Brian's team was playing Kevin's today. She pulled the station wagon alongside them.

"I'm so sorry I'm late. Thank you so much for waiting with him." She got out of the car and gave Brian a hug, and then another hug, because she loved him so much and because she was sorry she was late.

"I hit a homer, Mom!" he said, grinning. The two spaces where his front teeth had been missing were half filled in by his permanent teeth.

"That's great, honey!" she said, moving over to put her arm around Kevin.

"How are you doing, sweetheart? Feeling stronger?"

"Yeah, but I wish I could play, instead of being manager."

"We're just glad he's finished with the treatments for a while," Frances said.

Kevin was painfully thin, his hair a short, stubby cap, but growing in nicely. "I'm sure you'll regain your strength before long," Hillary assured him. She looked at Frances. They were both thinking the same thing, praying that he would not have a recurrence.

Brian tugged at her jacket. "Mom, can Kevin come to Passover?"

Hillary laughed, and looked at Frances, who shrugged. "Well, certainly, he can come if he'd like to. Would you, Kevin?" she asked.

He nodded eagerly. "In Sunday school they said it's the Lord's last supper. I wouldn't mind learning more about it, if it's okay."

She'd been so busy she hadn't given Passover much thought, but she really enjoyed preparing for this holiday. "It's next week, isn't it, Brian?" He nodded. "Kevin, I'll come and pick you up after school, and then someone will drive you home after dinner."

Kevin's eyes sparkled when he was happy. He was smiling and looking at her oddly. "Mrs. Robin, are you my secret pal?"

"What is that, Kevin?" Hillary asked.

"Someone who sends me letters and presents, or autographed pictures of baseball players; they're all from my secret pal."

"Guy, that's neat!" Brian pronounced.

"Sometimes it's a poem like this one:

'There once was a smart boy named Kevin
Who got sick at ten minutes past seven.
Though his illness was scary,
He said, 'Cure me, don't tarry,
'Cause I'm not sure I'm going to heaven.' "

He was watching her for any sign of recognition, but she shook her head. "I'm not much of a poet. But some-one out there sure likes you." It had to be Pam.

Brian was in the car. "Come on," he urged, "let's go."

Hillary shook Frances's hand and kissed Kevin, feeling the lightness of his body as she touched him. But he was growing, that was a good sign. "We'll see you next week," she said to him, as he and Frances walked towards their car.

Kevin waved back.

"He's really fine, Mom," Brian assured her, as she got into their car. He'd picked up the look of concern on her face. "I'm helping him get better, too. We do some arm wrestling, talk about things. He's my best friend, you know. So he's gonna be all right."

If only it were that simple, she thought.

Where was Mel? He should have been home hours ago. He wasn't at the office; she'd called at nine-thirty when her meeting was over. She'd cleaned up the Styro-foam cups, tossed the paper plates into the trash-masher, wrapped the cake and cookies up for the freezer for next time, and still he wasn't home.

He'd gone to work angry this morning, and she hadn't felt right all day. She hated it when they fought. Her stomach always churned and her shoulders went into knots. But he could go to the office and work as though nothing had happened, often coming home in the eve-ning whistling and unconcerned. That gave her two choices: either she could accept his mood and set aside the dis-agreement, or start talking about it again and risk his typical response, the icy shoulder. (*Cold* was too mild a term.) He was an expert at shutting her out, and after all these years, she still couldn't take it.

Today's disagreement wasn't a minor matter of his forgetting to have his brakes relined, or leaving the may-onnaise jar open on the kitchen counter all night. This was a fundamental difference between them that had to be resolved, only she didn't know how. And they'd been battling about it for over a year and a half, ever since she'd gotten involved with the problem of toxic waste.

"Can't you have those meetings somewhere else be-sides our family room? I want to come home after work and relax, not listen to the haranguing of some local yokel who thinks big business sucks. Big business pays our bills, Hillary. You and your friends will never get anywhere with this, don't you know that?"

"Damn your attitude," she'd yelled. "Where's your sense of responsibility?" But he just didn't agree with her that toxic wastes were spoiling their state and threatening their lives, or that it was up to her to do something about it.

How could he not agree? That question drove her crazy. It made no sense to her that because his territory had been invaded, he wouldn't support her. Why couldn't he understand? She'd let him run their lives for years; now it was her turn. Didn't all her devotion to him give her the right to expect some reciprocation? She wanted him to support her in this, the way her friends' husbands supported them. Early last year she'd been elected chairperson of a local committee, CCC—Crestmont's Concerned Citizens—and had worked all through 1978 and now into half of this year to make headway, yet he wanted no part of it.

"I want my old life back, Hillary. I don't want the phone ringing until one in the morning. I don't want to be ignored by the men on the commuter train because I have a crazy wife. Mayor Godfrey put pressure on the senior partner in my firm, for God's sake, to get you to back off. 'Can't you control her, Robin?' Addison Blake asked me. You know what a Wasp he is. He thinks Jews are tolerable because we do the accounting, the tax law, and hustle for new business. 'Control your wife' is the same to him as 'Curb your dog.'"

She was torn between her loyalty to him and her fanatical need to protect her children's lives. She'd always lived life the way her mother did; the husband's word was final. But her parents had common interests. They'd both believed in the causes they worked for, setting themselves as an example of commitment and togetherness as if those were aspects of a seamless entity. She'd never thought Mel wouldn't be behind her, but obviously he wasn't, and it was tearing her apart. She sometimes felt like Nora to his Torvald.

At 9:45 his car pulled into the garage. He was carrying

his coat; it was warm for mid-May. He looked the way Brian had looked when he'd borrowed Stephen's bike without permission and it got stolen because he hadn't locked it.

"Meeting over?"

She nodded.

"How did it go?"

She started to tell him, but when she saw his expression, all she said was, "We're making progress."

"I ran into Bobbie in the city. She just closed a deal on the Bateman house and was signing the papers at Chase on Madison. We went for a drink to celebrate."

"She sold the Bateman house, that's great. She's becoming Crestmont's top real-estate agent, isn't she?"

He gave her kiss on the cheek. Martinis. "She was really high. She makes a commission of twelve thousand—not bad, huh?"

"Where was Frank?"

"Home, I guess." He waited, looking at her. "You're not jealous, are you? Of Bobbie? She's your best friend."

"She's not as close to me as Pam and Trish, but no, I'm not jealous of your having a drink with her, or her getting rich. It's just that you and I had a fight this morning and you didn't call all day."

"How would you know? Were you home?"

"I called you."

"I'm sorry, honey, I didn't have time to get back to you. I saw Pam today; we're doing some more work for her. She's one of the firm's largest clients, thanks to me."

And thanks to me, Hillary thought.

He was locking the back door, checking the downstairs windows, going through the nightly ritual of locking up.

"Do you think Pam would bring her business to me if I went out on my own?" He started up the stairs.

"Are you thinking about doing that?"

"Well, I've *been* thinking about it. Bobbie thinks I'm being wasted at Lefferts, Bigman and Bates. They're billing a hundred seventy-five an hour for my time. If I could bill that myself, it would really make a difference."

"You'd have a high overhead, where you don't have any now. And you'd have to invest in a library." This wasn't exactly an unusual topic of conversation.

"So I'd take in some partners."

"Mel, you're avoiding the issue of this morning."

"You don't think I should go out on my own? I guess I know who my friends are."

"I'm your friend, honey. Why can't you be mine? I could really use your help, or at least your support. Your advice as legal counsel for CCC would be so important. The cost of this project is climbing all the time. We've got another bake sale planned, but they don't bring in much. Pam has been our main source of funds, but I can't keep asking her."

"I don't know anything about this kind of law, Hillary. Talk to the DEP, talk to the ACLU."

"I'm talking to you, Mel. My husband. My live-in counselor-at-law."

He stopped and took a deep breath, as much to calm himself as to gather his thoughts. She recognized the technique; her father used to light a pipe for much the same reason. "I don't think you have a chance, Hillary. Jersey Chemical is a major heavyweight in chemical disposal. They've got their building permits for Crestmont in spite of what your group tried to do. That's only an example of what you'll be up against all the way. The whole county is behind them, not just the town. Hell, the state wants them here, the locals want them here, the governor probably does too, everybody but my wife. *My wife,*" he said, with exasperation. "They're laughing at you out there, ringing doorbells, giving out leaflets, writing letters, asking for information from state officials."

"We're entitled to that information for our investigation."

"What investigation?"

"We're looking into Jersey Chemical's past history. If we can prove the continued environmental abuse is not only in the Elizabeth plant but in some of their others as well, we might be able to stop them here. Do you really want them here, Mel? In our backyard? Do you remember seeing those kids in the children's ward at Sloan-Kettering when we visited Kevin? Do you want that to happen to Brian or Stephen or Lori? Our kids might not make it to remission like Kevin."

"You're so melodramatic. You're playing a farce, only you won't see it. I find it embarrassing, a leftover from the sixties, only you're an aging hippie, Hillary, and it's unbecoming."

She cried herself to sleep, but Mel didn't hear her; he was already asleep.

10

Pam stepped out of her limousine at the Weymouth Hotel's carriage entrance. A crowd had already gathered, even though the hotel's opening wasn't scheduled to start for another hour. Camera flashlights flickered all around her as she emerged, wearing a white silk strapless beaded gown, a tiara of diamonds in her upswept hair. She'd thought about taking a suite for tonight's event, but then had decided it was easier to dress at home than bring her clothes here. There were so many last-minute details, she was afraid she'd forget something important, like her shoes.

She entered the lobby and glanced up at the gilded beamed ceiling, noting with satisfaction the enormous, sparkling crystal chandeliers imported from Czechoslovakia, and the frescoes painted by an artist flown here from Italy. Eight hundred guests would soon fill the lobby, entertained by a string quartet and served Louis Roederer champagne and beluga caviar. And among the guests would be her mother. Joanne was a different woman since Pam had moved her to New York. Having financial security for the first time in her life had brought Joanne some dignity. She'd lost that brassy look; her hair color was softer, and so were her mannerisms. And she'd stopped drinking. She had a job selling makeup at Boyd Chemists, and she'd acquired a group of friends, women near her age, whose lives she could emulate, who took her to lectures on Greek history, to theater openings, and for weekends in the country. It was an amazing transformation, one that Pam had never thought she'd see, and one that she was reluctant to take credit for. She believed that Joanne had done it on her own, and that all she herself had done was foot the bill. But Hillary told her she was too modest, that she was more responsible

467

for Joanne's transformation than she knew, because it was her generosity with Joanne that had gotten her started. In spite of all the pain Joanne had caused her·when she was growing up, Pam hadn't held it against her.

Pam went to check out the flower arrangements, magnificent bouquets more than six feet tall, nestled in four alcoves, two on either side of the elevators and two beside the entrance. The florist had outdone himself tonight. The hotel was supposed to have opened last January, and here it was September of 1979. Tonight's gala was the official opening, but they'd been doing business for weeks and the ballroom was booked into late 1980. She was glad she'd insisted on using the third floor for public rooms instead of more hotel suites. Nobody liked to stay on the third floor of a hotel in New York because of the noise.

Satisfied that everything was as she'd instructed, she was about to go into the office when she saw Frances Matthews coming through the main door of the lobby. Immediately, Pam's pulse began to race, hoping that nothing was wrong. Frances was wearing a navy print challis dress and had lost weight, or else she'd discovered how to choose clothes that flattered her figure. Pam wondered if Frances's improved taste in clothes had anything to do with her.

"You're not dressed for the party," Pam said. "I thought you were all coming tonight. I know Kevin was looking forward to it. Is everything all right?"

Over the past few years, Kevin had been in remission and had resumed a normal life; his hair had grown back, and he'd made up the schoolwork he missed, thanks to the tutor Pam had hired, and he was much stronger. But now that he was well, Pam had to find excuses to be with him. And lately Frances had made it increasingly difficult. There was always some reason why Kevin had to decline Pam's invitations to lunch, or other activities she thought he might enjoy. And Pam didn't push it. But tonight she had really looked forward to having Kevin here to see what she'd accomplished. The limitations were extremely frustrating, but it was all she could expect. The Matthewses wouldn't accept anything for Kevin or Su Mei but a few inexpensive gifts on special occasions such as birthdays and Christmas. Pam wished they would;

Kevin kept outgrowing his jeans. He was getting so tall, and even more handsome.

"Yes, everything's all right," Frances assured her. "But I wanted to talk to you, and I expected you'd be here."

Something was wrong; Pam steeled herself.

"I don't know a good way to say this to you, Pam, you've been so generous with our family. But I'd like you to stop seeing Kevin. I'm sure you don't mean any harm, but you are interfering in our family."

Pam's throat began to tighten so that she could hardly breathe. "I don't understand. How have I interfered?"

"You don't mean to, but you can't help it. Kevin is an impressionable boy, and you are a very rich woman. Your ways are not ours. You give him the wrong ideas about what he can expect. It's not fair to him, or to us, especially to Su Mei, who does not get the same favors from you. It makes me and my husband feel badly that we can't do for him what you can. I just don't like it." From the set of her jaw, and her prepared words, Pam could tell she'd rehearsed this speech. And that made it all the more ominous. They had ganged up on her, Gil and Frances. And they were the ultimate authority where he was concerned. *This can't be happening,* she thought. *I can't lose him again.* A wave of dizziness assailed her, but she fought it.

"How does Kevin feel about this? I'm sure he doesn't want to lose me as a friend. We get along so well." Every ounce of her was screaming in protest, *You can't do this!*

"Maybe so, but he's young. He has other friends. His own age, too."

Fury and panic battled within her.

Frances saw the look on Pam's face, and softened her tone. "I can understand how it happened. Your own child died, and you got attached to mine."

Pam felt a sudden coldness wash over her. "How did you know about my child?"

"When we first met, you said you had a child in the hospital, but then you never mentioned him again. I thought it was strange, and so I read some old newspaper articles. Look, I'm sorry for you. But my Kevin is not the answer. Maybe you could adopt a child of your own. Lots of single people are doing it these days."

"That's all I need," Pam snapped, nearly losing her control, "your advice on how to live my life!"

"I'm sorry, Pam, that is your business." Frances could see how offended Pam was, but was at a loss to understand her vehemence. However, she didn't back down. "Kevin is fond of you, you know that. We're all so grateful for your help. I mean, the money was one thing, but you devoted *time* to him. He told me it made him forget the nausea and the weakness; I'm sure that helped him get better. Gil and I didn't have time then for things like that, or the patience. We've never been readers. We like the tube. But Kevin's smart, he needs that extra bit. Maybe he could go to college."

Of course he's going to college, Pam thought.

"I'm sure you were a good influence on him, reading him the Oz books, and *Treasure Island,* and *King of Kings,* about the Arabian stallion, that was his favorite. Even getting him those old Jimmy Durante tapes was so wonderful. He loved watching them. So did I. Durante was my favorite. That must have been hard to do, even when you know important people." Frances was trying to be kind, to soften the harshness of her demands.

"This time it paid off." Pam tried to be calmer too. It didn't make any difference to this situation that an executive at the network was now living maintenance-free in a four-thousand-square-foot apartment in one of her buildings for copying the Durante tapes for her. No matter what ends she went to, she still might not be able to see Kevin. No, it was impossible!

People were starting to arrive for the party, and Frances was about to leave. Desperately, Pam said, "Please, can we go somewhere private and talk about this?"

"I don't think there's anything more to say." Now she was being stern again. "My husband and I talked till late last night, and we agreed. It's better for Kevin if you stay away." And she turned to go.

Pam was shaking so that she had to hold on to a nearby table to hold herself up, and she cried out as she almost fell. She gazed at Frances's retreating figure, barely seeing her. *I've lost him again,* she thought, trying to hide her pain from anyone else. Voices of arriving guests sounded hollow, barely penetrating the cotton in her brain. One of the happiest nights of her life had just disintegrated into dust. She prayed she could hold on until she could find somewhere to be alone, but there was a searing, unbearable pain wrapping itself around her. She couldn't let it end like this.

"Wait," she called to Frances, who turned back. Pam walked over to her, weaving her way through the antique style upholstered furniture. "Think about it for a minute. Is it wise to cut Kevin off from a friend, especially one he's grown so attached to, as you admit?"

"But being with him makes you a part of his life, and that's what Gil and I don't want." She gestured around the room. "This isn't us."

Pam dug her nails into her palms; she'd have to agree for now. Perhaps, sometime in the future, Frances wouldn't feel so threatened. "Then I'll stay away, Frances. But don't you think it should be done gradually, so we can make sure that it doesn't hurt Kevin?"

The strain of what Frances had gone through with Kevin had been harder on her than she let on. Pam knew that she was a woman who lived with the daily threat of losing her child; she had tried to be strong, to hold herself together for the sake of her child and her family, but her strength had been depleted.

"How does that sound?" Pam asked.

"I guess it's reasonable," Frances conceded.

"There's something else," Pam said. "You've got to let me keep paying any medical bills in the future. Please!" she begged. "Don't let your son suffer needlessly because of pride. It's too important."

"I can't take money from you anymore!" Frances said. "That's been the problem."

"You can't not take it," Pam insisted, "if he needs it."

Frances's helplessness was making her angry. "You always have to get what you want, don't you?"

"Lady," Pam said, "I hardly ever get what I want. But in this case, I have the means to help Kevin. For God's sake, Frances, it could mean his life!"

Frances stared at her, wondering about Pam's determination. When she spoke, it was with a kind of resignation one hears from a person who has lost, not won. "You can keep paying the bills. I'll send you a monthly report on his medical progress. You deserve that much."

"What about college? Can I pay for college? Please, Frances, let me do this. It's so small a gesture."

"That's enough," Frances said, exhaling slowly, making an effort not to lose her temper. "We'll discuss college if Kevin survives long enough to go."

"He will," Pam said, with every ounce of conviction she could muster. "Then we're agreed? I'll break away from Kevin over the next two weeks. I'll say I'm taking a trip, building a building in Europe, I'll work it out." How could she do it? she wondered. Only with the hope that she wouldn't have to stay away forever. "And you'll allow me to help financially."

"If I do, I want you to do something for me," Frances said.

"Anything," Pam offered.

"Swear on Kevin's life that you'll stay away from him."

Pam was taken aback, first by Frances's expression, which was almost cunning, and then by what Frances was asking. She could barely speak. Somehow she found the words, though she nearly choked on them. "I swear on Kevin's life, for his own good, I'll stay away from him completely." Pam felt that a part of her was dying.

A sense of relief showed in the way Frances held her head. She exhaled slowly, and then turned and walked out of the lobby, leaving Pam with a sense of loss so great she was afraid it would crush her then and there. And as she felt its weight pressing down on her, she prayed that it would crush her and finish the job.

She had to get away from prying eyes, and tried to reach the hallway outside the offices off the main lobby, but just outside the door her knees gave way and she nearly fell against the wall. Grabbing the door handle, as much to steady herself as to escape, she flung it open, pulling herself inside and slamming it behind her. But there was no shutting this out. It was like stepping inside a furnace. It's heat beat down on her, nearly suffocating her. *Kevin,* she cried, *I can't lose you again!*

11

"A friend of yours will be at the party tonight," Pat McGarrity told Trish. "He said he met you in the Middle East in the sixties."

"How nice," Trish said, trying to appear calm, while she was thinking, *It's Connor! God, I don't want to see him. I won't go.* But she'd already told Pat she'd be there. *Come on, Trish, he's just a man. You'll see him, talk to him, and that will be that.* But still she felt a slight chill of anticipation; it had been over five years since she'd seen him.

She wore white flannel pants, a wheat-colored wool sweater, and her turquoise jewelry from Santa Fe. And people looked at her when she entered the room, even one as full of celebrities as this. Recognition flashed in their eyes, and then, subtly, they turned to their companions to discuss who she was, some with envy, some with admiration. "Up and coming" no longer applied, she had Arrived. There were only a few newly recognized artists as well thought of as she, and commanding top dollar for their work.

The high-ceilinged room was overheated, with wall-to-wall people; a jazz quintet played soulfully, brilliantly. She looked around, but she didn't see Connor.

"The prime rate is down," someone said.

"Big deal, fourteen-and-a-quarter instead of fifteen. I still can't buy my apartment when it goes co-op."

"Have you seen *E.T.?*"

"I wouldn't wait in a line that long. But I liked *Chariots of Fire.*"

Trish moved among the crowd in the huge co-op, hearing snatches of conversation. "The industry suffered terrible losses this year, Grace Kelly, Ingrid Bergman, and

John Belushi." She noted events like that too, and dates, because sometimes she used them in her work. Last year, in 1981, Prince Charles married Lady Di, and Anwar Sadat was assassinated. This year, people in their thirties complained about closet space and private schools. In California, people were buying art and second homes, even though the cost of real estate had skyrocketed. New York collectors name-dropped what they'd heard at dinner with so-and-so, implying that they were friendly with the likes of Julian Schnabel or David Salle. Trish heard gossip about herself all the time, even read it in the paper. Little of it was true. She wondered what Connor would talk about.

Attending a party was rare for her; she spent most of her time with Pam or Hillary, or at her newly restored Victorian home in Middletown, New York. But she couldn't refuse Pat McGarrity, who had launched her career. In the last two years alone, she'd been in a group show at the Guggenheim, had been included in the "New Directions" show at the Hirschhorn, had had a one-woman show at the Denver Museum, which traveled to Fort Worth and Minneapolis, and had been featured in three articles: one in *Art in America,* one in *Art New England,* and, best of all, the cover of *ArtForum.* There was a waiting list for her work, which was up to twenty thousand dollars. She was exactly where she wanted to be.

She took a glass of wine from a passing waiter, thinking about what in tonight's event she'd replay later in her work. For nothing was lost, everything gestated, layer upon layer; she'd come to trust her subconscious, knowing that all her experiences were there, waiting to be used. It gave her a sense of peace.

The pain from her former life had subsided, except for her grief over Kelly, which was buried, avoided. But the attachment to Arthur was severed, the addictions laid to rest. And her success merely made her freer, able to reach greater heights than she'd ever reached before, without feeling threatened, or alternately, able to dig deeper into herself—whichever challenged her most. *Then why am I so nervous about seeing Connor?* she wondered, telling herself she didn't want any complications right now. Something wonderful was happening with her work, a creative growth that was about to burst forth, she could tell. The ideas were immense, all-encompassing; she had been thinking, planning, testing them, waiting until she was ready. The time was close while she hid this exciting new child within her, this creation about to be born. Being pregnant with a work of art was different from giving birth to a baby, though both were glorious. At least this new work would be healthy and whole.

She spent as much time thinking about her work as doing it, and sometimes longed for the days when she'd plunge naïvely ahead, heart palpitating as if she were meeting a new lover, and paint her way through the emotion. Experience had brought her thoughtfulness, wariness. Some called it being blocked, but she thought of it as maturity—or was it age? She wondered if Connor had aged, if he would find her different.

"It creeps up on you," she'd complained to McGarrity before the opening of her one-woman show at the New Museum in SoHo. "I'll be forty-three next year, and lately I can't think clearly unless all those spaces between my receding gums are cleaned out of tiny pieces of debris."

Pat McGarrity smiled, revealing his own set of crooked, yellowish teeth. "I know what you mean," he'd said.

Gray streaks were beginning to appear in her dark hair, lines round her eyes and mouth; she couldn't thread a needle without plenty of light; she felt her monthly ovulation as though something inside were about to fall out. She jogged now, took yoga classes, thought about lifting weights, but settled for lifting her canvases. What had the world done before sweat clothes?

Pat McGarrity's personal art collection was stunningly displayed tonight: Stella, De Kooning, Segal, Botero, Motherwell, Johns, and of course the artists he represented, who were all here at the party. She nodded to Jim Rosenquist, who was talking with Leo Castelli. She spotted several men she'd gone out with since coming to New York. Each budding romance had turned to friendship, her choice. Mary Boone was talking to Eric Fischl. Trish was glad to see them and waved hello; they waved back. Half the European art world was jammed into the library. Nikki de St. Phalle stood in a group with Pat Andrea, Bella Chagall, and Paloma Picasso. Trish saw several gallery owners whom she knew, and went to speak to them, but then she spotted Connor. He was standing alone near the bar. Their eyes met. She smiled and made her way toward him.

He took her hand. "Hello, Trish, it's been a long time. Or is that always my opening line?"

"I heard that you might be here," she said. A delightful happiness was washing over her, which she fought with all her might. A red danger light flashed, blocking out the clear blue of his eyes. He was so familiar to her, as if she'd seen him last week. But she just stood there watching him, trying to calm her shaking body, reminding herself of her resolve to say hello and then split.

He let go of her hand, studied her, noting her changes. He was older too, even more appealing, filled out. He wore a silk-wool blend shirt in a light brown color, and dark brown pleated pants. He was still stylish. She remembered the bell-bottoms he'd worn in Iran. The body tension that had been so much a part of him was gone. Had he been at ease the last time she'd seen him? She couldn't recall.

"I thought if you saw me, you might not talk to me."

Her resolve to be controlled fought with how glad she was to see him. "I was looking forward to it. How do you know Pat?"

"I've bought art from him." He took a step back. "Well, I just wanted to say hello." And he turned to go.

She was amazed, not expecting this at all. She almost laughed at the turnabout. "Wait!" she said, surprised that she was saying it. "Don't leave."

The look he gave her was so filled with gratitude and hope, she felt her heart thud; her hands were trembling.

The noise in the room faded into the background as she looked up at him. *Just keep it light, impersonal,* she thought. "The last time I saw you, I forgot to ask if you were still doing what you used to do. I think you called it computers? Or maybe you're not supposed to talk about it."

"Not really." Only a flicker of his eyes told her he was surprised she knew he wasn't really in computers. "Not anymore."

"Thanks for being honest. What are you doing?"

"Writing. Fiction, nonfiction, articles. I'm halfway through my first novel."

"About your work for the government?"

"Only as it applies to my psyche." He smiled, took her arm, and moved her away from a jostling group of people. "I'm not surprised at how celebrated you've become, and I'm glad for you. Must have built your confidence. Artists and writers never know the value of their work; no matter what kind of praise or prices paid, we always wonder: Is it good?"

His easy manner was calming her, her trembling subsided. "Guilty as charged," she admitted.

"I saw your show of scenes of the Middle East some years back. I thought it was wonderful. You managed to create a mystical quality, yet show the reality; I could also sense your confusion at the time. But then, I had inside information. Am I rambling?" He grinned shyly.

She laughed. "A little, I guess."

"What are you working on now?"

She rarely described her work, but she wanted him to know. "A new area for me, diptychs in mixed media— half painting and half assemblage construction. Way back in college I did freestanding construction, so it seems a natural progression."

"Let me ask you something," he said, totally absorbed; she remembered how he could make her feel that her words were the most important thing in the world to him. "When you complete a work, do you feel you've expressed what you were trying to say?"

"God, no," she admitted, without even thinking about it. "I always doubt that the work is fully realized. Emotions are such elusive things and I try to translate them into something tangible, but it's impossible. And maybe that's the way it should be. Perhaps seeing an artist's agony would be too painful." She turned away to hide the emotion in her eyes, and didn't see him reach out to touch her. She turned back as he withdrew his hand. "The same thing holds true for positive experiences, like the overwhelming joy and love I feel sometimes, or even adoration for life; those things elude me too." There was an awkward pause for a moment, before she went on. "But I keep trying." She shrugged. "Maybe if I wrote epic poems, composed symphonies, made films, and also painted and sculpted, I'd be able to express everything that's there."

"That would be a work of art to behold," he said.

"But would anyone really understand it?"

He was still listening intently. "Do you think that no one ever understands?"

"I've never known an artist who's satisfied. You're a writer, are you satisfied with your work?"

"No," he agreed.

"Maybe we should be linked by electrical impulses that feed our emotions back and forth at precisely the same moment."

"But then we would be confused as to whose feeling was whose."

She nodded. "Sometimes the need to connect is so strong and my inability to do it so great it makes me despair. But that's the basis of religious faith, isn't it? We tell ourselves that God understands."

"And if that brings us comfort, so much the better."

He was moving her toward the door, but she hung back. "Are you leaving?"

"I thought we could go somewhere else. I know you said you never wanted me in your life, but a cup of coffee or a drink isn't exactly a lifetime commitment, is it?" She laughed, feeling her cheeks flush with heat. She retrieved her sheepskin jacket from a pile in the entry, and he pulled one like it out for himself. They smiled when they noticed they were wearing almost the same coat.

She was embarrassed that he had remembered her words so well that he could quote her. She recalled how she'd felt that night in the restaurant in SoHo, still in so much pain over Kelly's death that the sight of him had struck terror in her heart.

They both said good-bye to Pat McGarrity, who nodded his approval at the two of them. But that didn't matter; she could not let herself get involved. And then a thought struck her: maybe he was remarried.

The elevator took them to the lobby, and then they were on a nearly deserted Madison Avenue.

"We could get a cab on Fifth," he said.

"Are we going downtown?"

"How about dessert at the Palm Court?"

She laughed. "I'd have thought Elaine's was more your style."

"Not until they seat me somewhere away from the kitchen."

"Maybe when your novel's published."

He took her arm and walked toward Fifth Avenue. "Trish, I have to say this. I still think about the death of your baby and what you went through."

The gentleness in his voice opened her up. She felt her throat constrict. "And I'm sorry for the things I said to you the last time we met."

His grip on her arm tightened.

She looked at him, suddenly remembering the way he made her feel. Desire gripped her, and she felt a wave of weakness wash over her. It terrified her. She forced herself to ignore it. "There's something I always wanted to ask you. How did you know I was pregnant?"

He didn't answer for such a long time she thought he hadn't heard her. Then he said, "I'll tell you later."

They had reached Fifth Avenue, and he hailed a cab.

"Where are we going?"

"How's my place? I'm on the West Side, Eighty-fourth." She stiffened.

"I just want to talk to you, Trish. Just talk."

She felt foolish and then eager. "Fine."

They didn't talk much in the cab. She learned that he was single and that Maureen was remarried, to someone in English society. She'd finally arrived.

"My parents became closer after the incident with Maureen," she said. "In a way, it made their marriage stronger. They left Iran in 1975. They're living back in Southern California now. My father's retired, and they seem happy. But the biggest change is that they've accepted my brother Tom's life-style. He's gay, and yet he sees them often. I'm proud of them for that. My mother opened a gift boutique in Santa Monica, on Montana, and it's quite successful. She has a career; she goes to gift shows, has Saturday tea in the shop, does a huge Christmas business. It's surprising what women are doing these days; the most unlikely ones have become liberated."

"Good for her," he said, paying the cabdriver. He waited for her to get out. He lived on 84th, off Columbus, in a brownstone that was divided into a triplex. They walked up to his floor. The apartment was masculine and comfortable, with a hand-loomed area carpet, a contemporary sofa, and Charles Eames leather chairs. An étagère dividing the living and dining areas held his collections of African statuary and artifacts. Mounted on another wall was a magnificent painting by Clifford Still, and above the sofa, in a place of honor with a spotlight on it, was a painting of hers. Seeing it there, knowing he'd had a part of her always with him, filled her with an indescribable joy.

"Is that what you bought from Pat McGarrity?" she asked.

"Yes. I've had it for a while."

He took off her coat, while she looked at her work. It had been done a few years ago, toward the end of her work on the female figure as goddess. She'd used a classical female figure painted from a live model, juxtaposed with contemporary scenes. The women were depicted as art-historical figures incorporating the past with the present. It was a natural outgrowth of that work to simplify into what she was doing now, contemporary America and everyday life. She'd discovered that the classical influence was inherent, and that she didn't need to be so obvious. But the work of that period did maintain a mystique. It was interesting to see it again, knowing what she knew now; but she was proud of it. She remembered where she was at the time, how she'd been feeling when she painted it, still dealing with so much pain over the baby, but so excited when it sold.

She turned to him and saw him looking at her. "I felt the emotion in it so clearly," he said. "I longed to comfort you, but I wasn't able to give to anyone at the time, either. I was too needy myself. I hoped it would help just to have a sale. You were just starting to get hot. Later, the gallery couldn't keep your work, it went right off the walls. I bought this right after I saw you. It helped me get over your rejection."

"I'm sorry." She felt the color rise to her face, feeling a new kind of sadness for wasted time.

She sat on the sofa while he went to get a bottle of wine from the refrigerator. "It's okay, I managed," he called to her. "I wouldn't have been good for you then, either. Went through some rough times myself."

She remembered the portrait collage she'd painted of him so long ago, how troubled he'd been. She'd have to show it to him; the contrast would be remarkable. She took a sip of the wine. "What happened?"

He sat opposite her in one of the leather chairs, slid down and put his feet up on the coffee table. "I had a kind of crisis. Suddenly I couldn't function any longer, doing what I'd been doing. My work had required manic behavior; I was always on the edge, observing everything, missing nothing. Yet my wife was cheating on me and I hadn't seen it. Not for a while. I found out just about the time you came to Iran. It shook me up that I had let that slip. My life depended on my seeing and knowing everything; other lives depended on it. I packed it in, went to Tahiti for a while, then to Tonga, where there's hardly any civilization at all. Lived in a hut, totally alone. I didn't know who I was, what I wanted. And I was a man who'd never questioned those things, who'd always known exactly what to do."

"You were wound pretty tight when I met you. I always thought of you as a spring about to be sprung. The twang heard 'round the world."

He smiled, sipped his wine. The lights were dim in the room, but she could see his eyes clearly. They looked right through her. It was a warm, comfortable feeling, like being in a soothing bath. She was more relaxed than she'd been in a long time. The need to keep him at arm's length had eased, but she was still wary. "Will you tell me now how you knew I was pregnant?"

He took his feet off the table, put the glass down, and leaned forward, elbows on his knees. His expression showed a concern that she would not believe him, or, worse, laugh. "I have to go back a bit. So bear with me." She nodded, intrigued. "In my previous line of work, every detail was crucial. What seems unimportant can mean life or death. Nothing's left to chance, *ever*," he emphasized. "But I never realized that I had the ability to figure out a situation before it happened. I took that behavior for granted, as though it was part of my work, a requirement. I depended on the part of myself that just *knew* things." When he talked about his work, she could see remnants of that old intensity emerge, but now he sensed it too, and calmed himself. He smiled at her for noticing. "I was cocky," he continued, "until I found out about Maureen and your father. I hadn't known about it myself, so I lost all confidence. That's when I realized something was really wrong with me. But I never questioned why I knew some things and not others."

"You mean like knowing I was pregnant?"

He nodded.

She was touched by his openness, his willingness to communicate.

"My loss of confidence had nothing to do with love or betrayal," he said. "Maureen was a detail in my life to control as I controlled everything else. I didn't have the time or the capacity to care about her. My work was too important, a way to prove the world couldn't get along without me." He smiled ruefully. "I discovered it got along without me very well." He sat back again. "When I finally got off the treadmill, I had to face it, that I was a failure."

"You were awfully hard on yourself, weren't you?" she interrupted, feeling a sudden need to be closer to him, but thank goodness he was all the way over there, and she was safe over here.

He shrugged. "In my world, to miss a major detail like your wife's infidelity is failure with a capital *F*. So there I was, a failure, with nothing to fall back on. I had to begin again. And when I finally came out of the worst period of my life, I was a different man. I discovered that the ability to know things almost ahead of time was not part of my work; it wasn't because I had been trained well, I just had that ability."

"You mean psychic ability?" She felt her body respond to his words with recognition. A kind of warmth flowed through her.

He smiled. "I don't like to name it. It sounds weird. Let's just say I know certain things about people, and they don't have to tell me. I'm not interested in pursuing it as a life's work, it's just something that's part of me. Every now and then it comes in handy. I don't know how I knew you were pregnant, I just did. Just as I knew that for you and me there was the possibility of a strong bond." He saw her stiffen. "But our timing had to be right," he assured her. "Obviously, the timing has been wrong. And since you and I were both needy at the same time in our lives, we would have been destructive for one another if we'd come together before. I had to rebuild myself, and so did you. I'll bet you had a lot of healing to do."

She nodded. "That's true." She tried not to be so obvious that she had to defend herself against his expectations. He seemed suddenly too sure of himself, maybe a little wacky. It wasn't as though she hadn't heard these conversations before. Her art, the mystical aspects of it, seemed to attract the crazies sometimes. Thank God, the critics didn't consider her someone with a stuck-in-the-sixties mentality.

"I don't blame you for being skeptical," he said, getting up from his chair and coming to sit beside her.

The nearness of him made her heart beat faster. She felt oddly frightened, and moved away. "I think we should get something clear between us, Connor."

"Uh-oh," he teased. "Here it comes."

She laughed, and that relaxed her a bit. "I don't want to give speeches, it's just—"

He interrupted her. "You don't want a relationship."

She nodded, once.

"Why not?"

She turned away. "I just don't." But that voice inside of her said, *Liar*.

"Those pesky emotions again?"

She turned back, her eyes filled with anger, fighting herself more than him. "You know nothing about it, nothing!"

He grabbed her shoulders and held her, gazing deeply into her eyes. "I know everything about it, Trish. I know pain, I know sorrow, I know loss."

She was trembling so that her whole body shook. She tried to move away from his hands, but he held her fast. The heat from his fingers warmed her, the intensity of his grip held her, and so did his eyes. She felt herself filling up; her eyes brimmed over. "If you know, then let me be. I couldn't go through it ever again."

"So you're not going to live? The passionate woman whose paintings show her inner soul, displaying the torture of the damned for all to see, is afraid to feel?"

He let her go abruptly, and she caught her breath, wiped the tears from her cheeks. "It's easy to judge when you haven't been there."

"And you haven't been in my life, either. Want to trade?"

For a moment she saw, etched in his face, the pain he had faced and conquered. It deepened the pools of his eyes, softened the muscles of his body, reshaped them in the image of suffering. He did know.

"If I can do it, so can you." His voice was deep with emotion. He reached for her again, but she pushed him away, almost violently.

"No!" she shouted.

He sank back against the cushions, defeated, watching her. And then he said, "What is it, Trish? It's not the fear of being hurt, it's something else, isn't it?"

She pulled away from him, caught by his words, by his knowledge, by his goddamned psychic connection to her. God, he was dangerous, the most dangerous man she'd ever met. She wanted to break and run, to leap away to safety, but something held her. His eyes on her, the gentleness of his voice. His presence. And her desperate need. Half of her wanted to be absolved, while the other half insisted that she rend her flesh to expiate this unforgivable aspect of herself.

He whispered, "What is it? Tell me."

She turned back. All her fear was in her eyes, and it was as painful to behold as it was to feel. "I can't," she cried out, her voice speaking for her on its own, her words coming forth from the depths of an agony long buried, but festering like a noxious sore. If it erupted, it would destroy her, she knew it, the pain would be like nothing she'd ever experienced before. She held it back with all her might, but there was another force working to let it free, his love for her. It had always been there, she'd always known it, trusted in its constancy. Now he was offering it to her, and all she had to do was take it. But if she did, she'd die in the process.

"Why can't you, Trish, darling, why can't you?"

Stuttering, frightened, she felt it pouring out, no matter how she tried to hold it back: "I can't love you, I can't love anyone, especially you, I don't deserve you. I don't, I don't," she cried. "It doesn't matter about me, about my life, about what I want. I can't ever love anyone, no one can ever love me." She was sobbing, hiding from him with her tears, but her face poured out her sadness from her eyes and nose and mouth.

The torrent couldn't be stopped. She could feel it coming, that aching, driving, searing pain she'd kept in for so long. She was terrified of it. All the crying and all the agony she'd felt over Kelly was nothing compared to this. She was afraid the strength of it would destroy them both. He reached out to hold her, but she pushed him away, almost screaming, "No! I can't ever be loved, I don't deserve to be loved, I don't deserve it. I'm the most despicable person who ever lived. I killed my own child." The admission came bursting forth out of the depths of her soul, that hideous, disfiguring, maiming secret she'd held in for so long, suspecting it was there, getting glimpses of it, inklings of it, never really being able to hide from it, but never really facing it, either. And now there it was, raw and naked, jagged edges scraping her flesh to the bone. She sobbed from the depth of her being, inconsolable sobs that ripped at her heart as she let herself feel the full force of the blame she'd hoarded for all these years. "I killed my child," she sobbed over and over again. "Oh God, I killed her."

She cried for a long time, through hours and canyons of pain, each estuary leading to a new store that bubbled forth molten lava, burning anew. If she stopped, or quieted, it began again. And Connor held her, touched her, gentled her, waited for it to subside.

Finally it did, but she was so exhausted she fell asleep on the sofa where she'd laid her head, in the pool of her own pain.

Hours later she awoke in his arms. He had been holding her as she slept. Some part of her was aware that he had scooped her up and held her to his heart, but she was too exhausted to protest. He sensed her stirring.

"Are you all right?"

After what happened, she couldn't look at him. "I think I'd better go."

"Do you really think you killed Kelly?" he asked.

She spoke low into his chest, hearing her voice echo. "I took drugs, I drank alcohol, I had a lousy marriage. And if that wasn't enough, I slept through the episode when she stopped breathing. I could have saved her, but

I didn't wake up." These were just words, but they awakened the pain again.

"I forgive you," he said.

His words washed over her. "It's not for you to do."

"Then who can do it?"

"No one."

"Can God?"

"I guess so."

"Do you think He forgives you?"

She nodded.

"Can you forgive yourself?"

"I don't know."

"Say it."

"Say what?"

" 'I forgive myself.' "

"But I don't know if I do."

"Just say it."

"I can't."

"Why not?"

"Not if you don't mean it."

"Maybe if you say it, you'll mean it."

She looked up at him. Already his face had become dear to her.

"Go on," he urged, "just say it."

"I forgive myself."

"For what?"

She shook her head, unable to go on.

"Say it all."

"I forgive myself for killing my child."

"That's not exactly right."

"What, then?"

"Say, 'I forgive myself for *believing* I killed my child.' "

"Is that what I'm doing?" she asked incredulously.

He nodded. "You didn't actually do it, did you? Is there anything you did on purpose?"

"No," she admitted.

"But you've blamed yourself for all of it, even though you know there was no direct cause, and no one was personally responsible. Isn't it time you stopped being a martyr?"

"A martyr?" She laughed. "I never thought of it that way. I hate martyrs." The laughter that bubbled forth was clear and bell-like, free from taint and spoil. She was amazed that she could finally give up her pain, but it must be because she was truly ready.

He picked up her hand and kissed her palm, almost with reverence. She moved her hand from his lips and touched his cheek. Then she whispered, "Thank you." In that moment, all of her resistance melted away; something in her poured out and blended with him. She raised her head up and looked into his eyes. Deep pools of calmness met her gaze, and love.

"Oh God," she whispered, feeling such gratitude that this was happening, for when she searched that place inside that had been filled with the deepest agony, it had been swept clean and clear. She breathed in and felt the clean winter air fill her to the brim. And then she lifted up her face and kissed him. In that instant she felt a kind of breathless envelopment, a joy so complete she'd never known anything like it. She almost lost consciousness, and then knew that it was herself she was losing in him. That hard knot of separateness she'd had for so many years was unraveling, coming untied, and now meshing with him. They were forming a new whole, a new being together.

When the kiss ended, they pulled apart and looked at one another, touched each other's face, unable to believe what had just happened, but not doubting it either. He smiled first, and then she did.

"You see?" he said.

And she nodded, tears of happiness filling her eyes. Then she held him to her again, knowing with the conviction of her soul that she'd never be alone again. They belonged to one another, and now it felt like the simplest, easiest thing she'd ever done in her life.

BOOK VI

Friends in High Places

1

The rain came down in sheets, letting up occasionally and then pouring again in torrents. Hillary's heartbeat kept time with the windshield wipers. When she used them, that is. She was afraid to leave them on for fear they might wear out the battery in the van. The huge, gray, elephant-like shapes fenced in across the road were nearly invisible except when lightning bolts lit up the sky. It was cold in the car, in spite of her warm clothes. She couldn't turn on the engine to start the heater; someone might hear her, or see the exhaust. She was parked among the trees across from the Chemicals for Safe Environment facility. The plant had finally gotten built; in spite of her committee's efforts, they'd only managed to delay it a year. As the parent company had promised the local leaders and the state environmental agency, it was built with the latest technology; at first everything had seemed to be right. Independent soil tests done by the state had shown no leaching problems. But then, last July, an entire crop of carrots had rotted in a field near the county line. Hillary and her friends suspected that CSE was receiving illegal mixtures of chemicals from other facilities and dumping them on nearby roads and farmlands.

If only we could prove it, Hillary thought. A group of volunteers had kept watch off and on for the past few months, but so far they'd found nothing. It was boring, tedious work, and each week there were fewer volunteers. But it was the only way they'd ever prove anything. Chemicals for Safe Environment was being extremely careful, or else they were waiting for rainy weather to do their dumping. That was why she was sitting here in this rainstorm; she was trying to prove her theory. One of her co-workers, Noreen Pelegrino, was supposed to be with her tonight, but had canceled. When Hillary couldn't reach Flo or Kathleen or anybody else from their committee, she'd decided to come alone.

She wrapped her arms around her body, trying to stay warm. *Think about something pleasant,* she told herself, and thought of her twenty-third anniversary last August.

"I want us all to be together at home," she'd told Mel, except that Brian was at Harvard, in their summer high school program.

They had a barbecue in the yard, with everybody pitching in and making his or her specialty. Lori made pasta salad, Stephen made garlic bread and fruit ambrosia, and she put together her famous sauce. Mel did the chicken.

"Mom"—Lori had put her arm around Hillary—"did I ever thank you for all you've done for me?"

Hillary smiled and kissed her tall blond daughter. "Every anniversary and birthday since I can remember. And especially on Mother's Day."

"Then you can add this to the rest." She leaned forward and put her cheek next to Hillary's. "I'm so lucky. You and Dad are always there for me, especially in the rough times—like trying to decide what to do with my life. Architecture school is a grind, but I know now it's what I want."

Hillary recalled Lori's indecision.

"I've always known what I wanted," Stephen said, placing the fruit bowl on the table. He raised his palms upward and shrugged with the optimistic confidence of his father, knowing it would get her.

"Oh, you're so great." Lori stuck out her foot and tried to trip him.

He caught himself, regained his balance, and grabbed for her, but she ducked behind Hillary, who insisted, "Leave me out of this."

Just then, Mel came out from behind the barbecue, a platter piled high with reddish, charred pieces of chicken. "It's ready," he called.

And from the side of the house they heard someone say, "Where is everybody?"

Hillary's heart did a fiip. "Brian?"

"Surprise," he said, coming around the side of the house, carrying a suitcase and a backpack, followed by a friend.

"How wonderful," Hillary exclaimed, throwing her arms round him and hugging him tightly. Then she noticed the tall, strikingly handsome, blond young man with him. "Kevin? My God, it's Kevin," she cried, reaching out to hug him too.

He smiled shyly, responding to her enthusiastic welcome.

"We haven't seen you in so long. What a surprise." Her family were all grinning, in on it.

"I ran into Brian in Cambridge," Kevin explained. "I've been going to the summer program too. When I heard it was your anniversary, I had to come." He saw the look of concern on her face. "I'm fine, Mrs. Robin, no recurrence of the leukemia. The doctors say I'm doing great."

"I can see that," she said, looking him up and down. There was some of Charles in his face, in the shape of his eyes, the square jaw, and a little bit when he smiled. But the gray-blue eyes, the expression of confidence, the aura of having the world where he wanted it and loving it at the same time, was all Pam. "I think it's time you called me Hillary," she said.

After dinner they wanted an update on Hillary's work.

"Last spring there was a crisis in Glen Ridge, Montclair, and West Orange," she explained. "The state had to remove contaminated earth from underneath over a hundred houses because it contained radon, a radioactive gas. Radon's decay products have caused lung cancer."

"That's when I finally became radicalized," Mel admitted, smiling at Hillary because of the sixties word.

"It took you long enough," Hillary commented, letting them assume he'd come around to her way of thinking on his own, but actually she'd threatened to move out of Crestmont if he continued to oppose her and not do something to help.

"This section of New Jersey was built on landfill once owned by the United States Radium Corporation, and people have lived there for years without knowing about the problem," Mel told them. "Now they've been evacuated, their basements dug up, and radioactive dirt removed. I personally know twenty families who were affected. If you think I'm worried, you should talk to them."

"It's too close for comfort," Lori said.

"But something good came out of it," Hillary said. "The CCC attracted new members. We've always had financial support, thanks to Pam, but for the first time since 1978, Flo Goldman, Casey Sullivan, and I have finally got a group clamoring for action."

"Pam?" Kevin said, picking up on the name. "Not Pam Weymouth, by any chance?"

Hillary started, realizing her mistake. Pam was her major financial supporter precisely because of Kevin; she'd wanted to prevent other children from suffering the way he had. Hillary glanced at Mel, who gave her a look as if to say, *You've really done it now.* "Pam and I went to college together," Hillary explained. "She's a very philanthropic woman."

Kevin smiled. "Yes, I know."

"She's practically our aunt," Brian said. "You know her too?"

Kevin nodded, and Hillary quickly changed the subject back again. "Anyway, we've gotten local support now because last month an entire field of vegetables rotted. We plan to catch them in the act of illegal dumping."

"What do you mean, 'we'?" Mel said, jumping on her comment. "I don't want you doing anything like that."

"It's D.D. again, Dictator Dad," Lori teased, and Mel glared at her, but then, when she glared back at him and crossed her eyes, he smiled.

"Do you want your mother hiding behind bushes like some private eye?" he asked. "Maybe endangering herself?"

"No, we want her barefoot and pregnant, just like you do," Stephen said, getting into the act.

"I do not!" Mel protested, going along with them so as not to show his concern.

Kevin grinned, enjoying the easy banter, unused to this kind of teasing.

"Is it dangerous, Mom?" Brian asked.

"I've read where organized crime is involved in waste disposal," Lori said.

"Terrific," Stephen commented. "It's Mighty Mom, here she comes to save the day."

Hillary didn't want them too aware of her plans, making too many objections, because if investigation and spying was what it would take, then that was what she would do, organized crime or not.

"I asked for it," she said out loud to herself in the van, shifting in her seat and rubbing her hands together to warm them. It wasn't as though they hadn't tried every other way before resorting to surveillance. Their committee had written complaints, called, lobbied every state official they could find concerning the matter. The Department of Environmental Protection was responsive, but they were inundated with problems throughout the state. And they wanted credit for the progress they'd made in other areas, such as fish and game, air pollution, wetlands, pinelands, and especially waste disposal. But somehow Chemicals for Safe Environment rarely came under their scrutiny, or if it did, someone was squelching the complaints.

Her back was aching as it did from time to time. The orthopedist said she had a deteriorating disc, and had recommended muscle-strengthening exercises. Yesterday the dentist had found three cavities, and even though she now weighed less than at any other time in her adult life, she had cellulite on her thighs and loose skin under her arms. *Falling apart, baby, that's what you are,* she thought. *Forty-five next May, and this is November 1985 already.* The last five years had flown by with terrifying speed. But she had a wonderful family and a job that gave her immense personal satisfaction. She put her head back and closed her eyes.

Another bolt of lightning startled her awake; she must have dozed off. Frightened and disoriented for a moment, she sat up abruptly and looked across the street.

Activity!

The side gates were opening. She leaned over and rolled down the passenger window so she could see into the compound. Three huge trucks were coming out of the gate, one by one. This was it! Her theory had been correct; they were waiting for rainy nights to do their illegal dumping, when there were fewer people around. The rain was their camouflage for pouring out toxic liquids.

The trucks were heading south. She just had time to snap a few pictures of them leaving the facility before following them. Finally, she could justify an expensive, super-fast lens. She forgot about the cold, excitement infusing her with energy as she turned the key in the ignition and pulled the van slowly out from between the trees where she had been waiting. Then she turned right onto the road, keeping a safe distance behind. She checked the gas gauge one more time; still a full tank. It occurred to her that these trucks could drive long distances before anything might happen, and she would have to follow them. This could go on all night. The clock on the dash said 11:10. In case Brian was asleep, she'd left Mel a note that she was going to a movie. Soon he would be getting worried about her. She drove with her lights off for fear of being seen by the truckdrivers. In the dark, on the sparsely lit highway, with the rain pouring down, it was nearly impossible for her to see at all. She realized she'd have to get closer to the trucks to see what they were doing. She spoke into her tape recorder, making observations of where she was, the time, and a description of the trucks; the CSE logo was clearly visible on their sides.

The trucks seemed to be headed for the agricultural area west of Crestmont. They slowed down and then turned right off the paved road onto a narrow dirt road between a row of tall trees on the left and a field on the right.

She pulled up to the edge of the dirt road and lowered her window. Luckily the rain had stopped, and the clouds overhead were breaking up so she could see better. A cold, damp smell of earth hit her and she shivered. She could see the trucks on the narrow road to the right of her. Three lumbering shapes, moving almost silently in the night. They were barely crawling along.

This must be it!

She grabbed the camera and opened the door of the van, cursing the dome light that came on automatically. She climbed out of the van, feeling the muddy earth squish beneath her rubber rain boots, closed the door, just so that the light went off, and headed down the road after the trucks. They weren't far ahead of her. She stopped and held her breath, listening to the night sounds, the wind rustling through the row of tall trees, water dripping from the leaves, the engine sounds of the trucks as they moved slowly along. And something else. Something that sounded like water gushing from a powerful hose. As she drew closer she could smell it, the rubbery, acid smell of chemicals. They were opening up the valves of their trucks right here in this farmland, next to fields where vegetables grew, vegetables that she and her family ate!

Crouching low, she ran along the road, trying not to step in mud holes. She took a few photographs of the field to her right, with the trucks outlined on the road next to them. Then she ran up closer to the back of the closest truck. She could see the noxious liquid pouring out of a large spout on the left side. She hurried back to the van and slid open the side door. Inside were a bucket with a tight-fitting lid, a shovel, and some protective gloves. She grabbed the bucket, put on the gloves, and ran back to the road, cradling the camera in the crook of her arm. The trucks had traveled a long distance by now, and she didn't think she could catch up with them on foot. She was relieved to see them so far away, because that meant they hadn't seen her. Using a flashlight, she hurried along the road, looking for evidence of where the dumping had occurred. In the dark it was nearly impossible to tell, with the earth so soaked by rain. But she made an educated guess, scooping up earth by the side of the road and dumping it into the bucket. She was so busy she didn't notice that the trucks had turned around and were coming back, until their headlights were bearing down on her; she grabbed her shovel and bucket and started to run.

Weighted down with the bucket of earth and her camera, the mud beneath her sucking at her feet, she could barely run. It felt as though she were in a nightmare, wanting desperately to escape her pursuers, but unable to move, sluggish and bogged down. The stench of chemicals was very strong in the moist air, and she realized that the trucks on their way back must be dumping along the other side of the road, but she couldn't stop to see.

The trucks were getting closer, their engines whining in the night, huge, modern beasts of prey bearing down on her. She could hear the lead driver close behind her now. He must have seen her; she couldn't be more conspicuous. Her only hope was that she was not in the direct line of his headlights and that her dark clothes kept her from being seen clearly. Should she huddle down and let them pass? She'd never make it to her van without being seen.

The van was just ahead of her, the trucks so close behind that she heard the shifting of gears, and sensed with a horrible reality that one of the trucks was heading right for her. She turned as she ran, glancing over her shoulder, and saw the dark outline of a man high up in the driver's seat, saw him turn the wheel and swerve across the road to head his truck directly at her. Frantically she put out her hand to stop him, and then turned and her foot slipped and she literally flew into a mud-filled ditch by the side of the road just as the truck passed by where she'd been only a second ago. And then she smelled that sickening odor again, only so strong it made her gag, as the chemicals in his truck sprayed over her.

The truck continued past her and she heard a loud crunching sound, metal on metal. Pulling her head up, she saw the lead truck careen over the edge of the ditch and smash into the front bumper of the van. Her heart froze. If the car was demolished, she'd never get out of here. They could kill her. They'd already tried. But the second truck in line gave a long, loud blast of its horn, and the first truck swerved to the right, away from the van, righted itself, and drove on down the highway, the other two following behind.

She watched them go, sobbing dry, terrified sobs. She felt violated, and began to tear off her contaminated clothes in spite of the cold, first the down jacket and then the jeans, and then the boots. She sloshed back to the van in her turtleneck and longjohns. Her socks were soaked from the water that had seeped into her boots when she fell. Her underwear was wet too, through her jeans; she prayed that only her outer clothing had been doused with chemicals.

She opened all the windows in the van, praying that it would start. Thank God, it did, but the front bumper was torn off. She picked it up off the road and tossed it in the back. Then she wiped off the camera with some Kleenex, turned the car around, and headed back to Crestmont, with the heater on full blast.

All the way home she was consumed with rage and fear. Those sons of bitches were contaminating the very neighborhood she lived in! Crying from fear and a release of tension, she kept pounding the steering wheel. *What did they dump on me?* She didn't know where to go first, to the police or to the hospital. She chose the hospital.

When she tried to tell the resident in charge what had happened to her, she got hysterical so that he had to guess. When he discovered she'd been sprayed with chemical toxins, he sprang into action. And like Meryl Streep in *Silkwood*, she was stripped bare and scrubbed all over until her skin felt raw.

When she was finally able to make a phone call, no one answered at home, so she called Casey Sullivan, who had loaned her the van. Where was Mel?

Casey was awake, which was very unusual, but Hillary didn't ask why, only told her in a rush what had happened. When she finished, there was a shocked silence on the phone.

"Did you hear me, Casey? I'm sorry about the van, but I need some clothes. Will you bring me some? Can you use your husband's car? I'm going from here right over to the police station. I've got pictures and samples of everything, even my own clothes are proof. We did it! We've got them this time!"

Another silence.

Then Casey finally spoke. "I'm so glad you're all right, Hillary. We've been really worried. I'll be right there with the clothes. It's good that you're going over to the police. That's where Mel is. He's been calling everywhere, looking for you."

"Why? Didn't you tell him where I was?"

"He didn't give me a chance. Mel's at the police station, Hillary, because he's been arrested."

2

Mel's face was a pasty white color, and the greenish glare of the fluorescent lights in the police station didn't help. His suit was rumpled, his hair every which way; there was dried mud on his shoes and on the edge of his overcoat. Gray circles lined his eyes. But his lost expression was the most frightening of all. The essence of Mel was gone, his warm smile, his self-assurance. Only a shell of him remained, deadened by misery.

He was sitting on a bench, his head lowered, his shoulders slumped forward, when Hillary entered. He turned and saw her, stood up and opened his arms. She came to him, held him, rocked him, until his head fell on her shoulder. He clutched her while his body trembled. The police officers behind the desk looked away in embarrassment. She could barely hold him up as she led him back to the bench, where he collapsed as he sat down.

"You were in the hospital, are you all right?" he asked, looking at her with such sadness her heart constricted.

She too was exhausted from her ordeal, but she forced herself to appear normal for his sake. "I'm fine. I'll tell you about it later. What happened?"

"An accident," he said, "in the car. It wasn't my fault. The guy ran a stop sign."

"Then what's the problem?"

"They don't know if he'll live, and I'd been drinking."

"Oh, Mel!" She looked at him closely. He didn't seem drunk. The thought of some unknown man injured, nearly dead, on top of her own close call, was nearly too much to bear. Death was all around her tonight. She didn't know how much more of this she could take.

"Were you drunk?"

"No! My blood level will show that. But they're trying to say I left the accident, even though I only went to call

500

an ambulance. Nobody was home in any of the houses nearby, and then I came right back. But still, they're being hard-assed about it."

"Why didn't you wait with the injured man until someone drove by?" she said sharply, turning fear into anger.

"For God's sake, not you too," he said. "It was pouring rain, the guy was bleeding, I needed help. I was on Bloomfield Lane, near those huge estates, and nobody was home, dammit."

"Okay, honey," she soothed, realizing how close to the breaking point he was too. "I'm sure you did the best you could."

"Listen, we can go home now. I have to be back tomorrow for an arraignment and a bail hearing."

This relieved her; she was nearly asleep on her feet.

"I finally got hold of Judge Barlow, and he gave them permission to release me on my own recognizance. He wouldn't have done it if Victor Godfrey hadn't helped."

He saw her reaction on hearing that name.

"I know you don't like our illustrious mayor, but he's a good contact to have at a time like this. And he never said anything about you or the CCC, even though he opposes it. Honestly, Hil, he sat with me for hours when I couldn't find you, until the judge came home and returned our call."

This was the last thing in the world she wanted to hear. "I can't believe you called Victor, of all people." She not only disliked Crestmont's mayor, the most vocal of all the opposition to CCC and the strongest supporter of the chemical storage plant, she detested him.

"I thought he was the perfect choice. His son's a police lieutenant, and he owes me a favor for that time his brother-in-law tried to take over his hardware store."

"All you did was write a letter."

"But I didn't charge him for it, and it saved him his business."

"He didn't deserve it." She remembered all the times she'd been insulted by Victor when she went into his store, the way he talked down to her as a woman, implying that she was too stupid to understand anything mechanical. "You tell your better half to call me and I'll explain it to him," he'd say, if she wanted to rewire a lamp. It made her want to laugh, because Mel was not good at that sort of thing, and she was a whiz. And then there were the comments about her religion. Self-righteous bigot. "You people," he always said, referring to Jews. And then he'd shake his head, implying that anything Jewish was really strange. She looked up and saw the officer behind the desk watching her.

"I'm Officer Daniels," he said. He seemed about Brian's age, with fuzz on his upper lip. "Hear you're havin' some trouble. Anything I can do for you?"

She nodded, praying for the strength to get through what was still to come. "I did have a problem tonight. I have to make an accident report. I was a victim of a hit-and-run. One of the tank trucks from Chemicals for Safe Environment rammed into the van I was driving, and then drove away. The damaged van is parked outside, behind my husband's Mercedes. The bumper's torn off. You'll find the bumper inside the van. I'd like you to investigate all the trucks at the chemical plant until you find the one that hit me."

When she mentioned CSE, she thought she saw a subtle change. She wanted him to believe her. If he didn't, would anyone? "I'll get on it right away, ma'am."

Now she realized another predicament. Any investigation of the accident would have to include an explanation of what she was doing there. She would have gone directly to the DEP except that it was the middle of the night. She wished she could discuss all of this with Mel, but he looked too exhausted, and so was she.

"Officer Daniels, when you go out to the van, you'll find some other evidence that I collected tonight, a bucket of soil from an agricultural field just five miles east of here. I saw the same truck that hit my car dumping toxic chemicals on the road during the rainstorm. My clothes are also contaminated. I'll need to take the soil and my clothing to the Department of Environmental Protection in the morning for analysis to see what they contain. From the smell of them, it's something very strong."

"I'm sorry, ma'am, but you'll have to leave those items with me. They're evidence in a criminal investigation."

"But what about the DEP? I have to get them analyzed!" This latest hitch in her plans seemed overwhelming, as near collapse as she was.

"We'll have someone take them to the DEP when

we're through with them," he assured her. He gave her a form to fill out. "I am sorry to hear about this," he said, dipping his head for emphasis.

When he came back, she was halfway through with her report, and he was wearing a fireman's suit to protect himself. He went out to examine the van and take the soil samples from the back.

Though she knew Mel was impatient to leave, he sat quietly next to her, slumped on the bench. She finished the report as quickly as possible, signed it, and handed it to the officer behind the desk. As she helped Mel out to the car, she passed Officer Daniels on his way around the back of the building, carrying her clothes and the bucket of dirt.

"Officer, please be careful with those samples. They're extremely important to me, to a lot of people. Will you get them to the DEP as soon as possible, please?"

His expression was unreadable as he said, "We'll do our best."

"How long will it take?" She felt suddenly anxious.

"I don't know, ma'am. But don't you worry, I'll make sure they're delivered all right."

It was nearly 2:00 A.M. when they got home. Mel had been silent, not wanting to talk, but he hadn't let go of her hand, even while she drove. She followed him into the house, so tired she could barely climb the front steps.

"This has been the worst night of my life," Mel said. "I sat there waiting for you for four hours, worried to death about you and terrified of what you were going to say about what I'd done. If I'd known what you were going through, I'd have been even more out of my mind."

"I'm sorry you had to wait, honey." She sank onto the sofa, not knowing if she could make it up the stairs. "It was a horrible night for me too. But I'm all right now. Why don't you tell me everything that happened?"

He sank down on the sofa opposite her in the family room, his soiled coat wrapped around him. "The train was on time, arrived in Crestmont at five past eight; I didn't feel like coming right home, so I stopped off for a drink. I had a scotch, and then a beer. I was driving down Bloomfield Lane when this guy ran a stop sign right in front of me. I didn't see him until it was too late. I hit him broadside, pushed his car across the intersection. I could see how badly he was hurt, and I ran up to the gate of one of the estates nearby. I rang and rang, but nobody answered. Same thing across the road. There are no streetlights there, it was pitch dark. I knew I had to get help. And I had a blood alcohol level that would register on a breathalyzer. Believe me, I thought about running, but I couldn't do it. I looked around for someone, but the road was deserted. I was afraid the man was bleeding to death or something. So I drove to the nearest phone and called the police, and by the time I got back, they were already there, prying the guy out of the front seat. He was conscious, and he looked up and saw me, and called me a sonofabitch before he passed out. And then Victor Junior, who was on the scene, asked me if I was the one who'd hit him and I said yes, that I'd gone to call for help. He made me do an alcohol test, and it came up point-ten and he arrested me for driving under the influence and felony hit-and-run. He almost got me for resisting arrest because I kept insisting the guy had run a stop sign." Mel's head was in his hands. "I'm in real trouble, Hil. If the man dies, it will be a felony."

"But you had the right-of-way. Someone will come forward and say so."

He looked at her, more frightened than before. "No, they won't!" he insisted. "It was raining, the streets were deserted, no one was around." She'd never seen him so defeated. "That poor man," Mel said, shaking his head. "Can you imagine what he's suffering right now? Maybe *he* was drinking. Do they check the victim's blood alcohol level?"

"Mel, you've never stopped off for a drink in your life. Why did you do it tonight?"

He looked away. "I just felt like it, that's all. I knew you weren't home."

"How did you know, if you didn't find my note?"

" 'Cause you're not home very much these days."

Her head was throbbing. She was so tired she thought she might pass out. She didn't have the strength to get into this with him now. She dragged herself up and helped Mel from the sofa to the stairs. "I pray that man recovers and that someone comes forward to say they saw the accident," Hillary said. "I'll go door to door if I have to. We'll find a witness. I'm good at that sort of thing."

He gave her a half-smile when she said that, which reminded her of Stephen at age ten. "I don't deserve you," he said, reaching the top of the stairs.

"Yes, you do," she said. "You deserve me and every aggravating thing I've ever done to you."

"But what about all the good things you've done?"

"Well, maybe you don't deserve all of those," she teased.

When they reached their bedroom at the end of the hall, he wrapped his arms around her, squeezing much too tightly. She felt his desperation.

"God, I love you, Hillary. I'm so sorry for tonight. I've never regretted anything so much in my whole life. If only I could erase it, make it go away. I'd give anything."

"We'll get through this, Mel, we've got each other."

"What if he dies, Hillary?"

"He won't." She kept saying it to him over and over, murmuring to him, soothing him. She helped him get undressed and got herself ready for bed, then climbed in beside him. He curled up in her arms and she stroked his head, his back, until she heard his even breathing, and then, even though her arm was going numb from his head resting on her chest, she finally fell asleep herself, but in her dreams she relived the nightmare, the rain and the truck, the smell of the chemicals, and running for her life. Sometime around five, she woke up to find Mel asleep on his side of the bed, and she felt lonely and depressed. *I should have given up this sleuthing long ago,* she thought. *I have no business risking my life when I have a family depending on me, needing me. If I hadn't been gone tonight, maybe Mel wouldn't have gone to a bar for a drink and had that accident.* She knew Mel's accident wasn't her fault, and she believed that he wasn't guilty of causing it, but that greedy, criminal chemical company was sure as hell guilty, of the most heinous acts. Now she knew that for certain, and her resolve returned. No matter what, she would continue!

3

Nothing had ever taken so long, Hillary thought, as waiting for the soil reports to come back from the DEP lab. But every time she checked, Officer Daniels seemed to be on top of it. "I was just about to call you with an update, Mrs. Robin," or, "I tried you this morning but you weren't home." Yet there were always some bureaucratic delays. There was a backlog at the DEP, Daniels explained. She had to be patient. And then it was Christmas and no one worked over the holidays.

At first, Officer Daniels was quite solicitous, apologizing, making promises. But as time went by with no report, she got more insistent, and he got more belligerent, to the point of not taking her calls or being extremely curt when she reached him. The more active members of her committee were as impatient as she. But the more they put pressure on the local police, the worse it got, until Victor Godfrey, the mayor of Crestmont, called Mel.

"I helped you out of a tight jam, Robin. A hit-and-run drunk driving charge is no easy matter. So tell your wife to lay off bothering the police. Daniels is a friend of my son's. He's a good man. She's making too much out of nothing, and she's angering some very important people. People who are my friends. And they don't like what she's been doing."

"I'll talk to her," Mel agreed, "but you know how women are, once they get their minds set. And she does have some strong evidence on her side."

"I'm telling you, Robin, she'll never get anywhere with this. She'll just make herself even more unpopular."

"The nerve of him," Hillary said, when Mel told her. "Do you think he was threatening me?"

"Victor's always melodramatic. But I think you should ease off. Don't be so hard-headed."

"I'll be damned if I'll let up, Mel," Hillary said. "Victor Godfrey's in CSE's pocket. I can smell it."

On the morning of January 8, the *New York Post* published the photographs she'd taken of the waste dumping; someone at the DEP had released them without her authorization. By afternoon, other New York and New Jersey papers had followed suit, and by the next day the photos had been picked up by the wire services and published all over the country. It was the hottest story of the day; no one had ever had such blatant pictorial proof of illegal activity. "Nightline" called to interview her, and all the national morning shows wanted her too. Hillary was besieged with sudden notoriety.

"Me and Ted Koppel. Should I do it, Mel? It's an opportunity to really bring our cause public."

"Hillary, for God's sake, I don't want you to go on national television and admit what you did. Those men tried to kill you, they could do it again. I know there is the theory that you could be safer by going public because if anything happened to you it would bring more attention to your cause, but what if that didn't work this time?"

"But I'm the only one who can testify to what I saw. I smelled those chemicals, tasted them. They've got to be stopped. They're polluting our food, our drinking water, the air we breathe, for God's sake."

"All right, think of it this way: you'll lose credibility. Without the soil reports, it's your word against theirs."

"You're always on everybody else's side," she said. But he was right. She turned down every interview.

On Friday, January 10, she decided she wouldn't wait one more minute, and drove over to the police station and demanded to see Officer Daniels. Instead she got Victor Godfrey, Jr., the eldest of Mayor Godfrey's three children, none of whom would ever be rocket scientists. Victor and his brother Tony had gone to school with Lori and Stephen. The boys were both bullies, their sister a troublemaker. To have Victor Junior now responsible for law enforcement in Crestmont was ironic. As a kid he'd always been at the edge of the law, and with his father as mayor he tended to be more an intimidating police officer than a helpful one.

He was tall and muscular, with close-set eyes like his father's, and short brown hair. His hand was on his hip, and a defiant look on his face.

"Here, Mrs. Robin," he said, a touch snidely. "I've got your report." And he handed it to her.

Eagerly she tore open the file and began to read. She couldn't believe it. The DEP had found nothing toxic in any of the soil samples, or in her clothing, except for some detergent residue. She glanced through all the technical jargon to the summary. The lab technician's opinion was that the rain had washed away any evidence, but most likely, what the trucks were dumping wasn't a toxic substance.

She looked at Victor Junior in disbelief. "I don't understand. I know it was toxic chemicals."

He shrugged. "Maybe you'd better leave investigating to people who really understand what they're doing, ma'am." The "ma'am" was drawn out for sarcasm.

She wanted to kick him in the shins. He was glad it had turned out this way, his father's son. To him she was just a hysterical female. Shaking with rage, she drove directly from Crestmont all the way to the headquarters of the Department of Environmental Protection and insisted on seeing Martin Cook, a deputy director, with whom she should have been dealing all along.

"I'm sorry, Hillary," he said, after reading the report, "especially since those damned pictures were already published. But there's nothing here to go on."

"Do you mean to tell me that in the dead of night, in a blinding rainstorm, those trucks were dumping pure distilled water?"

"Of course not. But without laboratory corroboration there's nothing we can do. It's a good thing you didn't go on TV. I hope you didn't make any statements to the press accusing CSE of anything. You could be sued."

"I don't understand. I know what I saw. The smell was sickening, dizzying. Even the medical resident who treated me in the emergency ward suffered dizziness from being around me. Won't his testimony mean anything?"

"Not if he doesn't have proof of what caused it."

"Oh damn." By now her head was pounding with frustration.

There was sympathy in Martin Cook's voice. "I've got the director's promise to keep a close watch on CSE, but that's all I can do. Since you had to let the police bring those samples directly to us, it might have been wiser for you to divide the soil into two containers and keep one, just in case. Our labs have the most sophisticated testing equipment, but we can't find something when there's nothing there."

"For God's sake, Marshall, do you think I was wrong to trust our local police?"

"Oh, I think that's going a bit far. I'm sure they made honest mistakes. Most people don't understand the seriousness the way we do. And to them, one bucket of soil looks just like the other."

"Well, you people were inept too, releasing those photographs without the soil reports."

"Again, I'm sorry about that, Hillary. I don't know how it happened."

She hated this feeling of failure. All her efforts, arising from her intense desire to prevent others from suffering the way Kevin had suffered, had done no good. She'd risked her life for nothing. That storage facility, and others like it, were still poisoning people. "Maybe it's just as well that the newspapers jumped the gun and printed those pictures; at least we got some good publicity." Still, she could hardly contain her disappointment.

"You'd better pray that that publicity doesn't backfire."

"You're right," Hillary said, afraid to think of the repercussions. "Keep me posted."

Tonight was the monthly meeting of the CCC. She dreaded having to face everyone and tell them she had failed. During dinner she told Mel what had happened. He was incredulous too.

"Somebody's covering up," she insisted. She felt like crying.

He could see how upset she was, but after his initial sympathetic reaction, he seemed to withdraw.

"Honey, would you go to the meeting with me tonight?" she asked, needing his support.

His expression tightened and he was about to say no, but she held up her hand. "Never mind. I'll go without you. Again. But I could really use you by my side to-night. The way I've been by your side since the accident."

He winced when she mentioned it, but he nodded. "Okay, I'll go. But don't expect me to participate, Hil. I couldn't possibly stand up in public and speak out in favor of anything. I hate even walking into the village. I know what everybody's thinking. 'There he goes, the drunk driver. Hanging's too good for him.' " He seemed so dejected.

She sighed. "Maybe you shouldn't go tonight, after all," she said.

"No, I said I would."

She handed him his coat, and touched his cheek. But he didn't smile. She wished she could help him too. Someone else she was failing. *Why do people I love have to suffer and I can't do anything to stop it?* She took his hand, but he pulled away. Lately he didn't want her to touch him. And that was the most painful of all. They had always been so physically close, taking pleasure in affection as well as lovemaking, but since the accident he didn't want to make love. He said he kept picturing the man slumped over the steering wheel, bleeding.

"Do you think someone at the police station switched the soil sample and laundered my clothes before taking them to the DEP?" she asked.

Mel got into the passenger's seat and buckled his belt. That was another change; ever since the accident he was reluctant to drive.

"It's possible. Maybe someone at CSE paid them off. People will do anything for money."

Hillary backed the car out of the driveway. "I'm sure those trucks were contaminating that soil. Why else would that driver have tried to run me over?"

Mel raised his voice. "Dammit, Hillary, enough with the trucks, and that report. Do you realize you haven't talked about anything else for weeks? In case you haven't noticed, my life is upside down. How about some concern for me?"

She clamped her mouth shut, startled by his outburst and incensed by his accusation. As much as she'd worried about her own problems, his had occupied her even more. But he was obviously too much on edge to remember. Fortunately, the man in the accident had not died, but he had sustained a serious back injury. The good part was that criminal charges against Mel had been dismissed. The blood alcohol test had been inconclusive, and he hadn't been held on the hit-and-run count since he had gone for help and returned right away. The bad part was that the injured man's insurance company wasn't willing to settle for the limit of Mel's policy, and could come after him personally. She understood why he was worried, and didn't say anything more.

Crossing the parking lot of the high school auditorium, she wondered if Victor Junior, working on his father's behalf, might have had anything to do with altering her samples. She wanted to ask Mel about it, but when she reached for his arm he was still stone-faced, so she let her arm drop. *I might as well have come here alone, for all the help he's giving me,* she thought. She had nearly been killed that night, and since then she'd yearned for his attention and care, the way he used to give it, letting her know how important she was to him. But his mind was only on the accident.

When they came into the auditorium, Hillary was surprised and pleased to see Bobbie talking to a group of people. Bobbie had never attended these meetings before, and Hillary was glad to see her here now. But then they ran into Mel's personal injury attorney, and Mel took him aside to talk.

"What's new, Bob?"

Bob smiled. "Your guy is out of the hospital."

"That's wonderful," Hillary said.

"But he's probably going to need a spinal fusion and laminectomy—that costs about seventeen thousand—plus several months of physical therapy before they decide whether or not to have the surgery; meanwhile, those bills keep piling up."

"Why are you smiling?" Hillary asked.

Mel answered for him. "He's been through this so many times it's a joke to him. Well, it's not to me." He ran his fingers through his graying curly hair.

"Come on, man, lighten up," Bob said, affable in spite of Mel's outburst.

"Is there more?" Hillary asked.

"What do you mean?" Mel asked, jumpy.

"There's always more, isn't there, buddy?" Bob said.

Mel was so nervous. "Get to the point, will you?"

"Your guy worked in a brick factory," Bob continued, "and he lifted heavy objects. But he can't do that anymore, so he can claim a loss of twenty-five thousand a year, over a lifetime. We're talking about eight hundred thousand, plus pain and suffering. He's got a seven-figure claim, all right. And if a jury is sympathetic to him, they could award him a million, which means you'd have to fork over half a million bucks above your policy. What you could use, buddy, is a witness."

Hillary drew her breath in sharply and looked at Mel, but he kept his eyes averted; she reached for him, but this time he walked away. It was such a blatant rejection that her cheeks burned.

She turned her fury on Bob. "Did you have to be so blunt? Can't you see how worried he is?"

Bob patted her arm, his voice full of confidence and good humor. "That's a worst-case scenario, Hillary. It's not going to come to that. I'll get them to accept Mel's policy limit. I don't think the victim was blameless, and I'll find a way to prove it."

"Why didn't you say that to Mel?" She wanted to shout her anger.

He smiled. "I like giving him a hard time."

"Well, I don't," she said, about to explode with frustration. "Go and find him and make him feel better." She gave him a push to where Mel was talking with Bobbie, and waited to see Mel's reaction, but he was absorbed in conversation so she went into the auditorium. Something wasn't right about this, but she couldn't figure out what it was. Why would Mel's lawyer tease him like that? And why was Mel so terribly upset about a situation that seemed to be getting better rather than worse? She had to find a way to assure him that everything would be all right.

The auditorium was crowded tonight; all the publicity from her photographs in the paper had brought the best turnout they'd ever had. She walked through a crowd of her neighbors and friends, smiling as people congratulated her, shook her hand, and patted her on the back. She hated to tell them it had all been for nothing. Then she saw Victor Godfrey. *Damn, he would be here tonight. Probably came to gloat.* He had a self-satisfied smile on his jowly face. And if that wasn't bad enough, for the first time in the history of Crestmont's Concerned Citizens, the press was here; now they'd find out firsthand how she'd failed. Yesterday famous, tonight infamous.

Flo read the minutes of the last meeting, and Kathleen discussed tonight's objective: whether or not their group should hold a mock funeral at Jersey Chemical's headquarters to bring attention to their cause. But Hillary couldn't concentrate. She kept looking for Mel, wishing he'd come and sit with her. And then Flo turned the meeting over to her.

She came up to the podium and gazed at the faces looking up at her. Only Mel's face was missing. He was still outside talking to Bobbie.

When she announced the results of the lab report, voices rose in protest. "I know you're outraged," she said, shouting to be heard above the noise. Then her heart sank as she saw Victor Godfrey standing up to speak.

"This takes the cake!" he shouted, pointing at Hillary, making himself heard with his booming voice. "I've seen a lot of foolhardy behavior in my time, but this wins the prize! For years your committee yelled their heads off about our evil local chemical storage facility, and now you admit that nothing's wrong. You've got your nerve, making fools of this whole town, libeling decent, taxpaying citizens! You waged a smear campaign against a law-abiding company. You've targeted the wrong people. You're the guilty ones! Why don't you people give up?"

Angry shouting nearly drowned him out. Hillary banged the gavel for order. "Mayor Godfrey has the floor," she insisted, wishing he'd shut up and sit down.

With some relief she saw Mel come in, but Bobbie was gone. He came down the aisle toward the front row and slipped into an aisle seat, still not looking directly at her.

"Since 1980," Godfrey said, "this state's toxic waste program has been unmatched by any other in the country. Indictments are brought every day against real offenders by the Department of Environmental Protection. We have to trust our officials; they're doing their job, I tell you!"

Some people agreed with him. Others shouted, "It's too little, too late. We're worried about Crestmont."

"We live near that place, and it's worse than living in hell," another woman shouted.

"We need more than Senator Lautenberg's help."

The press fired questions at her, and she answered them in rapid succession, stressing that Jersey Chemical, the parent company of CSE, had a statewide record of offenses. "Eventually, someone is going to prove this! In 1983, a *Newsweek* article estimated that fifty thousand dumps throughout the country are festering with toxic waste. One hundred eighty thousand open pits, ponds, and lagoons at industrial parks are like witches' brews. The EPA says that fourteen thousand of those sites are potentially dangerous, and that ninety percent of the eighty-eight billion pounds of toxic wastes a year are improperly disposed. In New Jersey, the chemical storage facility at Elizabeth exploded, releasing a toxic cloud into the atmosphere; radon was discovered next door to us, and there were twelve accidents involving a release of toxic chemicals into the air. I want it stopped! Don't you? We can make a difference. Look at what they did at Love Canal; the government was forced to evacuate five hundred families and buy their homes at fair market value. We know that CSE has committed offenses, and we'll prove it, no matter what it takes."

"You're on a witch hunt!" Victor Godfrey shouted.

This time she stared him down. "And you're protecting vested interests because of the taxes they pay and the jobs they provide. Are they following safety rules? No, they're dumping their wastes on us! Many of you are aware that organized crime is heavily involved in these activities." Mayor Godfrey's expression gave her a sudden feeling of fear in the pit of her stomach. "Organized crime has monopolized the trucking industry in this country because of its hold on the teamsters, and now it's monopolizing the waste-disposal business. Maybe that's who tried to run me over that night at Macauley's farm."

Mel was looking at her now, staring at her in disbelief. This was something they'd speculated about, but for her to say it in public was asking for trouble. Now he'd really be after her to quit. But at least she had his attention.

The press erupted with questions. "Only one more," she insisted, pointing to a young reporter with dark hair in a pony tail.

"Mrs. Robin. Any comment on Mayor Godfrey's announcement earlier tonight that he is a candidate for Congress?"

There was an instantaneous buzzing throughout the room. Hillary was outraged. *So, he came here for a forum.* Victor's arms were crossed over his wide chest; he raised one eyebrow to show how pleased he was to have caught her like this. *Think you're so smart,* his expression said. *I'll show you.* What was it about him that she so disliked? Everything. His prejudice, not only against Jews and minorities, but against people who lived in houses bigger than his, who had children smarter than his, who enjoyed their marriages more than he did, with his pinch-faced, intimidated wife. Anna Godfrey never smiled unless she looked at him first for permission. His face tended to redden whenever his thoughts were unkind; it was easy to read him, as easy as seeing his tanned scalp beneath his thinning hair, reflecting the light above his head. Hillary's attention was brought back to the reporter.

"Are you considering running in the next election, since Congressman Nutley has vacated this district's seat to run for the Senate?"

Hillary started to shake her head no, but before she could reply, Flo Goldman's voice called out from behind her on the stage. "Yes, she's thinking of running! We're forming a committee tonight, after this meeting, to sign up volunteers for Hillary Robin's campaign."

Mel's eyes met Hillary's, and they stared at one another for a stunned moment.

"For what office?" someone shouted.

Everyone spoke at once. "State legislature," was a suggestion. "Lieutenant governor," someone else said. And then everybody had something to say: "Not without some experience." "We need her in the Senate." "No! The Governor's mansion."

Suddenly, Mel stood up in the front row to make himself heard above the din. "Run for Congress, Hillary!" he called out, then turned to face the crowd. "The incident in the papers brought her national prominence. Besides, she's a leader with guts, brains, and, God knows, dedication. I should know that." He turned back to her. "I say go for it, baby!"

Hillary felt her stomach drop to the floor as she stared

at him. He was smiling at her and nodding. It was the happiest she'd seen him in months.

She was so surprised she didn't think any sound would come out if she tried to speak, but her voice was surprisingly strong. She raised her hand, calling for silence, and waited a minute for everyone to settle down. *Can I do this?* she was wondering. *Can I really do this?* But after her talk tonight, and the years of experience behind her, she knew she could—anything to keep Victor Godfrey out. She was so excited she wanted to leap off the stage and dance around the room.

"In answer to your question, Ms. Price, I do have a comment." She glanced at Victor Godfrey. "I am declaring my candidacy for Congress from the Fifteenth Congressional District of New Jersey. I'm willing to give Mayor Godfrey, and any other candidate, a real fight!" And as the enthusiastic applause rose around her, her excitement rose with it. She suddenly realized that she loved this feeling, she deserved it, she'd earned it. She was willing to do what it took for her cause, and if that meant running for, and maybe even winning, a public office, enjoying support as well as surviving the criticism, then that was all part of it. Her enthusiasm and excitement were so great that she raised her hands and applauded the audience back.

4

It was only May of 1986, and already she didn't think she could make it to the election in November. Nobody had told her about the exhaustion, about the cheek muscles so sore from smiling that they ached every night, about the bruises she'd get from shaking hundreds of hands, about the boring, fattening food, or about the threats. Every candidate got them, she was told. But she made certain to travel in groups, and tightened her security. Speaking in public had become second nature to her. She talked to strangers on the streets, workers coming out of buildings at five o'clock, gas station attendants, waitresses, and bus drivers; she made formal speeches to PTA groups, bridge clubs, country clubs, church groups, women's organizations, men's organizations, labor unions, and citizens' groups. She spoke at breakfasts six days a week, and lunches seven days a week. In the afternoons she stood on corners, drove around in a car with a loud-speaker, stood outside factories at seven in the morning, visited farmers at home. In the evenings her supporters invited their friends over for coffee and dessert to meet her; tonight, for example, Bobbie and Frank were hosting a fund-raiser. Campaigns needed a lot of money to buy advertising and pay for expenses; many times these speeches were an appeal for contributions as well as for votes. And all the effort had paid off. Tonight they were celebrating her winning the primary, along with Victor Godfrey, over six other candidates.

She'd always known it would come down to the two of them. The man gave her nightmares, not only because he was the front runner and had formidable backing, but because of the look of pure animosity he summoned whenever his small, dark eyes looked at her, and the way he shut it off so completely when being smarmy and slick

517

with his constituents. He would be difficult to beat. But she had several advantages in that he had a public record she could criticize, and his support of the chemical facility was unpopular, except that it brought him major contributions. She expected him to be a dirty fighter; already he was saying she had never done a day's work in her life, had no business running for political office, and had no moral anchor. What he was really saying was that she'd never been a party person. But the Democratic party was behind her now.

Bobbie and Frank's house was filled with spring flowers, banners were strung in open doorways, and there were campaign posters of her everywhere. Hillary had to admit that Bobbie had really put herself out. Six months ago she would have expected it, but lately Bobbie had been too busy to see her, or maybe she'd been too busy as well. And then last month Bobbie had called to say that if Hillary won the primary, Bobbie would invite her real-estate contacts and Frank's clients to meet her. Hillary was delighted, she'd missed Bobbie.

"Hi, toots," Bobbie said, giving her a careful kiss on the cheek so as not to muss either one of them. "Congrats. We're really proud of you." She nodded to Mel. Hillary was swept away by some of the people she knew, and Bobbie called out, "We'll get started soon, okay?"

Hillary nodded, wondering why she felt oddly uncomfortable with her friend. That easy friendship between them was gone.

After about thirty minutes, Frank called everyone to attention and introduced her. She gave her speech, and was quite pleased by the response. Kevin and Brian were with her tonight. As usual, she could count on them to solicit contributions like pros, but Mel had disappeared. And then, as she was talking to a group of doctors, she saw Mel talking to Bobbie. They were alone in the hallway between the kitchen and the dining room, unaware of being observed, but Hillary could see them reflected in the dining room mirror. Mel was angry about something. He was talking forcefully, and wouldn't let Bobbie get in a word. Hillary knew that behavior well. Then Mel grabbed Bobbie by the arm and almost shook her. Hillary was surprised that he felt familiar enough to treat Bobbie that way. It gave her a sick feeling in the pit of her stomach.

Later, when she and Mel and Brian were in the car on the way home, she was so tired she didn't want to bring it up. But Mel did.

"Bobbie and Frank are hypocrites," he said. "Here they give you this party, but I think they're supporting Victor."

"Why would you say that?" It was the last thing she expected to hear.

"Didn't you see me arguing with Bobbie?" he asked, glancing at her.

"Yes," she admitted. "I wondered what it was about."

"I saw it too," Brian said.

Mel explained, "Bobbie said she thought it wouldn't be so bad if Victor was elected, that he had more experience in public office than you did, and that some people might feel more secure with him in Congress. It made me furious. I think she's got her eye on running for mayor of Crestmont. If you win, Victor will still be mayor."

"That must be why she's been so distant toward me lately," Hillary said. "It makes sense. She's guilty about supporting Victor."

"I guess we all feel guilty," Mel said. "With this accident case still hanging over my head, I'm not much good to anyone."

It had been a while since he'd alluded to the distance between them, which had gotten worse in the last six months. She could blame it on the campaign, but she shuddered to think of what would be left after the election. They rarely made love, and when they did, Mel had problems, the kind that women's magazines discussed these days with such frankness. Either he couldn't sustain an erection or he couldn't get one to begin with. It bewildered her, though she was understanding, but he refused to discuss it. She knew it was the damned lawsuit, and he agreed. Not only could the lawsuit wipe them out financially, but whatever the outcome, the press would play up the negative, focusing on the arrest report, which accused him of drunk driving and leaving the scene of an accident. Even though he'd been exonerated, he'd look as guilty as hell. She was still not clear on Mel's motive for leaving the scene of that accident, but he was so sensitive about the subject that she couldn't ask him, especially in front of Brian. It was difficult not to fault

him. She worried, too, about how all the adverse publicity could decimate her campaign. Look at what it had
done to Geraldine Ferraro.

The next day, after speaking to a local Rotary Club,
she was trying to decide what to do about that, and about
Bobbie. *Maybe I'll call Bobbie and have it out with her,*
she thought, picking up the phone. But she was due at
her campaign headquarters in forty-five minutes, and
that gave her precious time to rest. Bobbie could wait.
She'd just taken off her blouse and skirt and lain down
on the bed when the doorbell rang. Cursing her rotten
luck, she asked who it was from her bedroom window.

"It's Kevin, Hillary," he called up, and moved out
from under the porch roof so she could see him. "I had a
free afternoon, so I drove over in case you needed me."

Since Brian and Kevin were both graduating from high
school this June, and Stephen and Lori were away, she
relied on the two boys. Kevin, especially, was full of
ideas and enthusiasm. He certainly had Pam's entrepre-
neurial skills. Lori had been home for spring break to
work on the campaign. Stephen had a job in New York,
where he was in law school. This summer, Lori, Brian,
and Kevin would be working for her full time. And she
did need them. Their energy and contributions were
invaluable.

She threw on a robe and came downstairs, feeling
every muscle in her body aching. Kevin handed her the
mail. He had a funny expression on his face.

"What's wrong?"

He shook his head, as though wrestling with a difficult
subject. Then he stepped aside and pointed to the edge
of the porch. His body had been hiding something there.
An open shoe box.

"I wasn't going to tell you about this, I was just going
to throw it away, but I figured you'd better see it."

She moved over closer and glanced inside, but the
smell was overpowering. A large dead fish lay in the box.
Then she noticed her name written in black letters on the
side. She looked away in disgust, and went into the
house. Kevin followed.

"Should I tell the police?"

"They won't do anything. They'll say it's some prank,

which it probably is. I thought these things would stop now that the primary was over."

"You mean it's happened before?" His young, guileless face showed his bewilderment.

"Promise not to repeat this to anyone," she said, going to her briefcase and pulling out a manila envelope. Inside were articles about people who had been found dead in connection with toxic waste investigation. And there were many. Forty people who were associated with disposal companies or chemical waste had been killed in the past few years. Across the articles were handwritten warnings like "You're next," or "Lay off," or "That's what happens to troublemakers." Kevin glanced through them and then stared at her.

"Why haven't you told anyone about this?"

"Some of my campaign people know. We decided to ignore it. I don't want Mel or the children to know, because they'd pressure me to quit, and I won't do that." Her eyes held his in a steady gaze. "I won't, Kevin. Other candidates get things like this; it happens all the time."

"The FBI should be informed, or even the local police."

"Certainly not them!" she insisted. "I've never trusted them after that incident with my soil analysis. Any complaint I make to the police becomes part of Victor Godfrey's campaign. I can't let him paint me as a hysterical female."

"Well, if it's only a few articles, I can understand, but this dead fish . . . Isn't that some Mafia symbol of a threat to your life?"

She felt suddenly cold. "I don't know. I'm not exactly an expert on the subject. It's probably just a prank, like the others."

"What were they?"

"Two of my tires were slashed when I was speaking at a luncheon one day. And the neighbor's dog was poisoned. Since he was in our yard, it's possible that whoever killed him thought he belonged to us. It's also possible that the dog ate insect poison." She shook her head. "I don't know. Maybe this dead fish is meant to be more serious. I just can't let them frighten me off. That would mean Victor Godfrey in Congress, and our environment would go straight to hell."

Kevin's brow was creased as he looked at her, trying not to show how upset he was. "I feel so helpless, and furious that someone would try to hurt you. It reminds me of when I found out I was sick and might die. There were times I was terrified to fall asleep, afraid I might not wake up again. Other times I was sorry when I woke up. There are some truths in life nobody should have to face, especially a kid, but we do anyhow. Like you getting threats." He blushed. "You know, I love your family as if we were related."

She took his hand and squeezed it. "We feel the same about you, too."

"Here I thought I was so mature. My mom says 'going on forty,' but this just throws me. Those bastards! I'd like to kill them. But then I'd be just like them, wouldn't I?"

"Look on the bright side. Here we are, the two of us, friends since you were a small boy. I've been there through your rough times, and now you're here for mine." She paused a moment, wondering whether or not she should say this. "I only hope it *is* some prankster doing these things, and not someone worse."

"That settles it, Hillary, we're calling the FBI."

"You promised, Kevin. I'm holding you to it."

"Then I'm going to stick close to you, Hillary. And that's a promise too."

She checked the time. Thirty minutes left to rest. "Come on into the den," she said, beckoning to him, as she stretched out on the sofa. She took a deep breath and exhaled, trying to relax, remembering the techniques she'd been taught by a stress-reduction expert. They seemed to help.

The phone rang. Hillary groaned, and Kevin answered it.

"Yes, she's here, Mrs. Levine, but she's resting."

Hillary motioned for him to give her the phone. "Bobbie? I was going to call you to thank you. The fund-raiser was a fabulous success. The contributions were substantial. It was wonderful of you."

"I have to see you, Hillary. Can I come over now?"

Maybe she wants to apologize for what she said to Mel, Hillary thought. She glanced at her watch. "I have to stop by the campaign office and then be at Brownfield's

Corners by four. My visit was announced in the local paper."

"I'll be right over." And she hung up.

Hillary gave a short laugh. "She's still the same as ever, won't take no for an answer." But there was an urgency in Bobbie's voice that alerted her. She sat up on the sofa, wishing she had another hour to rest. "I'd better get dressed," she said. But instead she lay back down and closed her eyes.

Kevin went upstairs to get her clothes, but she couldn't relax. The tone in Bobbie's voice kept gnawing at her. *Is she coming out in support of Victor?*

There was no use trying to sleep. When Kevin came back, she asked him about his parents.

"They're great," he told her with a grin. He always smiled when he talked about his family. "You know I'm adopted, don't you?"

She pretended she didn't know. "That must have been quite a surprise."

"It really was. Every kid thinks about being adopted, especially when his sister is Vietnamese, but I was amazed when I found out. Even though I'd wondered when I grew to be six-foot-two and blond and my parents were five-foot-four-inch Munchkins." Hillary laughed. "After they told me, I thought a lot about my natural parents. It was weird trying to imagine them. Then I got angry with everybody. At my real parents for giving me up, at my mom and dad for not telling me, even at the Lord for giving me another cross to bear. I gave everybody a hard time. It's no fun thinking your parents don't want you. My mom told me some story about my real mother being a high school kid in love with a soldier who was killed in Vietnam. Too easy. I didn't buy it."

Hillary's heart raced faster and faster as Kevin talked; she tried to keep her expression from giving away what she knew, and just listened.

"It took months, but I finally came to terms with it. Now I can even joke about it. I've got a better story about my natural parents than my mom's," Kevin said. "Want to hear?"

She nodded, almost holding her breath.

"My real mother was Princess Potch-in-Tuchas, which means 'a spank on the behind' in Yiddish—I had a Jewish girlfriend last year. She was in love with a frog who became a prince when she kissed him, but they couldn't kiss all the time. So one day he was captured and used for frog's legs. As his legs were being sautéed, they turned into the legs of a real prince in purple satin leggings and jewel-studded boots. The king who was served this delicacy said the chef didn't have a leg to stand on."

Hillary was laughing.

"She had to give me up for adoption, because with me the enchantment worked in reverse. Whenever she kissed me, I turned from a prince into a frog."

"You should be a writer."

"Naw, I'd rather make up stories for my kids someday, or read to them the way your friend Pam did for me. Pam's stories changed my life. I used to pretend I was brave, but I was one scared, sick little boy. And she'd come in, smelling of fresh snow or expensive perfume, and throw her fur across my lap for me to pet while she read wonderful stories to me. We'd talk about baseball and the building business. Sometimes she'd ask my advice, and then tell me about what happened afterwards. Boy, did I feel important, especially when she said I had good instincts. I may have had leukemia, but she gave me some happy times.

"I've thought about her often. I'm still planning to ask her for a job when I graduate from college. I've been reading about that project of hers, Weymouth City. It's going to change the entire face of the East Side; it's bigger than Trump's Television City. She's amazing."

Pam would be so thrilled to hear him talk about her like this, Hillary thought.

"I never could figure out what happened between Pam and my parents. We were all real friendly when I was sick, and then she just disappeared. My folks were hurt, you know. They said she was a snob, thought she was too good for them, so she dropped them. They'd get this nutty look on their faces whenever her name came up. My sister wants to be just like Pam when she grows up, tall and blond. But since she's a four-foot-eleven Vietnamese, I don't think she's got a chance, do you? Come to think of it, I'm the one who grew up more like Pam."

She couldn't tell him the truth, but her laughter was a

small consolation. She got up off the sofa and said, "Come here, you," then she gave him a big hug, took his cheek between two knuckles, and pinched.

"Ow," he said, grinning at her.

"See how lucky you are not to have a Jewish mother? We think pinching our children's cheeks is good for them. Jewish grandmothers are worse, they pinch tushies."

"I know," he told her. "I saw *Where's Poppa?*"

She had just finished putting her clothes back on in the powder room when the doorbell rang. Kevin said he was leaving and let Bobbie in. Just then, Mel's car pulled into the driveway. *Why is Mel home this early?* she wondered.

From the way Bobbie had sounded on the phone, Hillary had suspected something was wrong, but when Bobbie wouldn't even look at her, apprehension began to grip her.

"What's up?" Hillary asked, studying her friend. Bobbie had aged well, and plastic surgery had helped. Her black hair was in a short choppy style, slicked back over the ears with lots of hair on top—refined punk—her suit was couture, her earrings and bracelets architectural silver. Today her perfectly manicured hands, with their awfully long nails, were shaking.

"Why don't we wait for Mel?" she suggested, making her way into the living room and sitting on the edge of the sofa. It wasn't like her; Bobbie had always been a family room person. Hillary sat on the sofa opposite her.

Mel came in the back door and through the kitchen, taking off his coat. A look passed between him and Bobbie that made Hillary's apprehension turn to dread.

"Will someone tell me what's going on? What are you doing home so early?"

Mel kissed her and tried to decide where to sit. She waited for him to alight like a nervous bird. He pulled up one of the game table chairs so he was sitting between them, facing the fireplace. Why hadn't he sat next to her?

His hands were shaking too.

"Is this bad news?" she asked, feeling panicky. This couldn't be about Victor Godfrey.

"Everybody's fine," Mel assured her. He smiled, a frozen smile. "In fact, I have some tremendous news. We settled the case."

"What?" Hillary almost shouted. "How much?"

"He's not going after me at all. In fact, he's only getting what his own insurance company will cover."

"I don't understand."

"I had a witness, Hillary."

Hillary looked at him for a moment, and then at Bobbie. And then she knew. "That's what you and Mel were arguing about at the fund-raiser last night, wasn't it? You were the witness. You saw the accident."

Bobbie nodded, glancing away.

"Why in God's name didn't you say so before? Why did you let us sweat this out for months without coming forward?"

"Hil." Mel left his chair and came to sit next to her, taking her hand; his were cold. She wanted to pull away, but didn't. "Bobbie was not only a witness, she was with me in the car at the time of the accident. I left the scene to drive her home because she didn't want anyone to know we were together."

"Why?"

"Let me tell her, Mel," Bobbie said. "I didn't want Frank to know, because he was threatening to divorce me. He found out about my affair with Addison Blake."

"You were having an affair with Mel's law partner?" A more unlikely pair she couldn't imagine.

"Addison was my second choice, because I couldn't get the man I wanted."

"You wanted Mel, didn't you?" She'd known it all along, only she'd never let herself believe it. "And did you finally succeed? The night of the accident? Is that why you felt so guilty that you didn't want anyone to know you were in the car together, because you just fucked my husband?"

"Hillary, believe me, nothing happened. But Frank wouldn't have believed that, not after Addison. And with his best friend, too."

"You're some piece of work, Bobbie. Still the spoiled brat your mother raised. The only good thing I can say about you is at least you aren't supporting my opponent. So what were you doing together that night?"

"We ran into one another on the train."

"And you came on to Mel, for the hundredth time, only this time he felt sorry for himself because I was involved in my work, and took you up on it—is that what happened?"

"Something like that. It was all my fault. I tried everything, even bought him a double scotch, until he agreed to go to a motel with me. But when we got there he wouldn't make love to me."

"How far did you get before you turned her down?" she asked Mel.

He exhaled, and looked at the ceiling. "I kissed her."

"No grabbing tits, or ass, or anything like that? No passionate rubbing? Come on, if we're being honest here, let's hear it." The thought of them together made her furious. They had her at such a disadvantage; she hadn't even freshened her makeup. "Why did you even go?"

He looked so forlorn she almost felt sorry for him. "I couldn't say no. I thought I wanted to. Hell, I *did* want to. But not enough to really do it. It was 1972 all over again. Once I got there, it wasn't worth the risk. I'm long past the point of screwing around. But every now and then a guy needs to prove something to himself. I love you. I kept thinking about how I'd feel if this were you with another guy." He shrugged. "I realized I was making an ass of myself, I just missed you. I never appreciated everything you'd done for me until you stopped doing it. I was embarrassed to tell you. After all, your work is really important. And then that night when I found out you'd almost been killed and I'd been with Bobbie, I hated myself so much."

Things were beginning to make sense. No wonder their sex life had suffered and he'd pulled away from her for the last six months. He'd been feeling guilty. God, if only he'd told her. All that time wasted, all those terrible nights of trying to make love and failing. That was what hurt the most—not that he'd done it, but that he'd punished them both in the process. "Let's get back to the accident." She turned to Bobbie. "Were you ever going to come forward? And why now?"

"I know you won't believe this, but I waited until after the primary so this wouldn't hurt you politically."

"Oh, thanks. What do you think it will do for my election?"

"I hope to God that it won't hurt your chances. The accident is on public record, and it hasn't hurt you so far.

And nothing happened. People will believe that. Only my husband doesn't. Hillary, when Frank heard that Mel and I were together that night, he filed for divorce, just like I was afraid he would. I guess it was the last straw."

"If you care about your marriage, why are you still screwing around?"

Bobbie started to cry. "I don't know. It's about time I figured it out, isn't it? God, I don't want a divorce."

Hillary turned to Mel. "So you're Mister Gallant. You hit this man who runs a red light and Bobbie yells, 'No one can know I'm here,' and so you jeopardize your reputation and our financial security and take her home. And you expect me to believe nothing was going on?"

His stricken look told her more than his words. "It's the truth, Hillary, I swear to God, on the lives of my children. Nothing happened."

She shouted, "Why didn't you tell me before this?"

"I was hoping someone else had seen the accident and would come forward. And I felt guilty because of what almost happened. I was afraid I'd lose you."

Tears filled her eyes. "It would take more than a pathetic fumbling with Bobbie to make me leave you, Mel, don't you know that? You've been so distant; I thought you didn't love me anymore, and I wondered if I still loved you."

"You know I love you, how proud I am of you."

"Yes, I know." She turned to Bobbie again. "So what happens now? Are you going to pull in your claws and stop envying me—even start helping? You never could figure out how someone whose weight went up and down and had no interest in status symbols could hold a man like Mel, could you? It's no big secret. I just value myself, that's all. I value my children as human beings, too. That's why they don't take drugs or screw up their lives." She thought, didn't say, *Like yours.* "And that's why my husband values me enough to stay faithful even in the face of such a formidable opponent. For years I watched you trying to entice him, hanging out of your dress, putting me down in your subtle way. Sometimes I felt angry or threatened, but mostly I just felt sorry for you. And that's what I feel for you now. If you don't mind, I'd like to be alone with my husband."

Bobbie got up, and without looking back, she left the house. They heard her car drive away before Mel spoke.

"Can you forgive me?"

She nodded, and then started to cry. "I can forgive you for Bobbie. What I have a harder time forgiving you for is what came afterwards."

"You mean about not making love?"

"Mel, we had such a closeness, and you ruined it with a lie. That lie came between us as much as if you'd slept with her." She was so angry she wanted to pound her fists on his chest, to bruise his body as she felt her heart had been bruised. But she also felt such a tremendous relief that it was over. Perhaps now they could go back to what they had before.

"Hillary, I love you so much," he said, looking as though his world was shattering.

In spite of her anger, his anguish touched her and she went over to him and put her hand on his shoulder. "I'm so sorry," he said, burying his head in her waist.

It was the first time in months that there had been no barrier between them. She felt filled with such a sudden desire for him that it overwhelmed her.

"You have to forgive me, too," she said.

"For what?" he asked, looking up at her in complete surprise.

"There was a man I wanted to make love to, many years ago."

"When? Who was it? You went to a motel? Don't tell me it was Frank."

It was hard, but she kept a straight face. "He was gorgeous and young, and I kissed him. He was in a Broadway show at the time. Since then, he's become a big star. You're not the only one who lusts after someone other than his mate. Jimmy Carter did, and so did I."

He threw back his head and laughed. And then his laughter turned to tears. She pulled him to her again and held him tightly. "It's okay, honey, I really do forgive you. It's over. And best of all, the accident case has been settled. I say hallelujah!"

She held him until he had calmed down. "It's such a relief to have everything over with," he said. "The accident and this Bobbie business. I was really in a tough place. I couldn't force her to tell the truth at the cost of her marriage."

"Would you have let her keep her marriage while we lost everything we owned?"

He pulled back and looked at her with a sly smile and said, "No damn way."

And now it was her turn to laugh. Mel stood up and smiled at her, and then his smile turned to desire as he gazed at her. He reached down and lifted her up into his arms and kissed her. His mouth was soft and probing, filled with passion; she felt his erection full and hard against her groin. "Oh God," she moaned, every ounce of her responding, "it's been so long."

They tore at one another's clothes, their mouths still locked together, their excitement firing them like the young lovers they had once been, but with so much more wisdom. Mel pulled her blouse out of her skirt and unhooked her bra, revealing her full breasts. He bent his head and licked and sucked and touched and kneaded them with the heat of his hands and mouth until she moaned low in her throat. She wiggled out of her skirt and reached for him, placing him between her legs, feeling that exquisite part of him entering her as she stood there. There was no holding back, and no dysfunction. They pulled off the rest of their clothing and kicked it aside, until only the familiar rhythm and breathless outpouring from their mouths and eyes, their arms and legs wrapped around each other, filled their senses. They were both crying with emotion.

"I love you so much," Hillary breathed.

"I love you more," Mel declared. "I love you forever."

"This is forever, my darling."

"I'm so sorry, Hillary."

"Shh, no more. I love you. I love you."

And though saying it wasn't enough, making love to one another fully and completely was, for it was the only way they had.

5

Hillary rose from her chair on the bimah of the synagogue and came up to the podium for her summation. The congregation of Temple Beth Am murmured and shifted in their seats as Victor Godfrey returned to his seat after his speech.

She could feel her opponent's eyes on her. The plaid sportcoat he'd worn earlier in the campaign had been replaced by a blue suit and dark red tie. Because of Hillary's rating in the polls, he'd hired one of those expensive Madison Avenue campaign advisers. Tonight he was even more unctuous than usual, and in his speech he had asked his Jewish "friends" to be aware of the phony posture of the little lady running on the opposite ticket. "This lady may look like one of us, but she's a dangerous woman. She will take away your jobs and ruin this community."

So far, his attempts to discredit her had all backfired. Every time he tried a smear tactic, she released carefully researched evidence about his shady record. And he *was* shady. There had been many local favors granted to certain people; town ordinances that his friends were allowed to overlook; associations with members of organized crime; and best of all, the two years he hadn't paid all his taxes. No one could really clean up a lifetime of under-the-table deals. And the closer they got to the election, the more desperate he became, making wild, unprovable accusations against her that only brought her sympathy. She had climbed steadily in the polls and was now favored to win. She could almost hear him grinding his teeth.

"Next Tuesday's election is upon us," she began. "It's a crucial one. As I told you before, my record speaks for itself. But Mr. Godfrey plays both sides of the fence, depending on where he is speaking. Tonight he advocates support of environmental issues, but he is endorsed by the very people who are most guilty of polluting. Their contributions to his campaign are public knowledge. As for the car accident my husband was involved in last winter, which Mr. Godfrey's so eager to exploit, it's a non-issue. My husband was exonerated of any wrongdoing. He was not drunk, the other man ran a stop sign. A witness to this accident came forward to testify. I have said many times that I trust my husband completely. But he is not running for Congress. I am. And when I'm elected I am determined to help Governor Kean and the Department of Environmental Protection continue their excellent efforts in this crucial area. New Jersey needs strong advocates in Congress to make certain that federal funds for costly cleanup and prevention programs come our way. And let me assure you, I do not want to take your jobs away from you by closing the chemical storage facility in our area. I merely want it safe! I will work as hard to protect the quality of your lives and your health as I have worked all my life to protect and nurture my three children. I thank you, and *Shabbat Shalom.*"

Only four more days, she thought, as she climbed into bed that night, replaying the debate over in her mind. It had gone well. She wished Mel had been there, but he was in Los Angeles, helping his parents move to Palm Springs, and wouldn't be back until Sunday afternoon. Sunday night she was giving a speech at the Lutheran Church in Passaic; Monday there were three events scheduled; and then Tuesday was the election. It was lonely getting into bed alone. She tried to call Mel before she turned out the light, but there was no answer at his parents' new number, so she hung up and was soon asleep.

The sound of the telephone jarred her awake at three-thirty. She thought it was Mel, and grabbed for the receiver.

"Is this Hillary Robin?"

"Yes," she replied. "Who's calling?"

"If you don't resign, you will die!" The voice was raspy and low—mechanical-sounding. "Get out now, while you still can."

"Who is this?" Hillary shouted into the phone. But the caller hung up.

Heart pounding, pulse racing, racing, fear leaping to her throat, her entire body shaking, "Damn you," she said, putting the receiver back as if it were alive. She hadn't recognized the voice, but the message was clear. *Do they know I'm here alone?* The fear shot up to a higher level. Then she realized that the children were all here in the house to be with her before the election. There was no protection if someone wanted to hurt them.

She called the neighborhood patrol and asked them to notify her security people. They had wanted to put a twenty-four-hour watch on the house, but she hadn't thought that was necessary. But she barely slept for the rest of the night.

Somehow she got through her appointments on Saturday, and by Sunday, when Mel came home, the phone call was nearly forgotten. She didn't actually decide not to mention it to him, but was there a real need to worry him?

The lights on the sixty-sixth-floor penthouse of Weymouth Towers in midtown Manhattan blazed at 7:00 P.M. on Sunday, though the rest of the building had cleared out by six on Friday. Emptied of its office staffs, junior executives, maintenance people, secretaries, presidents, vice-presidents, even chairmen of the board, who'd mostly fled to the suburbs, the massive structure still held its power, its mystique. Tonight, Pam Weymouth felt that its girders supported only her, that its electric cables were her life force. She owned this building and eleven others like it—all of them fifty or sixty stories, in prime locations, fully leased, bringing in top rentals, appreciating in value at a constant rate. Every bolt and piling, curtain wall and elevator had been placed there by her order or under her control. And the hotels—starting with the Weymouth Hotel on 57th and the Weymouth House on 82nd, to her most recent, the Grand Princess, on Central Park South, the most elegant and prestigious hotel in Manhattan —ran at ninety-seven-percent capacity. All of her buildings were precious gems added to the diadem of this city, and tonight they sparkled. Soon she would be enshrined here for posterity; for when the most ambitious project of her career was completed, a nice piece of Manhattan would be named after her. She thought back over the years of her climb to this peak. So many along the way had found the city impenetrable, but she had slipped handlike into it, a perfect fit.

The people assembled at her conference table waited for her to get on with it; without the comfort of cigarettes, they fidgeted, watching to see what she was going to do.

She sat back in her chair, her elbows on the arms, fingertips touching, eyes narrowed, legs crossed in her burgundy suit, glorying in the moment, while the drama built. What a high! No champagne or white powder could induce this sense of euphoria.

Spread out on the table before her, in its final and most glorious version, drawing everyone's gaze to its magnificence, was the architects' scale model. Six feet long, four feet wide, completed after fifty other renderings, and after hashing and slashing, fighting over questions of concept and style, street access, and tile versus marble, she and her co-workers and the city bureaucrats had first disagreed, then compromised, and finally given birth to this ultimate version of a city within a city. Its magnificent twin towers rose to the south, the dome of the covered recreation park served as a focal point for the center, and the spokes of the streets and walkways branched out from that center. It would contain twenty-eight-million square feet of residential and commercial space, a multipurpose trade center, a European couture shopping center, street-front stores, townhouses, and a small lake. Weymouth City would cost two and a half billion dollars to build, and it was all hers.

Her eyes met those of Morton Fine, the city planner and architect with whom she'd battled long and hard to hammer out this design. He was flanked at the moment by three of his staff. He winked. She winked back. They'd worked together for so many years on this project that they'd become like siblings, scrapping and arguing until their love for it ultimately brought them in tune.

Next to her, Jake shifted his large bulk in his chair, filling its entire space, hinting at impatience as he chewed his unlit cigar. This would be their greatest achievement, and his eagerness to begin matched her own. It had taken eight years to bring them to this point, and now they were like a pair of racehorses at the gate. Around them were corporate attorneys, the Commissioner of the Department of Buildings, representatives from the Mayor's office, the Chairman of the Landmarks Preservation Commission, and the Parks Commissioner.

"It looks beautiful, Morton," she acknowledged. He nodded briefly, trying not to smile. He believed this final design was his victory because she'd conceded to many of his preferences; but that was her style, to get exactly what she wanted without letting anyone know it. Morton would rather be elsewhere on a Sunday night, they all would. But this was her night, she'd earned it, and she'd wanted them all here to witness New York's official christening of Weymouth City. There were few enough occasions in life just for celebration.

"Well, Craig?" She turned to Craig Stedman, the Commissioner of the Department of Buildings, whom developers in the city called the Inquisitor. He'd lived up to his nickname by wielding bureaucratic power to examine in minute detail every inch of the designs and proposals she and Morton Fine had developed. He'd picked them apart again and again, until she and Mort had despaired of ever fulfilling his demands.

"You've got it, Pam." Stedman spoke with a slight Bostonian accent. "I'm here to issue you your final permit. It's a bit unusual to do it like this, with a private ceremony, but for such an important development for the city, we wanted to do something special. Hear, hear," he said, raising his hand in a salute.

With that, everyone at the table started shouting, applauding, and slapping each other on the back, and then, as though they were of one mind, they all stood and applauded Pam where she sat, until, eyes filling with tears, she stood and accepted their acknowledgment.

Jake rang the kitchen to notify Arnold, the company chef, that they were ready, and he came in wheeling a cart glittering with a magnum of champagne, crystal flutes, and a pound of beluga caviar with a gold-embossed card from Petrossian's. It was a wonderful celebration, with everyone talking about the excitement this project had generated, about the monument it would be to Pam's career, and about how her determination and vision had made it all happen. But they were, after all, a group of business associates, and no matter how fulfilled and excited they were by this achievement, they all wanted to get home to their private lives and families.

All except Pam. This celebration was *it* for her. No family awaited her, by her own choice. How she missed Kevin tonight, especially knowing that he spent so much time with Hillary working on her campaign—yet Pam had to stay away from him. It wasn't regret she was feeling, the life she'd chosen long ago worked for her, and she floated on the excitement of this achievement, savoring it alone. She'd learned that sharing one's feelings with a mate didn't always make them more satisfying. But having Kevin with her tonight would have made her joy complete. Since that wasn't possible, her friends were an excellent substitute. She loved them deeply and looked forward to being with them. Ironically, Trish and Hillary would also be experiencing the most important events of their lives within the next few days. Hillary's election was on Tuesday, and tonight was the founders' opening for Trish's one-woman retrospective at the Whitney. *How far we've come,* Pam thought. *Not only have we survived, we've triumphed!*

Sunday night, Hillary wanted to have an early dinner at home with the family before delivering her speech at the church. Lori and Brian offered to order in pizza, but Hillary decided to roast a brisket, and invited Kevin to join them.

"You know what else she said, Dad, when Victor called her 'a bra-burner from the sixties'?" Stephen was bringing Mel up to date on Friday night's debate. He started to laugh as he quoted Hillary: "Mom said, 'For your information, I could never burn my bra. I wear a 36D.' "

Mel, who was finishing his coffee, started to laugh and swallow at the same time. The results nearly sprayed out into his cup. "You didn't!" he said, when he'd regained himself.

Hillary nodded, laughing with him. "It wasn't one of my prouder moments, but the audience roared. More people commented on it afterwards at the Oneg Shabbat than any other statement I made that night."

Mel shook his head. "I wish I'd been there."

"So do I," she said, thinking about the phone call in the middle of the night.

Just then the phone rang, and Hillary jumped. It was Flo Goldman. "She's calling from headquarters," Kevin announced. "The latest poll puts you two more points ahead."

Her family cheered, Brian whistled on his fingers, Hillary took a bow over her coffee cup. Then she noticed it was getting late. "If everybody's finished with dinner, we'd better get going."

"I'll go out and move my car," Kevin said. "It's parked behind yours."

"Why don't you drive me?" Hillary suggested. "We could leave now, while the others clean up."

"Not the dishes," Lori, Stephen, and Brian protested with a groan. Hillary looked up in surprise, and then they laughed because they'd caught her with their joke. They had been doing dishes since they were old enough to break them.

"Go with Kevin, honey," Mel told her. "You'll have some quiet time in the car without us all yakking. We'll finish up here, and be there in plenty of time."

She kissed him on the cheek. "I'll run upstairs for my coat and my notes, Kevin, and meet you in the car; that way you can warm it up for me."

Kevin came out the front door, zipping up his jacket against the November chill. His Triumph was parked in the driveway behind Mel's Chrysler sedan, and he headed for it. Just then, a man crouching low behind the driver's side of the sedan stood up and glared at him. He was wearing a knitted cap pulled low over his forehead, the collar of his heavy vest was up around his ears so that not much of his face was visible, but Kevin could see him clearly.

"Hey!" Kevin called. "What are you doing?" Immediately, he thought about the threats Hillary had been receiving, and how he'd promised to watch out for her. "Get out of there!" he yelled.

The guy took off running down the driveway, and veered to the right down the street.

Kevin ran after him. The guy was fast, way ahead, but instead of running on down the street, he ran towards a car parked by the curb two houses away, opened the rear door, and jumped in.

Kevin reached the car just as the door slammed. He pounded on the window. "Come out of there, you lousy jerk."

"What the fuck are you doing, man?" the driver of the car swore to his friend in the backseat. His window was partially open, so Kevin could hear him.

Kevin yanked on the handle of the door, trying to open it. "I caught you hot-wiring that car, didn't I? Or were you trying to get to Mrs. Robin? Are you the ones who've been threatening her?"

"Do something, man!" the driver shouted. "He's seen us."

And Kevin realized his mistake.

The back door flew open, shoving him off balance. The driver of the car reached out and held him so he couldn't get away, though he struggled with all his might; the man was too strong. And then he was grabbed from behind around the neck, his right arm twisted up behind him. Pain shot up through his shoulder to the top of his head. He couldn't breathe, couldn't move. He tried to yell, but he felt a knee slam him in the kidney and he cried out, then he did what he was told.

"Get in the car, fuckhead." The man in the knitted cap dragged him around to the backseat and shoved him in. He hit his hip on the door of the car and cried out.

"Shut up, kid. Or you're dead." And then something hard slammed him on the back of the head and he nearly lost consciousness. The pain was so excruciating he couldn't think; blood pounded in his ears. *What is it? What the hell's going on?* The pain was so intense he was afraid he would be sick. All he could think of was to pretend that he had passed out.

"Do it already, man, we've got to get out of here."

"I told you we shouldna done it this way."

"Shut up. I'm almost ready."

"Is he still out?"

Kevin felt a boot shove him in the back. He didn't react.

"Just watch the house, willya?"

"Hurry up, Leo, before somebody else comes. What are we gonna do with the kid?"

"How the fuck do I know? You set yet?"

Suddenly he knew. A bomb! These men were going to kill Hillary. He had to warn her!

"Oh Jesus, hurry up! The front door's opening, she's comin' out. Oh shit!"

Kevin's heart raced wildly, pounding so hard it felt as though his chest would burst open. *Hillary, no!* He had to do something now! Gathering all his strength, he gave a violent kick backwards with both legs. Something connected and he heard the man behind him grunt and lose his balance. As he kicked, Kevin screamed for help as loud as he could, and threw himself over the front seat, grabbing at the lever next to the driver intending to pull it loose, praying that he could stop the device from detonating the bomb. The man in the backseat had him around the waist, pulling at him, and the man in the front was smashing him in the head and upper body.

"Hit it!" the man in the back yelled. "Stop him."

Kevin looked up and saw Hillary halfway between the house and the car. "Hillary! Stop!" he yelled, crying out her name, sobbing with terror, but then the man who was struggling with him for the lever brought his fist down hard on the detonator. There was a blinding flash and a booming sound that pounded in their ears. And Hillary disappeared.

"You stupid fuck!" the man in the back yelled. "You killed her. We gotta get out of here. Move it, man, move it!"

Kevin heard the sound of the car's ignition. He fought with every ounce of his being, while his brain cried out, *Hillary, oh God, no!* But as hard as he struggled, he was yanked back into the backseat by more powerful hands, pummeled and shoved, feeling blow after blow slam into him until he was on the floor of the car again, unable to protect himself from getting hit on the back of the head, over and over, until mercifully everything went black.

The first of two gala evenings planned to honor Trish's retrospective at the Whitney was winding down when Pam left her office and finally arrived at the museum. Tonight's event was attended by a more select, elite group than would attend the larger opening-night party on Wednesday night for invited guests, press, and museum subscribers. Pam was sorry that her meeting with city officials had kept her from being here earlier, but on Wednesday she'd be here all evening. *Who knows?* she thought. *By Wednesday we could also be celebrating Hillary's election to Congress.*

As Pam stepped out of her limousine at the curb, she saw the chauffeurs of many of her friends, people who had some of the most prominent art collections in the world. She said hello to several of the museum's trustees as they came out of the building, and heard them exclaiming over the show. Smiling with pride, she showed her pass to the guard at the door.

"Evening's over, ma'am," he said. "Only a few people left upstairs."

"I know," she said, "but I'm a close personal friend of Ms. Baldwin's. I couldn't get here sooner."

Just then, the centermost of the three elevator doors opened, revealing a cavernous interior. Its only passenger, her small size even further dwarfed by the enormous space, was Trish. She was wearing a copper suede dress, beaded with copper-colored beads in high-tech designs; her long dark hair was pulled severely back, wound at the nape of her neck, and her topaz earrings caught the light. She had just been crowned queen of her domain on the fifth floor, and every inch of her looked regal.

She came rushing toward Pam, who opened her arms to greet her, but instead of euphoria and excitement, Pam saw terror on her face. "What's wrong, Trish?"

"Thank God you're here. I've been going crazy waiting for you." She was breathing hard; the panic and fear in her eyes shot terror through Pam.

"What is it?" Pam grabbed her hand, her own heart racing.

Trish was nearly in tears, her chest heaving. "Someone tried to kill Hillary. They planted a bomb in her car."

"My God," Pam cried out. Something with raw steel edges tore at her gut. "Is she all right?" *Hillary!* a voice was screaming in her head. The two of them stared at one another, trying to keep the terrors of hell from overtaking them. "We've got to get to her," Pam said, her voice vibrating with fear.

"Don't panic, you mean?" Trish's own voice answered with a shrill pitch, her hands clutching at Pam's were icy.

"I can't help it." Then she turned abruptly away, hurried over to the attendant, threw her token to him, and grabbed her wrap. Her hands were shaking so badly she couldn't fasten her cape. "Somebody at the party heard it on the news and knew I was a friend of hers. I've been trying not to panic for the last twenty minutes until you got here. I keep thinking these terrible thoughts. Oh God," she moaned, hurrying toward the door. Pam ran after her. "Your service told me you were on your way, but I couldn't get through on your car phone—maybe I dialed wrong, all those damned numbers." She started to cry. "I tried to call Crestmont, but the phones are out at Hillary's, and the police wouldn't tell me anything. What should we do?" She was sobbing, her chest heaving.

"Come on"—Pam said, pushing the door open for her, trying not to burst into tears herself—"let's go." Anxiety gripped her like a vise, and she longed for everything to just stop, this sickening fear, this screaming terror inside. *Not Hillary,* she prayed. *Anyone but Hillary.* It was too fast, too unreal. But that was exactly the way tragedy struck, suddenly, like a bomb thrown in the middle of your life.

Trish threw open the door of Pam's limousine and stumbled, but Pam caught her. Something in Trish's expression terrified her even more. "You know something else, don't you?" An even icier terror shot through her. "What is it? My God, tell me!"

"I didn't want to tell you, but I can't keep it in," she cried out, sobbing uncontrollably. "A woman was killed in that explosion."

Pam started to cry too, trying with all her might to hold on. "Was it Hillary?" She couldn't bear this pain.

"I don't know, but I'm terrified that it was."

Pam hurried Trish into the car and shouted to her chauffeur, "Jim, take us to Crestmont, New Jersey. Now!"

6

The limo trip from Manhattan to Crestmont was an agony of suspense. An accident in the tunnel prevented them from calling ahead for news. Forty-five minutes of imagining the worst sent their raw nerves into shock. First one of them would break down, while the other tried to calm her, and then the process was reversed. The thought of Hillary being taken from them and from her family was too cruel to bear. Finally they emerged from the tunnel and called the local police on the car phone, but still they couldn't find out anything. Hillary's phone continued to be out of order. "I know every goddamned politician in this state," Pam said, "and not one of them has been any help." It gave her some sense of control to keep trying to do something, to find out something. Trish envied Pam her power, her immense base of contacts, her ability to act, even when it wasn't doing any good.

"I've only felt helpless like this once before," Trish whispered hoarsely, "with Kelly."

As they arrived at Hillary's street, they were still trying to reassure one another that she was all right, but neither of them believed it, especially when they saw her house surrounded by barricades and police. Spectators and neighbors milled around, fire trucks stood by, their red lights turning. The blackened, twisted hulks of two charred cars stood in the driveway. The bushes, shrubbery, and lawn halfway from the driveway to the house were burned, and a corner of the house was blackened. Windows were shattered.

Trish moaned when she saw the house.

"Holy Jesus," Pam said, "this is a war zone."

The police wouldn't let them through the barricades. Pam showed the officer in charge her courtesy cards from the top police officials in New York and Mayor Koch's office. "Please," she insisted, "we're close friends of the family. I know they'll let us in." Finally he got clearance and let them through.

Lori, Stephen, and Brian were in the living room, along with Hillary's campaign manager and co-workers. Pam recognized most of the people whom she'd met over the years.

Everyone rushed to greet them, talking at once. Lori burst into tears when she saw Pam and Trish. Pam held her while Stephen told them what happened.

"Mom was thrown off the porch by the blast. They took her in an ambulance, she's in critical condition; Dad's with her. They're looking for internal injuries."

"Then she's alive!" Pam exclaimed, wiping away tears of joy. "Thank God."

"Who was killed?" Trish asked, unable to trust the news. "We were told someone died."

"Mrs. Carmichael, next door. She's seventy-eight. She was going to take her new puppy for a walk, and came outside just as the bomb exploded." He was holding himself together, behaving as his parents would have wanted, but he looked terribly vulnerable, couldn't hide that sick expression that always accompanies tragedy.

"What else did they say about your mom?" Pam asked. "Can we go and be with your dad?"

"I guess so," Stephen replied. "We all wanted to go with her, but the police said we should stay here. They want to protect us, now that it's too late."

"Who did it, do they know?"

He shook his head, fighting tears. "No. But I'd like to get my hands on them." He was bewildered and furious, unable to hide his grief. He looked at them with such naked pain that Pam winced and Trish took hold of his hand. Of the three children, he had the greatest need to talk, as if he could somehow make sense of what had happened. "She's going to win the election, you know. Wipe the floor with that guy. She's ahead in all the polls." He turned away, embarrassed at his tears. "She's got to be all right."

"She will," Trish said, putting her arm around his waist. He towered over her, but clung to her like a small child.

The phone rang, and Brian answered it.

"Have they finally fixed the phone?" Trish asked.

"I guess so," Lori said. "It's the first call we've had."

"Yes. Sure, it's all right," Brian was saying to the person on the phone. "You can come on over. We'll all be here." He said good-bye and hung up. "That was Mrs. Matthews. They wanted to come and wait with us. I told them they could."

Pam felt a shudder go through her body. *Kevin's parents?* "Frances and Gil Matthews?" she asked.

Brian nodded.

"Why are they coming here?"

Trish was watching her, picking up the note of fear in her voice.

"Didn't you know?" Brian said. "Whoever tried to kill my mom kidnapped Kevin."

A roaring sound filled Pam's ears. Something leering and evil flashed in front of her eyes, then jabbed her in the heart with poison talons. She stood there stunned, unable to think. Kevin, kidnapped? It couldn't be. There was no logical reason. All the years without seeing him had been so painful, with only secondhand details from Hillary, but she'd stayed away from him as Frances had asked. And now this. She was breathing in short gasps, about to pass out.

"Pam, what is it?" Trish asked, moving over to steady her.

She wanted to scream out loud, *It's Kevin!* But she had to hide what she was feeling. She held on to Trish; never had she exerted so much control over herself. "I'm all right. Everything is such a shock. Tell me what happened with Kevin. Do they know where he is?"

"No," Lori told her. "Let me get you something." She went to pour them each a cup of coffee from a thermos pitcher on the coffee table, but her hands were shaking so badly that Brian had to take over for her. Lori came back and sat down. "Kevin was going to drive Mom to give her speech, and he went out of the house to warm up his car. Mom went after him. Then we heard the explosion." She burst into tears again. "It was so awful. The crystal goblets in the dining room shattered, and the windows too. Glass was flying everywhere. We were all screaming. We knew something terrible had happened.

The police found Kevin's scarf in the street in front of the house next door. But no body. If he had been injured by the explosion, he would have been lying there. At least we think so. The police seem to think he planted the bomb, and then ran away. That's ridiculous. But we think he saw whoever did it and tried to stop them, and they took him."

"Dear God," Pam said. "They could kill him. He's been through so much, that poor boy, and now this."

"You know him?" Trish asked.

Pam nodded. "I'll tell you later."

The phone rang again, and Pam started. Everyone was afraid of what it might be. Lori picked up the receiver. "It's Dad," she announced, and then repeated what he was saying. As he talked, her worried face slowly lost its lines of concern, softening as they watched, and then they saw a tentative smile. "Mom's not as badly injured as they feared. Her X rays were good, no internal bleeding. She hasn't regained consciousness yet, so they don't know how bad her head injury is, or if her hearing was damaged. She suffered some burns, but mostly first degree. They're waiting for the EEG results and the brain scan." Tears of relief were rolling down her cheeks.

Brian hugged her, and then took the phone. "Any other news, Dad?" He listened. "No, we haven't heard anything else from the police either. No word on Kevin. The grandparents keep calling from California, and Uncle Bob, they want to know if they should come here. I told them to wait to hear from you. Pam and Trish are here. Yes, I'll tell them." He hung up and turned to them. "Dad says he's glad you're here, and he'll call later. He's going in to see Mom now."

Two hours went by before Hillary finally regained consciousness and opened her eyes, and the first thing she saw was Mel's face. It was blurry, but she could see his smile. She was afraid to move. In a jolt, all the pain in her head slammed down on her. She moaned. "Everything hurts." She wanted Mel to make it stop. "There's a terrible buzzing in my ears," she gasped. "Turn it off, please!" Her mouth couldn't form words properly. What was wrong? "Where am I?"

Mel said something to her, but she couldn't hear him.

That terrified her. She screamed. Or she thought she did; she didn't have the strength for a real scream. Her panic was real, though, she could feel it coursing through her. All she could remember was coming out of her house, and then nothing.

Mel held her hand, stroked her forehead. She couldn't feel his touch. *I must be dying,* she thought, and reached up. Her head was bandaged. Then she started to cry. "What happened?"

"You're all right, sweetheart," he said, over and over. "It's okay. You'll be all right. There was an explosion, a bomb. But the doctors say you'll be fine. No internal bleeding. The other injuries will heal."

"What day is it, what time?" she asked. It was a horrible feeling, not to know.

"It's ten-twenty Sunday night. You've been here a few hours."

"I've got three speeches scheduled for tomorrow," she said, trying to get up. Pain shot from her shoulder up to her head, and she cried out.

Mel held her back. "Honey, don't move. You've sprained your shoulder and you have a concussion. Not to mention the trauma of the explosion."

"What kind of explosion?" she said, not wanting to know.

"It was a bomb, in our car."

"Oh God, they said they would kill me. I want to go home." She started to cry again.

"Who said it, honey? Do you know?"

"Some awful voice on the phone, when you were in California. Can we go home?"

"Soon, baby. You're already doing better than they expected. Why didn't you tell me?"

She felt his anger; she could take anything but that. "I should have," she admitted.

Just then the phone next to her bed rang and she reached for it, but Mel grabbed it. "Damn, they're not supposed to put through any calls. Yes, who is it?" He listened for a minute, without saying a word.

Hillary strained to see him. Everything was still blurry and it hurt to strain so, but something about this call made her afraid. *It's them,* she thought. Her pulse began to race. She just knew it.

"You bastard," Mel said. "Who is this? If you hurt that boy, I'll kill you, I swear I will." But they had hung up, so he replaced the receiver on the cradle.

"What did they want?" she said, her voice rising, every muscle tense, tight. "I know what it is, they want to make sure I'm dead, is that it?" Her panic was close to hysteria.

Again he soothed her. "No, honey, no. They gave us an ultimatum. The police told me this might happen. I didn't want to tell you this, but the people who planted the bomb took Kevin with them. They're holding him somewhere. They just said if you don't resign from the congressional race they'll kill him."

This time, when the phone rang at Hillary's house, Brian answered it. He turned to Pam and Trish. "It's for you. My Dad again."

"I'll go use the kitchen phone," Pam said.

Trish waited until Pam was on the line. "How are you holding up?" she asked Mel.

"I'm okay, but something else has happened. Don't repeat this out loud to anyone, but Hillary has regained consciousness."

Trish started to shout with delight, but then was aware of the roomful of people who were watching her and she kept her expression blank.

In the kitchen, Pam said, "Why can't we tell them, Mel? The kids are terribly worried."

"Take them aside and tell them later. I've got a good reason." He told Pam and Trish about the ultimatum. "If everyone thinks Hillary is still unconscious, she can't resign from the congressional race. We have to have time to formulate a plan."

"You don't mean she'd stay in the race and risk Kevin's life?" Pam's voice rose to a high pitch. "You can't let her do that!"

Mel's voice was tight, desperate. "Of course not, but we can't give them what they want unless we're sure we'll get him back. We have to negotiate. That takes time, and they've given us a deadline."

"What is it?" Trish asked.

"She has to resign by tomorrow evening, in time to

announce it on the five o'clock news and give the papers time to print it in Tuesday morning's edition."

"Do the police know who's doing it?" Pam asked.

"The police think there might be a contract out on her because of the toxic waste issue. Somebody doesn't want her in Congress. In any case, we can't take any chances—not while they've got Kevin. I've never felt so helpless in my life." They could hear his anguish. "Apparently she's been getting threats all along. I didn't know how bad it was. She thought it was only scare tactics, that they wouldn't really do anything. I'll never forgive myself for not stopping her; I knew there was a problem. I should have made her withdraw."

"You couldn't do that, Mel," Trish said. "It's not your fault. If Hillary knew about the danger, she wasn't afraid, or if she was, she didn't let it stop her."

"But now she's put Kevin's life in danger," Pam said. She was losing control. "What are we going to do about finding him?"

"We have to leave it to the police," he said. "But I don't have much faith in these local guys, they're inept. If only we knew someone who had connections or inside information."

And then, suddenly, the old memories came flooding back to Pam. "I know someone whose former associates run the toxic waste disposal operation in New Jersey," she said.

"You mean Charles, don't you?" Mel said.

Her heart was pounding and her hands were sweating; there was a cold finger of dread snaking through her guts. In her most desperate nightmares, she'd always feared it would come to this. She had always told herself that there was nothing in the world important enough to make her deal with him again, but this was the one thing she'd never thought about. "If anyone knows who's behind all this, it's Charles." Just the sound of his name made her recoil. "He has the clout to do something about it."

"Absolutely not!" Mel insisted. "You can't have anything to do with him. Not after what you went through to get rid of him. That man hates you more than any of us can understand, and he's evil, Pam. Don't even consider it."

"But it's Kevin's life we're talking about, Mel." That cold finger of dread had turned into a hand squeezing her heart, chilling her whole body. "And Hillary's future, too. I'll have to see him." But the thought of being in Charles's presence again, asking a favor of him, made Pam wish the earth would open up and swallow her.

"He doesn't know about Kevin," Mel said. "If it comes out, he'll kill you, Pam."

Pam knew that was true. If Charles ever found out what she had done—stealing his son from him—he would kill her.

"What doesn't Charles know about Kevin?" Trish asked. "What are you two talking about? Pam hasn't seen Charles in years, has she?"

"Trish," Pam nearly shouted, "don't say another word." She could feel her temper and her fear rising out of control. "Please put down the phone in the living room, where everyone is listening to you, and come in here." She wanted to run in there and grab Trish, hold a hand over her mouth until she could get her in here, but she forced herself to wait until Trish walked through the kitchen door. Now they were alone. "You've got to swear never to repeat this, not to anyone, especially not to Kevin's family. Do you agree?"

Trish nodded.

Pam took a deep breath and let it out slowly, then she said, "Kevin is my son. Mine and Charles's."

For a moment, what Pam was saying didn't sink in. "But your baby died."

"No. I gave him up for adoption and told everyone he had died."

Trish stared at her as the truth began to dawn, thinking back over the years. All that mourning for a dead child, all that sympathy Pam had gotten for a child who wasn't dead, while hers really was. For an insane moment she was enraged with Pam for playing that role, for usurping what for her was nearly her entire being. And then she thought about what it must have been like for Pam to have to give up her child, never to be with him again. It was like dying. Trish shook her head to rid herself of these thoughts. There were more crucial issues at hand. "That's why you can't let Charles know."

Pam nodded.

"Then Mel's right," Trish insisted. "You can't see him. You'll be pleading with him to save his own son's life, and if he backs you into a corner, you might tell him."

"I won't," Pam vowed. "Never."

"I don't like it," Trish said. But she could see there was no other way. She reached for the receiver to talk to Mel. "I think I may be able to help too," she told Mel. "But you both have to swear not to breach my confidence, either." They both agreed. "Connor is an ex-CIA operative. I'd trust him with my life. In fact, he saved my life once. If I tell him what we're up against, he may be able to work on this from another angle."

Mel agreed. "It's a good idea."

"We'll get back to you as soon as we know anything more," Trish told him. "And, Mel, your kids are wonderful. They're being a real comfort. Give Hillary kisses for us. Tell her to get herself in gear, there's an election to win on Tuesday."

She heard the catch in Mel's voice as he thanked her, and then she hung up.

In all the years she'd known Pam, she'd never seen her so shaken, so frightened.

"It's been nearly eighteen years since I had any contact with Charles. A few years ago I beat him out of a piece of property that I needed. He still doesn't know about that. But I've always known Charles was out there, waiting to strike like a rabid dog. He controls my father's business. My dad is just a figurehead there now. I know William would like to get out, but he can't; Charles keeps him around just to humiliate him. Charles has tried to sabotage my jobs several times over the years, but Jake and I have always stopped him. I've heard that he's been salivating to get his filthy fingers into Weymouth City, but we've built a fortress of our organization. We have our own people who protect us, maybe not as high up as Charles, but we've kept him out. Oh God, he terrifies me."

"Is he still as powerful in the business?"

"Like a boa constrictor. When I first met him, he told me his family was involved in waste disposal in New Jersey. If anyone can find out who is behind this contract on Hillary, and negotiate for Kevin, it's Charles."

"Where is Charles?"

"If he's in town, he's probably at home. He moved to Staten Island."

"I could have guessed that's where he'd live."

"I'd better go there right now."

"Do you want me to go with you?"

"This is something I have to do alone."

Trish nodded. "I'll be here if you need me. I'll call Connor and tell him what happened. I want him to get started immediately."

Pam watched while she dialed, and said, "This is going to be a long night."

7

The house was Georgian, separated from the street by a wide expanse of lawn. Its next neighbor was two hundred feet away. A brick archway over the door and Gothic leaded windows gave it the appearance of a fortress. A sheaf of dried cornstalks tied with an orange ribbon, piled in one corner, and a basket of gourds in the other adorned the large front porch. Pam assumed they were decorations left over from Halloween, or an early anticipation of Thanksgiving. Decorating your entryway seemed like such a Protestant thing to do, not Italian-Catholic. Charles and Irma must have reached a new social plateau. Standing in front of the house, with all its normalcy, gave her a sense of security she knew was false, but she was grateful for it. She felt like Orpheus descending to hell. Eurydice had been worth it, and so was Kevin.

She glanced at Jim in the limousine. All through the long drive from New Jersey, his presence had given her some comfort. A video camera aimed its lens at her as she rang the bell.

After a long time the door opened, and Guido stood there, an older version of himself, even more huge, if that was possible, and still menacing. The sight of him made her stomach turn. He didn't say anything, but just stared.

"Is Charles in? I must see him."

Without waiting, she stepped forward, past Guido's bulk, wondering if he would grab her and throw her to the pack of snarling dogs that were sure to be lurking somewhere. But he closed the door behind her. She looked up, and there was Charles. He was coming out of what appeared to be a library off the entry, wearing an open-collared dress shirt. His belt was unbuckled, and he looked as if he'd been dozing. In the background she had an impression of 1940s furniture, dark Persian carpets, a brick-colored tile floor, mahogany everywhere, but Charles's presence riveted her. He'd lost much of his hair; what was left of it was combed back behind his ears. *He must be in his mid-sixties,* she realized, praying he'd lost some of his potency, but doubting it. She tried to hide her surprise; she'd expected him to be the same. He was heavier and jowlier, but still tanned, and he still had the piercing dark eyes. Without his handsome looks to distract her, his raw power was obvious.

"So," he said, without preliminaries, "what do you want?"

"This is private." She nodded to Guido.

"Are you kidding?" he said, indicating that, as usual, he never did anything without Guido.

Just then, Irma appeared at the top of the stairs, in a chenille robe. Her red hair, streaked with gray, was down around her shoulders, as though she'd unwound it from an up-do. She too was heavier. "Who's here, Charles?" she called. "Do you need Angie to make some coffee?"

"No coffee," Charles answered, never taking his eyes from Pam. That same hatred burned there, and the same passion. "This won't take long."

In defiance, Pam called up to her, "Hello, Irma. We've never been introduced, but I'm sure you know who I am. Pam Weymouth. I used to be one of your husband's mistresses."

Their eyes met, and for a moment Pam was embarrassed. In trying to show up Charles, she had hurt this woman who had never done anything to her.

Irma wrapped the robe more tightly around her ample waist, stared at her, and then said, "Yes, I know who you are." And to her credit, she turned, left the landing, and went back into her room, her dignity intact.

Pam looked at Charles and thought she saw the hint of a smile, as though he was remembering certain things about her. She hoped she appeared formidable. "Nice lady," Pam said, following Charles into the library, a book-lined, paneled room. A fire burned in the arched stone fireplace, the *Times* lay open on the floor. Charles sank down into the deep cordovan leather chair he'd been sitting in before. He flicked off the television. Guido went back to the card table to continue his game of solitaire. *The Vipers at Home,* she thought, fascinated to see how they lived, how they spent their evenings after the things they did all day. He looked up at her from deepset eyes ringed by puffy skin.

"So?"

"You're not surprised to see me?"

"I'm never surprised; that is a luxury of youth and inexperience. You got your final approval from the city tonight, I hear."

"And you must still have your stranglehold around the throats of all the small bureaucrats at City Hall."

He shrugged. "I'm interested in you. We have a score to settle over that property on Twenty-sixth. I figure tonight it's going to happen."

"How did you find out about that?" Some of her confidence was slipping. She'd forgotten exactly how cagey he was, how many tentacles he had.

"Eventually everything comes to me. You know that."

The antagonism he felt for her burned in his eyes, though his face was impassive. She found that more terrifying than his rage. "Does William know?"

"Not from me."

"What were you saving it for, some special coup de grace when you can rub his nose in it for full effectiveness?"

"You're a prize, you know?"

"I didn't come here to talk about that." She would not allow him to unnerve her. "I'm sure you're aware that Hillary Robin is running for Congress in the fifteenth district."

A nod.

"And you must be aware of her platform. She's been quite vocal and active in her opposition to environmental pollution. The polls show her ahead of her opponent, Victor Godfrey, but there are powerful people who don't want her elected, some of whom I'm sure you know."

"She's small fry," he said. "A flea on the hide of a dinosaur. A nothing. One congresswoman from New Jersey will have no power at all."

"Then why did somebody try to kill her tonight by planting a bomb under her car?"

Now she had his attention. His dark eyes glittered with reflected firelight. "I repeat: What do you want from me?"

"Can you find out who's behind it and get the contract nullified?"

He shrugged. "Maybe."

"She's in critical condition in the hospital, Charles. Not that the life of someone as kind and as special as Hillary would mean anything to you, but it means a lot to me. I've come here to bargain."

He allowed himself the briefest of smiles as he said to Guido, "Sooner or later, they all come around. All it takes is patience."

Guido raised his eyebrows, pursed his lower lip, puckered his chin, and gave a nod to show his agreement and superior knowledge of human behavior. If it weren't so chilling, Pam would have laughed.

"You've done real well for yourself, haven't you?" Charles said. "I'm impressed. Fucked your way right to the top, huh? But the trouble with you, baby, is you're too visible. You never learned the value of a low profile. Everybody knows it whenever you spread your legs. You and those other ego-jerk developers like Trump and Zeckendorf."

"Can the vulgarity, Meroni, or should I say, Your Assholiness. Those of us with nothing to hide are free to come out from under our rock." She paused to stare back at him. "You see, I can play any game you want."

Elbows on the arms of his chair, fingertips together, the professor was about to give his lecture. "I've done well for myself, too. I'm highly situated now, if you get what I mean. Just ask your old man. I know what's going on, and what isn't."

"Do you know who's behind this bombing, the contract?"

"I can find out."

"There's something else." She felt her bravado start to slip, an icy film coated the palms of her hands, beads of sweat broke out on her upper lip. She forced herself to keep every drop of emotion out of her voice, any extra concern and he'd notice. "A young man, someone who was working in Hillary's campaign, was kidnapped by the same people who planted the bomb."

"Has anyone been contacted?"

"Yes. Mel, Hillary's husband, received an ultimatum. If she'll resign, they'll let the boy go."

"You can write him off."

Pam gripped the sides of her chair, felt every muscle in her body stiffen and terror shoot through her. "Why?"

"He may have been a witness, and if he was, he's already dead."

"Then she won't resign and they will have to contend with her in Congress."

He studied her, absorbing this new idea. "I'll find out."

"When? Can you do it now? Tell them I'll pay anything. Hillary will resign and I'll send the boy out of the country. He'll never identify anybody, I swear to God, he won't." *Damn,* she thought, *I'm caring too much.*

His eyes narrowed, instantly picking up her tone. "What's he to you?"

"A good kid, that's all." She pretended nonchalance.

"Well, his life and Hillary's depend on what you do for me, baby." His enjoyment at having her where he wanted was so intense he couldn't hide it. If he was that obvious, maybe he didn't have as much control as he wanted her to believe.

"What do you want, Charles?" She stood up, feeling the walls of this tiny, overstuffed room closing in on her. It was so goddamned warm in here. A great time to have her first hot flash.

"I want the building contracts on everything Weymouth Development isn't handling in Weymouth City. I know you're subbing out the rec center and half the other buildings. You've never let us bid on any of your projects in the past. It's made a lot of people angry, people I want to keep happy. Now it's your turn to make it up. And besides, you owe me, baby."

She felt a sour taste rise up to her throat. The thought of doing business with him, of having to deal with him for years to come, was almost too much to bear. Life without him all these years had been so sweet; now it was turning to bile. She'd made some difficult deals in her career, compromises she'd hated making, fought against with every ounce of her being. But she couldn't utter a whimper of protest against this. She had to be grateful to hand her life over to him to do with as he chose. But if she gave in too easily, he'd ask for more.

"Are you crazy?"

"Take it or leave it."

"We haven't decided yet how much Weymouth Development is keeping in-house."

"If you want this job completed in five years, you'll be working at capacity if you only keep a third. Two-thirds will be just fine for me."

"Gray-Con can't handle that much. I won't let you be a subcontractor on my project. And I won't allow you to delay, to hold us up for ransom." Her voice was rising, showing her panic. She forced herself to speak normally. "Given that you're on the project, what guarantee do I have that you won't do damage, pull your same damned delaying, padding, sabotaging tricks, and drive us out of business?"

"You don't." This time his smile was broad, too broad.

She saw it clearly. Signing any deal with him was signing a death warrant for her career. She'd end up just like her father. Her mind sped through the details of ownership of her other properties, trying to see if they too would fall like a house of cards if Weymouth City went under. She was starting to hyperventilate, and again forced herself to stay calm.

"I can't make a promise like that on my own. I have partners. They have a say."

"No bullshit, lady!" he shouted, climbing out of his chair and grabbing the lapel of her suit. "You don't come in my house, insult my wife, and ask me for favors and then give me crap, you hear?"

She kept her eyes steady as she pried his hand away. "I'll have the agreement for you as soon as I can have it drawn. Will you start contacting your *friends* immediately?"

"Oh, I'll contact them all right. But nothing, I repeat, nothing will be done on your behalf until that agreement is in my hands."

"I'll get back to you in a few hours."

"No, you'll meet me in my office tomorrow. I'm not losing a night's sleep over this; that can be your pleasure."

"What time?" She was clenching her teeth so hard her jaw was aching.

"I've got a full morning, I can't see you until one

o'clock. My office! Gray-Con. Your father will be so pleased to see you bringing us business."

She couldn't stand the sight of him one minute more, and almost forgot to breathe until she was across the large entry hall and out the front door. But just as she reached her car, he called out to her, "This is going to be a sweet victory for me, Pam. Like I once taught you, nobody fucks with me and gets away with it."

Her entire body was trembling when she got into the car. But she held herself in control until they got to the end of Staten Island and were heading back into the city, then she let go and sobbed, crying with frustration and hatred for Charles, and anguish over Kevin.

By the time she had made her calls to Jake, her attorneys, her assistant, and her accountants and roused them out of bed, she was in control again. She explained the emergency and told them to meet her at the office in forty-five minutes. Trying not to think about Hillary in the hospital, or Kevin out there somewhere, maybe hurt, or perhaps already dead, she said the same thing to them she'd said to Trish. "It's going to be a long night."

It was after ten when Trish heard Connor's voice at the door. She went out on the porch to greet him. Nothing had felt as good all night as his arms around her; she clung to him.

"Thank God you're here. We really need you, though I know you don't want to get involved in these things anymore."

"You know I'd do anything to help you or the people you love." He pulled away and studied her, to make sure that she understood.

"What happened after I left the museum?" she asked.

"Everyone who was still there understood why you had to go. I'm so proud of your success tonight, baby. Seeing a lifetime of your work displayed like that was quite an experience."

She hugged him closer. "I can't fully enjoy it until Hillary and Kevin are both safe."

"I know," he whispered.

"I wouldn't ask you to help if there were any other way. We have to do everything possible." She told him about Hillary having to resign, and who Kevin was. "Now

Pam has gone to make a deal with Charles, to see if he can undo all this damage. Imagine what she's going through. The man is disgusting and evil and dangerous."

"I'll do everything I can, baby, but you know it's not my area of expertise."

"I thought some of your old associates might know something. Did you learn anything new?"

"Not yet. Honey, it's going to take time."

"We don't have time, Connor."

"We have to find a way to get information from the FBI. But I'm way out of touch; it's been years since I was inside. Everyone I knew is gone, or out on assignment. I have no status with the Agency, no official access to information, and that's nearly impossible to get, since I can't trade for favors; I don't have anything they need."

"Still, with your experience I know you can help. The local police don't seem to be doing anything. They haven't even searched the neighborhood or talked to the neighbors."

"Why not?"

"I don't know. They come and go like cloak-and-dagger types, whispering, talking to one another. But nothing's getting done and Kevin Matthews is out there somewhere."

"Pam must be frantic with worry."

"And his parents. You should see their faces, they're in the house."

She brought him inside. Over the years since they'd been together, he had gotten very close to Hillary and her family. Now he embraced all three of the children and gave them words of encouragement. Then she introduced him to everyone else.

"Is there somewhere we can talk?" he asked, after a while.

The downstairs was filled with people, so they went up to the master bedroom. Connor sat on the chaise in the corner, Trish on the bed. "If you had access to FBI or police information, could you help?" she asked.

"That would make a difference. But I'd need to get into a police computer for a list of all the places in northeastern New Jersey where explosives are sold. From there we might be able to find out who purchased the materials for the bomb. Every homemade incendiary device has something that makes it unique, more easily traceable."

"Won't the police give us that information if we want it?"

"No. They want to keep outsiders from interfering."

"I don't think they have that kind of information."

"But it's routine," Connor explained.

"I see," she said, aware that even in these dire circumstances, his presence made her confident. His way of getting directly to the crux of the problem reassured her, and his knowledge was extensive. "What else would you need?"

"A reading on the criminals in this area known for this kind of crime, the names of demolition experts. This bomb took some knowledge to construct. But getting information is another matter. Current operatives have contacts and informants they use to narrow the field. I don't have that. Besides, CIA people work abroad, not on U.S. soil."

It was finally getting through to her how complicated it was. "How could we get the FBI to cooperate with you?"

"I've been racking my brain."

An idea was beginning to form. "What if someone high up—say, the chairman of the Senate Committee on National Security—told them to," Trish asked.

"That would do it," Connor agreed. "Why?"

Now she was excited. "Because Calvin Bentworth, the head of that committee, is a major collector of contemporary art. He owns several major pieces of my work and is a friend of mine. I introduced you to him tonight at the opening; he's in New York."

"I remember, the tall man with the society wife."

"That's him. My point is, he's been trying to buy my contemporary history series. Told me he'd be in town until tomorrow for a fund-raiser."

Connor was leaning forward, staring at her intently. "He's not going to do you a favor for free."

"No successful politician would."

"Call him."

She tried the Waldorf Towers, where the fund-raiser was being held. When Senator Bentworth heard who it was, he took the call. "Trish Baldwin, calling me? This is a turn of events, isn't it? Your show tonight was phenomenal, by the way. But the best piece of all was the historical mural. What is it, about seventy feet long? Sixties to the eighties!"

"Cal, how badly do you want it?"

"You know how bad, Trish. But I can't beat the Saacchis' offer."

"There's also Eli Broad and Doug Cramer."

"Did you call me up to torture me?"

"You know what my reasons are for not letting it go to a private collector, or to England, don't you? I want it to be installed in an institution where the public can see it, but not in Washington, L.A., or New York, where it would be only one treasure among many."

"But private collections usually end up in museums someday. Or in private museums, like Kramer's."

"I'd like it more accessible. I've had an offer from the Ackerbergs in Minneapolis for the museum there, but it's far from where I live. I'd be thrilled to find somewhere closer, like Baltimore or Wilmington."

"My neck of the woods. You know my wife is a trustee of the new Contemporary Museum in Wilmington."

"Don't you live right near the museum?"

"Yes, I do."

"If you'll build a wing in the new museum for it, I'll sell it to you for a fourth off my best offer. You can retain ownership for as long as you like. All I ask is that it always be housed in that museum, and if you sell it, the buyer must agree to let it be housed there."

She heard him gasp. "You must need me pretty badly."

"How do you feel about owning it and still letting it be available for the public?"

"Well, having it in Wilmington would be almost like having it for myself. We're close enough so that I could show it to guests anytime I wished."

"You could even give parties in your own wing."

He chuckled; she could almost see him rubbing his hands together. "There's one thing," he said. "Since I hadn't anticipated the cost of a wing for the museum, I will still be paying more than I can afford. If you give me a third off, we have a deal."

She knew he would have spent that same money building a wing on his own home to house the work, and it wouldn't be deductible, but she didn't hesitate to agree.

Since she stood to make sixty percent of four and a half million dollars, six hundred thousand more didn't make that much difference. Of course, Pat McGarrity might not agree, but she had the final say. "It's yours, Calvin."

He shouted with pleasure. "I don't believe it. This is fantastic."

Then she explained to him what she needed.

"First thing in the morning, Trish, it's done."

"Not in the morning, Cal, now! There's a life at stake."

"But it's the middle of the night. This is going to cost me too many favors."

"Now!" she insisted. "Or no deal."

He groaned. "Give me your number and wait by the phone. I'll call you back."

"We've got it," she said to Connor as she hung up the phone.

"While we're waiting, I'm going to do some investigating of my own, just question the police downstairs, ring a few bells in the neighborhood before it gets too late. People are more apt to answer their doors pleasantly if they're not asleep."

Forty minutes later, after Connor had returned, the phone rang.

"My name is John," the caller told them. "I'm at the computer at headquarters in Washington. What do you need?"

And Connor told him.

Since Mel was at the hospital with Hillary, Trish and Connor were free to use their room. Each of them took turns dozing while they waited for news from John. Pam called to tell them she'd be at her office most of the night, working on the agreement for Charles.

"You have to give him contracts to build in Weymouth City?" Trish said. "You can't. Not after what you told me about him."

"I have no choice," Pam said. She was close to breaking; Trish could hear it in her voice.

"Hold on," Trish told her. "We're doing everything we can."

But the sound of defeat in Pam's voice told her that whatever it was, it might be too little and too late.

Trish finally did fall asleep on top of the bed, but never lost complete awareness of Connor on the phone with

John, going over lists and more lists of information. At one point he woke her to tell her he had made contact with an FBI agent who specialized in organized crime. "I suspected—and John's associate agrees—that the group controlling waste disposal in New York and New Jersey are the ones who want Hillary stopped, and are using Kevin as a bargaining tool. They have the most to lose in a congressional investigation, and Hillary's promised to do just that. Hell, she's been making it hot for them all along, with her fact-finding and nighttime sleuthing."

"Maybe Charles can help," Trish said. "But at what cost to Pam?"

Another time when she woke up, Connor said, "The strangest thing is happening. I keep getting a feeling of claustrophobia, of being closed in. I've never been afraid of small spaces before. I can't figure it out." He shook his head to dismiss it, but Trish wouldn't let him.

"Don't fight it, Connor, no matter how strange. I know from firsthand experience how intuitive you are."

He put his arm around her and kissed her softly, and then she fell asleep again.

8

By 4:00 A.M., Pam knew that if she didn't get some sleep, she'd never be able to hold her own in the negotiations with Charles later in the day. From what her advisers had told her, she didn't have much of a chance anyway. He held all the cards, and they were all aces.

Jake had barely said a word when she told him about Charles's demands. He'd just listened, then said, "You know he'll flush us all down his toilet."

She wanted to scream from frustration, but she held her temper. "He's got me, Jake. I can't sacrifice Hillary's career and my son's life by telling him to go to hell."

When they were on their way down in the elevator after the harrowing meeting, he said, "Isn't there anyone else who can intercede and free Kevin, assuming he's alive?"

"No one else has Charles's clout and his connections with this particular group. And even if there were someone, you know how the world works; it's tit for tat, scratch for scratch. Anyone who could grant a favor like this would hold me up too."

"We had such a sweet deal, Pam. God, all the work it's taken us to get this far, and now this." He threw away the stub of his cigar, and opened her car door for her. "What about your father? Is there anything he can do?"

She gave him a look. "You know how effective he is." She thought about it for a moment. "I've been noticing that in the past few years, my father's behaved differently toward me. Maybe it's time, maybe it's age, but I can tell he's sorry for the way we ended up. Frankly, so am I. But even if I made peace with him, he can't control

Charles, never could." She sighed. "I'm sorry, Jake. What else can I say?"

"I can't stand that fucking bastard Charles," he said as he helped her into the car, "and now you tell me I have to have his dick up my ass for the next five years. He'll chew us up and spit us out."

"Let's take it one step at a time. Think of it like a lawsuit. We've both been through those enough to know that by the time you get to court, anything can happen."

"Yeah, in favor of the other guy. You and your steps-at-a-time, that's how you conned me into your life in the first place. I'm beginning to rue the day."

"Like hell you are."

He grinned at her and winked. "Maybe that weasel won't be as smart as we think."

She nodded, feeling exhaustion creep over her. "Think positive, Jake; that's what I have to do."

"See you tomorrow," he said, then realized it was already Monday. "I mean, later."

Hillary dozed and woke. Each time she opened her eyes, Mel was still sitting in the chair in her hospital room. "Honey, why don't you go home?"

"I'm not going to leave you," he said.

"But there are guards at the door."

"I need to be with you," he told her.

She needed him to be here, too. "I keep thinking about what's going to happen in the morning, when I can't stall anymore. I'll have to resign as soon as we can call a press conference."

"I know you want to get it over with, but we have to give the police more time, Hil. The kidnappers may want to negotiate. We might even find Kevin in time."

"There's no way, Mel, and you know it. Those men have already killed one person. What hope do we have that Kevin's still alive?" She tried to shift in the bed, but every movement brought a new pain. Her head throbbed, as well as her shoulder. "I hate giving up, and I hate being coerced. We worked so hard, we had them beat. Now Victor could win, or my substitute might be less of an activist. And worst of all, our family and our community will be the biggest losers." She winced again from the pain in her shoulder.

"How's the ringing in your ears? Any better?" he asked.

"Not really," she admitted.

He came over and sat on her bed. "I'm so grateful that you're alive. The explosion knocked me out of my chair. For a moment I was completely paralyzed. And then, when I was finally able to move, I came outside and saw you lying there. I thought you were dead and I wanted to die too. I'm afraid I fell apart. I couldn't stop screaming, shouting. I wanted to lift you up, hold you. I would have done all the wrong things, maybe damaged you, but the kids calmed me down. Brian was the one who called the ambulance. Some father." Tears were rolling down his face. He put his head in her lap and she stroked his head.

"I know," she said. "I don't ever want to be out of your sight again. Now we've got to pray Kevin will be as lucky."

△   △   △

Kevin came to consciousness when the pain in his head woke him. He was lying on a bed in a dark room. A clock with a luminous dial on a nearby table said it was 5:20. He assumed it was A.M. because it was still dark outside. He knew he was in great peril and had to get out of here. The men had dragged him out of the backseat of the car, wrapped a blanket around him, thrown him over someone's shoulder and carried him up some stairs. And then they'd strapped his hands to his ankles behind his back. He'd pretended to be unconscious, but tried to keep his wrists flexed, so that when he relaxed there might be room to slip free of his bonds. After that he must have passed out or dozed off.

He listened for sounds, while his eyes grew accustomed to the dark. He thought he heard voices in the next room. That made him even more afraid. Any minute they might decide to come in here and kill him. He had to get out! He looked around. He was in a woman's bedroom. He could see clothes everywhere, as well as makeup bottles, a hair dryer, and curlers.

The urgency of needing to get out of here quickly made the panic rise in his throat. Stay calm, he told himself

*fighting the need to claw at the belts holding him prisoner.
He took a deep breath and prayed for strength.*

It was 5:55 before he managed to unbuckle his ankles.
He stood up slowly, feeling the exquisite relief of stretching the cramps out of his legs, but the throbbing in his
head was excruciating. He took deep breaths until it subsided to a dull ach, then, still trying to untie his wrists, he
walked over to the window. It looked out of the second
floor of the house, from the side. Craning his neck, he
stood on his toes, but the only thing he could see was the
car in the drive below him. If he could get out the window,
maybe he could use it to get away. Idiot, you don't know
how to hot-wire a car! Using the edge of the table behind
him, he twisted the belt on his wrists around so that the
buckle faced outward, then he turned his back to the
mirror above the dresser so he could see a way to unbuckle himself. Everything was backwards in the mirror,
but eventually he figured it out. And little by little he
managed, with cramped fingers and a stiff neck, to unbuckle the belt by holding his hands together and using his
fingers. Finally, he was free, rubbing the sore places on
his wrist. There wasn't a moment to lose. He checked the
bedroom window; it was nailed shut. To get out, he'd
have to smash the glass. The men would be sure to hear
him. He couldn't throw himself out of a window two
stories up. He might break his neck. And if he tied sheets
together to lower himself down, he'd still have to break
the glass and they'd be on him in a minute. He searched
the room; nowhere to hide. The closet was small and
square and stuffed with belongings. His heart pounded.
Any moment they might walk in.

He covered every inch of the room. There was no way
out. It was almost exactly like his parents' bedroom. This
house was old like theirs, too. He looked up. If that was
true, there might be an opening in the closet ceiling to a
crawlspace in the attic. He found some matches by the side
of the bed, went into the closet, and lit one.

There it was! A square shape in the center of the ceiling,
about three feet across. If he pushed up on it, it should lift,
revealing a space under the roof. Electricians and furnace
people used it. A hiding place!

To make certain, he grabbed a pillowcase off the bed
and stuffed it with every small, heavy object we could find

in the room—bottles, lotions, hair dryer, electric curlers, mirror, jewelry box—and tossed chains and necklaces in with the rest. Then he pulled a small stool over to the center of the closet, directly beneath the opening, and climbed up. The trapdoor opened easily. Remembering to tuck the matches into his pocket, we pulled himself up and crawled in. There was just enough room to lie down. He climbed back down and searched the room for something long and thin. There it was—a bathroom plunger, in the corner of the closet. He was ready.

He put the plunger up into the crawlspace, then took the filled pillowcase over to the window. He picked up the wooden stool, swung it back over his shoulder, and with all his might, slammed it forward into the glass. The window shattered outward, and we threw the pillowcase out the window, aiming for the car. Everything inside the case smashed and broke as it landed on the windshield with an enormous crash.

Without a second to spare, he raced back to the closet, climbed up on the stool, and pulled himself into the crawlspace. Holding on to the edge of the trapdoor, he stretched way down. He could hear voices yelling outside the door, the rattling of a key in the lock. He stretched as far as we could, aimed, and swung. Just as they burst through the door, he connected with the stool and sent it rolling under the bed. His heart stopped, but they were looking at the window and didn't see the movement of the stool behind them. Carefully, quietly, he pulled himself back up into the crawlspace and moved the cover into place.

"What the shit? I told you not to leave him alone, Leo."

"He's gone out the window."

"He musta broke his neck. Do you see him?"

"No."

"Well, there's something down there."

"Jesus, this is all we need. Vic Junior will have our balls."

"Let's go!" And they raced out of the room.

Kevin's heart pounded wildly, he was panting, out of breath. He tried to calm himself as the blackness closed around him. Soon it would be daylight and there was bound to be more visibility; light would come up through chinks in the roofing. But at the moment there was no light at all. Now that he was inside with the cover in place, he could barely move, he couldn't see anything, it was pitch black. The letdown of tension was tremendous. He could hear the two men shouting and cursing. Their voices carried from outside, though the sounds were far away, muffled. Were they sharp enough to figure out what he'd done? He closed his eyes and tried to rest, but the uneven ceiling joists cut into his back. The space was too narrow even to turn over, and the musty smell filled his senses. Suddenly the feeling of being trapped overcame him, and he broke out into a sweat. In another minute he would start to scream and try to claw his way out. Fighting for control, he inched his fingers along, looking for the edge of the trapdoor. If he could lift it just an inch to get a breath of air, he'd feel better. He moved his hand back and forth in the dust where he knew the trapdoor had been, but there was nothing there. The panicky feeling pressed down on him like huge bat wings. He felt suffocated, nearly ready to give himself up. Again he tried to find the opening of the trapdoor. He reached into his pocket and took out the matches, transferring them from his right to his left hand. He held the book and drew the match across the edge several times before it ignited.

He couldn't see very much; the space was so narrow, the light didn't travel far. He turned his head to look for the opening just as he felt the heat of the match reach his fingers. There it was, the opening of the trapdoor. It fit perfectly flush with the floor around it that he lay on. The only way to get it open was to push from below. He was trapped! A feeling of panic grabbed him around the throat and he coughed out a sob, swallowing it so no one would hear. Then the match died and it was dark again.

$$\triangle \quad \triangle \quad \triangle$$

By seven o'clock Monday morning, Connor and Trish were both showered and dressed in yesterday's clothes, ready to go, but still waiting for more information. She used the time to make him breakfast.

"The thing I find most odd," Connor said, sipping the last of his coffee, "is that the attempt on Hillary's life was bungled. Professional hitmen don't usually fail, although it can happen."

"Unless they were just trying to scare her," Trish said, glancing at him as she scrambled the eggs.

"That's quite possible," Connor admitted. Even with only a few hours' sleep, he was energized and alert, making notes on a pad, going over everything he knew.

"The other detail that bothers me is that the police didn't question the neighbors last night, and yet they provided a great deal of information. One neighbor gave me a description of a car that drove away right after the explosion. It was a dark blue, four-door sedan, small, like a Toyota or a Honda, and it had been parked in front of his house. There was one man in the driver's seat, and another behind him in the back. Another neighbor saw two men running down the street. The second man dropped his scarf. The witness thought they were joggers."

"That was Kevin!"

"Right. Kevin must have surprised them in the act. But the best information I got was that the car had a New Jersey plate and that part of the number was Z 4. When the DMV calls with a list of all blue sedans in New Jersey with those two numbers in the license, we're taking off. That's a real lead. But the police have ignored it. It's as if they don't want to solve this crime."

"Victor Godfrey, Jr., one of the local police lieutenants, might be dragging his heels for his father's sake."

"Maybe he's involved, along with his father," Connor said, suddenly getting an idea. "I think I'll check their financial records."

"But that's public information. After all, Victor's running for office."

He just smiled.

Connor had his own method of checking beyond the more easily available financial information that showed both men to have average incomes. And John, their computer expert, had found what Connor wanted. Mayor Godfrey had an insurance policy on a deluxe motor home valued at $75,000, yet he had no mortgage on the vehicle. He'd paid cash. And his son's wife had an insurance policy on a mink coat valued at six thousand dollars. Also paid for in cash.

"Think they're stealing from the campaign?" Trish asked.

"More likely it's a cash payoff for favors done for a mob-run chemical company."

"You think they're involved with the bombing?"

"After seeing their financial records, I wouldn't be surprised. In a way, I'm not sorry we're so short on time. In a case like this, most things happen in the first twenty-four hours. After that the trail gets cold."

"Do you still have that feeling of claustrophobia?"

"It was better during the night, but this morning about six, it was so bad it woke me up."

"Maybe you're just feeling the time pressure."

The phone rang. John had a real lead. There were only twenty blue, four-door sedans in the state with those two numbers, and in only four of them did the Z come before the 4. One car belonged to a teenaged girl in Paramus, another to a widow of sixty. The third had been nearly totaled in an accident just last week. The remaining car was a Toyota belonging to a man named Walter Hidalgo. Connor's voice rose with excitement as he relayed the best part. "Hidalgo's sister is married to Victor Godfrey, Jr."

Trish caught his excitement. "And Vic Junior bought his wife a mink coat."

"That's her. She may know where her husband is."

"Let's go." Trish grabbed her suede cape and purse.

"You're not going anywhere. I need you to stay by the phone in case the FBI agent calls with the additional information I'm waiting for."

"I'm coming with you. We can stop on the road and call from wherever we are. You know I'd go crazy here alone."

"This could get tricky, babe. I always work alone."

"We're wasting time, O'Brien," she said, refusing to stay behind.

Monday the third, the day before the election, was a cold, steel-gray November day. Pam slept until ten and awoke feeling revitalized, but her brain had never let go of the details of the all-night meeting: we'll give you x if you'll agree to y, and so on.

She put on her new rust-and-bone suit with its split wrapped skirt, and a rust silk blouse. It was bright and cheerful and gave her a lift. Her eyes were puffy, she noticed as she applied her makeup. But that was what happened when you stayed up all night and you were approaching forty-six years old. She checked with the hospital; Hillary was stable, but the official announcement was that she was unconscious. No word on Kevin. *Damn. Charles, you'd better do your thing.* Just as she was about to leave for the meeting, she remembered something from her past life with Charles that might come in handy today, and tucked it into her purse.

Promptly at 1:00 P.M. she met Jake and her attorneys, Michael Luckman and Addison Blake, in the lobby of the Pam Am Building, where Gray-Con had its offices. They entered the elevator together. Jake looked tired, his skin a grayish-white color. He wasn't smoking a cigar.

"This is it," Michael said. "I never thought it would come to this."

"Come on, Michael, buck up," Pam said. "We're not down for the count yet."

A receptionist got up from her desk and ushered the four of them into Charles's office. He was standing by the door to greet them. He looked jaunty, but Pam still couldn't get used to the change that age had made in him. In her mind he was still the powerful, dynamic Charles from years ago, but in person he had lost his physical appeal. The Italian suits didn't look nearly as good on him as they used to. Seeing him face to face, she suddenly recalled a dream she'd had in the early hours of the morning, and her heart began to pound. She and Charles had been negotiating, but Charles had looked the way he used to look. In the heat of their argument he had struck her with his fist, and to retaliate, she had screamed out the truth about Kevin, that he was Charles's son, that he had not died. Charles had advanced on her, put his hands around her throat, and started to strangle her, and there the dream had ended. She was terrified of that happening today. *He must never know,* she vowed. Nevertheless, she almost felt a compulsion to tell him.

Pam looked around. Charles's office had recently been redecorated; she recognized the fabrics and furnishings as the work of a mediocre designer. Charles indicated for them to sit on the sofa. Pam chose a separate chair, opposite Charles. She didn't want the disadvantage of sitting against soft cushions while she battled with him.

"What did you find out from your people?" Pam asked. "Can you get the contract called off and the boy released?" The muscles in her shoulders ached from tension.

"I talked to a few friends, who made some discreet inquiries. But before we begin, I'm going to insist that you and I negotiate alone, Pam. I want to be able to speak freely, without witnesses. No phone calls, no interruptions. Just you and me, or we cannot proceed." His face remained calm, but his tone said this was an ultimatum. He was tense about this request, too, as if there were something more to it than just the need for privacy. But what? She'd give anything to know.

His eyes bored into her, while her mind flew over the possibilities. She would be a virtual prisoner, no advisers, no one in her corner to help; he expected to out-negotiate her, alone. But she was prepared for this, in case he went for a divide-and-conquer strategy. But why no phone calls? If she refused, he might say, "Go to hell, let the kid die." He had that power. She had to agree, even though it was crucial to maintain some control. She recalled last night's discussion. At every juncture she must protest strongly, make him press for every concession, yet not drag on too long, not with Kevin's life in the balance. She nodded and looked up at Jake, who gave her a smile of support as he and the other two men left the office, and then it was just her and Charles.

"Is my father around?"

"Not yet. He'll join us in a while."

"I thought you didn't want witnesses." The last person she wanted here was William, watching Charles work her over. "If you have someone on your side, then I demand the same."

"He's your father, Pam, hardly on my side." His eyes had that cold, hateful stare. "That's the way I want it. It has more to do with William than with you. Your father has always taken the position that he kept you out of the business to keep you away from me. Now I want the pleasure of showing him that I've got you, in spite of his noble sacrifices."

"You haven't got me yet."

He gave a brief smile. "I've instructed my staff that there are to be no interruptions, even if King Kong climbs the Empire State Building."

"It takes a gorilla to know one."

"That's funny." But he wasn't smiling now. "I don't remember you having a sense of humor."

"It comes from being free of you."

"Coffee?"

"A Coke, if you have it."

"Still like them, I see."

He brought her the soda in a Baccarat glass with ice. He'd learned some things from her.

She handed him the standard AIA contract, which she and her lawyers had amended during the night, and he began to read.

9

Charles finished reading the AIA contract she'd given him, and tossed it on the table. "Now I'll tell you what I want."

"Before you say anything, I have to know," she interrupted, "what did you find out from your people? Is there a contract on Hillary's life? Can you get it nullified?"

"If she withdraws from the race, I might be able to get it revoked."

"She can't withdraw, she's unconscious."

"Then let her husband do it for her."

"The only one who can withdraw a candidate from a political race is the candidate, unless he—or she—is dead."

He gave her a look that sent chills down her arms.

"She's not dead, she's going to be all right, Charles. And 'might' isn't good enough for me. You have to get the contract on Hillary revoked, or I walk out of here now!"

"Go ahead," he said, crossing his legs and indicating the door.

She didn't move, and cursed herself for losing her temper. "What about the boy?"

"We'll get to him later."

"I've got to know if he's alive!"

"You seem awfully interested in him. What's he to you?"

Careful, Pam. She felt her heart skip as she feigned a look of bored disdain. "We're engaged to be married." He saw that she was joking. She shrugged. "He's a good kid, and his life is in danger."

"I'm waiting to hear about that. Now, to business." He pointed to the contract. "I asked to control three-quarters of this construction project and you've only given me fifty percent."

Oh, Kevin! She could not think of anything else, could barely concentrate on what Charles was saying. Did he really know about Kevin and wasn't telling her? Was Kevin alive? "I couldn't get my finance people to agree. Independence on a project costing two and a half billion dollars isn't as easy to come by as it is on a project that costs twenty million. My investors don't give a damn about my problems. Fifty percent was the best I could do."

He stared at her through half-lidded eyes, and she gazed back, deadpan. He could call her bluff. But he nodded. Her heart leaped with excitement. *Score one for our side.* She'd possibly just saved the life of the project.

"Now you tell me—what did you find out about Hillary and Kevin Matthews?"

"I told you, not until our deal is completely worked out."

She ached for the pleasure of dragging her nails across his face, and then she thought about her dream and instead crossed her arms and held in her rage.

"What's your estimate of cost per square foot to build?"

"A hundred a square foot," she told him. "That's a medium to low estimate, but we're doing it now."

"I need a hundred thirty-five."

"Are you crazy? That's ridiculous!"

He raised the corners of his mouth in a mock smile, and then shrugged.

"A hundred five," she countered.

"One-thirty-five." There was a look of calculation in his eyes.

"One-ten." She held firm.

He crossed his leg and watched her, the inquisitor dispassionately watching his victim being pulled on the rack. "Do you want to see Hillary remain alive, and that boy released? You know how hard it is to call off a contract?"

Only a sharp intake of air showed her fear. "One-twenty, Charles. The banks will rescind my loan commitments, we'll both have nothing."

He gazed out the window, taking his time. Finally he said, "All right, one-twenty-five."

She gave him a nod and a look of disgust. But it was about what they'd figured. *You're doing okay, so far.*

Then he hit her with it. "I want a fee of four percent over cost."

"But two is standard!" She ran her hand over her forehead, to cover her terror. "You're asking four percent of one and a quarter billion? That's fifty million dollars."

His body stiffened as he tried to hide his excitement. "You're figuring the budget to build Weymouth City will be two-and-a-half billion, and *my* fifty percent will cost one and a quarter?"

"Your half, indeed." *He's nauseating!*

"Well, won't it?"

"Charles, four percent is an outrageous precedent. You'll be stoned by other construction managers who understand the problems of the developer."

"They'll be thrilled," he laughed. "You're in no position to argue. I'll tell you what, how about a fuck on the couch for old times' sake, and I'll cut my percentage to three and a half."

She felt her blood pounding in her ears. God, she detested him. How she wanted to fling that gauntlet at him. *Your son is alive.* Instead she said, "I've had a bisexual lover, but I'd be most happy to pass on to you anything he might have given me."

He glared at her. "I hope it rots and falls off."

"That's my line." She was beginning to relax again. "Are we agreed on two and a half?"

"Three."

It was staggering, but she had to consent. Still, it was twelve-and-a-half million less than he wanted.

"You are a cunt, aren't you?" he said.

She paused for a moment, studying him. "You mean any woman who can match you in toughness and shrewdness is a cunt? To justify my success, you have to reduce me to a four-letter word? Well, that makes you a prick!"

He ignored her comment, but she could see it had gotten to him. "About the financial risk clause," he said. "If there's a departure from the plan, I get a higher fee, say four percent, and no risk."

She took a long drink of her Coke, trying to think of how to negotiate him out of this one.

*   *   *

Connor was unfamiliar with the streets and roadways into Newark, but by using a Hagstrom's street guide, Trish helped him locate the city of Bayonne and Walter Hidalgo's residence. The Hidalgos lived in a large brick apartment complex, and as soon as Connor saw it, he realized it was not a place where anyone would keep a kidnapped hostage.

"Wait here," he said to Trish.

But the moment he was out the car, she followed him and came upon him in the hallway outside the Hidalgos' door. He gave her a look and motioned her away; she moved on down the hall where she wouldn't be seen.

He pounded on the Hidalgos' door, until a woman's voice called out to him, "Cut the racket already, you want us evicted?"

"I'm looking for Walt," he shouted, like an outraged creditor. "He owes me two hundred dollars. I want it!" Again he pounded.

"He ain't heah," she shouted. "You're gonna wake the baby."

A sudden wail in the background meant she was telling the truth.

"Sonofabitch," she swore. "Get lost, mister, or I'll call the cops."

"Your cop brother doesn't scare me," Connor said. "Where's your weasel husband? With his girlfriend? He bought two fur coats, you know, not just one." He was fishing for information, hoping to find out anything he could use.

She pulled open the door and stepped forward, glaring at him, hand on hip. Trish could see she was full-bodied, with long dark hair, wearing a T-shirt and jeans. There was a family resemblance to her father, Victor Godfrey, from pictures of him Trish had seen.

"Who is she?" the woman asked. "That Bonnie, from high school?" Fury glinted in her eyes. "That little prick. How'd you know about the coat?"

"I monogrammed the linin' on both of 'em." Connor moved into her dialect, instinctively understanding that people responded to familiar speech patterns, tended to trust their own kind. Trish admired the way he worked.

"I'll kill 'im."

"Not if I find him first."

"Away on business all night, was he? Somethin' real big goin' down." She nodded her head as though she'd gotten his number.

"Where does she live?"

"I ain't tellin' you nothin', mister. This is family business. My brothers'll take care of it." And she slammed the door hard.

Trish thought that was it, but Connor wasn't giving up.

He called through the door, "Maybe you should know, Mrs. Hidalgo, your hubby bought you a mink, but he bought her a Russian lynx."

Brilliant, Trish thought.

This time the door flew open immediately. "Russian lynx for that bleached blonde? The bitch! She lives in East Orange. She's married, but her old man's away a lot on a freighter. He swore to me he never touched her, and I swallowed it." She wiped away tears in her eyes, and for a brief moment Trish was sorry Connor had had to lie to her.

"What's her last name?"

"Vicenzo," the woman said, closing the door more slowly. Before it closed all the way, she said, "Tell 'im I'm havin' the locks changed. Tell 'im he's a dead man. And tell 'im . . . No! Don't tell 'im nothin'. When you're shoving that monogrammed lining up his ass, give 'im a good strong one in the gut." She shook her fist. "And say it's from me!" And the door closed.

Trish raced after Connor back to the car, but he was furious. "The next time I tell you to stay in the car, you listen, you hear? If she'd taken one step out of that apartment and seen you, the whole thing could have been blown."

She apologized, sitting close by him in the car. She couldn't stop touching him. This was turning her on!

Time raced by as they headed back toward the suburbs of Montclair, Glen Ridge, and Crestmont, looking for Victor Junior, hoping he could lead them to Kevin. On their way, they drove by the Crestmont police station and then by the Godfrey house. Victor Junior wasn't apparently at either place.

"It's time to notify the FBI," Connor decided, "since

the local police can't be trusted. "I'll call them," he told
her. "You call John and see what else he's found out."

John gave her the number of a Dave Smith, who was
with the FBI. He answered on the first ring. "Trish
Baldwin speaking," she said. "Connor O'Brien and I are
working together. What have you got for us?"

"Are you the artist that Senator Bentworth told me
about?"

"I am."

"What's your mother's maiden name?"

"Huntington."

"Here's what I found out. There is no official contract
out on your friend from any organized crime family. The
family that's most involved in toxic waste disposal knows
about her, but they consider it a local matter between her
and a friend of theirs in the area who promotes their
interests. It's true that they want her scared away, but
they left it up to the local person to take care of it. That
left a wide range of possibilities."

"Then who tried to kill her? Do you know?"

"My guess is they were only trying to scare her, not kill
her, and that it's the man running against her in the
election, Victor Godfrey, or someone close to him. Mr.
Godfrey is on their payroll. It's in the best interests of
this particular crime family that he get elected, and not
her. They've backed him all the way, for years. But it's
not important enough for them to issue a contract. I
think that's why there were mistakes made, why an
unwanted hostage was taken and a bystander killed. And
frankly, it was smart of whoever took him to use the boy
to their advantage. But your friend can rest assured that
she's not in direct danger from the crime syndicate. They
only made their desires known, and some zealous person
took it upon himself to do them a favor."

Trish was stunned. "If it's not a contract put out by a
crime syndicate, then what should Mrs. Robin do? Should
she resign? How can we make them give us Kevin back?"

He was quiet for a moment. "Is Connor there?"

"Yes, but he's across the street on another phone."

"I would have preferred to tell this to him," Smith
said.

"You'll have to tell me," Trish insisted.

"Okay, then. The boy's chances are not good, even if

your friend does withdraw from the election. But tell her to stall until the last minute, and to insist, if she's contacted, that she be allowed to speak to Kevin. That way they'll keep him alive a while longer."

"You don't think they'll release him?"

"No," he said, "I don't."

Trish felt a terrible sadness fill her. "Are you certain, Mr. Smith?"

"I know what I'm talking about."

She thanked him and hung up, then ran across the street to the phone where Connor was just finishing his conversation. She told him what Dave Smith had said. "We're following the right man," she told Connor, "but we've got to get to Kevin somehow."

They got back in the car and headed for East Orange to where Bonnie Vicenzo lived, but the closer they got, the more Connor kept getting that claustrophobic feeling. It was so strong he couldn't ignore it.

"I have to stop a minute," he told Trish, and in spite of the time pressure, he pulled over to the side of a tree-lined residential street, turned off the ignition, and sat for a moment, trying to calm himself.

"What is it?" she kept asking, but he found it difficult to discuss.

Finally he said, "I keep wondering if what's stopping me is the fear of violence or the whole situation. I'm not a coward, but I sure as hell don't want to get killed. I should never have brought you with me," he said, grabbing her and holding her to him. "Dying didn't used to matter so much, but now it does."

"Neither of us is going to die," she assured him.

"When I was in the field and these kinds of strong negative feelings came over me, I'd ignore them, push right on through, singleminded O'Brien. But now that I've learned to trust my instincts and not ignore them, I can't do that."

He put his head back against the headrest and tried to relax. He took a few deep breaths and said out loud, "Why am I afraid?"

An image blasted into his brain. It was so clear that every detail stood out. "Someone's trapped in a narrow box," he told Trish. "He's hungry and thirsty. But most of all, he's terrified of being buried alive. Underground, they've buried him someplace, or put him in a box. I can feel the trapped person's terror, it's heart-wrenching, paralyzing. That kind of fear can kill you!"

"But it's not your own fear," Trish said. "It's someone else's. Do you think it's Kevin?"

Connor looked at her and nodded. The moment he understood it was not his own fear, it vanished and he gazed at Trish with total clarity and a feeling of lightness.

He started the ignition and headed directly for a phone book to find the Vicenzo address in East Orange, praying it was the right hunch.

Trish called the hospital to tell Hillary and Mel what she'd found out.

"Have you been contacted by the kidnappers?" she asked, hoping they knew if Kevin was still alive.

But there had been no more word at all, and it was getting close to three. Time was running out.

Hillary got on the phone. "I don't care what that man told you about delaying, Trish. I think I should withdraw now. If Kevin's got any chance at all, it depends on what I do. This election might be nullified anyway, because it's been tampered with. It will be up to the state board of elections to decide."

"You can't do that," Trish insisted. "You have to wait. The kidnappers may not be thinking of that and you'll give them our only advantage! We'll never see Kevin again."

"What if I made an appeal on television to say I'll withdraw, but only if they'll release Kevin."

"I don't know how that would affect their strategy. Maybe later, at around four-thirty, you could make an appeal. But now, officially you're unconscious. I'll get back to you if we locate Kevin. We've got a real good lead."

As she hung up with Hillary, it suddenly hit her. Pam was being blackmailed by Charles for nothing! She didn't have to give him a contract to build half the buildings in Weymouth City. She could get out of his stranglehold on her life. Charles couldn't call off a contract on Hillary that didn't exist. He had no control over Kevin's kidnappers. That lying bastard!

Heart pounding, hands shaking, she called Charles's

office. "It's a matter of life and death," she told his secretary.

"I'm sorry. Mr. Meroni left instructions not to be interrupted, no matter what the emergency."

"A kidnapped boy's life is in danger. They're going to kill him," Trish said, using anything she could to get through.

The woman sounded terribly upset, but finally she said, "I'm so sorry. I cannot put you through. I can't afford to lose my job."

"Then let me talk to Mr. Grayson."

"I'm sorry, the same goes for him."

Trish called the lawyers' office, but none of Pam's lawyers was there; they were with Pam. "I have to get a message to her, it's urgent!" Trish exclaimed. "I'll have Mr. Blake return your call the moment I hear from him," his secretary promised. "Can anyone else help you?"

She couldn't entrust this errand to someone she didn't know. She needed someone strong and forceful, who wouldn't be intimidated by Charles's henchmen outside his door. Jake Harrigan was nowhere to be found, either, probably with Pam. *I'm stuck out here in New Jersey,* Trish thought. *And Connor needs me. I'd never get into Manhattan in time to stop this.*

Joanne! Maybe she can get through.

But then she remembered that Pam had told her Joanne had gone to a cosmetics show in Dallas. Pam and Charles had been in negotiations for hours. It could be all over by now. She had to reach Pam. Would the police break up that meeting? Not likely. There was no one to do it but her, and she couldn't go.

10

Trish and Connor drove down the suburban street, looking for the address of Bonnie Vicenzo's house. But then,
up the block, they saw a Crestmont police car pull up and
park in front of one of the houses.

"Crestmont police have no jurisdiction here," Connor
said. He slowed down and they stopped to watch an
officer get out of the car and go into the duplex. There
was something familiar about him.

"That's got to be Vic Junior," Trish said.

"Obviously he's not here to make an arrest, or he
would have had a backup with him," Connor told her.
And then he noticed the car parked in the driveway; it
was a blue four-door Toyota with *Z 4* in the license
number. "There's the Toyota," Connor said, and his
heart began to race with excitement.

"Wait," Trish cautioned. "If the two men who took
Kevin are keeping him in that house, and now Vic Junior
is there, that makes three of them and one of you."

Connor looked at her with a sudden realization. "Some
hotshot I am, I haven't got a weapon! Damn, how stupid." He punched his foot on the accelerator and shot
past the house.

"Where are you going?" Trish asked, hanging on to
the dashboard of the careening car.

"To find a phone. There's one, on the corner, at that
White Castle," he said, jumping out of the car almost
before it had stopped. He dialed 911 and called in a
police emergency. "Officer down!" he said, giving the
address and jumping back into the car. "That will get
them here fast." He prayed it would be fast enough. He
drove back to the end of the street and stopped again.

"Get out," he insisted.

"I'm not leaving you," she argued.

"Trish, that's an order. I can't go in there with you! Now get out." He opened the door and shoved her. "Don't go near that house until the police are here and you see me come out safely! Is that clear?"

She nodded mutely, trying not to show him how terrified she was.

He was gone so fast she didn't have a chance to tell him to be careful.

Connor drove down the street and she followed on foot, but just close enough to see what he was doing. As he came within a short distance of the duplex where the police car was parked, he turned the wheel of their BMW right into the side of the police car. There was a loud crash of metal against metal.

"Connor!" Trish shouted, but he didn't hear her. She wanted to run to him, but kept her distance.

A man stuck his head out of an upper window of the duplex and shouted, "Vic, some asshole rammed into your car in front of the house, right in the driver's side. Holy shit! Now he's backin' up to do it again. No!" he yelled. "He's drivin' over the lawn, headin' for the Toyota. Stop him! You crazy bastard, stop!"

But Connor didn't stop, he did it again, ramming the BMW into the blue car parked in the driveway. Then, leaving his car where it was, Connor opened the door, folded himself into a tight ball, and rolled out onto the lawn, crouching low. Keeping down, he made his way to the back of the car, opened the trunk, and grabbed the tire iron, then ran to the porch of the duplex, positioning himself just to the right of the door, holding the tire iron like a baseball bat in both hands, waiting for the rats he'd just flushed to start running out. Trish watched from across the street, her heart in her throat.

Seconds later, the first man came charging out the door and Connor swung the tire iron, connecting with his abdomen and lower ribs. Trish could hear the sickening crunch where she was standing. The man grunted and pitched forward. But the next man was right behind him. It was Vic Junior, wearing a police uniform, with his gun drawn. Trish wanted to scream, but Connor didn't hesitate, or even wait for him to come through the door. He swung the tire iron with all his might into the opening.

The officer's gun discharged and flew out of his hand as the tire iron slammed into his extended arm. Vic screamed in pain as Connor lunged for the gun, grabbed it, and whirled around. Holding the tire iron in his left hand, the gun in his right, he shouted, "Hold it! Don't move! Down, and spread 'em!"

Vic turned to run back up the stairs. Connor fired, missing him by inches. But as the gun went off, someone screamed—Trish thought it had come from the duplex—and Vic turned back and dropped to the ground next to the first man, who was moaning in agony. Then he placed his hands behind his head.

A man's voice from inside the duplex yelled, "What the fuck's going on?"

"Get out of there!" Vic shouted from his place on the ground. "He's got my gun."

Connor went into the duplex, and Trish couldn't see him anymore.

Just then a police car screeched around the corner, siren screaming, and came to a stop in the street at an angle. Two officers got out and took positions behind their open doors, guns pointing at the two men on the ground.

Trish called out to them, "There's an armed agent in that house! He called for help! Those two men are kidnappers."

One of the officers yelled to her, "Get down, lady!"

Trish dropped to the sidewalk, crouching. "There's a kidnap victim in that house!" she yelled. "The agent's trying to help him!"

The two officers moved in and apprehended the men on the ground. When they saw Vic Junior's uniform, they were about to let him go, but Trish ran over and insisted that they hold him, at least until they found out what was going on inside.

They handcuffed the two men and placed them in the car; then, with their guns drawn, they went into the house.

△   △   △

In the crawlspace, Kevin couldn't tell what was happening. The gunfire terrified him. He moved away from the platform, but the boards beneath him made a cracking sound as the old plaster and ceiling insulation started to give way between the joists. Frightened of falling through the ceiling, he held his breath and tried to make himself as light as possible, inching his way back to the platform again, trying to stay on the joists. His hands kept getting splinters as he moved from slat to slat. The platform was so far away. He was concentrating so hard he didn't even hear the police sirens.

Then someone was climbing up into the attic. A man's head came up through the trapdoor. The man stared straight at him, and his heart thudded. It was one of the men who had kidnapped him. "So this is where you've been! You make a sound, you're dead," he said, pulling himself up. Kevin looked for a gun or a knife, but the man was unarmed.

"No, you're dead," Kevin said, kicking out with all his might. He connected with the man's head, and the man yelled. Falling back, he grabbed at Kevin's foot, twisting it as we hung on.

Kevin kicked with the other foot, again and again, trying to connect with an arm or a shoulder. "Get the hell off me, you bastard," Kevin shouted, and then he heard a voice calling his name.

"Kevin," Connor called, "are you here?"

The man hanging on to his foot was glaring at him. "I swear I'll tear you apart," he threatened.

"Who's there?" Kevin called.

"It's Connor O'Brien. I'm Hillary's friend."

Kevin's leg was throbbing where the man hung on, but he gave a kick with his other leg again, and this time connected with the side of the man's neck. The man let go with a grunt, and fell out of the attic. Connor was there to grab him.

"I've got him," he called. "Come on out now."

And just as the police got there, followed by Trish, Kevin crawled forward to safety.

△   △   △

Pam was concentrating so intently that when someone knocked on the door, she jumped.

Charles shouted, "Dammit! I told you not to disturb us."

"It's William," he said from the other side of the door separating their two offices.

Charles got up and unlocked the door.

William came storming in. "Why the hell have you locked me out? This place is boarded up like a fortress. Arlene says we've got people locked in the conference room too."

"Have a nice lunch?" Charles asked, ignoring his question. "We've been waiting for you."

His obsequiousness grated on Pam. She felt her cheeks flush; her father's presence made the meeting seem not only clandestine but dirty. She felt herself stiffen, waiting to see what would happen next.

"I couldn't get here sooner," William said to her. "How are you, Pam?"

"I've been better." Her rage against him reignited, flaring white-hot, flashing through her wildly, bringing back memories of a lifetime of neglect and rejection. His relationship with Charles had cost him so much, and now it was costing her.

William saw her disgust and turned away. He appeared older and sadder. His body was thin and gaunt, like that of an obsessive athlete or dieter, and the sharp lines of his handsome face were now blurred by softened flesh. His once-thick hair was all white and thinning on top. She could tell he wanted to approach her.

"I'd like to speak to Pam privately." He motioned for her to come with him, but she didn't move. Did they think she was going to fall for a good-guy-bad-guy routine?

"She doesn't leave this room," Charles snapped. "I mean it!"

William shot Charles a hate-filled look, which Charles ignored. Pam couldn't figure out what was happening, except that William and Charles were both her adversaries.

William came over, as if to kiss her on the cheek. She stiffened, and he said quietly, "Something's going on. You'd never offer us the building contracts on Weymouth City. Walk out of here while you still can."

So Charles hadn't told him what he had over her. She shook her head. The expression of pity in his eyes just made her angrier. The look she gave him back shouted, *Don't you dare pity me, this is your fault. You could never save yourself all these years, so how could you possibly help me?*

He moved away from her blazing eyes, his shoulders bent. For the first time she understood what his life must have been like, with Charles devouring him piece by piece. Perhaps he had tried to protect her, keep her away. But it didn't excuse the kind of a father he'd been, selfish and petty and weak. Maybe other fathers were worse, but that didn't mitigate his behavior. She'd heard about parents who beat their children and molested them, and still their children forgave them, even loved them. Not her. She thought of all the years she'd longed for him, wished he would be there for her, thought his love could make everything all right. What a cruel lesson it was to learn he didn't know how to love. Watching him, she knew he had no more hold over her. He was old now, close to seventy-five. The time for them to be father and daughter was past; all he'd become was a doormat for Charles. *I too am Charles's pawn,* she thought. Being a pawn of Charles's had turned her father's life into an absolute failure; the one thing he'd wanted to accomplish, regardless of his own ties to Charles, was to keep her independent of the man's tentacles. Now that too was impossible. Along with her resentment toward him, she felt a touch of pity.

"Sit down, William." Charles switched from hostility to syrupy sweetness, patting himself on the back in his superior role. "We're glad you've joined us."

"This is my company, you know." William sounded petulant. "What is going on?" He sat on the sofa, sinking into its cushions, and Charles's eyes glinted as he looked down on his partner from his place on the slightly higher chair. Pam stayed where she was, on an equal level with Charles.

"We're negotiating," Charles replied, returning to the agreement.

"Charles," Pam said, "you know I cannot control the possible changes in scope. Once we begin, there will always be more for us to do, like widen a street, or refurbish another subway stop, or build Con Edison an extra vault. Every job has those add-ons, and nobody holds us up like this."

"You bear those risks; I want my ass covered."

"That's a rather tough position," William commented.

"Bet your ass," Charles said, stopping him cold.

Again, she conceded. It was getting very late, and her optimism was deserting her. She still had heard nothing from Charles about Hillary or Kevin. For all she knew, Kevin was dead and some killer was stalking the hospital where Hillary lay right now.

"I want to take a break," Pam said, "order some tea, make a call to Mel and see how Hillary is doing, find out if there's any news." She tried to sneak it in casually.

"I said no phone calls until this deal is settled!" Charles snapped. "Or you can just walk, and let them both die."

At that statement, William sat up. "What are you talking about? Let who die?"

So Charles hasn't told him about this, either, Pam thought. She explained what had happened to Hillary and to her campaign worker, Kevin Matthews.

"This is monstrous, Charles." William's frustration came pouring out. "You're bargaining with people's lives, blackmailing Pam. I won't allow it, I tell you!"

"Shut up, William!"

Her father's outrage took her by surprise. For the first time she was experiencing what it felt like to have a father's protection, and it almost made her break down. William saw the look on her face, and got up to comfort her. But she held up her hand to stop him, and he sat back down. She could not allow his concern to weaken her position. Charles had brought her a sober reality. She would never be rid of him. In that moment she envisioned killing him someday. Coldly and calculatingly, she'd just blow his head off. *Nothing is worth this,* she thought. *If only I could find a way out!* She stood up and headed for the door.

"Are you giving up?" He was perfectly composed.

"Going to the bathroom."

"Use mine." He indicated a door to the left of his desk, making it clear she wasn't to leave the office.

As she closed the bathroom door, she could hear her father and William arguing.

Charles said, "Don't you dare interfere again with your stupid protestations about this being your company, or I'll tell her everything you ever did in our business dealings together. I'll drag you so far down in the garbage, you'll never raise your face out of it again."

"Everything I've ever done I was forced to do, the way you're forcing her."

"Mister Innocent," he mocked. "Want to try?"

But William didn't.

Charles picked up the phone and asked, "Are those people in the conference room still undisturbed? Fine, see that they stay that way."

"You're really wallowing in smugness today, aren't you?" William commented.

Charles just laughed. "Maybe I won't save the best for last. You've come to rescue your pure little daughter, but she's just as cutthroat as you or I have ever been. Remember our building on Twenty-sixth? The one we were forced to sell to get that job with Graham Weston? Well, little Pammy is the one who forced the sale. You handed her a cornerstone of Weymouth City, and I'm getting it back for us."

Trish left Connor and Kevin with the police, praying that her car would still run after what Connor had put it through. But the old beast managed to get going. The police didn't want to let her leave the scene, but she convinced them she'd make her statement later, and finally they let her go. She took off from New Jersey at 3:35, making it into the city and out of the Lincoln tunnel in a record fifty-five minutes. And then she began to crawl in afternoon traffic. Driving up Eighth Avenue from 40th wasn't too bad, but when she turned east on 50th, she was brought to a standstill in bumper-to-bumper. Some people were sitting there resigned, while others yelled, honked, raised their fists, and cursed each other, the city, and the mayor. She was jumping out of her skin, pounding the steering wheel, willing the truck up ahead to pull its damned rear end into the loading dock it was stuck in front of, so she could reach Pam.

Watching pedestrians make much better time than she was made her want to abandon the car and just run the rest of the way. But she was still wearing her high-heeled boots from last night's party. Being short, she often sacrificed comfort for height. At the moment she cursed her vanity.

Inch by inch she moved along, finally reaching Fifth Avenue. Only two more avenues to go.

And what will I do with the car when I get there? There are no garages near Charles's building. I'll just leave the damned car in the street, she decided. *Let them cart it away.*

"Is it true?" William was standing there when Pam came out of the john. Just being out of Charles's sight for a few moments had helped, even though she'd heard what they'd said.

"Yes, it's true. One of my better maneuvers. But it was strictly business, William, nothing personal. Not like the way you and your wife snubbed me for years, or the way you refused to help me get started when I first came to New York, or the way you let my mother and me barely scrape by all our lives, while you lived in luxury." She stood there face to face with him, staring him down. And damned if she didn't see surprise and then remorse in his eyes. She'd waited years for this moment, and it had a bittersweet tinge to it.

"I deserved that," he admitted. "I know what I've done to you is awful—"

"You have no idea," she flashed back, disdain in her eyes, but she couldn't hide her pain.

"I was weak and foolish when I was young," he said. "I left your mother when things got tough, and ran home. But I suffered for it, believe me. I loved my little girl."

She almost wanted to laugh, but sarcasm came out instead. "Some love. You never did anything about it. Did you? *Never!* And God knows you had the chance. You could have made up for it, you could have reached out! And you never did. For most of my life you meant more to me than anything else, but not anymore. Taking that building away from you was nothing, compared to what I wanted to do. I could have ruined you. There were times when I had the chance. I could have told your sons about you, about me, destroyed you in their eyes. But that would have made me just like you." Her fists were clenched so hard that her nails pierced the skin of her palms. She felt tears stinging her eyes, and willed them back. *Not now!* The look on his face was worth all her fury. He was truly sorry, ashamed, she could see it. But that only made her more furious. "It's too late to be sorry," she said.

"I listened to Jennifer when she told me to forget the past, to concentrate on our life together. I didn't realize how another wife and child threatened her, the scandal of it."

"She wasn't threatened," Pam scoffed. "She's a green-eyed witch, bitterly jealous, she wouldn't share you or her sons' birthright. And you went along. I saw it that day when I came to your home, your baronial mansion, asking to be your daughter, and got slapped in the face. You were such a weak excuse for a man. You did just what your friends advised, dumped your past mistakes, because that's what you wanted to do. I think you've used Charles all these years as a way not to blame your-self for what you've done."

"That's not true! I wanted to make it up to you when you came to New York, but what you wanted would have brought you great danger. And look how it turned out."

"So the final thing you have to say to me is 'I told you so'? Wonderful. Bravo." Out of the corner of her eye, she could see Charles smiling. She'd be damned if she'd give him any further satisfaction at her expense. And the problems at hand were urgent. "Charles," she said, dis-missing her father, which was probably the best revenge on him she could have ever had, "there are lives at stake. Let's get to it."

William seemed to deflate with her dismissal; he went back and sank into the sofa cushions. She would not waste any more time on him.

There was a plate of pastries on the coffee table, and Charles was eating one. She took a bite of cake for energy.

Something was different about Charles, she noticed as she sat down again. It galled her how much he'd enjoyed that exchange between her and William. Now he seemed ready to pounce. Every inch of her was alert.

"Only two items left," he said.

She could see how Charles loved rubbing it in. Each time he won another point, her father's expression grew tighter.

Charles continued, "I'm eliminating time extensions

due to unavoidable delays, the usual ten annual snow days, and strike days. We have a five-year deal, to the day. I get paid if the job goes overtime. And last but not least, I must have complete autonomy over the awarding of my subcontracts. You rescind discretionary rights."

"Under what pretense?" she asked. It made her skin crawl to think about giving up on this one.

"I don't want to ask for bids on a lot of this work; I'll award the subcontracts to people I've worked with. I need control and latitude."

"That's a license to steal! Without competitive bids, there's no control of price at all." She glared at him and then said, "It's pretty dumb of me to expect anything but larceny from you. To quote Shaw, 'We've established that you're a whore, we're just quibbling over price.' "

"Do you agree?"

How she wanted to wipe that look off his face. She stood up and walked over to his desk, trying to think. She needed Jake at this moment. Involuntarily she reached for the phone.

"No phone calls!" he shouted, leaping to grab the phone from her.

"That's it!" William said, jumping up from the sofa and crossing to the phone. "I've had enough of this."

But Charles blocked his path, daring him, William's fury increasing. Pam stepped in between them, remembering what Charles was like when he was enraged. "Please, he'll only hurt you!"

William took a deep breath, trying to control himself. His knuckles were white from clenching his fists. Pam gripped his arm, forcing him to relax a bit, then she turned to Charles. "You're enjoying this too much. Provoking us both. What do you know that I don't?"

"Do you agree to the last two points?" he insisted, ignoring her question.

But she was nearly at the end of her patience, her fear was growing by the minute. He had to tell her what he knew! "I cannot give up my discretionary rights! It's financial suicide."

"Then I guess that's it."

"Goddammit!" she shouted. "Tell me. Are you going to get the contract on Hillary's life called off and have Kevin released? Or is he already dead?"

"Hillary's a nice enough lady, Pam, but I don't give a fuck about some kid's life."

It was like a slap in the face. Every ounce of her longed to throw it back at him, *The kid is your son.* What pleasure it would give her to wipe that look of malice off his face, to show him how she'd beaten him, more badly than he was beating her today. But she'd vowed to go to her grave with this secret. He would not only kill her, but ruin Kevin's life. All her sacrifices would have been for nothing. "I know you don't give a fuck about some kid's life, Charles. As far as you're concerned, the world and everyone in it can rot in hell. But his life is important to me, and to others as well. And so is Hillary's." By God, she would force him to tell her what he was keeping from her. She crossed the room, reached into her purse, and pulled out the packet of photographs she'd brought with her that Hillary had taken of her so long ago. She handed them to William.

"I brought these along to remind Charles of what he once did to me, in case he's forgotten. I couldn't still press charges against him for assaulting me, but the tabloids would love the story. It would be worth any embarrassment to me, if it caused him some."

"You think I care about that?" Charles scoffed.

William glanced at the pictures and winced. "When were these taken? After the car accident?"

"No. The night he found out I was your daughter. I had just told him I was pregnant. But that didn't stop him from taking his rage out on me. After he beat me, I never thought I'd recover."

"My God." William seemed stunned for a minute, and then he lunged for Charles and grabbed him around the neck, squeezing with all his might.

Pam cried out, "No, don't!" and pulled at William's hands, amazed at how strong he was. Charles was gasping for air, his face red and perspiring, his hands clawing at William's. The three of them were locked together, struggling.

"You are scum!" William shouted, not letting go. "I want you out of my life."

"Don't do this!" Pam finally got through to William. She and Charles together succeeded in breaking William's hold. Charles fell forward, gasping for breath.

William shouted again, "You take this deal as payment for the ending of our partnership. Tell your bastard friends I don't care what they do to me, I don't care anymore, I tell you. I won't live with you in my life another minute! I've lived with what you've done to me, but when you beat up my daughter, it's too goddamned much. Do you hear me! Do you hear?" He was screaming, out of control, but Pam was able to hold him back.

"Will you accept his offer, Charles, if I agree to everything you ask for and sign the contract?" she said. "Will you leave him?"

"He was always free to buy me out, Pam." Charles was still breathing hard. He made his way to the bar to pour himself a drink. "It's in our partnership agreement. He said he could never afford to do it, but he could have found a way if he'd wanted to." He set down his glass and looked at her with the same loathing she felt for him. Then he shrugged. "Make the changes and sign it," he said. "And I'll be through with your old man." He turned to William. "You disgust me too, you hypocrite. Suddenly you're filled with family loyalty for a daughter you've barely seen in over forty-five years. It may not be much, but I beat you in that department, with all your social shit."

William's shame made him turn away, blotting out the hatred for a moment.

Pam moved over to the coffee table, sat down, and picked up the contract. Her hands were shaking so badly she could hardly write. She went through the pages clause by clause, making the changes Charles wanted, initialing every change. Each time it made her more and more sick. Her play for time had not worked. She had no more ways of keeping him from getting what he wanted. William was rid of Charles, but she was stuck with him now.

The last clause had to be written in by hand. Her fingers could barely form the words. *I rescind all discretionary rights of approval over all subcontracts entered into by Charles Meroni or Gray-Con Corporation.* "I'm doing this for Hillary and Kevin," she said. She held her breath and signed the contract.

Charles came over immediately and signed under her name; she turned to her father. "You have to witness this, William." And she handed him the pen. He had tears in his eyes.

A loud pounding on the door stopped him. It was followed by angry voices. She heard Trish's voice yelling her name.

"Pam, are you in there? Let us in!"

"That's Trish!" she said, grabbing the contract off the table. "If you hurt her, I'll tear this up. What's going on out there?" she shouted.

More pounding, then Jake's voice: "Don't sign anything, Pam!" he yelled at the top of his voice.

Charles tried to grab the contract from her, but she wrenched it away.

William unlocked the door and everyone burst in, led by Guido.

Jake spoke first. "Is it too late? Have you signed the contracts yet?"

She nodded. "Why?"

Trish interrupted, speaking in a rush. "There is no contract out on Hillary's life. The people Charles knows won't do us any good at all. Charles has no power to help her. And Kevin is safe. Connor rescued him!"

Pam's joy lit up her face, and she gave an excited cry. "Is he all right?"

Trish nodded. "Tired and scared, but safe."

"Thank God," Pam said. She turned to Charles, the truth suddenly dawning on her. "You sonofabitch! You were bluffing all this time, using this to get hold of my company."

He didn't reply.

Her hatred for him threatened to consume her. "That's why you wouldn't let me phone, wouldn't let anyone get to me and tell me what you were doing. Smart move, Meroni," she said. "I have to hand it to you, you almost did it. But your bluff was not as brilliant as the one I pulled on you years ago."

"What was that?" he said defiantly. His fury at being caught made his face flush a mottled red. How well she remembered that look.

"If I told you, then the bluff would no longer be effective. So it's for me to know and for you to wonder."

"Bullshit!" he said, grabbing for the contract. At the same time, Guido grabbed for it too.

But they were both slower than she was; she wrenched it back, and tore it up before anyone else could stop her.

"Attagirl," Jake said, rushing to her side to protect her.

The secretary was in tears. "Mr. Meroni, they overpowered me. This woman threatened to call the police. She said we were keeping people against their will. I tried to call you, Mr. Grayson," she said to William, "but you didn't respond."

"Shut up, Arlene," Charles said.

"What about Hillary?" Pam asked Trish.

"Reporters from all three networks are standing by at the hospital to hear her statement."

She turned to her father. "Is it true that you have a buy-out clause in your partnership with Charles?"

"Yes," he admitted. "But the way he skims everything out of the business, I've never been able to gather enough cash to do it. You know how builders are always leveraged."

She spoke to Charles, ignoring her father's excuse. "I'm buying you out on his behalf."

"Pam, it's a lot of money." William's voice shook with emotion.

"I still have my company. I can afford it," she replied, never taking her eyes from Charles. "Michael, Addison," she said to her attorneys, "look over the Meroni-Gray-Con agreement and conclude this buy-out by the end of today."

"Immediately, Pam," Addison Blake told her.

"This way," William said, leading them toward his office. "I have a copy of the agreement in here." But halfway through the door, he turned and came back to Pam. "I can never repay you for what you're doing." There was a catch in his voice, almost a sob of relief. "I don't deserve it." His face looked suddenly younger, free of burden, but his eyes were filled with tears.

"I know you don't," she said, dashing his sentimentality. "And I don't forgive you, either. I will not be your daughter. The irony of it is that now I own you."

He had a funny look on his face. "What are you going to do?"

"Nothing" she said. "You've done it all to yourself."

And she gestured for him to follow the lawyers into the other room.

As William left, Pam felt her own emotions welling up. The relief was enormous. She looked at Trish, and smiled. "D'Artagnan, I knew you'd come."

"Your Ladyship. Let's get the hell out of here," Trish said, grinning.

Pam was about to leave when she remembered the photographs. She went over to the desk, picked them up, and held them up to Charles for a brief moment. "Believe me, Charles, I really got you good." And without another word, she and Trish left the office.

11

The moment Trish and Pam were in the elevator, they threw their arms around each other and shouted for joy.

Trish inspected Pam as if she'd been in an accident, looking for bruises. "I'm all right," Pam kept assuring her. "It's over! The good guys won! Now tell me what happened with Kevin."

They were in Pam's limousine by the time Trish had finished telling the story. Then Trish remembered her car, the one she'd abandoned a block away. "I'm sure it's been towed by now," she said. "I'll have the garage claim it and do the body work. Connor really gave it a workout!"

They couldn't stop grinning, slapping each other's hands, going over the details of what each of them had gone through, and then basking in their success. "What a moment!" Pam kept exclaiming. "To hell and back in twenty-four hours."

"That was fabulous, what you did for your father, getting him away from Charles. Have you forgiven him?"

Pam shook her head. "But the bitterness is finally gone," she said.

"God, look at the time," Trish exclaimed. "The five o'clock news is on."

Pam reached over and turned on the television. The reception was wavy, going in and out as they drove, but still they could see the picture.

"This is Angela McBain, reporting to you from Montclair Hospital, where Mrs. Hillary Robin was taken last night in critical condition after a bomb exploded in her car. Mrs. Robin is running for Congress in the fifteenth district of New Jersey. Her condition began improving a few hours ago when she regained consciousness. But we were asked to stand by because she has an announcement

to make. The rumors are that because of the attempt on
her life, she's going to withdraw from the race. Mrs.
Robin has a substantial lead in the polls over her opponent, Victor Godfrey, mayor of Crestmont.''

"What do they mean, withdraw?" Pam said. "Doesn't
she know about Kevin? Didn't anyone reach her?"

"I don't know. Connor was supposed to call, or the
police. I'm sure someone informed her."

"You don't think they scared her off, after all, do
you?" Pam looked around. "Here we are, stuck in this
damned car again. But this time we're not in a tunnel."
She dialed the hospital.

Hillary came on the screen, trying to smile. Her face
was burned, and there was a bandage on her left temple.

"She looks awful," Pam said.

"No, she looks all right," Trish insisted, shushing her.

"Hello, I'm Hillary Robin." There were tears in her
eyes, and she turned away to try to compose herself,
reaching off camera for someone's hand. It was Mel. He
stepped into the camera's range next to her, his arm
around her. She turned back. "As you can see, this is a
difficult moment for me. For I had truly wanted to be a
representative of my district in Congress. We fought a
long and hard campaign."

"She doesn't know!" Pam said.

"The issue of toxic waste is of utmost importance to
our state and to this country. But for personal reasons I
have come to a decision."

"Oh God, she's really going to resign," Trish said,
"and then it will be too late."

They had pulled up to Pam's apartment building, but
neither she nor Trish got out of the car. Pam had reached
the hospital and was trying to get them to break into the
press conference. "It's a matter of life and death!" she
shouted. But the hospital personnel wouldn't interrupt.

"Get me your supervisor!" Pam ordered.

Trish seemed about to cry. "This is the most frustrating thing I've ever seen. Wait! There's a news bulletin."
She was staring at the television, holding up her hand to
keep Pam quiet.

The ABC logo came on, announcing a special report.
And then they saw Peter Jennings.

"There's been a break in the bombing incident that

injured a candidate for Congress in New Jersey last night,"
Jennings said. "We're going to Bram Claiborne at the
Victor Godfrey headquarters in Crestmont. Go ahead,
Bram."

"It seems to have happened already, Peter. Victor
Godfrey, candidate for Congress, has just been arrested
by the FBI. His son, Victor Godfrey, Jr., was arrested
earlier this afternoon, for the attempted murder of Hillary Robin, also a candidate for Congress, and the kid-
napping of one of her campaign volunteers, Kevin
Matthews, age seventeen. We have just interrupted an
appearance by Mrs. Robin on our local affiliate station,
where she was about to withdraw from the election in
order to save the life of the kidnapped boy. We are
waiting for word on his condition."

"He's safe, he's safe!" Trish shouted at the television.
Peter Jennings asked that they replay Hillary's speech.

Pam got through to the supervisor at the hospital and
explained that she had to talk to Hillary Robin or her
husband, even if they were on television.

"Victor Godfrey's a sonofabitch," Trish said. "Can
you imagine someone doing that, and then getting elected
to public office? I'd like to kill him myself."

"Why didn't they tell Hillary that Kevin was safe?"
Pam kept asking. "You don't suppose anything went
wrong, do you?"

Just then, the mobile cameras at the hospital came
back on and they could see someone handing Mel a
telephone. Pam heard him say, "Hello."

"Mel, it's Pam. What the hell's going on? Didn't you
know that Kevin was safe?"

The camera pulled back to reveal several people standing by Hillary. One of them was Connor. Mel stepped
out of camera range, so they couldn't see him on TV
anymore, but Pam could hear him.

"Yes, we knew," he told her. "But Hillary wasn't sure
she wanted to go through with the election anyway. She
was afraid of her enemies, afraid that Victor wasn't working alone, that someone else might come after her, or
hurt one of us."

"There's nobody else after her, Mel. And we'll get her
protection. Don't let her quit!"

"It's not my decision, Pam."

Someone was shushing him. The commentator's voice was speaking, telling about Hillary's reluctance to continue, and her family's support for her decision.

Then the camera focused on Hillary again. "I don't mean to make everyone wonder about what I'm going to do." This time her gaze was clear and she looked right into the camera. "Our community has been under siege. My next-door neighbor was killed yesterday and I was badly injured. My family's lives were threatened, and so was the life of a dear friend, by people who wanted to stop me from working against environmental pollution. But I won't be stopped. I'm going to continue my campaign and pay tribute to the memory of Edna Carmichael. My name is on the ballot, and I hope everyone in my district will vote for me!"

Trish and Pam cheered. Mel came on screen and kissed her, and handed her a phone. The station switched to the studio to comment on her announcement, but Trish and Pam had her on the phone.

"We're so proud of you!" Pam said.

"You did it," Trish told her, taking the phone.

"We all did it," Hillary said. "Connor sends his love. I have to talk to the reporters, I'll see you both later." And she hung up.

Pam hugged Trish good-bye, and sent her home in the limo. But when she came into the lobby of her building, she was shocked to see two people waiting for her, Frances Matthews and Kevin.

Pam glanced around to see if anyone was watching, still paranoid about Charles, but there was no one.

"Are you all right?" she asked Kevin. There were scratches on his cheek and bruises on his neck. He looked pale and disheveled, but happy. It had been so long since she'd seen him up close; he was a man now, a freshman in college, taller than she, and, thank God, healthy.

"They told me everything you did to try to save Kevin," Frances said. "We both wanted to thank you."

"You came all this way, tonight! You know it's not necessary," Pam said. "I did exactly what you would have done."

Frances squeezed her hand.

"Why don't you come up to my apartment, where we can talk?"

They took her private elevator up, smiling shyly at one another, while Pam's mind reeled. Kevin here with her was a dream come true. "It's been a long time," Pam said to Frances, and then smiled at her son. "I hear wonderful things about you from Hillary," she told him. "You got all A's on your midterms in your first semester at Princeton."

He smiled.

"You're as beautiful as ever," Frances said. "And still as generous."

When the elevator opened into the marble foyer, Kevin looked around, taking in all the sumptuous details, the tall ceilings and ornate moldings, the priceless antiques, the collections of small sculptures, the overstuffed furniture, the magnificent view of Central Park, and he sighed. "I knew it would look like this."

She wanted to take him in her arms, but she could only gaze at him, drinking him in with her eyes. How wonderful he looked, how alive, even with Frances holding on to his arm.

She offered them a drink while Kevin related how he'd escaped from his captors into the attic, and told her about Connor's rescue.

"Trish told me her side of it, but we wanted to know exactly how it happened and how you survived," Pam said, trying to keep her hands from shaking as she put ice in the glasses. "You were very brave."

"I've never been so happy to see anyone in my life as I was to see Connor, and then Trish," Kevin said. "You should have been there." He paused. "No, on second thought, none of us should have been there, especially me!"

Pam and Frances both laughed.

"Have you seen your father and your sister?" Pam wanted to know. "I'd feel terrible if this thank-you visit has taken anything away from the joy of your return."

"Dad and Su Mei came with us into the city. They went shopping so we could see you," Kevin told her. "Mom said she couldn't rest until then. I should have known you'd be involved somehow," he said thoughtfully. "You always show up for my worst moments."

Pam smiled, trying to keep the longing out of her voice. "We're very grateful you're all right."

Frances was looking at her, as though trying to work up courage. Then she set down her glass and stood up, straightening her shoulders, keeping a steady gaze. Finally she took hold of Kevin's hand and pulled him to his feet. He looked at her questioningly, but she brought him over to the sofa where Pam was sitting. Pam stood up to face them.

"There's someone I want you to meet, dear," Frances said. "Kevin, this is Pam Weymouth."

"I know who she is, Mom," he said, puzzled.

Pam and Frances's eyes met. "No, you don't, dear," Frances said. Her eyes were clear and direct, but her voice quavered. "Pam is your mother, your natural mother."

Pam felt a rush of fear course through her, as exposed as if she'd been stripped naked. "How long have you known?" Her knees felt weak, as though they might give way. So easily, a secret of a lifetime revealed?

"I figured it out some time ago," Frances said.

Kevin looked at Frances in shocked surprise, and then turned to Pam. He had been through a lot in the last twenty-four hours, but this was by far the biggest shock. He stared at her, trying to assess what he'd heard. So many expressions crossed his face, amazement, anger, betrayal. Pam saw them all and wanted to hide her eyes, but she forced herself to just stand there. Now that the moment had come, she would take every ounce of it, no matter how bitter.

He was trying not to cry, but his breathing was short and uneven, as though he was crying without tears. He spoke to Frances without taking his eyes from Pam's. "How long have you known?"

"It first occurred to me after you went into remission, because she was still as interested in you as when you were sick. Then I found out that Pam and Hillary Robin were friends and that Mel Robin was one of the attorneys who arranged for your adoption. And the resemblance is uncanny."

"Why didn't you ever tell me?" A sob caught in his throat.

Frances, too, was finally facing it. "I was afraid of losing you. Afraid that you'd choose her over me."

"Oh, Mom," he said, unable to understand. "And why

didn't you tell me?" he asked Pam. "You didn't hate me. You were my friend. I don't understand. You knew where I was, but you still didn't want me?"

Pam tried to keep the trembling from her voice, felt her eyes brimming full. "I couldn't tell you because I had to protect you. I gave you away to protect you. But, my darling boy, I always wanted you. With all my heart."

"Protect me from what?" Kevin asked with an anguished cry.

"From someone who would have ruined your life, who could still hurt you very much if he found out about you."

Now Frances was staring at her. "So that was why you never told him, why you stayed away when I asked you to."

"I had no choice," Pam admitted. "And I never wanted to hurt him. I believed you knew what was best for him. You were his mother."

"What about me?" Kevin cried. "Didn't I have a right to know?"

"Look at the life you've had," Pam said. "Would you have wanted any other parents? Would you have traded places with anyone else in the world?"

Slowly he shook his head, but now the tears he had held back streamed down his face. His anger toward her was fading as the memories returned; he was remembering the times they'd shared, his admiration for her. "You were my secret pal, weren't you?" He cried openly now. "You were a good friend. I always loved you."

"Oh, Kevin, I adore you." With a sob, she stepped up to embrace him. For the first time, she held her son in her arms while they cried together.

"I've imagined this so many times," Kevin said, holding her close.

"Oh God, so have I," she said.

"But it was never like this," he told her. "You were a bag lady. You'd plead with me to forgive you for what you'd done, and I'd find you a place to live and support you." He started to laugh and pull away, but kept his arm around her, not wanting to let go. "Can you beat that? Me, support you?" He glanced around the room and then at her, this beautiful woman, and shook his head in bewilderment. "No wonder I'm so fascinated with buildings that I'm majoring in engineering." He laughed again. "It runs in the family."

Pam laughed too, and then noticed that Frances was smiling with happiness and pride. "Thank you," Pam said to her, overwhelmed by her generosity. But then she realized it wasn't what Frances had done that was overwhelming her, it was everything; she couldn't hold back anymore, and broke down sobbing. She tried to talk, to tell them what this meant to her, but there was no way. All she could do was cry. There was no more need to fight, to keep the wolf at bay. She could let go of a lifetime of fear, and in its place would be enough joy to remake her world. And best of all, it was her own son who was comforting her.

Finally she stopped crying and went into the bathroom to splash water on her face. When she came back she was more composed. She said to Kevin, "If there's anything you want to know, just ask me, anything. But our relationship must still remain a secret."

"We understand," Frances said. Then she laughed, relieved that the tension had broken. "You've been so generous already, I can't imagine what it would be like if things were made public."

"Why do you keep saying generous, Mom?" Kevin asked.

"Pam is paying your college tuition and has set aside money for Su Mei's, too. Plus expenses."

"That was from you?" Kevin said, again shocked by the truth. "You mean my grades didn't earn it?"

"Of course you qualified for a scholarship, but why take money from some poor student when you have a rich mother?" Pam said.

And they all laughed.